MW01260214

# WHISPER

TAL BAUER

A Tal Bauer Publication
www.talbauerwrites.com

*This novel contains scenes of graphic violence.*

All rights reserved. No part of this publication may be reproduced in any material form, whether by printing, photocopying, scanning or otherwise without the written permission of the publisher, Tal Bauer.

Copyright © 2018 Tal Bauer
Print ISBN 9781980907008
Cover Art by Ron Perry Graphic Design © Copyright 2018
Edited by Rita Roberts
Published in 2018 by Tal Bauer in the United States of America

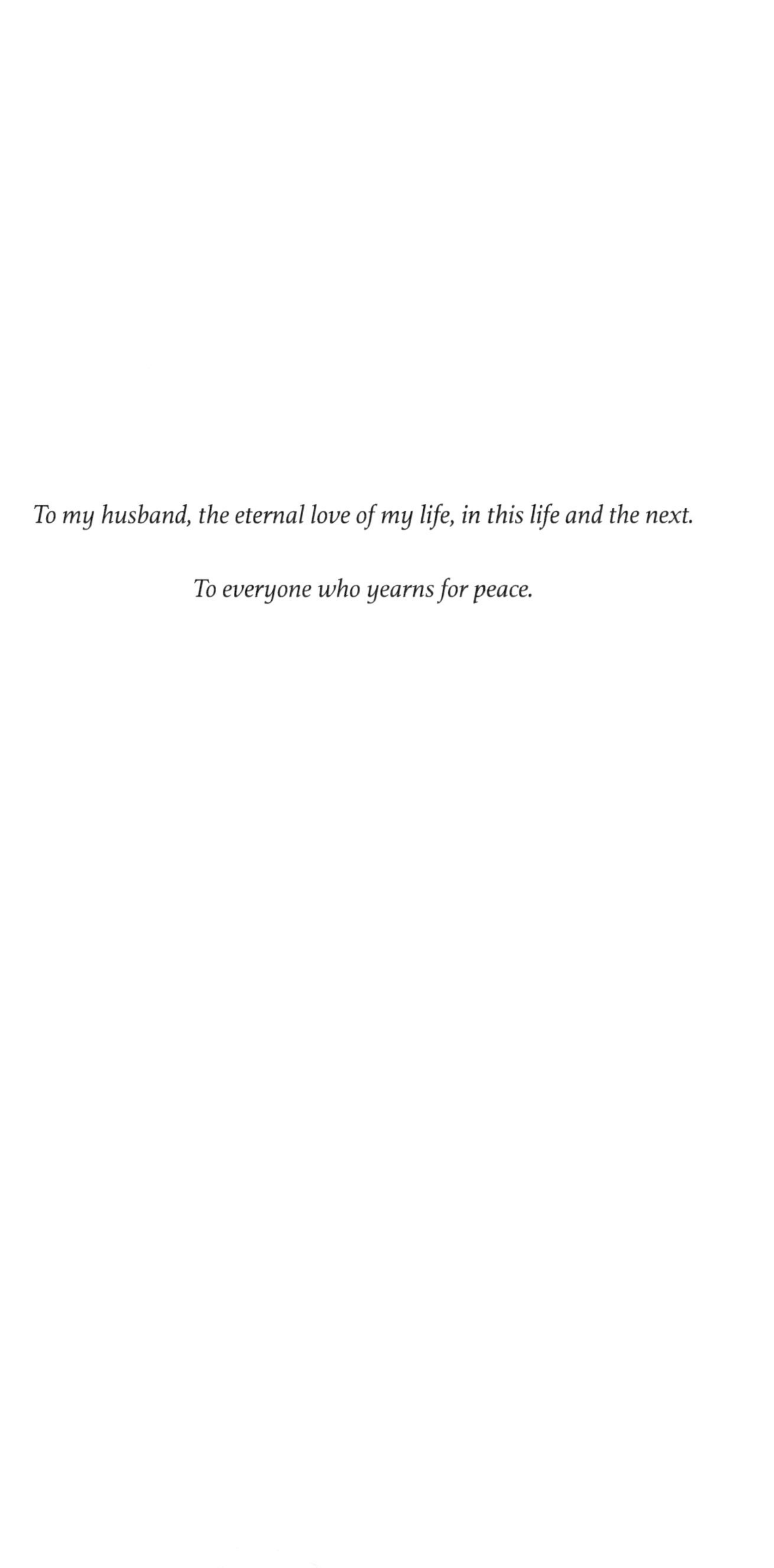

*To my husband, the eternal love of my life, in this life and the next.*

*To everyone who yearns for peace.*

What you think,
You become.

What you feel,
You attract.

What you imagine,
You create.

~ *Gautama Buddha*

## IMPORTANT NOTE

This story is, in part, inspired by actual events. Certain incidents, locations, and dialogue were fictionalized for dramatic purposes. This is a work of fiction. All characters, places, and events are from the author's imagination and should not be confused with fact. Any resemblance to persons, living or dead, events or places is purely coincidental.

*Then*

*September 11, 2001*

# 1

**CIA Headquarters, Langley Virginia - September 11, 2001**

It was supposed to be a good day.

Kris poured his creamer into his second cup of coffee. He heard feet pounding down the hallway. "It *must* be an accident."

"But it's such a clear morning. How did the pilot lose visibility?"

He hurried after his coworkers to the Counterterrorism Center, CTC, housed deep inside Langley. CTC looked like a Vegas sports bar: monitors spanned one giant wall with video feeds showing live TV, news, surveillance from a dozen overseas operations, status of forces deployed around the world, and more. In a pit before the monitors, lines of workstations stretched in rows. One wall was packed with racks of communication equipment. Radios, satellite phones on charging stands, humming servers that communicated with CIA stations around the world.

Everyone's eyes were fixed on the wall of monitors.

Every screen showed the same thing.

New York City. Lower Manhattan. Smoke rising from the North Tower of the World Trade Center.

Murmurs rose, the ebb and flow of uncertainty. More people

padded in. Analysts, officers, the deputy director. Clandestine Special Activities Division personnel.

Everyone waited for the news anchors to *say* it, to confirm it was an accident. A tragic, horrific accident, but still.

An *accident.*

One hundred CIA officers watched live as United Airlines Flight 175 slammed into the South Tower of the World Trade Center. The fireball filled the whole wall of monitors, stretching from one end of CTC to the other, as if they were right there in the center of the fury. Fire broke over the world, coloring CTC in waves from Hell.

Gasps rose, followed by screams. Kris dropped his cup. It shattered, coffee splashing his pants and the shoes of the analyst beside him.

No one noticed.

No one moved. No one spoke.

It was like the world had stopped turning, like time was frozen. Breaths seemed to take an eternity. Reality only existed in the billowing smoke, the flames roaring above New York. The desperation in the survivors' faces as they leaned out of the windows above the impact site and the roaring inferno. As they chose to jump, leap from the building, fleeing one certain death for another.

Twenty minutes later, American Airlines Flight 77 crashed into the Pentagon.

"Jesus Christ, it's al-Qaeda." Voices rose, comments over the din of the whispers. "This is their attack."

Kris started to shake, violent trembles as flashes of intel cables and reports he'd seen over the past two years came together like a terrible jigsaw puzzle in his mind.

*Too late. We were too late.*

"Will someone *please lead*?" a voice shouted from the back of the room. "Will someone *please* fucking do something?"

Clint Williams, Director of CTC, turned and stared. He blinked, as if trying to visibly restart his brain, as if he remembered he had men and women standing before him. "We're under attack!" he shouted. "And Langley could be a target! Evacuate! *Now*! Everyone out!"

---

Kris had woken up in a good mood.

The night before, he had lightly flirted with an attorney while watching *Monday Night Football* at a little bar in Georgetown. He'd cheered on Denver while the attorney rooted for the New York Giants, and they'd playfully jabbed at each other throughout.

At the end of the game, the attorney gave him a long, lingering stare over his slim chinos, his tucked-in button-down, open at the neck and showing off his undershirt and his shell necklace, the one he wore when he went out, to his spiked hair.

He'd bitten his lower lip.

"Wanna get out of here?"

Kris had thought he'd never ask.

They made out in the parking lot, pressed against the attorney's BMW, before trading blowjobs in the back seat. After, Kris straightened his clothes and headed to his car, going home. Alone.

He was a professional now, or trying to be. Holding down a job. His college days of waking up in a different bed almost every day of the week were behind him.

"Maybe I'll see you next week," the attorney had called after him.

"Maybe!"

Buoyed by the night before, Kris had wound his way through the North Virginia traffic to Langley early in the morning. He'd smiled at the guards who glared at him as he badged his way into headquarters, and then to CTC. The guards had shut up about the Monday night game as he passed. As if him hearing their conversation would somehow mean something. He'd smirked and twiddled his fingers.

At his desk, he'd read the overnight cables, shaking his head over the reported suicide bombing of General Ahmad Massoud of the Northern Alliance in Afghanistan. Massoud had been one of the better men in the dusty backwater of Afghanistan, a force against the Taliban.

He'd risen to get his second cup of coffee, wondering about the future of the tiny, forgotten country he was in charge of monitoring. Would the Taliban seize control of the entire nation? Would that be the end of the rebellion against the Taliban's chokehold? What about al-Qaeda, shielded by the Taliban? In the breakroom, he had to start a second pot of coffee. Everyone always let it run dry, down to the dregs that burned and stank.

He was pouring his creamer, wondering, for the thousandth time, about updating his résumé and getting out of the CIA when he heard the first whisper of a plane crash in New York.

The CIA was shaping up to be a rough career. Kris was surrounded by Type A personalities, people who stared unflinchingly into the darkness of the world and believed they could bend the globe's swirling maelstrom to their own will. Kris could barely get the security guards to say hello to him. Who was he to change the world?

He stood out, with his tweed sport coats and ascots and crisp button-downs. In a world of clandestine operators in rumpled khakis and polos with coffee stains, he was a Milan fashion model. In 2001, that *meant* something, in a man. Everyone, of course, noticed. Everyone talked. He could count on one hand the few people who spoke regularly to him, who were friendly.

Maybe that was why he was isolated on the Afghanistan desk.

Maybe it was time to start looking for another career.

Back in 1999, a man had stopped him outside his Advanced Farsi class at George Washington University. He'd hung in the corner of the hallway, keeping obsessively to himself, like he lived in the shadows by choice. He'd had two cell phones on his hip. In 1999, barely anyone had a cell phone.

"Mr. Caldera? Kris Caldera?"

"Who's asking?"

"I'd like to talk to you about a possible job." He'd handed Kris a business card with the CIA's logo on the front.

He hadn't known then what it meant that he was being sought out by the CIA. He was a gay Puerto Rican kid on a poverty scholarship to GWU and he didn't have a single ounce of blue blood in him, not one single connection or friend of his father's he could call on. It was only four years since President Clinton had rescinded the ban on homosexuals being allowed to hold security clearances, only four years since *people like him* were allowed to serve openly in sensitive national security positions.

Not that anyone *did* serve openly. The closet was still shut and barricaded from the inside.

"Why me?" He'd stuck out his hip, and he had lip gloss on and smudged eyeliner from waking up in Beta Theta Pi's frat house that morning.

"We hear you're good with languages. Particularly ones we're interested in."

He loved languages, loved the way the mind skipped and danced over converting rules of grammar, syntax, and expression, twists of phrase and linguistic layups. He'd grown up speaking Spanish at home and English at school, and a mix of everything on the streets, where he ran with other brown kids in Lower Manhattan. In middle school he'd crushed on older boys, writing long love letters in French that he dreamed of whispering to the shortstop on the school baseball team. In high school, he'd worn his school uniform the sassiest way he could, his tie just past scandalous, and regularly smacked on enough tinted lip balm to make it look like he'd been kissing for hours. He'd made it a point to stare at the football players until they barked at him. He'd laughed in their faces.

One had tried to kiss him after school, smearing his lip balm all over his cheeks. He kept the boy's secret, though.

Later, he'd crushed on a swarthy waiter from Rome who worked in a hole-in-the-wall restaurant while moonlighting off-Broadway, and he'd learned Italian just to flirt with him. As often as he could, he'd trekked up Broadway, ignoring the stares he got when the wealthy white people watched him flounce past.

Then one day, the waiter showed up with a white boy toy from the Upper East Side, and Kris never spoke another word in Italian.

The harder the language, the better he was. He'd taken Arabic throughout his junior and senior years in high school and earned a scholarship to George Washington University in DC.

Not Georgetown. They'd never accept someone like him.

But George Washington was only a few blocks away, and they offered as many languages as he could gorge himself on. He'd thought if he did well, maybe, just maybe, Georgetown's School of Foreign Service would accept him for a Masters. He could try to join the State Department, or the United Nations.

He'd maxed out of Arabic his sophomore year and switched to Farsi, taking courses until he had to do independent study with his professor to go further. He'd spent two summers on an exchange program in the Middle East, first in Egypt and then in Lebanon and Syria.

He was careful overseas, just to prove his doubters wrong. His professor hadn't wanted him to go. *"It's too dangerous, Kris. You advertise your sexuality."*

Of course he did. When the world looked at him, all anyone saw was a skinny brown gay boy, a kid full of attitude and trash. He had two choices. He could live out loud, take the hard world exactly as it came, be exactly who he was. He wasn't wrong; the world was. People moved out of the way on the streets for *him*. So what if they moved because they hated him? They still *moved*. So what if he was a scrawny Puerto Rican with too big a mouth and too little sense? New York was full of old gays who wanted little twinky white boys, anyway. He picked fights with everybody, with anybody. He had a sharp tongue and no patience for the sidelong looks he got. He just lived louder, filling up the space everyone left around him.

Or, on the other hand, he could try and bury everything, try and erase the gay and erase the brown and try to live a white bread kind of life. Put away the lip balm and stop cursing in Spanish. Learn Frisbee and golf and be like the upper-class private school white boys he saw in Central Park, and not the street soccer and football at his low-income school. He could make his world shades of white and pale, shades of sucking up and always trying to fit in, shades of never being enough, and being told, in a thousand, million, tiny ways, that he would never, ever fit in, no matter how hard he tried.

Fuck that.

He'd take his discrimination to his face, thank you very much. The world would acknowledge him. Somehow.

He'd left New York with the empanadas and platinos his mom had packed him, two suitcases, and a promise to never go back. Not to his father, who hadn't looked at Kris since he caught him jerking off to a picture of the Backstreet Boys, and not to the rest of his classmates who'd called him *princess* and *fairy* and *fag*. Not even to his mother, who'd dreamed of flying back to the island and living with her sister, escaping his dad and the endless nights of beer drinking and watching TV for hours on end. His mom was made for Puerto Rico, for wind in her hair and a salt breeze, and friends cooking together as music played over the sound of the surf and the birds twittering from tree to tree. She wasn't made for car horns and subway platforms, the stink of hot urine on Manhattan's blacktop.

He hadn't known where he was made for, either. Not New York. But where?

He'd never dreamed, never imagined, his path would take him to the CIA.

But then he'd dreamed of spies in luxury suits, seduction in far-flung lands, meeting a man's gaze across a crowded bar, swirling a Martini. Adventure. Intrigue.

And for once, someone wanted him.

A week after graduation, Kris was at Camp Peary, The Farm, the CIA training center.

He'd been certain, then, he had made the biggest mistake of his life. He was a bookworm, studious until happy hour, when he enjoyed his vodka and his cocktails and a man to go along. He had more clothes than sense and went to the gym only to show off his long legs in tiny shorts and ogle the beefy guys pumping iron. And for the sauna. And the blowjobs.

He liked first-world comforts: technology, comfy beds, and hot men waiting for him in them.

Halfway through the CIA's training course, he'd parachuted out of a plane and eaten worms for three days while trying to evade his trainers, career military officers, who had spent their entire lives hunting people.

He'd been captured in a swamp, hiding in the reeds. His trainers had hauled him back to The Farm for the next round of instruction: how to withstand an interrogation.

Kris had thought he'd be the first one captured.

He was the second to last.

During weapons training, he was the only one out of his class of twenty who had never fired a weapon before. Aghast, the instructors had begrudgingly started at the beginning of firearms training, all nineteen others, former military officers and federal agents, plodding along beside him as he fumbled through how to hold his weapon, load an empty clip, pull the slide back, dry fire.

Eyes slid sideways, staring at him in the cafeteria. The military guys stuck together, as did the LEOs, the law enforcement officers switching over to intelligence, in their own tight-knit fraternities.

There was no room for a twenty-one-year-old scrawny brown boy just barely graduated from college. Especially a twenty-one-year-old with a shell choker, distressed jeans, and tight t-shirts. He kept to himself, and the others seemed to prefer it that way.

The bulk of their training had been in the classroom, followed by the real world. CIA officers, for the most part, spent their time working to recruit foreign nationals to spill their secrets, betray their own governments. Give information to the CIA. That process was purely personal. Psychological.

Who was a good target to recruit? Were they vulnerable in any way? Reliable? How could they be approached? What aspects of their life could be exploited, for good or for ill, to develop the person into a source, an agent of the CIA? Were they, ultimately, friend or foe?

Kris had spent his whole life observing people—men in particular—and the exercises on targeting individuals, psychological analysis, the role-play of approach and ingratiation, were child's play to him. The military officers were too domineering, the former LEOs too interrogative, but he successfully recruited the assigned source each and every time.

He had excelled at his surveillance detection routes. Walking home from bars alone and being a single gay man in a metropolitan city—

Well, he'd learned how to watch his back long ago. It had been second nature to run the surveillance detection routes, the more complex the better, and pick out any tails following him. One of the military officers missed three of his tails on his final exam and was sent home that same day.

Kris didn't have to ever come out because he was never in. Everyone assumed, at first glance, what he was, and that was just the simplest for everyone. He heard a few comments, ignored the muttered curses. Gritted his teeth whenever "*fag*" was tossed around, a cultural synonym for *idiot* or *weak*.

It made him work harder, prove them wrong. He'd proven everyone wrong so far. He'd keep going. He'd never stop.

He excelled in most areas, passed in others. He'd have made a good case officer, going overseas to an embassy and pretending to be a low-level State Department official while trying to flip sources and foreign nationals. Maybe they would send him to Bahrain, he'd thought. Or Lebanon. Or Syria. He could work both sides of Sunni-Shia divide, target Iranian agents operating in Hezbollah and Syria as well as Hamas and Sunni extremists in Lebanon. He knew the culture, how to move around. He even knew how to find the right man in Beirut, or in Damascus. In Cairo, too.

He'd dreamed of adventure, of living overseas. Of making a difference.

Graduation day, Kris got his assignment: Alec Station, CIA Headquarters. Counterterrorism Analyst for Afghanistan, attached to the al-Qaeda team.

No adventure for him.

For years, Alec Station had long been the dead end for analysts, officers, and operators, especially those who fostered what the CIA's seventh floor, the executives, thought was an "obsession" with Islamic-based extremist ideology.

But in 1998, the United States embassies in Nairobi, Kenya, and Dar es Salaam, Tanzania, were attacked, devastated by twin suicide truck bombings. Al-Qaeda claimed responsibility. After those bombings, Alec Station became the hottest outfit in the CIA.

And they needed bodies. Officers fluent in Arabic in particular, with a good grasp of the culture, an eagerness to learn, and the ability to get up to speed with years and years of intelligence in a hurry.

Kris reported to Alec Station in 1999. He was assigned to Afghanistan, the only analyst in the entire unit.

In 2000, al-Qaeda bombed the *USS Cole* in Yemen.

---

After American Airlines Flight 77 plowed into the Pentagon, CIA police herded everyone out of headquarters.

The parking lots were crammed. Trucks led sedans over grass embankments and fields to side exits, pushing open gates that had long been chained shut. Kris inched forward in his clunker sedan, the best he could afford as a recent college graduate. To his left and right, drivers listened to their radios in horror, jaws slack, eyes vacant.

He got as far as the George Washington Parkway before traffic ground to a halt and refused to move. Smoke from the Pentagon rose ahead, billowing black rising and rising into the perfect blue sky. His stomach twisted, yanked, knotting until he had to throw open his car door and puke on the highway.

*It's a crematorium. Just like New York. It's all a fucking crematorium.*

The first to turn around was a truck, one of the lifted ones all the former Army Special Forces operators seemed to drive. Tires screeching, it bounced over the center embankment and forged a path over the tree-filled median to the highway going back to CIA headquarters. Another truck followed. Then a car.

Kris pulled his rusted sedan out of traffic and followed them.

---

Hundreds of officers poured back into Langley.

Names of potential suspects from CIA stations around the world flooded in, computers whirring and phones ringing off the hook. Names of people on watch lists, names passed along by foreign intelligence agencies, friendly and not-so-friendly alike. Names from each of the four flights, passengers and crew. Somewhere in those names were the hijackers, the murderers. They searched, poring through the lists.

Every cell in Kris's body fissured, fracturing and dissolving into a billion tiny pieces as he read the names off the flight manifests. The universe came to screeching halt as he came to two distinct names, halfway down the list:

*Nawaf al-Hazmi* and *Khalid al-Mihdhar.*

He felt like a marionette, a puppet with loose strings being manipulated by someone else. Someone else made him stand. Had him grab the printed pages with shaking hands. Something else made his feet move, carrying him to his boss's office.

His section chief sat at his desk with his head in his hands. The handset of his phone lay on the desktop. A circle of wetness smudged the desk beneath where he hung his head.

"Sir?" Kris barely breathed. "The hijackers... We know who they are."

His boss looked up.

Devastation poured off him, waves of anguish. Tears ran like rivers down his splotchy face, falling from red-rimmed eyes. "Al-Hazmi and al-Mihdhar."

Kris nodded, as if his head wasn't attached to his body. "Probably others with them," he whispered. "Sir, we have files on these guys. We were watching them. The FBI, they asked—"

His boss held up his hand. He squeezed his eyes shut, but that didn't stop the sob rising through him from breaking, cresting against the cold hard facts. His shoulders trembled, teeth clenched so hard

Kris heard them squeak and grind. A cry broke out of him, the sound of a soul shattering.

Grief wrenched into shame inside Kris. The weight of thousands of dead Americans pressed down on him, every one of their lives ended too soon. He couldn't breathe. He couldn't move. "Sir—"

"Get out, Caldera. Just get out."

---

Kris worked until he fell asleep in the middle of a name trace, trying to follow the rabbit back to its hole. Once every plane in the skies over the US was grounded, they were able to connect the dots that had been blazing constellations, if only they could have seen them from just a different angle. The monitors were fixed on the news, endless shots of the empty New York skyline, the burning Pentagon, the smoking crater in Pennsylvania.

Dan Wright, an analyst who worked a few desks down from him on Pakistani terrorism, woke him up with a cup of coffee. "You okay?"

"How can any of us be okay?" Kris scrubbed his hands over his face, pressed his fingers into his eyelids.

Dan sighed. He was a few years older than Kris and had entered the CIA in the mid-1990s. Ever since Kris had joined Alec Station, Dan had been his informal mentor. He'd just shown up one day, looking out for Kris. He'd never made a snide comment, or made fun of his paisley ascots. He'd been one of Kris's few friends, a constant at his side. Someone he could go to for a smile.

"People are saying we knew some of the hijackers?"

"I saw the reports myself." Vomit rose in Kris's throat. He closed his eyes. Tried to breathe.

Dan rested his hand on Kris's back. "I'm sorry."

Kris shook his head. His vision was blurring, tears he'd held back for over twenty-four hours building within him like his body was a dam. At some point, he'd burst. "We should have—"

Doors banging open cut off his words. Clint Williams, his boss's boss, stormed in, followed by a dozen officers and deputy directors. He scanned the room, scowling.

"*Caldera*?" he bellowed. "Kris Caldera?"

---

He was led to the basement, through twisting, winding corridors he'd never seen before. One-ton blast-proof doors slammed shut behind him and the dozen officers escorting him.

Williams brought him to a cavernous bunker that had been converted into a haphazard office. Long folding tables had been set up, lined with laptops, desktops, and printers. Cables fanned out in every direction, a spiderweb of internet and power cords. Fluorescent lights droned twenty feet overhead. Whiteboards had been wheeled in, scrawled with names and countries. *Bin Laden, Afghanistan, Pakistan, Sudan, Yemen. Mohammed Atef. Ayman al-Zawahiri*. Someone was trying to get a projector working. In the corners, men hunched over secured satellite phones, trying to hear through scratchy connections from across the planet.

Williams went from officer to officer, checking in, trading a few words here and there, passing papers back and forth. He was a storm, a whirlwind of action, somehow keeping everything straight. "Everyone!" he shouted. "Listen up!" The bunker quieted instantly. "This is Kris Caldera. He's the CTC analyst for Afghanistan. He knows the information you need!"

A hundred pairs of eyeballs rolled toward him.

"Use him! I want to know double what we know now by the end of the day, and double that by the next twelve hours, and double *that* by the next! Let's get to work!"

Seven people headed for him as soon as Williams left. "Caldera. What are the ramifications for the Northern Alliance following Massoud's assassination?"

"What are the Taliban's defense armaments? What is their status of forces?"

"How allied are the Taliban and al-Qaeda? Can the Taliban be persuaded to give up Bin Laden?"

"General Khan of the Northern Alliance has taken command following Massoud's assassination. What is your assessment of Khan?"

He couldn't breathe. *No one* had cared about Afghanistan before the attacks. He'd dived into Afghanistan intelligence, relishing the opportunity to examine a culture that had been isolated from the world, try to understand a people who had resisted being conquered for ages. Afghanistan was smaller than Texas. Twenty million Afghans spoke over thirty languages, were made up of dozens of tribal groups. The British, the Soviets, and even Alexander the Great had been humiliated in the Afghan highlands. Even the Taliban didn't control the entire country. The Northern Alliance, a festering association of fractious, infighting warlords, drug smugglers, and bitter rivals, fought the Taliban and each other for control of the country. The Afghan people were the ones who paid the price. They lived on less than a dollar a day and had the highest infant mortality rate in the world.

He'd been the Afghanistan nerd, teaching himself Dari, the Afghan form of Farsi, in order to read month-old newspapers flown in from Islamabad station and watch grainy videotapes the Taliban put out, preaching their firebrand fundamentalism and their blend of tribalism mixed with the most repressive interpretation of seventh-century Sharia law. He'd watched stonings in soccer stadiums, men and women get their hands and feet severed. Had seen pictures of ribbons ripped from cassette tapes, flying in the wind. Music was banned in Afghanistan, and all tapes had been stripped, their long black lengths fluttering at the borders, a signal to all who crossed into Afghanistan. *Here ye enter the seventh century. Here there be dragons.* Except they weren't dragons, they were men, and men were always far worse than any mythical monster.

The Taliban weren't religious scholars, and they weren't scions of Islamic learning and philosophy. They were men who had grown weary of the banditry and the robbery and the rape, the wild savagery and butchery that had seized Afghanistan after the Soviet withdrawal and the civil war. Mullah Omar, the Taliban leader, had rallied a group of villagers to enact revenge against a local warlord who had raped one of their village women. They'd hung him from the barrel of a tank. Their movement started as a means to bring order to the violent chaos of the country, and within two years, they controlled everything from Kabul to Kandahar, vigilante justice-seekers mixing Islam and tribalism that billowed into political control, control that was as repressive and violent as that which they sought to overthrow—just more organized.

*Everyone* ignored Afghanistan. Saudi Arabia and Pakistan sent their radicals there, offloading them from their own countries. The CIA and the State Department seemed happy to forget about Afghanistan as long as it was stable and the Russians were gone. Who cared about the world's backwater, anyway?

Sometimes, late at night, he thought the Afghanistan desk was a subtle snub. He still wasn't allowed in the big leagues, apparently. Was it because he was gay? Because he wore tighter pants and spiked his hair instead of buzzing it like the other guys? Because he didn't fit in with their fleece pullovers and their cargo pants and their ball caps?

But now, everyone wanted him, was trying to pull him in every different direction. If only he could cut himself into parts and pieces. Everything he knew, everything he'd ever learned, was rising inside him. He'd gladly saw open his brain, let everyone flick through his memories like files, parse information out of the nooks and crannies of his gray matter.

"Caldera, we don't have current functional maps of Afghanistan. What we do have is stolen from the Soviets back in the Cold War, or from Pakistan and their ISI. Everything is incomplete. Can you fill in the gaps for us?"

He squared his shoulders. "What day is it? What day is today?"

Someone blinked at him. "September thirteenth."

He hadn't been home in two days. He'd been sleeping under his desk, drinking coffee and eating whatever Dan brought him. "Okay." He breathed out slowly. "Okay."

He started talking, running through the recent history of the Northern Alliance, the loose, nefarious conglomeration of fighters arrayed against the Taliban. The CIA had given the Northern Alliance inconsistent support, helping them one week and pulling back the next. The Northern Alliance forces were arrayed across northern Afghanistan. The south was Taliban-controlled and heavily infiltrated by al-Qaeda.

He spoke for hours, until his voice was hoarse, moving from group to group, laptop to laptop. He translated Farsi, Arabic, and Dari documents, secured satellite calls between officers and Northern Alliance commanders, and processed incoming cables from Tajikistan and Uzbekistan. Williams appeared and disappeared, working the room, talking to the men in charge of the hive of activity.

Eventually, an officer in the operations side of the CIA led him to the far side of the bunker, to a darkened area where cots were set up with sleeping bags. People were hot racking, rolling in and out of shared cots as they needed. "Sleep," he was told. "Get some rest and refresh yourself. We all need you."

He was asleep before his head hit the cot. Nightmares plagued him: fireballs erupting in front of him, burning people alive, but he was trapped and he couldn't save them. Buildings collapsing, people leaping from the tops of skyscrapers that touched the stars, falling forever as he screamed and screamed.

---

Williams shook him awake. "Get up. We're going to see the president."

He stumbled out of the cot, almost falling on his face. Someone loaned him a fleece pullover with the CIA crest. He ditched his button-down and slid into it. The arms were too long, but it covered his unwashed stench, mostly. He shaved quickly and splashed water on his face, gargled some mouthwash, and met Williams at the east entrance.

A full motorcade waited for them.

"We're going to the White House with the director. He's in the next SUV."

"Geoff Thatcher? CIA Director?"

"Yes. The president wants to know everything about Afghanistan. Thatcher said to bring the experts. That's you." Williams shifted, the dark leather seat creaking as the motorcade pulled away from Langley. "Kris, the president is getting ready to make a decision. We're going to respond to these attacks, and we're going to respond quickly. The CIA is going to do something we haven't done since we were OSS, back in World War II. We're going to go to war, and we're going to lead this war. This is the last briefing before the president decides exactly what our response is going to be."

Kris sat, speechless. He wasn't ready for this. He wasn't a presidential briefer. He was just an analyst. A *junior* CIA officer.

But who was ever ready for their world to be upended, for planes to fall out of the sky, for buildings to tumble like blocks, and for the weight of thousands of lives to hang around their neck? Failure tasted like ash, like flame, like dust that filled his teeth and gathered at the junctures of his bones. Shame was his shadow.

He took a breath. "What do you need me to do, sir?"

"The president is a talker. He thinks with his words. Goes with his gut. Thatcher is good at talking him through things, thinking out loud. With this president, the last in-person briefing will usually be the deciding factor. He's going to be listening to what you say, to any answers you give, very, *very* closely."

"Who else will be there?"

"The vice president and the national security advisor."

Kris nodded. His mind whirled. It didn't get any higher than that.

"Listen, the national security advisor and Thatcher don't get along. She's a tough nut to crack. She and Thatcher are like oil and vinegar. The VP thinks he's the smartest guy in the room. He'll go behind all our backs and double-check, triple-check everything we say. Don't worry about talking to any of them. Speak directly to the president."

---

He could smell himself as they clambered out of the SUV at the secured entrance to the West Wing of the White House. Secret Service agents hustled them inside quickly, past a massive show of defensive force. Agents with snarling dogs, rifles, and heavy weaponry were on full display, ready to destroy any intruder who dared bend a blade of grass on the White House lawns.

Kris tried to keep his arms down to hide his unwashed stench. He couldn't do anything about the bags under his eyes, but hopefully the president wouldn't remember him as 'the smelly one'. He hadn't been home in three days.

In the Oval Office, the president and vice president sat side by side in the spindly armchairs before the fireplace, with the national security advisor on the sofa next to the president. They stood, shook hands tersely, and beckoned Thatcher, Williams, and Kris to sit on the other sofa.

"Break it down for us," the president said, lacing his fingers together. His Texan drawl was deep, a sign of his stress. "What do we have today?"

Director Thatcher spoke urgently, summarizing everything the CIA had learned in the last twelve hours. He'd been briefing the president three times a day or more since the attacks. Everything he shared, Kris had been a part of, working with the response team in the basement.

While Thatcher spoke, the vice president stared at Kris, watching him closely. Kris stared back.

The president pursed his lips as he frowned. "Musharraf in Pakistan has come around. He's decided the Taliban aren't worth committing political suicide over."

"Good. We'll need their full cooperation. Border posts and frontier bases along the border with Afghanistan opened up to American forces, a rescinding of all 'no-go' areas in Pakistan, unrestricted access to Pakistani airspace and full, unimpeded landing rights at all air bases and airports." Thatcher scrawled notes as he spoke.

"State is working on it." The national security advisor's voice was clipped, perfunctory.

The president's gaze flicked to Kris. "Director Thatcher says you're the agency's number one Afghanistan analyst. That you know that country better than anyone. Tell me. Do you think the Taliban will give up Bin Laden?"

Everyone looked at him. *Everyone.*

The president had issued an ultimatum to the Taliban the day of the attacks: give up Bin Laden, or your government will be destroyed.

Bin Laden had been granted refuge in Afghanistan since his exile from Sudan. As the president had said, as smoke still rose from Lower Manhattan and the Pentagon, any nation that harbored the terrorists would be treated as an enemy of the United States. *"You're either with us or against us."*

What Kris said next would shape policy. Shape the world. The unit secretary at CTC still couldn't remember his name, even after two years working there. He was *that* inconsequential. The security guards hated his guts. Yet here he was, briefing the president. Deciding the course of history. His palms slicked with sweat. Ice flowed down his spine.

"Mr. President, the Taliban will never surrender Bin Laden."

"Why?" The national security advisor frowned. "If they want to survive, they have to give him up."

"It's not the *Pashtunwali* way." Everyone frowned. "The Taliban blend tribal traditions and fundamentalist Islam into their repressive form of totalitarian rule. It has less to do with Islam and more to do with tribalism. *Pashtunwali* is their ethical code. It's so ancient, the tribes view Islam as a modern add-on to their worldview. That part of the world has operated on *Pashtunwali* for millennia. Specifically, *melmastia*, hospitality and protection of all guests, *nanawatai*, the right of a fugitive to seek refuge within the tribe, and, *badal*, blood feuds and revenge."

"Shit," the vice president grumbled. "So he's going to hide under Taliban skirts and claim tribal law?"

"The Taliban and al-Qaeda aren't friends. Mullah Omar repeatedly ordered him to stop antagonizing the US. To stop giving interviews and drawing attention to themselves, and to the other Arab jihadist training camps. When Bin Laden pledged his allegiance to Mullah Omar, he was trying to pave over Omar's complaints. Fix their relationship. But, right after his pledge, Bin Laden launched the embassy bombings in Africa. Mullah Omar was furious at him when the US attacked the training camps."

"Why didn't he kick Bin Laden out then?"

"Prince Turki of Saudi Arabia tried to convince Mullah Omar to hand him over, Muslim to Muslim. He flew to Afghanistan on a royal jet, big state visit. But Mullah Omar threw him out. He said he was sickened to see the prince of an Islamic state, and the guardian of the two holy cities of Islam, doing the bidding of the 'infidel West'. He accused the prince of being a *takfiri*, an apostate."

"Bet that went down well," the vice president grunted.

"Turki stomped on the feast Mullah Omar had spread for them and stormed out."

"So why not give him up this time? If he didn't want Bin Laden attacking the US, then why is he willing to die for him now?"

Kris swallowed, images from the attacks flashing in the darkness behind his eyes every time he blinked. Flame, smoke, and screams. Papers fluttering like rain, falling as if time had slowed. Ash blanketing the world. Bodies falling, jumping. He shook his head. "Bin Laden assassinated General Massoud on September 10. He sent two al-Qaeda bombers, posing as journalists, to his command center. They blew themselves up and decapitated the leadership of the Northern Alliance, and the one man who was a serious threat to Mullah Omar. Under *Pashtunwali*, Bin Laden paid Omar a blood debt, one the Taliban will be honor bound to return. They will never hand him over, Mr. President."

Silence. The president stared at him as if measuring his soul, taking the weight of his words. Finally, he nodded and sat back. "I don't want to give the Taliban any maneuvering room on the world stage. We're going to keep demanding they turn over Bin Laden. They're demanding proof he is responsible. What do we have that we can show the world?"

"Source reporting from Kandahar and Khost. Jubilation in the streets. Our intercepts before the attacks. We knew they were planning something. We just didn't—" Thatcher's voice croaked, choked, and died. He looked down. "Whatever we show as proof will be exposed, Mr. President. We cannot burn sources and methods at this time. Not right before a war."

Kris jumped in. "There's Yemen."

"Yemen?" The vice president frowned.

"The *USS Cole* bombings. The FBI is running a fusion cell in-country, working on prosecuting the attackers in Yemeni courts. They have an al-Qaeda operative there, someone who used to be Bin Laden's bodyguard, in jail. We could question him."

The president nodded. "Get on it. I want confirmation for the world that Bin Laden was behind these attacks. Something we can show off."

"Everything comes down to our response," the vice president said. "*Everything*. We have to find these terrorists and we have to stop them. Wherever they are. By whatever means possible."

"Geoff," the president said, turning to the CIA director. "I want the CIA to be the first on the ground. As soon as possible."

"Mr. President, we're on our way."

---

They hurried to the motorcade waiting outside the West Wing. Thatcher huddled with Williams as Kris followed, herded by hulking Secret Service agents.

Williams turned to Kris. "Great job. Take the last SUV back to your place and pack a bag. You're going to Yemen. You leave in three hours."

# 2

## Sana'a, Yemen - September 14, 2001

Kris sweated in the backseat of a creaking Yemeni government SUV, roaring through the capital, Sana'a. At one in the morning, the streets were deserted. Dust clung to Kris's hair, scratched his eyes, filled his nose. Even in the middle of the night, the heat tasted like the air was burning.

Since September 11, all Americans in Yemen moved at night, under the glowering auspices of the Yemeni national police.

Clint Williams had arranged for a private CIA jet to fly him directly to Yemen. He was the only passenger. He'd spent the fifteen-hour flight reading everything the FBI had on the incarcerated al-Qaeda terrorist.

Abu Tadmir was the former bodyguard of Bin Laden and the *emir*, the leader, of one of the guesthouses for Arab fighters traveling to Afghanistan to join with al-Qaeda. His guesthouse was connected to the advanced tactics training camp where the hijackers had most likely received specialized instruction.

On the flight, Kris received a cable from Langley. It had been confirmed: one of the hijackers had stayed at Tadmir's guesthouse. In fact, the hijacker was called "a friend" of the *emir*. They'd spent Ramadan together in 1999. They were close.

Finally, the SUV pulled up at the Yemeni federal detention facility. Two Americans in cargo pants, fleece vests, and ball caps waited inside the gates. Gold badges hung on chains around their necks.

"FBI," his Yemeni driver grunted. He didn't sound thrilled to see the agents.

Both FBI agents stared Kris down through the dusty windshield. They didn't say hello as he climbed out of the SUV or came to their side.

Kris hitched his duffel higher on his shoulder. "I'm here to see Abu Tadmir."

Nothing. It was like the FBI agents were statues.

One agent glared, his eyes narrowing to slits. "You CIA guys have anything you want to pass along? You know, anything you haven't shared that might save lives?"

The man's words eviscerated him, sliced him from belly to heart. Everything in him wanted to scream, to vomit, to rip his hair from his head. The names of the hijackers flashed in his mind, cartoon exclamations that followed his every footstep.

He forced his voice to remain steady. Forced steel into his spine when he just wanted to collapse and beg for forgiveness. "I am here on the orders of the president of the United States to get information from Abu Tadmir. I am here to do my job."

The FBI agents both snorted. "You guys really did a hell of a job already."

"I am here to help the president." Fireballs bloomed behind his eyelids. A scream hovered on the edge of his mind. "You can either help me or you can get the fuck out of my way."

The FBI agents shared a long look.

"The time for blame will come later," Kris whispered. And when it came, it would come for him.

"You're Goddamn right it will," one of the agents said.

They grudgingly led him into the prison, a dank square building of chipped concrete and cinder block. Sandstorms had blasted the dingy mustard paint to shreds, and dust-covered bare bulbs hummed behind rusted cages. Only every other bulb was lit. Down a long hallway, two Yemeni guards waited outside a door marred with black char marks and pocked with large dents.

Kris spoke to the FBI agents' backs. "I need to secure a confession that al-Qaeda is responsible for the attack."

"We already know they're responsible," one agent snapped as they stopped.

"The president needs this for the international coalition, and to pressure the Taliban."

"Anything else you CIA types think you can magically summon from Tadmir?" the second agent snorted.

"We need to know everything about the al-Qaeda camps in Afghanistan. Their armaments, their personnel. Capabilities, locations, numbers. Everything, for the invasion."

"We've had this guy for a year. We've been questioning him. Everything he's given us, we've sent back to Washington. He hasn't given up much, and, no offense, but I doubt *you* are going to be the one to crack him." The first agent looked him up and down, a cold glare etched on his face.

Kris bristled. Indignity pulled his shoulders back. "Things have changed since you captured him."

"The attacks? Yeah, they made most of the jihadis jubilant. Victorious. Hardened their resolve. You're not going to get anything."

"I'm going to try. You can participate or not. Observe or not. I don't fucking care. But I have my orders."

"Well, we'll go in after you're done. See if we can salvage the night." The agent shoved the door to the interrogation room open for Kris.

---

Abu Tadmir, whose *kunya*, or jihadist name, meant "father of destruction", strolled into the interrogation room in the company of two Yemeni prison guards. He was clean, his beard trimmed, and he was fat. Tadmir was obviously doing just fine. Yemeni prison agreed with him. He wasn't afraid.

The guards wore masks over their faces, hiding their identities, seemingly fearing Tadmir, or fearing him learning their identities.

Tadmir leached arrogance, power, intimidation. Kris had seen it all before, a world away.

Tadmir had been arrested by the Yemenis in a roundup of al-Qaeda suspects following the *USS Cole* bombing, at the behest of the FBI and the fusion cell working the case. He hadn't given up much in the year he'd been behind bars.

Tadmir pulled out the rickety metal chair on his side of the interrogation table and dropped into it, slouching. Kris stayed seated, silent. He let Tadmir stare and ignored the way he grinned, laughing, dismissive.

Kris pulled out a pack of cigarettes and offered it to Tadmir. Tadmir took one.

"*As-salaam-alaikum.*"

"*Wa alaikum as-salaam.*"

He flicked his lighter, igniting the end of Tadmir's cigarette. After, he lit his own and took a deep inhale. "My name is Kris. I am with the CIA." He spoke in Arabic, the words rolling off his tongue, clear and strong. Stronger than he felt.

Tadmir arched one eyebrow. "You speak God's language?" he asked in Arabic.

"*Nam.*" *Yes.*

"Yet you are an infidel?"

"*Nam.*"

"I will not speak to you in Allah's language." He switched to English. It was stilted, halting.

Kris followed him into English. "How are you? You look well."

Tadmir grinned. He puffed on his cigarette. "Very good. I am very good."

"I want to check. You are Abu Tadmir, al-Qaeda member and former bodyguard of Osama Bin Laden. *Emir* of the guesthouse, the House of Leaves, near Tarnak Farms?"

Tadmir smiled again. "I am Abu Tadmir." Pride shone in his eyes. "Of course I am he."

Over the past year, Tadmir had only confirmed, through questioning, all information the FBI had been able to gather about him from interrogations of other al-Qaeda operatives, captured al-Qaeda documents, and intercepted communications.

The file stated he admitted information he knew only after being called out in a lie, an arduous process of questioning, challenging, and then, finally, his admission. Back-and-forth, fact-based, closed questions had led to multiple dead ends when the intel the FBI knew simply dried up.

He had to try a different angle. "So, why join al-Qaeda? Why become a jihadi?"

"It is the duty of every Muslim to wage jihad. To fight for Islam. To defend Islam, when invaders and occupiers attack Muslims and take Muslim land. Islam also calls for the end of tyranny, as the Prophet—peace be upon him, all blessings and glory are his—showed in his example. We fight all oppression of Muslims. In Bosnia, in Chechnya, in Afghanistan against the Soviets, against Israel... and against you."

Tadmir's eyes gleamed. Kris filed that away as he took a drag of his cigarette. Tadmir enjoyed the spotlight. He enjoyed having an audience. "Where is the oppression?"

Tadmir threw his head back, laughing. Ash dropped from the end of his cigarette. "Where is the oppression? Oh, you are funny. You are a funny man. Muslim holy lands are under oppression. Occupied by filthy Saudi royals who are just puppets for your West. Infidels walk on the holy land of Arabia. Israel, and her Western supporters, attack Muslims every day." Tadmir switched to Arabic, seemingly not even noticing. "Throughout this century, Muslim lands have been invaded time and again. By soldiers. By the Soviet Union in Afghanistan, by Russia in Chechnya. Americans in the holy lands, fighting Saddam. We could have fought him! We did not need any infidels on our land! But that is what you do. You invade, everywhere. Western culture, Western ideas, Western innovations. We cannot look at the world and see anything but your invasion. This is why Bin Laden issued his fatwa. To liberate the oppressed."

"America also wants to liberate the oppressed. That's what we try to do. Did we not help Bin Laden expel the Soviets from Afghanistan?"

Abu Tadmir blew smoke into Kris's face.

Kris didn't wave it away. "We want to be a force for *good* in the world. To help the oppressed. Like it says in the Quran. *No man is free if one man is oppressed.*"

"You Americans want to be 'a force for good'. But all the world sees is *force*." Tadmir sat back, sucking his cigarette between two fingers. "Only Muslims can save other Muslims. Infidels cannot save Muslims. Besides, you are only interfering in Muslim revolutions. Leave us alone. We will make our own way in the world."

"How can we leave you alone if you declare war on us?"

"The war can end if you leave the holy lands of the Arabian Peninsula and submit to Islam."

"Americans are not all going to convert to Islam." Kris shook his head, smiling.

"Then the war will continue."

"How is this war, this jihad, fought? You kill anyone? Everyone?"

"No, no." Tadmir waved his hand, his cigarette wagging through the air. "There are rules to jihad. It must be declared. Bin Laden declared war upon the infidels. He told you how to settle the war. What to do to surrender."

"Yes, convert to Islam, leave Saudi Arabia."

"*Nam.*" Tadmir reached for a new cigarette. Kris had left the pack and the lighter in the center of the table.

Kris leaned back, crossing his legs. He took a drag, frowning. He wanted Tadmir to believe he was thinking hard about what he was saying. Let Tadmir believe he had the upper hand. "Okay, so tell me about tactics in jihad. Who can be targeted?"

"It is war. Jihad targets soldiers. Warriors. Governments. Those who are guilty."

"Like the embassies in Nairobi and Tanzania? American government buildings?"

"*Nam*."

"But there were women and children who died in that attack. Some of them were Muslims."

"Bombings and martyrdom operations are the weapons we are given in this great war. You have your missiles. We have our bombs. And, in all wars, there are casualties. Sacrifices must be made. Allah will accept these deaths as holy martyrs for the faith. He will reward them in Paradise. Any innocent Muslims will receive the rewards of jihad, as if they were martyring themselves. Their lives are given for the greater cause of jihad."

"I'm not sure they'd see it that way."

"They will be delighted in Paradise. What is the problem?"

"How many innocent lives is too many? When does what you're doing become murder?"

"Murder is not acceptable." Tadmir frowned, as if Kris had insulted him. "I am not a murderer. Casualties happen in war. But murder, taking innocent lives? That is forbidden."

Kris blinked. He flicked ash on the table. "Tell me about your friends. Your fellow al-Qaeda fighters. I want to know them. Understand them, like you're explaining yourself to me."

Tadmir smiled wide. "You see, I will show you the truth. You will believe."

Kris smiled back. He pulled a binder out of his bag and opened it up. Pages of pictures, headshots taken from passports and driver's licenses and ID cards around the world, appeared. "Your friends in al-Qaeda. These are their pictures."

Tadmir looked over the first page. He frowned. "No, I do not know these people."

"Yes, you do."

"Okay, maybe him." Tadmir pointed to one of the senior commanders, a man he'd already admitted to knowing in the FBI's files. "I recognize his face. But I do not know his name."

"Are you certain?"

Tadmir looked up, over the pictures. His eyes glittered. "Of course I am certain."

"Four months ago, you told my friend that this man is Abu Hafs, Bin Laden's trusted military advisor. Now you lie to my face? How can I trust you?" Kris laid it on thick, shaking his head and leaning back. Image was important, deeply important, to Arabic cultures and to Muslims. Honor and one's word were often all an individual had. Being called out as a liar was a stinging insult that left a deep cut of shame.

He'd use that. He'd use that all day long.

"Okay, I am sorry." Tadmir ducked his head, his cheeks flushing. "You are right. I do know that man."

"You are only admitting to things you think I already know. Abu Tadmir, I know *everything*. You have no idea which of your friends I have spoken to, who I have already arrested. Do you think I came to talk to you, all the way from America, because I know nothing? I want to trust you, but you make it difficult. How can I respect you when you lie to my face?"

"Okay, okay. Let me see the book again." Tadmir pulled the book close, studying picture after picture, shaking his head.

Kris waited, forcing himself to breathe slowly as Tadmir lit another cigarette. Ash filled his nose, his mouth. Echoes of shrieks hung in the silence, clashing like cymbals in his brain.

Tadmir was about to turn the page, move on to the next, when Kris slapped his palm down on the tabletop. "You lie to me again!"

"What?"

"You claim you do not know *this* man!" Kris pointed to one of the pictures, a small passport photo of a half-smiling Arab near the bottom third of the sheet. The man had glasses and a goatee and looked like a computer programmer. "You truly expect me to believe you do not know Abu Mahraj? The man you spent Ramadan with in 1999? You broke your fast with him every day, sharing your dates and yogurt. And yet you lie to me?"

Tadmir flushed deeper. "Yes," he said slowly. "I do know him."

"He is your friend?"

"*Nam.*"

"You are both in al-Qaeda together?"

Kris stared into Tadmir's eyes. Abu Mahraj, whose real name was Marwan al-Shehhi, was the lead hijacker of United Airlines Flight 175. The names of the hijackers hadn't been released to the public yet. Tadmir had no idea.

"This man is also your friend." Kris pointed to another photo. An unsmiling, square-jawed Egyptian with cold, dark eyes.

"Awag al-Sayyid." Tadmir bobbed his head. "He was very serious. He was with Abu Mahraj, and they were friends. But I did not like that he never smiled."

The serious man with the cold eyes, the picture Kris touched, was Mohamed Atta, hijacker of American Airlines Flight 11, which had slammed into the North Tower of the World Trade Center at 8:46 AM, three days before. He wanted to recoil, shake his hand until the evil of Atta left him, shake him off like he could shake off a bad dream.

"When did you last speak with your friends?"

"After Ramadan, they were away training for some time. Training with the Sheikh."

"Training with Bin Laden?"

"*Nam.*" Tadmir seemed proud, and he smiled as he blew smoke toward Kris. "I was happy for Abu Mahraj. He seemed happy. We did not talk about it, though. He left Afghanistan, and I came to Yemen on my own mission for the Sheikh. But I was arrested, and I have not spoken to Abu Mahraj since then."

A year. He hadn't spoken to al-Shehhi in a year. But the training had happened before that, in 1999. Kris's heart pounded. His breath sped up. All he could smell, all he could taste, was ash and flame.

"Have you heard about what happened in New York City and Washington?"

Tadmir hesitated. "*Nam.*"

"Do you know that thousands and thousands of civilians died in those attacks?" The death toll was still rising. Maybe it wouldn't ever be known. Kris swallowed back vomit. It tasted like ash. He stubbed out his cigarette. The towers tumbled like blocks every time he blinked.

Tadmir took a long drag of his cigarette. He nodded. "You have only yourselves to blame for Muslim hatred. Your foreign policy, your occupation of Muslim lands, your support of Israel."

"So you support the attacks?"

Another long drag. "No. Those attacks were not allowed under jihad. No Shura council would authorize that. Those are a crime. Murder. Anyone who knows jihad knows they were not allowable. Civilians are not to be targeted." He frowned. "Clearly, this shows those attacks were the work of Israel and the Americans, framing Muslims."

Kris stopped breathing. "How so?"

"To justify the invasion of more Muslim land. Where will you invade next? If you try to take Afghanistan, the mujahedeen will rise and they will slaughter you like they slaughtered the Soviets."

"I *know* who committed the attacks." Kris's voice was calm, soft. Almost a whisper.

"Then why are you here? Go chase them! Why bother me?" Tadmir scoffed.

"I *am* chasing who committed the attacks."

"You are not! You are bothering me!" Tadmir waved his hand, as if trying to shoo Kris away.

"*You* committed the attacks."

"*What*?"

"Al-Qaeda is responsible for the deaths of thousands and thousands of people. Innocent lives. Civilians."

"No—"

"Al-Qaeda hijacked these planes."

"No—"

"Al-Qaeda *murdered* all those people."

"*No*!" Tadmir slammed both hands down on the table. Cigarette ash went flying. "What kind of Muslim would do such a thing? The Sheikh would not! He is not like you Americans!"

"I *know* that al-Qaeda committed these attacks. I *know* it."

Tadmir snarled, "How? What proof do you have?"

"I was told al-Qaeda did it."

"By who?"

"*You.*"

Silence.

Kris pulled a manila folder from his bag and laid out nineteen photos. He placed Marwan al-Shehhi and Mohamed Atta's photos right in front of Tadmir.

Tadmir's eyes were wide, so round and huge Kris could see whites all around his dark irises. His gaze flicked from the photos to Kris and back, lingering on al-Shehhi.

"These are the hijackers who murdered thousands." He tapped al-Shehhi's photo. "Your friend flew United Airlines 175 into the South Tower in Manhattan."

Tadmir's jaw dropped. All the oxygen seemed to disappear, sucked out of the tiny, drab interrogation room. Shock poured from Tadmir, and he stared down at al-Shehhi's photo as he shook his head, over and over, his mouth hanging open. "How... how is this possible?"

"You tell me. You're al-Qaeda."

"Not like this... Allah forgive me, not like this. This is not what I believe in. The Sheikh... he's gone crazy."

"These men, they are all al-Qaeda?"

"Yes, all of them. I recognize them all. They were at my guest-house near Tarnak Farms..." Tears welled in his eyes. One hand reached for al-Shehhi's photo, his quivering fingers touching the image as if he could touch al-Shehhi's face so gently. "Why?" he whispered.

Kris stayed silent. His heart raced, pounding out a bassline drum-beat in his mind, hard enough to crack his skull. Blood burned in his veins. Ash filled his nose, his eyes, his lungs, searing everything until he could taste the flames, the jet fuel dripping through the Twin Towers' superstructure, could feel the singe on his own soul. Across from him, Tadmir wept for the friend he'd lost, and Kris tasted the bitterness of failure and shame.

Ashes to ashes, dust to dust.

Tadmir wiped his eyes, blinking. "I am sorry," he said slowly. "This is not right. It is not what I believe. They were supposed to fight in Israel, in Chechnya. Against soldiers. Governments. Not this. So I will help you. What do you need from me?"

"Everything."

---

The FBI agents, who'd been watching the interrogation on closed-circuit TVs, joined him. Together they asked Tadmir for details about the hijackers, their time at the al-Qaeda training camps, their connections to Bin Laden.

Tadmir gave them everything.

He smoked the entire pack of cigarettes, and his eyes kept straying to al-Shehhi's photo. He shook his head, every time, and then launched into describing al-Qaeda's defenses and marked on the map where he knew the Taliban had entrenched their own defensive positions.

After twelve hours of listening to Tadmir spill his soul, Kris ducked out. His hands were shaking, his legs, his whole body. He held himself up, one hand on the wall, as he walked toward a dingy window. He had to call Washington.

Williams picked up on the third ring. The satellite connection was scratchy, as if Williams were more than just a world away. "*Kris, great job. Really great stuff. Thatcher and I are on the way to the White House to brief the president. Come home. Fly back to DC right away. We need you for what's coming next.*"

# 3

**CIA Headquarters, Langley Virginia - September 15, 2001**

"The people in this room will be leading the first wave into Afghanistan."

Kris glanced left and right. He and about twenty others had been pulled by Williams into a side room off the basement-level bunker. Everyone around him was huge. Huge physically, hulking muscles and ripped bodies. Huge in reputation. Career officers of the CIA, men who had their names etched in iron, who had stopped more terror attacks than years Kris had been alive. They were legends in the CIA, officers used as training examples at The Farm. Men who didn't breathe oxygen, who didn't pump blood through their bodies. They were made of far sterner stuff, iron patriotism and pure American grit. It was like looking at one of the world's first astronauts. Who were these men who did these things? How did humans accomplish these feats?

And then there was him.

He'd managed to go home and shower after his flight back from Yemen. Change into a fresh pair of khakis and a burgundy turtleneck and repair the bird's nest his hair had become. Next to all these legends of the CIA, he had spiked hair, a shell necklace over his turtleneck, and shined Oxfords.

They looked like lumberjacks from American fables come to life, and he looked like a Gap ad. A member of a boy band.

He could feel their stares burning into the side of his face.

"The military says they will need at least six months to plan and stage an invasion of Afghanistan. That's not good enough for the president. He wants a response to these attacks and he wants it now. The director has told him we're the men he needs." Williams said.

Murmurs rose, grunts and acknowledgments from the room.

"Your mission is to insert into northern Afghanistan and link up with the Northern Alliance, the fighters aligned against the Taliban. You will convince them, any way how, to cooperate with us. You're also going to evaluate the Northern Alliance. Figure out what they need to become an effective fighting force on the ground, and an ally we can use when we invade."

"Will they cooperate, sir?" Ryan, a burly man with blond hair and a permanent scowl, spoke up. He was with the SAD, one of the clandestine super-secret soldiers of the CIA. The true James Bonds Kris had once dreamed of.

Williams turned to Kris, his eyebrows raised.

Kris chewed air for two seconds. He spun toward the rest of the room, his chair squeaking. "The Shura Nazar, which is the Northern Alliance's preferred name, has been trying to secure Western cooperation and assistance for years. The Taliban has pushed them back all the way into the Panjshir Valley, and if they keep pushing, the entire Shura Nazar will be wiped out or will starve to death. The Taliban will control the entire country. The Shura Nazar is the only military force in Afghanistan that is capable of taking on the Taliban."

"And, as Caldera briefed the president, the only way to get to Bin Laden is to destroy the Taliban." Williams nodded at Kris. A few eyebrows rose around the table.

"But this Shura Nazar has been pushed back by the Taliban. How are they any use to us if they're the losers?" Ryan asked.

"This is what the CIA does. We arm and train insurgencies. We topple governments," Williams said. "Normally, we do it in secret. This time, the whole world knows we're coming. And we're going to take out the Taliban, followed by Bin Laden. You will link up with the Shura Nazar and find out what they need to get the job done. Bullets, cash, food, bombs. Whatever it takes."

Nods around the room. Kris swallowed slowly. How was he supposed to fit in on the first wave of a war?

Williams kept speaking. Kris watched the men around him, saw their jaws tighten, their brows furrow. "The CIA hasn't fought in a frontline war since World War II. But this time, we're taking charge. You will be linking up with a small detachment of Special Forces soldiers on your way to Afghanistan. It's the most the military could spare so quickly. They will help navigate and prepare the battlefield for CENTCOM. You will be sharing everything in your mission. Everything."

More nods all around.

"And there's one last thing I want to make clear. There is a strong possibility that not everyone is going to make it back."

Silence.

"Not everyone is this room may come home. Maybe a third of you will pay the ultimate price. But we have to do everything we can do to bring these terrorists to justice. We owe that to the thousands of our people who were murdered four days ago. We have to act, for them.

"I want to go around the room, and I want everyone to speak their name. I want us all to acknowledge each other and what we're about to undertake. We will remember this moment when we're mourning our losses in the days and weeks to come."

Around they went, men grunting their names, their teams, their positions.

"George Haugen. Deputy Chief of Southeast Asia Operations. I'm leading the team going in. I speak Russian and Farsi." George was older, but obviously fit, built like an ox. His record in the agency was legendary. Kris could barely believe they were sitting at the same table. George was a former Army Special Forces officer and fifteen-year veteran of the CIA. Kris had learned about his counterterrorism operations in Greece and the Balkans, and his deployment with the CIA in the Bosnian wars, when he was at The Farm.

"Ryan Lawson. Deputy Chief of Special Activities Division. I'm deputy on the insertion team. I speak Russian and some Arabic."

"Phillip Nguyen. Communications. I'll do everything I can to keep us linked with HQ." Phillip looked like a linebacker merged with a wrestler, with a barrel chest and a shaved head, and wireless glasses perched on the end of his nose.

"Derek Bronicki." Derek had the sandy-haired good looks of a California surfer, and the laid-back attitude to go with it, even in this meeting. "I'm your pilot. We're taking a Russian-made helo over the Hindu Kush, higher than any helo has ever flown before. I'll try and make sure we don't die."

"Jim Lutjens." Tall and lanky, Jim looked like a basketball player, and had a deep baritone, as if he spoke through a long tube. He'd put Kris to bed in the cot a couple of days before. "Operations. I speak Russian."

Kris had no idea what to say for himself.

"Kris Caldera," he finally said, his voice a little breathless. "Afghanistan analyst and linguist. I speak Farsi, Dari, Arabic, and I can get by in Russian."

More eyebrows rose.

"Kris knows Afghanistan better than anyone in the agency. He speaks the languages we'll need in theater," Williams jumped in. "He's going to be your analyst and political affairs officer in-country."

Kris blanched.

"No medic?" Ryan frowned.

"Your medics will come from the Special Forces team. They're sending six men, half an operational detachment. One team medic, and the rest of the soldiers have full combat medic training as well."

Ryan and George shared a long look. George nodded once.

"Let's go through the operational plan."

Williams outlined the operation, codenamed Jawbreaker, that would pave the way for the invasion of Afghanistan. Separate teams of joint Special Forces and CIA would deploy into different regions of

Afghanistan, Kris's team being the very first. Once in Afghanistan, they would link up with Shura Nazar field commanders and convince them to cooperate with the United States.

Everyone going was former military, former Special Forces or Delta Force or Navy SEALs. They had all seen combat and had all spent time in third-world countries. They all had experience with covert combat operations.

Except for Kris.

"There will be nothing there. No footprint. You're first in. You will be creating that footprint." Williams didn't pull his punches. "You will be setting up joint intelligence collections with the Northern Alliance, or, the Shura Nazar." Williams nodded to Kris. "Everything you get comes back home and goes straight to CENTCOM. We want everything. Status of forces, Taliban defensive positions, numbers of foreign fighters. Most importantly, any and all intelligence you receive about the location and whereabouts of Bin Laden.

"You will work with the Shura Nazar to strengthen their front lines. Manage air operations to obliterate Taliban and al-Qaeda forces that engage you. You will be defining the battlefield for everything that follows.

"Here's what we're seeing so far. Satellite imagery shows the Taliban are digging in for a long fight. They're digging trenches and they're hoping for an early winter. If the snows start falling, we could be looking at trench warfare, the likes of which we only saw in World War I. Hundreds of foreign fighters a day are flowing across the borders of Pakistan into Afghanistan. They want to fight you.

"Afghanistan is one of the world's most difficult places to reach by air. Our bombers will be flying sixteen hours from the United States, one way, to drop their ordnance. We've got fighter jets based in the Gulf, but they'll be flying up to six hours to get to you for air support. In the Gulf War, we flew almost four hundred sorties a day. Here, you'll be lucky to get thirty, until we have the ability for air assets in-country.

"George, you're taking command of the Panjshir Valley."

Everyone nodded.

"You will link up with your Special Forces team in Tashkent, Uzbekistan, in one week. You're first on the ground in Afghanistan twenty-four hours after that. Following your insertion, if you're not all killed, we're debating sending in another team to link with General Hajimullah outside Mazar-e-Sharif.

"We can't move in the south yet. Taliban positions are too entrenched. That's their stronghold. It's a Pashtun-controlled hellhole down there." Williams sighed and folded his hands on the conference table. He looked down, for a moment.

"Make no mistake, gentlemen. The Taliban, and al-Qaeda, will be ruthless. Anyone captured will most likely be tortured to death. The Taliban love to videotape their executions, so if you're captured, your death will be recorded and broadcast. As part of this deployment, we've authorized the distribution of L-pills. If you are captured, and you believe you are about to be murdered, you *will* have the option to end your own life."

Kris heard Williams speak, but everything seemed to float by him, words like bubbles warbling in the air. He couldn't process it all, not yet.

"We here at CTC will do everything to support you. Anything you need, we will provide. The president will be receiving twice daily briefings on your activities. We're all behind you, everyone. The entire nation. Good luck."

---

George commandeered Williams's seventh-floor conference room as team space. He called everyone together for the first meeting, dumping a box of donuts and a takeout carton of coffee in the center of the table.

Ryan interrupted him before the meeting began. "George, can I talk to you?" He jerked his head toward the corner.

Kris plucked at one of the laptops, reading through the intel cables sent in from Islamabad, Tashkent, Dushanbe, and elsewhere. Anything and everything the agency could gather on the Taliban and the Shura Nazar. He was coordinating with Tashkent station while they met with Shura Nazar representatives and tried to secure permission from General Khan to allow them into their stronghold in the Panjshir Valley.

He, and everyone else, could hear Ryan and George's conversation.

"Are you *sure* Caldera is right for this team?" Ryan crossed his arms, glancing over his shoulder. Kris pretended not to notice.

"Clint personally picked him for the mission." George sounded as enthusiastic about Kris as he would about going in for a root canal. "Clint says he's good. He's the best analyst on Afghanistan. He knows the political lay of the land, the culture. We need that to build this alliance. And he knows the languages."

Ryan scoffed. "He looks like a hundred and twenty pounds, soaking wet. He won't be able to handle the physical aspects of this mission."

George shrugged.

"How is he going to be received in Afghanistan? We're going to *Afghanistan*. The Taliban murders anyone they think might be gay. And we're bringing *him*?"

Kris felt everyone's gaze slide to him. No one said a word. Everyone pretended they couldn't hear Ryan and George.

"Look, we need the language skills. He speaks Farsi and Dari. The other Dari speakers, all three of them in the agency, are going operational with the next teams. We need them on the front lines."

"But—"

"Look, Ryan, we're building alliances. Laying the groundwork. We're staging. We're not fighting. Clint believes in him, says he is the guy we need for building this alliance. Everything else... Well, Caldera has to figure out how to hold his own over there. At least until we get the ball rolling. Then we can send him home if we need to."

Ryan sighed, long and loud.

Mortification singed Kris's soul, burning him from the inside out.

He couldn't see the laptop screen anymore. Letters moved around in a haze, a fuzzy disconnect from reality. There was a fire building, that same flame he'd fanned throughout high school, throughout college, when people had told him *no*. He thought he'd banked that, turned the coals over on top of the rage and the hurt and the years and years of everyone telling him he wouldn't measure up, he wasn't good enough.

"I graduated third in my class at The Farm." Kris's voice rang loud and clear through the conference room. He stared at George, and then at Ryan. "I did better than two Special Forces guys and three FBI agents." He shrugged, going back to his cables. "In case that was important."

Silence.

George cleared his throat. That was the end of his and Ryan's huddle in the corner. He headed for the whiteboard at the head of the conference table. "We've got a lot of work to do and five days to do it in. What do we need to get to Afghanistan, and, more importantly, what do we need to stay alive while we're there?"

Weapons. They needed as many weapons as they could get. Handguns for every member of the team, long guns, ammunition as if they were going to war.

Food. MREs, water purification kits. Iodine tablets.

Computers. Lots of them. Field-grade laptops in indestructible bulletproof suitcases. Portable satellite dishes. They needed to be able to connect to both the CIA's geosynchronous satellite network in high orbit and access the low-orbit network, the communications satellites that tracked across the sky, circling the globe every ninety minutes. In the mountains of Afghanistan, the low-orbit satellites would be almost useless, the signal cutting in and out. But they had to have a backup. They also needed to integrate into the military's web of communication and observational satellites. Somehow, between the three systems, they'd have communication capability with the world outside Afghanistan. Hopefully.

Derek announced he'd been reviewing the specs on the helo they were picking up in Tashkent. It needed servicing and an overhaul before it could make the flight into Afghanistan. They'd have to do that on the ground in Tashkent.

"We're still working on getting approval from the Shura Nazar so we can even enter Afghanistan under their official invitation. If we don't get their cooperation, it will be a lot harder to stage in-country. We need their cooperation." George circled *Shura Nazar* on the whiteboard three times. "Caldera—" He turned to Kris, sighing. "—that will be our job. Political affairs."

"So, Uzbekistan is playing ball with us, but do we have clearance to fly over Tajikistan airspace yet? It would be far better to insert directly over the border of Tajikistan into Shura Nazar territory." Derek hunched over maps of the Uzbekistan-Tajikistan-Afghanistan border region. "Flying south from Tashkent and crossing the Uzbekistan border puts us right over Taliban territory. We'd have to fly over Taliban-held land for hundreds of miles until we get to the mountains and the Panjshir Valley. The Taliban have antiair weapons, right?"

Kris nodded. "The US gave the mujahedeen in Afghanistan about four tons of Stinger antiair missiles when they were fighting the Soviets. They're still around, all over the country. The Taliban seized most of them, so we can expect to be facing our own weaponry when we engage."

"Great." Derek snorted. "US-made shoulder-fired rockets."

Jim tried to lighten the mood. "At least it's tech from the eighties."

"A Stinger antiair missile is a Stinger antiair missile. It will shoot you out of the sky just as dead today as ten years ago—"

"That's *enough*." George silenced Derek and Jim. Derek shook his head, crossing his arms as he leaned back in his chair. "The seventh floor—" The political power of the CIA. "—is working directly with the Uzbekistan government on allowing us access. Understandably, there is some resistance to the idea of allowing the US to use their nation as a launching pad for a CIA invasion force. If they keep stonewalling, the director will go to the president. Apparently, Russia has offered to twist some arms in their old Soviet enclaves for us."

"*Russia* is offering to help *us*?"

George stared at Derek. "The Twin Towers are still smoldering. The entire world knows we are coming. Knows we're going to react, violently. What countries are lining up to oppose us right now?"

Derek's lips thinned. He looked down.

"What are our living conditions going to be like?" Ryan chewed on the end of a pen. "Are we talking camping outdoors? Living in caves? Will we be in mud huts? Are we going to have local food or will we be eating MREs the entire time we're there? If so, how long until we can expect a supply drop? We can't bring MREs for three months for twelve men. What are our exact conditions going to be?"

"Right now, we have to assume we're planning for bare essentials. Everything we will need, we have to bring with us. Everything," George repeated.

Kris breathed out slowly, flexing his fingers.

"George, the weather is going to turn nasty very soon. The Taliban are hoping to bog us down in deep snows. Will we be staying in-country throughout the winter?" Ryan asked.

"If it comes to that, yes." George looked around the table, into each man's eyes. "We're going on this mission with no end date. Come winter, the road through the mountains will close, and any helo that tries to make the flight over the pass will ice up and fall out of the sky. So, we'd be wintering in Afghanistan. The military has promised they will air-drop supplies to us if and when we need them. The best estimates right now say that we will spend autumn and winter working up the Shura Nazar, and then there will be a spring offensive mounted against the Taliban. We're going to move heaven and earth to do better than that.

"But..." George frowned, his tone turning cautionary. "But we need to be ready for the worst. I got the seventh floor to authorize each of us two grand to buy personal supplies, and another four grand for the mission. When it comes in, we're going shopping."

---

Two days later, the money arrived. George tossed each member of the team a folded envelope stuffed with cash. "Time to get our gear."

They rode together, piling into George's SUV and heading to the nearest camping store. Kris sat squished between Jim and Derek, with Ryan riding shotgun and Phillip in the back. When they arrived, Phillip and Derek disappeared, scattering to the far corners. George, Ryan, and Jim huddled at the front of the store.

"Kris, come over here." Jim waved him into the group. "Let's get what we need together."

They started in the clothing section, picking out cargo and tactical pants. Heavy snow gear for the winter. Layered shirts and zip-over fleece vests, fleece pullovers, and thick waterproof winter jackets. Wool hats and gloves, and leather overgloves.

George, Ryan, and Jim grabbed the basic colors: black, blue, and white. Kris riffled through the racks, coming up with burgundy and forest green, cream and burnt umber turtlenecks and layers. When they reunited to head to footwear, George and Ryan gave his cart a long, long stare.

"Well, no one will confuse your clothes." Jim elbowed Kris, chuckling. "Leave it to you to be the fashionable one."

Kris pulled his lips into a smile. Bared his teeth. Inside, he was screaming.

At the boot section, he saw Ryan nudge George and whisper in his ear, pointing first to Kris and then to the women's boots. Some were knee high, somehow combining hiking and sex appeal. In a different time, different place, Kris would have bought them just to spite Ryan and George, and then worn them until they fell apart, rubbing their faces in their own joke.

Afghanistan seemed the wrong place to rub someone's face in a joke, though. He tried to ignore their snorts and plucked a pair of ridiculously expensive tactical all-weather boots from the wall. They were heinously ugly, but they promised to keep his feet dry and warm, even in a foot of snow.

Phillip and Derek came back with tents and camp stoves, entrenching tools, compasses, tarps, camp twine, emergency field kits, water backpacks, day packs, and external frame rucks for everyone. The large rucks were wider than Kris was and came up to his chest. Empty, they were hard for him to hold. He felt Ryan's eyes burning into him, felt the words hovering over his head: *Caldera can't make it. Look at him, he can't even lift the empty backpack.*

He'd practice that night, practice marching around his tiny apartment, if he had to. Anything to prove Ryan wrong.

---

Crates of weapons arrived, lining the hallways outside Williams's conference room.

Ryan popped them open as everyone watched. He passed out AK-47s and 9mm handguns, handing them one by one to each member of the team. "We're using AKs because they're everywhere in the third world, especially in Afghanistan. We can pick up ammo easier for the AKs, if we need it."

Ryan hesitated when he got to Kris. "Know how to use this?" He held out the rifle.

Kris snatched it, spun the weapon muzzle-down, checked and cleared the chamber, and then disassembled the rifle, breaking down the stock and the barrel and laying everything on top of the crate. He kept his eyes on Ryan's the whole time.

Ryan smirked and passed him his handgun.

Holsters and ammo pouches followed, along with cleaning kits. They would each have a web belt and a drop-thigh holster, and a chest sling for their rifles. The rest of the crates were filled with bullets.

GPS units arrived that afternoon, along with the high-frequency encrypted radios for secured communications between the team once they were on the ground.

"We need to get all this—" George gestured to the gear piling up in the conference room and up and down the hallways. Food, weapons, survival gear, computers, radios, and more. "—packed and ready for shipping out. Remember, we only have one helo to get into Afghanistan."

"And it's not a magic helo," Derek chimed in. "We have serious weight restrictions. Between twelve men and all this gear, we're going to be scraping the mountaintops as it is."

"Well, Kris is light." Jim winked at Kris. Everyone laughed.

Everyone but Kris.

They spent hours breaking everything down, repacking it into the smallest spaces possible. Kris worked with Phillip, repackaging the comms gear and the computers. They worked in silence while the rest of the team cracked jokes and laughed.

It was almost midnight when they quit. George pulled them all together again, gathering them around the messy conference table. "We have two more days until we leave. Tomorrow, we'll go over our mission step by step. The next day, we'll stage everything for our departure and finalize our travel arrangements." He sighed. "But tonight, and tomorrow morning, you all need to take some time to get your personal affairs in order. You're going to be gone for at least six months, with no way to take care of things back home. Make sure your finances are in order. Your bills are set up to be paid. And..." He swallowed. "Everyone update your wills. Bring them in when they're done. The CIA will hold on to them for you. You'll get them back when you come home." He nodded to them. "I'll see you tomorrow. Take the morning to get your lives ready for this."

---

Eleven in the morning, and George was already up to some kind of bullshit. Kris could feel it the moment he walked into their workspace.

"Kris, follow me."

Kris clutched his cup of coffee and followed George out of their crammed conference room. They wove through the halls stuffed with crates until they got to George's office. George beckoned him in and shut the door.

Kris had exactly zero patience for what he knew was coming. His stomach clenched, and he wanted to throw up the latte he'd been drinking, fling the remnants at George's face, topple his bookshelf and stomp on its files and folders. His fingernails scratched against his cardboard cup.

George wouldn't look him in the eye.

He hadn't gotten enough sleep for this bullshit. He'd cleaned his apartment until two in the morning, trying to put off George's homework. At three thirty, he'd finally sat down at his laptop and typed seven words: *Last Will & Testament of Kris Caldera.*

What the hell did he have to give away? He was twenty-three. He had four grand in his bank account and a shitty car he'd managed to save up for in his last year in college. He had a closet that would make any self-respecting gay man weep, and enough hair product to open a salon. He didn't have stocks or bonds, investments or a retirement account. He was just a kid.

But the CIA wanted his will, his last requests, and he was going off to someplace where, more than likely, what he typed would be the last anyone ever knew of him. Between their mission and the conditions on the ground, he would be lucky to survive. If it wasn't the war, or the Taliban, then it would be a land mine. Hundreds of thousands had been buried across the country throughout the years of the Soviet invasion. And if it wasn't the war, the Taliban, or a land mine, it would definitely be a traffic accident. Roads were a fantasy in Afghanistan. New vehicles hadn't been imported since the Soviets pulled out.

*Mamá*, he tried to write. His eyes blurred. *I wanted to do good. I wanted to make a difference.* God, how spectacularly he'd failed at that. How he'd failed, so indelibly, so enduringly. He would never be free of that failure. *I love you to the ends of the earth, Mamá. Thank you for loving me, and never trying to make me feel bad about myself.*

They'd never spoken about him, about how obviously homosexual he was, especially in high school. His papi had shouted at her, loud enough to shake the walls of their apartment, screaming that his son was a sissy faggot and a fairy who jerked off to other boys. But his mamá had never said a word. Silence was, in a way, acceptance. Silence, and the way she'd still made him empanadas on Saturdays and lechon on Sundays, and had still wanted him to kiss her goodbye in the morning before school, before she left to clean office buildings in Lower Manhattan.

She'd flown to Puerto Rico, leaving his papi when he was a freshman at George Washington. When they talked on the phone twice a year, she sounded happy. He never called his papi. There was no reason to. His memories of Papi stank like beer and too many cigarettes, and the soundtrack was always shouting. Drunk shouting, sober shouting, it didn't matter.

His happy memories were of his mamá, or of being a punk teenager in Manhattan in summertime. He'd had short shorts and a tank top, and his skinny arms had swung with as much attitude as he could put into them. How many summer days had he spent on the stoop with Mamá, listening to Spanish music and watching his old Dominican neighbor wash his ancient Plymouth with a hose? The neighborhood kids loved to splash and play in the runoff. Once, he'd been one of those little kids, stamping in puddles. In all of his memories, the Twin Towers stood like beacons, like fireworks, like screams that ripped backward and forward in time, reminders of his failure for the rest of his God-given days.

In his will, he left his mamá half his bank account, and gave instructions to donate the rest to the Washington DC LGBT Center, along with his car. Maybe it would be best if he did die. The LGBT center would be better off with two thousand dollars. Surely the world would be better off without him. Surely.

He'd been too wired to sleep, so he'd pulled on his sneakers and running shorts, grabbed a hoodie, and headed out. He lived in Falls Church, Virginia, a postage-stamp suburb south of DC. His apartment was between the Whole Foods and the Circuit City. Just after four in the morning, the town was silent, smothered in darkness and sleep, but DC shone like a beacon on the hill beyond the Potomac River. He could see the Washington Monument, see the lights from the Lincoln Memorial. The dome of the Capitol, just barely, or at least the glow.

He'd also seen the floodlights from the search and recovery operation at the Pentagon. He'd tasted the smoke, still lingering in the air, the atomization of the beating heart of American military force. Never before had there been an attack on the US homeland.

He'd run faster, trying to outrun his thoughts. Feet pounding on concrete just starting to turn dewy with the first blush of autumn. *Slap, slap, slap.* He'd thought he heard the sound of construction trucks, of heavy machinery moving at the Pentagon. They'd be moving rubble, clearing debris. Searching for remains. Every time a body was found, work came to a standstill, every person present standing and removing their hard hats, placing their hands over their hearts, and watching as the fallen was escorted to an ambulance to be carried to the morgue.

*Slap, slap, slap.* Faster, harder. He couldn't outrun the images, the scenes playing over and over in his mind. The attacks, planes disappearing into fireballs, screams, shouts of horror. American flags were draped from every streetlight, every traffic pole, banners that seemed to drip crimson-red blood all over the pavement before him. *You did this. You let this happen.*

Ashes and dust hung in the air, choking his mouth, his nose. He hadn't been able to breathe, suddenly, the air too thick, too cloying. He'd stopped, doubled over, gasping. His fingers had clawed at his throat, at his face, trying to clear the ash, the dust, rip away the ghosts that tried to strangle him. *Ashes to ashes, dust to dust.* Every breath he'd taken inhaled more of the dead. *You did this. You let us die.*

He'd puked in the parking lot of Walgreens and collapsed in the flower bed on the corner. He'd squashed yellow daisies and pink ground cover, but hadn't cared. When the sprinklers had turned on half an hour later, he'd finally gotten up and stumbled back to his apartment.

So, at eleven in the morning, he was in exactly no mood for George's bullshit. He stared George down, willing him to look him in the eye. *Be a man, George. Say this to my face.*

"Kris..." George cleared his throat. Put his hands on his hips. Stared at the wall beyond Kris's ear. "You know there have been some... concerns about you on this team."

Kris ran his tongue over his teeth, sucking his lips together. His jaw ached, his teeth gritted. Holding back. His coffee cup trembled, his hand, his arm shaking.

"There are concerns about how the Afghans will react to..." George waved his hand over Kris, a sweeping motion that reduced everything that he was down to one adjective: *gay*.

"So—" George cleared his throat. Finally looked Kris in the eye. "I need you to keep your head down once we're in theater. Do your job. Don't—" He seemed to stumble, fumbling for the right word. "Don't advertise." He sighed, closing his eyes and shaking his head. "Look, Kris, it's a matter of safety." He spread his hands, and a helpless look crossed his face. "We need to get this done. We can't be also worrying about how the Afghans are reacting to you. We can't be worrying about whether you're in danger, or if they're planning on taking you out. So, please. Tone it down?"

Kris's voice was cutting, ice sharpened to razors. "What *exactly* would you like me to tone down?"

"That. That attitude. Right there. You don't have to fight everything all the time. We're just trying to help you."

"I don't need your help, George. I am just as qualified as every other member of this team. What I need is a little more confidence in my abilities, which have absolutely nothing to do with my sexuality."

"You're not as experienced. Everyone has been in the field before except you. You're coming because of your specialized knowledge of the country and your language abilities. And because you haven't been in the field before, in a hostile environment, everyone else is going to have to watch out for you. Watch your back. Pick up your slack."

"There won't be any slack for you to pick up. Not from me." Kris's blood burned. His molars scraped over each other, his jaw twitching.

"We still have to watch out for you. Because..." George waved his hand again, up and down Kris's body. As if he couldn't say the word. "Just... don't make it obvious what you are."

"Is there something I've done in the past week that screams what I 'obviously' am?"

George stared at him. He stayed quiet.

Kris broke first, pulling out a sealed envelope from inside his jacket. He held it out.

"You quitting? This your resignation?"

"It's my will. The only way I'm off the team is if you get rid of me. So either bench me and deal with Clint Williams or take this and let me get back to work. I have to call Dushanbe station today and check in with my contact in the Shura Nazar. Negotiations have been tense this week. General Khan is supposed to tell us today if we're allowed into their territory in northern Afghanistan." He shook the envelope. "So, are you going to take this?"

George snatched it out of Kris's hand. "Let me know as soon as you hear from your contact in Dushanbe."

# 4

**September 19, 2001**

"Hop in." Jim popped the trunk as he slid his sedan into park at Kris's curb. "I can help you with that." He unbuckled his seat belt and got one foot out of the driver's door.

"I'm fine." Kris hefted his ruck. He'd done the best he could getting everything packed. He'd whittled out as much as he could, too. But how did someone pack for a warzone when he had no idea how long he'd be gone? One sweater or two? How cold was *Afghanistan* cold? Was the jar of peanut butter really necessary? After six weeks of MREs, would he murder someone for a spoonful of Nutella?

He dropped his ruck in the trunk next to Jim's. His was smaller, leaner. Less full. They both had sleeping bags strapped to the top and thin sleeping mats on the bottom, but Jim had obviously stuffed his pack almost to bursting. Kris wanted to run back up to his apartment and grab everything he'd dumped. Clearly, he hadn't packed enough. But if he stuffed it fuller, he wouldn't be able to lift it. And then what would George say?

Kris slammed the trunk and came around to the passenger side. Jim stared. "Ready?"

"Are you?"

Jim handed him a cup of coffee, then held his own out for a toast. "Here's to the last cup of Starbucks."

The rest of the drive to Langley was silent. Fog shrouded the city, heavy with dew in the early-morning hours. Jim's headlights got lost in the gloom. Kris watched the yellow beams fall apart in the gray haze. It looked like smoke, like he was in the center of a firestorm. His heart sped up, beats pounding. He smelled fire, tasted ash. Heard the screams again. Was this what so many people had seen that morning, their last vision of the world? Dust and ash, forever? *Ashes to ashes, dust to dust.*

He leaned back, resting the side of his head on the window, and counted the minutes until they arrived.

Jim badged into the front gate and drove out to the long-term parking structure. He poured a bottle of fuel stabilizer into his tank. "Hope this car is still here when I get back. God knows how long we'll be gone."

They grabbed their rucks, Kris's shoulders screaming, his back aching. He forced his expression neutral, hiding the pain, the way it felt like his spine was compressing down to a single inch. He didn't speak as they made their way across three parking lots of people just starting to arrive. The newcomers didn't seem to care about two men hiking toward headquarters, looking like they were going off to war. Then again, it was the CIA. Weird things happened every day. And everyone knew the CIA was on the move, mobilizing to respond to the attacks.

The rest of the team was waiting with their gear and the crates that had lined the hallways and conference room for days.

In minutes, the truck rumbling across the parking lot would ferry the gear and crates, and the bulk of the team, to Dover Air Force Base, where they'd fly out to Germany that afternoon. Kris and George were taking a later flight from Dulles, rendezvousing with everyone before transferring to Tashkent to meet the Special Forces team.

Reality was starting to set in. The team joked loudly, trying to bleed out the adrenaline, fill up the quiet spaces that hung over their heads.

Maybe they'd never return. Maybe they'd never set foot in Langley again. Kris caught Ryan eyeballing him, his dark eyes watching from beneath the brim of his ball cap.

"Let's load up!" Ryan slapped the side of the truck when it braked. Hot exhaust fumes poured over the team. They moved fast, hauling the heavy crates into the back. Their gear followed. Kris loaded his ruck, grunting to heft it the final foot. Ryan grabbed it from him with one hand and swung it the rest of the way.

When everything was loaded, Ryan, Phillip, Derek, and Jim hopped aboard.

"We'll see you in Germany." George shook Ryan's hand. "Safe travels."

The truck rumbled away. Kris tried to swallow.

An hour later, he and George countersigned for a release of $5 million. The money was packaged in twenty-dollar and hundred-dollar bills, all used. There were bundles of $10,000, and bundles of those to make $100,000. Everything was loaded into two black duffels. The CIA accountant glared at them both. "You both will be the signatories for this cash. Keep track of every expenditure. Get receipts."

Kris snorted. George smiled. He took one of the duffels and gave the second to Kris. They'd never be able to get receipts from the Shura Nazar. The concept didn't even exist in Afghanistan.

Their last stop before leaving was to see Clint Williams.

Even though Kris was the least experienced, he was indispensable to the mission. His connections with the Shura Nazar, his language abilities, his familiarity with the culture, the way he'd become the Afghanistan expert in the CIA—if there was anyone else, literally anyone else who could go instead of him, Kris knew George would take them instead. But Kris was the man who had what George, and the CIA, needed for this mission. Which, despite Ryan's Special Forces experience and the team's experience in the field and in hostile situations, made Kris almost the most valuable man.

He could feel George's resentment, burning like a heat wave crossing the desert, as they sat in Williams's office.

"Gentleman," Williams said. He folded his hands. "The president has asked me to give you your final orders. You already know you are to convince the Shura Nazar to work with the CIA and the United States military and to accept US forces into the Panjshir Valley. We *will* be utilizing their territory as a base of operations for our war against the Taliban and against Bin Laden. They need to be on our side."

Kris shifted. George leaned forward, nodding.

Moving high speed into Afghanistan, coming on full throttle with demands to the Shura Nazar would be just about the worst way they could possibly approach building an alliance. In a culture built on reputation, on saving face, the US would be perceived as an invader and an interloper. They had to have a softer touch. They had to become allies. Friends. They couldn't go off like a misfired firework, or the entire mission would blow up in their faces.

"There's one more thing you gentlemen need to take care of. The president has ordered your team to do anything and everything you can to find Osama Bin Laden, and his senior leadership, and to kill them."

Silence. Kris froze. Beside him, he saw George go still, his spine stiffening. Kill orders, in the history of the CIA, were rare. Far rarer than the public believed. Rare enough that Kris knew it was George's first. His first, too.

"Bin Laden can't be captured. He can't be tried here in the US. He sure as hell can't be tried in some Sharia court in a Muslim country. Any al-Qaeda leader would turn into a symbol, a rallying point for every terrorist who hates America. No, the president wants Bin Laden *dead*. And I want to ship Bin Laden's head to the president in a box of dry ice. I told him you could deliver."

George blinked. Kris's gaze slid sideways. *What now, fearless leader?*

"Have I made myself clear?"

"Yes, sir."

"Excellent." Williams stood, buttoning his suit jacket. He shook George's hand, then Kris's. "You men have your work cut out for you. You'd better get going."

George and Kris shared a long look as they walked out, hauling duffels filled with $5 million in cash and heading to the farthest spot on the planet.

## Tashkent, Uzbekistan - September 21, 2001

Tashkent was every third-world nightmare Kris had ever had, rolled into one depressing, festering city.

Abandoned Soviet factories lingered like scars on the cityscape. Desperately poor Uzbeks huddled on street corners, their faces lined with weariness and the ravages of decade-old Soviet occupation, war, and endless struggle. Heroin traffickers from Afghanistan flooded the streets with the cheapest grade of their drugs, and high Uzbeks lay in a stupor in ditches and on the side of the road. The rest of the heroin was refined and sent on to Russia.

Everyone was armed. Everyone carried Russian-made AK-47s over their shoulder, and RPGs and machine guns rested on the back of nearly every rusted-out pickup. From the airport, Kris, George and the team sped through the capital to the US Embassy in a blacked-out SUV.

The embassy's political officer met them, ushering them into empty quarters the Marines had vacated for their arrival.

The political officer and ambassador fed them, spreading out American-style burgers and french fries on a long table in the conference room. There, they got their up-to-the-moment briefing.

"We got word that the Shura Nazar officially invited your team into their territory this morning. We received a cable from Dushanbe station. The Shura Nazar diplomat there gave our embassy coordinates for your entry."

George smiled. "Fantastic." He turned to Kris and nodded.

Kris tried to smile back, but it was tight, his lips pressed to his teeth, almost painfully so. Guess that was the only recognition he was going to get for making the connections with the Shura Nazar and guiding Dushanbe station through their negotiations with a completely foreign and unknown potential ally.

What else was new?

Iranian forces were already on the ground. Their Ministry of Intelligence had sent operatives and officers into Afghanistan following September 11 and were already embedded with Shura Nazar units in the south and the west. "Iran, and the Shia government there, hate the Taliban. The Taliban murdered eleven Iranian diplomats when they seized the Iranian Embassy."

George scowled. "We really don't want anything to do with the Iranians."

"They're staying well away from the locations where your team is planning on inserting. But they sent this through the French Embassy this morning." The political officer spread out an Iranian-made map of Afghanistan with detailed notes of al-Qaeda and Taliban positions labeled throughout the southern region of the country.

"We'll have to check this out. Get eyes on. We can't launch without confirmation that these are actual Taliban and al-Qaeda locations."

"The Iranians told the French to tell us to 'keep it'. We wanted you to see it first."

"Forward it to CENTCOM. See if they can get satellite coverage over the targets. Get them on deck for when the bombing starts."

"The Uzbeks have reported that the Taliban MiG fighters are grounded. You don't have to worry about air-to-air intercept. Just surface-to-air."

"MiGs? Who was flying MiGs for the Taliban? They don't have that military capacity." Ryan frowned, his brow furrowing hard.

Kris leaned forward. "Russian mercenaries were flying for the Taliban for a hundred thousand dollars a day. The Taliban could buy that with their drug-and-oil money. But Moscow has told all mercenaries to get out, and get out now."

"Thought Moscow said they couldn't control their mercenaries? Hasn't that been their line for years?" The ambassador's eyes twinkled.

"Moscow says whatever they need to say, whenever they need to say it."

The ambassador snorted. "And your Special Forces team arrived yesterday. They're bunking at the airport. With the way the weather changes, they want to be ready to move at a moment's notice."

Flying over the Hindu Kush and into Afghanistan was fraught with danger under the best conditions. The mountains pushed most helicopters to their upper limits. The helos shuddered in the thin air, fighting physics and wanting to drop out of the sky. Fog and snow sometimes blinded out the passages, leaving the pilots flying in total whiteout conditions.

"Smart. What's the weather like?"

"Looks like there's a break in the cloud cover tomorrow. If all holds, you'll fly out then."

---

The international airport at Tashkent looked like a haphazard series of shipping containers stacked together. Once, it had been painted powder blue, probably by the Soviets, who had a thing for pastels. The flight line was cracked asphalt, weeds filling the divots and cratered holes, never to be repaired. Sinkholes marred the expanse, filled in with cheap tar and sand.

Decrepit MiGs from the days of the Soviet Union languished next to mothballed military helicopters. Nothing had flown in years.

Light spilled from the open doors of a squat hangar, its windows broken, where a team of Special Forces operators sat around a mountain of gear.

The political officer pulled up in front of the hangar. A Special Forces team member stepped forward, a giant of a man with fiery red hair and a thick beard. He waited as they all piled out. Frigid wind whipped through Kris, cutting through his fleece jacket as he stood on the busted tarmac.

"Captain Sean Palmer?" George strode ahead, hand outstretched.

"That's me, sir. Special Forces ODA 505, at your service." Palmer and his small operational detachment of six men would be reporting to George, putting themselves, for the duration of the mission, at his and the CIA's command.

George introduced his team, Captain Palmer shaking hands as they went around the circle. George turned to Kris last. "And, this is Kris Caldera. He's the agency's Afghanistan expert, my political affairs officer, and our linguist on the ground."

Palmer looked him up and down before holding out his hand. Kris was less than half his size. "Sir," was all Palmer said.

Kris nodded as they shook, gave Palmer a half smirk, and then shoved his hands in the pockets of his jacket. He tucked his face into his scarf.

Palmer brought them into the hangar, to the circle of men they'd be operating with. Some cleaned their rifles and handguns. Others joked around. One was reading.

"Everyone, our CIA people are here." Palmer introduced them, going from man to man—Jackson, Warrick, Rodriguez, Cobb—before finally coming to the last. "And this is Sergeant David Haddad, team medic."

Haddad nodded to Kris and held out his hand, stepping forward to meet him halfway. Kris shivered, but Haddad's hand was warm as they touched. Unlike the others, Haddad didn't hesitate, or raise his eyebrows, or give him the skeptical once-over. "*As-salaam-alaikum.*"

"*Wa alaikum as-salaam.*" Kris tried to smile. His lips were still buried in his scarf.

Palmer spoke, pulling Kris's attention from Haddad. "Gentleman, I'd like to get on the same page with you ASAP. Do you have time for a briefing?"

George nodded and beckoned Kris and Ryan to join him and Palmer at Palmer's small command post—a map and a laptop open next to a flashlight—while Jim, Derek, and Phillip stayed with the Special Forces team. Kris looked back once.

Haddad caught his gaze. He smiled, nodding to Kris before turning back to his book.

---

"*Kif h'alek*?"

Haddad turned away from his book, looking up at Kris. A ghost of a smile curved one corner of his mouth. "*Wa'enta, shen h'alek?*"

Kris smiled. "I thought I placed your Arabic accent. Libyan, yes?" He'd said hello to Haddad in the Libyan dialect, with the softer Bedouin phrasing and the Egyptian-Tunisian influences of the Maghrebi dialects.

"I grew up in Libya. My mother is American, though." His eyes drifted, just over Kris's shoulders, for a moment. "We moved when I was ten." He peered at Kris. "You? I can't place your Arabic."

"I'm Puerto Rican, actually. Not Middle Eastern."

"From the island?"

"No, the other Puerto Rico. New York."

Haddad chuckled. "I didn't think they spoke Arabic in Puerto Rico."

As curiosity about his age went, it was one of the nicer, and subtler, questions. At Langley, one of the range officers who'd signed off on Kris's weapons qualification before the mission had stared at him and outright asked, "Aren't you a little *young* for this op?"

"I studied languages in high school and college. I pick them up easily. I was fluent in Arabic in two years, familiar with most of the dialects in three. Farsi a year after that. I taught myself Dari after the agency hired me."

"You speak Spanish, too?"

"*Sí. Y tú*?"

Haddad grinned. "I'm just the team medic. It's a good thing I already knew Arabic. You can't teach this dog any new tricks."

Something curled through Kris's veins, a familiar warmth. "Oh,

I'm not sure about that." He winked, his flirty nature naturally rising—

Mortification drenched him, sliding down his bones and under his skin like hot oil. What was he *doing*? Flirting? With a soldier, a member of the Special Forces? On a mission? His face burned, and he looked away, squinting at the open doors of the hangar and the flight line. Would the ground open up beneath him, please?

God, had George seen that? After his ridiculous spiel to Kris about keeping himself *contained* and to *not advertise*? There he was, flirting with the first hot soldier who gave him the time of day. Proving George's bullshit. *Fuck.*

Haddad reached for Kris's ruck, lying nearby. Their gear had been brought to the airport and dropped off, ready and waiting for the final flight into Afghanistan. Haddad dragged the ruck between them. "I added more gear you'll need."

Kris crouched, hiding his groan. Not more shit.

Haddad pulled out each item one by one. "Your headset and radio, extra ammo—" Kris already had his 9mm strapped to his thigh. "—compass, beacon, maps of all our areas of operations marked with escape routes, sleep sack, poncho liner, night scope, day scope, flashlight, backup flashlight, GPS, spare batteries, more spare batteries, and more batteries. And everything else you brought."

His clothes were squished in the bottom, next to a paperback he'd picked up in Germany and his all-weather CIA laptop. "Will two million in cash fit?" He still had one of the duffels under his control. For the moment, it was at the embassy, locked in the ambassador's safe.

Haddad stared at him. "We talking in ones or in hundreds?"

"Twenties and hundreds."

Shrugging, Haddad pointed to the bottom of the ruck. "In between the flashlights, maybe?" He grinned. "We should be able to make it all fit." He shoved everything back and stuffed the ruck closed. "Here, try it on."

The pack was definitely heavier than before. A radio antenna stuck out over one of his shoulders now. His sleeping bag pushed his head forward. He stumbled under the weight as he hefted it on his shoulders, but managed to get the pack settled.

It felt like he was carrying an elephant on his back. If he took a step, he'd collapse.

Haddad stared at him. "Good?"

"Yeah." Kris tried to smile. His eyeballs were going to pop out of his skull if he breathed too deeply.

He probably weighed one-third of what Haddad did. Haddad's biceps bulged out of his long-sleeved undershirt like he was a professional NFL linebacker. His chest was solid muscle, tapering down to a trim waist. Next to him, Kris wasn't a twink, he was a twig. He was a matchstick, and the ruck was going to snap him in half.

But Haddad smiled at him again, that small, tight smile.

Kris's knees weakened, and not from the load.

Shit. He was fucked.

Haddad was gorgeous. He'd recognized that immediately. Someone would have to be blind to not see Haddad's good looks. Bronze skin, a wide face, sweeping cheekbones, a jawline chiseled from granite. He was impressively built, with sculpted muscles that screamed of hours spent in the gym, training his body to perfection.

But, there was more, too. There was depth in his dark eyes, something that viewed the world unflinchingly. And something deeper. Something that seemed to tug at Kris, a force that made him want to fall into David Haddad. He had a presence, a pull, and it worked on every bone in Kris's body. Haddad had his own gravity well, and Kris was a shooting star, brushing too close to his orbit.

No, he couldn't go there.

Part of him felt like he was falling already, flying at the speed of light right at Haddad.

God, he was fucked. So fucked. He was here to fight a war. Avenge the people who had died, whom he'd let die. Try to fix, somehow, everything he'd done wrong, everything he'd let happen. Not crush on a Special Forces soldier. The Army frowned on men like him, anyway. *Don't Ask, Don't Tell* was the rule of law. Anyone in the military who was as gay as he was had to keep their mouth firmly shut.

That wasn't his style. And it didn't seem like Haddad's, either.

"Let's get this off you." Haddad helped him slough off the pack, taking the weight easily in one hand. It had to weigh at least seventy pounds. He tried to hide the deep breath he took, the way he rolled his shoulders. They felt like he'd ripped them off and tried to shove them back into their sockets the wrong way.

Pain wasn't sexy. Struggling wasn't sexy, either. He had to carry his weight. Not fall behind or slow the team down. He'd sworn he would shove George and Ryan's skepticism in their faces, rub their snide looks in his success. He'd sworn he would do the right thing, dedicate everything he had to the mission, to revenge.

He wouldn't have time for crushing on Haddad.

He'd broken out in a light sweat hefting the pack, but now that it was off, the frigid Tashkent wind chilled him to the bone. He shivered, shoving his hands back in his black jacket and tucking his face into his wool scarf.

Haddad pulled out a beanie from his cargo pants. "Here. This will help."

Kris frowned. His hair was his best feature. He'd actually been able to style it that morning. Maybe the last morning for a long, long time. He wanted to enjoy the feeling.

"Your hair is very stylish." Haddad winked. "But I promise you. You're going to want this. It's only going to get colder."

Cheeks burning, Kris took the beanie.

**Tashkent, Uzbekistan - September 22, 2001**

The weather cleared overnight. At daybreak, Kris, George, and the rest of the CIA team left the embassy, heading back to Tashkent airport. Derek, their pilot, had stayed behind, bunking with the Special Forces team.

When they arrived, the team was loading the squat, fat helicopter that would take them over the Hindu Kush and into Afghanistan. The rotors spun as the soldiers stacked the gear waist-high along the center of the cargo area, strapping everything down in a hodgepodge game of Tetris. Mini mountains of equipment and rucks filled the cargo area, almost butting into the fold-down canvas seats along the bulkheads. Kris searched for his, trying to find the smallest rucksack in the pile of gear.

"Caldera." Haddad's deep voice called out to him, barely audible over the roar of the rotors. Haddad beckoned him from near the front of the helo. He had Kris's ruck on the deck, next to his own.

Haddad's medic pack made Kris's ruck look miniscule.

Kris picked his way through as Palmer's men and his CIA coworkers crammed themselves into too-small seats and shoved their legs around the cargo. There was just enough room for the gear and their bodies if they kept their knees up to their chests.

Around him, the helo rumbled, vibrating like it was trying to shake them all out. He imagined every screw turning loose and falling out, the helo coming apart into a billion pieces on the tarmac and leaving them standing in the center of the rubble. The engines roared, the rotors sounding like the uptown express in Manhattan was rumbling over his head, over and over again.

Haddad passed Kris a headset with padded earphones. He slid them on, careful of his spiked hair. The roar faded, the volume on the world turned down. Kris still felt the vibrations in his bones, felt his organs rumble and pulse, but at least he could hear himself think.

Haddad's smooth voice came through the headset. "You're going to want to put on that beanie I gave you. The rear ramp and side doors will be kept open so the door gunners can hold position throughout the entire flight. It's going to be frigid."

Kris tugged on Haddad's beanie and zipped up his fleece. He had his thick outer jacket shoved in the top of his ruck, and he crouched down to grab it. As he did, the helo's engines turned over, spinning up with a wail. He pitched sideways and then forward, the helicopter shuddering and shaking. He reached for what was closest to brace himself. Both his hands wrapped around Haddad's thighs, his face mashed into Haddad's hip.

"Sorry! Shit, I'm sorry, I'm sorry..." Kris scrambled back, falling on his ass. He'd inadvertently hit on Haddad yesterday, and now this? He could practically feel George and Ryan's scorn burning into his back, feel the weight of judgment crashing down on him. This wasn't the time, or the place. He had assholes to prove wrong.

Gently, Haddad helped him up, holding his elbows until he was steady on his feet. Haddad grabbed the helo's handholds and pulled Kris's leather gloves and camo poncho liner, a silken, down-filled blanket that had felt like a slice of heaven when Kris had first handled it, out of his ruck. "Put on the gloves, too. And keep the liner near. You'll probably want to wrap up in it."

Kris nodded, looking away. Was bone-melting mortification going to be his default setting now, especially around Haddad? He was off to a great start.

He strapped himself into his seat, waiting stiffly as Haddad buckled in next to him. Haddad's muscles, wrapped up in his own layers of fleece and heavy jacket, pushed against Kris, their bodies pressing together from shoulders to ankles. He tried to shift away as subtly as he could.

Through the headset, he heard Derek talk through their takeoff, their route through Uzbekistan and Tajikistan, over the mountains and into Afghanistan. Derek spoke to Tashkent tower, CENTCOM, and CIA CTC directly, bouncing signals off satellites to reach three different places on earth simultaneously. The flight crew, bundled up in cold weather gear, took up positions at the massive machine guns mounted at the side doors and rear ramps as the helo lifted off.

Their mission had officially begun. They were on their way to Afghanistan.

They banked hard and turned south east, flying low and fast toward the border. Tashkent disappeared, turning to sprawling farmland worked over by stooped men with wooden hand tools and mules. They were flying through time, it seemed, gazing down at centuries past. Dirt roads cut between the farms, snaking through untouched steppe and rugged wilderness.

Kris pressed against his seat, pushed back by the force of Derek's acceleration. Rays of bitter sunlight spilled into the cabin, slipping through the freezing air. He squinted, fumbling for his sunglasses. Haddad, of course, already had his on.

Grassland and steppe faded, replaced by dust and scrub highland. Dirt roads vanished, turning to trails, then rutted tracks only camels could traverse. Part of Kris wanted to lean out and take it all in. These were ancient roads, caravan tracks used by Silk Road travelers, and before that, the first humans to cross the Asian continent. He wanted to revel in it, in history and sights no one had been able to see for years.

But he was too damn cold.

Ten minutes into the flight, he was a Popsicle. He shivered, huddling into his jacket as the temperature kept dropping. He burrowed under the poncho liner and tried to pull his beanie down farther. Tried to tuck his face into his scarf, the top of his jacket. The rest of the team was bundled up as well, but they all had at least a hundred pounds on him to begin with. He was the runt.

As if to spite him, Derek pushed the chopper faster, dropping altitude until they were running full speed down the length of a twisting wadi. There was nothing beneath them, no signs of life. The earth looked like the moon, like the oceans had been drained and they were the last humans on the planet at the end of the world. Ahead, the mountains on the border of Afghanistan soared, scraping the sky with peaks of snow and ice.

He left his stomach behind as the helo rose, a dramatic ascent that pitched them nearly vertical. He was strapped in, but still, he flailed. Haddad reached for him, wrapped his poncho liner tighter around him. The mountains seemed to encircle them, getting closer, closer, until Kris was certain they were going to crash. He flinched, screwing his eyes shut.

Haddad's hand landed on his thigh and squeezed once.

Kris heard Derek calling out altitude readings. He'd never heard Derek's voice go that high, that strained. Back at Langley, Derek had walked them through the ball-shriveling terror that was flying over the Hindu Kush. Few Soviets had ever done it and lived. No Americans had ever made the flight. The mathematics and physics alone almost suggested it was next to impossible.

Most helo pilots thought they were hot shit if they flew up to ten thousand feet in altitude. The Hindu Kush *started* at ten thousand feet, and then went straight vertical, as if they held up the sky, poked through the atmosphere and jabbed at the stars.

When he opened his eyes, they had leveled off and were flying between two massive walls of snow-and-ice-coated stone. At fourteen thousand feet, Haddad signaled the team, and everyone reached for the oxygen masks above their heads. Haddad pulled Kris's down and showed him how to hold it over his face. Cold oxygen flowed, frigid, but welcome. His head, which had started to ache, cleared.

Derek threaded the mountain passes, their rotors buzzing snow flurries off the sides of peaks, close enough that their revolutions whistled against the rock face. He could reach out and brush the mountain, if he wanted, the soaring, jagged peaks of untouched ice. Sunlight pierced the sky, falling through the mountains like samurai swords, like blades from a vengeful god. They and their helo were tiny, insignificant, and as far from humanity, from life as he knew it, as he'd ever been. Were there any humans on the planet more remote than them? If someone had told Kris they were actually on the moon, he would have believed them.

Did time still exist? Kris could hear his own heartbeat, the hiss of the oxygen, and the rumble of the rotors, but other than that, it was like being dropped into someone else's memory. Each blink lasted a lifetime, the world a smear that passed before his eyes.

Derek continued to call out elevation markers. Sixteen thousand feet. Sixteen-five.

He couldn't stop shivering. Haddad's hand on his thigh was the one warm point of contact in his whole body. He wasn't going to make it to Afghanistan. He was just going to freeze on this flight.

Haddad felt his shivers, he was certain. At 17,200 feet, Haddad pulled out his own poncho liner and a second jacket from his ruck and laid them both on top of Kris. Kris hid his face in his fleece and burrowed into Haddad. Fuck his pride. He needed the warmth.

Haddad wrapped one arm around him and pulled him closer.

The jagged peaks eventually gave way, turning to endless stretches of rumbling brown hills, snow snaking in waves across the higher elevations until that too petered off. Beneath them, as far as the eye could see, was the earth made wild, unimpeded wilderness, void of any human touch. Hills and valley, rugged and brown and filled with dried ravines and scrub brush. No humans. No life at all.

Finally, almost two hours after the flight began, the helo turned southwest and headed into the mouth of the Panjshir Valley.

The Soviets, during their occupation, had called the Panjshir the Valley of Death. They'd lost more soldiers in that valley than anywhere else and had come to a standstill in their occupation that had tried to press deeper into the Afghanistan mountains. They'd failed, and then they'd turned tail and run. The valley had been a graveyard of invaders for centuries, the Soviets only the most recent to meet their end at the hands of the Afghans. Before them, it had been the British. Before the British, Alexander the Great had been stopped on the land roaring beneath them.

Would America be the next great empire to find its end in Afghanistan? Would they themselves meet their ends in this Valley of Death?

From the sky, Kris spotted the remains of the Soviet occupation and endless civil war everywhere: rusted-out tanks and troop transports, bomb craters that had obliterated the roads, tattered remnants of minefield warning signs. Square-shaped mud houses riddled with bullet holes huddled together around the winding banks of the Panjshir River, its waters a deep, unfiltered sapphire. Green grass murmured around the tiny villages before slipping out to brown wastelands and dusty wadis. Beauty and desolation, life and death. Afghanistan.

Derek called over the headset, "*Three minutes to LZ!*"

Palmer and George popped up. The rest of the team turned on, going from sleepy laziness to full speed in a half second. Jackets and poncho liners were stowed, shoved into packs. Books and music players disappeared. They strapped on their gear, tightened their helmets, and readied their weapons.

Kris tried to keep up. His breath fogged in front of his face. He couldn't feel his cheeks. His lungs felt like they were frozen from the inside.

*"One minute!"*

Ahead, a bend in the river cut a wide, barren portion of the valley off from the rest of the villages. The helo banked hard and spun. Tilted, wobbled left and right.

Finally, they set down with a lurch on the dusty ground.

Kris felt like he was in a movie, stuck between too slow and fast-forward. He saw the rotors spin outside the open cargo door, the *whoosh-whoosh-whoosh* seeming to come from underwater, distorted and fractured. Men moved, scrambling, grabbing rifles. Running toward the cargo door.

They were in Afghanistan, with only the Shura Nazar, whom they had yet to make contact with, as their protectors. They had nothing other than what they carried on the helicopter. A scratchy satellite phone and the helo their only link to the world. After traveling over the pass, they may as well have landed on another planet, in another galaxy.

They were on their own.

Palmer started barking orders and the world snapped into fast-forward. Palmer's men burst out of the chopper, taking up protective positions. A group of three Afghans started for the chopper, AK-47s in their hands. Behind them, a ring of rusted and bullet-riddled pickup trucks waited, Afghans leaning out of the cabs and the backs of the beds, watching.

Each man held a weapon. Each man stared at the helo, at the team, his eyes dark, his gaze pinched.

George and Palmer strode across the grass-and-dirt field under the watchful eyes of the entire team. Kris saw fingers half-squeezed over triggers on nearly everyone. They were at the coordinates the Shura Nazar had given them. Was this their welcoming party? Or a trap? Kris searched the faces, looking for one he recognized, a photo from the files he'd read backward and forward at Langley.

He should be out there. He'd negotiated the bones of the alliance, had done the legwork to make this happen. He needed to be there with George and Palmer.

Haddad held him back. "Wait for the signal."

In the field, outside the bubble of wind kicked up by the spinning rotors, Palmer shook hands with one of the Afghans. George greeted him next. Their bodies were stiff, and the Afghan in the center glared at them both. He'd shouldered his rifle, but the others hadn't. Palmer waved to the helo. The signal.

"All right, now it's showtime." Haddad looked down at Kris, his deep eyes searing into him. "You're going to kick ass, Caldera." He guided Kris out of the chopper, jogging them both out to where Palmer and George waited. Haddad kept close, inside Kris's shadow, his weapon at the low and ready.

The rotors still spun, kicking dust into the air and blowing icy wind in cyclones around the raggedy group. Towering over them, steel-gray mountains soared, like the valley was the dungeon of the earth.

Kris spoke in Dari, holding out both hands for the Afghan man to take, to grasp. "Thank you for your hospitality. We're the Americans. We're here to help you destroy the Taliban."

"Welcome to Afghanistan. I am Fazl," the man said. He took Kris's hands and drew him into an embrace. He smiled, his teeth square and yellowed, gaps where some had fallen out. "The Shura Nazar welcomes you to our fight."

---

The rest of the team unloaded the helicopter as fast as they'd loaded it, hauling all the gear they'd packed for their invasion into the back of the Afghans' trucks. Haddad reappeared with his ruck and Kris's. He kept Kris's at his feet, even though Kris beckoned for it.

Fazl told Kris they had been sent by General Khan to pick up the

Americans. "We did not believe you would truly come," he said. "But you're here now. I will take you to your new home, in the village." Fazl pointed up the hillside across the river, past a switchback. Mud huts squatted close together, overlooking the valley and scattered fields with limp crops shivering in the cold. Higher up the hill, a compound had been built into the stone. Once it had been painted white, but shrapnel and wind had chipped the paint down to the concrete blocks. "The general will see you tomorrow."

One of the trucks didn't actually work. It was tethered to another by a length of frayed rope, which snapped under the combined load. Two of Palmer's men had to unpack a length of webbing and re-strap them together. The rest of the pickups strained to haul the gear, broken struts scraping as shocks compressed to the limit.

Palmer ordered his men to jog alongside up to the village. George and Ryan slid into the front cab of one of the trucks. Phillip and Jim nervously strapped the communications gear to the back of one and eyeballed the river. Derek volunteered to stay at the helo and shut it down. Someone would come get him later.

"Get on the back." Haddad nudged Kris toward the truck with the fewest bullet holes and the least scraping brakes.

"I'll walk, I'm fine."

"We're at six thousand feet above sea level. Going up that hill? We're all going to be puking in ten minutes. But we need you to be solid." Haddad took in the brakes and the suspension and the way the engine ground as the Afghan driver tried to move forward with the weight of their gear in the back. "This truck is the best."

"What about the river? How are you guys going to cross that?"

"We'll wade. I'll stay beside this truck. C'mon, get up in there."

"I can handle myself, Sergeant."

"I know you can. But you also have to handle all of us, too. We need you to be at your peak, especially now."

He could only hold Haddad's stare for so long. Even through his sunglasses, there was something there, some intensity that made Kris turn away. Haddad's gaze seemed to go right through him, like an X-ray that turned him inside out. He felt naked, down to his bones, under that gaze. "Fine."

The trucks lurched toward the river, kicking up dust that made them all cough. Palmer's men pulled their undershirts up, covering their noses and mouths and making them look like bandits from the Old West.

From the air, the river had seemed calm, almost tranquil. As they bounced and jerked closer, Kris spotted the whitecaps breaking around submerged boulders and the rush of the current swirling in eddies. He stared at Haddad, running beside him and the pickup.

Haddad frowned at the river. He looked up at Kris. "Hold on tight."

"What about you?"

The truck accelerated, its engine wailing as the driver floored it, heading for the riverbank. Jerking left and right, they bounced over the rocky embankment and plunged into the river. Water splashed over the cab, hitting Kris. He clung to his ruck, the truck, the crates jammed in beside him.

The engines screamed underwater as the trucks rumbled through the river, water rising to the doors. They had been modified for water crossing, but still. The river current pushed at his truck, and Kris felt the tires sliding off the rocky river bottom, felt them jerk and lurch more sideways than forward.

He watched Haddad, his heart in his throat, fingers scraping on the rusted frame of the truck. Haddad struggled in the water, his rifle up to his chest. He stared at Kris, striding as fast as he could against the current.

Kris wanted to reach for him. Pull him to safety.

Haddad was a two-hundred-pound super soldier. What could Kris really do to help him?

Still, he watched, holding his breath, until Haddad stumbled from the river and up the muddy bank after Kris's truck roared free. Wide arcs of frigid mud splattered over the truck bed. Kris felt it hit his cheek, saw it splatter his jacket.

True to Haddad's word, ten minutes into the drive up the hillside,

Haddad, Palmer, and the rest of the soldiers started puking. They didn't stop jogging, just leaned over and hurled into the dust. As the road rose and they climbed up the first ridge, they aimed their vomit for the gorge while trying not to slip and fall to their deaths.

The road could barely be called a road. On one side the mountain rose, sheer rock, and, far above, ice. On the other, a sickening drop, a ravine that went straight down, tangled with dead brush and a thousand lines of snowmelt meandering down the foreboding mountains. It was wide enough for one horse, barely wide enough for the trucks. Tracks etched into the earth over centuries showed lines and lines of single-file horses had marched up and down the ridge. Deep ruts where hooves had struck caught the tires, making them spin out, lurch heart-stoppingly close to the road's edge, nearly plummeting over. One driver spun out, and the rear passenger tires hovered over empty air and nothingness before he careened back onto the trail.

Kris would rather puke his guts out than fall to his death on the back of a bullet-riddled death trap, but when he tried to hop out, Haddad shook his head. He was right there, always right beside Kris and the busted gap where there should have been a tailgate.

Eventually, the convoy turned onto a smaller trail, winding into a narrow mountain pass that was ball-shrivelingly terrifying. The team walked single file behind the trucks as each picked its way through frozen mud and fallen rocks. Finally, they arrived at the village.

Stone huts squatted on either side of the dirt track. Mud covered the walls, insulating the homes through the bitterly cold winters. Gray dust swirled through the air, kicked up by the trucks' tires. Thin men leaned on hand-hewn wooden tools, watching the convoy as dirty kids played with deflated soccer balls with faded Chinese characters.

Beyond the village, tucked into the hillside, two buildings formed a larger compound overlooking the valley. A rutted, dead field, more dirt and broken concrete than anything else, spread in front of the compound. Decrepit tanks, remnants of the Soviet invasion, were parked at angles, pointing down the road and overlooking the village. If they tried to fire any ordnance, the tanks would blow apart.

Another team of Afghans awaited them, including an older man who was clearly in charge. He wore traditional kameez pants and a camouflage jacket. His beard was short and scraggly. After the convoy parked in the dirt field, Fazl and the Afghan warmly embraced.

Kris stumbled from the back of the pickup, every bone in his body jarred loose from the rough ride up the mountain. Haddad was right there, steadying him. Kris squeezed Haddad's arm and headed for Fazl and his friend. "*Salaam*," he said, one hand on his chest.

Both eyebrows on the Afghan's face rose. He stared at Kris, not speaking.

What was it? What about him screamed *gay*? He didn't think he was aggressively homosexual, not now with his double jackets and Haddad's beanie shoved on his head. He wasn't strutting a catwalk, wasn't catcalling like he was the wildest of drag queens from the Village. He didn't have eyeliner or lip gloss on. Frustration simmered within him.

There was a twinkle in the Afghan's eyes, though. He chuckled, and then embraced Kris, returning the greeting, speaking in Dari. "Did America send children to fight their wars?"

Goddamn it. Kris forced a smile. He rubbed a hand over his chin. Despite not shaving since he'd left DC, he had only a scattered few hairs poking through. "I am jealous of you," he said, pointing to the Afghan's beard. "Mine does not grow." And, of course, he was now in a country that judged men by the thickness of their beards.

The Afghan laughed again. "My name is Ghasi. I am the manager of this compound. It was General Massoud's Panjshir headquarters." Pride sang through Ghasi's words. His eyes glittered.

"We thank you for your hospitality. To stay at the headquarters of the great Massoud." Kris bowed his head. He held out both hands to Ghasi. Ghasi clasped his hands, squeezing his fingers.

Ghasi introduced his staff, mostly kids from the village who would be managing the compound for their stay. "They will clean, cook, do your laundry. Anything you need."

Fazl had summoned a group of Shura Nazar soldiers from seemingly nowhere, and they helped Palmer and his men unload the trucks. George and Ryan hung back, eyeing Kris as he chatted in Dari and held hands with Ghasi.

"May I introduce my fellow officers?" Kris beckoned George and Ryan over and introduced both men to Ghasi. George and Ryan shook Ghasi's hand stiffly.

Ghasi stepped back. "This main compound is yours." He pointed to a smaller hut set off from the main cluster. "That is where General Khan's men will stay. They will protect you. The rest is for you. Your headquarters in Afghanistan."

"Let's take a look."

Ghasi led George, Ryan, Palmer, and Kris around the compound. The first building was an old stable, a C-shaped line of bare concrete rooms with a dirt yard in the center. Palmer and George called out rooms for their equipment, storing the food and essentials on one side, gear and medical equipment on the other.

The second building, set beyond the first, was a rectangle of concrete with Soviet-style skinny double glass doors lining the front façade. The main floor was split, a long foyer overlooking the desiccated courtyard between the two buildings. Beyond the entrance, and down a handful of steps, a sunken central space loomed large, one wall lined with bookshelves and stuffed with old books, their spines etched in Arabic scripts.

Six rooms branched off the center space, with curtains nailed over their openings. A narrow hallway, with steps going farther down, led to two smaller rooms set off the main building by a breezeway. One was the tiny kitchen. The other had a square toilet—a hole in the ground—a spigot sticking out of the wall, and a bucket.

The center space was the perfect place to set up their nerve center. Radio and communications center, intel collection point, and planning station, their nerve center would have someone from the team present around the clock. They'd be able to get radio and satellite reception if they put their dishes and antennae on the roof.

The six rooms off the nerve center would be sleeping quarters for everyone. Two men to a room, plus their gear. It was going to be a tight fit all around.

Even though Palmer's guys had just puked their guts out, they were already hauling gear into the compound. Their crates of MREs and enough bottled water for an army went to the stables. All comms equipment went to the second building, their headquarters, and Jim and Phillip started working with Warrick, Palmer's communications sergeant, to set up the array of computers, radios, satellites, generators, and surveillance equipment.

Almost as an afterthought, everyone dropped their rucks in the room they claimed as their own.

Kris searched for his ruck in the dwindling pile of gear in the dirt courtyard.

It was conspicuously missing.

He caught sight of Haddad winding his way into their headquarters, hauling two rucks, one in each hand. Kris started after him, but stopped when he saw George pull Haddad aside, say some words, and gesture to Kris's pack. Haddad nodded, once, twice, and then again. He jogged down the concrete steps as George headed back out.

The Afghan soldiers loaned from General Khan, waiting with Ghasi, watched everything like they were seeing a feast spread out before them. Most Afghans lived on fifty dollars a year. Kris and the team had brought not just millions in cash, but millions of dollars' worth of gear.

Kris grabbed one of the money-stuffed duffels and slipped the first packet of mission cash out. "*Agha* Ghasi," he said, using the honorific *agha*. "I know these men are proud fighters, great men of your forces."

"They are, *Gul Bahar* American."

Kris gritted his teeth. *Gul Bahar* meant "spring flower" in Dari. "I would like to offer to pay them one hundred dollars a week to keep us safe. Us, and our equipment." He handed out cash to each soldier, pressing the crisp American bill into their palms. American foreign policy, hard at work.

The Afghan soldiers' eyes lit up.

"That is a good start," Ghasi said carefully. "But General Khan will want to negotiate. The rest of the army need provisions. Food, winter clothes, ammunition. Weapons. Salaries."

"We will outfit the Shura Nazar. I promise."

Ghasi squinted. "I've heard American promises before."

American foreign policy, with all its warts and wrinkles.

Kris held out his hand, palm up. "I'm here now, General. I keep promises."

Ghasi clasped his hand, shaking it gently. He smiled. "*Gul Bahar*, I have lived three of your lives. Your country makes and breaks promises as the sun rises and sets. You are here now, but for how long? How long until your promises start to break? I will never understand America. But..." He sighed. "You are here now. So we will see. General Khan will see you tomorrow."

---

Phillip and Warrick spent hours setting up the communications array, at least enough so that George and Ryan could send a message back to DC and to CENTCOM, confirming their arrival in-country.

The first order of business, after contacting Langley, was to set up the signals intercept array. With the signals intercept, they could break into the Taliban's radio frequencies and start listening in on their enemy. Back in the US, it would have been easy. In the Panjshir, working with a single generator and one helicopter's worth of gear, it was a laborious process.

Satellite dishes, from large to tiny, poked out from under camouflage netting on the roof of their headquarters, and a generator rumbled beside the dishes and antennae, next to a solar-powered battery backup.

The nerve center looked like a computer repair shop had exploded. Bare light bulbs strung from electrical cords hanging on nails cast long shadows over everything. Empty crates became stools and tables, lining the walls around the main room.

Kris finally found his pack, and Haddad, in one of the tiny curtained rooms as the sun was setting, throwing long lines of tawny light through the open patio doors at the front of the compound. The building had a musty scent, as if it had been locked up for too long, unused and unentered. George wanted the doors open, even though it was freezing.

The rooms were cramped and square, with dusty rugs stretched across the floors, faded and worn, and nothing else. The air was cold, damp. The musty smell was stronger in the rooms.

Haddad had emptied his ruck, and what looked like an entire pharmacy was spread out in the tiny room. Medicines, syringes, IV bags, lines, bandages, splints, surgical tools, and more. He had the same basic gear Kris had, a sixty-pound load, plus most of the medical gear for the team. How had he managed to pack all that?

Kris toed a bucket of pool chlorine powder, something that came off the shelf at any Walmart store. "Chlorine? For pools?"

"It will kill anything in the water. We can use it in the bathroom, too. Keep things sanitary. And for drinking. If we have to resort to using it, this will make the water safe to drink for us."

"I didn't think it was that easy."

"Well, it will give us a bad stomach upset. The cure is only slightly better than the disease." Haddad shrugged. "I'm going to set up a makeshift clinic down in one of the stables so everyone has access to what they need, whenever they need it." He frowned at the rest of the gear he'd spread around—his ammo and spare batteries, night vision goggles and scopes, clothing and GPS and electronics. "Kind of a tight fit in here."

Kris's stomach clenched. "I'll… I'll find somewhere else to crash. I just came to get this—" He hefted his ruck, holding his breath.

"All the other rooms are full." Haddad kept stacking medical supplies in his arms. He didn't look at Kris.

What had George said to Haddad? Had he warned Haddad away, told him to be careful of *the gay one*? Was all this gear, everywhere, Haddad's way of saying he wouldn't fit, he wasn't welcome?

Kris lifted his chin. Fine then. Add Haddad's name to the list of people he would prove wrong. "I'll figure something out. Thanks for bringing my ruck in, but I can handle it myself."

Haddad's hand on his elbow stopped him. "It's going to be a tight fit, but we'll make it work."

# 5

**Panjshir Valley, Afghanistan - September 23, 2001**

Kris was in Lower Manhattan, at Church and Barclay Streets. The World Trade Center, the Twin Towers, soared above. He'd thought, once, that the buildings held up the stars, kept the blue of the sky above from crashing down on the city. They were the pillars of the world, fixtures in his life from when he was a toddler growing up on the Lower East Side.

But the towers were on fire, billowing flames and black smoke rising and rising, clouds like shadows blocking out the sun. Planes kept flying into the towers, endless numbers of planes turning over Manhattan, flying too low over the city. He heard the roar, felt the rumble in his bones from jet engines only feet above his head.

He tried to scream, tried to bellow, but nothing came out. His voice was gone, and no matter how much he screamed, the jets kept flying, closer, closer, closer—

He fell to his knees as a plane slammed into the South Tower, again. His knees hit dust, a powder that felt like the moon. He pitched forward, burying his face in the desolation, his fingers trying to grab something, anything in the dust.

His hands closed around bone.

Rearing back, Kris tried to crawl away. Bones surrounded him, everywhere. A leg bone, a thigh, next to a skull, staring at him with vacant eyes, resting cockeyed in the dust.

The towers were gone, and so were the flames. All he could see, in every direction, was dust and bones. Bones, flung in every direction, a graveyard of bones, thousands and thousands of human beings. Ash fell from the sky, the remnants of the world, his world, coating his skin and choking his lungs.

He couldn't breathe. Ash clung to him, and dust. He screamed, trying to get the dust off. It was dust of the world, dust of the dead, dead he'd failed. The dust was trying to kill him, trying to turn him to dust as well. He wanted to give in, let them have him. He felt his soul begin to shatter.

Shapes moved in the gloom. He tried to reach out, beg for help.

Marwan al-Shehhi appeared, grinning, like in his passport photo. Khalid Al-Mihdhar followed, blank eyes staring Kris down.

Mohamed Atta strode out of the gloom, behind al-Shehhi. His square jaw, his dark eyes. A permanent scowl etched on his face, lines across his skin made from hate and endless wrath. Black flags flapped in a hot wind, snapping and cracking like gunshots, like planes slamming into buildings.

He had something in his hand.

Kris tried to back away, tried to crawl away. He screamed, flinging dust and ash at the hijackers' faces. "You did this!" he wailed. "You murdered everyone!"

"No," Atta said. He kept coming, rising over Kris, looming over him. He was as tall as the World Trade Center had been, as tall as the towers. His eyes were hollow, empty sockets, images of two planes slamming into the Twin Towers playing on repeat in the darkness where his eyeballs should have been. "*You* did this."

Atta's arm fell, slashing at Kris, cutting him to pieces, shredding him with the box cutter he'd used to hijack American Airlines Flight 11—

"Caldera. Caldera! *Kris*!"

Shaking woke him, rough jerks that ripped him from his nightmare. He gasped. Frigid air filled his lungs. The cold stabbed his insides. He rolled over, coughing into the floor. He expected to see blood.

Haddad hovered beside him. One hand squeezed Kris's shoulder. Kris could barely see the outline of Haddad's face. The world was dark, pitch black.

"What time is it?"

"Zero four hundred. Everyone is asleep." Haddad ran his hand across Kris's back, inside his sleeping bag. "You're shaking."

"I'm fine." Kris pushed himself up. He was tangled in his sleeping bag, and his jacket and fleece pullover were twisted, straightjacket-like. The freezing night air had slipped under his layers. His skin felt like a sheet of ice had frozen to him. He couldn't stop shaking. Shivers or his nightmare, he couldn't tell.

He heard a zipper, the long line of Haddad's sleeping bag opening. "Come with me." Haddad held out his hand.

Kris stumbled up, slithering out of his own sleeping bag and straightening his layers. He'd have to put on more clothes. Their stone headquarters did nothing to stop the chill. He wrapped his Gore-Tex jacket around him, burying his face in the turned-up collar.

Haddad guided him out of their cramped room and through the nerve center. Laptops whirred, and the radio was set on a low, soft crackle. Snores rose from the other sleeping rooms, behind curtains. After days of travel, the team was finally sleeping, and sleeping hard.

Haddad kept going, slipping out into the dead courtyard between their two buildings. Three Afghan soldiers huddled near a fire on the other side of the dirt patch, bundled in thick woolen blankets. They talked softly, AK-47s resting nearby. They were the night guards, keeping an eye on the team while they slept.

Haddad led him to the small fire ring, glowing with the last of the banked embers from their fire the night before. They'd all sat around the flames once Palmer and George had outlined their mission for the coming days. After the briefing, there hadn't been much to do except think.

Kris squatted, huddling with his hands in his armpits and trying to keep warm as Haddad turned the coals over, tossed more sticks on the fire, and blew on the embers. When the flames flickered to life, Haddad stepped back and moved to Kris's side. He wrapped his arms around Kris, briskly rubbing up and down his back.

The heat of the fire licked up Kris's body, but it was Haddad's warmth that seeped into his bones. He went limp, slumping into Haddad's hold.

"Better?"

"Mmmm."

"Want to talk about it?"

Kris shook his head. He couldn't even think. His nightmares painted images for him, screamed at him when he slept. He couldn't put the words together in his mind when he was awake. The attacks, and who was to blame—

What would Haddad, this vanguard of American fury, of patriotic fervor, a literal superhero sent to avenge the deaths of thousands, think if he could see Kris's nightmare? If he knew the truth?

Haddad kept stroking up and down Kris's back, his movements slowing, becoming softer. "You said you're from New York."

Kris nodded.

"The Bronx? Brooklyn?"

"No need to be insulting." Kris tried to smile. He couldn't. "Manhattan. Lower East Side."

Haddad breathed in and out, slowly. "I'm sorry.".

"I haven't been back since high school. I don't know anyone—" His throat closed. "I don't *think* I know anyone who was in the towers."

He thought back to his last year of school. Hadn't Junior and Mateo wanted to be firemen one day? Hadn't Celia said she was going to work in those towers, no matter what, even if she had to work as a cleaning lady or a food server in the McDonald's? Mr. Birmingham had always told her to dream bigger, to imagine herself in one of the offices up there, a corner office, with a view of the glittering sky. Celia said she'd never be smart enough for that.

But Kris hadn't ever thought he'd be in Afghanistan, or have jumped out of a plane, or have joined the CIA.

Sweet Jesus, who had he lost from his past? Celia was a mean bitch with a cruel streak, and she'd picked on him for years, taunting his eyeliner and the way he loosened his tie, his shell necklace and the shortest shorts he could get away with in the summer months.

But she was smart, and she could have made it, could have had that corner office, and no one deserved that day.

And he had—

He was going to vomit.

Kris shoved Haddad away, falling as he twisted, landing on his knees. His stomach flipped, turned itself inside out. Rancid vomit clawed its way up his throat, scalding his insides. Last night's dinner, prepared by Ghasi's teen Afghan boys, reappeared, weak broth.

Haddad stroked his back again, his large hand making circles from Kris's shoulders to his waist. He said nothing.

Kris sat back, trying to block out the memories, the years he'd spent growing up in the shadows of the towers. Years of being a barrio kid, imagining climbing out of the barrio and the tenements and up to those glass-and-steel towers. Every kid on the block had pinned their hopes somewhere on those towers. Every kid had a dream of escaping up the towers like ladders into the sky, all the way to the stars, catch a plane and fly away, disappear to a new life. Once, he'd thought he could climb to the top, to where they disappeared into the clouds, and search for a new home, one where there were people like him and he wasn't stared at for being brown, or gay, or young, or chided for having an attitude, or told he had to do better, had to be different. Somewhere, that world existed, he'd known it. He just had to find it.

Haddad wrapped an arm around his shoulders and pulled him close. Kris slid on the dirt, boneless, and fell into Haddad's arms and his chest, face-first.

He let the smoke wash over him, tasted ash on his tongue. Memories played, an endless loop, his childhood under the shadows of the

Twin Towers and the morning they came tumbling down. The fire crackled, flames sparking, snapping.

All he could hear were screams.

---

In the morning, Fazl, who stayed in the village with Ghasi and his family, walked over to the compound as the rest of the team was waking up. Groaning and huddling around the fire, everyone shared pots of hot water for their instant coffee and waited, sullen and tired, for Ghasi's staff to cook breakfast.

"General Khan will be here to see you at noon."

They moved into high gear after that. George pulled Kris into his and Ryan's room, where they had stashed George's duffel of cash. Together, they counted out $1 million.

"We'll give this to him to show him we're not fucking around. We're here to do business."

"George, Afghans are very proud people. They won't just take money from your hands."

"A million dollars? Yeah, he'll take it."

Kris kept his mouth shut.

Ghasi's staff started preparing lunch immediately after the breakfast of fresh-baked bread and eggs from the chickens that roamed the village and the hillside wherever they wished. Young boys ran everywhere in the morning, collecting eggs from nests hidden in ditches and under scrub brushes and bringing them to Ghasi for an apple or a tomato. Just before noon, Ghasi spread out a large blanket on the dirt in the courtyard and scattered flat, faded cushions along the edges. A breeze flitted through the village, cutting and cold. Most of the team hovered around the fire, still blazing in the courtyard. Phillip and Jim stayed up in the nerve center, trying to crack the Taliban's radio net.

A cloud of gray dust moving up the valley's single pocked road signaled the General's arrival. Kris stood with George and Ryan, the official political delegation from the CIA. Technically, Ryan shouldn't have been there, but he slid up on the other side of George, and Kris didn't have the energy to fight.

Haddad hovered behind the group, sitting on the steps leading to their headquarters building in front of an open patio door. He watched Kris, his face blank.

General Khan brought a security detachment of Shura Nazar soldiers, about twenty men. They clambered out of the bullet-riddled trucks in the convoy and positioned themselves around the General's Russian-made jeep. Palmer and his men stiffened, their hands reaching for the weapons strapped to their thighs.

Khan gazed at the compound. He held both hands cupped to the sky over his head, his eyes closed, before striding across the dirt and passing through the front archway of the stables.

He was shorter than nearly everyone on their team, but burly. Thick black hair spilled down his shoulders, beneath the flat-topped *pakul*, the woolen cap all Afghan men wore. He had a large, wiry beard, like a pirate from the days of old, and wore a Russian-made camouflage uniform. He stared at everyone, eyeballing them each for a long moment.

When his gaze landed on Kris, he broke into a wide smile.

"You must be *Gul Bahar*." He chuckled. "I see why the name stuck." He spoke in Dari. Fazl, Khan's translator, hung by his shoulder. "If you wore a turban, you'd be a beautiful Afghan boy."

George coughed, glancing sidelong at Kris. He knew just enough Farsi, the Iranian version of Dari, to parse out what Khan had said.

Kris smiled. "*As-salaam-alaikum*, General Khan." He pulled off his gloves and held out his hand, delicately. "*Chutoor haste*?"

Khan took his hand, placing his own free hand over his heart. "*Wa alaikum as-salaam, tashakor fazle khoda ast.*" *Thanks to God, I am good.*

Kris pressed his hand over his heart with a smile, then cupped Khan's hands in both of his.

"It has been some time since I was here," Khan continued in Dari. He looked over Kris and George's heads, to their headquarters. "This was where I last saw General Massoud. We dined together, in his house." He pointed to the building they now lived in.

"General Khan... We thank you for your honor. To stay in the General's home." Kris smiled, his breath shaky. "You honor us too much."

General Khan's eyes narrowed. One corner of his mouth curled up, an almost smile. "We will see if the honor is worth it."

On the other side of George, Ryan cleared his throat. He didn't speak a lick of Dari. He had no idea what was going on. His impatience was showing.

"General, may I introduce you to *agha* George and *agha* Ryan?" Kris used the deferential title to delineate the authority of George and Ryan over him. "We are CIA officers, here to help the Shura Nazar."

George held out his gloved hand and pumped Khan's once. Ryan followed suit with a firm handshake. Khan frowned. He stepped back.

"General, we have much to discuss." As George spoke, Fazl translated the English to Dari for Khan. Kris listened. "We need to coordinate with the Shura Nazar and prepare the battlefield for the US's invasion—"

"First, we will eat." Khan spread his hands to the feast Ghasi had laid out on the sheet in the yard. Boiled meat, dates, almonds, fresh yogurt, sliced tomatoes, fresh-baked flatbread, and watermelon. "Come. We will eat together."

Kris heard George's teeth grind, but they followed Khan to the blanket and crouched down, sitting on the faded, lumpy cushions. Khan invited his men to join them. He was relaxed, jovial on the surface, but Kris watched him watching George and Ryan with an intensity that rivaled a hawk's.

No one accidentally became a general in the Shura Nazar. Khan was not a young man. He'd been a warrior his whole life. Out of the mix and pull of rival generals in the fractious and bitter conglomeration that was the Shura Nazar, how had Khan become the heir apparent to Massoud?

Kris leaned into Khan's shoulder and asked.

Khan leaned back into Kris, smiling as he answered. He gestured wildly, great sweeps of his arms that matched how loudly and vibrantly he spoke. "After the assassination by those Bin Laden dogs, there was anarchy. Fazl was there." He gestured to Fazl, sitting opposite George. "He was injured in the bomb blast." Khan pointed to Fazl's head, to the scabs and burns healing down his face and neck. "No one knew what to do. Everyone was frozen. Massoud had been their general for their entire lives. Almost like a father." Khan's expression pinched. "They needed leadership. Strength, like Massoud. *I* provided it."

"General Khan arranged for the helicopter that evacuated General Massoud. We thought he might survive if he got to Dushanbe, but..." Fazl said in English, until his voice faltered. He looked down. One of the Shura Nazar soldiers wrapped an arm around him, squeezed his shoulders.

"I told them to say nothing. Not a word. We kept his death secret until I could radio all the commanders in the Shura Nazar. I told the other generals personally what had happened, and then asked for their pledge. I said we would avenge Massoud together. They wanted to be a part of that."

Stunned, Kris turned to George, translating quickly. George stared back at him, silent. Without Khan, the entire Shura Nazar could have fallen into fractious infighting, blood feuds and rivalries that could have allowed the Taliban to seize the entirety of Afghanistan in a matter of days. If the Shura Nazar had turned inward, fighting each other, there would have been nothing to stand against the Taliban, or against Bin Laden.

"And, after what happened. The attacks in America." Khan shrugged, switching to stilted English. "We knew the Americans would be coming."

"We are glad for your assistance." George smiled, full of teeth.

Khan's gaze turned sharp. He set down his cup of tea. "So. Tell me. What is it the Americans want in Afghanistan?"

Fazl struggled to keep up with the translation as George launched into his pitch, eagerly pushing the CIA's mission. They were there to establish a base of operations in the Panjshir, setting the stage for the US military's invasion force. They were also there to beef up the Shura Nazar, so they and the US military could work together to topple and crush the Taliban—and Bin Laden.

"So when will you leave?" Khan interrupted George's flood of words, his promises of support and cash, in his clipped, heavily accented English

"We're staying until the job is complete and the Taliban are gone. Until Afghanistan is safe again, and no longer a haven for terrorism."

Khan's glare seemed etched in stone as Fazl finished his translation.

"We have a gift for you, in fact. A show of good faith." George reached behind him. The double-wrapped plastic bag of $1 million rested in the dirt behind his back. He held it out to Khan. "One million dollars, General. To outfit your men. To buy weapons, ammunition, and clothing. Think of this as a down payment."

Fazl spoke softly as he translated. He stared down at the blanket. Khan gazed right past the cash, past George's outstretched hands. He acted as if it wasn't even there, like George hadn't even spoken.

The cash, and George, hung in the silence, waiting. And waiting.

Kris plucked the cash from George's hands and set it down, off to his side. He ignored it, and George's glare. "We plan on airlifting humanitarian aid to the valley as well, General," he said smoothly in Dari.

Khan finally smiled. He reached for Kris's hand. "Our people suffer. This feast is the nicest I have eaten in a year." The soldiers next to him looked scrawny in their Russian camouflage, and they'd picked clean the meal Ghasi had prepared. Every dish was empty. "The people need help. Food, clothing, water."

"We will provide that, and more." George spoke as soon as Kris translated. "General, we also want to set up a joint intelligence cell. Share intelligence between the Shura Nazar and the CIA."

"This intelligence will go both ways? You will share what you discover? Or will this just be my men giving you what you do not know?"

George faltered, hesitating after Kris relayed Khan's words.

Kris jumped back in, before Ryan could blunder the conversation. He'd been blessedly silent thus far. "We will share our intelligence with you, General Khan. There is much we don't know about Afghanistan, and we need your expertise to understand."

"*Gul Bahar, you* seem to understand a great deal." Khan's hand landed on Kris's knee, squeezing.

George stared at Khan's hand. Kris could feel the weight of his gaze, the heavy judgment.

"Our first mission, General, is to create a clear and precise map of the battlefield." Ryan leaned forward, around George. Kris sighed. Ryan just couldn't stay silent. "We need to understand precisely where the front lines are. Yours, and the Taliban's."

Kris translated before Ryan could make any more demands.

"We have maps." Khan motioned to his jeeps. Two young soldiers scurried away and jogged back with a stack of antique maps from the Soviet Union. Pencil marks had been drawn and erased and redrawn for years, the fluctuating lines of the front changing with each passing winter.

Like ghosts, Ghasi's boys cleared the dishes from the sheet, and Khan spread his map over the ground. Ryan and George pulled out their own maps, printed by the CIA before they left Langley, and laid them alongside Khan's. Khan's was far more detailed.

Kris translated, reading off positions of Khan's forces and the Taliban on the map and tracing the front lines that made the shape of a giant L across the northwest corner of Afghanistan, into Badakhshan Province and the Panjshir Valley. From east to west, crossing north of Kabul and bisecting Bagram Airfield to Jalalabad, and then shooting straight north to the Tajikistan border and into the mountains.

"Where are the Taliban?" Kris translated for Ryan.

"They are entrenched all along their front lines. Massive artillery formations. Antiaircraft battalions. And thousands of foreign fighters have been joining them since the strikes in New York."

The words stuck in Kris's throat as he translated. *Strikes in New York*. The American homeland, attacked. Americans dying inside their borders. Never before had that happened. Never, ever before. And he'd let it happen.

He forced himself back to the conversation, back to the Dari and English flying around him.

"What are your plans here, in our country? What is your timetable for destroying the Taliban? When will you bring in your bombs? How will you help the people here, who suffer the most under the Taliban? When will things get done? And when will you leave?"

Kris translated Khan's questions carefully, holding George's steady gaze.

George wasn't pleased. "We have an immense amount to do, and only twenty-four hours each day to work with. Before anything happens, we need to scope out the lay of the land. Send out a team to recon Taliban positions. Identify exactly where the Shura Nazar forces are. Create a map of the battlefield. We can only do one thing at a time. We have to do this right."

General Khan was scowling before Kris finished translating. "Right now, the Taliban and the Shura Nazar are at an impasse. Neither side is strong enough to break the other, *agha* George. But every day, thousands of fighters come to join the Taliban and al-Qaeda and to kill Americans, and anyone who helps the Americans. *My* people." Khan thumped his chest. "My people are the ones who have been fighting the Taliban for years. You say you need our help, but you refuse to help my people in return?"

Kris spoke in English to Ryan and George. "He's pissed. We need to give him and his people something, and soon."

"We just gave him a million bucks!" George frowned as Ryan scowled.

Kris smiled at Khan and bowed his head as he spoke in Dari. "We need to scout the terrain. Prepare for our forces, before they can arrive. To do that, we need vehicles." He nodded to the rusted hulks of scrap that had brought them up the mountain. "We won't take your trucks. You and your men need them. We will need to buy trucks. Will you find four trucks for us? We will purchase them at fair prices. And..." Kris grasped Khan's hand as Khan's frown darkened. "We will use these trucks to not only scout the lines, but deliver aid to your people. And as soon as we can, we will arrange for more food to be sent."

Khan stroked his dark beard. He squeezed Kris's hand, holding it on Kris's knee. "This will help my people, yes. Four trucks will be expensive, though. They will cost fifteen thousand each."

Fifteen thousand dollars for heaps of scrap. Kris smiled. "*Alhamdulillah.*"

"I will return tomorrow with your trucks, *Gul Bahar*." Khan held Kris's hand in the air, celebrating, and then released his grasp.

Ryan and George stared at him, their gazes hard enough to chisel stone.

Kris answered their unasked questions. "I bought us trucks. We need to get around. I also said we would deliver aid as we scouted the front lines."

George kept his face neutral, a practiced skill. "What aid?" he asked carefully.

"We're being fed by Ghasi every day. We can spare the MREs we brought until we schedule a humanitarian aid drop."

Ryan leaned across George, eyes wide as he seemed ready to tear Kris a new asshole.

George held him back. "We'll discuss this later." He took a deep breath and smiled at Khan. He spoke to Kris. "See who speaks Russian. I want this joint intel cell set up ASAP. I need the people in it to speak Russian so I can communicate with them."

Kris translated, turning away from George. The back of his neck burned. Why did George need to speak directly to the intel cell? He was the translator on the mission, wasn't he?

"Several of my officers speak Russian," Khan replied. "They were educated in Tashkent and Dushanbe and in Yekaterinburg. I will send them to you tomorrow."

Kris relayed Khan's words, then frowned at George. "George, we're going to be limited to the top range of the weakest Russian speaker." He left out his concerns that the weakest individual could be George himself. "I can translate Dari for the intel cell."

"No, you can't, Kris." George gave him a thin, strained smile. "Because you're going to scout the front lines."

---

David watched the meeting from the compound's entrance, manning the point position on the team. Palmer had spread out everyone, encircling Khan's party and the CIA team, creating a security bubble for their people. Everyone on David's team had their weapons in hand, fingers curled around the triggers. One wrong move, one hint of subterfuge, or an attack—

His gaze kept dragging to Kris, no matter how he tried to look away. Kris, speaking fluent Dari and connecting with Khan in all the right ways, as courteous and respectful as the suavest socialite in Benghazi or Beirut or Cairo. He knew the rhythms of the people, that was obvious. He knew how to move and breathe with Islam, how to live in the religion in a way that David only barely remembered. Kris had spoken Arabic to David like it sounded in David's dreams, his earliest memories. David had thought he'd covered his accent, had made it purposefully bland, purposefully Gulf with faint hints of Egyptian. He'd thought wrong, if Kris could uncover him so completely from their first hello.

But that was just one more thing to bury.

Sixteen hours, they'd been in Afghanistan. He'd kept his mind occupied from the moment they'd entered Afghan airspace. Running through the mission, over and over. What would happen when they landed, who would take the lead. Palmer's orders, his mission plan. Their contingencies. Their contingencies' contingencies.

Kris.

Palmer had told them all, before the CIA showed up, that they would have to take the lead in securing the CIA officers with whom they were partnering. They had to make sure none of them got shot, kidnapped, or executed. Who knew what the circumstances were on the ground? It was up to them to keep everyone alive, keep the mission going. So far, the situation seemed far better than their most dire predictions, back in Tashkent, had imagined.

But still, he'd kept close to Kris. Shielded him in the helo. Watched over him on the journey to the compound. Delayed and delayed, until there was only one choice left for a roommate and a sleeping room.

Kris was both the mission and a distraction, a man David was obligated to protect, to defend, and a man who called to him. He could feel his blood stirring, his body turning, waking in ways he'd forbidden, other than the briefest, most fleeting encounter.

That, and Kris, were distractions. But not just from their mission.

Afghanistan, as a land, as a people, had been mythic, larger than life. During the run-up to the mission, Palmer and the rest of the operations staff had spoken in cold, clinical terms, briefing the team on the landscape, the environment, expected hostilities. He'd been awash in preparations, reeling, like everyone had been, and consumed with a sense of purpose.

*Go. Do. Act. Revenge.*

Purpose had drowned the hidden shadows that lingered in his soul, slid between his bones, caressed the spaces between his ribs. Twenty-one years ago, he'd fled Libya hand in hand with his mother. Fled the sand and the sun and the Arabic, the daily rhythms of Islam. The calls to prayer, and the way the sun slanted through the morning windows, bursting the prayer rugs he and his father kept side by side to vibrant, vivacious life. There were worn spots on their prayer rugs at the knees and where their foreheads hit the rug together. His father's prayer rug, older, more used, had a bald spot where his forehead rested, five times every day, for the length of David's memories.

Twenty-one years and twelve days. That was how long it had been since he'd thought of Islam, thought of his father. Thought of the words of the Quran, the prayers that used to slip over his lips in time with his father's voice.

Memories lived in shadow, buried in his bones, pushed down so deep he was a smuggler of his own existence, his own past.

Until twelve days ago.

September 11.

To be Arab, to be Muslim, after September 11, especially in America, was to be full of questions. Confusion. Horror. Rage.

To have the words of the Quran inside of him, the rhythms of Islam in his soul, so long dead and buried he'd thought they'd atrophied and atomized into a billion pieces of sand and had blown away, was a slowly opening abyss.

*"We're going to go over there, and we're going to kill all those towel-headed motherfuckers that think they can get away with this. We are going to avenge the deaths of our countrymen. Hoorah!"*

Palmer's commander, their unit colonel, had led them all in a raging speech shortly before they'd taken off for Tashkent. *"We're going to kill every one of them. Every single one."*

Twenty-one years ago, David had left it all behind. He wasn't a Muslim. He wasn't an Arab. Not anymore.

The muezzin's call to isha prayer, the nightly prayer, after the sun had set and the stars unfurled above, their first night in Afghanistan, had struck his soul like lightning. His memories were a weathervane, a lightning rod. Images flickered in the dark as he lay in their new compound, surrounded by his team and with Kris sleeping two feet away.

Images of his father, praying, the night before *it* happened. Their bodies moving as one, folding, bending, kneeling. In his mind, he wasn't thirty-one, he was ten, suddenly, from the first note of the muezzin's wail until sometime late in the night, when his soul was released and he floated back through space and time, back to the man he'd become.

Kris, with his fiery eyes, his flashing smile, sharp enough to cut, to hurt, was like an oasis in the Sahara. *Take me from these memories*, he thought in a small voice, his ten-year-old voice, whispered. *I'm not*

*Muslim. I'm not Libyan. I'm American. I'm here to do my job, serve my country. Complete my mission.*

His gaze drifted back to Kris.

Twenty-one years ago *and* twelve days ago—simultaneously—his world had been ripped apart. Certainty became a chasm. Truths he'd stood on for years had vanished, leaving only questions. A boy after his *after*, and an Arab after September 11. As a child, he'd nurtured a love of silence, especially *after*. Stillness. The thought that if he didn't move, didn't change, nothing would happen. Nothing would move on from that moment. As a man, he charged ahead. The only way through was forward. The way back was lost, gone forever. Answers, if there were any, belonged to someone else.

But now a man had walked into his life, a slender young man, barbed and pointed and fighting tooth and nail. In Kris's life, there were no questions. How could there be, when he was so vividly alive? A man like Kris, who lived life out loud but who had joined the CIA to work in secrets and silence, and who concealed nothing of himself except everything that mattered. Who *was* he?

Why did David want to crawl to him? Stay by his side until his heart stopped beating?

Like a wave trying to curl up the sandy shore, beating against the earth ceaselessly, always trying again, parts of David reached for Kris.

*Foolish,* his mind whispered. *So foolish.*

But he had questions. So many questions.

And maybe Kris had answers.

# 6

**Panjshir Valley, Afghanistan - September 27, 2001**

War, like all things, moved slowly.

Scouting the front lines was delayed. The trucks Kris ordered from Khan arrived through Ghasi and Fazl, hulks of scrap metal with bullet holes and overheating engines. Each had a bucket of water in the bed and old mounts for a Russian PK machine gun. They'd been technicals once, the light cavalry of warlords and sanctioned countries the world over: old, beat-up pickups retrofitted with machine guns.

"Captured from Taliban," Fazl said, pride in his voice. "Now they are ours. Yours."

Despite General Khan's insistence that he wanted to move quickly, he still seemed to operate on Afghan Time. George, Ryan, and Palmer fumed as one day bled into the next and the Shura Nazar officers still hadn't arrived for the joint intelligence cell.

"The culture isn't based on linear thinking, George." Kris tried to calm another of Ryan and George's rants. They paced on the concrete porch as they drank cups of instant coffee. "The culture is based on relationships. Impressions. Time is an afterthought to the importance of relationships."

"We don't have time to waste on relationships," George growled.

"You're going to have to make time. You can't force this. We're guests in their country asking for their help."

Ryan snorted. "We can do this without their help. We really can."

George's jaw worked, his teeth grinding. "What do you suggest, Caldera? As the Afghanistan expert?"

"Slow down. Connect more with Khan, with the Shura Nazar forces."

"Speaking of connecting—"

George shot a harsh glare at Ryan, shaking his head sharply. Ryan held up his hands, but he stared Kris down.

"How are the intercepts coming?"

Kris sighed. He squeezed his eyes shut, trying to block out the headache that lived behind his eyeballs. "Good, so far. We're getting a shit ton of traffic. I'm going as fast as I can, but..." He trailed off. His fastest still wasn't enough to keep up with everything they were getting.

Half a day in-country, Phillip had broken into the Taliban radio net. Every Taliban radio transmission in range of their receivers was vacuumed up and recorded. Kris spent hours listening in real-time and to the recordings, translating endless conversations in Dari and Arabic.

Al-Qaeda used a different radio frequency, and Phillip hadn't had as much success breaking into their radio net. Yet. Part of the problem was that the team's headquarters was so far from al-Qaeda's base of operations. The Taliban front lines were much closer.

"Sergeant Haddad has been helping you translate?" George's voice went thin. His gaze was guarded.

Kris nodded. He said nothing.

Haddad stuck to him like he was Kris's personal shadow. From sunrise, when the team rose, all through the day, and into the evening. When the radio transmissions started piling up, Haddad jumped in, grabbing a set of headphones and listening in to the

Arabic transmissions, the Taliban communicating with al-Qaeda, or foreign fighters within the Taliban ranks.

He and Haddad hadn't spoken much. Translating radio intercepts wasn't a talkative job. After, Kris was so brain-dead and exhausted that he usually stayed quiet throughout dinner and the team meetings. But Haddad was always right there, at his side. Most evenings, he sat close enough that Kris could slouch into his side. He could almost rest his head on Haddad's shoulder.

But he didn't.

Not because he didn't want to.

It was Ryan who stopped him, and George. The eyes that followed him at headquarters, the snide comments behind his back. The guys from The Farm, even, in training, who'd thought he'd never make it through, would never graduate and become an officer. Everything and everyone stopped him.

Ryan's eyes glittered, the way he watched Kris, like a predator stalking a gazelle on the savanna. One wrong move, one mistake, and Kris would prove everyone's worst imaginings, their worst prejudices, right.

And what would Haddad think if he folded into Haddad bodily the way his soul was folding into his care and comfort? What was this, between them? He didn't know, and he couldn't know. Couldn't imagine anything, either. There was no time, no space to wonder, or to dream. Each day was spent living one hour at a time, doing what they had to do. Building an alliance. Starting a war. Striking back.

Every night, Kris retreated to his sleeping bag early, collapsing for a few hours of fitful sleep. He woke in the middle of the night, inevitably, and crawled out to the radio room. If he was up, then he might as well translate some radio intercepts.

Haddad had followed him, about an hour later, the first night. He hadn't said anything, just sat beside Kris and started working on his own translations.

Every morning, as the first beams of the cold marigold sun began to peek through the mountains, Haddad brought him a cup of instant coffee and insisted he take a break. The rest of the team woke up to them sitting around the fire, sometimes talking softly, sometimes just staring at the flames.

Occasionally, Haddad asked about life at the CIA. What Kris did at Langley, and how he liked working there. Kris asked him about the Army, about the Special Forces.

Haddad said training was awful, he loved the camaraderie and brotherhood, and that he'd deployed to Somalia and survived the Battle of Mogadishu. He didn't say much after that.

There was no privacy in their compound, or in the village. Everyone saw how Haddad stuck by him, how close they were becoming. Every meal was eaten side by side. They all ate together on a wide blanket spread in the corner of the main compound, surrounded by cushions. Occasionally, Haddad slid a piece of meat to Kris's plate, or gave him two apples and his hunk of fresh-baked bread. Every night, they retired to the same sleeping room.

Their sleeping bags were islands in the little stone room, though. As much as Kris might wonder what was happening between them, the six inches of empty space between their sleeping bags was answer enough. To Haddad, he must be someone to protect. A part of the mission, something catalogued and itemized and checked, like his medical equipment and his rifle.

Should he be bothered that Haddad thought he needed so much caretaking?

The truth was, he didn't want to fight it. He liked Haddad's protection, his quiet care. A part of him even craved it.

*Dangerous ground*, he warned himself. *Dangerous territory. Focus on the mission.*

*Besides, you're not worth someone like him. He should do better than the likes of you.*

Kris slipped up to the roof of their compound in the evenings to watch the sun set. Phillip and Jim were up there five times a day, cleaning the fuel filter of the generator and trying to keep their power up and running. The fuel in Afghanistan was so poorly refined that it clogged their generator, shutting everything down. When Derek saw the condition of the generator's filter, he booked it back down to the airfield and checked their parked helo. Both fuel filters were clogged, almost completely. Had they flown any farther during their initial flight, they would have stalled and crashed.

Afghanistan's war-ravaged past littered the country as far as the eye could see. The village they were in had been captured six out of the eight times the Soviets had invaded the Panjshir Valley. It was the high-water mark of their invasion. They'd never succeeded in advancing any farther. The Afghans had pushed them back each time, devastating the Soviets. For months, the village had been shelled and bombed day and night during the invasion, almost fifteen years before. Every building had crumbled. The rubble of old houses stood beside the new square mud homes, the entire village shifted ten feet to the left. Resilience in its purest form.

Massoud had led his fighters against the Soviets and against the Taliban. He'd been an Afghan nationalist for longer than Kris had been alive. His presence, his influence, his leadership, was everywhere in the Panjshir, permeating the people and the nation.

Al-Qaeda had succeeded where empires had failed, extinguishing the life of the strongest warlord in Afghanistan. Massoud's death had been their opening act to September 11.

If September 11 hadn't happened, if it had been stopped, would Masood still be alive?

Could it have been stopped? If his team, if he, had shared what they knew of Marwan al-Shehhi, Nawaf al-Hazmi and Khalid al-Mihdhar? Could the hijackers have been stopped?

He tried to rein in his morose thoughts, tried to stop the tumble and slide of his mind into the darkness of shame.

"Caldera?" Haddad's voice cut through the miasma, the fog that surrounded him. Kris turned. Haddad strode across the empty roof. Jim and Phillip had left, probably long ago, through with cleaning the fuel filter. They'd be back in a few hours, at it again.

"Hey." The sun had almost set, the sky streaked with watercolor pastels, lilac and periwinkle, persimmon and cornflower. Stars winked overhead, burning points that speared through the sky, undaunted by city lights or pollution. When the night turned black, and the only light came from the fire and the red night-vision bulbs they switched over to, the sky looked like a beachhead of the universe, the stars like the sand of the galaxy twinkling as waves and waves of darkness rolled over the world.

Staring up at the stars made him feel like he was the only human on the entire planet. For once, the universe appeared as lonely as he felt, seemed to echo inside all of his empty places.

Haddad stopped at Kris's shoulder, close enough that their arms, their thighs, their hips brushed, swayed back and forth. In a moment, Haddad would step away, cough and look down, shift, and try and play the touches off. Kris saw it all the time.

"It's pretty here." Haddad's voice was soft, deep. "Sometimes it's hard to imagine the worst atrocities happen in the most beautiful places. Somalia was like that, in a way. And—" He stopped. Swallowed. "Makes you wonder sometimes. Why the world's like this."

Kris sighed. "Everything's connected. It's all one big web. A butterfly flaps its wings in Brazil, and the stock market crashes. We thought we could ignore Afghanistan, but we were wrong. Where does it all begin, though? Where's the beginning of this hate?"

Massoud fighting the Taliban. Massoud fighting the Russians, the communists, America's enemy. There was a thread connecting everything together, he knew it. History was a flow that tumbled all things to their end, consequences and outcomes frothing up from the actions and reactions of time. What were they creating now, in their moment? What would tumble forth, ever onward, from their actions, this time?

Haddad sighed. He shoved his hands into the pockets of his jacket. He didn't step away. Kris felt every inch of his breath, the slow rise and fall of his chest. "Whatever beginning there is, it was long before now."

Kris's soul flinched, his insides carved out so suddenly he almost collapsed. His mouth moved. He tried to breathe, tried to speak. Couldn't. Black flags flapped in the distance, on the edge of the horizon, and in the back of his mind, burned into the backs of his eyelids.

Haddad stared at him beneath the stars. In the darkness, his eyes were stars themselves, too close to Kris, burning through him, exposing him. "Caldera?" His words puffed in front of his face, the chill of the night trying to freeze their bones.

Kris stepped back. "We should get inside." His breath fluttered, as if it could escape him. "Ryan... He'll wonder where I am."

Haddad said nothing, just walked with Kris down to the landing and then into the compound.

George and Ryan both looked up as they walked in together. Kris saw them trade long looks.

At his side, Haddad stared back.

---

In the morning, Khan's promised officers arrived: Wael and Bashir. They got to work and connected with the Shura Nazar radio operators across the Panjshir, started receiving detailed intelligence and information reports from each outpost. Taliban frontline positions, fortifications, fighters, and armaments. Observations of troop movements. Even what some of the Taliban ate for breakfast.

Kris helped tack up a wall-sized map of Afghanistan in their command center. George and Ryan marked off the positions Wael and Bashir identified, setting pins wrapped with colored string around the Taliban and Shura Nazar positions. Ryan faded away after, hovering over Phillip as he transmitted the morning's reports back to Langley over the fussy secured satellite interlink.

"If we start bombing, and we don't have exact GPS positions on the Shura Nazar forces, we're going to be killing a lot of innocent people." George scrubbed his face. "Kris, the GPS positions are critical. We have to know exactly where they are."

"I know. I'll get it done." What was this, him being given possibly the most critical job on the team? George, for all his criticism, his dark glares and veiled stares, wanted the mission to succeed. Wanted the US to wash Afghanistan in righteous vengeance, destroy the Taliban, and al-Qaeda, and even bolster the Shura Nazar.

"You're the best linguist of us all, Kris. And you understand the people more than the rest of us. You've connected with Khan. You're the only one who can make sure nothing is missed." Over his coffee, George's eyes looked like sunken pits, eyeballs falling into sagging crevices of exhaustion. "Ryan, Jim, and Palmer are going to take the Special Forces guys and survey the Shura Nazar forces. See what kind of support they need. Supplies." He pinched the bridge of his nose, squeezing his eyes closed again. "We—the team, Langley, CENTCOM, even the president—can't do anything until you get back with those coordinates."

"I understand, George." Pressure coiled around his spine. Was it not enough he had thousands of souls on his conscience already? Should he add the nation of Afghanistan to his guilt? "What about the MREs? I told General Khan I would be providing aid to his people."

"And you'll be bringing it. All of it. God help us, I hope we don't starve."

"Ghasi is taking care of us."

"For now. I've requested a resupply from Langley. They have to fly the MREs to us from Germany through Tajikistan. It will take a week. I hope our goodwill with the Shura Nazar lasts that long."

*Don't be an asshole, and it will.* Kris bit his tongue. "When do I leave?"

"They're packing everything into your truck now. The driver who brought Wael and Bashir is taking you down to the front as soon as that's done. Are you ready?"

He'd been packed for days, since George had first told him he was going. Kris nodded.

"Good luck. We're all counting on you." George shook his hand, the firmest he'd ever had, as if George meant what he was saying. "If anyone can do this, it's you."

He didn't know what to say.

Haddad appeared at their elbows. "Truck is packed, sir."

George's eyes skittered away from Kris. "Good. Time for you both to head out."

"Both?" Kris looked from Haddad to George and back.

"No one goes anywhere alone. You two seem to work well together. Haddad will provide security and backup while you're scouting positions with General Khan."

Haddad gave Kris the tiniest smile.

---

Within the hour, they were bouncing down the loosest definition of a road, ever, in their truck. It was a bone-shattering one hundred miles to the front lines, but it might as well have been a thousand. The mountain track winding through the Panjshir was one lane wide, big enough for horses or camels. Any width added by the Soviets during the invasion had long crumbled away into ruin. Craters and remnants of artillery and splintered bombs littered the mountains, the roadside, the road itself. Dust, millennia of dust, blew around the truck until Kris couldn't see. He couldn't brace himself when the truck inevitably careened into the craters, the pits in the road. Each jolt felt like a car accident, felt like he'd been rear-ended by a semi.

He sat in the front while Haddad sat in the back with both their daypacks. Kris had packed all his cold weather gear—sweaters, neoprene undersuit, wool gloves, scarves, Haddad's hat—water, and a few MREs for himself. Haddad's pack was larger. The MREs for Khan were in the truck bed.

Two hours into the drive, just over halfway to the front, the road curled around a blind bend in the mountain and then opened up, descending to a verdant, wide river valley, the mouth of the Panjshir Valley. The river that wound through the village collected tributaries and creeks through its passage south and had widened to a flat delta spread between the mountains. Mudbrick homes, ringed in apple orchards and small farms, squatted between the peaks on the bank of the delta. They were a million miles away from home, but, for a moment, it seemed like a scene from President Lincoln's childhood.

On the opposite peak, fluttering above the valley, a line of green flags waved in the wind. Martyr's flags. Sunlight splintered into the mountain, streaks of light that hit each one.

"General Massoud's grave?" Kris's stomach knotted.

Their driver nodded but didn't look up. His hands clenched around the steering wheel until the old plastic squealed. He refused to wipe away the tears rolling down his cheeks as he sped them out of the valley and toward the Shomali Plain.

An hour later, after speeding along the northern edge of the Shomali Plain and hugging the mountains and cliffs, their driver turned toward a compound surrounded by a chain-link fence twined with barbed wire. Blocky concrete buildings, reminiscent of Soviet architecture, loomed within. T-72 Russian tanks and Soviet artillery lay parked in even rows. Sandbagged machine gun positions hovered before the compound with antiaircraft positions dug into the hills above. Soldiers in crisp, clean uniforms manned guard posts, watching their approach with an eagle eye, weapons at the ready. They recognized their driver, but gave Kris and Haddad long, lingering looks.

Radios on the guards' waists chirped, spitting out Dari. The guards listened, and then opened the gates and waved the truck through. A delegation of officers waited across the clearing, at the compound's entrance.

"This is... much more organized than we expected," Haddad said under his breath. "I've seen Army bases run with less precision."

Kris met his gaze through the rusted rearview mirror. A motley band of guerilla fighters, these people were not.

General Khan waited at the steps. He beamed when he spotted Kris through the filthy passenger window.

"*Gul Bahar*!" Laughing, Khan held both his hands open as Kris climbed out of the truck, shaking his limbs loose and trying to reseat joints banged up and bruised from the brutal drive. "I am pleased you are here." Khan hugged him tight and kissed both of his cheeks. He held one hand over his heart.

Haddad waited behind Kris. "David Haddad," he said simply, holding out his ungloved hands. He clasped Khan's hand in both of his as they shook, bowing slightly. "Thank you for your hospitality, General."

Khan's chest swelled. His smile grew. "Come, come, we will share tea," he said in his stilted English. He beckoned them both into the compound.

Kris turned back to the truck for his pack. Haddad stopped him. "There's only one pack."

"What? I packed mine and loaded it into the truck myself. Did it get left behind?"

Haddad shook his head. He hefted his own, much larger than it had been when they left. He didn't strain, didn't flinch. "I repacked everything. Into my bag."

"*Sergeant*—"

"The general is waiting for us."

Khan called from the doorway. "Come! The tea will be cold!"

He wanted to scream, rip the pack from Haddad's shoulders and shake out all his belongings. He could carry his own weight, Goddamn it. Wasn't that his vow from day one? He could handle himself. What right did Haddad have, butting in and sweeping everything away from him? Wrapping him up in... What was this? Consideration? Or condescension?

Haddad nodded for him to follow Khan. Kris sighed, a promise that they would revisit this later, that the conversation was not finished. He had to put his foot down before Haddad ran right over him and his convictions.

Khan eyed Haddad shouldering their shared pack. He smiled again at Kris. "*Agha Gul Bahar*."

*Agha*, the honorific title for a man of respect. A leader, the man in charge. Kris stared at Haddad.

Haddad smothered a smile as he looked down, keeping behind Kris's shoulder. Deferential.

Damn it, he'd done it on purpose. He'd known what message shouldering the pack would send, what General Khan and the others would see out of his actions. Haddad had just shown Khan, and all the Afghans, that Kris was his leader, his superior. That Kris should be treated as an equal to General Khan.

Kris followed Khan, winding through corridors and up narrow

staircases until they arrived at the top floor, General Khan's private office and quarters. The room provided a panoramic view of the Shomali Plain, the former breadbasket of Afghanistan. Once, it had been a lush garden, fruit orchards and farmers' fields from the eastern slopes of the Hindu Kush to the desert edges of western Afghanistan, all the way to the gates of Kabul.

Now, armies ringed both sides of the Plain, Taliban and Shura Nazar. Decades of war had ravaged the land, turning the fields to desolate wastes, as pitted and pocked as the moon, and just as welcoming. Only the dead lived in the Plain now.

Khan called for tea and bread to be brought out. Young soldiers, no more than boys, scurried in, balancing trays of tea with chipped Russian glasses and plates of hot, fresh-baked bread. Apples and dates followed, and fresh yogurt. Kris could smell the milk, the tart skin of the apples.

Khan sat beside him, right next to him, on floor cushions before the window. Haddad settled down a respectful distance away.

They spoke gently, chatting back and forth over tea for almost an hour. Khan wanted to know how Kris liked Afghanistan and the Panjshir, the valley Khan had called home for over forty years. He could name every tree, every creek, every fruit that grew. He knew the horse and camel tracks like he knew the twists of veins on the backs of his hands. The land was in his soul, and his bones were made of Afghanistan's dust, his blood her waters.

Kris spoke honestly, telling Khan he thought the country was breathtaking, the land beautiful, but scarred by conflict and brutality. Haunted by sadness. Khan agreed, and their conversation shifted to what his people needed, and the supplies Kris had brought. Khan grasped his hand and held on, their hands resting on Khan's knee. The entire time, Haddad sat silently nearby, sipping his tea and calmly watching their back-and-forth in Dari.

Finally, Khan shifted to the business of why Kris was down on the front lines. Had George been there, Kris thought, he'd have crawled out of his skin long before, stepping all over Khan's friendship and relationship-building in his quest to get things done immediately and ferociously.

"We must travel my front lines, yes? Plot positions of all forces?"

"Yes, General." At Kris's nod, Haddad passed over the GPS units. "We need exact positions of your forces."

"This is so your planes can bomb the Taliban? So you can destroy them completely?"

Kris nodded. "We want to make sure none of your people are mistakenly targeted—"

"If you destroy the Taliban, and my people fall while fighting beside you, it will be an honorable death. As long as the Taliban are wiped from Afghanistan in the end. Them, and their al-Qaeda allies," Khan growled, spitting out his last words. "Those al-Qaeda dogs, they are filth in this land."

Stunned, Kris sat silent for a moment. Haddad stared at him, eyes burning into Kris's profile. He'd sensed the change in the conversation, the ebb and flow, though he couldn't understand the meaning.

"Khan is fine with collateral damage," Kris breathed, passing back the GPS handheld. "As long as we obliterate the enemy."

Haddad's eyes narrowed, but he said nothing.

Khan let go of Kris's hand and stood. "Let us begin this survey. The sooner we get it done, the sooner you begin dropping your bombs."

---

Khan led them to a convoy of trucks in the courtyard and guided Kris and Haddad to the back of his truck, giving the signal to move out. As they drove, Haddad started taking photographs, snapping pictures of the fortifications on the hills, dug into the mountains above, and across the dreary plains toward Kabul.

"Our front lines are not what you imagined, yes?" Khan twisted around in the front seat. For Haddad, he spoke in his heavily accented English. "It never is, for you. From the West. Journalists, they come sometimes. They are disappointed. We are no savages, guerilla fighters around campfires, shivering as we starve." Khan laughed.

On their right, the hills bled upward into the northern mountains. Khan's soldiers had fortified positions running up the slopes, embedded fighting positions, machine gun placements, and antiaircraft positions. Bunkers ran along the ridgeline. "We own the high ground here. The hills, the mountains. We have built bunkers in place and have solid firing positions for miles across the Plain. Our lines run down into the Shomali, across Bagram Airfield."

"With the high ground, you can see all of the Taliban movements in the Shomali?" Kris asked as Haddad took more photos.

"Everything they do, we see. We have tanks and artillery. To keep them in place. If they break out of the Shomali and try to cross our lines—" Khan grinned. "They will be destroyed."

"You're organized, you're armed, you have the high ground. Why do you not attack?"

Khan sighed. The truck bounced and swerved, weaving and climbing along the hillside. He slipped back to Dari. "We hold them in place. But they hold us in place as well. I do not have the men or the arms to mount an attack. I only have the strength to repel their attacks and hold the Taliban out of the Panjshir." Khan nodded to Kris. "This is where you come in. Why we have invited the Americans to help us."

"We have a common enemy, General."

"The people of Afghanistan have been enemies of the Taliban for years, *agha Gul Bahar*. But now the Taliban are your enemy, too. The Taliban killed thousands of Afghans for years before they killed your Americans."

Kris kept his mouth shut. The taste of ash filled his mouth, acrid smoke that seemed to fill his soul. He closed his eyes, rocking sideways as the truck slipped past a boulder in the road.

They pulled to a stop at the base of a winding hillside track. "We go up." Khan pointed to the steep, narrow track zigzagging past boulders and through low scrub. They'd continue on foot to the crest of the ridge overlooking the Shomali. "The front is there. We will follow the front and plot your maps. Come!"

Kris struggled to keep up with Khan. He slid out on the loose dirt, the rocky soil, falling to his hands to steady himself. They were climbing a mountain, but the base was already at almost ten thousand feet of elevation. He felt like he was sprinting up the Rocky Mountains. Each breath seemed thin, as though there wasn't enough air left in the world for him to survive.

Haddad followed behind, carrying their pack. Kris heard his grunts, his labored breaths, his soft curses under his wheezes. He wanted to offer to share the load, carry the pack for half of the climb. If he did, he'd die, though. He would tip over backward and slide to the bottom of the hills or collapse like a tin can under the weight of the pack. He wanted to do more, be more, especially for Haddad. But it was all he could do to cling to the dirt and keep climbing, following behind General Khan, who roared up the mountain like it was his morning walk.

It probably was.

Finally, they arrived at the top. Khan politely waited, looking away as Haddad pulled out his canteen. He offered it to Kris first. Kris refused, and Haddad downed half the bottle as Kris hovered beside him, breathing hard with his hands on his hips. Haddad passed over the canteen and wiped his face, dripping with sweat.

"You okay?" Kris muttered, after drinking. "That was..."

"Awful." Haddad chuckled. "That was terrible." He spat in the dirt, rolled his shoulders. "But I'm good."

"You shouldn't have repacked everything. You shouldn't have had to carry everything up by yourself. I can carry my own weight."

Haddad's gaze pierced him, again seeming to look right through him. "I know you can. I didn't do this because I thought you were weak. I wanted the General to see you right. To treat you the right way."

"What way is that?"

"As the leader. The man in charge, and the expert. I'm just your muscle here."

"Sergeant—"

"No rank. Not here, not now."

Khan called out, "Are you ready to carry on?"

Haddad raised his eyebrows, waiting for Kris.

"Yes, General." Kris turned away from Haddad and joined Khan. From above, the Shomali was a blurry mess of brown, all the shades of brown Kris had ever seen, from oily tar to dusty, smog-filled air choking the distance. Kabul was a smudge, a rub of dirt on the horizon, surrounded by fallow, empty farmland and desert. Dirty snow rose on the Hindu Kush to the east.

"This is the eastern end of my front lines." Khan spoke in English and waved over the ridgeline, the Shomali Plain below. "We will follow the front to the west. You will see our positions and those of the Taliban. You can see them now, in fact."

"Can they see us?"

He waved his hand in the air, a vague, *kinda-sorta* gesture. "They like to shoot off rounds of artillery if they think strange things happening. They are sometimes lucky."

Haddad stepped up to Kris's back, like he could protect Kris with his muscles, shield Kris from an artillery strike with his presence alone.

Khan led them down the front lines, following a well-worn trail behind his men and their fighting positions. Dug-in foxholes and sandbag-reinforced berms shielded Shura Nazar fighters. "Everything in the Shomali, the Taliban have destroyed. Farms, houses, villages. All gone. They took over the villages outside Kabul. Everyone who used to live there is gone." He mimed shooting a gun as if he were executing someone. "They use these villages as bases, bunkers. Artillery can hurt them, but to truly fight the Taliban there, you need either close fighting, village by village, or—" He smiled. "Or, your American bombs must fall on them."

Haddad peered across the plains. "What about al-Qaeda?"

"The Arab fighters are embedded in the Taliban. They keep to their own units. They fight better than the Taliban. They can aim. They are fierce fighters, especially those from Chechnya and Central

Asia. They want to die fighting. They love death. The Taliban keep the Arabs out of range of our artillery, in a line that circles Kabul, beyond the outer villages."

"You can show us where they are?"

"Come. We will begin plotting." Khan waved them both toward a bunker built into the hillside, behind the fighting positions and beneath the artillery. It was a concrete box with slits for windows, built to withstand Taliban artillery fire. Inside the dark, musty, frigid room, wooden beams, cut from thick trees, propped up the concrete ceiling. Lanterns burned on a central table laid with maps of Afghanistan in Russian and Persian. Khan spread his hands wide. "Let us begin."

Haddad dropped their pack and Kris pulled out their maps, marked with rough information about the front lines. As Khan read off the positions of his own forces, Kris translated those to their map, marking exactly where Khan's forces were placed. All three maps were in different scales: American, Persian, and Russian geographic scales all using different measurement systems. After Kris jumped through the conversions and marked Khan's positions on their map, Haddad input the coordinates into the GPS system, saving each entry as "friendly forces."

Khan checked each coordinate, approved each input into the GPS.

Every few hours, they moved down the line to the next bunker. In the afternoon, Khan radioed for lunch, and they sat with Shura Nazar fighters, sharing mystery meat roasted over a fire, and apples, rice, and tea. Haddad was drenched in sweat, even though the temperature hovered in the upper thirties. Kris offered to carry something, anything, to lighten the load. Haddad refused.

At the end of the day, they had half of the Shomali Plain mapped. Khan called for them to quit as the sun began to descend, and a hoarse Shura Nazar soldier started crying the *azan*, the call to prayer. Kris and Haddad stood to the side as Khan joined his soldiers, everyone kneeling and facing southwest to pray.

"Are you a believer?" Kris leaned into Haddad's side, whispering in his ear. Haddad wasn't praying with the Shura Nazar.

Haddad hesitated. "I was raised Muslim."

Kris frowned. "With a name like David, I thought..."

"It's actually Dawood. I changed it when we moved to America. And I stopped going to the mosque then, too." He smiled, but it seemed strained, almost forced. "There were too many other things to do, especially in high school."

Kris chuckled. His own high school years had been a blur of hormones and hot boys, pimples and his gangly body growing in too fast. He'd wanted to inject New York City straight into his veins, live the fast life, but he'd been all mouth and legs and pimply sass. It had taken college to blunt those edges, and then a few years of government grind to force him down even further. A few years of stares and glares and socialization, being ostracized from the herd when he was too loud, too gay, being welcomed when he was conforming just enough. Psychology 101, Pavlovian responses, building a life.

And one attack to shatter his soul.

"So you don't still believe? Or pray?"

Haddad shrugged. "Feels like a lifetime ago. A different person. You?"

His mamá had dragged him to Catholic mass when he was a boy, licking his hair into place and forcing him to wear those awful shiny shoes that pinched his feet. He tagged along until he was old enough to stay out Saturday nights, just late enough that he could whine and bitch about not wanting to get up early to go to Mass. Mamá had soured at him, her lips pursed like she'd sucked on a lemon, but after three months straight of that act, she never asked him to go with her again. At the time, it had felt like a weight had been pulled from him, like Atlas had set down the world. Not having to pretend, to endure the stares, the whispers, the questions about when he'd bring a sweet girl to Mass with him and Mamá.

He hadn't had to think too deeply about things like eternal guilt, hellfire, and damnation. He'd flat-out refused to believe he'd burn in hell for liking dick. That was ridiculous.

But murder? Three thousand souls hung from his soul. Their screams shredded his bones, the sobs of families ripped apart drowned him in his nightmares. *I'm getting revenge*, he'd whisper. *I'm avenging you.*

*It's not good enough. It will never be good enough.* Like a constant refrain, the words echoed up from the nothingness, the pit within him that had opened at 8:46 AM, Tuesday, September 11.

"No. I don't believe." Kris crossed his arms. Shook his head. Looked away.

Haddad stared at him. Said nothing.

After prayers and another meal of mystery meat, fruit, rice, and tea, Khan led them to the soldiers' sleeping quarters, caves chipped into the hills behind and above the bunker. Some of the Shura Nazar had been living in the caves for years. The sleeping nests looked permanent, and lanterns hung on the rock face. Fire pits dug deep holes into the dirt, dark smoke blackening the cave walls and ceiling.

Kris and Haddad received their own cave, next to the others, but for their private use. Two cushions lay next to a fire pit.

"We will meet again after morning prayers." Khan, as gregarious as he had been that morning, shook their hands and bade them good night, disappearing to his own cave to rest. Echoes of soldiers' conversations in soft Dari floated on the twilight.

Haddad dropped their pack with a heavy sigh. He closed his eyes and rolled his neck, groaning.

"Sit down. I'll unpack."

For once, Haddad didn't fight him. He slid down the rock face to the dirt as Kris pulled out their sleeping bags, extra sweaters, and water bottles.

Kris eyed the small cave. The fire flickered, throwing off enough light to scatter glittering shadows into the darkness, an amber glow that seemed to conceal more than illuminate. The cave was warm, enough that they wouldn't freeze. But when the fire burned low, they would be cold. Very cold.

Should they bracket the fire? Sleeping bags on either side, and try to keep it going all night? Would Haddad insist on staying awake and trading shifts to watch over it?

"We'll need to sleep side by side. For warmth." Haddad tugged at one of the cushions, dragging it across the dirt and sliding it beside the other. "We can lay the sleeping bags next to each other. It will help, especially when it drops below freezing."

Silent, Kris laid their bags out as Haddad directed. He felt Haddad's gaze on him, heavy, weighted with something. It was almost like Ryan's stare, but it moved through him in a different way.

He didn't want to run from Haddad.

---

Haddad crawled into his sleeping bag and passed out almost immediately. Kris stayed awake, watching the flames flicker on the cave walls, watching the shadows turn to puppets and plays, images dancing in front of his unfocused gaze.

As the soldiers went to sleep, the front lines quieted, a silence that seemed to saturate time. Without the noisy snores of George and Ryan, without Phillip and Jim working on the radios, or the soft chirps and whirrs of the computers in the nerve center humming away, or the groan and chug of the generator, it was as if the world had gone adrift. Three weeks ago, he'd been at Langley in the United States, and now he sat before a fire on the front lines of a war in a corner of the world that wasn't on most maps. Somewhere, sometime in those three weeks, he'd bungee jumped from the edge of reality, and he was still falling. When would he snap back?

Or was he going to fall forever?

Eventually, Kris slid into his own sleeping bag, his back to Haddad. Haddad had spread out, sprawled on his back, one arm over his head and the other flung wide, as if waiting for someone to crawl in next to him, curl into his side. He'd look amazing with a sweet girl against him, someone kind and gentle who thought he was her Superman. Kris could see a perky American blonde, someone with a button nose and a cheerleader's outfit from high school in her closet. She'd have porcelain skin and blue eyes, the classic American beauty, the look that had been force-fed to him his entire life as the impossible standard. She'd be someone who scrunched up her nose at him, winked over coffee. Someone who held his hand as they walked through a farmers' market together, picking out weird fruits and farm-fresh flowers and homemade breads, getting suckered into buying local honey. Haddad would protect her, shield her, be her hero against the world. He'd be gallant, her knight in shining armor.

He'd be like he was with Kris, a personal guardian angel. Except he'd be hers, and she'd know it. And she'd love him for it every day.

Kris lay on the very edge of his cushion, his head just barely resting over Haddad's outflung arm. He stared at the flames. The heat prickling his eyes was the scorch of the fire, too bright for his eyes. Nothing else.

Haddad's arm fell across his waist, and his body scooted in behind Kris. Sleeping bags rubbed together, nylon whining as Haddad pressed as close as he could, separated by the vast distance of compressed down. Haddad nuzzled his face into Kris's neck. His beard, unshaven since Tashkent, tickled Kris's skin. His breath smelled of black tea and ghee, the Himalayan butter. His snores were soft, gentle puffs of breath that tickled Kris's ear.

Kris let his soul pour backward, let his body go limp, let everything he was fall into Haddad's sleeping hold.

Just for this night. Just until dawn.

---

The scratchy, off-tune wail of the soldiers' muezzin calling the *azan* woke them as the first ray of sunlight split the horizon and peeked into the cave.

Kris woke bundled in warmth, wrapped in two arms of solid muscle, strength and power that kept the world and darkness at bay. His cheek nuzzled a scratchy beard, a warm face. Safety flowed through him, and a flicker of contentment. Happiness. From his head to his toes, Haddad was pressed against him, spooning him, only their sleeping bags separating their bodies.

His eyes popped open. *Shit.* At least it wasn't as awkward as it could have been: their bodies uncovered, pressed together, uncomfortable truths exposed against bellies and thighs. He *ached.* God, he hadn't woken with morning wood in weeks. Now, in a cave in Afghanistan, his body was acting up? He tried to edge away, slip from Haddad's hold.

"Five more minutes," Haddad mumbled.

Kris froze. Haddad must be dreaming still, lost in his memories of home and the sweet American girlfriend. "What?"

"It's what I told my mom every morning. When I was in high school." Kris felt Haddad's smile, the shift of his beard on the back of his neck. His sleepy breaths, his soft voice.

He shivered. "Sergeant, we need to get up."

"You can call me David." Haddad swallowed. "If you want. We usually drop rank when we're operating in-country. Try to blend in. Use our first names only."

Kris tried, he really tried, to control his breathing. Keep from hyperventilating. His body ached, straining against melting back into Haddad's—David's—hold again. "You can call me Kris, then. Kris with a K."

"I like your name. It fits you."

"Do you prefer David or Dawood?"

David was quiet for a long moment. "They're two different people. I'm David now." His breath caught, hitching against Kris's neck. "But I like the way you say it."

"Joking about my accent?" He was as American as New York City, as Coney Island and heat baking off the asphalt in Lower Manhattan. His mamá's accent was as thick as the day she'd flown out of Puerto Rico. He, however, had been socialized on cartoons and New York streets. His accent was sass and snark, with just a dusting of his mamá, a touch of island.

"I had an accent when we moved from Libya. The kids made fun of me. I spent all summer getting rid of it." David's voice changed, shifted. Went flat and nasal, his sound dropping to the back of his throat. "I was ashamed to be who I was. I had to change everything I could."

David's body burned through the sleeping bag, everywhere they were pressed together. They hadn't moved, not even an inch. "I know what you mean," Kris whispered.

David's breath fluttered against Kris's hair, his jawline. The *azan* faded, the muezzin's caterwauling finally finished.

"I think that's the first bad muezzin I've ever heard." David chuckled. "Usually they're chosen for their voice."

"He sounds like he wants to be doing it as much as we want to be hearing him."

"Let's win this war so he can give his duties to another muezzin."

"Sounds good." Kris laughed and felt David squeeze him, just slightly, an almost hug. He didn't know if he should hug back, wrap his arms around David's, hold on to his hold. Or pretend it never happened? What if he was misreading it? What if that was just a stretch, and not a hug at all?

David let go, rolling back and sighing, stretching on the cushions Khan had provided. They were softer than the ground, but lumpier. Kris's hips ached as he rolled over. "How's your back?"

"Stiff. But it's nothing like training. I'm good." David smiled. "I can go another hundred miles. And you can add another hundred pounds to the pack."

"You're crazy."

"Just a little." David winked, and then peeled himself out of the sleeping bag. They'd slept in their clothes, added layers of warmth, and David readjusted as he stood and stretched.

Kris watched it all, the ache in his body growing. David caught his gaze, blushed, and looked away. "I'm going to check on what's happening out there." He slipped out of the cave.

Groaning, Kris dropped his head, rolling over and face-planting into his sleeping bag. His promises to be distant were growing thinner every day. Every moment he spent with David.

It was one more thing to add to the guilt pile, the avalanche of shame rolling through him.

---

Plotting the rest of the Shomali Plain took the entire day. They broke for the night at the western end of the Shura Nazar lines, celebrating with Khan and his officers. The battle lines turned and followed the White Mountains, the spine of Afghanistan's north, to Taloquan and Mazar-e-Sharif, cities in northern Afghanistan that had once been Shura Nazar territory, but were seized by the Taliban.

"Whoever holds Mazar-e-Sharif holds the north," Khan said, sitting across the fire from Kris and David. He spoke in halting English, saying he wanted the practice. "Whoever controls the north controls Kabul."

"What makes that city so special?" David sat next to Kris, reclining against the pack, his legs crossed, boots tucked under him. David pressed into Kris's side.

"It was the most brilliant city in Afghanistan before the Taliban destroyed it. The rest of the country was devastated by the Taliban's bombs. They wanted to erase everything, start over, build from the time of the Prophet, *salla Allahu alayhi wa sallam*. But! They also needed the money to be seen by the rest of the world, yes? Mazar, she has oil and gas outside the city. Russians wanted to drill it. They let them." Khan held his hands up, as if in defeat. "The longest paved runway in Afghanistan is in Mazar. And the people in Mazar, they are the best of Afghans. What they have endured, under those dogs."

"How did Mazar-e-Sharif fall?"

"The Taliban came. They destroyed everything. They had so many fighters. General Hajimullah, my commander in Mazar, he had to take his people and run south to the Darya Suf river valley. The Taliban took Mazar-e-Sharif and took the high ground around the city. Right away, they slaughtered six thousand people. Any man who refused to join them, any man or boy who hid. Any woman caught out of her home. They castrated the men, cut the heads off everyone they arrested. They left the bodies in the street to rot."

Silence. David's molars ground together. Kris heard them over the crackle of the flames.

"You must tell your government that we *must* bomb the Taliban in the Shomali to advance on Kabul. But we must also free Mazar-e-Sharif. Or the Taliban will use the city as a northern base. Squeeze Kabul between Kandahar and Mazar. And the people there. They will be slaughtered. Again."

"What forces do you have in the north? Outside Mazar?" Kris took notes as fast as Khan spoke.

"General Hajimullah is there now with his fighters. They are trapped in the Darya Suf, surrounded by the Taliban in the hills. The villages have been destroyed, bombed. In some, the Taliban locked the people in their homes and burned the village to the ground. Only ash remains."

Kris's vision went double as he wrote, flames leaping out of the fire and scratching across his eyeballs. Smoke choked him, filled his nose, his eyes, his throat. Screams echoed, screams of Afghans, screams of Americans. The roar of an incoming jet, flying low, too low—

"We fought in Safid Kotah in summer and into autumn. The Taliban dug into the mountains there, with their heavy weapons. Hajimullah's people tried to storm them, but the Taliban shot them down. They tried to climb by hand, but the snows came, and we could not get supplies to Hajimullah. They tried to fight the Taliban hand to hand, in the snow. His fighters climbed the mountains with only five bullets in their rifle each.

"We turned to raids before you Americans came. At night, climbing the ice and snow, Hajimullah's people drove the Taliban's tanks, their artillery, off the mountains so their brothers would live in the next battle. But it is not enough. The Taliban have more weapons. More tanks. With the oil money, they have been able to buy enough weapons to take all of Afghanistan. If you Americans want to help Afghanistan, you must help us here. Give us this help so we know this is not just your war. That we are not your puppets. Muslim lands have been playthings for the West for generations. Show us this is different. That you are allies. Before we are exterminated by the Taliban."

"*In shaa Allah*, we will help you. We will." David's voice was firm, hard. "You won't be exterminated, General."

Kris stared. The Arabic vow, the Muslim vow, falling from David's lips was a shock to both him and Khan.

"I have heard American promises before. *In shaa Allah*, you are different, this time. You are either the answer to our prayers or the last trick of the devil."

# 7

**Panjshir Valley, Afghanistan**

Khan brought them back to their compound, deep in the Panjshir, by the middle of the next day. He traded hellos with Fazl and Ghasi but didn't wait for George and Ryan to finish with their satellite call to Langley.

"*Agha Gul Bahar*, you will tell them what you learned. What we spoke about."

"Of course, General."

"We will wait for your bombs to drop from the sky and for Mazar-e-Sharif to be liberated." Khan gripped his and David's hands, hopped into his truck, and headed back to the front lines.

Exhausted, Kris and David trudged for their compound. Two figures burst from within, heading for them.

"Here we go," Kris murmured, watching Ryan and George run pell-mell.

"Where's General Khan?" Ryan shouted as soon as he was in range, pulling ahead of George. "Where did he go?"

"He left. Back to the front."

"We wanted to speak to him. Damn it!" George kicked a baseball-sized rock, hurling it down the flinty road.

"What did you do?" Ryan pressed into Kris's space, glowering. "What did you do to piss him off, Caldera?"

"I didn't do anything!"

"Back up!" David dropped their pack and shoved his way between Ryan and Kris. "You're out of line!"

"Stand down, Sergeant, you've done your job." Ryan shoved back, pushing David away. David didn't budge. He loomed larger, spreading his shoulders, his legs, bracing for a fight.

"Enough!" George bellowed. "All of you, enough!" He glared at Kris. "What the fuck happened? Did you get the GPS data?"

"That and more. We got the entire front of the Shomali Plain mapped. Shura Nazar forces *and* confirmed Taliban positions. Khan also tipped us off about Mazar-e-Sharif. He needs help there. Wants us to send forces."

"Langley is thinking the same. CENTCOM wants to use Mazar-e-Sharif as a northern outpost. A staging ground to shuttle supplies in-country from Uzbekistan."

"Khan will be delighted to hear that."

"Why the fuck didn't he stay to talk to us?" Ryan still fumed. "Why the hell is he so captivated by you, Caldera?"

"I'm not an asshole, Ryan! Maybe that's why!"

"Both of you. Shut your mouths, right now," George growled, his hand slicing through the air. "We're not doing this in front of the Afghans." Eyes followed them everywhere. "Ryan, get back inside. Kris, hand over the GPS data. Ryan and I need to send it to Langley."

Kris rifled through their dusty pack, ripping out the GPS handhelds. He shoved them at George, ignoring Ryan's fixed stare, his rancid glower. "Everything is in there."

George passed the GPS units to Ryan, who took off, heading back for their nerve center.

"Get washed up." George looked back and forth from Kris to David. "You look like you brought the entire battlefield back with you."

---

Kris took a splash bath out of a small bucket of frigid river water, scrubbing the dust from his face and his hair and splashing his pits and crotch as clean as he could. Someone from the village had washed his left-behind clothes while he and David were on the front, and he slipped into crinkled cargo pants and a thick turtleneck, trying to warm up. David went next, and he met Kris after at the fire pit with two cups of instant coffee.

David stared into his coffee cup, a deep frown etched on his face. His beard twitched, lips pursing as his jaw clenched. "Why does Ryan dislike you?"

"Isn't it obvious?"

David stared at him.

Kris turned away, back to the fire. "I'm gay," he said quickly. "And I don't have any business being here. Being a part of this operation. Ryan's always known that I'm going to fuck it up, somehow, someway."

"Is that what you think, or is that what he says?"

Kris shook his head.

"I didn't know you could be out in the CIA."

"Well... I'm not sure you can be, really." Kris shivered, more than just the Afghanistan cold seeping under his skin. "You didn't know?" How was that even possible? Everyone knew just by looking at him. Everyone knew, with a single look, that he wasn't worth their time.

"From the moment I shook your hand, all I've seen is a CIA officer who knows his shit. Who is an undisputed expert in this country, in Islam, and who consistently performs exceptionally. That's all that matters."

Kris couldn't breathe. He couldn't look at David, either. His stomach knotted, and knotted again, coiling tighter than a spring about to snap. "You're the only one."

"General Khan sees that too."

"*Caldera*!" George's voice boomed from the compound's entrance.

Kris twisted. George waved to him, ordering him inside.

"The principal is calling. Wish me luck," Kris murmured, rising. David said nothing, just watched him stride into the compound, following George.

Jim and Phillip were gone. Maybe on the roof. Derek was nowhere to be seen. Even Palmer was gone, though he normally shadowed Jim and Phillip on the radios. It was just Ryan and George, standing in front of the giant map he'd helped hang.

"Kris... We need to talk." George stood beside Ryan, arms crossed, scowling. "We think it's time you head back to the States."

He'd known it was coming. He'd known from the first moment Ryan had protested, back in Langley, September 14, that this would come. His ignoble removal from the team, sent packing, don't let the door hit his ass on the way out.

He hadn't thought he'd be so enraged. Fury billowed through him, an inferno that sucked the air from his lungs, from the room. "*Why*?"

Ryan and George shared a long look. George opened his mouth.

Ryan spoke first, cutting George off. "You're a liability. Whatever is going on between you and General Khan is interfering with this mission. We're worrying that an Afghan general is going to sexually assault you instead of focusing on the mission."

"*What*?"

"We needed the GPS data and we knew you could get it quickly. Khan connected with you, we believe, inappropriately. But we knew we could use that connection to get the intel we needed, fast," George said, his voice heavy with something.

"Are you fucking kidding me?" Ruby rage colored Kris's vision. He could feel his hands slicking, his muscles tightening throughout his body. "You think Khan wants to fuck me?"

"Are you inviting it from him? Your behavior around the general is concerning," George said carefully.

"I am behaving exactly as the culture prescribes! Which you would fucking know, if you bothered to learn anything at all about it!"

"Holding his hand, being touchy-feely with him, being all up in his business? That's culture?" Ryan snorted.

"This isn't a machismo culture!" Kris roared. He'd never shouted this loudly, never bellowed like this. Not at his drunkest, not even when he was thrown out of beds in college or dumped by the older men he'd slept with on weekends and ditched on Monday mornings. Never, ever had he been filled with this much rage, this much sizzling-hot blood. "In Muslim cultures where there is a strict division of the sexes, men form close emotional bonds with other men. They aren't concerned with posturing or proving who has the bigger dick in a perpetual 'who is the bigger asshole' contest! *Yes*, men here hold hands! *Yes*, men here hug! Being physical is a sign of trust!"

"That's just Khan. We haven't even started on you and Sergeant Haddad." George sighed.

"What the fuck do you mean about me and David?"

"Oh, it's *David* now, is it?" Ryan shook his head. "Of course it is."

"Ryan." George cut his gaze to Ryan. His expression had gone dark, a frown worrying his forehead. His fingers dug into the sleeves of his jacket, his knuckles white. "Look, Kris…" Sighing, he pinched the bridge of his nose. "*I* asked Sergeant Haddad to look out for you. To keep an eye on you. And I think you may have gotten the wrong message from that. We're concerned you've taken his protection as something it's not. And we're worried about what the Afghans will think about how you are around him."

"How I am around him…"

From the inferno of his wrath to the frozen pit of his soul. He'd *known*. He'd known that all of this, everything, was only a test he was bound to fail. That no one was on his side.

George kept going, hammering the nails through his wrists. "We've all seen how you are with him. If we've seen it, the Afghans have seen it. We can't waste our time and our energy worrying about how the Afghans are going to react to you. To your—" George waved his hand over Kris, as if he could encompass everything Kris was with one limp-wristed waggle.

"It's time for you to go." Ryan's glare could cut diamonds, could cut Kris's soul to shreds. "We're contacting Langley. Tonight."

There was nothing to say. Nothing he could do. If he gave them the satisfaction of his rage, they'd win. If he tried to argue, they would say he was belligerent, combative, and it would prove their point even more: that he wasn't fit to be there. His life, again, was being decided by other people, others who had ideas about who and what he was. His only choice, his only power, was in his reaction.

He said nothing, just turned and walked away.

David waited for him outside the compound, hovering by the dusty glass doors leading to the dirt courtyard and fire pit. He was like a gargoyle without a ledge, waves of morose frustration coming off him. His frown lines were etched deep into his face, canyons that held something dark, something secret.

George's admission repeated inside Kris's skull. *I asked Sergeant Haddad to look out for you... taken his protection for something it's not.*

He hadn't hoped for anything with David, except for maybe a friend. But that in itself was too much, too audacious a wish. He'd forgotten the rules of the world: he wasn't allowed to befriend these men. He wasn't allowed to befriend any men.

"What happened?" David pounced as soon as he fled the compound, falling into step with Kris as he thundered across the cold dirt.

He just had to go, walk away, be alone. Not let anyone see how much it hurt. Or they'd win again. They'd always win.

"Don't. Don't worry about it."

"Kris, something happened. What? What did they say to you?"

"Sergeant, it's fine—"

"*Sergeant*?"

Kris slipped around the edge of the stables and collapsed against the mudbrick wall. He threw his head back, staring up at the peaks encased in ice and dusted with snow, down almost to their compound. Another week or two, and they'd be getting snow falling on their heads. But he wouldn't be there to see it.

David followed, standing too close. He hadn't stopped staring at Kris, peering at him like he was trying to decipher a riddle, read the way Kris fought to keep his chin from trembling, stop his hands from clenching. "I thought we were past 'sergeant'."

"George told me about your agreement. That he asked you to keep an eye on me." Kris exhaled slowly. His fingers scraped the wall behind him. "It's fine, I understand. I appreciate all you did. But—"

David's frown, if possible, grew deeper. There was an intensity to him, a star hovering on the edge of a supernova, as if everything that he was had compacted deep down inside his body. Rarely, so rarely, parts of him escaped, solar flares thrown off, intense enough to fry the sky. Kris had only seen hints of that intensity.

"Sergeant, you don't have to do this anymore. I'm going home. They're sending me back."

"*What*?" The world narrowed to David, to his shock, the way his jaw dropped and his eyes widened. He stepped closer, almost boxing Kris in against the wall. Kris tried to shift away.

"They're sending me back." His voice went thin. He grunted, dug his fingers deeper. "I'm leaving. As soon as they can get me out of here."

"Why?"

Kris laughed, hysteria straining through him. "Because they think my cultural sensitivity is inviting sexual assault. That it's too risky having an openly gay officer here. That I'm too close to you, and the Afghans will see that. I'm gay, and that's *the* fucking problem. For everyone. They don't want to worry about me, they say." Dry mud flaked from the wall, coming apart beneath his fingernails. Like the dirt, his control crumbled, and Kris felt the first sob bubble up in his chest.

No, not in front of David. Let him keep a sliver, a shred of dignity. Just one tiny piece.

"That's bullshit!" Rage poured off David, an explosion of it, the sun shedding its outer layers. Kris could almost feel the heat, the power. "You're the best officer the CIA has in-country. You get the Afghans, more than George and Ryan combined. You know the culture. General Khan respects you. You were his honored guest at the front!"

"Even if I told them all that, they wouldn't listen."

"You didn't tell them?"

"Their minds are made up. They don't want me here."

David's jaw squared and set. He pulled back. Glared over Kris's head, over the roof to the compound beyond. "Then I'm telling them. They need to know what you did."

"Sergeant, please. Don't." Kris grabbed David's arm, trying to stop him. It was like trying to stop a bull. "Don't make this worse," Kris called after him.

"How can it be worse? They're sending away their expert. You leaving would be the worst thing for the mission. The absolute worst thing."

"Won't you be glad you don't have to babysit me anymore?"

That stopped him. David spun, the fury on his face darker, the edges of his scowl harder. "I do not babysit you!"

"You were told to watch out for me—"

"I was already watching you. Before they asked."

"Why?"

David said nothing. He turned and kept walking for the compound.

---

David burst into the nerve center. George and Ryan were conferring, their heads leaning close. Phillip was at the radios, starting the switchover to convert to the secured satellite uplink back to Langley.

"We need to talk." David stared right into George's eyes. "Now."

"Are you kidding me?" Ryan rolled his eyes. "You too? What the hell?"

"Ryan." George closed his eyes, for a moment. "All right, both of you. Ryan, Phillip. Out."

"Sir—"

George cut off Ryan's protest. "Out. Now."

David waited while Ryan filed past him, brushing too closely, staring him down. David kept his eyes fixed on George. Ryan was an asshole, but he was just the voice in George's ear. George made the calls.

"What's on your mind, Sergeant Haddad?" George had a pained expression. He spread his legs and crossed his arms, as if he were waiting for the executioner's bullet.

"You're making a mistake. Don't send Caldera home. He's the best officer you have on the ground."

Everything in George slumped, a puppet whose strings had been cut.

"General Khan respects the hell out of him. He was Khan's honored guest. We've been at the front for two days, embedded with their fighters. Not once, not once, during that entire time was he treated with anything other than the utmost respect and deference."

"What was your role during the scouting? Did Khan speak to you?"

"I carried the backpack and I wrote what Caldera told me to write. I was muscle. That's it. If you're going to try and say I was the one Khan worked with, you're wrong."

"What about the Shura Nazar fighters? Did anyone... perceive anything?"

"You're asking if the Afghans are freaked out about Caldera?"

"Yes."

"Why? What did he do? What about his performance is causing you to question him? What has he done to earn this skepticism?"

"His performance has been fine—"

"Then where is this coming from?"

"You know where! We took a chance bringing him because of his knowledge base, but it's too big a risk! We shouldn't have done it to begin with. We don't bring female officers because of the risks, and we shouldn't have brought Caldera! I'm sick of worrying that he's going to be attacked! That someone is going to take offense to his existence! Or, if things go wrong, and he's captured by the Taliban! I can't sleep, I'm spending all my fucking time worrying about him!" George turned away, pacing to the far wall. He stopped in front of the map and dropped his head. "I don't want to lose anyone I'm responsible for."

"You're willing to banish the best man you've got on the ground?"

Turning, George peered at him. "You really believe that?"

"I've seen it. Firsthand."

George withered. One hand rose, covering the mark on the map where their village was.

"Your fears and your prejudice are going to ruin the mission. And they're hurting Caldera."

"I'm not prejudiced." George glared. "I have nothing against Caldera. Nothing."

"Except you're judging him on all the wrong things. For all the wrong reasons. Start looking at what he's doing, not who he is. Start looking at his performance. At how exceptional he is here." David snorted. "Stop listening to Ryan."

George's glare turned sour. He squeezed his eyes closed. "What about—" He hesitated. "—him and you? What's going on there?"

"Nothing. Nothing is going on. You're so focused on Caldera and worrying about him, you haven't even realized that he and I are exactly the same."

George blanched, rearing back. His jaw dropped open.

"I mean, we're acting the same." David fumbled his words, stuttering once. "We're behaving the same. If the Afghans don't have a problem with me, they don't have a problem with him. With our friendship. It's probably closer to what they're used to seeing. Frankly, you're just reading into everything, seeing what you want to see and thinking the worst."

"I thought you were coming out, Sergeant." George chuckled, shaking his head. He groaned. "I couldn't take double that stress. Not now."

David kept his mouth shut. His fists clenched, the leather of his gloves squeaking, fingertips digging into his covered palms.

"I know he's the best. That's why I sent him to the front, to Khan. I thought, 'once he's done, once he's got what we need, he can go home'. Does he need to be here still?"

"Do you want this alliance to really work? Do you honestly think everything is just fine, it will go perfectly smoothly from here on out? What about when something happens that you can't fix, or when you've pissed Khan off so badly he wants to throw you out of the country, and Caldera is ten thousand miles away?"

"Damn it." George scrubbed his hands over his face. "All right, he stays. You guys obviously work well together. I'm going to keep you partnered up. Captain Palmer says he's fine with that, that the rest of your team is making good progress with their appraisal of the Shura Nazar forces. Are you good with it?"

"Yes, sir."

"Watch out for him, Sergeant. Don't let anything happen to him."

"Sir, can I speak freely?"

George grunted.

"You need to think about why you believe Caldera needs protecting. He's a CIA officer, the same as you. You both went through training. He's stronger than you give him credit for."

"That's enough, Sergeant."

"And you need to think about why it took me barging in here to make you see reason. Why couldn't Caldera himself tell you this? Why don't you see his accomplishments? Why did you only listen to me?"

"I said that's enough!"

David's jaw snapped shut.

"Get out of here. I've got to go over the intel you guys brought back from the front and get on the horn with Langley." The dark circles beneath George's eyes seemed to grow, spread, turning to pools where all the sleep he wasn't getting stacked up like spilled ink. "Send in Ryan when you leave."

David didn't speak as he strode out of the nerve center. Ryan waited just outside, leaning against the wall and smoking a cigarette. He stared at David, his cheeks hollowing when he sucked in a deep breath of smoke.

"What happens is on you," he said, puffs of smoke billowing around his every word. "You wanted this. You own it."

David kept walking. Kept his shaking hands balled into fists. Shoved them into the pockets of his jacket. He needed to get away. Get clear of everything.

Get away from Kris, especially. Just for a little while.

Palmer and his men had set up a makeshift firing range in the hills above the village, shooting into the dirt and dust against the slope of the mountains. Snow crunched under David's boots as he climbed the narrow goat track leading to the range. Sounds faded, falling away, until it was just the snow and his breath, the sounds of himself, his own life, that surrounded him.

He pulled his handgun and lined up, taking aim at the debris his team had dragged in for targets. Old water canisters and broken furniture. Decrepit Soviet jeeps, half blown apart. Moldy tires, more than half disintegrated.

He breathed with each bullet he fired. Slowly, in and out. His mind cleared, going blank, until there was nothing left. No thought, just breath. Just the squeeze of the trigger and the bullets slamming into their targets, and then into the snowy hillside. *Thump, thump, thump.*

The isolation suited him. Fit him like a glove, a perfect pairing of his soul and nothingness.

He'd always been alone, always been an *other*, from ten years old on. He'd been a boy without a home, without a father, a history, a people, or an identity, a boy apart from all the others. He'd learned early to carve and mold and cover the parts of himself that didn't fit into the world. Keep the fractals of himself hidden, the way he came up at harsh angles to everyone else. He was a kaleidoscope, shifting and changing in the light. What was true was kept in the shadows, the same shadows that lived in his bones, that covered the memories of praying beside his father in the sunlight, murmuring the Quran.

He'd practiced hiding so many parts of himself so many times, that when he became a man and there was something else to hide, it was only too easy, and oh so natural, to bury that as well.

Bury everything.

It was harder to keep everything hidden here, in Afghanistan, the land of secrets and death, the graveyard of eternity. His seams were coming apart, the latticework he'd laid over his soul to contain everything he *never* wanted the world to see. At night, truth rose like stars, like the moon, bathing him in things he didn't want to see, to feel. The rhythms of Islam were pulling on him, the daily calls to prayer, the whispers that saturated the air, made the country thick with the presence of Allah. Something was tapping at him, something he had thought had been cut out and he'd left behind in the sands of Libya. Something that had been forcefully ripped from him, twenty-one years ago.

And something else, too. Something he'd found when he was a teen in America, a part of himself he'd walled off instantly. But between Afghanistan and Kris, between the prayers and the whispers and the pull toward Mecca, toward Libya, toward his memories, and between the tug in the center of his being toward Kris, as insistent as the constant of gravity, he was splitting apart.

He kept firing until he was out of bullets, and until the whispers and the pulls on his soul were buried again.

---

"Kris? Can you join me on this call to Langley?"

Numb, Kris followed George to the waiting satellite connection that would be the end of his tenure on the team. His jaw locked, closed around words he couldn't speak. Shame scraped his insides like a rake.

He felt David's eyes on him. David had stayed scarce until dinner, no longer haunting the halls of their compound or lingering by the bonfire.

Kris had stayed outside until his fingers went numb, knuckles stiff from the cold and fingertips turning blue. He'd wanted to soak up as much Afghanistan as he could, feel the life of the people, the land, one last time. Khan's voice, his fractured words, detailing the deprivations and degradations his people had endured at the hands of the Taliban, across the crackle and spit of the fire, looped in his mind. How did the world stop bad people from hurting good ones?

What kind of person was he? Where did he fit on the scales?

He couldn't answer that. He just didn't know.

He'd spent the afternoon typing up a report on his and David's time on the front lines. Everything had gone in, from David's analysis of the Shura Nazar to his photos of the front and of the Taliban. Khan and his forces, not so starved and helpless as Langley had once believed. Their conversation by the fire and Khan's quiet plea for help for the people of Mazar-e-Sharif. He'd turned it in earlier and started to pack.

George had the satellite phone on speaker, and the hisses and pops, the scratch-filled background to their tenuous secured connection, filled the empty nerve center. It sounded like they were talking to the past.

"*Kris*!" Clint Williams's booming voice powered over the pops and screeching wails. "*Fantastic report on the front. This is outstanding. Excellent job.*"

"Thank you, sir."

"*Give me your no-bullshit assessment, Kris. Tell me about the Shura Nazar. Can they fight*?"

"Absolutely. They *have* been fighting, for years. The Taliban have pushed them back because they have more money and they can buy off rival warlords. Or buy secondhand military hardware from Russia or China. Right now, the Shura Nazar and the Taliban are at a stalemate, but the balance is tipping toward the Taliban with the rush of foreign fighters pouring into Afghanistan to offer their assistance. With no intervention, the Shura Nazar will fall next spring."

George nodded along with Kris. "I concur with Kris's analysis, Clint."

"*So does Langley. We've had our analysts here dissecting your report, along with everything else we have, and they came to the same conclusion. Gentlemen, what is the plan*?"

George raised his eyebrows at Kris. "Thoughts?"

What was this? Hadn't he been ignobly told to pack his bags and clear out, be on the next chopper to Tashkent? Kris hesitated, holding George's stare. "The Taliban front lines are exposed. They defend against artillery and small arms fire only. Taliban positions are target-rich for an aerial bombing campaign. If the US can pound the

Taliban positions and break the front lines, the Shura Nazar will be able to storm through. We just need to open the door for them."

"We need to bring the rain, Clint. If we do that, the Shura Nazar will win the war. And it could happen fast."

"*Which means we need to be ready to capture the foreign fighters and al-Qaeda members when this whole thing blows up.*" Williams sighed over the line, a long string of static. "*Kris, CENTCOM agrees with your assessment that Mazar-e-Sharif is the key to northern Afghanistan. Mazar and Taloquan both. The current strategy is to liberate both of those cities, and then move on Kabul.*"

"That will bolster the Shura Nazar, thin out the Taliban, and cut off their attempts to pinch the Shura Nazar when they move on Kabul."

"*And the military is tickled pink about having Uzbekistan so close to Mazar. CENTCOM is already working on propping up field bases there for resupply and combat missions,*" Williams said. "*So you guys need to get up to the northern front and get another GPS survey done. We need to know where the lines are outside these two cities. Where we can start dropping some bombs. And where we can insert a second CIA team outside Mazar.*"

"We'll get it done." George scribbled notes as Williams spoke. His gaze darted to Kris. "Sir, there's one more thing."

Kris closed his eyes.

"Sir, Kris has made significant inroads with the Shura Nazar leadership. He's become the liaison between the Shura Nazar and our team, and the CIA as a whole. During their negotiations, Kris learned of the Shura Nazar's need for humanitarian resupply. There's a famine in the valley and people are struggling. He's promised an airlift of food. What can we do about getting that filled?"

Williams was quiet. Static filled the line. "*I'll make some calls. We'll get the Air Force to make a drop within forty-eight hours. I'll send you the coordinates when I have them. Kris... Well done. Really. Well done.*"

"Thank you, sir." Kris stared at George, jaw hanging. He tried to speak, but George shook his head.

"We'll call you with an update in twelve hours, Clint."

"*Keep up the fantastic work. The president is impressed. So am I.*"

The line cut.

Silence.

Afghanistan was an unnaturally quiet place. The snowcapped mountains, the icy peaks, all seemed to encase the valley in a stillness, a separation from the real world. Without the static of the phone, without the rustle and bustle of the rest of the team working in the nerve center, the quiet of Afghanistan seemed to seep into the room, fill up the corners, swim down their throats until Kris was drowning in thick, weighted silence. He could hear his own breath, his own heart beating.

"I owe you an apology," George finally said. His voice was low, almost grinding in his throat. He flicked a pen against his palm, over and over. "You have done exceptional work here, Kris."

"You're not sending me back to Langley."

"No." George grimaced. "I want to. But I want to send you back for the wrong reasons."

Kris waited.

"My first team lead was on counterterrorism operations in Greece. When it was bad. Greece was a nexus for all flavors of terrorism, from the rising Islamic terror to right-wing fascist neo-Nazis to extreme left anarchists. It was a violent, unstable place. And I lost someone. Someone young, and new, and brilliant. We all thought we had a handle on the risks. We all thought we knew how bad it was. But... we lost her. A neo-Nazi countersurveillance operation discovered she was working for the CIA. They lured her into a trap, and—" The pen kept slapping his palm, faster. "I promised myself," he said carefully. "That I would never, ever sit in an officer's house and tell their family that one of my people had been killed. On my watch. It is... the worst feeling anyone can ever feel. That you let someone else down like that."

Something grabbed Kris's heart and squeezed, kept squeezing. He couldn't breathe, couldn't think. The echoing roar of an airplane filled his soul, the too-low whine of a jet engine accelerating over Manhattan.

George finally met Kris's stare. "You are a good officer, Kris. A *very* good officer."

Kris said nothing.

"You are. Which is why you and Sergeant Haddad are headed to the northern front. I radioed Khan this evening, told him we wanted to expand operations, and that you would be there to map out the lines. He was overjoyed. You both leave tomorrow. Get it done and come back safely." George nodded and turned away, done with the conversation. He tossed his pen onto their makeshift work table, into the clutter of papers and floppy disks and old coffee gone cold. "Keep up the good work."

---

Kris escaped to the roof to watch the stars wink over the Panjshir, appear in a flood of scattered paint across the arc of the sky. To the south, faint echoes of artillery sounded, like the roar of a subway rumbling beneath the Upper East Side after midnight.

He finally headed down late, after the rest of the team had turned in. Days were long, frigid, and rough. Everyone went to bed early. He hoped David was already sleeping.

No such luck. David was awake, propped against the cold cinder block walls of their tiny room, reading by the light of his headlamp. He looked up when Kris slipped around their dingy curtain, blinding Kris.

"Sorry." David set his headlamp on the floor. The light cast long shadows up the walls, claws that curled over and reached for Kris, trying to drag him down, tear him apart. "Everything okay?"

"I'm not leaving. But I guess you already knew that."

David nodded.

"Why? Why did you say anything?"

David took his time answering, closing his book and tucking it back into his pack. Kris watched him, searching for something, anything. An opening, an answer.

"Never let anyone else define your life, Kris. Never let anyone else define who you are. They will always get it wrong. Never settle for that."

Kris shook his head. He'd learned to give up, long ago. Give in. Sniffing, he grabbed another jacket, tried to wrap up in it.

David watched him. "We're going to the northern front tomorrow. It's going to be cold."

"It already is cold." Kris had slipped on another sweater earlier and was bundled in his thick jacket. He'd pulled on his gloves, wool and leather, and wrapped one of the black-and-white scarves Khan had gifted to him at the front around his neck and head.

"You can sleep next to me. If you want." There was an empty space beside David, his gear shoved away, cleared out to the other side of their room. "For warmth."

Kris had seen porn movies that started this way, probably a dozen. If he hadn't been so exhausted, so bone-weary, his heart so shredded, he might have mustered a flirtation in response to the invite. Or at least a joke. Something to blunt the choking tension, the cloying hesitation, the stink of anxiety that permeated their room.

But he was too tired.

He dragged his mat and sleeping bag next to David's and crawled inside, bundled in all of his clothes. David waited, hovering, propped up on his elbow as Kris settled in. As his head hit the bundled sweater he used for a pillow, Kris felt David settle in behind him, felt his body through his sleeping bag when he curled into Kris's back.

As he fell asleep, the weight of David's arm settled over his waist.

---

He was choking on smoke and bone dust, jet fuel and atomized concrete. A billion pieces of burned paper falling on him, smothering him. Massoud's body, broken and bloody and bombed, the leader of a parade of ghosts led by Mohamed Atta, with his box cutter and his black flag and his empty, evil eyes.

This time, George was there, watching it all, along with Clint

Williams. *We thought you were good*, they said, though their lips didn't move. *We thought you were the good guy.*

He tried to run, but when he turned, David was right behind him, closer than his own shadow. Kris couldn't get around him, couldn't get away from him.

*I thought you were worth—*

He woke before David finished, gasping and clawing at his sleeping bag, at the arms holding him tight. David clung to him, burying his face in Kris's neck, both arms around Kris like he was David's teddy bear. He snorted and stretched, but let Kris go long enough for him to escape.

Kris stumbled out to the nerve center, to the hum of the computers, the snores of the rest of the team, the soft murmurs of the radio. Dari and Arabic floated through the static, live captures of the Taliban's radio net. Kris picked out the words for *apple* and *pomegranate*, *rice* and *goat*. *Hunger* and *cold*. The enemy was struggling, hungry, cold, and lonely, talking into the night about what they wanted to eat.

*Eat an airplane*, Kris thought. *Eat an airplane, dropping bombs until you're full. Until you're so full you explode. Until you're one of three thousand, a name that can't be remembered because there are too many.*

He tried to breathe, tried to stop the shaking that came over him, crawling up from the bottoms of his feet, all the way up his skin. He hadn't felt this before, hadn't yet run face-first into the same furious, crackling rage the rest of his team nurtured. He hadn't joined in on the calls for revenge, the bloodthirsty hunger for retribution against al-Qaeda, against the Taliban. He'd kept the blame for *himself*.

"Kris?" David yawned as he slipped out from behind the curtain to their room. "You okay?"

Fury roared through him. Blinding, aching fury. His bones seemed to scream, his skeleton shaking, burning to every last inch.

"Kris?" David was right there, reaching for him. His hands landed on Kris's arms, gently.

Kris jerked free. "Stop!" he hissed. "Just stop!"

David stepped back, hands up, surrendering. His eyes glistened, pools of silver in the flash of the radio lights. "I'm sorry."

"You shouldn't help me! You shouldn't care about me! You shouldn't do any of this!" Kris waved back to their room, to David, trying to wrap everything David had done, all that he was, up as one. "I am *not worth* anything!"

"What?"

"I am not worth *one moment* of what you've given me! Not a single moment! Your care, your concern, your coffee? Stop wasting your time on me!"

"Kris..." David slowly inched forward, his voice a whisper. "Why are you saying this?"

"Because—" His heart screamed, the same pitch, the same tone as the planes that had flown over Manhattan, that had slammed into the Pentagon and Pennsylvania. Ash coated his throat, and in his hands, he felt the dust of thousands upon thousands of bones sift through his fingers. "Because *I* am responsible for nine-eleven!"

David froze. His eyes narrowed. "What?"

"My section, my unit! We were tracking Khalid al-Mihdhar and Marwan al-Shehhi. We had them on our radar. The FBI, earlier this year, they asked for what we had on them! We refused to share the intel. We knew they were al-Qaeda. We knew they were connected to the embassy bombings in Africa. We were tracing their connections, their meet-ups with other al-Qaeda operatives. Money that was exchanged. But we wouldn't share what we had! The higher-ups, they thought the FBI would fuck it up! We wanted to see how much higher we could go through the chain. Didn't want to risk blowing our intelligence if the FBI just arrested them! But no one knew, no one fucking knew, when they needed to know! To stop what happened!"

"Kris, what—"

"Their names were on *my* desk! *Mine*! If I had just passed those names along, if the FBI would have alerted someone, anyone, about those two... American Airlines Flight 77 and United Airlines Flight 175 wouldn't have slammed into the Pentagon and the South Tower!"

"You don't know that. You can't say that—" David sputtered, shaking his head.

"They would have been detained when they entered the US! Questioned. They wouldn't have been on those flights. Maybe al-Qaeda would have had to call the entire operation off! Maybe they would have had to cancel it! If they'd had to cancel it, then Ahmad Shah Massoud would still be alive. Bin Laden wouldn't have had to murder him! Everything, all of this! It's my fault! Because *I* didn't—"

His voice cracked, and Kris collapsed, the bones in his body no longer able to hold him up, keep him standing under the weight of three thousand dead souls, under the years of unlived lives, under the shame that grated his heart to slivers, to dust, to ash. He fell to his knees, curled over, and pressed his forehead to the dirty floor, to the threadbare carpet covering the cold concrete.

He couldn't breathe. He gasped, his throat closing, choking off like he was being strangled. Tears flowed, cascading down his cheeks, falling from his chin into pools beneath his face. Snot and spit dribbled from his nose, his mouth. He was disgusting. A disgusting human being.

A hand rested on his back, gentle, warm. Another landed on his head, fingers sliding through his hair. The hand guided him up, cradled his head until he was sitting, staring into David's stern face.

Kris waited for David to snap his neck, to rip him in half. To end everything.

"It was *not* your fault," David breathed. His voice, a whisper, shook. His eyes burned, slamming into Kris like brands. "It was *not* your fault. You did *not* hijack those planes. You did *not* fly them into the Towers, into the Pentagon. You did *not do* this."

"I let it happen..."

David gripped his skull, pulled Kris closer. His hands shook, his arms, and Kris trembled with him. Kris's teeth started to chatter. "Do not take on this blame. You are not them. You are not a murderer. You are not part of their hate. You are not to blame."

"I am..."

"You are not the beginning of this, Kris. You are not where all of this, all of the hatred, all of the fighting, comes from. Don't do this to yourself."

"All I can see, when I close my eyes," Kris gasped, "are the Twin Towers. The planes. And their faces. Looking up at me from my desk." He squeezed his eyes closed. Tears spilled from his eyes. "How can you even look at me?"

"Because I see what you don't. I see the smartest man I've ever met. A man dedicated to the fight. To stopping the Taliban, to capturing Bin Laden. I see a man focused on doing the right thing. On being the best he can be. I see a hero, Kris."

"No..." A sob built in his chest, and he tried to pull free of David's hold. "No, I'm not."

"I see a man who came to Afghanistan, and despite everyone's judgments, everyone's prejudices, did his job perfectly. You built an alliance with General Khan. You did that. You built that. The people of Afghanistan will have hope, and a future, once we get rid of the Taliban. And we will, because of what you've built with Khan. How is that not heroic?"

Kris shook.

"I see a man I care about," David whispered. "Someone I—" His lips clamped shut. His thumbs stroked over Kris's cheekbones, wiping away tears. "I see you. I see someone exceptional."

He pulled Kris in, slowly wrapping his arms around Kris until they were one, huddled on the floor and wrapped around each other, arms and chests pressed so tightly together there was no space between them. Kris trembled, shaking until he thought his body would just fall to pieces. David held him, a fierce hold that surrounded Kris, enveloped him completely, and held him up. Held his bones and his soul in place.

He didn't know how long they stayed there. It felt like an eternity, listening to Arabic whisper over the radio and Ryan and George snoring in counterpoint. Finally, David pulled him up, guided him back to their room. He unzipped his own sleeping bag and laid Kris inside, deep in the warm folds that smelled like David, that radiated his presence.

Hesitation. David stared into Kris's eyes, deep into his gaze.

Kris reached for him. His hand shook.

Silently, David slid into the sleeping bag beside Kris, their bodies aligning, folding into each other. A sob caught in Kris's chest, and fresh tears spilled over the edges of his eyelashes. Arms wound around him, held him close. "It's not your fault," David whispered. "It's madness, it's hatred, it's murder, plain and simple. It's history that got all fucked up. It's a thousand things other than you. It's not you, Kris."

Kris pressed his face into David's neck and, for the first time, let himself weep.

# 8

**Panjshir Valley, Afghanistan - October 14, 2001**

"We came here thinking we'd be with the Shura Nazar until April, getting them up to strength. Well, good news. They're already there. With a little more money, more ammo, and supplies, they're actually quite fierce. They just need a little extra *oomph.*" Ryan briefed the team as they sat in the nerve center, struggling against exhaustion.

Ryan grinned, the Special Forces warrior rising within him, poking through the CIA officer. "So, we change the war. We strike first, and we strike now."

Everyone sat up, suddenly awake, focused on what Ryan was saying.

"CENTCOM is going to begin bombing the areas we've designated on all fronts." Ryan deigned to nod toward Kris and David, sitting together at the back of the semicircle next to the radios and Phillip. They'd mapped the northern front like they'd mapped the Shomali Plain, ducking mortar fire and artillery rounds for three days as they snaked through the mountains with General Hajimullah. "When the first bombs drop, the war will begin."

George took over. "CENTCOM's strategic plan is to bomb the Taliban into such an obliterated state that the Shura Nazar can walk right over them. Estimates put the capture of Kabul occurring within days of the first push by the Shura Nazar and General Khan." He fixed each of them with a long stare. "Which means we need to be ready to move fast. Stay ahead of the fighting and make sure we're identifying, targeting, capturing, and/or killing senior al-Qaeda members. We capture anyone who can lead us higher for interrogation. We kill the leaders."

"We fight now, or we're stuck here through the winter." As Ryan spoke again, icy wind whistled through the cracks in their compound. Frozen mud clung to their boots. They were all in their warmest clothes, dressed in layers, but it wasn't enough. The concrete box they were living in was a freezer. They could see their breaths, big puffs in front of their faces.

It would be a long, miserable winter locked in the valley, with no evacuation and no resupply until the snows melted.

Unless they won the war early.

"Is everyone ready? Really ready for this?" George went around the room, asking everyone individually. Twelve people, George's team and Palmer's, deciding to start a war.

Kris was the last to speak. "Yes." George gave him a ghost of a smile.

"Then that's it. I'll tell Langley we are ready for CENTCOM to begin combat operations."

---

Excitement flooded the valley, electrified the Shura Nazar. Khan drove up personally and shook George and Ryan's hands, inviting them to feast with him and to watch the bombs fall. George accepted, and after Khan left for the afternoon, he pulled Kris aside and asked for specific advice on how to be a better guest and friend of Khan's.

Ghasi and Fazl appeared later in the afternoon, buzzing about the imminent combat. "Would you like to watch the bombs? The news reports? We can build a satellite to capture the TV signal," Fazl offered. Reporters were embedded with the Shura Nazar forces along the front and in occupied Kabul, and just like in the Gulf War, there would be grainy video footage of the bombs falling and flaming clouds rising into the dark night.

Ryan's eyes boggled. "What took you so long to ask? *Hell yes*! Here, I'll help you make it!"

Within hours, Ghasi and Fazl taught Ryan, who'd brought in Jim and Phillip, how to make an Afghanistan satellite dish. Flattened beer cans, completely illegal in the country, were bent around Chinese rebar left over from half-finished reconstruction projects into a crude metal saucer. Odds and ends of wires were strung together, loops tied and twisted into a spaghetti array. Phillip managed to get it linked to their power system, creating a power cord from scratch and connecting it to the generator.

Khan arrived just after evening prayers with his staff and a banquet for the team. They ate together, everyone jovial and exuberant at the thought of the war finally beginning in just a few hours. It seemed impossible that it was all coming together.

They all gathered around the satellite and the boxy, static-filled TV after dark on the roof. Khan's men watched with binoculars to the south. British commentators from the BBC narrated the anxiety-filled darkness, the patch of black that was Afghanistan on the grainy TV, as everyone waited for the first strike.

"It will be the end of the Taliban," Khan said. "My forces are ready to move at dawn. Afghanistan will be liberated at last."

The first flash appeared in the sky, a yellow blink that seared the clouds. Another. And another. Cheers rose, and the team clapped and hugged as Khan's men cried *Allahu Akbar* to the sky and held each other as they cried tears of joy.

David wrapped an arm around Kris's shoulders and held on, not letting go. Kris rested his head on David's shoulder.

No one said a word.

The revelation of Kris's secret, the sharing of his burden, his anguish, had bridged them together in a way he hadn't expected. He'd thought David would discard him, drop him like the trash he was, pull back in revulsion. He was a monster, a murderer. No better than the hijackers themselves.

David had held him through every tear, through every "but", until he'd exhausted himself, was nothing but a bag of bones and snot. When the moon had set, he'd started to whisper, breathing into Kris's ear. "*I felt like this before. When I was a kid. Something happened. And, I knew it was my fault, all of it. I knew it. If I'd been better, if I'd done something different. But I had to convince myself, I wasn't the one who pulled the trigger.*"

He'd stared at the line of David's jaw, the scruffy beard there.

"*I thought the same after Mogadishu. How many died because I wasn't good enough? Didn't do my job right? I failed, and those deaths are on me. Right?*"

"*That's not true—*" Kris had sputtered, between his sniffles.

"*Then it's not true for* you, *either. Not in this.*"

David had held him until dawn, when the intrusion of the sunlight forced them out of their shared sleeping bag.

Every night since, David had cradled him as they slept.

Kris didn't know what that meant. He knew what he wanted it to mean. But he was exhausted, run through with the invasion, strained until he was nearly broken. He didn't have any bandwidth left to wonder about David, about the way David looked at him. About how his face curled into Kris's neck in the middle of the night, and how their hands found each other's when their eyes were closed.

Was it comfort? Simply human need, the pull to connect to someone in their upside-down world? God knew he'd read lip-biting stories when he was a high schooler about soldiers seeking illicit comfort in the arms of their brothers. He'd jacked off to fantasies like that when he was a teen. But now that he was living it—

He just couldn't puzzle through the mystery of David, not while bombs were lighting up Afghanistan and David was holding onto him like he was a shield against the darkness.

"A month after September eleventh. Here we fucking are." Ryan and George shared their own hug, muttering into each other's ears as they hugged like they were grappling.

Khan's radio chirped.

The first reports from the front trickled in, anxiety-filled Dari from the Shura Nazar spotters.

Khan's disappointment, his frustration, his look of disgust tinged with exhaustion, hit Kris like a punch to the gut. Even George froze.

"Your bombs have hit only their storage depots! Old staging grounds! Empty compounds! Your bombs have hit *nothing*!" Khan bellowed in his stilted English. Rage silvered Khan's eyes, made them shine in the night. "After your mapping! Your insistence that you would destroy the Taliban!"

"They were supposed to hit the front line!" George went pale, as white as the moon.

"Nothing on the front has been hit! The Taliban, al-Qaeda, they are rejoicing at your stupidity!"

"General, this is not what we were told. Our bombers were supposed to strike front line targets. Take out everyone in your way."

"More American duplicity! Lies!" Khan cursed, but the fight seemed to go out of him. He sagged, sighing as he shook his head. "I put my trust in you Americans time and time again. Always, the same outcome. You never keep your word. Never."

"No, not always. We're friends." George scrambled, reaching for Khan's hand. Khan didn't accept. He stayed still, a silent statue. "We brought food. The aid drop, it went great. We can bring more. I'll schedule more food, more supplies for your people. We are friends, General."

Khan stared him down. "You will do that, and you will destroy the Taliban like you said you would. Or you will leave my country."

---

Days later, and the nightly bombing runs from the US fighters were still weak. Taliban radio intercepts laughed uproariously at the pitiful might of the Americans, the unintelligence of the most powerful nation on earth bombing dust-filled, abandoned shacks into oblivion.

George and Ryan railed at Langley on the satellite, almost every hour. George had Kris on the calls, too, since he was still the main liaison with General Khan. "The Shura Nazar expect our bombs to raze the earth, Clint! They expect the sun to be blocked by the number of our bombers!"

"*They are going to have to adjust their expectations, perhaps permanently.*"

"What the fuck does that mean?"

"*Look, the Russians, the Pakistanis, and the Iranians are making noise about the Shura Nazar taking over Kabul. They think General Khan and his fighters are going to slaughter the Pashtun minority once they're in power. Your Shura Nazar forces are mostly ethnic Tajiks. You ready to put a different ethnic tribe in power? History shows what happens next.*"

"General Khan has absolutely *no* plans to engage in ethnic cleansing." Kris's voice shook as he spoke up. "The Tajiks and Pashtuns have existed together for centuries. The Pakistanis just don't want to lose their influence in Kabul. ISI in Pakistan props up the Taliban, you know that!" Oh, the twisted web of international relations: Pakistan was America's ally today, the Taliban's yesterday. Maybe their ally still.

"*The president is working to ensure the UN takes control of Kabul. You have to get your Shura Nazar forces to stay* outside *of the city. We won't move forward unless they agree to stop advancing on Kabul.*"

Kris's stomach sank. Khan would be furious. More than furious, he would be *betrayed*. His entire life had been forged around securing Kabul, on saving his country and his people. The team, Kris, and by extension the Americans, were there to help him do just that.

There was no way he could tell Khan that he wasn't allowed to take Kabul. That men in briefing rooms on the other side of the world were changing his fate, curtailing his destiny. Kris shook his head at George, not saying a word.

"We'll discuss that here, Clint. That's a big fucking ask, though.

For someone we've spent Goddamn weeks convincing we're his allies that he can trust."

"*We can find another warlord, George. There are dozens. He's a tool, a means to an end. We can find a new tool.*"

Kris walked away, frustration building in him until he wanted to lash out, cut Williams down, kick a chair, scream about the trickle-down effect of constant American lies and a foreign policy of duplicity and double-talk, of changing sides when it suited their mercurial mission. *This is why the world hates us. This is why Khan is waiting for our betrayal.*

George growled something and ended the call. "Kris..."

"We *can't* turn on General Khan. We just can't."

"I know." For a moment, George looked like he'd been stabbed, like he was facing the worst possible decision in his life. "I think I have another way."

## Panjshir Valley, Afghanistan - October 20, 2001

Snow flurries blasted Kris's face as Derek spun up their helo. He squinted. David shifted, sliding the bulk of his shoulder in front of Kris, as if he could block the onslaught. As Derek lifted off, David and Kris sat with their legs dangling out of the open cargo door, the wind and the snow blitzing past them. David's arm wrapped around Kris's waist, out of sight and hidden beneath Kris's jacket.

Afghanistan's weather had turned, shifting from the chill of autumn to a frigid winter that locked the country in an icy stalemate. Snow fell in the Panjshir, storms that left inches on the ground and turned the dirt to sucking, ice-filled mud. In the mountains, blanketed peaks closed the pass to Tajikistan by land and by air.

As they flew to the Shomali, descending in altitude, the snows grew lighter. At the front, the snow had softened the harsh mountains and craggy hillsides, blunted the bare, desiccated earth. From the air, it almost looked serene, peaceful.

Derek dropped them near Khan's compound. Khan wasn't there to meet them. One of his deputies, a major who spoke only Russian, guided them to a jeep that bounced and slid down the snowy track to the front. The snow slowly vanished, stretching until it turned to frozen dust.

Khan was in a forward-fighting position between two of his soldiers, peering across the Shomali Plain through a pair of binoculars. "*Gul Bahar*," he called, not looking back. "Do you see what I see?"

"I see the Taliban, General."

"Exactly!" Khan twisted, glaring at him and David. "They are all there, hundreds of Taliban positions and foreign fighters, al-Qaeda embedded within them! Your bombs have hit nothing! The Taliban laugh every morning when they wake and nothing has been damaged."

He climbed out of the fighting position and strode right up to Kris. "*Gul Bahar*... My men are ready. I am ready. We can take Kabul as soon as you break the Taliban lines. My men, they will not last another winter in these snows, in these mountains." He looked up and down his lines at his fighters. "If your country does not fulfill your promise, we will attack the Taliban. We will not wait. We cannot wait, not any longer."

Kris swallowed. David shifted, pressing into his side, silent support. "General, that will be suicide."

"What choice do I have? Your country has abandoned me and my men."

"No, we haven't. We have a plan to help." Kris squared his shoulders. "We need to start laser-targeting the Taliban positions, General."

Khan frowned.

"We're here with a laser-guided targeting system that communicates directly with our pilots. We can paint each target with this laser, and then—" He smiled, patting the backpack David held. "The bombs will go exactly where they are supposed to go."

A new light glittered in Khan's gaze. "How soon can we begin?"

"Take us to Bagram. To the very front, General."

---

Khan piled them into his truck, but he dismissed the fleet of vehicles and the guards who had ridden with them before. "We will be riding through the Shomali. The Taliban attack anything they can down there, and they hold a ridgeline to the south. I won't give them too many targets."

Khan's driver pushed the pedal to the floorboards. The old engine whined, coughed, and spewed dirt as the truck's wheels spun, sliding on melting snow and mud. Door panels rattled, windows shivered and shook almost hard enough to fracture. They slipped down Khan's front lines, down the hillside, and dropped into the Shomali.

Desiccated earth, the dust of a ceaseless famine, blustered by the truck. Snow blown down from the mountains mixed with the dust, creating an alien landscape, a desolate expanse of dead land. Crops had long withered, whatever vegetation long shelled by bombs and turned to craters and ash. Broken villages and the remnants of homes littered the windswept land.

"The Taliban punished the Shomali when they first took power. The Plain, it resisted. So the Taliban smashed the farms, destroyed the homes. Burned villages to the ground. They blew up the water pipes and dams and poisoned the wells. Murdered anyone who did not fall into line." Khan nodded to the devastation.

David was ripcord taut next to him.

"Even Allah has forgotten Afghanistan," Khan rumbled. "Now there is no water, no food. The people starve and the animals die." Weariness weighed heavily on the general, etched into the growl of his voice.

An hour later, Khan guided his driver to the northern side of Bagram Airfield. It rose from the Shomali like a concrete ghost town, decrepit bunkers and shattered buildings, twisted rebar and broken glass, an apocalyptic nightmare.

Khan's driver stopped at a line of low bunkers reinforced with sandbags along the front. He stayed in the bunkers' shadows.

Kris poked his head around the side of one. A long runway

stretched toward the south end of the airfield. More bunkers hovered at the end of the runway, sandbags and a dirt berm beside them.

"That, *Gul Bahar*, is the Taliban. We are one runway away, here. The front line goes across this airfield." He pointed to the northern end of the base, where the ravaged pillar of the air traffic control tower still stood, windows long blown out. "But we have the high ground."

Three cracks sounded, fast snaps that broke the cold air. Whizzes whistled by. Dust sprayed off the bunker wall.

"Careful, *Gul Bahar*. We trade fire here often." Khan guided Kris and David into the bunker, a former Soviet military office. The broken windows were blocked with sandbags, only narrow firing slits open at the very tops. Soldiers peered through binoculars at Taliban positions. One soldier passed his binos to Khan.

"They are watching us. Wondering who you are and what you are doing. They will be attacking this afternoon."

As Khan spoke, the dull thump of a mortar round launching from the Taliban's line rumbled. It whistled, flying low, and hit the top of their bunker. The walls shook, dust and sand falling from the ceiling. David grabbed Kris with both hands.

"Do not worry. The roof, it is reinforced. We are hit many times. We will patch the damage tonight."

They slipped out of the bunker and back to the truck. Khan's driver wound through the remnants of buildings, rotten metal and twisted frames collapsed in on themselves. Destroyed aircraft decayed on the tarmac and in front of hangars, tires long gone flat, frames dented, metal missing, wings torn off. But each wreck was still in a neat line, famous Soviet military discipline still on display, even in an abandoned base at the end of the world.

They idled for a moment at the edge of a long runway, hidden behind a hangar. "You both should duck," Khan said.

His driver floored it, whipping around the hangar and hauling down the runway. The engine roared, and David pushed Kris down across the back seat, covering him with his body. Kris felt David's breath against his cheek, felt his fingers dig into Kris's arms. Bullets pinged off the runway, snapping like firecrackers. One shattered the rear glass.

"The Taliban hold the village in the hills above the base!" Khan shouted. "They can fire on this runway from there. Unfortunately, this is the only way we can drive to the control tower! You will have to take out that village with your lasers!"

Finally, they pulled behind two bunkers, riddled with shrapnel and bullet holes, and parked in the shadow of the tower. The upper radar dish, the overhang, and the antennae were gone; only the observation deck remained. There was no door on the tower. It had been destroyed long ago. A spiral stairway went up to the observation deck and more bullet holes ringed the inside of the tower. The tower had seen a hell of a fight.

Inside, Shura Nazar forces had telescopes set up for targeting and range finding. Maps covered the floor, marked up with Taliban posts and positions.

Khan introduced Kris and David, and the Shura Nazar fighters eagerly looked at David's pack once Khan explained what they were there for.

"You can destroy them from here?"

"Between the scope, the coordinates, and the laser, yes. We definitely can." Kris smiled.

---

Kris had spoken too soon.

George called on the satellite phone that evening. "*Targets on deck for the night are situated around Kandahar, Jalalabad, and Mazar-e-Sharif. They want to pound al-Qaeda strongholds and loosen up the Taliban around Mazar for Hajimullah's forces.*"

"We've got a village infested with Taliban. They're picking off Khan's men at the airport. We've got the coordinates mapped and a laser on them as we speak."

"*CENTCOM is refusing to release a fighter for your targets unless you can triple guarantee that there are no civilians in the village. We're not flattening a village of women and children at the start of the war."*

"Khan assures us the Taliban have moved all civilians out. It's only fighters."

*"Not good enough. They need visual confirmation before they'll approve the mission."*

Kris saw David shake his head. His eyes pinched, concern warring with determination. Sneaking behind enemy lines, infiltrating enemy positions? That was David's bread and butter. He and his Special Forces team were trained to do just that.

But David was alone, with only Shura Nazar forces to back him up.

Alone, except for Kris.

*"We'll have visual confirmation tonight, George. Tell CENTCOM to have their fighters ready."*

---

"Are you *sure*?"

David squatted on a pile of crumbled cinder blocks in front of Kris, holding a compact of camo paint. Half of Kris's face was darkened, the shading breaking up the lines of his humanity, enough to blend in with the darkness.

"Very sure."

Sighing, David painted a long streak of black over his nose, across his cheek. He wouldn't look Kris in the eye. "Kris—"

"Out of everyone, you have never doubted me. Not once. Are you doubting me now?"

"That's not what this is."

"Then what is it?"

Finally, David looked at him, really looked at him. David had applied his own camo paint first, streaks of brown and black across his face until just his eyes were visible in the dim light of the bunker, in the corner where they had set up their sleeping bags.

The air shivered, hovering around them, weighted with whatever David was about to say next. Expectancy was thick, pressing on Kris.

But David looked away, and in that moment, he closed up, rolling up the expectancy and his hesitation as he cleared his throat. The air in the bunker seemed to suck into David, vanishing with a *pop*. "I don't want you to get hurt," David said. He dabbed brown paint on his fingers and reached for Kris's cheek.

"Neither of us will get hurt. We're in this together."

David nodded. Kris watched a barrier go up in his gaze, watched him shift, start piling up block after block within him, barricading the world away. He was going operational, putting himself into the mindset of the mission. Kris could feel him disappearing within, going deep into the center of himself.

Closing his eyes, Kris followed, tipping back and falling into his training. The mission plan, their objective, played over in his mind. Their route, how to get to the village. Time on station, and a rehearsal of their actions, their moves, step-by-step in his mind. His breathing leveled out, going flat, going even.

"Done."

---

They waited until the dead of night. Other than a few fires lit by frozen Shura Nazar fighters, well off the front lines or buried in bunkers, there was no light after dark in Afghanistan. Certainly not at Bagram. Only the stars gleamed above, beneath a quarter moon.

Kris crept behind David, stepping exactly into his dusty footprints. They were on a grazing path that goats and horses had used before the fighting. To the left and right of the narrow dirt track, buried mines and unexploded ordnance littered the ground. Spent shell casings and dirty brass covered the dust, reflecting a glinty green in Kris's NVGs.

Neither the Taliban or the Shura Nazar had night vision capabilities. Both sides were blind after dark. Kris and David were ghosts, slipping unseen into the Taliban's village.

Fixed gun positions pointed down at the airport, manned by sleeping Taliban soldiers. Heavy machine guns, mortars, and larger artillery pieces were covered in rough camouflage. Broken homes, their mud roofs caved in and walls shattered, blown apart by years of bullets and bombs, squatted behind the guns. Soft Dari wound out of the wreckage, carried on the low light of banked fires.

They slid silently through the village, moving house to house, quiet as smoke. There, a group of soldiers slept. There, guards, huddled around the fire. Beyond, in a house set off the center of the village, what looked like a group of mullahs, the senior leaders of the fighters, sat together around a pile of orange coals. Radio antennae cluttered the roof of their hut, and weapons leaned against the side walls.

A convoy of trucks waited behind the village. Two Russian tanks lingered beyond the gun positions with fresh tracks in the dirt. Soon, they'd be firing on the airport with tank rounds.

No civilians. Not a hint of life, other than the infestation of fighters. Who had lived there before? Where had they been taken when the Taliban moved in?

David shifted, sliding around a mudbrick home, the last in the village. Its roof had caved in more than the others, and its walls had crumbled almost to the ground. Burn marks and soot licked up the sides of what remained. Crouching, David scanned the ground, peered inside. Kris followed, hovering beside him. Something must have caught David's eye,

He spotted it a moment after David did.

Bones.

Chipped, brittle bones, burned and snapped in half. Small bones, the size of a child's. The size of a young woman. Kris could pick out femurs and jawbones, ribs and shoulder blades. He tried to count them by twos. At least twelve—no, fourteen, eighteen—

Too many. Too many for this to be an accidental fire, a tragedy of fate.

If they sifted through the ash, they'd no doubt find a bar that had held the door closed, locked from the outside. They might find a grenade, or a canister of fuel.

David stayed down, kneeling beside the burned wall as he reached for a bone. It fit in the palm of his hand, gently curved. Once, it must have wrapped around the chest of a child, a young boy or girl's rib.

Footsteps, coming out of the house where the mullahs had been. One of the leaders walked their way, toward the edge of the village, the darkness just beyond this house. He carried a rifle, but lazily, slung over his shoulder like a teenager would slough a backpack at school.

Kris ducked, his back to David's, one hand on David's thigh. *Freeze.* Beneath his touch, David went completely still.

He lifted his rifle, the folded stock pressed to his shoulder, sights tracking the mullah's every footfall. They were in the darkness, in the shadows, completely blacked out. But if a star happened to shine on the lens of his NVGs, if a flicker of flame winked across their bodies, arced around their presence, the game was up. Kris's finger half squeezed the trigger.

The mullah sighed as he faced the darkness, feet from Kris. He fumbled with his robes, eventually adjusting to relieve himself. They heard everything, the splash and spray, the mullah's stream as it hit the dirt and then petered off. After, he muttered a quick word in Dari, prayers of the ultra-faithful following urination, and headed back.

David's hand covered Kris's, still on David's thigh. He squeezed.

*Time to go.*

---

They didn't speak until they were out of the village and back down the path, lying against the dirt berm beneath the Taliban's gun positions. From where they lay, they could hear Taliban fighters speaking in Dari in their foxholes.

David pulled the laser targeting array out of his backpack. "Call it in," he breathed in Kris's ear. "I'll hold the target."

Kris skidded down the berm, to the very base. He was maybe sixty feet from the Taliban. He pressed his radio to his lips. "Eagle Eye, this is Jammer Three. Request priority strike on confirmed enemy position with senior Taliban leadership. Target is laser designated."

Static whistled in his ear. He pressed on the earbud. "*Jammer Three, confirm. Are civilians present*?"

"Confirmed. No civilians present."

Static. He waited.

"*Jammer Three, two aircraft inbound. ETA, twenty minutes. Standby*."

He clicked his acknowledgement and crawled back, sliding in beside David. "Two inbound," he mouthed along David's ear. "Twenty minutes. Probably Navy."

"Quick strike then," David breathed. "They have to get back to the carrier before they bingo fuel."

Kris nodded. He settled in to wait, leaning into David, almost on top of him. He felt the rise and fall of David's back, each inhale and exhale. They were close enough that they only had to turn their heads and they would be speaking in each other's ears.

The first *whoosh*, the deep scratch against the night sky that was the fighter honing in, screamed in above. Kris's earbud whistled with an incoming radio transmission. "*Jammer Three. Aircraft on deck. Patching to pilot now*."

A whine, and a new voice came on, a woman. "*Laser target locked on*," she said. "*Bombs away*."

"Now," Kris breathed. He and David flicked off their NVGs, plunging the world into pitch black. Kris counted, barely breathing. David pushed his face against Kris's, their cheeks pressed together.

They could hear the Taliban laughing at the sound of the jet, cursing the sky and the inept American fighters who had yet to hit them with their bombs.

A fireball bloomed, erupting with a crack and rolling thunder rising over the berm and enveloping the Taliban-occupied village. The shock wave followed, rushing wind like a slap, burning heat pushing him and David into the dirt. Debris rained, smashing down like hail. A shattered turret from one of the tanks landed straight up, embedded in the hillside, still smoking.

Broken bodies and screams split the night in every direction. An inferno raged, consuming everything blown apart by the strike.

"*Jammer Three, R-T-B*," the pilot said. "*Good luck*."

"Good strike," Kris replied. He didn't have to whisper, not anymore. Not with the screams of the Taliban loud enough to hear all the way in Kabul. "Finally."

# 9

**Panjshir Valley, Afghanistan - November 7, 2001**

The war accelerated, moving at breakneck pace.

High on adrenaline after the first strike, Kris and David stayed up all night long, sitting in front of a small bonfire behind the control tower, talking down the shakes in their hands. David spoke softly as the fire burned low and the coals glowed, casting the hollows of his face into shadow.

"I've lost count of how many children's bones I've seen. You'd think that would be something you'd remember. But... there are places in this world where hearts don't beat. Where humanity is just... gone. I thought I'd never see that kind of hate again. But now, with New York, and here... It's all coming back, isn't it?"

Kris took his hand, lacing their fingers together. Side by side, they watched the coals turn to ash, hands clasped, heads resting against each other.

Should he ask? Should he squeeze David's hand and ask what that was before, when they were rubbing camo paint over each other's faces? What it meant that David slept with him every night, drawing him close and into his arms? What it meant that they were never far from each other anymore, always a hand's reach away?

Would asking end it all?

Inertia was a powerful force. Kris didn't want it to end. The hand-holding, the surrender into David's arms, the warm breath on the back of his neck. Maybe it was just Afghanistan, the war, the cold. Maybe they were clinging to each other because they were alone in this craziness, untethered from reality, trying to navigate warlords and terrorists and battle plans from caves and concrete bunkers via a scratchy radio and a homemade satellite dish, as snow fell and froze their fingers and toes. Maybe nothing would leave the valley.

He should keep his mouth shut and soak it in, just be glad for the human connection. For the beating heart he'd found on the surface of Afghanistan, the dark side of the moon.

General Khan was overjoyed with the first laser-targeted strike. He arrived at dawn, just after prayers, effusive in his praise for both Kris and David. "We must have more, many more, of these strikes."

Every day, Kris and David worked with the Shura Nazar to scout targets from Bagram's control tower. At night, they slipped out under cover and crept close to the Taliban and al-Qaeda targets, painting each with lasers until Navy or Marine Corps fighter jets arrived and obliterated them in fury.

"They are no longer crowing about how weak the Americans are, how pitiful your attack is." Khan held Kris's hand, grinning ear to ear, after days of constant strikes around the airfield. "We will use Bagram as a secondary headquarters when we break through the Shomali."

In the north, the Taliban tightened their grip on Mazar-e-Sharif and Taloquan. From the hills overlooking the two cities, they began shelling the outlying villages, civilians who supported Khan and the Shura Nazar, and who had escaped the wrath of the Taliban's choke-hold. General Hajimullah struggled to save his people and keep the pressure on the Taliban.

"We must have these bombs in the north," Khan said one morning. "And more help. We must have more CIA assistance, *Gul Bahar*."

After a week straight of clearing Taliban out from around

Bagram, George ordered him and David to meet up with Hajimullah outside Mazar-e-Sharif.

*"Kris, Langley has sent a second team for Mazar. They're inserting tonight, and I want you and Haddad to show them the ropes. How to work with Hajimullah. The intricacies of the front line. Get up there, ASAP."*

Mazar-e-Sharif hugged a valley in between a gorge of mountains. The Taliban controlled a majority of the highlands and the city itself, and Hajimullah's men were pushed back into the valley below, stuck like fish in a shooting barrel. They were a ragged army; most soldiers didn't have socks or gloves, but they still fought in the snow as winter closed over Afghanistan.

Hajimullah's men also fought on horseback. Ethnically Uzbeki, his men had been raised on horseback, like their Genghis Khan and their Mongol ancestors.

When the second CIA team scampered off their helicopter out of Uzbekistan, General Hajimullah had six Afghan horses waiting for them.

Afghan men were smaller than most Americans. Famine, lack of quality nutrition, not enough protein, and a host of other maladies had left the Afghan population more diminutive, leaner. Afghan horses, likewise, were smaller, more compact.

Smaller Afghans and smaller horses meant smaller saddles, made of wood and stiff leather and right angles. Kris fit easily into his, and he copied Hajimullah's standing riding style, keeping out of the saddle as much as he could.

The rest of the CIA team, by the end of the day's ride to Hajimullah's base camp, were nursing sore asses and bleeding thighs, skin rubbed raw from squeezing into the too-small saddles. David, too, limped when they arrived.

Hajimullah enjoyed the Americans' discomfort like he'd feasted on fine Russian caviar. He laughed, barrel chest shaking, roars echoing off the mountains ringing his camp. "You Americans," he cried. "So soft. If you stay here for one week, I will make Afghans out of you."

With the promise of covering fire from the US fighter jets and a significant bombing campaign guided in by Kris and David, Hajimullah and his deputies formed a plan to capture Mazar-e-Sharif and cut off all Taliban escape attempts. The US would obliterate the Taliban in the hills, paving the way for the Shura Nazar to enter the city without fear of strikes from above.

Two days later, David and Kris huddled on a flinty shale slope in the White Mountains, casting lasers at Taliban targets pinpointed on maps and GPS. The Taliban had concentrated their forces, building into the mountain in the hope that they would be safe, shielded by the rocks.

They were so very, very wrong.

Kris relayed his conversation with an American B-2 stealth bomber coming in from the south at high altitude, flying out of Diego Garcia in the Indian Ocean. He could just make out the white contrails streaking the very top of the cornsilk sky, as if dragging stardust down from space. "Time to target, two minutes." Everyone on the radio net heard him.

Far above in the bomber, someone was getting ready to deploy the Daisy Cutter. Non-nuclear and designed to instantly clear a landing zone in Vietnam, the bomb had found a second purpose destroying caves, bunkers, and deeply buried fighters in combat zones around the world.

"Weapon away!" Kris called.

Across the valley, the position he and David had painted disintegrated, disappearing in silence into a mushroom cloud that shot higher than the ice-covered peaks. A second later, a *boom* shook the earth, a thunderclap that rumbled Kris's organs and pushed him physically down the mountain. He clung to David, both of them sliding on shale as the ground trembled and quaked.

"Second target commencing." David shifted the laser to the next Taliban position as the first cloud continued to grow. Everything that had existed where the bomb landed—Taliban, weapons, tanks—was dust, blowing away.

After three Daisy Cutters, Hajimullah, his horseback fighters, and the CIA team charged. Kris watched from above through his binos. Taliban survivors, stunned by the blast, crawled toward their weapons, bleeding from everywhere—their eyes, their ears, their mouths. Wailing, they tried to fight, firing wildly and without aim at the charging Shura Nazar.

Hajimullah's men rode them down.

Outside Mazar-e-Sharif, Hajimullah roared over the radio, broadcasting to the Taliban, "*I have the Americans*!" he shouted. "*They brought their death ray! Surrender, or you will die*!"

The remaining Taliban fell over themselves to be the first to surrender.

November 10, Hajimullah entered Mazar-e-Sharif on horseback. David followed Kris into the city on horseback, finally used to the cramped, stiff saddle. They watched as Hajimullah marched his fighters to the Blue Mosque, the holiest mosque in Afghanistan and a place of pilgrimage.

"Ali, the Prophet's cousin, is buried there." David breathed in slowly, staring wide-eyed at the mosque. "It's a holy site in Islam."

"Do you want to go in?"

David flinched, squirming down the left side of his body. "I don't think I can," he whispered.

Kris sidestepped his horse until he was alongside David's. Their horses snorted, nipping at each other's faces. Afghans flooded past them, following Hajimullah to the mosque, cheering and celebrating. Out of sight, he squeezed David's hand, laced their fingers together.

Kris's radio chirped. "*Jammer Three, Jammer One. Come in.*"

George, calling from headquarters in the Panjshir. The signal was weak, scratchy over a dozen repeaters and mangled towers. "Go ahead Jammer One."

"*Great job with Mazar. General Khan wants you both at the Shomali front, ASAP.*"

---

The Taliban collapsed, from Mazar-e-Sharif to Taloquan and all the towns in between. The Shura Nazar chased them down across the northern front.

Kris and David joined Khan on the Shomali Plain, and the last front line against the Taliban. Finally, they were reunited with Captain Palmer and the rest of David's Special Forces team as they waited for the bombing to shift to the Shomali. Palmer greeted David with a handshake and a quick, backslapping hug. "Great job, Haddad. You hanging in there?"

"Yes, sir."

Kris thought having Captain Palmer and the rest of the team back, surrounding David, would *change* things. Would change whatever they had fallen into. He expected David to shy away from him, shift his focus, turn to his team and forget whatever he'd made with Kris.

But the first night, David laid Kris's sleeping bag right next to his in the middle of the team's dug-in fighting position. As the stars came out, David's arms wrapped around him and his face tucked into the back of Kris's neck.

Other members of the team also huddled close together, spooning their sleeping bags in rows to share warmth. Maybe it was just that, just the cold and nothing more. Maybe everything was in Kris's mind.

He felt the squeeze of David's arms around his waist.

November 21 dawned a perfect morning, crisp and clear, edged with frost and the scent of snow, but covered by an endless blue sky, so clear Kris thought he could see the curvature of the earth that encapsulated Afghanistan. He and David were up at daybreak, used to the rhythms of the muezzin and morning prayers after being embedded in the Shura Nazar for weeks.

Khan drank tea with Kris, watching over the Shomali. "After Mazar-e-Sharif, after Taloquan, you promised the Shomali Plain would be next. That you would break the lines and I would lead my people into Kabul."

In the distance, Kabul was a muddy smudge, a blur of brown and smog. "They're coming, General. The bombers are on their way."

They watched the fighters and the bombers fly in, streaks of contrails dragging behind triangles of black and grey and brown. They watched the sky ignite, saw the flash of bombs and heard the roar of the eruptions. The earth quaked, and the skies split, jets breaking the sound barrier after they'd dropped their ordnance and bugged out back to their bases and their carriers.

In the silence after the attacks, they could hear the echoing screams of the Taliban and al-Qaeda, burning, suffering, and dying in their foxholes.

As each bomb dropped, Shura Nazar fighters fired their rifles into the sky. Captain Palmer and his men watched the bombs drop through their scopes, confirming targets hit and destroyed and marking each on their maps.

Kris saw the reflection of the bombs, of the destruction, in the shine of David's eyes. The backs of their hands brushed.

George's call came midmorning. "*Jammer Three, come in.*"

"Go, Jammer One. What is it?"

"*Kris, we just got word. It's happening. The Taliban are completely collapsing. They're evacuating Kabul. We've got to* go, *push hard,* now."

Khan heard every word. Kris hadn't seen a man look so joyful, so ecstatic, ever in his life. "We move out, now!" He shouted up and down his lines and over the radio. His fighters took over, repeating his orders from foxhole to foxhole. Trucks zipped out from the rear, loaded with machine guns and fighters.

Khan rode at the head of his convoy. Dust spewed up from the Shomali, hundreds of tires and men storming across the dead and haunted plains.

Palmer and his team followed in two trucks. The massive convoy of Shura Nazar fighters rode in a single file toward Kabul. Kris rode in the back of Palmer's truck, beside David, his scarf tied around his face, sunglasses on, trying to keep out the dust.

As they advanced, they came upon the craters of their bombs, large enough to destroy the entire width of the single road to Kabul. To either side, decades' worth of mines were buried. Nervous drivers inched forward, trying to stick to the remnants of the road as much as possible and avoid certain death.

Mangled corpses littered the Plain, broken and bloody and fallen across torn black flags, half buried in shattered rock and dust. The Plain, so harsh and gray, desiccated and windblown, was wet with blood, the end of the Shomali's drought.

Kris's gaze swept the devastation, the death and destruction.

"*Stop,*" Khan called over the radio in Dari. "*Everyone, stop. We must see to the dead.*"

"General... These are the Taliban. And al-Qaeda," Kris radioed back.

"*Leave al-Qaeda to rot. They are apostates, and no longer Muslim. But we will bury our Afghan dead. They are still our people.*"

Khan's men dragged the Taliban together, making piles of corpses. They covered them in rocks and stones, the Afghanistan tomb, and whispered prayers over their graves.

When they restarted, there was no resistance on their drive across the Plain.

Khan's convoy roared up the hills, heading for Kabul.

In hours, they'd be in the capital. Washington had insisted, again, that Khan *stop*, not advance into the city. That the UN be allowed to fly in and take over. That Khan not get the victory he'd worked for, had struggled for, for decades, working with Massoud and now on his own.

Kris kept his mouth shut and watched the clouds billow behind Khan's SUV.

---

Kabul was a city of dust and ghosts, of blue burqas whispering out of sight.

The city sprawled, dusty streets and cobbled-together buildings, mud huts and cinder block rows of houses lined with rusted steel fences topped with barbed wire. Some houses were empty, ransacked, belongings scattered into the streets. Bloodstains drenched the dust on street corners, but there were no bodies. No movement. No people.

Khan's army stormed into the city, rolling down the streets in their trucks and tanks. The soldiers honked, cheering loudly, their entrance a celebration.

Kris, David, Palmer, and the rest of the team kept their heads on a swivel. The city was silent, far too silent.

Kris watched empty homes pass by, decrepit streets and blocks of stores and buildings that had burned to ash and the skeletal remains of rebar. The city felt heavy, the weight of thousands of unlived lives and decades of sorrow embedded into the foundation, down into the sewers and into the tangled and broken power lines overhead.

General Khan led his army to the steps of the Taliban's intelligence headquarters, their former seat of power in Kabul and in Afghanistan. Burned papers blew in the wind. Doors banged, opening and closing on broken hinges.

Khan and his senior command staff exited their vehicles, rifles at the ready. Palmer ordered his men to form a security perimeter, but David stayed at Kris's side, dogging his footsteps as he followed Khan into Taliban headquarters. Kris watched tears fill Khan's eyes as he strode up the burned and shrapnel-scarred steps.

He'd done it.

---

"*We came to liberate, not to conquer.*"

General Khan issued his orders to the Shura Nazar as he instructed them to maintain peace and order in the capital. Checkpoints cropped up throughout Kabul. Hesitant civilians began poking their heads out from behind their gates. Slowly, men began to congregate on street corners, gazing at the Shura Nazar soldiers and the city with wide eyes, like they were seeing something brand-new, something they'd never seen before.

By afternoon, the bazaar was open again, chicken and goat roasting over open fires inside fifty-gallon metal drums, and limp vegetables and bruised fruit were hawked from every other stand. Kids gathered in clusters, hiding whenever the soldiers would try to say hello. Tangerine sunlight twirled with the smoke and haze over the capital and lapped the mountains ringing Kabul.

Kris and Palmer's team watched everything from the Taliban's former governmental guesthouse, their old living quarters. They were woefully outnumbered, the only seven Americans in the city.

"Any word from George?" David leaned against the open window opposite Kris, watching Kabul come alive on the street below.

"Not yet."

George's last message had been that he was on the move, breaking down in the Panjshir and taking a chopper to Bagram to set up a secondary headquarters closer to Kabul.

Greasy chicken and diesel fuel mixed with rapid Dari and Pashto, the laughter of children, and cheers that rose from groups of men. Women in burqas moved silently through the crowd.

"I thought they'd take the burqa off." David frowned.

"They're out without a chaperone. Before, they were imprisoned in their homes." Kris nodded to a group of women meeting on a street corner, their burqa-covered hands clutching each other's. He saw their burqas tremble, the fabric rustle. "It's the first day. Let them feel safe first. Let them realize the religious police aren't going to beat them this afternoon."

Palmer and his men lay on every available horizontal surface in the guest room they'd been given. There were two single beds, a thin love seat, and a writing desk. They were trying to soak up all the sleep they could. It was amazing, how sloth-like Special Forces soldiers could be when at rest. As if they knew they had to capture every moment, stack it up like a savings account they could draw on in the future.

"I've got to call George. Let him know we're in Kabul." Kris rolled his neck.

"Think Washington is going to shit?"

"Probably. Which means I'm going to get it all."

David squeezed his shoulder, then dragged his hand up, stroking up his neck until he cupped the back of Kris's head. He said nothing, just stared into Kris's eyes.

Six weeks they'd been at each other's side, from the frigid cold of the mountains, the lonely nights of the front with only the dust and the stars and each other, to the frenetic chaos of combat, of air strikes, of decimating the Taliban all over Afghanistan. And now they were in Kabul, surrounded by David's team and Kabulis learning how to live again.

Was there ever going to be time to talk about the way David looked at him? Kris had already hardened his heart to the possibility that there was nothing there. A passing moment in a life, a blip of human connection in the horrors of war. Warmth, physical, perhaps even emotional.

But not hunger. Not need. Not desire.

Not what Kris dreamed about, despite his ceaseless recriminations.

David took a breath. Opened his mouth. "I—"

*Ring ring ring.*

The shrill scream of the satellite phone Kris kept on him at all times, in the front of his thick jacket, ripped the evening apart. Soldiers groaned, rolling over to avoid the noise. David pulled back, dropped his hand.

"Shit. I'm sorry." Kris fumbled in his jacket, finally found the phone. Groaned when he saw the caller ID. "It's George." He pressed to answer and cringed. "Caldera."

"*Kris! Are you in Kabul with Palmer's team*?"

"Yes, George."

"*Is everyone all right? No injuries*?"

"No injuries." He hesitated. "Khan wasn't going to stop outside the city. He never even slowed down. And I wasn't going to tell him he couldn't win his war."

*"You did the right thing, Kris, going with him. Washington is screaming about it, but you did the right thing, and I'm telling Clint that. They are imagining a bloodbath in the city. Tell me what's really going on."*

Kris almost couldn't answer. He blinked. "Uh, the market is open. We're in the old Taliban guesthouse overlooking one of the bazaars in the main square. Kids are outside. Women are out, talking together. Men are cheering. Khan stationed his soldiers at intersections to keep the peace. There were some reports of looting, but that was mostly Kabulis trying to destroy former Taliban homes."

Wonder filled George's voice. *"My God, we did it. We took Kabul."*

"General Khan and the Shura Nazar took Kabul."

*"Our alliance took Kabul. Which wouldn't have happened without you."*

Kris stayed quiet.

*"We need to move into Kabul, ASAP. We need to search the Taliban and al-Qaeda facilities there, start interrogating prisoners the Shura Nazar have captured. Do you have a facility we can move into?"*

"This guesthouse is huge. It could hold us all, and room for more."

*"Good, because Washington is already talking about sending in more teams to Kabul, to the north, and to the south."* There was a lot of work to be done in the south, near Kandahar, the ancestral home of the Taliban. Taliban and al-Qaeda forces were still rampant there. *"Any word, any intel on Bin Laden?"*

"Not yet."

*"I'll get the team ready to move out to Kabul. It will be good to get us all together again. See what you can do about setting up a headquarters there for us."* George paused. *"And good job, Kris. Really, great work."*

---

George arrived with the rest of the team in a convoy of trucks, lugging all of their gear that had once been set up in the Panjshir, then moved to Bagram, and finally to Kabul. Derek had stayed behind at Bagram to coordinate incoming CIA and Special Forces teams from Pakistan and the Gulf. Kris got the okay from Khan to convert the guesthouse into the first CIA station in Afghanistan in over twenty years, since the closing of the US Embassy.

They spent the first night setting up operations again. Jim and Phillip spent hours with the generator and the communications equipment. Ryan seemed to be in a thousand places at once, hauling gear, setting up workstations, poring over maps of the country and the capital. George had walked in with the satellite phone glued to his skull, given Kris a one-armed bear hug, and then spent the next six hours talking to everyone from Langley, to CENTCOM, to CIA station in Islamabad, and the White House.

Jim, Phillip, and George had seemed happy to see Kris, shaking his hand and smiling. Ryan studiously avoided him, even avoided looking at him. His eyes slid away whenever Kris neared.

By morning, after a solid night of work, the station was up and running. George called a break and gathered everyone—CIA officers and Special Forces teammates—together for breakfast.

Thirty people squeezed in, scooping fried eggs and strips of goat, yogurt, flatbreads, and apples onto their plates, and grabbing instant coffee. For the first time, since nine in the morning on September 11, everyone seemed content, and confident in their work, their mission. Laughter broke over the group, jokes flying back and forth. Smiles stretched everyone's faces.

David's smile, the way it crinkled his eyes, carved furrows into his face, made Kris's bones weak. Out of everyone in the room, David burned the brightest, laughed the loudest, transfixed Kris in ways he couldn't describe. He almost couldn't breathe, watching David. The thin air of Kabul seemed too weak, too light, to contain all that David was. He was exhausted—they all were, worn through from six weeks of war—but there David was, hamming it up with his team.

Kris fled before breakfast was through. He couldn't take it, couldn't take David's effect on his heart.

---

George found him a few hours later. “We’re going to head over to the US Embassy. Want to come?”

George, Kris, Jim, and Phillip hopped into one of the trucks they’d driven from Bagram. Ryan drove, and they wound their way through Kabul’s bustling streets to the boarded-up embassy.

The embassy had been locked up for fifteen years, closed and abandoned after the bloody civil war started tearing Afghanistan to shreds following Soviet withdrawal. Ryan cut the chains off the front door and broke through with an axe.

The seal of the United States lay under a thick carpet of dust, welcoming them into the gloom. Pictures of President Reagan and Vice President George Bush hung on the walls, and rotary telephones still sat on desks. Broken picture frames and glass covered the marble floors.

Kris stooped to pick up one photo, half buried in dirt and the dust of decay. President Jimmy Carter watched over a casket, his head bowed.

“Ambassador Dubs’s funeral.” George spoke over Kris’s shoulder. “He was murdered in Kabul. Kidnapped under suspicious circumstances, supposedly by terrorists. The Soviets forced their Afghan puppet government into a rescue mission, despite the US wanting to negotiate. Dubs was executed when the rescuers stormed their hideout. His death, and his kidnapping, was never fully explained. But his murder poisoned our relations with Afghanistan for decades. We withdrew completely.” George sighed. “He was murdered in February of ’79. By that autumn, the communist government of Afghanistan was in shambles, the country was in open revolt. In December, the Soviets invaded Kabul to prop up their communist allies. We, naturally, wanted to fight communism and avenge the death of our ambassador, and provided covert aid to the enemies of communism: the Muslim fundamentalists.”

“Bin Laden came to Afghanistan in 1980.” Kris felt his stomach turn, felt it knot. “All this—” He nodded to the photo, the time capsule of the embassy, perfectly preserving 1979. "—was part of why he set off down this path. He was so enraged by the Soviet invasion of Muslim lands, and the signing of the Egypt-Israel peace treaty. He was furious, lashing out. He wanted to fight the enemies of Islam, and we helped him. And then we dropped Bin Laden once the Soviets pulled out. And we became the enemies. It's all a vicious cycle, isn't it?"

"'What a tangled web we weave...'" George smiled sadly. "But we're not the arbiters of the world, Kris. We're just here to gather intelligence. Our job is to see, to listen, and to know. It's not up to us to shape the world."

"But here we are, fighting a war." Kris brushed the dust off Dubs's funeral photo. He set it on the edge of the ambassador's desk, propped up against the rotary telephone and next to an old cigarette ashtray. "And everything we've done here? What you just told me? We absolutely shape the world. We've made all of this, everything, happen."

"Is that a bad thing? Would the world be better if it were more American?"

He thought of Khan by firelight, asking for American help yet convinced it would all end in betrayal, the same end to the same song replayed a thousand times in the Arab world. And of the Shomali, the dusty, blood-soaked drive to the capital. Corpses blown apart, mangled body parts strewn across cratered roads. The women whose hands had shaken under their burqas, walking outside unaccompanied for the first time. The thousands who had been murdered by the Taliban, and the village of bones he and David had found. The shape of a child's rib bone in David's palm.

"War is hell, George. No matter what."

"Some things are worth fighting for."

"That's what everyone says."

Footsteps echoed on the marble, drawing close. "War makes men." Ryan, his hands propped on his hips, glared at Kris. "It defines a man. He's at his most connected with himself. And of course this is worth fighting. There's nothing more just and right than exterminating these murderers. They deserve everything that they get. And more."

"Ryan, did you cut your way into the old CIA station?" George ignored Ryan's outburst. The old CIA station was housed in the basement of the embassy, and it had been abandoned at the same time as the withdrawal.

"It's empty. Some old cash in the safe, but they burned everything before pulling out."

"Good. Then there's nothing for us here. State will take over the embassy when they arrive."

---

"We're suddenly the most popular people on the planet." George smiled ruefully at the team, back at their new station. "Everyone is coming to visit. CENTCOM is sending a huge deployment of humanitarian aid. We're keeping the lead in the Bin Laden hunt. Islamabad station says their sources claim they have a credible lead on Bin Laden. We need to see if it pans out. If they're right, we have to strike.

"Ryan, I want you and Jim to head east. You can't go alone, though. East is al-Qaeda country. This morning, a group of armed fighters slaughtered a village where the men had decided to shave their Taliban-mandated beards. We may feel safe in Kabul now, but you step one toe to the east, and you're in a world of hurt without the right kind of support."

He turned to Kris. "What do you know about the eastern provinces? Are there any warlords affiliated with Khan that we can turn to? Whose loyalty we can buy?"

Kris blew out a long breath. "I'll ask Khan for an introduction. You're deep into *Pashtunwali* in those regions, though. No matter how much you pay, you're going to run smack into their tribal code. If Bin Laden is hiding in the tribal areas, he's going to rely on *Pashtunwali* to shield him, especially from infidels such as us."

"We have to try. See what you can do."

Kris nodded.

"And I want you to head to wherever the Shura Nazar are keeping their prisoners. They captured al-Qaeda training camps, bases, and fighters. I want them interrogated, as soon as possible. We need to know what they know. We need to dig up everything at the camps. Everything they were up to."

"George, may I take Sergeant Haddad with me?"

"Can't be without your little friend for even a day, can you?" Ryan grinned. Jim chuckled once, but sucked in a breath and shut down immediately after.

It had been seven hours since breakfast. Not that Kris was counting. "Medical care in the Shura Nazar is minimal at best. They're not going to spare anything for captured al-Qaeda fighters. They didn't even bury them on the Shomali. If we bring medical care, they might be more willing to talk."

"Good thinking." George nodded. "I'll let Palmer know we need Haddad for this. Let's get moving."

---

He and David were guided to a bombed-out warehouse in a dark and destroyed sector of Kabul. Broken windows let in snow flurries and icy wind. It was too cold and dry for the snow to stick, and it felt like a thousand blades hitting his skin. The al-Qaeda fighters were kept in shipping containers with holes drilled in the sides. They stayed in the dark until pulled out by Shura Nazar guards for Kris to question.

Kris's stomach turned as the first prisoner came to them. He had a shrapnel wound on his face, over his cheek and curling up to his forehead. Blood and pus matted his head. His face was swollen, his eyes glassy.

"He won't be able to answer any questions. Not until he's recovered," David said softly.

"Offer him medical care. It's what we can do."

The man was Saudi, and he gratefully accepted David's offer to clean and bandage his wounds. He sat stoically through it all, never once flinching. He seemed surprised when Kris revealed he and

David were from the CIA. He claimed he had been studying the Quran in Afghanistan and had been caught in the war. That he was innocent.

"You were in Afghanistan studying the Quran?" Kris asked in Dari.

The Saudi frowned, confused. "What did you say?"

Kris switched to Arabic. "Why come to a Dari-speaking country to study an Arabic text?"

The Saudi said nothing.

Kris and David sent him back.

Word spread that the interrogators were giving medical aid. They had dozens of volunteers willing to speak, scores of young fighters lining up for David's care.

Man after man repeated the same line: that they were in Afghanistan to study the Quran. That they had lost their passport. That they had never heard of Bin Laden.

There simply wasn't any reason for Arabs, Chechens, Chinese Uighurs, Burmese Muslims, or Central Asian Islamists to be in Afghanistan other than as fighters. Certainly not hundreds of them studying the Quran in a language the Quran wasn't even written in. How had all these students been so grievously wounded by bombs and bullets? Weren't they supposed to be studying?

Al-Qaeda had prepped their people well, giving them the same line to use in detention. As long as no one broke, their answers were impenetrable, and without any actual hard evidence—impossible to come by in a warzone—their answers couldn't be challenged.

David patched them as best he could and sent them back to their cells.

Kris kept questioning each fighter. He could recite their answers now, and he mouthed along with their protests as they delivered the same line again and again.

Until an older Yemeni sat before him.

"Why were you in Afghanistan?"

Silence. Kris frowned.

"I came to fight the infidels," he said slowly. "The Americans. We knew they were coming for the Sheikh."

"The Sheikh? Bin Laden?"

"*Nam.*" David had stitched together the Yemeni's face, plucking out a bomb fragment. Stitches ran up his cheek, down his throat. He'd narrowly avoided death. Kris's eyes kept drifting to the stitches, squiggly lines that moved when the man spoke, like he had two mouths, two voices.

"Where is the Sheikh now?"

"He is waiting for you. Where he killed the Soviet infidels. He will kill you, too."

---

"George, Bin Laden is retreating to Tora Bora. Where he fought the Soviets in '87 at Jaji. If we don't stop him now, he can slip over the border to Pakistan through the mountains."

"This lines up with our intelligence, too. We've got reports coming in from on the ground that Bin Laden was seen heading east to Jalalabad. Dining with tribal leaders. Praying at a mosque in Jalalabad with the Taliban governor there. He left in a convoy of trucks and jeeps that stretched a mile long, they say." George pointed to the map Ryan had tacked to the wall of their station's command center. Bin Laden's sightings were pinned in a row, stretching east from Kabul toward the border with Pakistan. "There's also a news report of a convoy of trucks passing through the village of Agram. Qurans in one hand, AK-47s in the other. Multiple nationalities." George handed over an article from the *Times*. Some reporter had trekked all the way out to Jalalabad for the article.

"This reporter is lucky to not have been killed."

"It matches what we're getting from the sources on the ground." George fingered the pins, moving east, and then south through the Agram village and Nangarhar Province. He kept going, and his finger ended up dead center on Tora Bora against the base of the Spin Ghar mountains straddling the Pakistan-Afghanistan border. "Where are we on getting support from Khan to head east?"

Kris sighed. "Khan and Fazl have been dragging their feet. They're content in Kabul. They want us to take care of the south, and the east, and al-Qaeda. They think their work is done."

"We helped them get here." George's eyes flashed. "Kris, you have Khan's ear. His trust. Use your relationship with him. Get us the support we need to go after Bin Laden, before he slips away!"

# 10

**Kabul, Afghanistan - November 22, 2001**

"Listen up!" George bellowed over the mess of bodies stuffed into one of the bedrooms at their CIA station. True to George's word, Kabul—and Kris's CIA station—had turned into the hottest place on the planet. The station was buzzing, electric with energy and trilling satellite phones and bodies moving in and out at all hours of the day. George had peeled off his core team and pulled them into a tiny bedroom. "The men in this room are going on the hunt for Bin Laden."

Silence, instantly. The hushed voices, the whispers, the side conversations, stopped.

Kris stood next to George on a rickety chair. Palmer and his team were there, along with Jim and Ryan.

"We've pinpointed Bin Laden's movements. He's headed east-southeast. He's moving with a large contingent of al-Qaeda fighters. Kris has secured the allegiance of a warlord in the east, a man named Shirzai. He's been paid handsomely to help us set up what we're now calling the Eastern Alliance. He's gathered together some friendly warlords of his own, and they're laying the groundwork for our entry into Jalalabad."

"Isn't Jalalabad where those journalists were murdered?" One of Palmer's men called out.

The Taliban had melted into the countryside and the mountains following their withdrawal from Kabul, turning to wraiths. Roving bands of fighters moved outside Kabul, swooping down on roadways and villages and serving swift retribution.

"Yes. A van of six journalists was stopped by what we believe are Taliban- or al-Qaeda-affiliated fighters. They were marched off the van and executed. Jalalabad and the rest of Nangarhar Province are white-hot right now. Filled with fighters. But we're on the move. You will be Team Bravo. Shirzai has sent his deputy, Naji, to Kabul. When he arrives, you all are deploying with him to Jalalabad. The Eastern Alliance has already started working in Nangarhar and Jalalabad. They've pushed back on the fighters there. They, and you, will fight your way to Tora Bora and find Bin Laden."

Excitement thrummed through the tiny room, exultation mixing with exhilaration, with adrenaline, with the thrill of the chase, the hunt. They'd come to Afghanistan for this reason: to exterminate Bin Laden and al-Qaeda, make sure they could never attack the US again. Kris could see it in everyone's eyes, the commitment, the finality. They'd put their boots on the ground in Afghanistan less than two weeks after September 11. They would be the ones who saw this through to the end.

---

Naji arrived just after noon. He had four trucks with him, filled with fighters, everyone dressed in a mishmash of kameezes and fatigues and turbans. Every fighter had an AK-47, a bandolier of grenades, and at least two knives. These were not the organized, professional fighters of General Khan and the Shura Nazar. These were mercenaries, tribal fighters under a true warlord's banner.

Palmer and his men loaded up one of the trucks and climbed in.

Ryan tried to talk to Naji, but he didn't speak anything other than Dari and Pashto. "Kris!" Ryan waved him over, irritation flooding out of him. "You need to stick next to Naji. Translate for us."

David jogged over before Kris slid into the front seat of Naji's truck. His face was hard, expression fixed, eyes cutting through every man around them. He leaned into Kris, growling into his ear. "Be careful." His hands flexed, clenched, at his sides, like he wanted to reach out.

Kris grabbed David's arm. He felt David's trembles through his layers. "I will see you in Jalalabad."

David nodded once. Palmer shouted, calling him back. Running backward, David kept his eyes on Kris until the last moment, until he climbed into the truck bed.

Naji spoke in gutter Dari, the kind of slang and street lingo a gang member back in the US would use. It took Kris a while to catch up with him, but he followed along with the map Naji had, tracking their route east and into the mountains. It looked like a short trip. They would be off the road before dark.

---

The drive lasted all day, and well into the night.

Switchbacks and curves that pushed the trucks to the edge of dirt tracks, roads that careened around mountain passes, washed-out sections of mud that had collapsed under snowfall, and rockslides that blocked the pass slowed them to a crawl, and then to stop when they had to clear the road. Each time the convoy stopped, Palmer's men were up and armed, scanning the road, the hills, the valley, anywhere and everywhere.

Finally, they crept into Jalalabad.

The city, like the mountains, the countryside, everything they'd driven through, was gray. Surface-of-the-moon gray, alien-landscape gray. Like all life had been sucked out of the land, and only an endless stretch of desolation remained. Narrow streets crowded stone homes together. Limp power lines sagged across alleys, and some hung torn and frayed on the dusty streets. Fires burned on street corners, and men huddled around the flames. Their eyes stared from beneath their flat wool caps, gazes dead and cold.

Once, Jalalabad had been one of the most beautiful cities in Afghanistan. Lush with greenery, it had been an emerald in Central Asia, a Shangri-La of Afghanistan. Now, it looked like the dark side of the moon, inhabited by refugees of the fall of Earth.

Armed men stood on every street corner, glaring menacingly at the trucks as they rumbled through the city.

"These are our men," Naji said. "We control this city now."

"What about outside the city?"

Naji didn't answer.

He drove them through the winding Jalalabad streets and turned south, out of the city. The sun slipped behind the Spin Ghar mountains, behind sheets of ice and snow along the peaks. The countryside plunged into darkness, more quickly than Kris was used to. There wasn't a hint of electricity in Nangarhar Province, not a light bulb for miles and miles. The truck's headlights flickered and faded, stretching to the dusty road just in front of their tires and no farther.

"Where are we going, Kris?" Ryan's agitation was tangible, his jaw muscles clenching hard. "Where the fuck are we going?"

Naji wouldn't answer.

They pulled off the dirt road and bounced over the rough, rocky track of the Afghanistan hills. Shale slipped beneath their tires. Ice crusted the edges of the truck's chipped windshield.

Hours later, Naji pulled up to a blasted, half-bombed brick building, squatting against the base of the mountains, nestled in the flinty foothills. The truck's dim headlights caught on the figure of a lanky man in a salwar kameez and camouflage jacket, a bandolier, and a turban. He clutched an AK-47 and watched them drive closer, never blinking. Fighters in turbans, their faces covered, loitered around the blasted building.

Over the team's radio, Palmer ordered his men to raise their weapons, to take cover.

"What the fuck is happening, Kris?" Ryan vibrated next to Kris in the truck. Kris could smell his fear, the stink of his adrenaline.

Naji pointed to the man, the leader. "Shirzai," he said. "Our commander."

"It's our ally." Kris put his hand over Ryan's, fisting his handgun. He radioed the team. "This is Shirzai. Our contact."

When the trucks stopped, Kris was the first out, striding with Naji to Shirzai. "*As-salaam-alaikum,*" he said, one hand over his heart.

"*Wa alaikum as-salaam*," Shirzai responded. He eyed Palmer's men, and Ryan and Jim, hanging back. "These are your fighters?"

"The rest of our fighters are up in the sky. The Air Force and the Navy."

"Ahh, yes." Shirzai smiled. His narrow face, hawkish with a beaked nose, creased in deep lines. "Your bombs." He pointed up. His smile disappeared the next moment. "Your men will stay here. I have fighters guarding this place. The rest of my men, and Majid's men, have pushed into the mountains. They are in the villages." He pointed to the mountains, rising above them like claws ready to slash at them, destroy everything in a moment. Only the peaks shone, starlight reflecting off shimmering tips.

"Majid?" Kris asked.

"Another warlord. He will need one hundred thousand from you. Cash. Tomorrow."

Kris sighed. American foreign policy, again. "*Nam.*" Yes. "But not tomorrow."

Shirzai gazed at the darkness, squinting. "The Arabs have gone up the mountains," he said. "Into the Black Dust." The Black Dust. Also known as Tora Bora.

Kris's heart pounded. "We need to go up there. We need to find Bin Laden. You will you take us? Up into the mountains, to where we can find them?"

"Yes. Yes, we will do this for you. Tomorrow, we will go up the mountains."

---

Daybreak dawned crisp and frigid, the frozen air shivering snowflakes in a dry dusting around their shattered forward base. It had been a long, chilly night.

Shirzai had left with Naji the night before, disappearing on a bouncing track that took them up into the foothills. Ryan had kicked into command gear, throwing his weight right and left, barking orders at Jim and Kris and Palmer to get their forward operating base up and running. Palmer and his men had done what they could to reinforce the decrepit building. Everyone managed to catch a few hours of sleep before dawn, Palmer and his men keeping watch.

Instead of the wail of the muezzin and the call to prayer, Kris woke to Ryan and George going back and forth over the radio.

"*How confident are you in the situation there? In Shirzai and his alliance*?"

"We've met Shirzai so far, and we're rendezvousing with Majid, another warlord. We're at the foothills of Tora Bora. Bin Laden is here. I know it," Ryan insisted.

"*Take a forward team into the mountains. I want eyes on this al-Qaeda camp where he's hiding out, and on his fighters. As soon as you do, radio back. I'll bring the entire air power of the US military down on that camp.*"

"Yes, sir." Ryan clicked off the radio.

David appeared at Kris's elbow, a thermos of hot coffee in one hand. "Morning."

The war had gone so fast, so furious, that Kris couldn't remember getting more than four hours sleep in one stretch since before they had landed in Afghanistan. Since before September 11. He felt like something the subway had run over and dragged for three stops. David's morning cups of shitty instant coffee, thick like tar and bitter enough to make his molars scrape together, were manna from heaven.

"Thanks."

David, too, seemed exhausted. Looked exhausted. His eyes were sunken, deep, dark circles lining their orbits. His bags had developed bags, a double-layer paunch of exhaustion that aged him beyond the young thirties he was. Dirt creased in the furrows of his face, the lines of his frown and his cheeks above his beard. He smiled, though, as Kris sipped his coffee. "We built a fire out back and boiled some water. And—" He passed over an energy bar from an MRE. "Breakfast."

"Mmm, I actually miss the eggs fried in ghee and seared goat."

"You mean the shoe leather?"

"I thought it was a bit like jerky."

David laughed. "Remember pancakes? And French toast?"

"Mmm... There's this diner on the Lower East Side, in my old neighborhood. Made the best pancakes. It was island flavor, a Spanish fusion hole-in-the-wall. The pancakes had a piña colada twist to them. Pineapple and coconut, with guava syrup and sliced mango."

"That sounds so fucking amazing." David's eyes were burning, miniature suns spinning in the blackness of space. "We'll have to go there when we get back."

Kris's smile faltered. "David—"

"Everybody, listen up!" Ryan barked. "Gather around."

Frustration filled David's gaze. He held out his hand, helping Kris stand. "Later, we'll talk," he said softly.

"We're moving out." Ryan crouched in front of a map of Eastern Afghanistan, Jalalabad, and the Pakistan border. "Everyone but Caldera and Jim. We're moving into the mountains with Shirzai and Majid." He tapped on a village, high on the side of the tallest mountain. "Milawa, here, above the snow line. That's where al-Qaeda's base camp is. We need to get eyes on. Find him there."

David had gone ripcord taut, his spine straightening, muscles clenching, when Ryan said Kris wasn't deploying forward.

"Caldera, Jim." Ryan glared at Kris, then addressed Jim. "You both will maintain Team Bravo base camp. We'll be able to radio you, but no farther. You're our link to the outside world. Kabul, CENTCOM, Langley, everything."

"What about translation? On the mountain, you're going to need someone who speaks Dari."

"Majid speaks fluent Russian. He did time in a Siberian gulag for drug smuggling across the border during the Soviet invasion. I'll provide translation for the forward team. Caldera, you'll provide translation for the base camp."

He couldn't argue with that, much as he wanted to scream and shout and rail at Ryan for leaving him behind. For taking David into the mountains. Separating them.

They hadn't been separated at all in this war. Not once. Every mission, every moment, they'd been together. The longest they'd gone apart was seven and a half hours in Kabul. And now David was going into Tora Bora, into the den of al-Qaeda, to hunt Bin Laden... alone.

It wasn't like Kris was David's vanguard of personal security and safety. David's entire team was with him, and Kris wasn't a Special Forces soldier. Ryan was. He knew how to move, how to fight. Kris was a graduate of The Farm at Langley, and he could field strip an AK-47 and put it back together in under a minute, but he was no James Bond.

But... the thought of being away from David's side, especially now, at this moment, at this juncture, when everything they'd all planned for, worked for, had struggled and sacrificed for, was lining up like a constellation before them all...

He didn't want to be apart from David. Not in the quiet mornings, sharing terrible coffee, and not in the heat of combat, the electric chaos of battle. What did that say about him?

God, he'd gone and done it. He'd fallen for a teammate.

What was David going to say to him before Ryan interrupted?

"Caldera? When is Shirzai due to arrive?"

Kris shook his head, scattering thoughts of David as far into the corners of his mind as he could. "He said he'll come down from the village after morning prayers."

"He'll be here soon, then." Ryan stood, folding the map. "Everyone, get ready to move out. Once we go up the mountain, we're not coming down until we have Bin Laden's body." He nodded to Palmer. "Captain, would you like to address your men?"

Palmer stepped up, reminding his team to check and recheck

their gear, and then do a complete weapons and ammo inventory. Kris watched as David's expression hardened, turned to stone.

After, he had to coordinate with Ryan and Jim on radio frequencies and secured channels and mandatory report-in times. By the time they were finished, Shirzai and Majid were rumbling down the track, dust rising behind their trucks in a thick cloud.

Kris searched for David as his teammates repacked their gear and loaded their ammo into their combat vests, snapped their helmets into place, and fixed their radios and throat mics. They'd painted their faces with lines of dark camo paint and had transformed from the men Kris had joked around with, had laughed with, to fierce hunters.

He spotted David slipping out back to the rocks behind their base camp.

He followed.

David waited for him. He reached for Kris, pulling him close. Their foreheads brushed. Kris smelled the coffee they'd shared and David's musk, his sweat. He shivered.

"Be careful," Kris whispered. "This is..."

Everything. What they'd come to Afghanistan for. The most dangerous mission they'd undertaken.

Except, it wasn't them undertaking it. It was David, without Kris.

"I wish I could come with you," he breathed.

"You have to be careful here." David's gaze seared into Kris, burning his soul. His eyes were brighter now, suns going supernova, set against the blackness of his face paint.

David had always been unreadable, a star fixed in the heavens, something Kris could see and feel but never touch, never know. He lived like he was an event horizon unto himself. Everything seemed to fall into David and get swallowed up in the churn of his heart, his soul. Kris had no idea, none at all, what was going on. What David thought, or even felt.

"You and Jim, alone here. I don't like it. Make sure you have tight security. Keep an eye on Shirzai's guards. Be careful." David's hands closed around his. "Keep an extra weapon on you at all times."

Kris had his handgun strapped to his thigh and an AK-47 next to his pack. He nodded.

"Kris… I'm coming back." David's voice rumbled.

"You'd better."

David reached for him, for his cheek. His big hand cradled Kris, one thumb stroking his cheekbone. His hands were cold, dry, roughened from being in the field for six weeks. Kris tried to stop his whimper, his gasp, but he couldn't. He melted into David's touch, turned into his hand. His lips grazed David's wrist, chapped skin barely kissing his pulse.

"I'm coming back to *you*."

Finally, David let him see, when Kris looked into his eyes, *everything*. Desperate hunger, aching need, a raw, almost painful yank toward each other. Days and nights by each other's side, David's constant attention, his physical touch, the way their souls had curled into the other. "I'm coming back to you," David whispered, his voice shaking. "If you want that."

Kris grabbed him, both hands wrapping around David's face, his head, and pulled him the last inch until their lips met. Their lips were chapped, dry skin catching, and David tasted like bad coffee and Afghanistan's dust, dust that clung to his mouth and his beard and his skin. But Kris didn't care. He kissed David like he was trying to bring him back to life, trying to resuscitate his soul. Trying to merge, in some way give David a part of Kris to carry, bury a part of David inside of him. David's arms wrapped round him, all the way around, encircling him and drawing Kris against David's bigger, stronger body. He could spend forever in David's arms, fall into David, live each day beginning and ending with David's lips and his arms around him, just like this.

"*Haddad*!"

David pulled back, breaking their kiss. He didn't let go of Kris.

Palmer, leaning out of the building, stared at them. "We're rolling out in five, Haddad. On the move."

"Yes, sir." David never looked away from Kris. Palmer disappeared back inside.

David's face paint was smeared, black and green and brown smudged together around his lips and chin, his cheeks where Kris had grabbed him. "I'm sorry," Kris breathed.

David kissed him again, a soft peck on the lips. "I'm not." He licked his lips. "I've wanted to kiss you for so long. I didn't know if you — And it wasn't the place, or the time."

This hardly was, either, at the penultimate moment of their hunt for Bin Laden. But what if everything went wrong after this moment? What if all their good luck, every roll of the dice that had come down in their favor, turned once David went into the mountains? What if this was all they ever had?

"I'll be waiting for you."

David smiled, and it was like watching the sunrise over the Hudson River in March, when the light struck the first buds of spring and the last snow melted into a dizzying spray of rainbows, and the air was bursting with potential, with everything that could ever happen in that one golden ray of perfect light. Forget that they were freezing, standing in dust and rock and dry snow, with wind whistling through the shattered mudbricks of their camp at the base of Bin Laden's last stand in the mountains. Kris would remember this moment, this smile, this kiss, this feeling, for the rest of his days.

A tinny horn honked. David cursed. "Gotta go."

They jogged back inside, David grabbing his pack and running to Shirzai's trucks. Palmer and the rest of his team were loading up in the beds. Ryan sat in the lead truck, next to a scraggly fighter with one milky eye and a long, jagged cut, fresh and oozing blood, going down one side of his face. Ryan and the fighter spoke in fast Russian, gesturing back and forth to a map.

"You, uh, have paint on your face." Jim sidled up beside Kris. He waved to Kris's mouth. "Might want to wipe that off before Ryan sees." Jim's lips quirked in a tiny smile.

Kris scrubbed his jacket sleeve over his mouth, rubbing away streaks of green and brown and black just before Ryan hopped out of his truck and jogged over. He handed Kris a marked-up map, a duplicate of his own. "Here's our route. Shirzai and Majid say we're staying off the main roads 'cause they're mined. We're driving to this mountain, and then hiking up the rest of the way."

"We'll wait for your radio check-ins. Be safe."

Ryan studied Kris. "You too," he finally said. Turning, he jogged back to the truck.

"Good luck!" Kris called as the trucks pulled out, skittering on rocks and shale. Jim ducked back inside, but Kris watched the trucks slide along the track and climb the rough trail up the mountain until he couldn't see their dust cloud any longer.

# 11

**Tora Bora, Afghanistan - November 26, 2001**

"*Just over those rocks. Point the laser down, right on top of them.*"

Ryan's voice whispered into David's earpiece as he crawled on his belly up the ice-crusted stone of Tora Bora's tallest peak. He breathed hard through his mouth, trying to suck up all the oxygen in the air. At almost twelve thousand feet, the air was thin and frigidly cold. His nose ran constantly. His lips were cracked, bleeding.

It had taken four days to climb to the al-Qaeda camp at Milawa. Shirzai, Majid, and their rabble of fighters had led them up the shale slopes, through farms that seemed trapped in the Middle Ages, primitive villages and communities that hadn't seen a foreigner ever. David and his team might as well have been aliens. The Afghan farmers stared at them like they weren't even human.

Up they'd climbed, farther and farther, passing through the snow line and into shin-deep drifts, at times plunging down to their thighs. Scraggly trees stretched for the sky, and frost clung to the boulders, tree trunks, even their packs and their clothes.

Earlier that morning, Shirzai had led them to an overlook above a valley, beside a mountain peak that cast long shadows over the hills and the farms. They'd been climbing into the peak's dark hollows for days.

Majid had pointed to a military camp, built into the side of the mountain and covered in snowdrifts. Mudbrick buildings lay scattered along the ridgelines. Flat spaces around the homes looked like fields for crops, now covered in snow. An unused obstacle course squatted between three structures that looked like warehouses or barracks. Lookout posts and gun turrets were manned by guards watching over the valley.

"They do not look up," Majid had said, smiling. "Only down. This is why we came this way."

Ryan had barely been able to contain himself. "This is Milawa?" he'd asked. Everyone had seen the shine of his eyes, the bloodthirsty gleam.

"*Da*," Majid had said. "Milawa. Al-Qaeda's base camp in Tora Bora."

Ryan and Palmer had dispatched them all to observation points above the camp, ringing the mountain's peak. Cover was sparse, just snow and rocks and scraggly trees. They'd moved slowly, hauling the laser-guided targeting system as carefully as they could.

To call in air strikes, they needed laser-targeted coordinates to feed to their fighter pilots. The jets' bombs would ride the laser down, a perfect strike.

But in order to paint their targets, they needed to be *close*. Especially in the mountains.

David and his partner, Jackson, slid to the boulders perched at the top of a rise overlooking the Milawa camp. They ditched their packs and crouched, peering over the rocks. "We've got eyes on," David radioed back to Ryan. He listened to the other two teams—Warrick and Cobb, Rodriquez and Palmer—ringing the camp report in. He couldn't see them, but he knew they were there.

"*Establishing communication with Bravo Base Camp*," Ryan said. "*Time to light them up.*"

The radio scratched, signal struggling to bounce back through the mountains to the crumbling shack where Kris and Jim were working. Majid had told Ryan it had once been a school for girls; the Taliban had destroyed it years ago.

And then Kris's voice crackled across the line. "*Team Bravo Forward, come in.*"

David hissed. Kris's voice, a physical ache, like his insides had been scooped out raw. He closed his eyes, holding his breath. *Kris...* What was happening at base camp? Was Kris safe? He could hold his own, but he and Jim were alone in the dangerous reaches of Afghanistan with nothing and no one around.

He wanted to be there, with Kris. And not just to protect him. He wanted to be at Kris's side, through every moment. Kris seemed to have a part of him, like a kidney or a lung or his right hand, and David hadn't even known he'd been missing something integral until he'd met the slender, shivering man with the spiky hair on the runway in Tashkent.

"*Bravo Base, we have lasers painted on the al-Qaeda base at Milawa. We are ready for air strikes.*" Ryan called out the coordinates, and Jackson turned the laser on, lighting up the center of the al-Qaeda camp.

"*Bravo Forward, acknowledge. Will get online with CENTCOM and theater air support. Standby.*"

Dead air filled the radio, whistles and pops and crackles. David clung to Kris's last words, the sound of his voice.

"*Bravo Forward, bombers on station in twenty minutes. Hold your position. I will patch the pilots through to you when they're in range.*"

Seventeen minutes later, the adrenaline-infused voice of the bomber pilot broke over the radio, calling out his vector and time to drop.

"*So, Bin Laden is here*?" the pilot asked.

"*We believe so*," Ryan answered.

"*For New York*," the pilot said. "*Bombs away*."

They could see it, when it hit. The bombs fell like cars, like rotund VW Bugs, screaming from the sky and slamming into the camp. The mountains had been peaceful, serene, almost beguiling in their lassitude, if David didn't think too much about how they crawled with men who wanted to murder every American on the planet. When the bombs fell, the air split, cracking like the earth's crust had broken in half. Huge walls of dirt leaped into the sky. Buildings blasted apart, trees shredded into toothpicks. Mangled trucks and tanks flew in every direction. Even where they were, high above the camp, David and Jackson ducked down, taking cover.

"Fuck yeah," Jackson cheered, rising up to watch the chaos below. Dozens of al-Qaeda soldiers had been blown apart and killed, parts of their camp destroyed, and the survivors moved in a daze. Some tried to help their fallen, their wounded. Others ran for cover. Leaders emerged, trying to rally their fighters to defend up and down the slopes around their camp. Fighters still alive in the lookout posts wildly fired down the mountain and into the air.

Blood spread through the snow in Milawa, pools of it. Screams rose, cries in Arabic, shouts and prayers and screams of fear and rage and anguish.

"*Haddad, translation.*"

Swallowing, David started translating the agonizing last words of their enemy.

---

They called in air strikes for almost sixty hours straight, obliterating the Milawa camp and the valley. Ryan kept them going, calling in air strikes every two hours until the valley was *gone*, wiped from the earth. They didn't sleep until daytime on the third day, while Shirzai and Majid kept watch.

Broken bodies, blood-drenched snow, and upturned mountain lay scattered for miles. Craters dozens of feet deep swallowed all light, holes that seemed to reach for the center of the mountain.

By the third day, it was obvious.

"There's nothing alive down there," David radioed.

"*Think we got them all?*"

"No. We saw fighters escaping into the mountains. At night,

between the strikes, they could have moved hundreds of fighters without our knowledge. OBL probably moved out that first night."

"*Which direction did they all head*?"

"East. Toward Pakistan."

Shirzai and Majid sent small teams of scouts forward while everyone recombined in the remains of the Milawa al-Qaeda camp. They clambered in and out of craters, pulling out debris, checking bodies.

David went with Ryan, picking through the burned and shattered remnants of the warehouse, the training facility and barracks at the end of the camp. Military manuals on how to build bombs and IEDs. Close-quarters urban combat. Infantry tactics, weapons, evasion, and counter-interrogation tactics. Chemistry textbooks, including formulas for chemical weapons and poisons.

"Jesus," Ryan breathed. "This is a Goddamn professional training system. They could have churned out thousands of fighters, all educated in how to fucking kill us." He threw one of the manuals, hurling it into a patch of bloody snow.

David flipped through page after page of chemical formulas. The recipe for anthrax sat in his hands.

Printed fatwas blew on the ground. He grabbed one, read it. His eyes ground over an Arabic word, *takfiri*, over and over again. *Takfiri, takfiri, takfiri.*

Apostate.

His stomach squeezed, like a black hole had opened inside him and was sucking him away, belly button first.

Bin Laden's body was not in the remains of Milawa's camp.

---

It took three days, but the scouts found al-Qaeda's deepest mountain hideout, stretching across three peaks.

Ryan and Kris got on the radio with George in Kabul, poring over the maps they each had, trying to triangulate Bin Laden's specific position, and his next move.

*"He's going to try for the tribal belt in Pakistan. It's as lawless as any place on the planet. He can disappear there."* Kris's voice made David's bones ache.

"How do we stop him from getting there?" Ryan, covered in dirt and buried in the mountain, relied on Kris and George to guide them all.

*"We have to plug the passes. Pakistan says they're staging thousands of soldiers in the mountains, blocking the routes from Afghanistan, but we're not seeing it on the satellites. Langley says the back door to Pakistan is still open."* George sounded dog-tired, like he hadn't slept in days.

*"What about CENTCOM? Can't they deploy Rangers into the mountains? Behind al-Qaeda?"* Kris asked.

*"I've got the request in. The military is running the show now. CENTCOM has been silent so far. I'll push harder."*

"We can't let him get away, George." Ryan's voice shook. David saw his knuckles go white around the radio, saw his arm tremble. "We *can't* lose Bin Laden."

---

Kris smiled down at David, sunlight wreathing his spiked hair, crinkles framing the pinch of his eyes. They were warm, basking in sunlight and lying in a field of green grass. Green, everywhere he looked, lush with life. The air was thick with humidity, a weight that filled every space between them, the inches between their lips and eyes and smiles. He was going to kiss Kris, *finally*, and Kris was happy. Smiling, laughing, deliriously happy that they were there, together, and David was about to kiss him. There wasn't a shadow anywhere. Not a question or a doubt. He felt certainty like it was solid thing, an organ in his body that had been lost sometime, somewhere, but was back where it belonged, now.

Kris opened his mouth, and David waited for the sound of his voice, the sweet, lilting edge, teasing and powerful in one, a voice that could build or destroy. He wanted to hear his name fall from Kris's lips, wanted to feel the way his soul shivered whenever Kris looked at him and spoke to him in just that way.

Hushed Arabic spilled from Kris, throaty and guttural. He frowned. It wasn't right; that wasn't what Kris sounded like. But it kept coming, harsh Arabic in whispers and hisses, a conversation in two parts that Kris was carrying on by himself.

"What about him?"

"He's *kufir*. He doesn't know anything."

"He dies with the others?"

"*Nam*."

Wrenching free of his dream was like falling to earth from space, a rush of flame and fear that ripped him back to reality. David's eyes flew open, but he didn't move.

Behind him, and behind a rocky outcropping on the western face of another icy peak in Tora Bora, two of Majid's fighters, scouts who had slipped forward during the day, whispered beneath the slivered moon. David felt frost on his exposed cheeks, felt his lips crack. He listened.

"What did you tell them?"

"That the Americans were coming. They had to act fast."

Roaring, David launched from his sleeping bag, flying to the two Afghan mercenaries. He tackled them both, pressing them into the frozen earth and grinding their cheeks into the dirt. "Who did you fucking speak to?"

Both men looked up at David, trembling. Their mouths moved, but no sound came out.

He woke Ryan and the whole camp, and Ryan called Majid to come for his men. The two were stripped of their weapons and boots and tied together, left under guard.

Majid, when he arrived, seemed unperturbed.

"My soldier heard your men say they *talked* to al-Qaeda. What the fuck is going on, Majid?" Ryan fumed.

"These men have family in al-Qaeda." Majid shrugged. "It is their Pashtun responsibility to give their family a warning before we arrive."

"More of the Pashtun tribal code *bullshit*?" Ryan seethed. "Did your men give away our position? Did your men tell al-Qaeda where we are?"

One corner of Majid's mouth quirked up. "You have no idea how this place works, American. These men here were paid to dig the trenches al-Qaeda now sits in." He pointed to his fighters. "And this? Where do you think I received this?" One finger traced the scab curving down his cheek, hairline to jaw. "Three weeks ago, I was huddled in a trench on the Shomali. Facing you."

David watched Ryan's face go bone white, lose all of its color. David's heart flip-flopped, squeezed and squeezed until all of his blood was thundering into his muscles, until he was a trigger poised to fire.

"Why the fuck are you here?"

"For the moment, you are our allies. You are paying and paying well. The future has changed in Afghanistan. It makes sense to be here with you. For now."

Ryan's gaze flicked to Palmer's, then to David's. David could see Ryan's thoughts, as if projected inside his skull through the windows of his eyes. Did they keep Majid and his men close, despite their connections to al-Qaeda and the Taliban? Or did they cut them loose, run the risk they'd turn right back to Bin Laden?

Breathing hard, Ryan pushed into Majid's face, staring down the burly, war-ravaged fighter. Ryan, in his Gore-Tex jacket and combat boots, seemed out of place, comically so, against the mujahedeen fighter and the primal Tora Bora mountains. "You *will* lead us to Bin Laden. To his personal caves. At dawn. Do you understand me?"

Majid shrugged. "*Da.*"

---

Majid's scouts led the way to Bin Laden's caves with David's rifle pointed at their back.

"There," one said, pointing to slits cut into the snow-covered limestone. "His caves begin there. They go toward the sun." He pointed west.

They peered up the mountain. Fighters huddled around fires in front of the slits, and more waited in trenches dug into the dirt and shale. The fighters were cold and bundled in robes and turbans. Weapons lay in stacks, everything from rifles to RPGs.

Ryan pulled out the radio and started calling in air strikes.

---

It was David's turn on the radio. The snow kept falling, just enough to slow down air strikes, but not stop them entirely. They'd pushed forward, obliterating cave after cave, and were pushing al-Qaeda and Bin Laden deeper into the mountains.

It was bitterly cold every day, and only getting more so. December had rolled in, sometime between the constant air strikes and the never-ending snow. He dreamed about Kris and the warm field almost every night, the endless waves of green, every shade imaginable. Kris was always at the center, always smiling at him. Always happy. Always warm against his skin.

Hearing Kris's voice through the radio was almost as torturous as it was cherished. "How's it going down there?"

"*Well, our secret is out. Base camp is now journalist HQ.*"

"Shit."

"*Majid's men have found a new source of revenue. He's shuttling journalists out to the Milawa camp for a hundred bucks a drive.*"

"Enterprising warlord." David huffed, and clouds billowed in front of his face.

"*Villagers are coming down with bodies, too. They're trying to sell them to us.*"

"Jesus."

"*It's gotten crowded here. The journalists are camping outside our camp, and they're now paying Shirzai's men to keep the entire area secure. Jim and I try to stay out of sight. But it's safer now. Which is good. How are you?*"

"Cold." There was so much David wanted to say. They were on a secure radio, impenetrable by al-Qaeda or any journalist, but every member of the team had an open earpiece and could listen in to whatever was being said. "We keep moving forward, but we're only moving inch by inch. Any luck with CENTCOM? We getting Rangers to plug the rear?" What was the point of pushing Bin Laden toward Pakistan if no one was there to stop him?

Kris was quiet. "*CENTCOM is refusing to deploy Rangers behind Bin Laden. General Faulkner says the Pakistanis have it covered. Hold on.*" The channel clicked, Kris switching to another frequency back at base. Dead air filled David's ear, static and pops, whines and whistles.

Kris came back. "*Be advised, fighters on station in two minutes.*"

David relayed the message to his team, holding position with their lasers trained on another cave, another trench. There was always another cave, it seemed. Always another bolt-hole for al-Qaeda fighters to run to.

He was *tired.* Tired in a way he hadn't been since he was a child leaving Libya, when he'd been exhausted of life and shattered from the inside out. Somalia and Mogadishu had made him weary, his first return to Africa since he was a boy and he'd been faced with, yet again, all the ways humans could tear into each other, hurt one another until the soul was raw.

The world spun differently once all the horrors men could inflict on other men were revealed. The colors changed, the sounds, the sights. *He'd* been changed, initiated into the world of terror and gut-wrenching truth when he was a boy.

Air tasted different when it was saturated with death.

He still felt the hands of ghosts on his shoulders. Muslim dead. African dead. The sound of his father's voice, too, along with the hands. He couldn't make out what his father was saying. It just added to the maddening pressure, like a push. A pull.

He was left to his thoughts in the quiet moments of the battlefield, between the bombs and the bullets, and when he tried to fall asleep. The backs of his eyelids were screens, replaying the days, the weeks, of violence, the onslaught of savagery he was a part of, the circle of life and death. Not just death, but terrible, agonizing death. Suffering.

Al-Qaeda was their enemy. Al-Qaeda fighters zeroed David in on their rifles, on their artillery, fired at him, tried to blow him off the mountain. They wanted him dead, like they wanted every American dead. They tried to kill him.

He, and his team, killed them first.

But who were they?

Men, Muslims, al-Qaeda.

He was two out of the three.

What had created the battlefield, had carved such hate into the faith he remembered his father teaching him in sun-strewn gardens, whose first precept was to submit and to love?

*Whoever slays a soul, it is as though he slew all men.* His father had taught him that verse from the Quran when he was four.

Every day, David counted new blood splatters in the snow and measured the depth of the craters by how many bodies were stacked within.

Was the world black and white, evil and good, horror and righteousness, or did Majid and his shifting loyalties understand the world better than anyone else?

What about Khan and his quiet pleas for American aid, yet his certainty that he would be betrayed? Every Muslim in Afghanistan had stared at them the same way, from Khan to Majid, from the Taliban David spied through his binoculars to the Kabulis on the streets. That look of uncertainty, of wariness. Of expectant betrayal. Of hesitant, hidden hatred.

Was he too American to be Muslim now? Forever outside the rhythms of his youth, the faith of his father, once passed down to him? Twenty-one years he'd been away from his faith. Yet the whispers of prayers came back to him in dreams, the same dreams he had of Kris, bathed in sunlight and smiling down on him.

*Kufir*, a dark part of his mind hissed. *Takfiri*. Unbeliever. Apostate.

He wanted to burrow into Kris's arms and ask questions David wouldn't even whisper to himself, ask Kris all the whys and hows and whens. Let Kris explain the world until it made sense again. Listen to Kris's sharp-edged voice until time ran out, until he found the answers, and found the end.

When the dust cleared from their latest strike, David clambered down the sliding rocks with Ryan and Palmer, sifting through the craters. Obliterated rifles and shredded Arabic books littered the blasted rock face. Bodies smeared into the ground, the earth the color of a bruise.

He heard tinny Arabic mixed with static coming from a crimson patch of snow.

Digging through, David peeled a handheld radio out of the near-frozen clutch of a dead fighter. "*We need water!* Yallah, *you must melt more snow. Hurry*!"

Another voice answered. "*Is the Sheikh all right*?"

"Allahu Akbar, *the Sheikh is fine.* Bismillah."

"Guys!" David held out the radio. "This radio is tuned to al-Qaeda's frequency. And it's unscrambled."

---

They kept the al-Qaeda radio powered on at all times, patched a dedicated line into it so it would transmit down to Kris at base camp. As a giant gunship circled over Tora Bora, plugging the mountain full of thousands of rounds of hot lead, they listened to al-Qaeda fighters scream and run, scramble for hiding spots deep in the caves. They listened to the fighters declare a series of caves lost, trenches abandoned and move on, farther to the west. They heard the fighters call out for more food, send out scavenger parties for roots and twigs, leaves, anything at all that was edible.

And then, they heard *his* voice.

David recognized it immediately. He'd heard the voice before, in training, in briefings before the mission, in the Panjshir when Kris would play old recordings from the late '90s, back when he was issuing fatwas and warnings and promises to strike.

Osama Bin Laden.

"*My brothers, keep fighting,*" Bin Laden said. "*We will vanquish the Americans. They are weak, and their bombs cannot destroy us. When they come up these mountains, they will be cold and alone and afraid, and we will beat them. Fight, my brothers. Fight.*"

Ryan called in an air strike with a Daisy Cutter, the same superweapon they had dropped on Mazar-e-Sharif, that had decimated the Taliban so completely. They waited, watching the skies, and counted the minutes until the giant bomb was pushed from the giant plane.

When it blew, the mountains themselves seemed to shake, shudder, and nearly collapse, trembling down to the center of the earth. Snow and ice toppled from the peaks and avalanches sloped downhill hundreds of miles away. All the air in the Tora Bora mountains seemed to suck inward, a giant, rushing *whoosh*, pulling toward the center of the impact zone. Dirt and flame rose, shooting high into the air.

Everything that had been there before was now vaporized.

Frantic screams and shouts blurred over the radio. As the Arabic speaker, David had been charged with listening to every cry, every bitter curse, every desperate plea.

In the aftermath, he heard one voice shout. "*The Sheikh's trench, it was hit! It has been destroyed! The Sheikh, the Sheikh! Is he okay?*"

Next to David, Ryan clenched dirt and snow beneath his hands, gloved fingers digging deep into the frozen earth. Palmer gripped his shoulder, not breathing, waiting on the words coming out of the radio like he needed them to breathe.

"Allahu Akbar, *the Sheikh is alive!*" another voice cried. "*He was not in his trench when the bomb hit. He is alive! He is okay.*"

As David shook his head, Ryan cursed, collapsing forward. His hands made fists in the ground, squeezing around mud and snow. Palmer turned his face away, glaring into the darkness of the mountain.

---

"*We wish to negotiate a cease-fire, to prepare to surrender.*"

Majid's man held out his radio, identical to the al-Qaeda model David kept on him at all times, but tuned to a different frequency. Why Majid's man had it, how long he'd had it, who he was communicating with, those were questions without answers.

"That's al-Qaeda?"

"*Nam*," Majid's fighter answered. He'd spent time with the Arabs, with al-Qaeda, long enough to learn Arabic.

David's teeth scraped, molars grinding. "I'll relay the message."

---

In Kabul, George blew his lid. David and Ryan almost heard his bellows in Tora Bora.

"*No fucking cease-fire*!" he hollered. "*Fucking murderers don't get cease-fires! DC and CENTCOM agree! Keep up the pressure! Keep fucking attacking*!"

Kris, as always, was the voice of reason. "*They might be using a cease-fire as a pretext for slipping away. Bin Laden would never surrender, especially not now. Not after his victory on nine-eleven. This is the beginning of the end times for them. This is their Armageddon. He won't give that up*."

"*No cease-fire*," George seethed. "*I want you to keep killing those bastards*."

---

The tentative cease-fire lasted five hours, from the time Majid's fighter relayed the message to the time George put his foot down. CENTCOM sent their fighters back into theater, dropping thousands of pounds of bombs onto al-Qaeda's location.

When the fighters appeared overhead, their silhouettes perfectly outlined against the sky, Bin Laden's voice boomed from the handheld radio. "*The time is now*!" he cried. "*Arm yourselves! We destroy the infidels now*!"

As the sun dipped beyond the western peaks, flames rose from the mountains, bomb after bomb after bomb exploding in the caves of Tora Bora.

Late at night, David heard Bin Laden's voice again. Bin Laden sounded tired, worn down. Weak.

He radioed Kris at base. "Are you hearing this?"

"*I am.*"

Bin Laden, his voice weary, spoke slowly. "*My brothers, our prayers were not answered. The* takfiri *apostates did not come to our aid, and instead sided with the infidels. They will pay for their crimes against the faith, my brothers. We will rise again, after this battle.*" Bin Laden broke off, and static squealed, wailed. "*My brothers, I am sorry for leading you into the mountains.*"

They kept bombing all night long, and all the next day.

The day after, the radio sounded again with Bin Laden's voice, but this time, it was a prerecorded sermon, extolling the wickedness of America and proclaiming a fatwa against the Great Satan. It was the sermon he'd used when he had first declared war on the United States, on Friday, August 23, 1996, and when the collision course between Osama Bin Laden, David Haddad, and Kris Caldera had begun.

---

In the following days, disheartened and gravely wounded al-Qaeda fighters were captured fleeing Tora Bora. Some barely clung to life, nursing ragged field amputations that had long gone septic. Others cursed Bin Laden with every breath, accusing him of abandoning them and the battle. Some fighters, when surrounded by Majid's or Shirzai's soldiers, or Palmer and his men, would pull a grenade from beneath their robes and detonate it against their chest, screaming "*Allahu Akbar*!" with their last breath. David was spattered in blood and brains and splinters of bone, digging into his frostbitten cheeks, the exposed skin on his arms.

By December 17, 2001, the battle was over.

Over a thousand fighters had gone into the mountains with Bin Laden. Four hundred bodies had been recovered, and fifty-five prisoners were taken, a mixture of surrenders and the capture of those too wounded to flee. Hundreds had escaped, vanishing, melting away into the mountains, into the tribal regions of Afghanistan and Pakistan.

And Bin Laden was *gone.*

---

David came down from the mountains on December 20, with Ryan, Palmer, and the rest of his team. Through it all, they hadn't lost a man, but Kris had relayed the murder of a CIA officer in the north of Afghanistan while they were in the mountains.

Majid's fighters had walked away as soon as the al-Qaeda fighters had, and Palmer had been the first to question whether they'd been al-Qaeda's allies all along. Had they just been slowing the Americans down? Redirecting them in the wildness of Tora Bora, a mountain range so hopelessly complex, they never would have managed without guides?

Ryan was sullen the entire journey down, through the frigid ranges back to Milawa, and then in the bouncing, rusted-out jeep Shirzai's men sent. They drove down the one road in Tora Bora, the road from Milawa camp to Jalalabad that Bin Laden had built in the early '90s, in silence.

At the end of the road, waiting outside of their shattered base camp, was Kris.

For David, the world finally began to spin again.

# 12

**Kabul, Afghanistan - December 23, 2001**

"To the finest men I have ever served with."

George raised a bottle of Russian Baltika beer, Number 7, and held it high. "I am honored by every single thing you gentlemen did. Every moment you spent here on the ground. Every ounce of blood, sweat, and determination you gave. Everything you did was heroes' work." He pumped his bottle as his chin wavered. "We will get him. I swear it. We will get Bin Laden. Not today. But we will."

In the corner of the command center at the CIA station in Kabul, in the same old Taliban guesthouse, Ryan turned away, hiding his face in the shadows. Kris watched him blink fast, wipe his nose. Sniff hard as his jaw muscles clenched and held.

At Kris's side, David leaned into him, their bodies touching from shoulders to ankles. One of David's arms wound around Kris, his hand disappearing beneath Kris's sweater, palm against the skin at the small of his back. His thumb ghosted over the baby-fine hairs on Kris's skin, hairs he hadn't known he had until David strummed them, made him shiver. Made his bones melt.

He'd wanted to fling himself into David's arms when he'd seen their jeep bounce down the mountain, sliding and shaking on flinty shale and the jeep's broken shocks. They were more mud monsters and frozen swamp creatures than men when they'd arrived, covered in dirt like they'd burrowed through the mountain. David's burnished skin, rich like bronze, had seemed ghostly, a deathly pale, and Kris had wiped his hand down David's cheek, ostensibly to clean the dust away. He'd just wanted to feel David's warmth, his presence, to know that he was alive.

Beneath his palm, David had trembled, a grenade shivering before it exploded. He hadn't said anything, but Kris saw the supernovas in his gaze, the burn of his soul blasting through the tattered remnants of his control.

David, like Ryan, like Palmer, like the rest of them, had come back defeated. Wounded. Empty.

Jim had arranged for transport straight back to Kabul, from their base camp through Jalalabad and back though Nangarhar Province. In the weeks they'd been in the mountains, Jalalabad had turned from a war-ravaged ghost town to a vibrant trading city, full of honking cars, rickshaws, bicycles, and people moving in every direction. After staring at the bleak moonscape of Tora Bora, the explosion of life, of color, of humanity, was almost too overwhelming. David had hidden his face, tucking his head sideways against Kris's shoulder, and they'd hidden the clasp of their hands between their thighs for the entire drive.

Kabul had changed as well. As vibrant as Jalalabad had become, Kabul was a hundred times *more*. More people, more color, more traffic, more horns, more life. More women in hijab, fewer burqas. More children playing games and flying kites. The movie theater, shuttered under the Taliban, had reopened, and lines stretched for hours.

George had met them at the CIA station and had promptly ordered Palmer and his men to continue driving to Bagram, to the new Army's Unified Command Center. They needed to be debriefed and seen by medical, and the Army insisted on doing it their way. Kris almost hadn't let go of David, and their fingers had clung to each other until their arms would have pulled apart if they'd held on any longer.

"Don't worry, Kris," George had murmured. "They're coming back. We've got a new mission coming up."

He'd taken a lukewarm shower and tossed and turned on his thin mattress all night, his thoughts consumed by David.

But, just after breakfast, as he was trying to coax resurrection out of a cup of shitty instant coffee, Palmer had led his men back into the CIA station. "Reporting as ordered, sir," he said to George, who'd been sitting two seats down from Kris.

"Pull up a chair, gentleman. Dig in."

Palmer's team had torn into the breakfast the Afghan cooks had made. They'd eaten like they'd never seen food, shoveling breakfast into their mouths at world-hot-dog-eating-championship pacing.

David had come around the table and sat in the empty seat beside Kris.

He'd showered, and his cuts had been bandaged, and there were stitches above one eyebrow. Bruises along his cheeks and jaw. His knuckles were raw, his skin cracked from the cold. But his eyes still burned every time he looked at Kris. Need pulsated from him, like gravity, like the oceans' tides, pulling Kris in.

George had called a meeting after breakfast, carting in a crate of beers and passing them out individually. "From Uzbekistan." He'd grinned. "I heard this is the strongest Russian beer an American can drink. The rest of the brews are fermented engine oil." Chuckles rose, halfhearted.

After he'd thanked them all and had extolled their heroics with hearty cheers, he led the team in the first round of drinks. George sputtered after his first sip, nearly choking on the thick, dark brew, far more robust than a Guinness or a black stout in the States. Palmer laughed and clapped him on the back.

"I told you we were going to find Bin Laden, and I meant that. We, the people in this room," George said, nodding to each and every man, in his team and in Palmer's. "And we have a new mission. We are the team charged with hunting down and capturing Bin Laden, wherever he is, no matter how long it takes. And we'll capture every other high-value al-Qaeda leader, too.

"Which means we're moving shop. Al-Qaeda isn't in Afghanistan anymore, at least not in any real presence. They fled, or they're trapped in Kandahar, which means the Marines are going to smoke them out. Most of the high-value leadership made it out of Afghanistan overland to Pakistan. They're either hiding in the tribal areas, or they've made their way to Peshawar or Kashmir. So, we're on the move. In two days, the entire team is moving to Islamabad station." He took another sip of his beer, cringing as he swallowed. "The next two days are yours. I'm sorry we can't give you a better Christmas vacation. But the Army has set up some facilities at Bagram for their soldiers. There's the theater, showing Bollywood's finest from a decade ago. And there's plenty of beds, hot chow, and secured internet here. Sleep, eat, and call home."

"Sounds great, sir." Palmer held out his hand. George shook it. Jackson and Warrick were already cheering, talking about plans to eat until they puked and then sleep until they couldn't physically sleep another minute. Jim and Phillip had their heads together, muttering about Bagram and the facilities there. Ryan stayed in the corner, his arms folded, staring at the ground.

David's gaze met Kris's.

Two days, all to themselves.

Visions tumbled through Kris's mind, dreams he'd nurtured through the scant few minutes he'd slept at base camp, always clutching the radio close in case David or the team radioed in. Finally, after all this time, after everything. He could see his own eagerness reflected in David's eyes.

"Kris, Sergeant Haddad." George stopped in front of them as the rest of the team peeled away, off on their own adventures. "I... wanted to say something to you, Kris." He swallowed, his Adam's apple rising and falling. "I am very proud of you. You proved everyone wrong. Really rose above all of the challenges you faced." He smiled and held out his hand.

*Never let anyone else define your life, Kris. Never let anyone else define who you are. They will always get it wrong.* David's words came back, slamming into his skull like gongs being struck, like fireworks shooting off into the night sky.

"George, the only real challenge I faced here was *you*. And Ryan." Kris felt that fire that had always burned in him reignite, felt the flames grow larger. Something had slipped, between the boy he'd been, who'd refused to hide, and the man he'd become, who had let other people set barriers for him. When had he given up? "The only thing I had to prove wrong was *your* prejudice. I knew what I was doing. I was confident in myself. I didn't struggle with what I could do. No, George, I am proud of *you* for finally seeing that I was working my ass off, that I was doing everything I could. That I knew what I was talking about and really was put on the team to be the subject matter expert."

George stared. His jaw hung open.

Kris put the cherry on top. "I'm proud of you for finally seeing the real me, George."

"That's... one way to put it," George said slowly.

"It's the right way to put it."

George's gaze darted to David. David stood beside Kris, silent and sentinel. He stared at George, daring him to disagree.

"I think I was right about one thing, at least," George finally said, his voice low. He stared pointedly at them both, holding each of their gazes for a long moment.

David straightened. Kris heard his vertebrae crack, felt his muscles tighten until they started to tremble.

"Which brings me to my next question." He cleared his throat. "State wants to reopen the US Embassy in Kabul after the new year. They want someone to go through it first, get an assessment of the damage. I... was wondering if you two would be interested. It's a big, empty building. Might take two days to go through."

Kris's head swam, like he'd been plunged into the ocean, tossed on waves after falling from a high cliff. George was... giving them space? Privacy? Calling them on their fledgling relationship, and, inexplicably, enabling it? In all of Kabul, in all of Afghanistan, was there any place he and David could possibly be together without any fear of discovery or of reprisal?

"We'd be happy to," David rumbled. "We'll start immediately."

"Good." George looked like he'd just shit his pants. "I expect you back here in two days."

---

The doors to the embassy had barely shut behind them when David first pressed Kris against the wall.

David's body surrounded him, covered him completely, devoured him. David pressed his forehead to Kris's, lips hovering microns apart. Their breaths shook, tiny gasps keeping the last of their bodies separate.

"You want this?" David breathed. "You want me?"

Kris saw the spark of hesitation, of fear, in David's eyes. He reached for David, his hands on David's hips, pulling him closer, tighter, as if they could melt into each other's bodies then and there. "I want you, David."

David shuddered, his eyes squeezing shut as he drew in a breath, as he pressed into Kris. Had anyone wanted Kris before? Truly wanted him, like everything in David wanted him?

Finally, David's lips brushed Kris's, a tentative kiss, so unlike their bruising clash at the base of Tora Bora. Their lips caught, stuck, clung together. David tasted him slowly, like Kris was made of honey and David was tasting his soul. Kris had had hundreds of first kisses in his life, from high school to college and beyond, hundreds of kisses at parties and before one-night stands, with men he'd wanted and men he didn't care for. No one had ever kissed him with the tenderness of David's touch, the intensity of his desire. Kris shivered, shook. His knees went limp.

David caught him. Their bodies aligned in just the right way.

"The ambassador used to live here," Kris gasped. "His apartment is on the top floor."

They kissed their way up the stairs, bouncing from wall to wall, pushing each other back and molding their bodies as one. Hands cradled faces, jaws, wrapped around waists. At the top floor, they started stripping, shedding mud-spattered jackets and dusty sweaters. In two months, they'd never seen each other's skin, had never seen beneath the contours of a thick sweater. Kris's bare skin puckered as the cold air hit him, his thin chest contracting. David was there instantly, wrapping his arms around him, pressing his furred chest to Kris, a primal connection completed when David closed his lips over Kris's again.

Their bodies had changed. Kris had come to Afghanistan slender and waifish, his strength always of the lean variety. Weeks of mountaineering and combat missions had molded his upper body, given him strength where he'd never had any. David's strength had ebbed thanks to the weeks in Tora Bora, the deprivation and harshness eating away at his reserves. Bruises and scars marred his skin from impact blasts, slides down the mountain, times when he'd had to duck for cover when al-Qaeda had fought back, sent their artillery raining down near David's position. His body was a map of the war. Kris's hands roamed, covering every mar, every battle, as if he could heal him with his touch alone.

The ambassador's apartment had been left unused since Dubs's assassination. They kissed their way into a time capsule, a replica of the late '70s, dust-covered and forgotten. The windows were slim, near the ceiling, only to let in light. No one could see as they shed the last of their clothes, boots, pants, and briefs. No one saw Kris pull David on top of him, into the ambassador's bed. No one saw David slide onto Kris, cover him completely, begin to rock against him, like he wanted their atoms to merge, like he was trying to disappear within Kris's being. Like he was the ocean, coming in for Kris's shore.

---

David lay between Kris's legs, his head pillowed on Kris's chest, ear over his heart. Kris's hand stroked up and down David's back. They'd made love until they'd thought they would die, until Kris had thought he'd combust, explode, become a star in the heavens.

Outside, the sun had dropped beneath the mountains, and the last rays of light sent long shadows through the thin windows ringing the room. Kabul hummed beyond the empty embassy, car horns and wagon wheels and donkey snorts mixed with shouts in Dari and Pashto.

"Does this come with us to Pakistan?" Kris whispered. "Or do we leave this here?"

David's shoulders tightened. He looked up, his beard scratching against Kris's chest. Kris tried to lock down his emotions, shield his heart. Tried to throw up walls behind his eyes, just in case.

"We both have experience loving and leaving, I think." Kris tried to smile. He recognized in David the same love-them-and-leave-them style he'd had back in America. Ships passing in the night. The rush of combat. Adrenaline, close quarters. Too much had happened, too fast, and they needed to burn through it somehow. "If this is just what it is, I understand."

David's chest rose and fell, his breath quickening. He pressed a kiss to Kris's chest, over his heart, and spoke into his skin. "I don't want to stop."

Relief was physical, the unclenching of Kris's heart, the rush of giddy joy, the way he squeezed his fingers into David's back, nails biting into his skin.

Smiling, David slid up the bed, tangling his legs and arms around Kris. He tugged a blanket up with him, a dusty wool cover, and snuggled close. "I don't ever want to stop this. Us."

"I had no idea," Kris said, turning to face David. He propped his head on one elbow. "I never thought you were gay. You confused me. But I never thought—"

"*Don't Ask, Don't Tell* is the law of the land. I can fight and die for America, but they can't handle me loving another man." David shrugged. He laced his fingers through Kris's, stroked his thumb over Kris's knuckles. "I've lived my life like a kaleidoscope. If you look at me one way, I'm the Army Special Forces soldier. Stern. Solid. American." He chuckled. Kris grinned. "But I'm also Arab. Muslim, in some part of me." He swallowed, squeezed Kris's hand. "And... gay. Even though no other part of me can accept that. It feels like I'm different people all in one body, and I don't know how to be everyone equally, or if I even can."

David pressed his forehead to Kris's, turned those burning, starlight eyes into Kris's soul. "When I am with you, I feel parts of myself come together. Parts I thought couldn't ever mix. You make me want to be everything I am. For you."

Kris couldn't breathe. "I'm... just—" He was just a kid, a skinny, brown Puerto Rican who had been underestimated his entire life. He was just a side-eyed snort, an afterthought, someone people consistently expected nothing from. Hadn't George *just* proven that?

How was he everything to David? When David had become everything to him?

"You're like a part of me I didn't know was missing. Part of my mind, or my soul. Like you have the thoughts I haven't thought yet, feelings I haven't felt yet, waiting for me. Inside you. You feel like a part of me I've been craving." David's voice was a whisper, a breath.

"David..." His vision swam. He couldn't breathe. He cupped David's cheek. Words wouldn't come, not through his strangled throat.

"Ever since we got here, things have been upside down. What's right and wrong. According to the others, we're here to kill all the Arabs, get revenge for what happened. But I'm Arab. And I'm not saying I condone or understand what the hijackers did, or anything about al-Qaeda, I don't. Not at all. But I do understand... Arab pain. Muslim pain. Libya—" He hissed, and everything in him tightened. "I saw it in Somalia. And I see it here. There's this collective pain, this ache, in the Muslim soul. And now I feel the world turning even more against us. Are we supposed to shoulder the collective guilt, the blame for nine-eleven, too? When the Muslim soul is already shattered?" He buried his face in Kris's neck, shallow breaths warming Kris's skin. Kris stroked his back, tangled his fingers in his dark hair.

"What do you think is going to happen?" David whispered. "Now, after this?"

Kris chewed on his lip. "This isn't just a battle to capture Bin Laden, or to avenge the deaths from nine-eleven. Or to get rid of the Taliban to make a free Afghanistan and eliminate terrorist safe havens. Bin Laden spent years building the narrative for this attack. He's framed his entire movement around *one* hadith from Abu Hurairah. '*When you see the black banners coming from Khorasan, join that army, even if you have to crawl over ice*'."

David spoke the last half of the hadith with him. "'*For no power will be able to stop them, and they will reach Jerusalem, where they will erect their flags*'."

"The Islamic end times, Armageddon, begins with the fighters coming out of Khorasan, after striking a fatal blow against their enemies. Bin Laden's declaration of war against the US was signed from 'Hindu Kush, *Khorasan*, Afghanistan.' He's used the Khorasan hadith in all of his speeches, his videos, his recruitment. He believes, and the people who join him believe, that they are fulfilling the Islamic end times prophecies." Kris stroked down David's back, fingers dipping into the valley of his spine, mapping the bones of his vertebrae.

David exhaled. "There's too much pain. Too much Muslim pain." He swallowed. "Are you going to stay in?"

"I have to. The hijackers, their names were on my desk. And we should have known. With Bin Laden's '96 declaration of war and his fatwas. His three warnings, like the Quran prescribes, for declaring war. We should have put the dots together. I should have seen..." Kris chewed on his lip. "I bear some responsibility for what happened."

"Kris—"

"I do. I knew Bin Laden and al-Qaeda were dangerous. I knew they wanted to hurt us. The embassies in Africa, the *USS Cole*. I just didn't think... I never imagined they'd do what they did. I didn't think it was possible." He sighed, biting his lip and rolling it back and forth. "I need to spend the rest of my career making up for that. And always think about what is possible. What is coming next. I have to." Kris scooted close to David, hitching one leg around David's calf. "What about you?"

"I have another few years left on my second enlistment. Sounds like my unit is linking to the CIA. Happens, occasionally. I'd never been part of a CIA secondment before." David stroked Kris's leg, his palm circling Kris's thigh. "I want to stay with you," he said softly. "I'm afraid I'll get lost in this war." His eyes were black holes, and the burning edge of his soul peeked out, just barely. Like the shadow of a crescent moon, or a whisper against Kris's skin.

"I think the whole world is going to get lost in this war."

# 13

**Islamabad, Pakistan - March 29, 2002**

The web stretched across an entire wall in the CIA station. Spindly lines crisscrossed each other, tracing points back to the dead center.

Someone had drawn a reticle around the photo in the center. A black marker sniper's scope circled the black-and-white passport photo of a thin, young Saudi with a close-cropped beard and moustache, his hair hidden under a neat keffiyeh.

Abu Zahawi.

Langley said he was al-Qaeda's third-highest officer, third in command after Bin Laden and his deputy, Ayman al-Zawahiri. He'd been the external *emir*, the high commander, of the Khaldan training camp in Afghanistan before the invasion. The Khaldan camp was where the hijackers were trained, where Bin Laden regularly visited. Where all high ranking al-Qaeda operatives transited.

They needed Zahawi.

And they would have him. Tonight.

In January, Kris, George, and the rest of their combined CIA-Special Forces team stepped out of a helicopter in Islamabad and started fighting the CIA's next war.

"We have a new position at the CIA," Bill, Islamabad's chief of station, had told them all during their first briefing. "Targeteer. These guys are going to be the most important people in the agency. They're hunters. Anything and everything we get on a high-value target gets routed straight to their desks. The targeteers package all of that intel together. Make sense of it. And then they find our targets." Bill thought fast and spoke fast, and his eyes peered around the room, dancing over each person on the team. "It's part forensic psychology, part jigsaw puzzle, part sifting through haystacks, and part voodoo. You've got to be a cultural anthropologist, a translator, a psychologist, and a psychic. So. Who is going to be the targeteer on this team?"

George hadn't hesitated. "Kris Caldera. That's made for him."

Bill's stare had pierced Kris. He'd had a thick stack of folders on the table in front of him stuffed with CDs and DVDs, papers and photos. Bill had pushed it all toward Kris. "Here's your first target. Abu Zahawi. He's in Pakistan. And we have to find him."

*He's in Pakistan* turned out to be the agency's most popular line. Everyone was in Pakistan, from Bin Laden to the most minor al-Qaeda recruit, and they were supposed to find every last one of them. Pakistan was the size of Texas but had the population of the United States. Karachi was the fourth-largest city in the entire world. Finding anyone in the crushing mass of humanity, much less someone purposefully hiding, was a near impossible task.

Zahawi's name, and about a dozen phone numbers associated with him, kept coming up in documents and debris recovered in Afghanistan from destroyed al-Qaeda camps, captured fighters, and picked from the dead. From Marines and soldiers, combing through the remains of the Taliban and al-Qaeda in Afghanistan, to Islamabad, hordes and hordes of information flowed.

Not all of it was intelligent. There was just too much of it, too many bits and pieces and names and addresses scattered across thousands of leads.

Kris nearly buckled.

Palmer's men hit the streets, going to Lahore, Peshawar, and Karachi, trying to scour the cities with a small passport photo, searching for Zahawi like they could pick him from the millions and millions of people crowding the streets. David came back from each trip frustrated and filthy, and always exhausted.

"I need more resources," Kris told George at the end of January. "I can't make a man appear with nothing but luck."

"What do you need?"

"Give me an entire electronic net over Pakistan. Zero in on the numbers we have of known al-Qaeda agents. The phone numbers connected to Zahawi. If anyone calls those, who do they call after that, and then after that, and then after that. We need to build a web."

The invisible electronic net dropped. Calls were vacuumed up, scrubbed and searched for names and keywords. When calls to Zahawi's known numbers didn't connect, America's digital eyes tracked the calls they made next, asking for instruction, and then again, and again. Everything went on the wall, a giant web of connections, of unrelated people trying to live in hiding, exposed by the pattern of their phone calls.

Finally, they found Zahawi's new numbers.

Zahawi had fourteen new numbers tied to fourteen locations. Thirteen in Faisalabad, the third most populous city in Pakistan, and situated far from the Afghanistan border, south of Islamabad. One in Lahore, a city almost on the Indian border.

They hit the streets again, winding through the tangled, twisted alleys and dirt roads. Faisalabad was a rough, dangerous, and hopelessly poor city. A never-ending sprawl of shacks, dump lots, and precarious slums. Children played in raw sewage. The stench of rot slipped under their clothes, into their noses, down their throats, gagging them all. Cars and rickshaws and bicycles and donkeys and camels crowded every inch of the roadways. Walkers glided in and out of traffic lanes and passed angry cabbies shouting in thirteen different languages.

Most people living in Faisalabad lived on less than five dollars a day. And most were fierce adherents to a firebrand fundamentalist Islam, married to a violent rage. Life in Faisalabad was epically shitty. Why not desperately wish to turn to the past, to the golden days of Islam, when life was vibrant, peaceful, and Muslims were regarded as the enlightened intellectuals of the world? Why not crave that historical power again? Everything to blame in Faisalabad was the West's fault, anyway. For putting them at the bottom of the world order.

Going into Faisalabad meant working undercover. David and his team dressed in salwar kameezes, breezy tunics and linen pants. They'd kept their thick beards from Afghanistan. David blended in the best, with his bronze skin and his native Arabic, and he played the part of a foreign fighter working the streets. He was the point man for all of Kris's operations.

Kris watched David take to the mission like a fish to water, seamlessly blending into the passionate Islamic fundamentalism. Even in Faisalabad, David moved like he knew how to live in a city on the edge, under the thumb of oppression and desperate poverty. There was something there, something Kris wanted to ask about, but couldn't. Not yet.

Kris, slender, even with his added muscles from the war in Afghanistan, played the part of David's wife. He donned a hijab and the head-to-toe *abaya*. He tied a *niqab* around his face, peered out of the narrow eye slit, and kept his body hidden from view under the sweep of black. His *abaya* collected filth from the streets as he swept over puddles of sewage, walked up and down dusty alleys. To add to the disguise, Kris lined his eyes with kohl, like the local women did.

David couldn't tear his eyes away.

Kris and David walked the streets as if they were married, scoping out all thirteen properties. They found squat mudbrick homes, small one-room huts with corrugated tin roofs, and shacks on the edge of slums. Hatred seethed from the slum, like a physical pulse.

"We can't take the entire slum. But there are al-Qaeda fighters in there, for sure."

"Zahawi is the target. We have to find him."

The last location was a large house, almost a villa, built of cinder blocks, three stories tall and surrounded by an eight-foot privacy fence. Every window was closed and shuttered. In the sweltering one-hundred-degree heat and humidity, that stood out like an electric sign in the sky, pointing straight down. All of Faisalabad had thrown open their doors and windows, trying to cool down with the limp, rotten breeze.

All of Faisalabad, save for them.

"Bad news in there." David leaned into Kris.

Sweat poured down Kris's back. He was roasting, nearly passing out under the *abaya*. "No one keeps their windows closed. Not in this heat."

"Let's get back to the safe house."

George had rented a safe house in Faisalabad, paying cash for a villa in the wealthy sector of town. The mansion had fourteen bedrooms, twelve sitting rooms, and a huge plot of land, surrounded by a giant fence that kept all curious onlookers far away. From the roof, they had satellite connections with seven different communications relays, from the CIA to the military. The team lived in the safe house and rotated surveillance on each of Zahawi's locations.

A backup team from Langley was sent in, too, to help share the load. They'd arrived while David and Kris were off in Faisalabad's reaches, hunting for al-Qaeda.

"Kris!" Dan Wright, Kris's mentor at Langley, jogged to him when he and David returned to the safe house and wrapped Kris up in a hug, holding on for longer than Kris would have expected. "God, it's good to see you again."

They caught up that night, sitting together on the roof. Dan had brought three bottles of wine, and he and Kris downed shitty chardonnay as they sat in lawn chairs and tried to breathe through their mouths, tried to not smell the fetid stench of Faisalabad.

"You blew the door open, Kris." Dan held out his plastic cup of white wine for a toast. "You blew the door for all us gays open. Going to Afghanistan and kicking ass."

Kris's jaw dropped. "*Us gays*? Dan?"

"I entered the CIA before you. When it was still not allowed."

It was only in 1996 that the law had changed, allowing homosexuals to legally possess security clearances. Prior to 1996, any gay man or woman was considered a liability, someone who could be blackmailed, someone untrustworthy. Someone not allowed into the hallowed halls of the national security establishment.

"I loved that you never played the bullshit games." Dan smiled at him, his eyes bright. Glowing. "You never tried to hide. I wanted to help you. Wanted to see you succeed. And, *Goddamn*. Did you ever."

"I just did my job."

"You did a hell of a job. You're a fantastic officer, Kris. And you're paving the way for everyone after you. No one thinks twice anymore about us."

"You going to come out?"

Dan winked at him over the rim of his cup. "If there was someone to come out for."

Kris froze.

"I always wanted to ask you to dinner. Back in DC. I've always wanted to get to know you better." He leaned forward, fiddling with his wine. "Maybe, after this is over, we could try? The Marriott in Islamabad isn't the Capital Grille in DC, but..." Hope infused Dan's words. "I just really want to spend some time with you."

"Dan..." Kris squeezed his eyes closed, leaned forward. His head hung between his slumped shoulders. "Dan, I'm sorry. I'm seeing someone."

Shock pushed Dan back. "Oh. I didn't know. I thought you were single, in DC—"

"I was. It's... new."

"In Afghanistan?"

"It's secret. We're not out. We're—" Kris fumbled for words, stumbling over his exhaustion and the wine.

"He's military." Dan nodded slowly. He stared into his wine. "I understand." He sighed. "Whoever he is, he's a lucky guy. But I hope we can still be friends."

"I'd like that."

---

The night before the raid, he and David lounged in a tepid bath surrounded by stubby candles. The safe house had sunken mosaic tubs in most bedrooms, playthings for the wealthy who had lived stratospheres above the rest of the city's inhabitants. David rubbed his feet, massaged his legs, kissed his way up and down Kris's body. They made love silently, Kris riding David as his hands traced David's chest, his body, mapped the terrain of his lover. Candlelight flickered over their skin, threw shadows against the walls. Kris came with a muffled cry, his head thrown back, David's hands clinging to him, his arms wrapped around his back. David's lips kissed every inch of his chest.

Their teammates were on either side of the paper-thin walls. Kris could hear their laughter, their conversations, between his gasps, his muffled moans.

Who knew about them? George, for sure. Had he told Ryan? Ryan was still his deputy. Jim and Phillip were wrapped up in their own projects. Derek had stayed in Afghanistan. Jackson? Palmer's team had to bunk together, and Jackson was David's roommate.

David spent all his time in Kris's room, though. What did Jackson think about his absent partner?

And Palmer? He'd seen them kissing back in Tora Bora.

David had become distant from his team since moving to Pakistan, moving with Kris and on the ground instead of holding surveillance and going on night raids with the others.

They weren't supposed to be doing this. David's entire career could come apart, shatter under the *Don't Ask, Don't Tell* rules of the military.

Sleeping with a partner on an overseas mission happened, but it was generally filed under "ill advised" by the CIA and "disastrous" when it went all wrong.

It was illegal to be gay in Pakistan. Illegal to love another man. They were in Pakistan on diplomatic cover, but the bond between Pakistan and the United States was tenuous, a daily negotiation of threats and bluster. A scandal like this, which the Pakistanis could use to claim the US disrespected their culture, their laws, and flagrantly violated their beliefs, could tear their alliance apart.

And, for the first time, Kris had some measure of respect. Dan's words haunted him, repeating in his mind on an echoing loop. His name was said with praise. People believed in him. Thought he could do something. That he wasn't just a *fag* or a limp-wristed gay people put up with. His whole life, he'd been treated like half a man.

Until now.

But for how long? Should they stop? Should they just put it aside, focus on their mission? They were risking too much, with this.

But he *couldn't.* He couldn't set David aside, couldn't put him out of his mind. David had become linked to him, inextricably linked, like two stars orbiting each other. Words like "combat stress" and "adrenaline bonds" tried to nip at him from the darkness, but he pushed them back.

David was in his bones, in his blood. He set his heart by the moments he stole with David. He'd never let that go, not unless David was ripped from him. And even then—

David held him after they finished, cradling Kris close with his forehead pressed to Kris's temple as they caught their breath. Sticky Pakistani heat clung to their sweaty skin. A limp ceiling fan circled overhead, lazy circles that moved stale air and the stench of sex. Could their teammates smell what they did? Could they smell David on Kris, like Kris always could?

Much later, Kris pulled the curtains back and stared out their bedroom window. He'd wrapped up in a silk robe, a gift David had bought for him during one of his undercover trips into Pakistan's twisting cities. He'd bought Kris a small mountain of gifts since they'd arrived in-country. Silk shirts and linen suits, long robes, and the finest salwar kameezes. A gold necklace, a filigree of the Hand of Fatima, that he wore under everything, every day. Now that they weren't in Afghanistan, they got to change their clothes every day, actually look decent again. David, it seemed, had taken it upon himself to make Kris's wardrobe the finest in all of Pakistan. Kris reveled in David's gifts, in the luxury. In the knowledge that every day, no matter where David was, Kris was on his mind.

David stood behind him, kissing his bare shoulder where the robe slipped down. The call to prayer sounded, the wail of a hundred muezzins across the city rising as one. There were no stars above Faisalabad, no moon in the sky. The stars were spread below, a blanket of lanterns and fires that turned the air to wood smoke and musk.

Across Faisalabad, somewhere in the darkness and the smoke, Abu Zahawi prayed.

His last prayers as a free man.

---

"In three hours, we leave the safe house in our breach teams. At zero one thirty, each breach team will stage outside their target location." Kris pointed to the giant map on the wall, with each of the fourteen targets marked and surrounded by surveillance photos. "Pakistani police will meet you at each target."

An FBI agent, from a team that had been flown in from DC overnight, interrupted. "Is ISI involved?"

"No. ISI has not been briefed." Pakistan's military intelligence, ISI, had been caught leaking information to al-Qaeda, both during the Afghan invasion and after. Kris kept them iced out of his entire operation. The FBI agent, jet-lagged and clinging to a mug of coffee, nodded.

"At exactly zero one fifty, each team will stage at the outer breach marker for each site. Your team leads have your specific coordinates for your site in their packet. At precisely zero two hundred, at all fourteen sites, we breach simultaneously. The order of entry is as follows: The Pakistani police enter first and subdue any resistance. They separate the women and children from the men. The FBI enters second and preserves the scene for evidence collection. The CIA enters last."

The FBI, appraised of Kris's operation to catch Zahawi, had insisted on inserting into the takedown team. The September 11 attacks were considered an active criminal investigation in addition to being an intelligence failure and the new target of an independent Congressional oversight investigation. Jurisdiction was overlapping, and messy.

"I and my team—" Kris nodded to Dan, David, Ryan, Jackson, and Palmer. "—will accompany the breach team at Target X-Ray." The last target on the list, the villa he and David had found with the windows closed and locked.

"You think Zahawi is at that location?"

"We think there's something bad going on there, yes. It could be Zahawi. It could be another cell of al-Qaeda fighters. Whatever is going on, it's bad news." Kris, standing on a coffee table in the middle of the safe house's living room, met everyone's gaze. Nearly sixty people stared back at him. Listened to him give orders. "Any questions?"

---

0155 hours.

They were well into zero dark hundred, the dead of night when Special Forces loved to operate, when the CIA always made their moves. Kris breathed through his mouth, huddled against the privacy fence around Target X-Ray, behind David and in front of Dan. Ryan and Jackson brought up the rear of their breach team.

His body armor tried to pull his shoulders off. The thick ceramic plates weighed at least forty pounds each. He felt tugged toward the ground, like he should just tip forward, let gravity do its thing. His backpack full of gear counterbalanced the weight, just barely.

Zero one fifty-six. At thirteen other sites, breach teams were waiting, following Kris's plan to the letter. There was no room for error in this. No room for one team to strike early, give a target time to make a phone call or start screaming—or worse, shooting. In Faisalabad in the middle of the night, only the dogs were out. The city was silent, five million people locked in their houses. Unless something went wrong.

Zero one fifty-eight. The check came down the line. *All good?* David reached behind him, tapped the side of Kris's leg. *All good.* He sent the signal back, tapping Dan. Heard Dan reach for Ryan. Then it came back, two taps from Dan on his thigh. *All good.* He reached forward for David. David intercepted his hand. Squeezed. Kris squeezed back.

Zero one fifty-nine. They'd synchronized their watches to the second. He watched them count down.

*Three. Two. One.*

Pakistani police at the head of the breach team blew open the lock on the privacy fence and wrenched the heavy metal gate open. Boots slapped concrete and dirt, thundering toward the front door. Kris heard echoes of *booms* across Faisalabad, bouncing through the warren of the tangled city. He followed behind, running with David and stacking at the fence line as the Pakistanis prepared to break down the front door. Shouts rose inside the villa. Lights flicked on inside the third floor.

*Clang.* The Pakistani police officer who'd swung the battering ram stumbled backward. Another rushed forward, grabbing the battering ram and trying again. *Clang.* "It's reinforced!" he shouted. "They reinforced the door with steel!"

*Slap slap slap.* Dirt shot up from the ground, geysers from bullets slamming into the dust at their feet. Glass shattered, rained down on their heads. Dark muzzles, the bores of AK-47s, poked out of the upstairs windows.

"Take cover!" David grabbed Kris and hauled him around the side of the house, away from the windows and the shooters above. Ryan and Dan retreated behind the privacy fence.

"Grenade!" one of the police officers shouted. Glass shattered. A *thud* as the grenade bounced and rolled inside the house. Frantic Arabic, shouts that rose in pitch, until—

*Boom.*

Scrambling, David poked back around the corner, looking down the barrel of his rifle. The shooters in the upper windows were gone.

Police officers were going through a ground-level window into a smoke-filled hallway.

"Open this door! Open this fucking door!" Two FBI agents banged on the front door, their backs flat to the wall. They'd been trapped on the other side of the gunfire from above, totally exposed.

The front door burst out of its frame, kicked open by the largest police officer on the team. Cursing, the FBI agents ran inside. "Hands up! Hands up!"

"They have to say it in Arabic," Kris growled. "Did they forget?"

"We gotta get in there." David nodded to the front door. "I'll cover you."

Kris ran, David following in his footsteps, his rifle trained on the empty third-floor windows. Whoever had been shooting at them was gone. For now.

Dan, Ryan, and Jackson met them at the door. Shouts barreled through the house. Flashlight beams crisscrossed the smoke. The FBI agents were stuck in the front room, hollering at someone to put their hands up.

Shouting, again, in Arabic. This time, from outside. Kris turned. "The roof. They're on the roof!"

David and Jackson flattened themselves to the villa's wall, looking up their rifle scopes at the roofline.

Scuffling, above. Frantic Arabic flew back and forth. Two—no, three voices.

Kris followed David, holding his weapon up, keeping it steady on the roofline. Dan covered him, moving close. Ryan slipped away from the villa's walls, sliding into the courtyard.

*"Hnak hu alan! Ha hu! Ha hu!" There he is now! There he is! There he is!*

"Shit!" Bullets peppered the courtyard, the dirt at Ryan's feet. He ran for the shadows, ducked behind a pillar for cover. The shooter on the roof chased him to the edge.

David slid out of the shadows and squeezed his trigger. Three bullets spat into the night, catching the first man on the roof in the shoulder and jaw. He tumbled forward, limp, spilling over the edge.

He hit the ground like a broken doll, headfirst. Kris looked away, flinching.

He'd remember that sound as long as he lived.

*"Qafz! Qafz!" Jump! Jump!*

Two men scurried across the roof, heading for the edge. David, Jackson, and Kris stepped over the broken body in the courtyard and followed the sounds. Behind the house, the closest neighbors were nine feet away, across a sewage-filled alley. An improbable jump, but not impossible. Not with adrenaline coursing through the men's veins.

They heard feet slapping against concrete, gaining speed. Heard a man approach the edge. Saw him leap.

David and Jackson fired together, two shots. Both tore through the jumper. Shrieking, he fell to the ground, bones in his legs cracking on impact. He wailed, screams loud enough to wake the dead, knives that sliced through Kris's eardrums.

Using the distraction to cover his attempt, the last man jumped right after his friend.

Kris saw him. He raised his weapon. Fired.

His shots caught the jumper in his hip and his stomach. He lurched, tumbled, and fell, slamming into the top of the privacy fence before sliding to the ground.

Inside the house, the frantic shouts from the FBI had subsided. Kris heard boots running up and down the stairs, heard calls of "*Clear*" from within. Heard more boots on the roof, and shouts of "*Police*!"

"Friendlies!" David bellowed. "Friendlies, down below!"

"We heard gunshots. What do have?" One of the FBI agents poked his head over the roof's edge. He blanched when he saw the first man from the roof spread in a wet mess across the courtyard.

"Three jumpers. All down." David and Jackson had formed a loose perimeter, keeping all three bodies in sight.

Kris called up, "Zahawi in there?"

"No. Is he one of them?"

"We're checking." Kris and Dan ignored the first body. There wasn't anything left to ID. He didn't have the right coloring for Abu Zahawi, either. The man who'd tumbled was Pakistani. Zahawi was Palestinian, fair skinned and slender according to the passport photo they were working with.

The second jumper was still shrieking. Blood pooled beneath one of his broken legs. White bone stuck out of his torn pants. Strips of skin clung to the jagged ends of his shattered femur. Dan shined a light into his face.

"Not him." Kris waved to David. "This one needs a medic. He's going to bleed out."

As David kneeled next to the broken-legged man and opened his medkit, they moved on to the third jumper. Heavyset with a round belly, thick legs, and wild, springy hair, almost to his shoulders, he was clean-shaven, almost as smooth as Kris. Blood smeared across him, from the shots in his belly and his impact with the fence, his slide to the ground. Pools of ruby liquid formed beneath him, soaking the dirt. His eyes were closed, and he didn't move. Still, they kept their distance.

"This can't be him." Dan frowned.

"His jawline looks similar…" Kris reached for the man, turned his head left and right. The man groaned. "I think it's him. I think it's Zahawi."

"How do we know for sure?"

Kris turned the man's head to the side again and held it still. "Take a picture of his ear. Everyone's ear is unique. Just like a fingerprint."

Dan arched an eyebrow at him, but snapped the photo. Kris pulled out his field laptop from his backpack and plugged in the camera. Downloaded the image, and sent it via satellite link to Islamabad. "We'll know in a minute."

Sirens blasted across Faisalabad, Pakistani police coming out in force. Rickshaw ambulances followed behind the police. David, through with putting a tourniquet on the broken-legged man, jogged over to Kris. "I thought this one was dead."

"Not yet." Kris grabbed his medical kit from his backpack and pulled out a wad of field dressings and gauze bandages. He pressed them into the man's bullet wounds, over his stomach and his thigh. Blood saturated the dressings, soaking through almost instantly. "We need to keep him alive. This is Zahawi. I'm certain of it."

His sat phone rang. Dan reached for it. David grabbed it first. "Hello?"

"*Where's Caldera*?" George barked.

"Holding pressure on a wounded al-Qaeda man."

*"If it's the same man whose ear he just sent, then he'd better do everything he can to keep him breathing.* That *is Abu Zahawi. And we need him. Alive."*

---

"We need a doctor!"

Kris ran backward into the Faisalabad Emergency Department, carrying Zahawi's legs. David carried his arms, tried to support his shoulders, and Dan ran beside them, holding soaked gauze over Zahawi's gunshot wounds. Ryan, Jackson, and a dozen police officers followed, all shouting for a doctor.

Two young Pakistani men in white doctor's coats poked their head out from a dingy office. Overhead, fluorescent lights flickered. Kris skidded on the floor, almost slipping. He looked down. Grease, oil, and blood smeared on the cracked linoleum. As they jogged farther into the hospital, the stench of rotten meat, of putrid, festering wounds, slammed into them. Ryan gagged, fell to the side. Kris heard him puke into the wall.

The Pakistani doctors' eyes were as wide as the moon. Twenty men were barreling into their ratty emergency department, all armed to the teeth and wearing bulletproof vests and helmets with tactical backpacks and gear hanging from them. Kris's rifle banged against his thighs as he ran. "We need you to save this man!"

Blood dropped from Zahawi, a long trail leading back to the dirt parking lot and the truck they'd screamed across Faisalabad in.

One of the doctors finally unfroze, grabbing a filthy gurney from along the wall and running it toward them. The sheets were stained, a mottled mess of old-blood brown and pus yellow. Kris and David dropped Zahawi on the gurney. His head lolled to the side, limp. His skin was gray as ash.

"Two gunshot wounds. He's lost a lot of blood." Kris jogged with the doctors as they frantically ran the gurney toward surgery. "You have to save him. You have to keep him alive!"

"He's already dead," one of the doctors said, shaking his head. "You want us to cut into a dead man!"

"Stop the bleeding! Keep him breathing!"

---

They waited in the emergency department, pacing between the beds. A third were full, one man in a leg cast and three elderly people who looked like they were disintegrating into their beds. Grime was slick beneath their feet. Mosquitoes and flies buzzed in from the open windows, hovering around the fluorescent lights and feasting on raw wounds. The hospital had an "end of the world" aesthetic. If a hospital from the 1950s had been catapulted to zombie land, it would look like this place.

A bar of soap rested on the bedside table of each patient. Syringes were jammed into it, sticking up at crazy angles. It came to Kris after a moment. That was how they sterilized their needles.

David found chairs scattered around the hospital, and he brought them back for everyone. Dan and Jackson collapsed, both falling asleep sitting up. David wrapped his arm around Kris, trying to hold on to him and look like he wasn't.

Ryan refused to sit, pacing as he growled into his phone on fifteen different calls. "What do you mean you put his cell phone in evidence?" he shouted at one point. "His cell phone is a *communication device*! That belongs with us!" He apparently didn't like the answer he received. He flung his phone down the hallway, watching it skitter and glide through the grime and dirt.

"Fucking FBI put Zahawi's phone in an evidence bag. They're

refusing to open it up. Damn thing's been ringing off the hook since the raid." Ryan seethed in front of Kris.

Kris scrubbed his hands over his face. David's hand was on his back, out of Ryan's sight. "Damn it. That means they know we have him."

"And they're going to be coming for him."

---

The gunshots started two hours later.

A truck screamed by the front of the hospital, kicking up dirt and swerving through the near-empty parking lot. Bullets popped. Glass at the front of the hospital exploded, raining shards into the hallway and the lobby.

Kris and David hit the floor. Dan landed beside them, eyes wide. Ryan and the Pakistani police officers drew their weapons and took cover, aiming for the dark parking lot. The truck peeled away.

"We have to get him out of here." Kris staggered to his feet. "They're going to keep coming. They'll try and get him back. And kill us."

He got on the phone with Islamabad. "We have to get out of here. They're coming for Zahawi, and if they realize there's only a handful of us, we're done for."

"*I'll make some calls,*" George said. "*We'll get you out, Kris.*"

Five minutes later, another truck came barreling toward the hospital. Bullets spat from the passenger window.

Ryan and the police fired back, again.

The truck veered off, swerving wildly.

Ryan shouted that he'd seen the shape of an RPG as it passed by the light of a streetlamp. "They'll come at us with technicals, next!" he hollered. Pickup trucks, usually Toyotas, outfitted with heavy machine guns in the beds. There was no way they could stand up to a force of technicals. Or even just one.

Finally, eight minutes after Kris called George, his sat phone rang. "*Kris, the Pakistani military is on the way. They're going to pick you guys up and bring you to Pakistani Air Base Chaklala, in Rawalpindi. The base's medical team is waiting for you.*"

"They'd better be fucking fast. Al-Qaeda is coming. *Now.*"

"*Get out of there!*"

David and Kris jogged together to the surgery suite and burst in. "Wrap it up, doc! We've got to move!"

"He is still bleeding internally. We have not given him enough blood!"

"Make him stable for transport. We're leaving, now!"

"He will never make it!"

David grabbed three units of blood, a transfusion kit, and a wad of gauze and dressings. He prepped a line for Zahawi and slid a unit of blood into the transfusion port on his arm. "I'll watch him during the flight."

The doctor threw his blood-soaked surgery apron on the ground. "He will never live! Never!"

---

David hovered over Zahawi the entire helicopter flight. Kris cradled Zahawi's head in his lap, keeping him still while David fed all three bags of blood into his body. Pools of blood formed beneath him, saturating Kris's pants and the helo's deck. He pressed where David told him to, held pressure over Zahawi's wounds for the hour-long flight.

A medical team met them at the air base, a full Pakistani military trauma team and an ambulance. Kris and David climbed into the back with them. Kris ended up perched on David's lap for the drive across the base.

After the medical team whisked Zahawi into the Pakistani military hospital, Kris turned in to David, folding into his arms outside the doors of the emergency department. For the moment, they were alone. Ryan, Dan, and Jackson had stayed behind with the helo and were on their way back to Islamabad and the CIA station.

"You did great," David breathed. He pressed a quick kiss to Kris's hair, as fast as he dared.

"I shot our target. The one man we wanted to capture alive. I shot him, and he's nearly dead."

"You planned this entire takedown. The coordination, the operation, everything. You did that." Pride shone from David's gaze. "I think George is starting to believe in you."

"The CIA way is to ride competent people until they break."

"I thought that was what you did to me." David winked.

"Let's get out of here. I want to change, shower, and get in bed with you for a whole day."

David's eyes gleamed, that look he got when he wanted to lay Kris down, spend hours devouring him, tracing his skin, the contours and curves of his muscles, until he finally brought their bodies together. David could turn him inside out, make love to him until his bones wept. He'd never thought his soul could ignite, but when David's hands cradled his hips, ran up his back, drew him close until they merged...

Some days, he thought David was the fire he needed to live.

Kris's phone trilled. He groaned.

It was George.

"Caldera."

"*Kris, Langley has sent orders for Zahawi. He's twenty-four-seven, CIA-only eyes on. You've gotta stay at the hospital with him.*"

Fuck. Of course. "What's the plan?"

"*Langley is picking up the top trauma surgeon from Johns Hopkins tonight and putting him on a plane. He'll be there tomorrow to patch up Zahawi. Then you're off to Site Green.*"

"Me?" A chill slithered down his spine. Site Green was their newest, darkest black site. Exclusively for interrogating high-value al-Qaeda prisoners.

"*He's* your *target, Kris. You know him better than anyone else alive, probably better than he knows himself. And... out of everyone here, you're the best I've got.*"

"Sounds like that was difficult for you to say, George."

"*Only because you make liking you difficult, Caldera.*" There was a ghost of a smile in George's voice, though. "*You're a Goddamn pain in the ass.*"

"That's my charm. It's my appeal."

"*You're lucky* he *seems to like it.*"

Kris's gaze flicked to David. "Request permission for Haddad to remain assigned to Zahawi? We'll need a qualified medic if anything goes sideways. Here, or at Site Green."

George's sigh could have toppled Tora Bora, could have blown away the Hindu Kush. "*Caldera, I swear to* fucking *God, if it comes out that you've manipulated us all into covering for your bordello...*"

Kris, for once, kept his mouth shut.

"*Haddad can remain. You'll need a backup Arabic translator anyway. Send him back for supplies before you leave for Site Green.*"

"Thank you, George."

# 14

**CIA Black Site, Detention Site Green, Thailand - April 2002**

Rain poured from the sky, soaking the detention facility. Steam rose from the concrete pad, the facility's attempt at an outdoor pavilion. Heat smothered them, like a sauna Kris couldn't escape.

Zahawi slept fitfully in his makeshift medical suite, hooked to machines and monitors, bandaged like a mummy halfway through his mummification.

---

Kris's shot had been perfect. He'd shattered coins in Zahawi's pocket, sending shrapnel throughout his hip and stomach. The bullet had also torn apart bone, and shards were lodged in the organs of his pelvis, along with fractured coins and bullet fragments. The Johns Hopkins surgeon had spent thirteen hours in surgery with the Pakistani doctors. Zahawi had bled out more than twice the blood he'd been given before he was finally stabilized.

Kris had stayed with him the entire time. He'd watched the

surgeons, had followed Zahawi into the recovery ward. Sat by his side, his hand wrapped around Zahawi's wrist when he fell asleep.

David had gone back to Islamabad to meet with George and returned with both their bags packed, nearly all of their possessions, and a crate of intelligence. Dozens of Zahawi's journals had been picked up in the arrest. Kris pored through them as he watched Zahawi sleep.

The first time Zahawi woke, in Pakistan, he'd opened his eyes and saw Kris staring down at him. His gaze had wandered from Kris's face, down past his sweat-stained undershirt from the raid to his black combat fatigues.

Kris saw the moment recognition had settled into Zahawi that the United States *had* him. That Kris was his enemy. His heart rate had spiked, climbing from one hundred beats per minute to one-fifty to one-eighty, to over two-hundred. He'd pushed back in his hospital bed, trying to escape, gasping, trying to scream. Stitches had torn, and blood had poured from his side. Nurses had rushed in, screaming at Kris to back off, to get out of the room.

He'd stayed, holding Zahawi's glare until Zahawi passed out from shock.

The next time he'd awoken, he'd stared at Kris for a long moment, not speaking. Kris spoke first, leaning in and saying, in Arabic, "Abu Zahawi. I know who you are. And you know who I am. We found you and we've captured you. You were wounded when we arrested you. But we're taking care of you." Kris had held Zahawi's stare. "I will be right here, the whole time. I won't ever leave your side."

Zahawi had answered in English. "Don't desecrate God's language with your infidel tongue."

"Rest. You need your strength."

"Please... Let me die."

"No. I want to know you, Abu Zahawi. We have so much to talk about."

"I'll *never* talk with you."

Zahawi had passed out again shortly after, weak and barely able to stay awake. He'd waxed and waned in and out of delirium, sometimes reaching for Kris and clasping his hands, other times praying in Arabic as he sobbed. Kris fed him sips of water and read his diary, seized after the arrest, and held his hand when Zahawi flailed, reaching out for someone nearby.

David camped on a cot at the foot of Zahawi's bed, out of sight. When Zahawi slept, David and Kris passed his diaries back and forth, sharing thoughts and ideas. David had a perspective Kris couldn't have, and needed: an Arab view from an Arab mind, and an Arab experience of Zahawi's childhood, his years growing up as a Palestinian refugee and part of the diaspora in Saudi Arabia.

"Funny, isn't it. He and I are the same age. Thirty-one. His family life was better than mine. But here I am. And there he is."

"A better family life?" Zahawi's father had been a teacher in Saudi Arabia, a Palestinian expat, and his mother had taken care of Zahawi and his brothers. He'd had a middle-class upbringing, far better than many other Palestinian refugees.

David didn't answer.

David spent long hours in the dead of night watching Zahawi. Once, Kris woke and saw him staring at Zahawi, hunched in a bedside chair, contemplating the man as if he wanted to climb into Zahawi's skin, possess his mind, his eyes, and understand him like he could breathe in his soul and devour his memories.

When Zahawi finally wasn't in danger of shattering into a million pieces, he was brought to the base's airfield and loaded onto a private jet. He was hooded and shackled to his gurney, sedated for the flight.

He woke up in Thailand, in the steamy heat of the jungle and in the remote clutches of the black site.

He was the CIA's detainee number one.

---

*Everyone* in DC wanted in on Zahawi's interrogation, it seemed. When Kris, David, and Zahawi arrived, the facility was already crawling with suits from DC. CIA analysts, paramilitary officers, and a host of brand-new interrogators, fresh from a three-week training course. Even the FBI was there, in a joint-agency information sharing capacity, they said. Kris recognized one of the FBI agents.

"Agent Naveen." Kris held out his hand. "Good to see you again."

Agent Naveen, part of his welcoming committee in Yemen, days after September 11, stared him down. Finally, he shook Kris's hand. "I have heard a lot about you, Caldera. Seems you kept your word. You were there to help."

Kris lifted his chin. "And I still am. You?"

"This is a CIA-led operation. We were sent here by our director to offer assistance. I'm one of the FBI's trained interrogators and I specialize in Middle Eastern terrorism. I know how these guys work. How they think. What they expect. I'm happy to lend a hand."

"What do you suggest would be the best approach to Zahawi?"

"Has his medical situation been seen to?"

"Yes."

"Then we should engage in rapport building. Try to get a baseline understanding of his motivations. See if he throws up a cover story, and if he does, use meticulous details to break through the eventual lies and double-speak." Naveen smiled wryly. "You know, like you did in Yemen."

Finally, Kris had smiled. "Seems we're on the same team after all, Agent Naveen."

Having everyone who was anyone there at the facility was both a blessing and a curse. Kris wasn't used to so many people. So much oversight. So many eyeballs wanting to be read in on what he was doing. He, somehow, still maintained the lead on Zahawi. He was still the targeteer, and thus, the main interrogator. Everyone looked to him for direction on Zahawi's case.

He waited for someone to try and wrestle his authority away, try to say he wasn't qualified for the Zahawi operation.

The base was bursting at the seams, and practicalities had to be seen to first. There wasn't enough space for everyone to have their own rooms. Kris *volunteered* to bunk with David in a tiny, dank hut, built out of corrugated steel and a thatched roof lined with plastic bags. Their shared toilet was an outhouse. Humidity turned the toilet paper soft. Snakes crept into the outhouse, and into their hut. The first time one had, Kris had jumped onto his bed, shrieking, until the security team had busted in, weapons up and ready to fire.

They'd exchanged long looks when they'd seen David and Kris's metal beds pushed together to make one large bed. Oops.

---

Kris started questioning Zahawi the third night after they arrived at Site Green.

He started slowly, taking up his vigil by Zahawi's bedside in the hospital room they'd put together. Zahawi lay on a gurney draped in a mosquito net under a thatched roof. At dusk, monkeys sounded in the trees. In the morning, bird calls echoed for miles in the empty jungle. Vibrant orange extension cords snaked across the wooden floor, over the edge of the half wall, and disappeared into a maze of bundled wires and underbrush. The entire facility was being run on industrial generators, buzzing far away on the other side of the base.

Zahawi lay propped on pillows, hooded. For once, the sheets beneath him were clean, not stained with blood. His chest rose and fell quickly, trembling.

Kris pulled the hood off his head. Zahawi's hair was still wild, falling in long strands around his face. His beard had grown in, patchy in places. One eye was covered in a green film, clouded and milky. Zahawi stared at Kris.

"*As-salaam-alaikum.*" Kris pressed his hand to his chest.

"*Wa alaikum as-salaam,*" Zahawi whispered. "You are still here."

"I promised you I would be. How are you? Are you in pain?"

Zahawi shrugged. He looked away.

"We are not here to hurt you. What do you need?"

"There is some pain," Zahawi whispered. His chin wavered, but he held it high.

"Let me get that seen to."

An entire team was listening to the interrogation through the mic Kris wore, piping their conversation into a dozen different recorders.

Cameras watched them from every angle, hung in Zahawi's secured medical hut. Kris waved to one.

A moment later, David walked in, carrying his medical kit. The Johns Hopkins surgeon had flown home and the CIA medical officer wasn't allowed to interact with Zahawi while he was awake. David was Zahawi's medic.

"*As-salaam-alaikum*," David said, offering Zahawi a small smile. Zahawi tried to smile back. A tear spilled down his cheek. David prepped a syringe of morphine and slid it into Zahawi's IV bag. "This should take the edge off. I'll come back to check on you in a little bit."

"*Shukran*," Zahawi whispered. His fingers played with the edge of his sheet.

David gave Kris a long look before he strode out of the room.

"Is that better?"

"Why are you doing this? Why did you keep me alive? Why..." He waved to his IV bag, the door David had walked out of.

"I told you. I want to talk to you, Abu Zahawi. I want to know what's in your mind. Understand you."

"But you are American."

"Yes." Kris crossed his legs. "I'm not what you expected?"

"Not at all."

Kris let the moment stretch long, let silence fill the room. "I have questions, Asim." He used Zahawi's birth name, his given name. "Help me understand you. Help me understand the pain you're in. Not the physical. Help me understand your Muslim pain."

A trail of tears ran down Zahawi's cheek and fell from his chin. "I will never be free, will I?"

"That really depends on how much you help us, Asim. Help us understand."

Zahawi nodded. "I will answer your questions," he whispered.

*Jesus fucking Christ*. Kris could only imagine the faces in the control room, the expressions on the other officers' and interrogators' faces. For days, he'd had to fight off demands to go in hard, treat Zahawi brutally from the moment his eyes opened. He'd pushed back, insisted over and over on sticking with his methods.

Everyone had waited for him to fail.

"You were born in Riyadh. Your father is a teacher." Kris walked through Zahawi's childhood, his early years. Zahawi seemed shocked at some of the things Kris knew, lifted from his diaries. Good. Kris needed Zahawi to think he knew everything, that lying to him about anything was pointless. "You were married, once, after your studies. But you divorced her. Tell me about that."

Zahawi cringed. "She was obsessed with sex. But I did not want her that way." He looked away, his eyes skittering to the corner.

"Abdullah Azzam's sermons lit a fire in you, after that. Made you want to travel to Afghanistan?"

Zahawi nodded. He took over, detailing how he'd joined the mujahedeen in Afghanistan to fight against the Soviets. How he'd been filled with fury over the attacks against his fellow Muslims, the occupation of the Soviets in Muslim lands.

"Tell me. How did you feel?"

Zahawi squirmed. "What do we have left of ourselves? Everything in the world is touched by the West. Corrupted by you. From cars to clothes, washing machines to food. Everything in our life is corrupted by you. You've taken it all. We have nothing left. We are totally dependent on you. It is shameful. *Humiliating*. Once it was exactly the opposite. You Westerners once looked to the Arabs and saw the *best* of humanity. Now you look at us like we are dogs. Filth."

"I understand. You may not think I do, but I do. I *know* what it's like to be hated by the West."

Zahawi squinted.

"I know what it's like to be hated for who you are. To have your life dictated by others, your choices made for you. To have that rage in your chest, all the time. That scream, that says you are more than this. The desire to prove everyone wrong."

"*That* is Muslim pain," Zahawi breathed.

They stared at one another, silent for a moment.

"Tell me about your injury, years ago," Kris finally said.

"I don't remember it. They say a mortar came into our position.

That I was hit in the head. My brothers took me to the hospital. When I woke, I did not remember anything. Not even who I was."

Kris held up one of Zahawi's journals. Zahawi's heart monitor beeped, pulsing faster. "You started keeping journals after your injury." Zahawi nodded. He never took his eyes off his diary. "These are very important to you?"

"Yes."

"They are safe. They will be returned to you after questioning. And we'll arrange for a fresh notebook and pen to be provided to you."

More tears spilled from Zahawi's eyes. "*Shukran*."

They kept talking. After Zahawi had recovered from his head wound, and had pieced together most of his memories, he'd gone to work as an instructor at an al-Qaeda-run training camp. He'd worked on the firing range, and he had cooked and maintained guesthouses for the recruits. He was back in the arms of a community again, embraced by his brothers. He had felt at home.

But he'd wanted more.

Finally, he was given the chance. He was ordered to a new training camp to join with Tajikistani rebels fighting against the Russians. When Zahawi mentioned the name of the rebel group he'd joined, Kris silently cross-checked his own notes. Zahawi's rebels had been one of the groups the CIA had directly funneled money to, back when fighting the Soviets using mujahedeen had been the most popular game in town. Had Zahawi been considered an ally then?

When did history shatter into hatred?

"It was that operation that showed me what al-Qaeda had become. That they were the future of Afghanistan, of the jihad. I wanted to join. Be a part of their community."

"And did you?"

Zahawi had been given the position of external *emir* of the Khaldan training camp. He'd managed the recruits, the trainees, and the guesthouses, as well as the recruits' travel arrangements. Forgeries had been required, as attendees wanted to evade any attempts to track their whereabouts. Zahawi became al-Qaeda's best forger. After the attendees graduated, he'd sent them back out to the world, to Europe, to America, sometimes with missions, sometime to lie in wait for an opportunity to strike.

"Who came through the Khaldan training camp?"

"Many people. But... what you are asking is, did the martyrs who did the planes operation go through the camp?"

"Yes, Asim, I am asking that."

Zahawi nodded. "They were chosen by Mokhtar for the operation, and then sent to Khaldan. For advanced training."

Mokhtar. They'd heard that name before. In videos taken from captured al-Qaeda camps in Afghanistan, the name Mokhtar kept coming up. Bin Laden himself, in one video, praised Mokhtar for his part in the "planes operation", al-Qaeda's name for September 11. He was everywhere, in the inner circles of al-Qaeda.

But no one in the CIA knew who he was.

Did Zahawi?

"You said 'chosen by Mokhtar'. Why was Mokhtar choosing the operatives for the planes operation?"

"The planes operation was his idea. He brought it to Bin Laden and asked for his support. His blessing. And his money. He needed five hundred thousand dollars, he said, to pull it off."

"So the idea for the attacks was Mokhtar's?"

"*Nam.*"

"But Bin Laden supported it? Financed it? Trained the operatives at his camps?"

Zahawi nodded. "Some did not want Bin Laden to support Mokhtar's plan. They said he was crazy. That the attacks were not allowed by Allah. That we shouldn't attack the US. The US helped Muslims in Serbia and Bosnia. They said we needed to focus on jihad close to home, where Muslims were being killed every day. In Chechnya. Israel. Russia."

"What did you think?"

"I *hate* America. I wanted Mokhtar's plan to go ahead, and to succeed. I dreamed about it with him, for months. We dreamed of the day of the attacks." Zahawi exhaled, his voice shaking. "I hate America. Because of America, my life was shredded. I am an exile from this planet, a man without a home. I wasn't a person to the world until I was a brother with my mujahedeen! Because of America, and Israel. My life, my history, has been taken from me."

Kris was quiet. "Tell me about after the attacks."

Zahawi spoke softly, almost reverently. After September 11, after the celebrations, the parties, and the dancing in the streets, the gunshots into the air in celebration, the giddy, almost drunk feeling of exultation, Zahawi, in Afghanistan, had joined together with the rest of the foreign fighters and had begun making preparations for defending their camps and cities from the coming American invasion. "Bin Laden, he had told us that the Americans would only launch missiles, like they did after the embassy bombings in Africa and the attack in Yemen. We did not think the Americans would invade. When we realized they were coming, we tried to buy weapons. Build defensive lines."

"What happened then?"

Zahawi's fists clenched the sheet. His heart monitor beeped faster. "The Americans dropped their bombs. The brothers… So many were killed. Death was everywhere we looked, everywhere we turned. We couldn't bury all of our bodies. We couldn't find all of our brothers. And we couldn't survive against the bombs. We had to run."

How many of those bombs had been guided by Kris and David's own hands? They'd spent weeks around Afghanistan, painting Taliban and al-Qaeda targets with lasers for the bombers and jets above, had walked the entire front line of the Northern Alliance, meticulously mapping coordinates of enemy positions after staring through their binoculars.

And here they were, from opposite sides of a battlefield at the end of the earth to sitting together in a makeshift hospital in the jungle of Thailand.

It was almost dizzying.

In shaking words, Zahawi detailed the collapse of the Taliban, the collapse of al-Qaeda, and the scattering of their forces. Bin Laden's exodus to Tora Bora. How Zahawi and so many others had stayed behind, trying to save Kandahar. Kandahar fell, and they escaped over the bodies of their dead, fleeing into Pakistan through the tribal regions. From there, he made his way into the underground al-Qaeda safe house network he had built.

"I hid from everyone. I did everything I could to hide. The American bastards wanted me. I had to stay free."

"Why do you think the Americans were looking for you?" Kris picked up on Zahawi's splitting of the Americans from him. In Zahawi's mind, the Americans were still bad. But Kris, sitting in front of him, offering him water and medicine, listening to his story, seemed to be different.

Zahawi shook his head. "Tell me," he whispered. "Have the Americans invaded Iraq yet?"

Kris frowned. "Iraq? Why would America invade Iraq?"

"It's next, in the prophecies. To fall. The armies of Khorasan will come through Iraq. The final battle with the West will be there. America is going to invade."

"I don't think—"

Zahawi shuddered, and shame filled his gaze. He looked down as a smell wafted from him. He groaned. "I am broken," he whispered. "I am shamed. I cannot—"

Kris grasped his hand. "You are healing." Zahawi had soiled himself. A dark stain of urine spread on the sheets. "It is not shameful. We will help you." He waved to the cameras.

David walked in again, with towels, a bucket of water, and clean sheets. Together, Kris and David lifted Zahawi from the bed, wiped him down, and changed the sheets. Zahawi curled against David's chest, hiding his face. "*Shukran*, brother," he whispered. "You are Muslim?"

"*Nam*," David said, gently settling Zahawi down on the clean, remade bed.

Confusion tangled in Zahawi's eyes. "*And* American?"

"Yes."

"Rest, Asim." Kris gathered his notes and Zahawi's diaries. "We will talk again soon."

## CIA Black Site, Detention Site Green, Thailand - May 2002

"He's *expecting* brutal treatment! They all are! They live on the worst fears and conspiracy theories about the US, and they expect to be proven right. If you want to rock their world, then you give them what they're not expecting. Humanity. Compassion!"

It was an endless argument, *the* endless argument, at Site Green. Every day, Kris had to defend his approach to questioning Zahawi.

Kris, David, and Naveen stood on one side of their messy command center's worktable, completely covered with the detritus of the interrogation so far. Stacks of folders, Zahawi's bagged and tagged possessions, his diaries, transcripts and tapes of the interrogations, follow-up intel, leads chased from Zahawi's information. Names of his former recruits. Graduates of the training camps sent to America and Europe. Targets al-Qaeda were surveilling. Plans that were still in the dreaming stage, but had to be checked.

Photos and charts hung on the walls, a cornucopia of intelligence and information, all gifted from Zahawi.

Paul, a senior officer fresh from Langley, snorted at Kris. "There's no compassion for these animals. They're murderers. Every last one of them. And here you are, becoming best friends with him. Caring for him!" He sneered.

"I am getting information out of him. He is cooperating!" Kris waved to the stacks and stacks of intelligence piling around their command center. "He's giving us actionable intelligence."

"He's playing you," Paul snapped. "He's giving you what he wants to give, to keep you happy. To keep sucking on the American tit."

"Paul—"

"Why is he even on pain medication? Who authorized that?"

"You would withhold medical treatment?" David pushed off the wall, where he'd been standing in the background, half in shadow. Arms crossed, he stormed to Kris's side. "That's torture. Keeping someone purposely in pain. Interfering with their medical treatment. You know that, right?"

"What constitutes torture is an open question. The definition is up for debate," Paul said smoothly.

"No, it's not!" Kris cried. He shot a glance across the table to Agent Naveen, his FBI partner for the ongoing interrogations.

Naveen had a scowl on his face, his lips pressed firmly together, eyes narrowed as he stared at Paul.

Kris glared. "The US has signed treaties against torture. We *don't* torture people."

"You won't be making that call."

"What the fuck did you say?" David, again, stepped closer. He started making his way around the table. Kris stopped him, one hand on his arm.

"Things are changing in Washington. This 'buddy-buddy-with-the-terrorist' bullshit isn't flying. The president is not amused. Get ready. Your little Muslim friend is in for a world of hurt."

---

Days later, an unmarked private jet landed on the runway outside Site Green. One passenger clambered off, adjusting his glasses. Paul strode up to a middle-aged man, professorial and lean in a tweed sport coat and holding a briefcase. They shook hands warmly.

Kris and David watched from an overhang, out of the way of the steadily falling rain. Monsoon season had come, and with it, torrents of water, like the world had turned upside down and the oceans were drenching the land. Puddles the size of buses covered the pavement. Leaks had sprung across the compound. The air they breathed was soaked.

They met the newcomer in the command center. Paul escorted the new arrival in like he was a guest of honor. "This is Dennis. He's a psychologist who's worked on the SERE program. He's studied how to break recalcitrant detainees in interrogations. Washington has sent him to fix this situation."

"Fix what? The interrogation is going great. Zahawi has given us years' worth of information. Yesterday, he confirmed Mokhtar's identity," Kris snapped.

Dennis peered at Kris. "He gave up Mokhtar? The guy who planned nine-eleven? I haven't heard about this."

"You've been flying. It's brand new. We spent all day talking about his and Mokhtar's years-long friendship. They were both on the periphery of Bin Laden's network. Associated with him, close to him, but not sworn to him."

"Allies, you mean."

"Of a sort. Mokhtar wouldn't swear allegiance because he didn't want to have to obey if Bin Laden called off the attacks."

"Jesus Christ." Dennis swore under his breath, shaking his head. "How does Zahawi fit into this?"

"He prayed every day for the attacks to succeed. He and Mokhtar dreamed about them together."

"They're close? Very close? Zahawi and the architect of nine-eleven."

"Yes," Kris said simply.

"Who is he?"

"Khalid Sheikh Mohammed."

"The same guy who wanted to blow up flights from the Philippines five years ago? We've got an open case on Khalid. Jesus..." Dennis cursed again. "All the puzzle pieces were there to see this coming, weren't they?"

Kris stayed silent, even as his soul shredded.

Paul, quiet through the exchange, finally spoke up. "All this time you've been best buddies with your little terrorist pal, and he hasn't given up Mokhtar until now. Why the delay? Why was he holding back? What did you give him for this?"

"Nothing," Kris hissed.

"If he held this back, what else is he holding back? This is just proof that he's playing you."

"We were going after critical plots against the homeland first," Naveen said, jumping in. "We wanted to stop anything in the works before playing who's who in al-Qaeda."

"He's giving you just enough to keep the sweet treatment going," Paul sneered.

"Which is why I am here." Dennis spoke before Kris could. "Like Paul said, Washington wants to change the nature of this interrogation."

"Change it how?" David, at Kris's elbow, frowned.

"*Who* are you?" Dennis frowned back at David. "I don't recall seeing you on the list of cleared personnel."

"Him? He's just the medic," Paul said.

"And the medic is in the command center?" Dennis's gaze bounced from David to Kris. He scowled.

Kris held his glare. Behind him, he felt David's fury build, felt it grow and press on the walls, until the room was choked with his raw emotion.

"What's the nature of this change?" Naveen asked Dennis, cracking the tension. "What exactly are you planning on doing here?"

"We're going to force him into submission. Send him the message that we know he's been playing games. We know his little tricks. His pretense. He needs to know that his games are over and we're not going to indulge him any longer."

"But he's been cooperating!" Kris shouted.

"He doesn't know what cooperation is. He sees you as a tool, someone to manipulate, and he's been successful so far. He's got a comfy bed, blankets, food. Why should he do anything differently when he's in the best space he's ever been in?" Dennis glared at them both, but most especially at Kris.

"He's fucking miserable! He's away from his brothers, he's been captured by his worst enemy. He sobs at night when he thinks we aren't watching on the cameras. You think he's fucking happy?"

"He's doing a hell of a lot better here than he would be in some cave in Afghanistan. Of course he's happy." Dennis seemed shocked Kris had talked back to him, challenged him.

"He'd give anything to go back. Be with his brothers. You're so fucking ignorant. You have no idea what the hell you're saying."

Dennis scoffed. "Well. He's certainly convinced *you* of his little act, Mr. Caldera. But that ends. Now."

"What do you really know of Zahawi?"

"I've read the reports."

"That's all?"

Dennis stayed silent.

"Why don't you try to understand him first, spend a moment actually listening to him, before you tell me what he's like. I've been by his side every day for two months now!"

"And that's the problem. You've gotten too close." Dennis shook his head, like he was shaking Kris off. "We're changing his world. He needs to earn his comfort, his care. He needs to understand that we *own* him. We *control* him. When he's good, he gets rewarded. But when he's bad, and when he doesn't cooperate, he gets punished."

"He's not a fucking dog!" David shouted. "He's not a fucking animal or a slave! He's a human being!"

"He's a terrorist! He'd kill you if you gave him a knife! Slit your fucking throat! Didn't you see what happened to that journalist in Pakistan? You think Zahawi would think twice about beheading you?"

"Do you have any experience with Islamic extremists? With ideologically driven hatred? With anyone incarcerated in the third world or in repressive regimes?" Kris groaned, clenching his hands. "He's prepared himself for all of that and more. He's expecting to be tortured, to be beaten, to be sodomized, for his family to be attacked and killed in front of him. He's ready to die for his cause! What can you possibly do that will break that resolve? He came apart when I was kind to him. That was unexpected to him."

"It's human nature," Dennis said simply. "He'll collapse. They always do."

"You are going to reinforce what he expects. You will harden him."

"Caldera, listen," Paul interrupted, spreading his hands sanctimoniously, a smug look on his face. "Washington has made the call. This isn't your show anymore. Dennis is in charge."

Dennis took a breath, visibly trying for calm. His cheeks were red, his eyes bright. "Tomorrow, Zahawi's interrogation changes. Caldera, you're staying here because we need your knowledge base on Zahawi. But you're not going in there again. His friendship with you is over."

"It wasn't friendship—"

"Boyfriends, then?" Paul quipped. "Looked like you two were having a hell of a time together."

David burst around the table, charging Paul and shoving him against the wall. Pictures of Zahawi crumpled behind Paul's back. David fisted Paul's shirt, grabbing him with both hands until his knuckles went white.

"Whoa, whoa!" Paul held up his hands, disgust crawling over his face. He glared at David. "What the fuck?"

Naveen, at the end of the table, had his hand on his hip like he was reaching for his weapon. He wasn't armed, though. Not at the CIA site. He froze, his eyes darting from David to Kris and back.

"Understand this," Kris hissed, his voice, his body, shaking. "I will do whatever it takes. Anything at all. To prevent another attack. I will never, ever watch our people die again. Not while I can do something, anything to prevent it. So, if I have to joke with Zahawi? If I have to sit at his bedside? If I have to hold his fucking hand, be the one human being he thinks understands him? I will *fucking* do it. I will do it every Goddamn day!"

Silence.

Kris felt Naveen's stare, the burn of his eyes into the side of his face. Once, months ago, Naveen had spit fury at Kris, blaming him for the attacks. He'd been right, of course. It had been Kris's fault.

But it never would be again.

Paul shoved David back. "Get the fuck off me," he growled. "And get the fuck out of the command center. You shouldn't even be in here."

Without looking at Kris, David stormed out. The room trembled, concrete walls shaking, as he slammed the door behind him.

Dennis straightened his shirt. "Washington has made the call. I'm in charge now. Starting tomorrow, we're moving him out of his hospital room and into a real cell. Make him feel like the criminal he is. We're taking everything away. He has to earn what he gets. All the way down to his clothes."

---

Days passed.

Kris watched, over the monitors, as Zahawi was sedated, stripped, and moved into a dirt-floored cell. Four brilliant halogen lights hung above him, burning on Zahawi around the clock. He was given one metal chair. The temperature was dropped, the air conditioning cranked up until it was frigidly cold.

Paul had taken over the questioning at Dennis's command, donning all black and covering his face with a balaclava. The first day of Zahawi's new interrogation, Paul had strode in and bellowed at Zahawi to *get up, get up against the wall.* Zahawi had scrambled, moving as fast as he could hobble with his still-healing injuries.

"We know you're playing games with us, Zahawi!" Paul had roared. "We know you're lying! We know everything about you! We own you! And we're going to break you, until you tell us what we want to know!"

"I have told everything—"

"You haven't! You're lying!"

"I have told everything—"

"When you lie to me, you will get punished."

And Paul had left.

Cold, alone, and naked, Zahawi had huddled against the wall for hours.

Zahawi stopped talking the third day Paul barged in, all hours of the day and night, demanding information and calling Zahawi a liar. He stared beyond Paul, eyes vacant, trying to hide his nudity, cover himself as best he could.

Paul scoffed, snorting as his attempts. "I don't care about your little dick, Zahawi. We grow them bigger in America."

"We need to rattle him," Dennis said one day. "I'm going to blast music into his cell. Until he begs for us to turn it off."

Zahawi didn't beg. He sat on the floor, eyes closed, stone-faced, until Paul stormed in again. Every time Paul entered, Zahawi jumped up against the wall. He stopped trying to cover himself. He held his chin high.

Kris was torn between staying and enduring alongside Zahawi, and fleeing, escaping to the other side of the compound, the silence of his shared hut with David. But, even there, the walls shook, reverberating off the quiet force of David's rage.

As much as Kris hated Dennis, hated Paul, David's hatred went deeper. Darker. Kris felt earthquakes in David's soul, tremors in his body every time they touched. Darkness filled David's gaze.

But he refused to speak about it.

When the music failed, Dennis ordered Zahawi be kept awake. Sleep deprivation, and lots of it.

"How the fuck will you know that you're getting any real intelligence or just the firings of an exhausted mind?" Kris snapped.

"That's your job," Dennis snapped back. "Aren't you the Zahawi expert?"

Zahawi was kept awake for two days, forced to sit upright on the metal chair, his hands cuffed behind him. Anytime he slouched or his eyes slipped closed, Paul, or another all-black-clad officer, was there to scream at him, force him to wake up.

Once, Dennis uncuffed his hands, offered Zahawi a crayon, and held out a notepad. "He'll write intelligence down, and he won't know he's doing it."

Zahawi stared at the crayon, and then at Dennis. He dropped the crayon.

"Start it all over," Dennis said. "The music. And then the sleep deprivation. He gets sixteen hours to rest before we begin again."

---

"*Why the* fuck *has the intel from Zahawi stopped*?" George, in Islamabad, shouted over the phone at Kris. "*What the* hell *is happening down there*?"

"Ask your friends at Langley. They sent some clown here from Psych 101 and told him he would be the one to make Zahawi talk. Never mind that Zahawi's been talking to me just fine." Kris paced away from the command center, sucking down his cigarette.

In the distance, David jogged around the airstrip, shirtless, his running shorts sliding up his thighs. Sweat slicked down his skin. Kris wanted to get lost in his back, press his face to David's skin until he could transport out of there, reappear on a beach somewhere, where the sweat was from the sun and the sand and not the humidity and the rage, the futility of watching their interrogation go to waste.

David had gone quiet since Dennis had thrown him out of the bunker. Rage pulsed off him constantly. Kris spent most of his time in the interrogation cells, watching the monitors as Paul and Dennis tried to break Zahawi. Dennis kept the interrogations random, going at all hours, trying to disrupt Zahawi's sense of time and place. Kris was keeping to the same schedule, awake for almost twenty-two hours a day. When he finally collapsed in their bed in their hut, David was usually gone, out pounding the runway or working out in the makeshift gym he and the rest of the Special Activities Division —SAD—guys had created. Steel rods with concrete on the ends were the dumbbells and barbells, along with old tires and pieces of chain.

"*The word on the street is that Zahawi is the number three man in al-Qaeda. He needs to give up the goods on Bin Laden. Where is he hiding? What plans have they set in motion? What's the next play?*"

"He's given up all their current plans. He's given up what he knows about the leadership. He doesn't know where Bin Laden is, though. He says no one does. Bin Laden's in hiding. From everyone."

"*That's* bullshit. Someone *knows. The number three in al-Qaeda* has *to know. They have an organization to run.*"

"George, I'm telling you. He doesn't. I think we've tapped him dry for actionable intel. Now we need to focus on operations. Understanding what's what in al-Qaeda. Who's who, and what their history has been. Who believes what, who is married to whose sister? Where are the loyalties, where are the weak spots? What can we exploit? We need a picture of their organization from the inside. He won't tell us that while he's sleep deprived."

"*What are you saying?*"

"This quack and his crazy attempts to break Zahawi are only doing harm. Zahawi has given us what he knows."

"*Kris... Are you willing to put the lives of everyone in the US at risk for that statement? Are you positive,* dead positive, *that he's said everything?*" George sighed. His breath crackled over the scratchy cell connection. "*Are you willing to risk another nine-eleven?*"

Fire bloomed behind his eyelids, concrete dust and ash falling from the sky. Tumbling Towers, blocks falling down. The Pentagon, one side gone, and a tower of black smoke rising over DC.

He stopped, tipped his head back. Stared at the sky. It was gray, rolling with monsoon clouds that threatened torrents of rain, storms that would shake their world to the foundations.

"*There's a new directive that's come from the White House. Straight from the lips of the vice president to Director Thatcher. 'If there's a one percent chance that something is possible, we act like it's a certainty.' There's no room for error anymore. If it's possible that Zahawi is holding back...*" George trailed off.

"What they're doing, George... It isn't right. They're on a dangerous path. How far will they go?"

George sighed again, long and low. "*What else can we do? How can we know for* sure? Really *know?*"

He watched David run, watched his shoulders heave, his chest rise and fall, as the skies split open again and the rain started to pour.

---

Another jet landed on the rain-soaked runway. The tires sprayed an arc of water, sluicing over the wings of the jet. Rain pounded the soaked compound in a never-ending staccato drumbeat. It sounded like the rock music Dennis blared into Zahawi's cell. Like Zahawi, they couldn't turn it off.

Kris waited under the overhang. David wasn't with him. They'd been by each other's side for eight months straight, day in and day out, through combat zones and undercover operations, from Afghanistan to Pakistan to Thailand. But David had slipped away over the past week, disappearing from his side like the humid mist of the jungle bleeding away. Kris ached for him, felt his absence like a physical hole he might fall into.

Two familiar men came off the jet, running through the rain to meet Kris.

"George sent us. Said you might need some help." Ryan shook his head. Water droplets went flying. His duffel was soaked, just from the run.

Dan, beside Ryan, smiled at Kris. His sunglasses had fogged from the humidity. He pushed them up, into his wavy black hair. Rain dripped from his jaw, highlighting the angles, the sharp square of his bones. Kris had never seen Dan out of a sport coat. His polo clung to his surprisingly broad shoulders. Raindrops traced down muscled forearms, raced over his smooth skin. He was a handsome man; Kris had never noticed.

"The prisoners are running the asylum." Kris guided them through the compound. "Dennis, a psychologist who has never worked with Islamic radicals, or even interrogated anyone before, is in charge. He's trying to break Zahawi."

"What's the problem?" Ryan, as usual, was gruff. "We're not feeding this detainee milk and cookies."

"No, but my interrogation was going just fine. I got mountains of intel through rapport building. This is bullshit."

"We're all on the same team here," Dan jumped in as Ryan opened his mouth, a scowl on his face. "We all want the same outcome. Good intelligence. The homeland protected. Let's figure out how we can all get that."

Ryan's mouth snapped shut. He glowered, but didn't argue.

Dan smiled at Kris behind Ryan's back.

Two giant security guards, SAD officers who hung out with Paul, stopped them outside the interrogation bunker. "You aren't allowed in."

"Excuse me?" Kris, though not actively involved in questioning Zahawi any longer, still was on the command team of the detention site. "What the fuck did you say?"

"Paul's orders. You're not allowed in today."

Ice wrapped around Kris's spine, a ribbon that twirled down his bones and squeezed. What were Dennis and Paul doing? What didn't they want anyone to see? "Get out of my way," Kris growled.

"Sir—"

"Sir! That's right! Because I am fucking in charge of Zahawi, no matter what the fuck Dennis or Paul told you! Who are you to keep me out? Get the fuck out of my way!"

The SAD officer's eyes slid sideways to Ryan. Ryan nodded. Finally, the guard stepped one half step to the side. Kris had to squeeze past him to open the door.

The stench hit him first.

Human feces. Sweat. Adrenaline. The stink of pure terror, animalistic fear.

Whimpering, and then screams. Shrieks and babbled Arabic, nonsensical.

Paul's voice, bellowing. "I want the *names*, *email addresses*, *phone numbers*, and *safe houses* of *all* your fucking brothers who are planning on attacking the United States! *Give me the information I want*, Zahawi! Give it to me, or your life gets worse!"

"*I don't know*!" Zahawi wailed.

Kris ran.

The interrogation bunker was long, with only one entrance. At the far side, they'd built Zahawi's cell inside a freestanding isolation room. Outside the isolation room, banks of monitors showed the inside of his cell from every angle, in vivid Technicolor.

Dennis stood before the monitors, watching Zahawi's tearstained face grimace and wail.

Kris ran, shouting. "What the fuck are you doing? What the fuck is going on here?" Footsteps echoed behind Kris, Ryan and Dan racing after him.

Dennis shoved a single sheet of paper right in Kris's face. "White

House authorization. The president has authorized enhanced interrogation techniques against uncooperative detainees."

Kris's eyes darted over the classified memo. "Slamming into walls? Beating him? Confinement? Stress positions?" He read on. "You're using his fears against him! Putting insects in a confinement box with him?" Zahawi had told him, weeks ago, his biggest fear was bugs, especially ones that stung or bit. He'd been petrified of the desert scorpions, of the bugs in the mountains of Afghanistan and Pakistan. Of the spiders.

His gaze skittered to a stop over the last two techniques. "Mock burial?" he breathed. "*Waterboarding*?"

Ryan appeared beside him in time to hear Kris's last words. He snatched the paper out of Dennis's hands.

"He's not giving up all that he knows! *This* is how we protect the homeland, Caldera! *This* is how we get through to these people that we mean business!" Dennis snarled.

"This isn't legal—" Dan began.

"It is now. Straight from the White House. Zahawi doesn't fight for a nation or belong to any country. The Geneva Conventions don't apply to Zahawi. He's an enemy combatant. And we can do whatever we want to him."

A piercing wail rose over the monitors, scratching out of the speakers. On the screen, Zahawi collapsed, falling almost into Paul. Paul had a towel around Zahawi's neck, wrapped like a sideways noose, and was flinging him against the wall. Zahawi's head, his naked shoulders, bounced, sharp cracks breaking over the speakers.

"Are you this fucking weak?" Paul roared. "I thought you were the fucking prince of al-Qaeda! You were someone big and bad, weren't you? Not so big and bad now, huh?" *Crack.* Zahawi hit the wall again.

A long box was in the cell, standing against the bars. It looked like a coffin. Paul swung Zahawi around, grabbed his hair, forced him to look at the box. "Do you want to go back into your box? Your new home?"

"No..." Zahawi moaned. "No, no, no..."

"You only have a few minutes to tell me what I want to know, Zahawi! Only a few minutes before your life gets even worse!"

A puddle appeared beneath Zahawi, a trickle down his legs. He tried to double in half, tried to shrink, moaning.

"You pissed yourself again? Jesus Christ, you are a fucking mess. Fucking pussy, that's what we say in America. You already shit yourself in your box!"

Zahawi's foot slipped on his urine on the floor. He hit the wall headfirst.

Kris was trapped in a nightmare. This wasn't happening. Time fractured, the words coming out of the speakers broken into consonants and vowels that he had to reassemble, had to try and parse meaning out of. It was like Paul was speaking a foreign language, something he couldn't understand. Images collided, smeared, the world moving too slowly and too quickly all at once. Zahawi hit the wall in slow motion. His urine spread on the floor. Kris's heart stopped beating.

"You are asking me to hurt you, Zahawi. Do you know that? You are asking me to make your life worse. You're asking for this! Tell me what I want to know and your life will get better. What are the *names, email addresses, phone numbers, and safe houses* of the brothers who are going to attack America?"

"*I don't know*!" Zahawi shrieked. His bones seemed to give out, and he sagged against the wall, shivering. "*I don't know*!"

"Remember, Zahawi. You asked for this." Paul let go of the towel, his makeshift collar noose, and walked away. Zahawi slumped, sitting in his urine.

Once, Zahawi had told Kris how much he hated being dirty. He hated feeling unclean and loved his daily prayers, loved the way he made himself pure and clean before Allah. He'd fought to control his bowels, his bladder, after that first session, despairing whenever he lost control. Kris had helped him, encouraged him. Helped him relieve himself during breaks in their interrogations. Built up his strength again.

Zahawi pitched sideways, lying in his piss. Blood seeped from one of his reopened leg wounds, trickling down, mixing with the urine. Zahawi pressed his face into the dirt. His lips moved, scraping over the dust.

Paul reappeared, wheeling in a thin platform. Thick straps went across, obviously to restrain someone. A bucket of water and a black hood lay on the surface.

"No," Kris breathed. "You can't."

"We absolutely can," Dennis said. "The president authorized it. You just are too weak to do what the United States needs."

"I gave you the opportunity," Paul told Zahawi. "I gave you the opportunity to save yourself. All you had to do was tell me what I want to know." Paul grabbed Zahawi and hauled him to his feet. Zahawi wilted, almost collapsed. Paul dragged him to the platform.

Someone else watched Paul strap Zahawi down. Someone else who inhabited Kris's body, his mind. Someone else who could comprehend what was happening. Kris felt Dan and Ryan beside him, bracketing him. Dan was frozen, staring. Ryan had gone bone white. His hands had fisted, crumpling the memo Dennis had shown them. Only the top line was visible. *Enhanced Interrogation Techniques Authorized.*

"You can stop this, Zahawi. Tell me what I want to know. Tell me how the United States is going to be attacked." He held Zahawi down with one hand as he tightened the straps around Zahawi's wrists, his ankles.

"I told Kris. I told him, I told him everything. Ask Kris. *Please*, ask Kris," Zahawi whimpered.

"No, I know you didn't tell Kris everything. You are lying to me, Zahawi. And you know what happens when you lie?" Paul yanked on the strap over Zahawi's thighs. It cut into his open wound again. Blood poured down Zahawi's leg. He screamed. The speakers cut out, warbled, not able to process the intensity of the sound.

"I'm telling the truth," Zahawi sobbed. "I don't know anything... *I don't know anything!*"

Paul pulled the black hood over Zahawi's face. Zahawi screamed, shrieked. "*Please! Please!*"

Paul grabbed the water bucket.

"Holy fuck..." Ryan breathed. His voice shook.

Kris wanted to close his eyes. He wanted to run. He wanted to disappear and reappear on the far side of the moon. He wanted to time travel, go back to when he was nineteen and walking out of his classroom at George Washington, and tell his younger self to ignore the man with two cell phones who said his country could make use of his talents. He wanted to stop breathing, stop seeing, stop feeling anything at all. Stop his heart from beating. Stop time, and stop the pour of water as it fell from the lip of the bucket. He watched, every moment a lifetime, as the stream fell onto Zahawi's hood-covered face.

Zahawi thrashed, wailing. Paul kept up a constant litany, telling Zahawi he could stop this anytime he wanted, that all he needed to do was tell Paul the truth. "What is your secret, Zahawi?" Paul called out, almost mocking. "What is the *one thing* you are holding back? What is it that you don't want me to know? Just tell me, and this will stop!"

Water poured. Blood seeped down Zahawi's leg. He thrashed. The sounds he made weren't human. They were primal, animal. Something beyond terrified.

Paul let up the water. Zahawi sputtered, for a moment. Until Paul started pouring again.

Kris forced his eyes open, forced himself to watch, the seconds turning to years, until his eyes watered and he couldn't see, until he couldn't breathe, until he felt like he was under the stream of water, the endless, ceaseless stream pouring from Paul's hands. Paul's voice was a monotonous call, a chant, a promise of salvation if Zahawi *just told the truth.*

Zahawi jerked. Went wild as a scream slithered from beneath the hood and his legs and arms went rigid.

And then he went limp.

Water poured, overly loud in the sudden silence.

Dan leaned forward, peering at the monitor.

"Is he—" Ryan's voice choked.

"*Get David*!" Kris bellowed. "Get David *now*!" He shoved Ryan, pushing him back toward the entrance. "Get him! Get David!" Ryan took off, racing for the door.

Kris shoved Dennis out of the way and barged into the interrogation cell. Paul was still pouring, still talking to Zahawi, still trying to get him to tell the truth. Kris felt like he was running upside down, like he was trapped in a carnival of horrors. Paul was pouring water on a dying man, trying to interrogate a soul that was disappearing.

He swung, his fist slamming into Paul's cheek and jaw, decking him from the side. The bucket clattered to the ground as Paul went sprawling across the dirt on his face.

Kris worked the restraints, yanking on the ties and freeing Zahawi. He pulled the naked, filthy, bleeding man to the ground, kneeling next to him as he ripped off his hood.

Zahawi's eyes and mouth were open. A bubble rose from his throat and hit the back of his teeth. It grew, ballooning out of his lips.

Kris laced his hands together, one on top of the other, and pushed his palms down into Zahawi's unmoving chest.

Paul stared, frozen on the ground, as Kris pushed on Zahawi's chest, over and over.

Shouts rose outside the cell, boots running through the bunker. He heard Ryan's voice, and then David's voice. He screamed, "In here, David!"

David flew into the cell, Ryan and Naveen on his heels. Both Naveen and David came up short, their heads swiveling from left to right. The last time they'd seen Zahawi had been with Kris, when Zahawi was resting, healing in his hospital bed with a view of the jungle, listening to monkey calls. But David had been banned from interrogations and Naveen had been disinvited, pending CIA review, Dennis had said.

Now, Zahawi was naked, covered in his own urine, stinking of the shit from his confinement in the coffin box earlier, and not breathing. Water and urine and blood soaked the dirt floor of the cell, and Zahawi.

Naveen froze at the door.

"Hold his head," David growled at Ryan. He kneeled across from Kris taking Zahawi in, from head to toe. Shock, sheer disbelief, bled from him. Kris had never seen him so raw, so open. Not ever.

"Halt compressions," David choked out. He tilted Zahawi's head back and dropped his chin. Leaned forward and closed his mouth over Zahawi's. Pinched his nose. Breathed into Zahawi, twice.

"Resume compressions."

Kris kept going, counting under his breath. Ryan stared at Zahawi's wet hair as he held his head, stared at the way his ribs puffed out, his body shook, limp and unresponsive. Had they killed him? Had the CIA killed their first detainee?

Sputtering, Zahawi coughed, hacking up water mixed with vomit, bits of rice and beans and bile falling from his lips and across his face. He gasped, struggling to inhale, to exhale, and coughed up more water. David rolled him on his side, facing Kris.

Zahawi's eyes were glazed, unfocused, but slowly, they tracked up Kris's hands, up his arms, until Zahawi's gaze landed on Kris's face. He started to shake, to tremble, and he curled toward Kris, wrapping himself up into a ball as close as he could get to Kris's knee.

---

Kris leaned his forehead against the metal door of his and David's hut. Rainwater soaked his skin, spilled down his hair, his face. He closed his eyes. What would he find on the other side of the door?

After Zahawi had started breathing again, time had seemed to snap forward, every moment Kris had spent frozen in horror watching suddenly zipping ahead, fast-forwarding reality. David had started shouting, hollering at the top of his lungs, shouting at Paul, at Dennis, at everyone in the room. Ryan had manhandled David out of the cell before David could get his hands on Paul and rip him in half. David had bellowed, calling Paul a fucking murderer, a torturer, a disgusting human being.

Kris had helped Zahawi up, cleaned him, dried him off, and got him a blanket and his clothes. Zahawi slumped against the wall, huddled in his blanket, and tried to cling to Kris.

Naveen had disappeared. Dan and Ryan huddled off to one side, talking amongst themselves softly. Paul and Dennis locked themselves in the command center.

Now, there was no sense prolonging the inevitable. If David wanted to throw Paul in jail, what must he think of Kris, who had stood by and watched it happen, frozen, unable to stop the torture that went too far? Taking a breath, Kris pushed open the door.

David sat on the floor, leaning against their bed, his head in both hands. His legs were spread before him, as if he'd collapsed, fallen to the ground when they gave out. He didn't look up.

"David," Kris whispered. "I—"

David's red-rimmed eyes lifted, found Kris's. Dried tear tracks stained his rage-ruby cheeks, twisted over his clenched jaw. The air burst from Kris's lungs, punched out by the depth of anguish in David's gaze, the bottomless abyss of agony he saw in the black of David's eyes.

He didn't know what to say. What to do. He stood immobile, stunned, as frozen as he'd been before, watching Paul slowly kill Zahawi.

"When I was a kid," David said slowly. His words ground out of him, halting, as if physically ripped from the center of his soul, or deeper, from a place where he'd buried them forever. He stopped, and started again. "When I was a kid… in Libya…"

Kris felt like he was on the edge of the abyss inside of David, about to tip forward and fall into something he wasn't ready for. He wasn't ready for this, wasn't ready for the secrets David kept buried.

"Qaddafi's men arrested my father. They said his faith was turning him against Qaddafi. Against the state. Because he believed in Allah too strongly."

The more David spoke, the more his voice seemed to fall from his body, to come from somewhere else. As if he wasn't speaking any longer, but something else was. Something that lived inside him, and he'd tried to bury. To forget.

"My father was taken. To Qaddafi's secret prison." David shuddered, his whole body spasming, like Zahawi's had spasmed. Kris felt rain falling on his skin, felt it splash on his face. No, not rain. Tears.

"My father... *was tortured...*" David tried to breathe. His mouth was open, and Kris saw his throat work, saw him gape like a fish out of water. "He was tortured, and then executed," he whispered. "We fled." He gasped, as if he'd been given permission to breathe, as if he was coming up from being held underwater. As if he was taking his first breath after drowning.

Finally, Kris moved, breaking free from the force that held him immobile. He couldn't save Zahawi, not in time, but he'd go to David. He wouldn't leave him to drown in the memories, the horror, the torrents of hate and fear and water that flooded them all, united them. He crouched beside David, curled into him. Wrapped his arms and legs around David, as close as he could get. David folded into him, like a child would, like a ten-year-old boy would in his father's lap.

"I try never to think about what happened to him," David whispered. Tears poured from his eyes, landed on Kris's skin. He could drown in David's tears. "If I imagine it, if I think about what he went through—"

"Don't. Don't do that to yourself."

"We tortured him. I don't even fucking like him. Zahawi. He ruined his Islam, made his faith ugly. He destroyed the best of what he had. A life. A family. A *father*."

Kris tried to swallow. He couldn't, not past the shame, the bile.

David's words were bullets, fired on breathless gasps as he clung to Kris, like Kris was his anchor to the world. "I. Saw. My. Father. In. There. I saw my father on the ground. In the dirt. Covered in his own piss and shit, drowned, beaten. I saw *him*. I didn't see Zahawi."

"David—"

"We came to America, and my mother said we'd never have to worry again. America was free. America was safe." He pressed his soaked face into Kris's chest. His hot breath burned through Kris's clothes, scorched his skin. David's confession was burning him alive, turning him to ash and dust. "But today, I *saw my father.*"

Kris curled over David, wrapping his arms around him, holding him as tight as he could. "It will never happen again," he choked out, each vowel, each consonant struggling to escape through Kris's own tears. "Never, David. I swear."

---

"Enhanced interrogation techniques will resume in thirty-six hours."

Dennis and Paul squared off against Kris and Naveen in the command center. A single memo rested on the table between them. The rest of the intelligence, everything Kris and Naveen had built between them and with Zahawi's help, was gone.

The memo from CIA Director Thatcher's office started:

> *Resume EIT on subject after sufficient recovery period from incident reported in previous memo. All previous EIT techniques authorized.*

"You're *not* fucking torturing him again," Kris growled. "You almost killed him."

Dennis tapped the memo, the third paragraph. "Read on."

> *Regarding subject's disposition. All contingencies must be planned and prepared for, including the subject's potential death while in custody. Regardless of future disposition, subject will be held incommunicado for the rest of his natural life.*

"We will resume in thirty-six hours," Dennis repeated. "He has information. And we're going to get it. He will break. You'll see. Especially after the last session. He'll break when he sees the waterboarding table again. We'll use what happened against him. He'll break out of fear. I guarantee it."

Naveen stepped back, away from the table, until he turned and walked out of the bunker.

"I am calling Langley," Kris hissed. "I'm calling the president. I'm calling fucking everyone. You are not torturing him!"

Paul, quiet throughout the confrontation, finally spoke up. "Who do you think authorized us to continue? Why do you think anyone at all will care about this terrorist? When he dreamed about nine-eleven? When he was best friends with the architect of the plot? When he rejoiced and danced in the streets when he heard the towers had collapsed? Do you think anyone at all will give a fuck?" Paul peered at Kris. "Why do you? Maybe you should think about that."

The only answer he could give Paul, after that, was a slap to the face. He restrained himself, *just*.

Following Naveen, Kris strode out of the command center, his mind whirling. He was going to call George, then Clint Williams. Work his way up the chain of command until he got to the director, then the White House. He'd make everyone see reason.

Naveen waited for him outside, leaning against one of the half walls and watching the rain. His face was twisted, like he'd seen something he'd wished he'd never, ever had. A duffel was by his feet.

"Caldera." Naveen's gaze flicked to him, then back to the rain. "I'm leaving."

"No, we've got to stop this. I need your help. We can go together, to Langley and the FBI—"

"I already called FBI headquarters. Spoke to my director, right after... *it*... happened. My director called your director..." He trailed off. Squeezed his hands together. "The CIA isn't changing their mind. They told Director Mueller to go fuck himself." He shook his head. "I've got a choice. I either arrest them in there—" He jerked his head back, toward Dennis and Paul. "Or I leave. The FBI... It's like Mueller said. We don't do that. Ever. And we won't be associated with anyone who does."

It felt like a chasm had opened up between them, like a ravine had been rent into the earth. Naveen on one side, Kris, and all that he'd seen, all that he'd watched unfold before him as he stood silently, on the other. Kris, and the CIA, all the way up to Director Thatcher, and further, to the president.

"Why don't you arrest them?" Kris finally said. His voice cracked.

Naveen blew out a long breath. "Arrest two Americans on a base that doesn't exist, in a country that pretends we're not here? While I'm surrounded by other CIA officers who support what those two jackasses are doing? I wouldn't make it out alive." Turning, Naveen grabbed his duffel, slung it over his shoulder. "Watch out, Caldera," he said. He didn't offer his hand to shake. "This isn't right. And it's all going to come out one day. It's going to be a fucking mess when it does. Justice always comes."

Turning, he headed for the vehicle bay, the concrete slab where they parked their four-wheelers. It was a grueling six-hour drive through the mud and the jungle to get to the nearest city. They were off the map, purposely. Off the edge of the world, in more ways than one.

"Wait. Wait."

Naveen stopped, but he didn't turn around. "I'm not staying, Caldera. Don't try and stop me."

"I'm not staying either. Can you fit two more in your jeep?"

# 15

**Islamabad, Pakistan - June 19, 2002**

The sound of rain, of water dripping from the faucet, the toilet bowl filling after a flush, flashed David back to Thailand, every time.

He hadn't seen it happen. Hadn't seen Zahawi be smothered with the water, drowned, until Kris had interrupted and brought him back to life. But his mind could fill in the gaps, rewind reality and paint too-vivid pictures, working backward from the moment he'd appeared in the cell door.

Untethered, his mind worked overtime, building images from his memories, dredging through his soul for the raw material. He'd been through SERE school where Dennis had studied, had based his interrogation techniques on. He'd been mock interrogated, forced to sit nude while someone tried to crack him. It had been a game, an endurance test. He'd known there was an end, a point at which it would all evaporate. It hadn't ever been real.

He'd *never* thought of his father.

His memories fractured, a broken kaleidoscope, or the carved wood fractals of his childhood mosque, honeycomb filigrees of bursting sunlight, a million tiny rays. His father's face, smiling at him after prayers, reaching for him, rubbing his head. His father's face on a naked, piss-covered body, drowned in a puddle on a dirt floor.

He'd never put his father back into his life. Not in twenty-one years, not since leaving Libya, leaving Africa, and washing the sand and the sun and the memories away. He'd left it all behind, his history, his name, his religion. *Everything.* He couldn't be an Arab in America, certainly not a Libyan, not when they'd arrived. Pan Am exploding over Lockerbie had still been fresh for most people, as was President Reagan calling Qaddafi the most dangerous man in the world.

Never mind that David and his mother agreed. Never mind that the worst victims of Qaddafi were the Libyan people.

To be Libyan in the nineties was to be the enemy. He'd seen it on TV, in the movies, *everywhere.*

He'd buried it all, fragmented the memories until they were grains of sand, blown to the corners of his soul.

September 11 had brought the world to a standstill, had shaken the foundations of the globe, and everything he'd buried had come uprooted. He'd worked so *hard* to become American, but in a *moment*, one morning, he'd turned right back into a dirty Arab, someone dangerous, someone suspicious, the epitome of the *Other* in so many people's eyes.

Collective blame was heaped on his and every other Muslim's shoulders, the hatred of the Western world heaped on a billion people for the actions of nineteen men and the hatred of their small cult.

How could al-Qaeda undo the world so completely? Poison the minds of so many? Tarnish a people, and a faith, so entirely? How had their pain led them to dream about death, crave annihilation? Men like Bin Laden, like Qaddafi, like Zahawi and his best friend, Khalid Sheikh Mohammed, they ruined the world for *everyone.*

And were ruining David's world, spinning it around like a Ferris wheel that wouldn't stop.

Kris had pulled him out of Thailand, pouring him into the jeep with Agent Naveen in the middle of the rain. He'd still been unbalanced then, still fighting to keep the past and the present right in his mind.

Ryan and Dan hadn't come back with them. He'd thought they would. But Kris had said, when he got into the jeep, "Dan promised he'd watch them. He's going to take over the intel analysis. Ryan... He's taking over the facility."

They'd shared a long look at that. Ryan, in charge of the detention facility, overseeing Zahawi's interrogation.

Six hours through the rain, and they were back in the city. He and Kris had spent a full day in a rundown motel, turning off their cell phones and their satellite phones and making love until they couldn't breathe, until they couldn't think, couldn't hear the rain turning to water being poured over a black hooded face. When he'd wanted to sleep, he'd rolled Kris over, slid into him again. When he couldn't breathe, when the memories were too strong, he'd kissed Kris until Kris had breathed for him.

Twelve hours later, they were back in Pakistan.

He was sent to the streets, back to Islamabad and Peshawar, back to being undercover in the teeming masses. Pashto, Urdu, and Arabic washed over him. The sun, a physical burn, blasted him from above. He tasted dust and sweat, and walked between streets, between alleys, into and out of markets. Overhead, sunlight split into streamers between swaying bands of fabric stretched across alleys and market stalls. He moved from shadow to shadow, watching and waiting.

*Living*. Listening to the people around him speak of Allah every other sentence. Hearing the muezzins call the city to prayer, over and over again. Mothers and sisters moved around him. Fathers and brothers called to one another. Soccer balls rustled in the dirt. Tea and cinnamon floated on the air, above the sewage and the manure.

Pakistan, on the surface, wasn't anywhere close to Libya. People pressed in on him from every side. Pakistan was full, crowded with humanity, whereas Libya was spacious, more sand and sun than people. Empty stretches of the desert concealed Libya's secrets. In Pakistan, there were no secrets, only gossip and scandal waiting for the right moment.

But it was a Muslim nation, with the rhythms of Islam embedded in its bones, in its blood, and old men walked the street with their slow, careful gaits, watching the sky and waiting for the time to pray.

If his father had lived, would he look like this man, or that man?

He stayed out of the US Embassy from before the sun rose to after it set. He returned late, after driving for hours, shaking any tails he might have picked up, and blending into the obscurity of the millions and millions of other Muslim men.

Time was no longer linear. The past lived in his present, extruding from his pores, his lungs, his eyeballs. He was saturated in memory, in time, drowning in it. At the wrong moment, he'd hear a note, the lilt of Arabic, a portion of the *azan*, and be back in his childhood. Catch a glimpse of the sun burning the sky to the color of an overripe orange, the look in a stranger's eye, or the skyward gaze of a man in prayer.

He saw his father in the face of every old man.

He had to *stop*. Focus. His mind was like a broken sieve, leaking everywhere.

Kris spent a lot of time with George, especially in the evenings, when they were in meetings with Langley and Washington DC. He needed Kris, his lighthouse, his anchor. He was drifting out to sea without him.

David tried to get back in tempo with his team. Since Afghanistan, since he'd splintered off and stayed by Kris's side, a gulf had emerged between them. His team had been his family, his brothers-in-arms, even despite their wildness, the bloodlust that had seized Jackson and the others, and the way their colonel in Germany had talked about killing *those fucking Muslims*. They were his family, as screwed up as some of them were.

Or, they *had* been.

He couldn't fall back into the endless bullshit Cobb and Warrick threw at each other. Couldn't muster the interest to kick Jackson off the junky game system, take his turn at shooting up the bad guys who dressed suspiciously like Middle Easterners, like Arabs, even Libyans.

Their noise moved around him, through him, as if he were an alien in their midst.

Palmer crashed down on the couch next to him, creaking the old springs. They hadn't spent much outfitting their living quarters in Islamabad, a sprawling house near the embassy. The furniture was on the verge of collapse. "Haddad. Squared away?"

He nodded. "Yes sir."

Palmer kept staring at him. "You sure?"

He blinked. "Is this Captain Palmer *asking*, sir?"

"No, Sergeant, there is nothing that I want you to *tell* me. This is a friend checking in." Palmer's voice dropped. "Something's got you shook. We can all see it. You've been off since Afghanistan. Ever since you were pulled off to go one-on-one with the CIA."

"I'm good to go." David tried to brush Palmer off.

Palmer wasn't taking it. "Look, I got a WARNO for you." A WARNO, a warning order, a heads-up. David's hackles bristled as Palmer leaned in closer, speaking into David's shoulder. "Some people are asking questions. Making comments. Wondering about you."

"About *me*?"

Palmer stared. "Jackson let it slip you aren't racking out in your own bed."

He turned away. Stared at the TV, at the video game. Rodriguez was mowing down the bad guys in a tank. The bad guys looked like his neighbors from when he was seven, his neighbors who'd run a restaurant on Abdullah Bala Street in Benghazi and gave him pomegranates. His seven-year-old fingers would be ruby red, stained down to his fingernails by the time he was done. In his memories, the pomegranate juice turned to blood, the same blood on the TV screen.

"You gotta watch your six, Haddad. It's almost time to pop smoke."

"What?"

"We're coming up on nine months we've been deployed. They're gonna pull us back soon. Rotate us out. I'm sure you've heard the rumors."

"What rumors?"

"Iraq, man. We're taking Iraq out next."

David bit his tongue, hard enough to hurt. He'd heard about Iraq from Zahawi. The black flags of Khorasan coming over the hills, through Afghanistan, through Iraq. The prophecy, the prophecy.

"We gotta rotate out to start workups for invading Iraq. You know we're always the tip of the spear."

"When?"

"I'm waiting for the orders. Any day now."

---

It was late when Kris finally came back to his—their—bedroom. David had already halfheartedly shared a beer with Jackson and Palmer, tried to shoot the shit with Warrick a bit. Had showered, standing in the cool water with far too little pressure as images of Zahawi and his father, Pakistan and Libya, and the burning sun beating down on a dry, dusty landscape, burst like fireworks behind his eyelids.

Kris looked like he'd been up for days, had stood before Goliath himself. Unlike the mythical David, though, he hadn't succeeded.

Collapsing onto their bed, Kris slumped forward, burying his face in his palms. The knobs of his spine stuck out through his rumpled button-down. David trailed his fingers down each of them, pausing at every furrow. He felt Kris's breath, the shudder of his lungs.

"I'm sorry," Kris whispered. "I tried."

It had always been a foolish promise.

Kris couldn't stop the US government, couldn't stop the might of the biggest bureaucracy on the face of the planet. Especially not from itself. "They won't stop."

Kris shook his head. His face was still hidden. He spoke to the darkness of his fingers. "George told me I was making a mistake. I was ruining my career. The detainee program is the next big thing in the agency. That anyone who is anyone is jumping to get on board."

David's fingers trailed down Kris's back, tugged at the loose fabric until it was free from his pants. He slid his hand up Kris's skin, ghosting over the small of his back, the taut warmth there. The small of Kris's back had become his holy land, his Mecca, a place he craved and worshipped, burying his face deep in nightly prayer. The secrets of his soul were in Kris's body, he knew. He just had to find them. He'd spend his whole life searching, on his knees in prayer before Kris.

He knew what Kris's answer to George would have been. He knew it like he would have spoken it himself. "You told him to go to hell."

Kris snorted. Finally, he pulled back, his fingers revealing his red-rimmed eyes. "I said a little more than that." He sighed. "I swore I would never be a part of the detainee program. That one day it would come apart and I would fucking cheer when it came down around the agency. I would fucking cheer." Kris rubbed his eyes. "George said I was damn close to being a traitor."

"You're not a traitor."

Kris slumped, falling backward against David. "I'm being sent back to CTC. To Langley." He rolled into David, burying his face in David's chest. "I leave in a week."

Relief bubbled through David, and he wrapped his arms around Kris, pulling his body completely against his own. They fit together like a puzzle made of two pieces, their bodies made to conjoin in a million different ways. "Palmer said we're rotating out, too. Soon, he said. Very soon. I'm going back."

"Where are you based in the States?"

In all the time they'd been together, they'd never spoken about home. About the United States and what life was like for them back there. It hadn't seemed real, as real as their days in Afghanistan and after. Going back to America seemed like a movie he was about to see, something that was going to happen to another person.

It felt exactly like he'd felt when he was ten years old, fleeing Libya with his mother. Then, like now, he'd clung to another person to make the journey.

America wasn't a place to go alone. He'd die if he were alone there, suffocate under the pace and the energy. But Kris would be there. His palm found the small of Kris's back again. He spread his fingers, stretched his hand open until he swept down Kris's ass.

"I'm at Fort Bragg. North Carolina. It's a little over a four-hour drive to Langley." He swallowed. "I've already looked it up."

Kris smiled, that sly curl of his lips that crinkled the corners of his eyes. The smile sounded like the shape of his laugh—sardonic, but warm at the center, for the one who mattered. For David. "Have you? Think you're going to be coming up to visit?"

It slipped out, before he'd thought it through. Days and days of hearing Arabic, of hearing his language, his father's faith, saturate the air around him. "*In shaa Allah*," he said.

Kris's eyes went wide. David's breath stuttered, stopped. "I mean—"

Kris pressed his fingers to David's mouth. His lips followed, trading places with his fingers. David drank him in. Pulled Kris on top of him, until Kris was everywhere, until his arms surrounded David like a veil and his body was the moon over David, rescuing him from the sun, from the memories, from everything.

## Falls Church, Virginia - July 1, 2002

Kris's apartment smelled like dust and old age.

Thank God for automatic bill pay. His checking account, abandoned save for his paychecks deposited by the CIA, had dutifully pumped out payments for his apartment, his utilities, and his insurance for the near year he'd been gone. But not a soul had entered his cramped home. Dust over an inch thick coated everything. His windows were covered in grime. A forgotten spoon in his sink lived under a cover of green fuzz.

He cleaned for days, scrubbing every room from top to bottom. In the background, the television hummed, tuned to CNN all hours of the day and night.

None of his old clothes fit. His body had changed, broadening in places, tightening in others. He had an empty closet and a stack of designer clothes to donate. The only things that fit were combat pants and worn field jackets that always smelled like gunpowder and woodsmoke. His Pakistani clothes fit, too, thanks to David. Kris spent the days cleaning his apartment in breezy kameez pants and his silk house coat, the necklace David gave him nestled against the hollow of his throat.

The day before he reported to CTC, he went on a shopping spree, frantically buying out Banana Republic and Abercrombie & Fitch. He blew thousands, but came home feeling like a runway model, like all those days spent enduring mismatched camo and unwashed shirts were vindicated. CIA money would make him the most fabulously dressed officer. He'd helped win the war for them. They would make him look fabulous again. And no one would make him feel badly about it now. Not after everything.

CTC hummed like a beehive had been kicked over. Shifts worked around the clock, targeteers and analysts and operations officers stacked in working groups and zeroing in on anyone who was anyone in al-Qaeda. Kris plugged into the Afghanistan group, avoiding the Khalid Sheikh Mohammed group, the detainee interrogations group, and the Zahawi group.

In the evenings, he worked out in his apartment's gym, watching CNN on the televisions over the treadmills. After, he fixed dinner in his apartment, throwing together a protein shake and a chicken breast while CNN kept droning. He fell asleep to the shifting lights and the dull susurrus of the TV.

Finally, eleven days after he'd set foot in his apartment, his phone rang. The incoming number looked like a credit card, long digits stretched across the display. An international number.

"Caldera." His heart pounded.

"*It's me. We're in Tajikistan, at Camp Alpha. We just got word. We're going to Germany, then back to the States.*"

"When will you be home?"

"*Three, four days, at the most.*" There was a pause. Static. "*We'll have three weeks off when we get back. Stabilization. I can be anywhere. I don't have to stay at base.*" Kris heard David swallow. "*Can I—*"

"Yes." Yes, David could come. Yes, David could stay. Yes, David could spend every day and night at his apartment, in his life. Yes, he wanted David. Forever.

---

Three days later, as fireworks bloomed over DC, David pulled into Kris's apartment complex in his truck. He was still in his uniform, his green military bag on the floorboards and a duffel beside him in the passenger seat. David jumped out, jogged to Kris, and wrapped him up in a hug, lifting him from the ground and swinging him around, like they'd been apart for months and not two weeks. Fireworks kept bursting overhead, red, white, and blue falling like glitter over the city. Music blared from the radio, the National Anthem and God Bless America. It was the first Independence Day since September 11. Patriotism was in the air, so thick Kris could taste it.

Every *boom* sounded like a mortar blast, a dropped bomb in Afghanistan, an explosion blooming over the Shomali Plain, Bagram Airfield, Tora Bora. Every fizzle of firework was a scream, every hiss of a rocket rising into the air a wail. Kris had closed his blinds, shuttered his windows, as soon as the fireworks started.

David flinched in Kris's arms as a massive shower of ruby sparks burst above their heads, sizzling into streamers that fell like tracer rounds.

They huddled in Kris's apartment through the long weekend, not coming up for air until Kris had to report back to CTC.

---

David spent all but two days of his stabilization time with Kris. They made love until they couldn't, laid in each other's arms until they started and finished each other's thoughts, each other's sentences. Kris took David into DC, to the National Mall and the Smithsonian, to museums and restaurants. They were as careful in DC as they were in Kabul and Islamabad about being seen together, about being physically affectionate in public. Furtive handholds hidden in close bodies, quick clasps of fingers beneath tables. Some nights they slipped out to one of the handful of gay bars in DC, where they could sit side by side, kiss, dance together. Make out in the bathroom until they had to slide into a bathroom stall and relieve the pressure before making out in a taxi all the way back to Kris's apartment.

David had jeans and t-shirts in his duffel, and nothing else. Kris took him shopping, opening up his wardrobe to shorts and chinos, breezy tees and linen button-downs, casual cutoffs and fitted polos. Low-cut flats and airy sandals squatted side by side with tan work boots and boat shoes, and David's cracked combat boots, still gray from Afghanistan's dust. David got a corner of his closet, then a bar, then one entire half. David's toiletries cluttered one side of Kris's sink. For three weeks, they lived together in all the ways they'd wanted to and hadn't admitted out loud.

Two days before he was due back, David kissed Kris and made love to him for hours, until he thought he'd die. After, he drove away, heading for Richmond, Virginia, and his mother. He spent hours on the phone with Kris that night, lying in his teenage bed in his mother's home.

"Does she know?" Kris asked.

*"No. She asks me every time I come when I'm going to make her a grandmother. When I'm going to bring home a nice girl for her to meet."*

"Think you'll ever tell her?"

David sighed. *"My mother wears the veil and goes to the mosque three times a week. She's one of the masjid's main sisters. I used to think it was just my father who believed so strongly, but..."*

Kris kept his mouth shut. He didn't say any of the false platitudes, like, *"You're her son,"* or *"Her love for you will be stronger than anything."* Because that wasn't true, not most of the time. Passive avoidance was better than the explosion, lies that were kept in the head and the heart better than the certainty of banishment. Kris and his mother had never said the words. Did she know? Or did Kris delude himself into thinking he would still have her love if he told her the truth?

"Come back next weekend, if you can?"

*"Of course."*

---

Summer turned to fall. On September 12, the president, speaking to the UN General Assembly, announced his intention to go to war in Iraq.

In October, Congress passed the Iraq Resolution, giving the president the authority to use any means necessary to remove Saddam Hussein from power.

At CTC, *Iraq* was the word on everyone's lips, a hum that started softly, whispers in dark corners that grew to a dull roar, a headache that couldn't be ignored. Pressure mounted from the White House, demanding a link between al-Qaeda and Iraq. Kris was pulled into the special working group, ricocheting between the White House and Langley.

*"Find the connection,"* he was ordered. *"Find it now."*

All he could think was *Zahawi*. Zahawi and his certainty America would invade. Zahawi muttering the hadith.

*It's next, in the prophecies. To fall. The armies of Khorasan will come through Iraq. The battle with the West will be there. America is going to invade.*

## Fort Bragg, North Carolina - November 2002

"Haddad, you have new orders. You are joining Detachment 391. Their linguist is out and you've been tapped as their replacement. They're already in training. Report immediately to Captain Diaz." His colonel, bright and early in the morning, pulled him and Captain Palmer into his office.

"Colonel, what is 391's mission?" David's stomach sank as Palmer went unnaturally still, his legs and jaw locking.

"Don't be a moron, Haddad. You know exactly where 391 is going."

## CIA Director's Conference Room, Langley Virginia - December 2002

"I have to say, I am incredibly disappointed." The vice president scowled across the table. "I expected more from the CIA."

Kris, sitting to the right of Director Thatcher, stiffened. The vice president, in a shockingly unusual visit, had come to the CIA. He'd walked into headquarters, strode through the halls, and had sat with Director Thatcher's handpicked team in the strategic heart of the CIA, where every major operation had been decided for decades.

"I cannot understand why the CIA hasn't uncovered the intelligence the Pentagon has." The vice president stared at Director Thatcher. "There are mountains of information proving a link between al-Qaeda, Bin Laden, and Saddam Hussein. Why don't you people see the connections?" He shook his head. "The CIA has got some real problems."

"Sir, we'd like to go over the intelligence your office has developed, step-by-step, and compare it to the sourcing and analysis our office has collected," Thatcher rumbled.

From behind, Kris saw the director's hands clench, his fingers lace together until his knuckles went white. The Pentagon's intelligence office had been micromanaged by the vice president, twisted and twisted until it put out exactly what the White House wanted to hear.

"I hoped you would say that, Geoff." The vice president flicked open his padfolio. Top Secret folders lay inside, and a classified memo rested on top. "What about the Iraqi intelligence officer's meeting with Bin Laden in Sudan in 1996? Or the meeting between Atta and the Iraqi intelligence office in Prague? Al-Qaeda and Iraq's discussions about explosives and chemical weapons training? The Salman Pak terrorist training facility in southern Iraq? I mean, Jesus, Geoff, this is just the tip of the iceberg!" The vice president tossed his pen onto his folders and sat back. "Can your people provide *any* credible intelligence?"

Silence.

Throughout the conference room, Kris heard the inhalation of breaths, and the sudden quiet of air being held inside lungs. All eyes slid to Director Thatcher.

"My people have been working extremely diligently—"

"Where's the *proof*?" the vice president cried. He spread his arms wide, scoffing. "Where is your intelligence?"

"Mr. Vice President." Kris leaned forward. "Regarding your claim that an Iraqi Intelligence Services agent met with Bin Laden in Sudan in 1996. We've also seen that intelligence report. It was passed to a foreign government's intelligence service from a thirdhand source through an unverified network of informants. In the vernacular, Mr. Vice President, it's a *rumor*. Furthermore, this rumor states that the Iraqi agent met with Bin Laden in July 1996. That's a problem."

All eyeballs in the conference room snapped to Kris. The air vibrated, almost enough to make the water glasses sing.

The vice president stared. "Why is that a problem?"

"Bin Laden left Sudan in *May* 1996. By July, nothing of al-Qaeda was left there."

"And how do you know this?"

"I personally interrogated the individual responsible for transporting Bin Laden and his men from Sudan to Afghanistan: Abu Zahawi."

The vice president's eyes narrowed, dangerous slits. "What's your name?"

"Kris Caldera, sir."

"Mr. Caldera is one of our foremost targeteers and al-Qaeda experts—" Thatcher said, his voice rumbling.

The vice president interrupted. "I know who he is."

Silence.

Kris barreled ahead. "Furthermore, allegations that there is a 'terrorist training camp' at Salman Pak in Iraq are erroneous."

"The Iraqi Intelligence Service is running a state-sanctioned terror training facility at Salman Pak," the vice president insisted, speaking over Kris. "Two airplanes were spotted at the facility. A Boeing 707 and a Tupolev Tu-154. Both were used to train foreign terrorists in how to hijack airplanes. This report has been confirmed by three Iraqi sources."

"Yes, I know the sources." Kris read off the names from his own notes. He heard Director Thatcher's quick inhale, a hiss of breath, beside him. "Two of the men are associated with the Iraqi National Congress, a political lobbying group that has for years peddled misinformation in an attempt to foment political support for regime change within Iraq. Their claims, up until this year, have been roundly debunked. There is no proof that their claims of a terrorist training facility at Salman Pak are anything other than fiction this time around. They are opportunists, manipulating information and outright faking intelligence."

"And the third source?"

"The third source, a former captain seeking asylum in a foreign nation, stated in his debrief that Salman Pak was a *counter* terrorist training camp for the Iraqi military. But the *counter* portion of that phrase seems to have gotten lost in translation. I have the original debrief from his petition for asylum here." Kris tossed a folder onto the conference table.

The vice president did not reach for it.

"Reports of a plane in the desert south of Baghdad have been confirmed," Kris continued, his voice softer. "It was a plane crash out of Baghdad Airport. The plane is a wreck. It's not a training facility. Satellite photos show it has mostly been picked apart by civilians desperate to sell the metal and the wiring for a few bucks."

"Mohamed Atta, the lead hijacker, met with an Iraqi intelligence agent at the Iraq Embassy in Prague in April 2001." The vice president stated the information like it was fact, chiseled in stone.

"That intelligence was provided by the Czech intelligence service. They refuse to give up their source for this report, so we cannot verify the credibility of the reporting. However—" Kris took a breath, folding his hands together. The pressure in the conference room had increased a thousandfold. It was as if only the vice president and himself were there. Even Director Thatcher seemed to have faded away.

"However," Kris continued. "We have worked backward and created a day-by-day profile of Mohamed Atta's movements in the year before the hijacking. Atta was photographed at an ATM in Virginia Beach on April fourth. On April sixth, seventh, eighth, tenth, and eleventh, cell phone records place him in Coral Springs, Florida, where he and Marwan al-Shehhi had an apartment together. We've checked every airline. Every route into and out of the US. Every passenger manifest. Every passport entry recorded for the first fifteen days of April. There is no sign of him ever leaving the United States, entering the Czech Republic, or returning to the United States."

"There are no records of Atta's movements on the ninth of April."

Kris licked his lips. "That's true. We don't have any cell phone activity on the ninth. No email activity. No images of him captured at any bank or closed-circuit TV in the Coral Springs area."

"Then that's the day he was in Prague."

"We also have no evidence of him leaving the United States."

"He most likely traveled under a false passport."

"A false passport we have never uncovered, using an alias we have never discovered, despite a year of turning this man's life upside down, investigating every part of his existence? I can tell you what food he bought three times a week at the grocery store and how often he bought toilet paper, Mr. Vice President. I can tell you what movies he watched repeatedly and what his favorite drinks at his favorite strip club were. The brand of toothpaste he used and how often he brushed his teeth."

"But you cannot say where Atta was on April ninth, 2001. Can you?"

Kris exhaled. "It was a Monday. The pilots responsible for the hijacking had completed most of their training. Their funds were fine. No one was experiencing money problems. The so-called muscle hijackers were about to enter the United States. There had been no issues with their plans so far. Everything had gone perfectly for a strictly compartmented mission that only a few members in the senior al-Qaeda leadership knew anything about.

"Mr. Vice President, there simply is no reason for this meeting to have taken place. And Atta hated Saddam Hussein. His journals show that he hated the secular dictatorship, as most members of al-Qaeda, Bin Laden included, hated Iraq. Saddam Hussein was, to them, an apostate. They wanted him destroyed. They didn't want him as an ally. There is no reason for Atta to have flown to Prague or to have met with an Iraqi intelligence agent. There is no proof, none, that it happened."

"If Bin Laden and his followers hated Saddam, then why did Saddam order his military to Alert G, the highest military readiness level, two weeks before nine-eleven? Why did he move his wives to the most protected compound in Iraq? Why did he seem to know, ahead of time, that a major attack was imminent?"

Kris swallowed. "I don't know, Mr. Vice President."

The vice president swooped forward, hovering over his padfolio. "You don't think it's strange at all that in August 2001, one of the United States' main opponents was expecting a massive attack to occur?"

"I do think that's strange, sir."

"Iraq was the only nation to not offer condolences to the United States after nine-eleven. Every other nation on the planet offered their sympathy to us. Even tribesmen in Kenya, who didn't hear the news for months, responded to the attacks. They gave us cows. Fourteen cows. And the Iraqis said we *got what we deserved*." The vice president spoke quickly, his words like rapid-fire bullets aimed straight at Kris.

"Saddam Hussein is an incredibly paranoid and monstrous human being," Kris said slowly. "No one disputes that. But to use his psychopathic tendencies and his hatred of the US in an attempt to force a connection to al-Qaeda..." Kris trailed off. "Mr. Vice President, I *can't* support these findings."

Director Thatcher spoke up, clearing his throat. "We have human source reporting from within the Iraqi government, Mr. Vice President. A source claims that after nine-eleven, there were fierce debates within Saddam's inner circle. All of Saddam's officials were counseling him to reach out to the US to make it clear that

Iraq had no connections to the terrorists who perpetrated the attacks."

"But they *didn't*," the vice president spat. "They *didn't*."

"Saddam Hussein has been opposed to Islamic fundamentalism for decades. When the Taliban took control of Afghanistan, he refused to open an Iraq Embassy in Kabul. Whenever Saddam discovered elements of Salafi or Wahhabi Islam sprouting in Iraq, he ruthlessly executed anyone associated with the fundamentalist sects."

The vice president stared at Kris. "Caldera," he said slowly. "Kris *Caldera*." He nodded slowly, pursing his lips. "I doubt you've reviewed our *other* intelligence linking Saddam to al-Qaeda."

He *couldn't* get into an argument with the vice president of the United States, no matter the dig, the potshots that the vice president might take. He lifted his chin. "I have, Mr. Vice President. In fact, I took a special interest in the report, chiefly because of its origins."

The vice president arched a single eyebrow. He sat back, holding his pen in both hands, spinning it in front of his chest. "You cannot dispute this intelligence."

*I absolutely can. I can and I will. I'll scream and shout and dance on this table, call the newspapers, go public–*

Kris kept his shoulders still. Didn't move a muscle. Stared at the vice president. Director Thatcher's foot nudged his, under the table.

"You're talking about the torture of al-Shayk."

"The *questioning*," the vice president snapped. "Under enhanced interrogation techniques."

"Al-Shayk was captured in Pakistan in November 2001. He was questioned at Camp Cobalt in Afghanistan, but someone thought he wasn't giving up enough information. Despite him detailing plans to attack naval infrastructure in Yemen and Bahrain, and despite providing information that helped point to Zahawi's capture."

"Kris," Director Thatcher said softly.

"Al-Shayk was rendered to Egypt, where the Egyptians took over questioning. I've reviewed the cables. It's astounding how, in early 2002, months after September eleventh, just after the war in

Afghanistan, al-Shayk was questioned about al-Qaeda's ties to Iraq. The focus of his interrogation changed completely. The questions weren't about protecting the homeland anymore. They were exclusively focused on determining what connections al-Qaeda had to Saddam Hussein."

"Uncovering the links between al-Qaeda and Iraq *is* protecting the homeland! Saddam Hussein is a state sponsor of terrorism! You can see for yourself!" The vice president waved to his files.

"What I see is a man who confessed under torture to whatever his interrogators wanted to hear!"

"*Kris—*" Thatcher hissed.

"Al Shayk confirmed it. In 1999, al-Qaeda sent two operatives to Iraq for Saddam to train in chemical, biological, and nuclear weapons systems!" The vice president slammed his hand down on his padfolio, over the Top Secret folders. "He admitted it!"

"He confessed to *stop* the torture!" Kris snapped. "Egyptian prisons are notorious for their torture and their forced confessions! They're fingernail factories!"

"*Kris*!" Director Thatcher glowered at him.

"*I was there,* in Afghanistan!" Kris barreled ahead. "My team walked through the remains of al-Qaeda camps. We read through the training manuals al-Qaeda had for their chemical and biological weapons program. You know where everything came from? The United States. Most all of their manuals were reprinted United States military training manuals. Not a single piece of information we picked up from their training camps came from Iraq!"

"Al-Shayk is a senior al-Qaeda officer and in charge of military operations. He is exactly the right person to know about external outreach attempts by al-Qaeda."

"And his information is dead wrong, obviously falsified to stop his abuse. He only said that two people were sent. He can't say who. He can't say where. He can't say who in Iraq he planned the training with. He can't say when these two trainees supposedly returned. His intelligence, for all intents and purposes, is worthless!"

"The information is exactly what he said it was. Al-Qaeda and

Saddam Hussein, working together. Saddam, sharing his chemical and biological weapons technology with terrorists."

"Mr. Vice President, al-Shayk intentionally misled his interrogators. He lied."

Flashes of memory came at Kris from all sides, monkey trills in the jungle and the sound of rain, Paul's sneer. Water being poured. "In my experience questioning Abu Zahawi, I discovered that al-Qaeda is anticipating the United States' invasion of Iraq. Zahawi asked me if the US had invaded yet. They're waiting for your attack. They want you to take out Saddam. They're no friend of his."

"And why would they want us to take out Saddam?" The vice president's voice had dropped, like he was suffering through a conversation with a child.

"Because their apocalyptic prophecies foretell it."

The vice president tossed his head back and laughed.

"'*If you see the black banners coming from Khorasan, join that army, even if you have to crawl over ice; no power will be able to stop them*'." Kris quoted. "'*And they will finally reach Jerusalem, where they will erect their flags*'. Khorasan. Afghanistan. The land of the Hindu Kush. Bin Laden has been using this hadith for years, drawing his fighters to his vision of a holy war. He's always wanted to push the fight toward Iraq. To turn Iraq into the next Afghanistan, and then onward, until they strike Jerusalem. Until they take out the West."

The vice president stopped chuckling.

"This is the fulfillment of their prophecies, Mr. Vice President."

He blinked. Stared at Kris from under his furrowed brow. Tossed his pen onto his folders. "Tell me, then, about Saqqaf."

Kris's gut clenched. The floor seemed to drop away, a swirling vortex opening beneath his feet.

"You, out of everyone, know about Saqqaf." The vice president's head cocked to one side. "I've read all the cables."

"Saqqaf is a thug. According to the Jordanian Mukhabarat, he was a drunk and a gang member, and when his family tried to straighten him out with religion, he went overboard. He found a new addiction and a new outlet for his rage and his cruelty. He went to Afghanistan and he begged to meet Bin Laden. Wanted to join up. But Bin Laden was disgusted by him." Kris flipped through his notes, cables from Jordanian intelligence, reports from his interrogations of Zahawi. "In my interrogations, Zahawi said there was a man named Saqqaf who operated a training camp near Herat. He was unsophisticated. Crude. He didn't have a good command of Islam, Zahawi said. He wanted to be a part of al-Qaeda, but al-Qaeda wouldn't have him. He promised to open a foothold in the Near East if they backed him. He was put on a probation of sorts. They asked Saqqaf to set up a training camp. They'd provide the funds if he provided the training. They wanted to see what he could do."

"They provided the funds," the vice president repeated. "He was affiliated with al-Qaeda."

"No. He never swore allegiance to Bin Laden. Bin Laden wanted nothing to do with him."

"But he came to Kandahar to fight against the Americans. With al-Qaeda, during the invasion of Afghanistan."

"We attacked all foreign fighters in Afghanistan—all the fighters allied against us. That included other units besides al-Qaeda." Majid, in the mountains with David, had fought both for and against the Taliban, both against and for the Americans. Alliances had shifted faster than the sun rose and set. It had seemed like any choice could have been made there, on the roof of the world. Any choice, any direction. Nothing was clear, nothing.

"After Kandahar, what happened to Saqqaf?"

Kris felt like his words were nails, broken glass he had to chew through. "Saqqaf made his way through the mountains of Iran to northern Iraq," he said slowly. "Our intelligence places him in Kurdistan right now. He's joined Ansar al-Islam, a radical Islamist group."

"A radical Islamist group aligned with al-Qaeda. Operating within Iraq's borders."

"Ansar al-Islam operates in the Kurdish north, in an area out of reach of Saddam. It's protected by our no-fly zones, Mr. Vice President."

"Saddam has given sanctuary to this group, and to Saqqaf. He's allowed a known member of al-Qaeda freedom to operate in Iraq, to continue to operate an al-Qaeda-affiliated terror group on Iraq soil."

"Saddam has barely any presence in the Kurdish north. He has no control there. We've kept him out of the north. We gave room for Ansar al-Islam to take root and grow. We protected the area from any incursions through our no-fly zone after the first Gulf War."

"Mr. Caldera, where did this intelligence on Saqqaf originate?"

It felt like a trap, suddenly. Because it was. Kris fumed. "From my own interrogations of Zahawi."

"During your *personal* questioning of Zahawi?"

"Yes."

"Before any enhanced interrogation techniques were applied?"

"Yes."

"If I understand your personal political position correctly, Mr. Caldera, from the numerous screeds you submitted to the White House Counsel's Office, only intelligence gained outside of enhanced interrogation techniques is considered valid. Useful." The vice president paused. "Is that correct?"

"Torture is completely ineffective, Mr. Vice President. Once you go down that road, everything you get is tainted. There's absolutely no guarantee that anything revealed is truthful—"

"That's not what I asked."

"—Torture goes against everything this nation stands for—"

"The detainee program has stopped attacks from happening in Yemen, Singapore, Saudi, and right here, in DC and New York City and Chicago. It's broken up cells all across Europe—"

"—torture violates the Geneva Conventions and goes against the Declaration of Human Rights—"

"Kris!" Director Thatcher grabbed his elbow.

"*They don't have human rights*!" the vice president bellowed.

Silence. The director gasped, quietly. He kept his hand on Kris's elbow.

"Animals that murder thousands of innocent civilians don't get human rights! They don't get international protections! They don't get to go crying to the Red Cross for nicer treatment. Not when they want to murder every American on this planet!" The vice president's voice shook the bulletproof glass in the windows, rattled the water glasses on the table. "They don't deserve anything more than what they're getting."

Kris's fingernails dug into the folders he gripped, scratching against the manila cardboard. "What is the status of Zahawi's interrogation?"

"That's *enough*, Kris," Director Thatcher said quietly, leaning into him. "You've made your point."

"What is the status of Zahawi's interrogation? Did you send him to Egypt like al-Shayk? Or have you finally succeeded in killing him? This government was trying its hardest to!"

"*Caldera*!" Thatcher barked.

The vice president sat back, his seething rage replaced by the visage of a man who had sucked on the sourest lemon. He gazed at Kris like Kris was a traitor. No, was worse. Was one of *them*. Was a terrorist. "The interrogation of Zahawi has ended."

Dan. He came through. He ended it. "He didn't give you anything after you tortured him, did he? Not a Goddamn thing."

The vice president didn't blink. "What he did give us through your questioning was Saqqaf. An al-Qaeda operative who went to Iraq. Who is working in Iraq, under Saddam Hussein."

"You're twisting the intelligence around. That's not an accurate representation of what Zahawi told me, or of Saqqaf's current status in Iraq."

"What does it matter, Caldera?" The vice president sighed, shaking his head. For the first time, he let his exasperation show. "What the fuck does it matter that we want to take him out? Saqqaf murdered our diplomat in Jordan two months ago. He is committed to killing Americans. Waging war against the West. So is Saddam. Now they're in the same country, sharing resources."

"He's not al-Qaeda. He's not even a big player. He's a low-level jihadi flunky who has been searching for an outlet for his reckless criminal activity and his murderous fantasies. He's isolated in the

Kurdish region. If you want to take him out, send in a strike team, or a half dozen ICBMs. Both will eliminate him and solve the problem."

"Look, Caldera, if there's a *one percent chance* that they are working together, even just one percent—" The vice president spread his hands, as if to say the decision was out of his hands. "We cannot lighten our vigilance. We cannot take our foot off the gas. We have to win this war."

*It matters because David is going to be fighting this war of yours. David, and a hundred thousand other men like him. Fighting for reasons that aren't truthful. Fighting a war that can be won another way. Fighting enemies that are propped up, made larger than life. Fighting for the wrong reasons, and fighting based on lies gained from torture. A lot of people are going to die for this, and if they die for lies, then what are they dying for? It matters because they want us there, they want us to take out Saddam, fight in Iraq, help them create the eschatological hellscape they crave, bring out the end of the world through bloodshed and the apocalypse—*

But he didn't say anything. He couldn't get the words out. His wrath, his fury, gummed up his throat, ground his voice to silence.

"I want everything on Saqqaf. Everything the Jordanians have. Every intercept we have on the man. Every source on the ground, every rumor, every whisper of this man. I want to know where he is. I want to know what he's doing. I want to know what time of day he eats. What time of day he takes a shit. When he goes to sleep, and where. Got it?"

*This is how the war will begin.* Kris gritted his teeth, biting down so hard his jaw hurt. There were other reasons for the invasion—the administration had tasked another team with tracking down Iraq's weapons of mass destruction—but the link between al-Qaeda and Saddam Hussein was the vice president's holy grail.

"We're going to nail this son of a bitch." The vice president stood. Everyone followed.

Kris was the last to rise.

The vice president nodded to Director Thatcher, reached across the table and shook his hand. He turned to Kris. Glared, and said nothing.

The Secret Service was waiting for the vice president and his staff outside the conference room. They swept him up, passing him his Blackberry and his cell phone and escorting him through the building and back to his motorcade.

Director Thatcher slumped forward, bracing both of his hands on the table. He hung his head, his back bowing, shoulders slumping like the weight of the world was pulverizing his spine.

"Caldera..." He snorted. "That was a bold fucking career move."

# 16

## CIA Headquarters, Langley Virginia - February 5, 2003

*"Iraq today harbors a deadly terrorist network headed by Abu Saqqaf, an associate and collaborator of Osama Bin Laden and his al-Qaeda lieutenants."*

The secretary of state spoke as Saqqaf's face appeared over the UN Security Council on a giant projector screen. Saqqaf glowered down at everyone, wrath and murder in his gaze, the image of a hardened devotee to an austere and ruthless brand of Islam, twisting the words of the faith until his followers believed they were walking in the footsteps of the seventh century.

*"Iraqi officials deny accusations of ties with al-Qaeda. These denials are simply not credible. Al-Qaeda has bragged that the situation in Iraq is 'good', and that Baghdad can be transited quickly."*

Kris's chin hit his chest. He wilted, slumping in his seat as his coworkers in CTC shook their heads and groaned.

Once again, he was alone, off in the corner, in a desk no one visited. Once again, his coworkers stared at him. This time, not for the clothes he wore, or the rumors about his sexuality.

But because everyone knew—everyone—that he was the vice president's most-hated American.

That he'd bitched out the vice president.

And that he'd lost.

*"Saqqaf and his network are responsible for the murder of an American diplomat in Amman, Jordan. After this despicable act, we demanded that Saddam Hussein turn over Saqqaf so that he can stand trial. However, Iraqi officials protest that they are not aware of the whereabouts of Saqqaf or any of his associates. These protests, again, are not credible."*

The secretary of state went on, outlining the United States' case for invasion. Images of mobile weapons production facilities, storage bunkers, and surveillance overflights at Iraq's nuclear sites were shown to the world.

On Kris's computer, Saqqaf's image stared back at him. Dark, soulless eyes, void of spark or life. A diffuse rage seemed to linger in his stare, a promise of brutality.

By all accounts, Saqqaf had been born a monster. The Jordanian Mukhabarat hadn't been able to contain him. Twice he'd slipped their bonds, running off to Afghanistan.

Kris tapped away at the finishing touches on his report, a projective analysis of post-Saddam Iraq.

*Without significant post-war planning and an immediate transition to a functioning, representative government, chaos and discontent will open the door to sectarian tensions. Chaos and sectarian tensions may be capitalized by foreign jihadists searching to destabilize both Iraqi reconstruction and/or any American/Western-allied endeavor. We should expect to meet significant numbers of foreign fighters in post-war Iraq if security and stabilization operations are not immediate benchmark successes.*

An intercept from Jordan had picked up a message Saqqaf had sent days before. The printout lay on Kris's desk, underlined over and over until his pen had gone through the paper. "*Iraq*," Saqqaf had said over the scratchy phone line sucked up by the Mukhabarat listeners, "*will be the graveyard of the Americans*."

## ODA 391, Fort Bragg, North Carolina - February 7, 2003

"*Haddad*!"

David bristled. He waited for his sergeant, his stomach clenching.

"Haddad, you aren't bringing it. You're consistently lagging behind the rest of the unit. In the last exercises, you failed. You aren't making it, Haddad. You're a fucking embarrassment." His sergeant's vitriol burned into him, bellows that were more appropriate for a recruit than the fourteen-year veteran he was.

Nothing had gone right since his reassignment. His new unit hadn't deployed to Afghanistan. They'd stayed in the homeland, watching as anthrax attacks paralyzed the nation in fear, as a Muslim shooter opened fire at LAX, as paranoia and hostility ratcheted higher and higher, turning to a hatred against Arabs and Muslims so thick and rancid David was choking on it. The guys talked about "*getting some*" and "*taking their turn*" at the "*jihadis*" and the "*camel jockeys*". The "*goat fuckers*".

And worse.

Haddad, the outsider with the Arabic name, the quiet one, the weird one who left on the weekends, wasn't invited to their testosterone party. Willfully obstinate in the face of idiots, purposely distant and hostile toward people he found distasteful, he'd widened the gulf between him and his new unit into a canyon.

"I swear to God, Haddad, you act like you don't even want to be a part of the Army anymore. You getting soft for your little Arabic friends? Wanna 'conscientiously object'? When we get over there, you gonna be with us or against us?"

The countdown was on. The invasion of Iraq wasn't a *maybe* any longer. *When* was the only question.

David's eyes narrowed. "I have nothing to prove, Sergeant. I've served honorably for fourteen years. All of a sudden, I need to prove that I'm not a bad guy? 'Cause of my skin? My last name?"

"No, 'cause of your piss-poor attitude and your fucking abysmal performance."

David didn't have the energy for this. He didn't have the energy for anything anymore. He was in the field more nights than he was at his shitty apartment. They trained for days, weeks. Leaping out of helicopters, storming pretend Iraqi villages, taking down pretend Saddam army checkpoints and bases and installations. Planning for assaults on Baghdad and fighting street by street. Urban warfare was drilled into them, and they spent their nights occupying buildings in their pretend Iraqi training city, taking out the entrenched Saddam forces, red team members from another unit posing as Iraqis.

For the first time since he'd joined the Army, he didn't believe in the mission. Didn't care about his team, either. The bonds between him and his unit were a tattered mess. The mission rang hollow to him. Zahawi's words, his interrogation, kept replaying in his mind.

He'd thought Zahawi's question about the US invading Iraq was insane, was ridiculous and naive. No way would the US entrench itself in a two-front war. No *way*.

But here they were. Practicing for an invasion.

How had Zahawi's trembling lips foretold the future of American foreign policy?

Was everything a giant circle? One big Möbius strip, taking him looping like a roller coaster, around and around and around again? Was it prophecy? Destiny? Or a hideous cosmic joke?

He just wanted to go *home*. Back to Kris, make the long drive north to Falls Church and let himself into Kris's apartment. Plant himself face-first in their bed and wake up curled around Kris.

Something, somewhere, must have shown. He'd lived his life never letting anything slip, not ever, but after Afghanistan, and Kris, and Zahawi, he wasn't so good at keeping everything hidden anymore.

Maybe he should have been mad about that. Mad about his past becoming his present and his secrets becoming known. A petty part of him sometimes lashed out at Kris in his thoughts. *If it weren't for* you, *in Afghanistan, being so fucking perfect, being like pomegranates and honey for my soul. If it weren't for your take-no-prisoners attitude and your fucking amazing brain, the way you knew your shit and made everyone respect you. If it weren't for the fact that you're perfect, in every way. And I'm so fucking lucky you even look at me. If it weren't for all of that.*

His sergeant was slowly turning purple. David hadn't responded to him. "I've *heard* things about you, Haddad," his sergeant hissed. "Heard you like to suck cock. Is that why you're a Goddamn disgrace? That why my men can't stand you? I get more complaints about you than every other soldier put together. I don't have time to make you a man, turn you into what you need to be." His sergeant looked him up and down, like Paul had once looked at Zahawi. "Get your shit together, Haddad. I have exactly no room for fuckups."

The "*or else*" hovered unspoken between them. *Dishonorable discharge* seemed to burn into his forehead. Almost half his life had been given to the Army. Would that be his grand exit?

Would he even care anymore, if it was?

They finished processing the gear and checking out for the weekend. David ignored the stares, the snorts, the barely concealed ill humor sent his way. He hopped into his truck and hit the road.

Hands shaking, he grabbed his phone. He nearly cracked the case, nearly shattered the screen. His vision blurred, rage distorting the edges. His foot floored the gas. His engine roared.

The phone connected after three rings. "*Captain Palmer.*"

"Captain. It's Haddad."

"*Haddad?*" Shock colored his former captain's voice. "*Uhh... what's up?*"

"You free? Can I buy you a beer?"

Palmer's silence was heavy.

"I need your advice, sir," David breathed. His voice shook. "I need your help."

"*I'll be at the Liberty Bell at eighteen-thirty.*"

"Thank you, sir."

---

David had shredded his napkin and the label on his beer by the time Palmer sat down across from him, exactly at eighteen-thirty at the

Liberty Bell bar off base. Palmer took in the mountain of shredded paper, the nearly empty beer bottle. David called for another round.

"I need to talk to Sean," David said quietly. "And ask his advice from Captain Palmer." He looked up, through his eyelashes. He was asking to talk off the record, keep whatever was said between them out of the Army. *Don't ask, Don't Tell* hovered over him like the sword of Damocles.

Palmer had kept his secret in Afghanistan. Had covered for one of their former team members when he'd gotten drunk and stupid with a sailor once, four years back.

Two moments in his history with Palmer. Was it enough to trust him?

"You in some trouble about you and your CIA friend?"

The waitress brought over two fresh beers. David grabbed his, downed a long draught. He picked at the label as he set it down. Nodded. "That, and some other bullshit. My new sergeant is an ass." He took a deep breath. "He said he heard things."

"Shit." Palmer glared.

"You think one of the guys?"

"Maybe. Someone said something, someone joked around. I'm sure they didn't mean it. But who knows who heard?" Palmer screwed up his face. "No one cared, though. I mean, yeah, we all saw."

Fuck. David buried his face in his hands and groaned.

"C'mon, Haddad, you can't be like what you two were and *not* have guys talking. You were fucking crazy about—" Palmer's jaw snapped shut. "You were head over heels," he finished. "It was obvious." He took a drink, watching David. "Is it still going?"

David nodded. He batted his beer bottle back and forth, sliding it across the table. He'd just handed Palmer the ammunition to drum him out of the Army.

"Serious?"

"I think so."

"He going to Iraq, too?"

"I don't— I don't know." Panic, the same panic that lived in his guts, that crawled up his ribs, rose inside him. Another war was around the corner and he was lined up to go. How long would he be gone this time? Separated from Kris, back in the Middle East, in the middle of everything he'd run from. In the middle of a reality that had stopped making sense.

"You guys aren't going to try what you did last time again, are you?" Palmer snorted. "I don't think that's really going to work. Iraq is gonna be a whole lot bigger than Afghanistan. Too many people will be eyes on."

David shook his head. He scrubbed his hand over his face again. "I don't know what to do," he confessed. He felt like vomiting.

Palmer stared at him. "What do you want most in the world, man?"

*Kris. I want Kris.*

Did that make him a shitty person? Was he turning his back on his brothers, on the military, on his nation? The nation that had adopted him, had taken a broken, lost boy in and made him a man? Was he giving up, turning away when his country needed him?

Palmer leaned across the table. "By your silence, I think I can guess your answer. Look..." His eyes darted around the bar. "There's this friend I have. Buddy from ROTC. He *hated* the Army. Did the whole thing for college money. As soon as he could, he popped smoke and got out. He landed at this real crazy company. Under the radar. They do secret squirrel shit. Work with the CIA, DIA, NSA, you name it. Called Blackcreek." Palmer jerked his chin toward David. "I think you should give them a call."

"Thank you," David whispered. "Thank you, Captain."

"Be careful." Palmer eyeballed him, not blinking. "Be *real* careful, Haddad."

**Washington DC - February 8, 2003**

"You brownnosing little shit." Kris chuckled, throwing his balled-up napkin across the table at Dan. Dan batted it away easily.

Dan was back from Islamabad, rotating through on a four-day, in-person briefing with the director before flying back to Pakistan. He'd flown in for the secretary of state's presentation to the UN, and to watch it with the director, too.

"Look at you, in with the big boys now. Moving on up in the world. Making waves with the White House. Riding the gay fame card." Kris smirked.

Dan pretended to bow. "I learned what *not* to do from watching you." He tried to smile. "How are you doing?"

Shrugging, Kris sighed, deflating against his chair. He toyed with the remains of their bruschetta. "It's the first time they've let me out to see the sun, so I suppose that's something."

"Oh, stop."

"Bitching out the VP was great for my career. I recommend everyone do it. Everyone. You'll rocket your way along the career ladder. There's no faster ride in the CIA."

"You mean plummet, right? Straight to the basement?"

"At Mach ten."

Dan sipped his wine, a light white, and stared at Kris. "I'm sorry—"

Kris waved him off. "Don't. Stop." He stared out over DC, over the bustle of the Capitol. He'd come into the city to meet Dan. "I never got a chance to thank you for taking over in Thailand. After I pulled out. I heard they stopped everything after seven weeks. You *must* have had something to do with that. And with closing that place down."

Dan looked away.

"I can't even imagine what it was like after we left. With Paul and Dennis, and Ryan in charge? Jesus..."

Dan spun his wine glass. "You guys did the right thing. Leaving, when you did."

"I'm just glad it finally ended. Zahawi didn't reveal anything, did he? In those seven weeks?"

Dan peered at him. "Not a thing," he said carefully. "Everything he gave, he gave to you."

"Do you ever think about blowing the whole thing open? Calling the *Times* or the *Journal* or the *Post*? Do one of those tell-alls?"

"Go to prison?" Dan snorted. "They'd lock you up and throw away the key."

Kris shrugged. He watched the cars roll by, the blacked-out SUVs. Watched the flag flap over the Capitol. Cold sunlight fell, turning the city a banal smear of gray. "Would it be worth it, though?"

"You would be the one to make that call?" Dan stared at him, eyes narrowed. "Out of the whole government, out of the whole world, you'd be the one to decide what is and isn't worth it? Which lives are worth saving? What costs are too high?"

Vibrating in Kris's pocket made him jump before he could answer. He pulled out his phone. No one called him anymore, except for David. He was the CIA pariah. He didn't usually get calls in the middle of the day. "David?"

"*I'm on my way.*"

"Here? Now?" There was something off in David's voice, something wrong. "What happened? I thought you were going back to the field."

"*Not anymore. In fact, not ever again.*" A car door slammed over the phone line. "*I resigned. I quit. I couldn't—*" His voice broke off.

"Oh my God..." Kris's jaw dropped. His gaze darted from the bruschetta to his wine glass, up to Dan, across to the Capitol. "What now?"

The worst of the CIA and a Special Forces soldier who'd quit. They were certainly a power couple on their way up in the world.

"*I got the number of a contractor. I'm going to try to call them.*"

Dan stared at Kris, frowning.

"Call me when you get closer. I'm in a meeting right now, but I'll be home soon."

David grunted and hung up.

Dan's frown turned to a smile. "Your lover from Afghanistan? David Haddad? The Special Forces soldier who was glued to your side, closer than your own shadow?"

"He's not Special Forces anymore. He just resigned."

"It's hard to be gay in the military."

Kris blinked. "You?"

"Navy intelligence. Before joining the CIA." Dan shrugged. "I wanted to get out of where I was. So. What now? He's picked you over the military, huh?"

"I..." The air fled Kris's lungs. "That's not what it was."

"I'd have done the exact same thing. If I were him."

The burn was back, the same burn he'd felt in Pakistan when Dan had confessed he'd wanted Kris, had wanted more between them before David and before Afghanistan. He thought Dan would have moved on now that Kris was the CIA's worst and Dan was on the path to becoming Director Thatcher's new star. "Dan—"

"I know." Dan held up his hands. "I'm just saying. I'm glad he recognizes what he's got. What's the plan?"

"He said something about a contractor—"

"Call George," Dan interrupted.

"George does not want to talk to me. He doesn't want to see me. His last words to me in Pakistan? '*Take your bleeding heart crusade somewhere else*'!"

"If you're not calling him, I'm calling him. He's here in DC. Getting promoted to the head of the Middle East division."

"Jesus Christ. What about Ryan?"

"Ryan is getting a bump up, too. Chief of station in Afghanistan. But George is going to be in charge of us all, soon. And he knows the head of the contractor that gets all the CIA business. Blackcreek. They're everywhere we are. You want him with you, right?"

---

Kris waited on the stairs to his apartment, huddled in a pair of sweats and a hoodie David had left at his place last month. The temperature had dropped when the sun set. He rocked back and forth, chewing on his upper lip and flicking a marker against his thigh.

"*Fucking Caldera*," George said, picking up on the fourth ring. "*I thought they fired you*."

"You can't fire the gays, don't you know that?"

George didn't laugh.

"George… I'm calling for a favor."

*"I figured as much. I just don't know why you think I'd be willing to even take your call, much less give you anything."*

"You're still on the line, aren't you?"

Silence.

"It's David. David Haddad—"

*"I know who he is."*

"He's left the Army. He was told to look at this contractor."

George's voice changed. Lost the hard edge and turned almost thoughtful. *"Blackcreek. They're hiring everyone they can right now. Especially former Special Forces, and* especially *Arabic speakers."*

"Can you get him a CIA contract? If he's hired? Can you—" Kris exhaled, looking at the floor. *Can you please keep him near me?* He was close to begging, close to groveling. Asking the powerful for a token of grace for him and David. Shame bent his back. He couldn't sit straight.

*"Have Haddad call this number tomorrow."*

Kris wrote the number on his arm. "Thank you. Thank you, George."

A heavy sigh. *"Caldera… Try and stay out of your own way, okay?"*

The line clicked.

Snowflakes drifted in front of Kris's face. He burrowed into David's hoodie. Any minute. Any minute, and David would be there. Would be home.

Finally, David's truck lumbered into his apartment parking lot. Twin headlights bounced over the speedbumps, slowed in front of his building. The door opened.

He'd recognize that shape, the slope of those shoulders, anywhere.

David jogged to him and wrapped his arms all the way around Kris. He loved it, loved how David's arms could completely encircle him. David buried his face in Kris's neck and breathed him in.

Behind David, the truck idled. Kris spotted boxes in the truck bed, duffels stuffed in the cab. "You brought everything?"

"I'm never going back." David's gaze slid sideways. "I can find my own place. I'll start looking tomorrow. We didn't talk about this, and I'm not trying to—"

Kris squeezed his hand. "Stay here. Stay with me." It would be cramped, but they'd make it work. Maybe they'd get something bigger, together. The thought stole his breath. They could live together.

"You sure?" Hope shone from David's eyes.

"I'll have to tell all my other boyfriends to stay away." Kris sniffed, lifting his chin. He tried to look playful in David's hoodie.

David took both of Kris's hands. The snow kept falling. "I don't have anyone else. It's just you."

Was this *the* conversation? They'd never discussed it. Kris was too busy during the week with war preparations, being the CIA's doom and gloom pariah, and keeping an eye on the Bin Laden cables, to do anything other than go home and crash. Sometimes he fell asleep in his clothes. There hadn't been anyone else, not since David came into his life. There hadn't been anyone else since September 10, 2001.

He didn't want anyone else.

"It's only you, David." Snow stung the backs of his hands. "I want you to move in with me. I want you to stay. For as long as you want. And I hope that's a long time."

David nodded. Flakes stuck to his eyelashes, the corners of his lips as he smiled. "I think it will be."

They kissed until the snow burned their cheeks and Kris started shivering, despite David's arms around him. David made him go inside, and he ran bags and boxes from his truck to Kris's living room, seven trips in all.

Half of Kris's studio filled up with David's stuff. Snow melted onto the carpet. Kris didn't care.

He pulled David to his bed. "Welcome home."

They came together, and apart, in pieces. Clothes fell away, and then more, the last barriers separating them from joining completely. Kris imagined turning his chest inside out, placing his heart outside his body for David to hold. He felt David's trembles as their skin brushed together. He felt like a naked star, like every one of his dreams was laid bare for David.

Kris's body burned as David made love to him. His bones scorched him from the inside, and he felt David in every cell of his being. David hovered over him, his hands mapping Kris's body, his eyes memorizing every expression. He drank in each of Kris's moans, his sighs. He kissed every gasp that fell from Kris's lips.

David's lips found a home on his neck, spent hours lingering at his jaw and below his ear. His breath branded Kris, exhales matching the tides of their bodies. "Kris," David breathed, chanting his name. "Kris... I love you. I love you." His buried his face in Kris's neck, pressed his lips to Kris's collarbone. "*Ya hayati, ya habib alby*." *My life, love of my heart*. He gasped. "*Ashokrulillah*, Kris..." *Praise Allah for you.*

Kris grabbed his head, fingers digging into his scalp, sliding through his hair. All the parts of David, all the pieces that made him the man Kris loved, were tumbling within him, slipping inside of his soul. Vows of love in Arabic and English, prayers to Allah, Kris's name, the name of his lover, a *man*. David shuddered, his body quaking in Kris's arms. Who was David when he bared everything?

"*Habib albi*," Kris breathed. "*Enta habibi*." *Love of my heart. You are my love.*

David pulled back. Their eyes met. "*Ya rouhi*," David whispered. *My soul.*

Kris kissed him. Their bodies were still joined. David still filled him, body and soul. "You are my soul, too."

# 17

## Falls Church, Virginia - August 2003

Kris stared at his ringing Blackberry. He blinked.

Why the fuck was George calling him at nine o'clock at night?

He pushed off David and sat up on their couch. They'd been watching the news, another nightly report of rising tensions in Iraq and Washington DC.

Five months after the invasion of Iraq, the moral undergirders of the war had collapsed. No weapons of mass destruction had been found. The image of an Iraq armed to the teeth, ready to support every jihadi in the world, had fallen apart. The supposed links to terrorist groups, the narrative that Iraq was a broad state-sponsor of terrorism that imperiled the world, had turned to dust and smoke. No al-Qaeda camps were found in the country. No terrorist training facilities. No documents outlining an alliance, no proof of cooperation, no indications anywhere.

Even Saqqaf had vanished from Kurdistan before the invasion began.

But online, his reputation had never been greater. The man Bin Laden had refused to meet, the thug Zahawi had decried as being too unintelligent for al-Qaeda, had turned into the darling of online jihadis. Moments after the secretary of state's speech to the UN, jihadist message boards had lit up with praises and blessings.

Saqqaf had gone from third-string nobody to the new terrorist superstar, thanks entirely to the United States.

David shifted, muting the TV. "Who is it?"

"George." Kris stared. His phone kept ringing. Should he answer? Or should he just toss his phone behind the couch?

He squeezed his eyes shut as he answered. "Caldera."

"*Took you long enough. Hope I didn't interrupt anything.*"

Kris snorted. "Should I tell you what you interrupted? Detail it out for you?"

"*No thanks.*" George's voice was thin, strained.

"Why do you guys always think the gays are hosting sex parties in dungeons, or about to blow a clown car of dick? Why do you straights always think it's some wild insanity? Can't we just be eating dinner? I mean, fabulously, of course—"

"*I'm regretting I called.*"

"Why *did* you call?"

"*'Cause now* I *need a favor.*"

"I really don't understand why you think I'd even be willing to take your call, much less give you a favor."

"*You're still on the line, aren't you?*"

Kris smiled. Was this friendship? George was an asshole who played politics with Langley, with Capitol Hill, but he'd come through for Kris more than once. He'd turned a blind eye in Afghanistan, in Pakistan. He'd hooked David up with his new job. David was finally finished with his Blackcreek training and was assigned to Langley, helping on the range with weapons qualifications and special training for advanced tactics. He spent a lot of time with the junior CIA analysts getting shuttled off to Iraq. Every night, he came home to Kris. Kris's apartment had become *theirs*. Cramped and too small, but *theirs*. George had helped make that happen.

"What do you need, George?"

"*You have an inescapable talent for slicing through any and all bullshit that comes at you, Caldera. It's one of the reasons you're so popular.* Especially *with the vice president.*"

"So we're acknowledging now that everything was bullshit?"

"*It's always been bullshit. We just all knew to keep our mouths shut.*"

"Well... you know me. That's *always* been my problem." He put as much sass into his voice as he could and turned the whole thing around, knowing George would go straight to what he was suggesting.

George coughed. "*Jesus, Caldera. I thought you were with Haddad now. Together forever, or isn't that why you wanted him at Langley?*"

He stayed quiet. George was still George. He didn't need to hand deliver his weaknesses to George. Not gift wrapped like that.

"*How soon can you be in Baghdad?*"

"Baghdad?"

"*The White House is shitting bricks over the situation on the ground. The chief of station in Baghdad wrote a report, and he used the word 'insurgency'. The White House went nuclear. Pushed back. No one has used the insurgency word, not yet.*"

"It's fucking obvious, isn't it?"

"*Someone is pumping the National Security Council up with stories of renegade Baathist loyalists and scattered pockets of violence. But our soldiers are being picked off. We're up to ten dead a week now, from snipers and IEDs. The White House is petrified this is turning into Vietnam.*"

"I believe I tried to warn them that could happen."

"*In fact, you did.*" George read the title of Kris's prewar analysis. "*'Security Challenges in a Post-Saddam Iraq—Navigating the Political Battlefield.' I fished this out of the agency's black hole.*"

"Glad it was taken seriously."

"*I need you here. I need your eyes, and your brain. I need your analysis. I need you to find out exactly what's going on. This is your specialty. Putting the pieces together like no one else can. Getting into their minds. Understanding the world from every dimension.*" He sniffed. "*I need your* help, *Caldera.*"

"And then what?"

"*I'll take what you say and force the White House to understand. No bullshit. Not this time.*" He sighed. "*Too many lives are on the line.*"

"That's always the justification, isn't it? 'Lives are on the line'. 'We're saving lives'. 'It will be better this way'."

"*Caldera. This is important. And yes, we can save lives. If we understand what's going on, we can fix it.*"

"Could have saved lives if someone had read my report before the war."

Silence.

"Book two tickets on the next flight to Baghdad. I'll be there."

"*Two*?"

"If you think I'm flying in without backup, without security, you're out of your mind. I'm bringing someone I trust."

"*Let me guess.*" George snorted. "*Haddad*?"

"We'll see you soon, George."

"*See you soon. And... thanks, Caldera.*"

**Baghdad, Iraq - August 2003**

Baghdad in August was like landing on the surface of Mercury. Heat blasted him in the face, as if the sun had been given a magnifying glass and was intent on burning Iraq off the planet. He squinted behind his sunglasses. Grabbed his bottle of water and downed the whole thing. Nothing helped.

A pair of F-15s roared down the next runway. In the heat haze, they seemed to melt as they lifted off, shimmering into the dull blue sky. Dust and sand filled the air, a grit Kris could taste between his teeth. Everything was dulled by the sand.

George had sent a car for them. They blazed through the Baghdad streets to the Green Zone in a blacked-out SUV, racing past Iraqis struggling with their broken-down sedans and dusty bicycles. Sullen stares from Iraqis waiting in long lines for food and fuel followed them.

"Those people look happy we're here?" Kris peered out the window. "They look happy with their liberators?"

David, silent since before they'd landed, stared at the people. "Their eyes are hard. They look like what my people looked like. Under Qaddafi, when I was a kid. A quiet rage against their oppressors mixed with a powerless void." He licked his lips. "It creates an impotent rage. Being someone else's afterthought."

"They've been abandoned." Kris saw it in the faces of the men and women they zipped by. "What kind of world have they been given now? We asked for their trust. And we've given them this."

There wasn't enough food. Most families relied on handouts from the UN, when before the war their cupboards had been full. Power was rarely on. Security blockades chopped the city up, leaving neighborhoods cut off from one another. Shadowy attacks on American soldiers and patrols had turned a creeping paranoia into a full-blown American-run police state. Instead of Saddam, the Americans were now the occupiers, controlling Baghdad's every move. And yet still, near-daily bomb blasts ambushed the military patrols and sniper fire rang from almost every neighborhood.

The Green Zone was Baghdad's riverside district, and the occupation's headquarters. The curving bends of the Tigris walled off the Green Zone, limiting the entrance to one six-lane highway. Concrete barriers guarded by tanks and Humvees and dozens of soldiers greeted them as they snaked their way through the entrance.

Saddam's palaces had been taken over and turned into the US Embassy and military command posts. Inside the Green Zone, verdant gardens stretched long, with scattered fountains spurting water in lazy arcs and dazzling flower beds sprawled in roaring bloom. Imperial palms reached for the sky, towering at least forty feet overhead. The Green Zone was manicured, ordered, and peaceful. The headquarters of the occupation was worlds apart from the Baghdad the Iraqis lived in.

Humvees shared space with SUVs. American flags flapped from every building, at the doors and on the roof. Helicopters roared overhead, sweeping low over the city. Some landed at the hospital. Others kept going, turning for the airport.

George met them on the steps of a grand former palace, marble and gold stretching as far as they could see. "Pretty incredible, huh?"

Kris peered over the top of his sunglasses at him. David hitched their duffel on his shoulder.

George scowled. "C'mon. I've got a lot to show you."

---

"We've had three major bombings that have made everyone sit up and take notice."

George personally walked Kris and David through the devastation and destabilization that had seized Iraq over the summer months, following the invasion. They spoke in his secured office, on the top floor of the palace overlooking the Tigris and the gardens. The air conditioning churned, keeping the room just on the wrong side of too cold. It was good to be the head of the CIA in Iraq.

"August seventh. The Jordanian Embassy was hit. Car bomb. Remote detonator. The driver parked his van and walked away. The blast tore a thirty-foot hole in the embassy. Destroyed cars up and down the street. Seventeen Iraqis were killed."

George slid photos across the desk. Kris and David looked together, flipping through images of bodies on the streets, crumpled cars, and the destroyed embassy. It looked like someone had taken an ice cream scoop to the building.

"This was the first time civilians were targeted. We don't understand why this target was picked. We don't know who ordered the bombing, either. We've been going through who was there that day, trying to see if it was an assassination that went large. Took out a bunch of collateral damage."

Kris stayed quiet. His brain churned.

"After, rumors ripped through the city. Some said an American helo had fired on the embassy. There were riots."

Sighing, George passed over a second set of photos. Another building destroyed, flattened by a bomb blast. A burned UN flag lay on the heaps of shattered concrete. “August nineteenth. Twenty-two people were killed at the UN headquarters here.”

“In the Green Zone?” David frowned.

“No. The UN kept their headquarters outside of the Green Zone.” George shook his head. “This was a suicide blast. The driver drove a flatbed up to the building and detonated. The head of the UN mission in Iraq was killed.”

“A suicide blast rules out the White House’s theory that this was the work of Saddam loyalists and disgruntled former Baathists.” Kris squinted.

“They have conceded that ‘foreign fighters’ are in Iraq. But nothing else.”

“Where are you on the investigation into the bombing?”

“We turned up electronic surveillance all over the country. NSA’s been vacuuming up all cell phone calls. We picked up a series of calls that are obviously coordinated attempts to relay messages. There’s no chatter. Just coded phrases, and then the callers hang up.”

“Have you started a phone web?”

George smiled. “Like you did in Pakistan? It was the first thing we did. We’ve got a network of numbers, but no names.”

“Where do the numbers come from?”

“Stolen prepaid SIM cards from Germany. God only knows how they ended up in Baghdad.”

“So that’s a dead end.”

“For now. We’re still listening to everything. Every call through those numbers.” Grimacing, George passed over the last set of photos, scenes of carnage and death that eclipsed both previous bombings. “And a few days ago. Friday, prayer day. The whole city, it seemed, was trying to go see Sheikh al-Ahmad, who had just returned from exile in Iran. He was a beloved Shia cleric. His sermon was on forming a unity government, on building bridges throughout the country.”

“*Was*?”

David looked down. Fisted his hands over his mouth.

“Twin car bombs killed eighty-five people at the mosque, and after, more were crushed to death in the stampede of panic. Al-Ahmad was vaporized. We only found a foot."

Kris closed his eyes.

"Riots have been going on for two days now. The Shia in the city and across Iraq are outraged."

"As they should be."

George shot him a look. "I've set you both up with rooms in the Green Zone. Caldera, you're in the secured wing of the embassy. CIA, FBI, NSA only. Haddad, you're with the contractors." He sketched a quick map, three lines showing the major roads and the river, and *X*s for buildings. He tapped a square he'd drawn, over a mile away from the embassy palace. "Here. The contractors are here. In the Imperial Palm Hotel."

"*George*."

"It's policy, Caldera." George held up his hands, shrugging. "No nonsecured personnel in the secured wings."

"So you're telling me that all the spouses, when they visit on the CIA's conjugal tour, stay in some hotel? And not a single CIA officer has brought someone back to their 'secured room'?" He made air quotes with his fingers as he snapped.

"I don't believe you two are married." George held Kris's icy stare.

"George—"

"These are the rules, Kris," George snapped. "I've gone to bat for you a hundred times already! Saved your job, and your ass! Before, and now. I'm not putting my neck on the line for this."

"Nice to know where your lines are, George." Kris stood. "I'll be at the Imperial Palm Hotel."

---

George gave them a bulletproof SUV and boxes of intelligence. Evidence reports from the FBI and military police, NSA intercepts, CIA and military intelligence analyses of the bombings.

George had hooked David up with a decent room, at least. Once, the hotel might have been something. Fifties art deco style seemed out of place in Baghdad. The hotel felt uncomfortably close to one Kris had spent Spring Break in one year on Miami Beach, sleeping his way through what seemed like an entire fraternity.

Instead of frat boys in popped collars, contractors swarmed the hotel, hanging out in the hallways and the lobby and in their jeeps and SUVs. They wore baseball caps and had weapons strapped to their thighs and under their arms, and their polos all had some security company emblem emblazoned on the chest. Every single one stared Kris up and down as he walked in, with his man bag and his linen suit, his pale-pink button-down, and his spiked hair.

It would be one of *those* places, one of *those* deployments.

David shouldered close to him, walking inside his shadow. Kris watched him glower back at the contractors, hold their stares until they were forced to look away. He put one hand on Kris's back, low, protective, possessing.

He smiled. Maybe it wouldn't be so terrible after all. Not this time.

Even though David was exhausted, he helped Kris set up the intel. The Jordanian Embassy bombing, the UN bombing, and the mosque bombing, each on a different wall. Kris pinned and taped evidence in clusters. Bomb fragments and wiring diagrams. Witness statements. Victim profiles. NSA intercepts and a copy of the phone web went on another wall.

As Kris started working through the intel, mumbling to himself, David lay down and started to snore.

---

Hours later, David woke, jet-lagged and out of sequence. A helicopter was rumbling by, flying low and rattling windows. Darkness stretched outside the Green Zone, spreading over Baghdad. Electricity was still off, except for the generators the Americans kept running to light up the highways and overpasses. Dots of illumination flickered throughout the city, a mix of generators and fires that built a paint-by-numbers canvas of post-invasion depression.

Inside the Green Zone, floodlights kept night at bay, lighting up the central roads and gardens in fluorescent daylight. Neon spilled into their hotel room.

Kris was on his fourth cup of hotel coffee, brewed from the bathroom coffeemaker, a relic of the seventies. David came up behind him, wrapping his arms around his waist and burying his face in his neck. "What have you found?"

"The bombs are the same. Old aircraft munitions, probably raided from one of Iraq's military bases during the invasion. The wiring fragments recovered are the same at each location."

"It's one person?"

"One bomb maker, or one organization being taught by a single bomb maker, yes. All three blasts were the work of a single entity."

"Any thoughts on who?"

"I have an idea. I want to connect more dots, though. Like these." Kris took David to the NSA intercepts. "We're seeing more of the relay messages. These callers are definitely using a code. '*Praises were given to Allah today*.' And the calls are going to the same numbers they went to after each of the other two bombings."

"We need to break into this cell. Find someone who is making or receiving these calls."

"There might be someone." Kris grabbed a folder, stamped with the Army's military police emblem. *800th MP Brigade* was emblazoned in bold, all caps. "This Saudi was picked up in a nightly sweep two days ago. His cell phone was confiscated. The Army just uploaded his cell number to the database."

"A match?"

"For one call. He called another number after the mosque bombing. He was recorded saying '*eighty-five pomegranates have fallen*'."

"Eighty-five people killed."

"His cell number doesn't show up after the other bombings, though. Could be unconnected. Could be something."

"We have to go talk to him. Where's he being held?"

"Abu Ghraib Prison."

---

Abu Ghraib stank like death, like terror.

Mass graves from Saddam's era were being dug up outside the walls, filled with bodies of political prisoners rounded up in sweeps during his reign. Hundreds had been executed at a time. Old bloodstains marred the dingy concrete, the brown sandy walls.

Silence, heavy and filled with secrets, surrounded Kris and David as they followed a young Army MP soldier through the prison wards. Kris felt a weight on his chest, like something was trying to get out, claw its way free. He felt eyeballs on him, prisoners watching him and David. Men in filthy orange jumpsuits sat with their backs against their cell walls.

He heard every squeak of his boots against the old linoleum.

"In here." The MP guiding them spoke for the first time. "Prisoner number seven-nine-three-tango." He gestured to a locked cell, and a man inside. "Tango for suspected terrorist."

Kris nodded. "We'll take it from here."

"I'm not allowed to leave anyone alone with the prisoners, sir."

"I *said* we'll take it from here."

"No, *sir. No one* is allowed to have unsupervised or unrestricted access to the prisoners. Especially the tango prisoners." The MP squared his shoulders. He spread his feet, intent on staying.

Kris rolled his eyes. His job was that much harder, suddenly. How did he build a conversation with a prisoner while his jailer was standing over his shoulder? He stepped up to the bars. "*As-salaam-alaikum.*"

The MP's eyes flashed. He stared at Kris.

"*Wa alaikum as-salaam,*" the prisoner said. The words seemed dragged from him, reluctantly. But he still said them. For true believers, it was heretical to refuse to respond to the blessing and greeting used by the Prophet.

"Your name is Rashid?" Kris spoke in Arabic.

The man stared at Kris.

"Can you tell me about the call you made on your cell phone right after the mosque bombing?"

"*Allahu Akbar*, we sent the innovators to the grave."

Innovators, a fanatical Sunni insult against the Shia sect. Rashid was definitely a fanatic, a fundamentalist, and a violent extremist, influenced by twisted ideology.

"He only ever says nonsense like this," the MP grunted.

Kris arched his eyebrow at the MP. "You know Arabic? But you have no idea what he's saying?"

"He's probably insane." The MP shrugged. "It's probably all meaningless."

Kris shook his head. Tried to come up with something to say to the MP, something that could cut through the shocking ignorance, the complete lack of knowledge, at all, about the culture, the religion, the million myriad nuances that defined a people and a region that couldn't be brushed aside and ignored, or destroyed and cast aside. But where to begin? Where on earth to begin?

His job was Rashid. The bombings. Kris turned back to the cell. "Why are you in Iraq?"

Rashid smiled. "I came in the name of the holy warrior. The fierce one, the lion who will rip the throat out from the Americans."

"You came to wage jihad? Fight the Americans?"

"We will destroy the Americans. Death to America."

"Who is the holy warrior?"

"His name will be on everyone's lips. He will be known to all."

"Perfect. Then tell me his name now."

"Saqqaf. The man who will destroy the Americans."

Fuck. Kris had known, from the moment George started talking about the Jordanian Embassy bombing, that it was Saqqaf. Saqqaf, the devil the US had built up to justify the invasion, had hinged their war on.

"Did Saqqaf give you this phone? When you got to Iraq?"

"Death to America!" Rashid shouted. "*Death to America! Saqqaf! Saqqaf!*"

The MP pushed Kris out of the way. He ripped out his baton and slammed the stick against the bars. "*Shut it,*" he bellowed. "Shut your mouth!"

Rashid bared his teeth. He trembled, and his fingers clawed at the stone wall behind him. Echoes of shouts reverberated through the prison wing. Other voices rose, repeating Rashid's shout. "*Saqqaf! Saqqaf*!"

The MP turned on Kris. "It's time for you to *leave*. Now."

---

They were deposited outside the prison gates by a silent driver, left in the dust in the visitor parking area. Sand blew, the fine grit coating every inch of every exposed surface. Hot air blasted Kris, like standing in front of his blow-dryer set to high.

"Something's off in there." David squinted back at the prison, rising behind the tall brick walls. Concertina wire gleamed in the punishing sunlight. The American flag flapped weakly over the prison. "Something's very wrong. Did you see the blood?"

"On the ground? Walking in?"

"In his cell." David had leaned against the wall, standing on Kris's right. He'd been able to see into Rashid's cell at an angle, something Kris couldn't. "On the walls. Close to the bars. Fresh bloodstains, and older ones."

"From Rashid, you think?"

David nodded, once.

Kris squeezed his eyes shut. Zahawi, bloody, soaked, and screaming, flashed behind his eyelids. The shrieks, the sounds he'd made as he'd struggled. The way the blood had flowed with the water pouring over him. Red swirling in the water, like ink or paint, indelible confessions of what had happened, written on Kris's memories for the rest of his life. Onto his soul.

"You think—"

"Something is very wrong in there."

"The Geneva Conventions apply here." Kris's palms slicked with sweat. "The Red Cross, they've been to the prison. This prison. They've done inspections. It's not happening again. It's not."

David stared at him. Even through his sunglasses, Kris could see his squinted eyes, his disbelief.

"We need to get Saqqaf. We need to find him, destroy his network. Put an end to his attacks before they spiral out of control." Kris peered at the horizon, lost in a heat haze and the burning sand. Baghdad shimmered beyond, still and silent, but humming with a searing fury. He could taste it, between the diesel fuel and the rot, the *eau de invasion*. The smells of an occupier unable to provide for the nation. "This city, this country, is on the brink."

"We need to talk to the Iraqis. Listen to them, and what's really going on."

---

The CIA was focusing most of its angst and anxiety on the region north and west of Baghdad, nicknamed the Sunni Triangle. Extra military units were sent to the region. Kris scanned the multitude of files, the military's catalog of the region, until he found a name.

"Omar Abu Hussain. He's a tribal leader outside Ramadi. He was named the local negotiator with the Marine Corps unit. Things haven't gone well."

They drove out that afternoon, heading west on Highway 1, the highway going straight through the desert to the Syrian border. They passed Fallujah, passed military checkpoints and slow-rolling convoys, until they reached Ramadi on the edge of the western desert.

Hard stares greeted them—long, lingering looks from men in checkered keffiyehs and billowing robes. One man eventually gave them directions to Abu Hussain's ranch. They bounced along a dusty road until they pulled up to a low-slung dwelling of sandstorm-blasted concrete. Sheep roamed in a wire pen, chewing on scrub desert grasses. Few trees dotted his land, casting slender parentheses of shade on the baked desert ground.

A stooped man stared at them from the doorway.

Kris and David greeted Omar Abu Hussain with blessings, and he invited them in for tea. His wife and daughter, triangles in black robes in the kitchen, scurried into the backroom. Kris spotted his daughter peeking around the hanging carpet that divided the home.

"Please, Abu Hussain, will you share with us what you have experienced? What is happening here, with the Americans?"

Abu Hussain looked away, staring at nothing and everything. His eyes pinched. "The Americans don't understand anything," he murmured. "Nothing, nothing."

"Please, tell us of your experiences." David set down his tea and leaned forward. "Please."

"Iraq used to be the center of the Islamic world. Baghdad used to be the home of learning, of science, of mathematics. This desert, this land, gave birth to language, to algebra, to astronomy. To law, even. Iraq, this land we stand on, is not just some land between lines on a map. The Americans, they believe that history begins with them." Abu Hussain shook his head. "Iraq, the tribes that make this country, the families who have built this land, have existed for over six thousand years. But the Americans are undoing all of that."

"What happened?" David spoke softly.

"Promises. There were so many promises. Life would be better after Saddam. But curfews! And roadblocks. Checkpoints. How am I supposed to deliver my meat and my wool to the market with these restrictions? I cannot travel in the morning when it is cool and when the meat can stay fresh. I cannot travel in a large truck, which means I cannot transport enough to sell to make a living. And no one can buy anything! The markets are bombed! No one comes out any longer. People go hungry and my meat goes bad. How can this country function if food cannot be brought to the people?"

"There was a protest against the curfew," he said slowly. "It was peaceful. But the Americans..." His eyes squeezed shut. "They got scared. They shot at the protestors. A dozen men and boys were killed." Abu Hussain's eyes drifted to a picture hanging on the wall, a picture of his son with Arabic circling the frame and written onto the stark walls. "We tried, we *tried* to keep calm. To not create problems with the Americans. Finally, we, as a tribe, agreed. We would ask the Americans to give us a tribal solution. They should pay *diyya*."

"Blood money," David whispered, nodding.

"Pay to support the families, we said. Pay to help them with the loss of their fathers, their husbands, their sons. Pay to help the families and to show them you mean no harm. That you are sorry. Pay so that the sons will not grow up to hate the Americans and turn to the fighters."

"Did the Americans pay?"

Abu Hussain spat. "They offered. We refused. The amount they offered..." Tears filled his eyes. He cupped one hand over his mouth. "They offered a thousand dollars. For a life. Only a thousand dollars. We saw how little they value us. What they thought an Iraqi life was worth." He rocked back, mournful prayers bursting from him.

David joined in, reaching across the carpet for his hand. He recited the prayers for the dead with Abu Hussain, bowing his head.

When his eyes finally dried, Abu Hussain walked them out. He held David's hand for a long moment, staring at the ground. "The killings will get worse," he said softly. "There is no trust, not anymore. Not for the Americans, and not for the Shia. Some in my tribe have formed secret groups. For self-defense, they said. But now, self-defense is also going on the attack. Against American troops."

"That will not help, Abu Hussain." David squeezed his hand. "That will not help anyone."

"There is a Jordanian. He pays the Iraqis who join his movement. He pays lots of money. Far more than the Americans offered."

"Saqqaf?" Kris's stomach tied itself in knots, waiting for the answer.

Abu Hussain nodded. "He is building an *army*."

---

"It's Saqqaf."

Kris crossed his legs and stared at George. The air conditioning in George's office was still too cold. The marble floors and gleaming columns, holding up the vaulted ceiling, reflected the cool air into the massive office.

George tossed his pen onto his desk and cursed. He sat back in his chair.

"It's Saqqaf. The man the White House used as a pretense for this war. Who was supposed to be killed in the invasion? But now, thanks to the *amazingly* impressive job you all are doing, he's become empowered. Thanks to the complete abrogation of the American military to secure the country, he's found himself a whole new battlefield." Kris pretended to think, squinting as he tapped his chin. "I believe I predicted something... exactly like this."

"How do you know it's Saqqaf?" George looked like Kris was telling him to eat glass, chew nails, go pound sand until Kris got tired of watching him.

"The bombs come from a single entity. A single organization using the same munitions, the same wiring. The intercepts tracked a cell phone to a recently arrested prisoner in Abu Ghraib. We went to talk to him. He came to Iraq from Saudi to fight for the 'holy warrior' who would kill all the Americans. He named this inspirational holy warrior: Saqqaf. He started a chant in the prison. Then we drove to Ramadi. Talked to one of the tribal elders outside the city. He said Saqqaf is paying big bucks to anyone who joins him. And that there are cells of fighters forming out there in Anbar Province fighting with him. You invaded, and you swore it would be better, you swore to the world. And now you've given an actual terrorist the means to build an army."

"Why these targets? Why these three?"

"Saqqaf hates Jordan. His homeland. He hates everything about Jordan, the monarchy, the royal family, the Mukhabarat. He wants to destroy Jordan. Jordan was the first Arab nation to open an embassy in Baghdad. He could take out two birds with one stone. Foment unrest and suspicion and attack his most hated government. The UN? Destroy any hope of NGOs and aid organizations that wanted to enter the reconstruction space. How many have pulled out since the UN was bombed? How many won't come now? How much hurt will the Iraqis feel now that humanitarian aid, the most critical piece of reconstruction, isn't coming?"

“And the mosque?”

“He planted a bomb inside the cracks that were already splintering in the sectarian divide. He’s trying to divide the country, George. Put the US in the center of a three-way civil war. Us against the Sunni and the Shia, and against Saqqaf and his army. And it’s working. He’s succeeding.”

George leaned forward, hunching over his desk as he scrubbed his face with his hands. His hair, graying, stuck up at every angle.

“The White House is going to shit. Actually shit,” George breathed.

“This isn’t a victory, George. This isn’t *Mission Accomplished*. This is the start of a fucking nightmare.”

# 18

**Baghdad, Iraq - March 2004**

The walls shook, windows rattling. Glass tinkled. Everyone looked up. Froze.

Beyond the Green Zone, a column of black smoke rose above a pillar of flame, a billowing fireball that stretched for the dusty sky. Three more columns of dark smoke, not yet put out from earlier conflagrations, dotted the horizon, just to the north.

"Another one." The duty officer in the joint intelligence command center, inside Saddam's Republican Palace in the heart of the Green Zone, called. "Mark it."

One of the junior enlisted soldiers scurried to the main white-board front and center in the cavernous ballroom converted for the intel cell's use. He dutifully ticked off another attack in the running daily tally, then marked the time in a separate grid. He waited, pen poised, for the radio to announce the target, the location, the victims. Facts, numbers, points on a map. Quantifiable costs in the insurgency.

David looked down. His fists clenched. Every column of smoke, every roaring fireball, was another broken life. Broken US soldiers and broken Iraqis, trying to keep going in the day-by-day hellscape the country had fallen into. Forty-three attacks, on average, every day, by the command center's official ticker. Forty-three attacks, killing dozens, sometimes hundreds, wounding thousands.

Baghdad was a city of widows and orphans, of tears and shrieks and lamentations. The smell of death and rot hovered over the city, a festering, fetid miasma. The city, the country, was dying, day by day.

The White House pushed for the removal of the CIA station chief in Baghdad after Kris's report. George took over running the CIA in Iraq, and his first act was to beg Kris to stay, beg him to lead the hunt for Saqqaf.

"You're the expert in hunting these guys. You captured Zahawi. You wrote the book on how to hunt these guys. Everyone copies what you did there, in Pakistan. But this is Iraq. And you're the one who predicted all this shit, predicted Saqqaf. We need you again. We need you, Kris."

It was praise Kris hadn't wanted, and David watched him seethe as he accepted it, and accepted the assignment.

"I really hate '*I told you so*'," Kris had said. "It's used against me too many times. '*I told you he was gay. I told you he couldn't do whatever, because he's gay*'." He'd shaken his head, staring down over Saddam's fountains, lips pursed, eyes narrowed. "But *I fucking told you so*," he'd hissed. "And I fucking told the vice president, too!"

Kris went back on the hunt.

Saqqaf was his prey.

Being in Iraq was like being in a Salvador Dali painting, with reality melting on all sides, slipping and sliding away. Iraq, with its dusty air and faded light, the stench of rot and death and diesel, the concrete barriers that rose and rose and rose, dividing the city into siege zones, into sectarian crises and splinter cells. Life was cut off, constrained, checkpointed. Life was suspicious. Seething hatred filled the streets, as thick as Baghdad dust, heavier than the diesel fumes and the sweat. Hatred was a stench that couldn't be washed away.

David existed within and outside the hatred. Driving in Humvees, in bulletproof SUVs, the glares on the streets turned hard and cold toward him. He was an occupier. He was one of them.

Walking on the street, undercover, dressed in jeans and a long-sleeved shirt, leaving behind the bulletproof armor and the polo emblazoned with the Blackcreek logo, and leaving behind the weapons strapped to his thigh and under his arms, he became human again.

It was his Libyan blood, his burnished skin, his dark hair. It was Arabic that came effortlessly to his lips, with an accent that couldn't be faked. It was the way he moved and flowed with the Arab culture, slipping back into the tides of his youth, living in his memories in the present all over again. It was the thousand and one judgments that came at him, from a thousand and one stares. To be American, and to be Arab. To be a collaborator, and, later, to be one of the dirty Arabs on the street, sweating under the gaze of the American soldiers, hidden behind their sunglasses and their tanks. To be viewed, by everyone, as something other than what he was. A thousand and one stares. A thousand and one ways to be perceived. The kaleidoscope of his soul shifted, twisted. Who he was changed again.

He was a puzzle that the world constantly played with. His soul twisted and turned a hundred times throughout the day.

Every night, he returned to Kris's arms. Kris was the one person in the world who didn't demand something from him, didn't judge him for the way he listened to the *azan* with his eyes closed. Who never asked him to choose, American or Arab, gay or Muslim, him or them. Kris let him exist, in all his mismatched parts, even if his existence felt like an ink blot stain or a bug splat against a windshield.

Kris seemed to want nothing from him except his blemished life, and his whole heart. He could give those to Kris.

Iraq *demanded* his anguish, his rage. The CIA and Blackcreek *demanded* his wrath, his fury, his vengeance.

Whispers from the desert scratched at his soul.

But his heart quieted when he returned to Kris, when they rejoined at the end of the day. Kris, exhausted after his hunting, his managing an intelligence operation that rivaled the size and scope of what they'd built in Pakistan, had time to smile at him, hold his hand. They drank Baghdad Martinis—boiled water—on their balcony and watched the sun set, listened to the call to prayer as they held hands.

Words from the Quran came whispering back to him, out of nowhere, in the quiet moments he shared with Kris. *And of everything, We created pairs. Heaven and Earth. Night and day. Sun and moon. Sea and Shore. Light and darkness.* David gazed at Kris. *You, for me.*

*Subhanallah*, he loved Kris so much. Loved him for loving him, and never demanding. Loved him for knowing parts and pieces were broken or missing, tarnished or destroyed.

Kris had those parts within him, too. They'd never spoken about it, but it was just something they knew. He loved Kris for that, for the shared ways they'd moved through the world and had each gotten kicked a dozen times or more. Coming from nothing and fighting for more, being brown in a world full of white, being gay in a world full of straight. Kris had the same bruises on his soul that David had, all the sighs and side-eyes that came with growing up poor, brown, and gay. They'd both been outsiders, both been relegated to the margins. They'd both fought for everything they'd had, every single scrap. Like recognized like, it seemed. They'd never had to fight each other. They were survivors together, them against the world. The whole world seemed to be dividing into lines, into demarcations, into *us* versus *them* versus *the other*.

But not between him and Kris. They were the same, as if half of David had been split off and put into Kris, like the Quran said about the souls of lovers. That soulmates had known each other before life, before time, and once on the earth, they were searching for each other again. Kris was that, to him.

And Kris, like David, seemed to want nothing more than to be loved for who he was. And, by Allah, he loved Kris for all of who he was, and more.

He tried to care for Kris the best he way could, repay Kris for the peace his presence brought to David's existence. He made love to Kris until Kris screamed his name, until he was limp and spent and grinning ear to ear. He rubbed his shoulders every day, tried to relieve the strain of carrying the weight of the CIA's hopes and the White House's fears on his shoulders. He held him every night, whispered *I love you* into Kris's hair before he fell asleep.

If he could have, he would have bottled those days and nights, kept them hidden away, able to be lived in and remembered, like slipping into a dream as easily as one could slip into a lake.

But autumn turned to winter, and then to spring.

Ramadan came, and with it, the bloodiest surge of the insurgents. Fury boiled over. Hatred turned against everyone and everything.

Kris took command of a fusion cell, working in tandem with General Ramos and a joint task force of Special Forces operators responsible for finding and striking at the cells of fighters aligned with Saqqaf. David saw some of his old friendly teammates, and some who hated his guts. Every night, Kris and General Ramos sent teams into the cities, raiding houses, searching for fighters. Searching for Saqqaf.

David spent the mornings with Kris, working through the raw intelligence gained, assessing the men arrested during the night before they were sent to Abu Ghraib.

"We need more intelligence!" General Ramos constantly bitched. "We need more actionable intelligence. People to arrest and get off the streets. Terrorists to interrogate."

"We need *better* intelligence," Kris snapped back. "Not more garbage. Better *quality* intel. We need more people on the streets, more people building bridges. More people willing to talk to us."

General Ramos snorted at him, and then called Abu Ghraib, demanding more information be extracted from the prisoners. "There's eight thousand terrorists in that prison," he barked. "Get them to talk!"

Interrogators flew in from Guantanamo Bay, from the CIA's detention center and interrogation unit. Trainers arrived, sent to help at Abu Ghraib. Information began flowing.

Most of it was useless.

In the afternoons, David hit the streets of Baghdad and the Sunni triangle, sliding into the rhythms of the occupied city and the tides of fury, rage, and impotent helplessness. On the streets, he was Dawood, a displaced Libyan who used to work in the oil fields and in the refineries, but had been ousted, like so many others, thanks to de-Baathification. He listened to the rage, the street corner wailers, the coffee shop arguments with other out-of-work Iraqis and bitter denunciations of the occupiers and the Americans.

"The Americans, they're rounding everyone up. Everyone. Not just the Islamists and the insurgents."

"Dawood, you should be careful." An old man, a former teacher, who smoked and sat in the same café everyday drinking coffee and chatting with the neighborhood men, called out to him. "The Americans, they're arresting all unwed men! Anyone from this high up!" He held his hand just above his waist. A boy's height.

He played soccer in streets overflowing with sewage alongside high school dropouts and smoked cigarettes on street corners, beneath gas hawkers bellowing their prices for fuel, a hundred times any affordable rate.

"I heard we're not supposed to play on Karraba Street on Thursday." One of the players passed him the ball. He juggled it between his feet, kicked it down the block. It bounced off a burned-out car, bounced in a pile of sewage.

"Where did you hear that?"

The player shrugged. "Around. Things get said, you know?" He chuckled. "I don't want to get—" He made an explosion sound, and his hands burst open. "You should stay away too."

David hid from American convoys and felt the burning gaze of a Humvee's turret gunner zeroing his sights on the center of David's forehead.

"Do you ever wish things would go back to the way they were?" Samir, another out-of-work young Iraqi, smoked with him on a street corner, hidden away from the American convoy blazing down the Baghdad street. Car horns blared, and the Americans fired warning shots into the street, forcing the Iraqis to drive over each other to get out of the convoy's way. Cars crunched. Glass broke. Curses and shouts filled the air.

"There's no going back."

"There's no going forward." Samir shrugged. "What do we do? We have nothing. No country. No jobs. No pride." He grabbed David's shoulder. "At least we have today, and each other, my friend."

Hatred, a palpable, pure thing, grew like cancer, like a tumor David could hold. Could taste, choking him and everyone in Baghdad.

He felt, with a surety of rage, what Saqqaf was tapping into on the streets of Iraq. There was a blood haze rising, a fury cresting, that was going to swallow the world.

## Baghdad, Iraq - March 31, 2004

*Where are you?*

The text came in midmorning. David had slipped out of the Green Zone early, heading to one of his meeting points. He ducked into an alley, skipping over a puddle of sewage and discarded shell casings.

Kris kept texting. *Where are you? Answer me. I need you to text back, right now. Right now.*

*[I'm here. I'm on Karada Road.]*

*Thank fucking God. Get back here. Now. Please. PLEASE.*

*[What happened?]*

*Get back here.*

He pocketed his phone and turned around, heading for the Green Zone. He twisted and turned, ducked into a café for a coffee and smoked two cigarettes on two different street corners, making sure he wasn't followed, before entering the Green Zone cordon. Half a mile of concrete barriers topped with razor wire funneled all pedestrians into a single file line. Barely anyone wanted to enter the Green Zone that morning. David, dressed in his Iraqi street clothes, moved quickly past the overwatch posts, the tanks and giant machine guns glaring down onto the pedestrians in the concrete tube.

At the first of three checkpoints, a soldier ordered him to his knees fifty feet from the sandbag barrier. "Get the *fuck* down! Hands on your fucking head! *Now*! *Now*!"

Twelve rifles centered on his head.

David slowly dropped to his knees. Placed his hands behind his head.

Four soldiers tackled him, pushing his face into the ground. One stepped on his cheek, the sole of his boot digging into his skin.

Old pain, the remembrance of his childhood, flared. *You are worth less than the filth I step in every day*. He winced and closed his eyes.

"What the fuck are you doing here?" One of the soldiers, a squad sergeant, bellowed. Hands rifled over him, roughly searching his body. They lifted his clothes, grabbed his chest, his stomach. Grabbed his crotch and fisted around his cock. "What the fuck are you doing here, huh? Come to blow yourself up? Come to kill more Americans? Huh?"

"Sergeant!" One of the soldiers searching him found the badge he kept sewn inside his jeans, his contractor badge and his CIA ID. The soldier passed them to his sergeant.

"Are these fucking faked?" The sergeant bellowed. "Did you fake these credentials?"

His cell phone, lying next to his head, buzzed. Every soldier whirled, pointing weapons at him and at the phone.

"It's a CIA officer calling," he said slowly. "Please answer it."

"Shut the fuck up!" The sergeant gave him a love tap with the butt of his rifle, slamming the stock against his cheek. His face ricocheted off the ground, gritty sand coating his mouth, his nose, his eyes. He tasted blood. "You want us to pick up the phone and blow ourselves up?"

Another soldier had disappeared back to the Humvee with his credentials. David saw him on the radio, frantically gesturing to David and then to the creds, lying on the passenger seat. After a moment, he jogged back to the sergeant and whispered in his ear.

"You fucking wait right there," the sergeant spat at David. "Fall back," he grunted to his men. "Keep eyes on him."

Nine minutes passed as David tasted his blood and smelled the fetid fumes of Baghdad's streets. Felt the dirt and the filth seep into his body. Felt the hatred of the American soldiers burn into him, and felt the weight of their half-squeezed rifles pointed at his head. Never, in his whole life, from Afghanistan to Somalia to escaping Libya, had he felt closer to death.

He breathed in and out, keeping his eyes closed. *Kris. You will come. You'll always come. I didn't answer your call. You won't ignore that. You'll come for me.*

Another voice rose inside him, a voice he recognized, and yet did not. It sounded like his father, but not. Like the voices of a thousand old men and old women combined, like wisdom and experience and age. Like humanity, but more than humanity.

*Call on me, and I will answer you.*

His breath faltered. His gasp blew a puff of dust from the street. Sand collected on his bloody lips.

*If Allah should aid you, no one can overcome you.*

*Years.* It had been years and years since he'd prayed. The last time he had was before flying out of Egypt, before heading to America. He could barely mumble through the tears, then. He'd never had to pray without his father beside him.

In America, his mother turned deeper into her faith while David spun out into the waters of MTV and football and his first fumblings with another boy.

*Allah*, he whispered. How did he even begin? What did he even say? What did you say to someone you had ignored for decades? Had turned your back on? What did you say to your God who had let your father be taken and killed?

Tears burned through him following a burst of rage, white-hot agony at the memory. The afternoon when the men had come, had dragged his father out of their house. His mother, sobbing, trying to plead with them. The Mukhabarat had backhanded her, pushed her down. His father had tried to break free, tried to run back. He was like an animal, desperate to get to his wife, to get back to his home.

"*Dawood!*" He'd screamed. "*Dawood! La hawla wala quwwata illa billah!*" *There is no power nor strength save in Allah.*

The Mukhabarat had punched him, knocked him down again.

A week before, his family had celebrated David's tenth birthday. His father had given him prayer beads and a djellaba, a mini replica of his father's, to wear to the mosque. He'd loved it, had worn it night and day, trying to look like his father. All he wanted, when he was nine years old, was to be the perfect replica of his father when he grew up.

"*Dawood...*" His father had locked his gaze on him, lying on the sandy ground, blood splattering his white djellaba. "*Habibi...*"

Those were his father's last words to him. The men, the Mukhabarat, had grabbed him and shoved him in their car, driven away.

He had become his father, beaten and bloody in the street, put on the ground by another man.

"What the fuck!" Kris's shrill screech, his outrage, shredded the memory. David's eyes flew open. He was still on the street, still cheek-down in the blood and the sand.

But not in Libya. In Iraq.

And Kris had come for him.

"Put your *fucking* rifles down," Kris shrieked. "Put them fucking down, now!" He held his ID in front of him like an indictment, like a warrant for the soldiers' souls. A proclamation, declaring they had done fucked up. "He's fucking CIA, you assholes!"

One of the soldiers, a young private, helped David stand. The kid was maybe eighteen. Maybe younger. He had baby fat in his cheeks and pimples on his nose. When David looked like that, he'd been at football practice, watching the track team in their running shorts. He'd gone to high school dances. He hadn't held a rifle.

"Sorry," the kid mumbled. He wouldn't look at David.

Kris appeared at his side, his hands everywhere, putting David's clothes back to rights, running over his skin, holding his face.

"You fucking assholes hit him," Kris snarled. "What the fuck!"

"We're on high alert," the sergeant growled. "You know that. You put it out."

"He's fucking one of us." Kris smoothed back David's hair.

David held his wrists. "What happened?" Sand and blood smeared on his lips as he spoke.

Tears simmered at the edges of Kris's eyes. His lips moved, but nothing came out. He cupped David's cheek, his thumb stroking over David's growing bruise, the knot from the sergeant's love tap. "Fallujah," he whispered. "*Everything* has changed."

---

The command center was deathly quiet.

Sixteen video cameras played different angles of the same scene. Two dilapidated SUVs, burning to a husk. Their metal frames were ashy skeletons, engulfed in an inferno.

Charred bodies, Blackcreek contractors, pulled from the flames. Beaten. Dragged through the streets.

"Oh God, they were Blackcreek contractors," Kris whispered. "They were *Blackcreek*! Do you have any idea what I thought, when the first reports came in? Do you have any idea—"

He grabbed Kris and pulled him into his arms, held him as Kris sobbed, his muffled cries against David's chest the only sound in the command center. Kris clung to him, his fingers digging in to his skin, as if David would disappear, as if he wasn't really there, was only a figment of Kris's imagination.

"I'm okay," he breathed into Kris's hair. "I'm okay, Kris."

The screens kept playing, revealing the barbarity of the morning. Blackened bodies dragged across the road. A riot had formed around the bodies. Chanting, cheering, faces bursting with excitement. The madness of a mob. Insurgents, jihadis, masked men in black, in the center. Taking the burned bodies, the corpses. Dragging them to a steel lattice bridge, notated on the military's maps as landmark "*Brooklyn*".

Sometimes, it looked just like America, like looking at the steel girders of the Big Apple, and it was easy to imagine the Hudson or the East River was just beyond, instead of the endless wash of desert.

Ropes were thrown over the girders.

Kris squeezed his eyes shut. He wouldn't watch. His lips thinned, pressed together until they went white.

David had to see. He had to see the swing, the strain in the rope. Had to see the crazed crowd cheer, chant wildly, convinced they had just done something wonderful, something to celebrate. He had to see the bodies, broken and suspended, left for all to stare at, to judge. And for the world to judge them, in return.

He had to see.

He'd seen bloodlust consume people's soul, their humanity, until there was nothing left.

He'd seen a man hung before.

**Baghdad, Iraq - April 28, 2004**

*"This is a picture of an Iraqi prisoner of war, and according to the US Army, Americans did this to him."*

The man stood on a crate, hooded, with wires stuck to his fingers, his penis, and shoved up his ass.

His image went around the world in four seconds.

More pictures followed. Iraqis in dog collars and on leashes. Naked, and forced to masturbate. Naked, and staked in pyramids. Covered in feces. Bound and stretched against metal bars. Hooded, and forced to simulate sex with one another.

Humiliation screamed from the images. Ravaging, aching, burning humiliation.

Every Arab felt it, in their bones. The past and the present, eternally connected in the Arab soul, twisted again. A thousand years of Western aggression distilled into a series of photos, proof positive of a thousand years of mistrust, betrayal, and anguish.

Iraqis flooded the streets. Riots erupted around the Middle East. US Embassies locked their gates.

"It's Abu Ghraib," David breathed, watching the news report for the fifteenth time. "We walked down that hallway. We saw those prisoners."

If Kris hadn't come for him that day he was on the ground at the military checkpoint, would he have been taken to Abu Ghraib? He was nothing but an Arab to the soldiers, and Arabs were just targets. Humiliation had washed his soul on the street, shoved to the ground and stepped on, treated like an animal. They would have thought nothing of sending him to Abu Ghraib, where he would have been treated the same way.

David rewound the tape and watched the news report again.

Once, when he was a boy, he'd looked at the United States of America with hope. His tearstained soul had lost his father, and he'd been promised that things would be better in America. Everyone told him, *America is free. America is good. America is where you will have a better life.*

He'd had *so* much hope, flying cross the ocean to a land that seemed almost mythical. If it was true, if he could really live a free life in America, then he'd give everything back to America, he'd promised as the plane slowly descended into New York City.

Thirty-four years old and a lifetime later, it was next to impossible to resurrect that same hope he'd once felt. His soul felt dirty, tarnished with the buildup of things he'd done, the things he'd seen. Things he'd condoned, for being a part of the silence.

He froze the video, staring at the image of the hooded man on the crate.

Could his father be under that hood?

Could *he*?

What was the difference between that man and him?

Was he—were they—on the wrong side of history?

Where had *everything* gone wrong?

---

Abu Ghraib was the chip in the dam, the first domino to fall.

George, ashen and shaking, called them to his office nearly every day.

They didn't like each other, not really. David looked at George the way he looked at most spineless bureaucrats. Medical marvels, humans capable of existing without spines or the guts to do anything meaningful at all. Afghanistan, all they'd been through there, was a distant memory, Pakistan and Thailand far more vivid.

"There's been a leak," George told them. His voice shook. "Director Thatcher called. Said it's going to hit tomorrow's papers."

"There are a thousand leaks, George." Kris smoked inside George's office, blowing his cigarette smoke over George's desk. "What are you talking about now?"

"I'm talking about what doesn't exist!" George snapped. "The detainee program! I'm talking about Zahawi."

Kris's chuckle was dark, the kind of laugh the devil made when he came for Faust. "Out of everything that is leaked, *that* deserves to be made public. It deserves a Congressional inquiry and a fucking indictment."

"Are you so Goddamn naive that you think it was just a handful of people? Some cabal of evil that needs to be taken down? It fucking went to the top!" George trembled, from his fingers to his toes. He tried to clench his hands, ball them up. His fists shook on his desktop. "And *you* were there. You both were."

Kris blew smoke in George's face.

## Washington DC - May 2004

The president admitted the detainee program existed.

He admitted to enhanced interrogation techniques.

He admitted to waterboarding detainees in the CIA's detainee program.

Director Thatcher resigned from the CIA, in the outcry that followed.

But it was the vice president who came out swinging, insisting that the United States did not torture anyone. "*Look, waterboarding is not torture. Based on the legal definition of torture, we do not torture anyone.*"

"*The legal definition as defined by this administration*?" the interviewer asked.

The vice president ignored him. "*We use aggressive interrogation techniques. And I do not apologize for that. Not ever.*"

**Baghdad, Iraq - May 2004**

The video was five minutes and thirty-seven seconds long. It was uploaded to a jihadi website that had been a clearinghouse of Saqqaf's. They watched it together in George's office.

The video opened on a man dressed all in black, his face covered in a balaclava, standing over a pale man in an orange jumpsuit, his arms and legs bound.

"*Nation of Islam, great news*!" the man in black boomed. He read from a script that he held in both hands. "*The signs of dawn have begun and the winds of victory are blowing*!"

"It's him." Kris fought back a gag. "I know the voice." He reached for David.

"You're *sure*?" George hovered over Kris's right shoulder, General Ramos over his left. "We *have* to be sure."

"It has all the hallmarks of Saqqaf's messaging. It's his style."

"Why the orange jumpsuit? Saqqaf doesn't keep prisoners," Ramos asked.

"It's because of Abu Ghraib." David, finally, spoke. "In Abu Ghraib, you put prisoners in orange jumpsuits. He's drawing a direct line between the two."

Ramos glowered at David. "When you say 'you', do you mean the military, or do mean Americans? Because I thought you were American."

David blinked at Ramos.

The video kept playing, churning onward in George's office. Saqqaf issued a blistering tirade, berating the Americans and their occupation.

"*How can a free Muslim sleep soundly while Islam is being slaughtered, its honor bleeding and the images of shame in the news of the abuses of the Muslim men and women in the prison of Abu Ghraib? Where is your zeal and where is your anger?*"

David's gaze bored into Ramos.

*"O, to the president of the Great Satan, I deliver this warning. Hard days are coming to you. You and your soldiers are going to regret the day that you stepped foot in Iraq and dared to violate the Muslims. The dignity of the Muslim men and women in the prison of Abu Ghraib and others will be redeemed by blood and souls! You will see nothing from us except corpse after corpse, casket after casket, of those slaughtered in this fashion."*

Saqqaf drew a machete from his belt and grabbed the prisoner's hair—

Kris slammed the laptop shut. "I'm not fucking watching this."

He shoved back from the desk, toppling his chair. Ramos and George jumped out of his way, giving him space. He ran to the line of garbage cans by the door and heaved. Gagging filled the office, retching.

David stared at the marble floor, the cream and beige tiles.

Kris rose, wiping his lips. He glared at George. "I fucking told you," he hissed. His voice shook. "I fucking told you we shouldn't torture anybody. I fucking told you, I fucking told Director Thatcher, and I fucking told the Goddamn vice president!" His shaking finger pointed at George's closed laptop. "You, and everyone who sanctioned the detainee program, who sanctioned torture, caused this. This blood is on you."

General Ramos stared out the windows, his eyes narrowed as he watched the setting sun beyond the Tigris. George's jaw pulsed, clenching and unclenching.

Kris ripped open George's office door. David followed him down the marble hallway.

"He's got a new nickname," George called after them. "The 'Sheikh of the Slaughterers'. We've got to take him out, Kris. I'm fucking begging you. We've got to get this son of a bitch."

"I can't unfuck what's been fucked, George." Kris stilled, but didn't turn around.

"The White House is serious now. And the president wants to hear what's going on, from you. We're going to DC. They are going to put everything behind you, Kris. Everything."

## Washington DC - June 2004

"Do *not*, under any circumstances, shoot your mouth off." George growled into Kris's ear. "Do not make a scene in front of the new CIA director. Do not, for the love of fucking God, say 'I told you so'."

"I wasn't going to say it. My plan was to do a tap number on the center of the table, belt out, '*I fucking told you so*' at the top of my lungs, and end in the splits in front of the VP. So he could suck my dick."

George gaped at him.

"Do you think I should do an opera rendition, or should I stay more along the lines of Bernadette Peters? More Broadway, you think?"

George's face slowly turned purple. David smirked behind his hand.

"What do you think the VP's face will *be* like when he sees me walk in?"

"You are your own worst enemy. I swear to God," George finally choked out.

"I didn't invade Iraq and fuck up the entire Middle East. I didn't fulfill the hopes and dreams of al-Qaeda, and a prophecy they cling to."

"Caldera, I swear—"

The door to the Situation Room opened. The new director of the CIA, Christopher Edwards, stepped out. His gaze bounced from George to Kris.

"You must be Kris Caldera." Hand outstretched, Edwards smiled broadly.

Kris shook his hand, coy smile on his face. Just what had the new director, ushered in after Thatcher's fall and the conflagration of the prisoner abuse scandal, heard about him? His head tilted. "My reputation precedes me? Or my fashion?"

To really stick it to everyone, just everyone, he'd bought a new suit for this, a charcoal Brunello Cucinelli, on a layover in Rome. A fuchsia pocket square puffed out of his chest. David had helped him pick it out, and had nearly torn the suit off him in the dressing room, fire in his eyes as he dropped to his knees.

That was a memory to carry while wearing the suit. While meeting the new CIA director. Briefing the president.

Instant swagger.

Edwards chuckled, and, not missing a beat, said, "A bit of both. Director Thatcher warned me about you on his way out."

"Warned you about me?"

An aide poked her head out of the Situation Room. "The president and the national security council are ready for you."

Edwards led them into the president's Situation Room, the storied command center of presidents waging war.

*Thought it would be bigger.* The room was cramped, dominated by the conference table and a bank of monitors along one wall. Kris recognized everyone in the room, all the big names and faces of the administration. Secretaries of state and defense, the national security advisor, the joint chiefs. Other generals and admirals. Military aides and officers squeezed beside their generals, and civilians in suits juggled calls and emails on Blackberries and bulky laptops balanced on their knees.

They were given three seats near the head of the table. George sat along the wall as David and Kris settled next to Edwards. Dim lights hummed above while the wall monitors were on, illuminating the table but keeping the occupants' faces bathed in shadow.

The president stood behind his chair, talking fast and furiously with someone who looked like they wanted all of their bones to liquefy and to drop to the ground, and then slink out of the room.

The seat across from Kris pulled away from the table. Hands appeared in the light, holding a coffee cup, and then arms, a body, sitting down. A face.

Kris stared as the vice president sat across from him.

It took a moment for the vice president to recognize Kris. He frowned, like he was sifting through his memories. The frown shifted, turned to a scowl. His lip curled. He looked away.

George sighed, just loud enough for Kris to hear. Edwards, next to

Kris, turned and gave him a slight—very slight—grin. The ghost of a smile.

David squeezed Kris's hand beneath the table.

"We all here? What are we waiting for?" The president settled into his leather seat at the head of the table. "Let's talk about Saqqaf."

Edwards guided the room through Saqqaf's biography, a report Kris had written the month before. He stopped, though, just after Saqqaf's move to Afghanistan. "I brought the agency's Saqqaf targeteer here today. He's the CIA's expert on Saqqaf. I look for his reports first, every day." Edwards looked at Kris. "Mr. Caldera."

All eyes were on him. No pressure. Kris's eyes flicked from the president to the vice president. Did the president remember him, smelly and sweaty and unwashed after September 11?

David laced their fingers beneath the table.

"Mr. President." Kris nodded his hello.

"Go on, Mr. Caldera. If Christopher here thinks you're all right, then we want to hear what you have to say."

Kris walked everyone through the timeline of Saqqaf's rise, from his backward days in Jordan to his sideshow days in Afghanistan, kept at arm's reach from al-Qaeda, a curiosity more than an asset. His flight to Iraq, and the administration's use of him to help justify the invasion. His subsequent rise, following the invasion, in the lawless, hopeless wasteland that Occupied Iraq had become.

His savage butchery since, and his stirring of a sectarian civil war that was pushing Iraq to the brink of collapse.

David spoke next. "Mr. President, my name is David Haddad. I work with Mr. Caldera on the ground in Iraq. Saqqaf has taken over the global jihadist movement where Bin Laden has fallen short. Bin Laden has been relegated to near obscurity, issuing dry pronouncements from caves and spending his days in hiding. His claim to fame, after nine-eleven, is that he's evaded us. Saqqaf, on the other hand, is captivating the world with his brand of jihad. Where Bin Laden looks old and dreary, Saqqaf is seen in videos as a young man, actually fighting. He looks like a John Wayne jihadi, and his violent rhetoric, his promises of freedom and revenge, and his slick propaganda are pulling the disenfranchised to him."

The vice president's gaze narrowed. "How many do you believe are with Saqqaf?"

"About ten thousand active fighters, pulled from around the world. Iraq, the near east, north Africa, Saudi and the Gulf states, Afghanistan, Chechnya, even as far as Tajikistan. About half of those are designated for martyrdom operations, suicide bomber training. He preys on feelings of guilt and shame, promising recruits who martyr themselves they'll be forgiven for everything. That martyrdom will also avenge the shame of the entire Muslim community from the occupation. For people, youth especially, who are attracted to the promise of a better world, but feel they've broken the strict moral code of the jihadis, the promise of a cleansing martyrdom and a rich afterlife is a potent recruitment tactic."

"They're just kids?"

"Many of them are. Teenagers and young adults. College age. After arriving in Iraq, they're sent to suicide bomber schools and kept purposely isolated from everyone and everything. The first time they see an Iraqi or an American soldier is right before they blow themselves up."

The president's eyes narrowed. He shook his head, lips thinning. "We've got to stop this."

*Shouldn't have created the problem to begin with.* Kris kept his thoughts to himself, though. "Saqqaf's silent support, the Iraqis who have welcomed him and his men, are the people we need to reach. They're stuck, forced to pick a side in this ongoing civil war, and we haven't given the people of Iraq enough to want to pick our side."

"We Goddamn got rid of Saddam for them," the vice president growled. "We gave them their country back. What the hell else do they want?"

"To not be tortured," Kris snapped. So much for keeping quiet. "They wanted us to bring electricity back, but they didn't want us to shoot it up their asses. I don't think that's too much to ask for. They want to live in a secure country. To not have to face a sectarian civil war, an occupation, and a rising jihadi army all at the same time. Safety. Security. Jobs." He started listing off the country's woes until he ran out of fingers. "Should I keep going?"

Behind them, Kris heard George's heavy sigh. Edwards looked down at his notes, shuffling papers.

"What does Saqqaf want? The end of America? To get us out of Iraq? He want to be the next Iraqi prime minister?" The president looked tired.

"No, Mr. President. Saqqaf isn't even Iraqi. He's Jordanian. He doesn't care about Iraq, not like you think. He wants to destroy Iraq, because after the country is destroyed, he can take over and institute a new way of life. He wants to fulfill the prophecy. Bring about the end times and usher in the Islamic Caliphate."

"Don't the Iraqis have a problem with that? They want their country back. Not some medieval Islamic empire."

David nodded. "Yes, they do. There's some evidence of resistance. An awakening, of sorts, against the brutalities of Saqqaf. No one wants suicide bombers in Iraq. No one. But, there just isn't enough safety on the ground for people to turn against Saqqaf and his people. He's controlling the areas he and his fighters hold through brutal repression, a firebrand fundamentalism that is holding the Iraqis hostage."

"Mr. President," Kris said, "We're looking at post-al-Qaeda terrorism now, led by Saqqaf. It's not just targeting us. It's targeting everyone. Once Iraq, as a country, as an idea, collapses, Saqqaf will attempt to create an Islamic Caliphate from the ashes. He believes that by pushing Iraq to fail through civil war and through terrorism, he can control and shape the chaos that will follow. And it's working."

"They've started referring to the cities and the desert they control as the Islamic State," David said.

The president sighed. "So, what are we going to do about him?"

Farther down the table, a general stood. "Mr. President, General Terry Carter, sir. I've been assigned to join with the CIA in hunting, capturing, or neutralizing the Saqqaf threat. Please allow me to present our strategy."

Carter, a picture-perfect military officer, spit-shined and polished, starched and stacked, delivered a slide-by-slide presentation on his new counterterrorism strategy. "We developed this strategy after reading the intelligence supplied by the CIA, by Mr. Caldera." Carter's words were bullets, his movements as precise as a drill sergeant's. Kris felt like saluting. He sat up straighter. Carter was a man to whom details mattered, he could tell. His underwear was probably all the same brand, folded and organized in his drawer, his socks rolled neatly beside his squares of white briefs.

"Saqqaf, up to this point, has been in control of the tempo of battle. He sends out attackers. We respond. He strikes civilian targets. We attempt to harden them. We cannot be reactionary any longer." Carter spoke directly to the president, as if the room were empty. "We have to be faster, stronger than his people.

"I propose the formation of a joint operations unit, led by Mr. Caldera and myself, where we strike Saqqaf's people *every single night*. Relentless pressure and constant attacks that will keep Saqqaf and his fighters off their game. We press them, continuously, until they're consumed with just trying to stay alive. Until that's all they can do; be on the run, trying to escape. But we'll keep coming. We will exhaust them. And then we will destroy them."

The president and Edwards's heads swiveled to Kris. "What do you say, Mr. Caldera?" The president asked. "Think this will work?"

Kris shared a quick look with David. "Yes, Mr. President. We think it will work."

"Then you and General Carter are in charge of the hunt. Form this joint strike force. Take out this son of a bitch." The president stood, and everyone followed, waiting while the president buttoned his jacket and strode toward the door. The vice president followed, but not after giving Kris a long, hard glare.

The rest of the room scattered, officers and aides slipping out or pulling out their cell phones to make a dozen calls each. Edwards and Carter stood apart, discussing shared resources and budgets for the joint strike force. George leaned forward, poking his head between them.

"This is huge, Kris. Bigger than me, even. If you take this guy out, you'll probably end up taking my job."

"I don't want your job. I want this all to end."

And, he wanted David, and a home of their own. A place to go to that wasn't a tiny room in a fracturing country. He wanted to not have to conceal their relationship all the time in public. He wanted the CIA to recognize them. He wanted to be heard, listened to the first time. Not have to pick up the pieces of a broken country, not have to sing *'I told you so'* at the top of his lungs. He wanted a lot of things, but none of them were George's job.

George appraised him, peering at him the way a parent might look at their grown child, surprised to see an adult for the first time. "You've always been made for more than what the CIA could give you. You take this guy out, and you'll save Iraq. Maybe the whole region."

"It's *that* kind of thinking that got us in this mess in the first place. One person isn't the key to anything. Ever. Everything's connected, George. Saqqaf has set off a movement, and even after we kill him, we'll be dealing with his children, his devotees, in ten years. It's all just a circle, a never-ending circle."

# 19

## Joint Strike Force, Sunni Triangle, Iraq - March 2006

2100 hours. Time for last checks, tightening the straps and checking gear. Jackson and Warrick, Special Forces guys from David's old team, smoked their last cigarettes alongside David.

Kris had briefed the team an hour before. For months, their Special Forces strike force, with David attached, had hit Saqqaf and his fighters and hit them hard, crushing blows to his burgeoning Islamic State.

Most of the jihadis were now on the run.

Every night, they swooped in on another safe house, another location uncovered by meticulous hunting through emails, text messages, and cell phone calls. Every night, Kris stripped the jihadis they arrested of all their belongings, taking the pocket litter and the safe house computers and the jihadis' notebooks, and spent the next twelve hours perusing everything, combining it with intercepts and drone overheads and human intelligence from on the ground. By afternoon, Kris had another list of targets, another night of work for David and the strike team.

General Carter and Kris had turned out to be a potent, formidable pair.

Tonight, Kris had told them to "*expect resistance*", which meant "*expect a firefight*".

Everything in David raced. His mind, his heart, the tapping of his finger against his rifle. Details thundered through his mind. The sequence of events, the breach order. The call signs, the signal to go. Where to set up perimeter locations. The targets.

Cool professionalism warred with nervousness. He'd been on a hundred raids, had been on a hundred different missions. But today, his skin was too small, his bones too large. Everything was ultracrisp, like the world had been sharpened before his eyes.

Kris stamped out his last cigarette and stood before David. His eyes ran over David's blacked-out face, his black fatigues. A few hours ago, they'd woken up in Kris's cot beneath his plywood table-turned-desk in a curtained-off section of the warehouse the strike team used as a base. The sun set and they ate breakfast for dinner, sitting side by side on the cot. Their workday started at sundown.

"You've got this." Kris smiled. "You'll get him."

David nodded. They were going after Saqqaf's senior lieutenant, a man named Mousa. A month before, Mousa and Saqqaf had ordered a pre-dawn raid on the Askari Shrine in Samarra, one of the most revered mosques in the Shia faith.

At dawn, as the sun splintered the sky, explosives planted by the fighters had ripped the mosque apart. The golden dome, a shrine in the hearts of millions, lay in a pile of rubble and dust, and all that remained was broken concrete, twisted rebar, and screams.

Blind rage followed, fury and anguish that split the city and the country. Reprisal killings rolled in wave after wave, bands of Sunni and Shia gangs murdering and beheading their way across the country.

Thousands were killed. Morgues started turning away the dead. There was no more room.

Bodies were left in the streets. Severed heads rolled in gutters, lay on their side next to piles of trash and bloodstained mud.

David wondered if the end times were upon the world. If the Apocalypse had truly come. Months of decimating cell after cell after cell, flipping low-level and mid-level fighters. Siphoning all phone calls, all emails. Everything they could scrape from any of Saqqaf's associates. They'd choked off his ratlines into Syria, choked his supply routes. And yet, Saqqaf had managed to throw jet fuel on the bonfire of Iraq's sectarian tensions. The end truly did seem nigh.

The radio crackled. General Carter's voice rang out in David's ear. "*Everyone, form up. Prepare to move out.*"

Kris grasped his hand. David squeezed his fingers. It was the most they allowed each other around everyone. Neither in nor out, they existed in the in-between space. Neither acknowledging nor denying it. Hiding, and yet not. Sharing a room, but never holding hands, never kissing in public. "See you in a few hours," Kris said softly. He smiled, the same smile David saw in his dreams when they were separated, the same smile that lived in the center of his heart.

"*Ya rouhi.*"

### Joint Strike Force, Sunni Triangle, Iraq - 0230 hours

Mousa sat in a cell, hands bound behind his back, hood covering his head. Halogen lights burned down onto him, turning the night to the brightest day. David stood outside the cellblock, watching.

"You okay?" Kris frowned. He sucked down the last of his cigarette, blew out the smoke quickly. David had been quiet since the team had come back, since they'd dragged Mousa in, screaming curses and raging about hellfire and infidels.

David couldn't tear his eyes from Mousa. "I'm fine."

"You sure you want to do this?"

"I have to do this."

Kris stamped out his cigarette. "Then we need to get started. It's after zero two hundred already."

Slowly, David nodded.

Kris led them in. He'd been the lead interrogator for the strike team, picking apart low-level fighters and senior commanders, breaking them down one by one. Mousa was the most senior commander of Saqqaf's they had captured alive.

He moved behind Mousa. Gripped his hood. Waited.

David stood in front, feet spread, arms crossed. He nodded at Kris.

Kris ripped the hood off.

Mousa's dark eyes shone with hatred, with pure, wretched fury.

David was stuck in Mousa's stare, pulled in like gravity, falling into a black hole. He couldn't breathe. Couldn't look away. Couldn't escape the clawing dread rising through him, a wave trying to pull him under—

Revulsion, like acid, tried to drench him, drown him. He wanted to gouge Mousa's eyes out. He wanted to grab him and throw him down, punch him until he bled, until he choked on his blood, his tears. He wanted Mousa to feel one ounce of what he'd made so many others feel, taste the fear, the helplessness, he'd help unleash upon the world.

Twenty-six years. It had been twenty-six years since he'd felt that same touch of evil, wave after wave of hatred and despair. The raw whisper of twisted darkness reaching for him, grabbing onto his soul.

David clenched his hands into fists, dug his fingernails into his skin.

Mousa spat at David's feet. "*Kufir*," he hissed. "Traitor. You pretend to be Arab, yet you're only a dog for the Americans. The blood of Muslims is on your hands. Hell awaits you, my brother." He grinned, savage. "The abyss of *al-Nar*, the fires, awaits you and all hypocrites. All who have turned against the Prophet, *salla Allahu alayhi wa sallam*, and Allah."

"Have you heard of the Amman message?"

"Do not *speak* to me, infidel—"

"The Prophet, *salla Allahu alayhi wa sallam*, said, 'My *ummah*, the nation of Islam, will not agree upon an error.' Do you know of this hadith?"

"Do not speak his blessed words, infidel! Your tongue is not worthy to speak his sayings!"

"Five hundred Islamic scholars and imams from over fifty countries have condemned your butchery. They have issued a binding ruling, a fatwa, against you. The *ummah* has spoken."

"Lies, from a hypocrite. True Muslims know what we're creating and believe in the struggle for our Caliphate."

"Muslims around the world gag against your savagery, your barbarism. You do not speak for the *ummah*. The scholars have defined who a Muslim is, who a believer and follower of the Prophet, *salla Allahu alayhi wa sallam*, is. I have news for you, Mousa. It's not you."

"Do not dare accuse me of apostasy!"

"You have no idea what it means to be a Muslim. What it means to follow Allah, and to worship Him."

Mousa sneered. "The *Amman* message. The Hashemite King of Jordan is an American puppet and a CIA spy! He has Muslim blood on his hands, too! He aligns himself with the infidels and allows Muslim blood to soak the world! He is *takfir*! A hypocrite and unbeliever! He will join you in *al-Nar*!" Mousa's bellows bounced off the cell walls, physical blows that hit David in the center of his chest. "The Sheikh is the future, the head of the Caliphate!"

"The imams have turned against you. Muslims are disgusted by you. Before Saqqaf, no Iraqi cared about Shia or Sunni. Friends and families joined together. There was harmony—"

"The innovators, the bastard Shia, should be wiped from the earth with their apostasy!"

"Your Islamic State has no Shura council. No religious guidance. Your 'Sheikh of the Slaughters' isn't even literate. He pulls lines from the Quran without understanding their meaning, their context. He has no idea what he's saying. He sounds like an idiot, Mousa."

"*Lies*!" Mousa tried to lunge at David. "The Sheikh has a guide. An *allamah*, a high scholar! He reads the signs of the end times! Guides the Sheikh's designs!"

Behind Mousa, standing out of sight in the shadows, Kris stiffened. David kept his face impassive, tried to look bored, even. "And who is this *allamah*? This learned scholar?"

"He is known as Sheikh Jandal." Mousa hocked spit at David's feet. "Because he will bring the death of the infidels, the disbelievers, and the *kufirs* Like you!"

"You disgust Muslims. No one wants you, or your death cult."

"We are *loved*!"

"*La*," David shook his head. "I do not love you."

"You are a dirty *kufir*," Mousa spat. "You mean nothing. You should be killed where you stand."

David's throat clenched. His fingers dug into his folded arms, his elbows, again. The world spun, like a top out of control. "I had to postpone isha prayer because I had to capture you. I haven't said my night prayers yet. But, as you know, the Prophet, *salla Allahu alayhi wa sallam*, prayed for the entire night, giving thanks to Allah as often as he could. So, I will go pray. You should pray too. Pray an *istikhara*. Ask Allah for guidance. Ask for his forgiveness."

His words tasted like rot, like decay. Like lies.

Mousa tried to surge out of the chair, tried to rush David. His restraints held him back. He looked like a chained dog, foaming at the mouth, fury in his cold eyes. "You are no Muslim!"

"*Taqabal Allah*." *May God receive your prayers*. "You need to repent, Mousa. The *ummah* has abandoned you. Allah has abandoned you. Why do you think you are here, with us, tonight? Allah delivered you to me."

He walked away.

Mousa bellowed curses at David's back, struggling to break free. He cursed David's existence, called down Allah to burn him alive, condemned him to death. His shouts descended into blind wails, growls of fury, of frustration.

David watched from the observation room, waiting.

Kris, standing behind Mousa in the shadows, slipped around and stood in front of him. Mousa jolted. He'd thought he was alone.

Kris wore the same black fatigues as the strike team. He stared Mousa down, crossed his arms over his chest. "I am going to question you about your involvement with Saqqaf."

"I have no involvement with Saqqaf."

"I know everything about you, Mousa. I've listened to all of your calls. I've read all of your emails. I've listened to your wives' phone calls. I listen to them call their mothers, their sisters, in secret, even when you've forbidden them to. I know things about them that you do not."

Mousa bared his teeth. Pulled at his restraints. "I have nothing to do with Saqqaf," he spat.

"I am trying to respect you. Honor your position as Saqqaf's right hand. Did you not help plan the destruction of the Askari Shrine?"

Mousa's eyes flashed, but he said nothing.

"Of course you did. Mousa, I know you. I've captured all your friends. Every one of your brothers has sat in that chair. They've all told me so much about you. So much, in fact, that it feels like we are brothers as well." Kris let a tiny, wry smile curl his lips. "Tell me, how is Abu Abdel? Has he recovered from his injuries?"

Mousa shifted. The first crack appeared. Unease spilled over his features.

"You cared for Abu Abdel. Personally carried him from the battle. The brothers speak highly of you, you know. They say you are their leader. Their *emir*. That you are the Sheikh's right hand, his favorite of all the brothers. But now, you're telling me that you don't even know him?" Kris feigned disappointment. He screwed up his face. "How loyal are you, truly? To turn your back on the Sheikh? On your brothers?"

"I *love* the Sheikh!" Mousa shouted. "Saqqaf is the future! He will lead the Caliphate to the final battle, to the day when Islam will triumph over the armies of the cross! Until all infidels are destroyed, and the rivers overflow with your blood!"

"Ah." Kris smiled. "So you *do* know him."

Mousa fumed.

"We will find your Sheikh. We will find him. We're getting close. It's only a matter of time. We'll find him, like we found you. We'll capture him. I'll sit him in the same chair you're sitting in."

Mousa's eyes blazed. His uncertainty vanished. A slow smile pulled his lips apart.

Outside the interrogation cell, David cursed. *No, damn it.*

"The Sheikh will fight you until his last breath. He will sacrifice himself in the battle against the *kufir* and the *takfir* and your infidel West. He will bathe in your blood and dance on the dust of your bones, spread the ashes of your body, and the bodies of those you love, across the corners of the world. You will *never* capture him alive."

---

Kris tried to restart Mousa's interrogation three times during the night. Mousa refused to speak any further, shutting down and retreating into himself. He chanted prayers, calling down Allah to punish the wicked and the infidels. Kris left him for the final time as Mousa asked Allah to strike Kris down where he stood.

David, exhausted, paced in Kris's makeshift office. The strike team's command center was quieting, the day shift coming in to monitor drone feeds and open-source intel, scoop up phone calls and emails and pick through the raw intelligence from the night's raids. The strike team, and Kris and General Carter, were going to rest before it all started again at sunset.

"I slipped up. I gave him an opening to reinforce Saqqaf's appeal for martyrdom."

"He was always a long shot. Mousa's a true die-hard believer in Saqqaf's brutality."

"We had him on the edge, though. You did. You rocked him hard with the faith angle." Kris sat beside David on the cot, slumping against the warehouse wall.

David felt Kris's stare on the back of his head.

"Did you actually pray?" Kris asked, his voice strained.

David twisted. He stared at Kris. "What do you think?"

Kris shrugged.

"*No*, of *course* not." Snorting, David whipped around, paced faster. There was an itch in his bones, a heat in his blood. Four steps took him back and forth across Kris's small office. The world was still spinning, had never stopped spinning, not since he'd fallen into

Mousa's gaze. Faster, faster. He was going to be sick. He was going to die.

"Even if—" His lips clamped shut. "There's—There's no one to pray *to*."

Kris stayed silent.

"Not *here*. Not with these monsters." David's voice cracked, warbled. "They've ruined it. They all have! Mousa, Saqqaf, Bin Laden, Qaddafi, all of them!"

Memories tore at David. Sunshine and his father's voice. His little djellaba, a miniature of his father's. His father's hand in his, teaching him the prayers. *Every chapter opens with the love and mercy of Allah, ya ibni.*

"None of this, *this shit*, is my father's faith! *None* of it! He taught me about... submission and gratitude and love and thanking Allah for life and joy and living in peace—" His voice choked off. Heat rose in his chest, behind his eyes, a volcano erupting within his soul, so suddenly he couldn't tamp it down. "*Nothing* here, none of what they've built, is from Allah. My father would *never*—"

His voice, his body, his soul, quaked. He couldn't stand any more. The world was spinning out of control, spinning off its axis, spinning into space. He was ten years old, and his father was on the TV, in a basketball stadium Qaddafi had built in Benghazi.

"This isn't Islam because *Allah has abandoned us*! He's gone, he left, and we're all just fighting over the Hell He left behind! And that's fine! I want nothing to do with Him!"

Where was the world he'd glimpsed when he was nine years old? Where was the faith his father had taught him, had shown him through quiet devotion and whispered prayers? Where was the future of warmth, of his soul filled with light and gratitude, secure in the knowledge that he was loved, by his blood father and the Father of all? What had happened to that life? To that love?

Ten years old, and he'd watched his father's faith, his peace, be turned into a crime.

Days and nights after his father was taken he'd spent in prayer to Allah to deliver his father back to him. To bring them together, to make them a family again. The prayers of a child, the simple pleading, the offers of exchange. He'd be the best Muslim, the best worshipper. He'd never talk back to his mother again, and he'd eat all his dinner, even the disgusting vegetables. He'd always listen to Baba, always. Just please, *please*, bring his father home.

His prayers were answered by a screaming mob in a basketball stadium and a rope tied in a noose, swinging from one of the bright orange hoops. Thunderous applause, shouts and cheers, thousands of Qaddafi loyalists screaming for his father's blood. Over the TV, over the live broadcast he and his mother were forced to watch, guns held to the backs of their heads by the Mukhabarat, the roars had faded in and out, overpowering the tinny speakers, the shitty microphones.

His father had cried as they forced him to climb the ladder to the hoop. To the noose. He'd prayed, too, steadfast in his faith until the end, not even stumbling on his tears. David had watched his lips move, had recognized the shape, the movements.

He had memorized the shape of his father's prayers as he sat at his side, his little body trying to grow into the image of his beloved father.

His mother had screamed when they shoved him from the ladder's rungs, let his body swing. The Mukhabarat agents in their home had let her hide her face. But a ten-year-old boy was old enough to watch, to experience the seconds that stretched for hours, the minutes turning to years, to an eternity that still lived in the base of his brain. Hands had held his head forward, forced him to keep his eyes open.

The drop from the hoop wasn't long enough. His father struggled to breathe against the noose. Someone grabbed his legs, hung from him. Pulled him down.

He'd watched the rope stretch.

And the crowd wailed, wild with exultation. With a mob's delight, and the glee of being safe from the wrath of Qaddafi's mercurial mercy. They screamed for his father's death, and screamed for their own lives.

It was not the first, and was not the last, televised execution Qaddafi put on.

But it was *his father's.*

He'd been murdered for the crime of loving Allah more than he loved Qaddafi. He'd loved Allah with his whole heart and soul, and the only thing he'd wanted in his life was to share that love with his son and his wife.

No one and nothing had saved him from the pain, the humiliation, of his murder. He'd lost control of his bladder, his bowels, as he died. David's last image of his father, the best man in his life, was a piss-and-shit-stained djellaba swinging on the end of a rope, eyes bulging, tongue protruding, tears and snot smeared over his once-proud face.

No boy should see their father, their ideal, struck down, destroyed by hatred and violence.

Somehow, he fumbled enough words for Kris to understand, for Kris to *get* it. He watched the truth hit Kris, the weight of David's confession, a truth he'd *never* spoken aloud, not once since sneaking out of Libya's sandy desert, smother Kris's soul.

Evil, the truth of it, was a weight that a soul could barely carry. They'd already shouldered so much together. When would they break? When would the world, and all of its evil, shatter them?

Kris's jaw dropped. He reached for David, stumbling, falling himself, as if they were now together in freefall, in the vortex of evil destroying the world. His lips moved soundlessly as he tried to find words, find something to say. "David..."

"I want—" Tears choked him. David grabbed Kris, tried to hold on. Tried to stop falling. "I want my father's faith—"

*I want my* father.

There was a permanent hole in his soul, in his life, and nothing could fill it. His father had been ripped away from him.

He clung to Kris, burying his face in Kris's chest, as his bones collapsed, no longer able to carry the weight of a man who hadn't mourned his loss. His baba, the man he wanted to become, the man he looked up to more than anyone else in the world. His faith in

Allah had shattered that day, and the pieces, the refuse of the first ten years of his life, had blown like litter through his existence, debris that kept piling up against his heart.

Had Allah been murdered that day as well? In David's soul, and also the world? Were they just continuing to murder Allah every day since, every incarnation of evil in the world another blow against Allah and His love? Could even the Father of All stand against so much hate and so much evil? Something was broken, fundamentally broken, in the universe. What if it was Allah that they'd broken?

Had their hatred finally killed God? Was that why He was gone?

What would his father say about this world, if he'd lived? He *needed* to know. He needed that guidance, his father's presence in his life.

What would his father make of the man he'd become? The choices he'd made? The man he loved?

Would his father have ever looked at him with hatred? Would he ever have called him a sinner, a *kufir*, a disbeliever? Set against the horrors of the world, all the ways big and small that people could inflict horror and anguish on each other, was David's heart beating for Kris so evil? Had Allah made him this way? Or was it just emptiness and chaos, his genetics aligning in one of a million different possibilities?

David had always put his faith in biology, in genetics, in his high school science teacher who had belabored the point, over and over, that being gay was *not* a choice. It was who you were, how you were made. David's friends on the soccer team used to joke that Mr. Whitley talked about gay stuff so much because he was gay, obviously gay, with his skinny body and his pastel button-downs and his lilting voice.

But what if he'd seen the truth about David, and maybe others, and he'd spent the nine months he'd been given as their teacher trying to give them a gift that they'd cling to for the rest of their lives?

How did anyone feel loved for who they were, in the face of so much agony? How did anyone reconcile the world with a dead and absent God?

He struggled to breathe, dragging in ragged breath after breath. He was shaking, quaking, as if his soul was about to burst apart. Kris stroked his hair, pressed his lips to David's temple. He hauled David to him, pulled him into their cot. Wrapped his arms and legs around David, holding him as close as he physically could.

David wanted to crawl inside Kris, press their souls together. Reunite with Kris in the way they were meant to be, before time, when Allah had made them as one. He believed that, to the marrow of his bones, the center of the atoms that made his being.

But if he believed that, if he believed he and Kris were the same soul made by Allah, then what else was true?

Could Allah give him Kris and take his father?

Could both be true?

What did that mean?

Damn it all. Damn Mousa, and Saqqaf. Damn the president for invading Iraq. Damn Bin Laden, and Khalid Sheik Mohammed, and the nineteen men who hijacked four planes on September 11. Damn Qaddafi. Damn all of the hatred, all of the anguish, that had set the world on this path, had twisted lives and history and faith, had killed Allah and scattered all hope until no one could find the truth anywhere, no matter how hard their heart beat or their soul bled.

The one, the only man, who could have ever found the answers, who could have ever put the world back together, had lost his life in a basketball stadium, swinging from a rope as a crowd cheered. He'd loved too much, too strongly, for the world, especially a world that had killed God. His death had created a void, a black hole, and David imagined all the love, all the light in the world disappearing into the void his father's life had left behind, like water disappearing down a drain, spiraling away into nothingness and infinity.

David had watched it through his tears on TV, the day the world killed the one man who held Allah in the center of his heart.

## Joint Strike Force, Sunni Triangle, Iraq - June 2006

"Hey. We've got something on the drone feed."

The sun was still up. Kris blinked, bleary eyed. He and David were tangled in his cot beneath his plywood desk. The Iraqi sunlight burned through the blinds, through the sheet Kris had tacked up to block out the spears of light.

Groaning, David face-planted in the cot as Kris struggled to his feet. Carter's deputy, a Special Forces captain, kept his gaze purposely up, not looking at the two of them entwined, half naked. It was too hot to sleep in anything but the bare essentials. David wore his tiny running shorts, black nylon that hugged his upper thighs. Kris slept in his briefs, outrageously colored neon and brilliant patterns that cupped his ass and crotch. The captain turned in the doorway, giving him privacy.

For a military that had beaten out modesty in basic training and that treated nudity as commonplace as being fully clothed, the privacy granted to David and him felt like a shun. Carter had insisted that he be given a private office and private space to sleep and had quietly put out a gag order on discussing him and David. It was the biggest open secret in the strike force. The man leading the hunt for Saqqaf was as gay as the day was long.

"Imagine Saqqaf's face when he finds out it was a gay guy who tracked him down," Kris heard once in the mess, two Special Forces soldiers with their heads together, eyes flicking toward him.

Kris grabbed his black fatigue pants and pulled them on, threw on a black t-shirt. "What's going on?"

"We have movement on the spiritual advisor."

Kris tossed David's pants at him. "Gotta move, babe."

Since Mousa's slipped confession about Saqqaf having a spiritual advisor, Kris had devoted a huge amount of the strike team's intelligence collection and targeting toward finding the *allamah*.

*Sheikh Jandal* was a *kunya*, a jihad name that translated as the Sheikh of Death. They went through everything, every phone call, every email, every possible lead. Religious leaders across Iraq were fractured, most decrying the savagery and violence of Saqqaf, his bloodlust and his fanaticism. But some celebrated the 'Son of the Desert', the 'Emir of the Resistance against the West'. They focused in on those imams, put them under the microscope of the US intelligence machine. Undercover officers went to their mosques, listened to the sermons. Watched them, everywhere they went, followed by the drones that hovered over the country.

The captain filled them in on the way to the command center. "One of our drones monitoring imam delta-seven tracked him leaving his house this morning. He ran his errands, dropped his kids off at his wife's mother's house. Standard behavior."

"Until?"

"Just past noon, the imam diverted from his usual path and started driving through four separate Baghdad neighborhoods. He executed a series of turns and curbside stops, backtracks and pauses."

"He was checking for surveillance," David said.

The captain nodded to David. "We think so. He drove onto the Baghdad highway, but pulled off on the onramp. One minute later, a blue pickup truck pulled in behind his original car. He drove away in the blue truck."

"A car swap." Kris's heart pounded.

"Yes sir. We're following the truck now. It's heading north, leaving Baghdad."

They badged through the electronic locks and swept into the command center. The lights were dim, but the monitors along one wall were bright with live video. Black-and-white images, thermal scans, high-def video footage. All feeds showed the same image. A blue pickup driving along the highway.

Banks of analysts and drone operators worked in long lines before the main monitors, tapping away at their laptops and working the radios. David peeled off, heading to the back where five coffeepots percolated twenty-four hours a day. Kris joined General Carter, still shaking off his own sleep. He'd rushed in, wearing his PT shorts and his Army undershirt, crisply tucked in. Kris had never seen the general so underdressed.

"Caldera." Carter nodded to him. "What do you think?"

"The behavior is consistent with someone attempting to shake surveillance and throw off a tail. Whatever he's doing, he doesn't want anyone to know."

"Think he found our undercover agents? Think he's spooked and is running?"

"He could be. But someone on the run doesn't spend hours trying to shake a tail. They run, as fast as they can." Kris watched the pickup drive on, miles of highway disappearing beneath its tires. The sun blazed down on Iraq, burning away shadows. Everything was brilliantly lit, perfect clarity. A desert day beneath the harsh sun. A day for revelations.

David appeared at Kris's side with two cups of coffee. They watched, expectancy hushing their voices, their breaths, as the truck pulled off the highway and wound through the countryside northeast of Baghdad. Palm groves and farms blurred past the monitors.

"Maybe he's just going to visit a farm," one of the analysts offered.

"And shake a tail to do so?" Kris scoffed.

"Maybe he's going to the Iranian border. It's only seventy miles away." Carter arched one eyebrow.

"Saqqaf despises the Shia, and this imam supports him. He's stirred sectarian violence for months. No way he goes to Iran." Kris pursed his lips. "He's going to meet Saqqaf."

Carter *hmmed.*

The truck turned, heading for Baqubah. Analysts sprang into action, pulling up all information that they had collated on Baqubah. Who was who, who was there, what attacks the city had suffered. How many informants they had on the ground.

"He's stopping," David said. "Another vehicle is approaching."

A white sedan pulled alongside the truck. The imam hopped down from the truck and slipped into the backseat of the white sedan. Both vehicles drove off, sand arcing behind their tires as they sped away in opposite directions.

"It's him. It's definitely him." Kris's blood turned searing, burning the inside of his body. *This is it. We're going to get Saqqaf.* His gaze met

David's. David's eyes were wide, as round as dinner plates. *I'm going to get him. For you.*

Carter shouted orders, calling for air support and for the Special Forces team on standby to get in their choppers and get ready to go. It was a thirty-minute flight from their base to Baqubah, if they left now.

Every monitor was filled with the white sedan driving along the desert road. "He's still heading north," an analyst narrated. "Moving at thirty-three miles per hour."

"What's out there?" Carter barked.

"Three villages. A handful of ranches. Not much, sir. We haven't spent much time looking. There was nothing strategic there, we thought."

"Well, we thought wrong."

The white sedan pulled off the desert road at the village of Hibhib. Built around an oasis, the village was a shock of green situated in the rocky hills and dusty north of Iraq. Palms and ferns crowded the ground, jockeying for position. Houses were low, whitewashed and blocky. The car kept driving, passing through the village.

Until it turned up a narrow drive, lined with thick palms that towered overhead. The car disappeared from the feed, lost in the foliage.

"Get the visual back!" Carter barked. "We cannot lose this car!"

The images bucked and wove as the drone pilots swerved, changing altitude, axis and orbit, searching for a better angle. Images appeared through the mess of palm fronds. A two-story house with a flat roof. A long, gravel drive. The sedan, parked in front of the entrance.

Two men embracing in greeting. The imam was one of them.

And a stout and stocky man in black combat fatigues, with a short beard and a black *taqiyah* was the other.

Carter's gaze flicked to Kris.

"It's him," Kris breathed. He knew that shape. Knew that man. Knew everything there was to know about him without having spoken a word to his face. He knew Saqqaf, from the inside of the man out. “It’s him.”

Carter’s deputy spoke up, bracketing Carter. “We don’t know that for sure. We can’t get a definitive visual verification from this angle.”

“Get the strike team in the air and on target, now!” Carter barked. “We are not losing this opportunity.”

David leaned into his side. “I’m going with them.”

A thousand different half thoughts poured through Kris. There wasn’t time to think, wasn’t time to talk. “Go.”

David tore out of the command center as they kept watching the house. Kris imagined the frenzy of activity as the team prepared to launch from the airfield.

*David... be safe.*

“General, the chopper pilot is reporting engine trouble. They need time to fix the problem.”

“They don’t have time! They need to get in the air, now!”

Minutes turned to years.

The two men on the monitors went inside the two-story house, talking amiably, warmly.

Silence filled the command center.

Grainy images of the house filtered through the palms, disappearing and reappearing.

“How long will they spend together?” Carter leaned into Kris and asked softly.

“We have no idea. Could be minutes. Could be hours.”

“We could miss him, then. If we don’t get on the ground immediately. If he thinks we’re onto him, he could duck out into the palms and we’d never find him. He could run and disappear. We could lose this chance.”

Kris nodded. “We do have fighters overhead.” Two F-16s held position over Iraq twenty-four hours a day in case any US forces needed immediate air support.

“Do you want to capture him or do you want to kill him?” Carter asked. “What’s the CIA’s position on this?”

Kris's eyes slipped closed. Mousa's viciousness, his rabid brutality, replayed behind his eyelids. David's shattered faith. A hundred bombs exploding, a thousand scenes of carnage. Beheaded bodies and destroyed mosques. The shattering of a nation, of a region. A faith ripped apart with every act of savagery. The slow march of time toward a final point, Saqqaf's plan to bring about the end of days. Anguished families on both sides of the world, mourning the loss of their loved ones.

He'd been Saqqaf's specter, his judge and jury, and his shadow confessor. He'd become as close to Saqqaf as another human could be, peering inside his skull, his mind, his psychology. Reading his emails, snooping through his laptop. He dreamed of Saqqaf at night, long dreams where they spoke across a river of blood as the world burned and airplanes crashed into the ground, but they were speaking different languages and nothing made sense.

Was he to be Saqqaf's executioner, too?

"Sir, there's movement in the house." An operator zoomed in on the thermal scan. Two figures inside. One was moving toward the door.

"We need to go. Now." Carter's eyes blazed. "Caldera. What's your call?"

He breathed in. Sounds faded, blurred together, smeared. He stared at the monitors, but all he saw was David. *There is no Allah, not anymore*. "Get the fighters. Bomb the son of a bitch."

Carter gave the order, an immediate redirect for the fighter pilots on standby to the tiny village. The pilot's voice crackled over the command center's speaker. "*ETA, three minutes*," she said. She repeated the coordinates of the house. "*Confirming target*."

"Target confirmed."

The house wove in and out of the palms, circled on the monitors. Kris held his breath. Everyone leaned forward, eyes peeled to the screen. No one spoke. No one moved.

The radio crackled. "*Bombs away*."

Drones didn't transmit sound. One minute the house was there, between two palm fronds. The next moment, it was a plume of dust, shattered concrete and broken trees, a cloud of debris rising and rising into the sky.

"*Target destroyed.*"

Cheers erupted, soldiers and analysts bursting from their seats, pumping their fists and screaming. In the center of it all, Carter stared at the monitors, his jaw clenching, his arms crossed over his chest. Kris sagged, bracing his hands on the table in front of him before he collapsed.

"Sir! The strike team is ready to go!"

"Get them to the location right away. We need to confirm it was him."

---

Dust choked the air, miles outside of Hibhib. David and the others pulled their scarves up, checkered keffiyehs worn around their necks. Iraqi police from Baqubah were on the way to the destroyed house, police sirens wailing as the chopper overtook their convoy.

They set down at the end of the gravel drive. Where the house had been, only a crater remained. Palms that had encircled the house had toppled, shattered in half and splintered apart like broken toothpicks. A thousand years of sand and dust hung in the air, upturned by the fighter's twin bombs.

"Start searching. Gotta find the body."

They sifted through the rubble, stamping out fires as they turned over broken chunks of concrete. Smoke made David's eyes water. Six Iraqi policemen showed up, but hung back at the driveway. No one wanted to interfere with the Americans sifting through the rubble of a bombed house. No good came from that.

David saw it first. A hand poking out of the ruins, blackened by soot. "Over here!"

They flipped concrete like they were flipping Lego bricks, cleared the debris from Saqqaf in under a minute. He lay half buried in the crater, covered in dirt. Soot and burns painted his face, his body. Blood poured from his ears, his nose, his mouth. The bombs' pressure wave had ripped apart his internal organs, liquefied them inside his bones.

Saqqaf's eyes flickered open. His gaze landed on thirteen American Special Forces soldiers standing in a circle over him. He mumbled something. Blood trickled past his lips.

David crouched next to him. "*Nam*?"

Saqqaf reached for David, his hand trembling. He shuddered, coughed blood. David leaned closer. An observant Muslim would whisper the *shahada* before they died, the statement of faith. *Allah is the one God, and Muhammad is his messenger*. It was supposed to unite the faithful's soul to Allah at the moment of death. Would Saqqaf speak the words? Did he imagine, somewhere in that twisted brain, that he was on the way to eternal Paradise?

"*Ayree feek*," Saqqaf bubbled. He coughed again and went limp. His last breath shuddered form his chest.

David shook off Saqqaf's hand and stood. No Paradise for Saqqaf. But David had already known that.

The strike team's sergeant frowned. "What'd he say?"

David snorted. "He said, 'Fuck you'."

---

When the team got back, they brought Saqqaf's body bag into the operations center. A gurney waited, and the strike force's medical staff.

General Carter and Kris waited while the captain of the team unzipped the bag. Carter had a sat phone in one hand, connected to the Situation Room. The president, Director Edwards, the national security advisor and the secretary of defense hovered on the other end of the line.

"It's him." Kris nodded. "It's him."

He thought he'd feel something. Anything. The satisfaction of a job well done. The joy of removing a mass murderer, a butcher, from the world. Revulsion, finally seeing him face to face. He thought he'd feel a hundred different things.

He felt nothing.

Carter spoke to the waiting Situation Room. "Confirmed, Mr. President. Saqqaf is dead."

The medical team wheeled Saqqaf away for an autopsy and a full investigation into his death, and what they could learn about his life. The strike team headed back to their part of the base. General Carter marched into the command center, still on the phone with the Situation Room.

What would happen next? When would the announcement of Saqqaf's death be made? What kind of reprisals would his fighters, the children of Saqqaf, attempt? What would happen to Saqqaf's movement, his death cult that wanted to remake the world in shades of hatred and gore?

What would the president do? What was the US's role now? What could they do to right this U-turn of history and despair?

David interrupted Kris's swirling mind, taking his hand and drawing him close. Dust from Saqqaf's death house clung to his black fatigues. Blood stained his sleeve, his knee. Saqqaf's blood. David pressed their foreheads together.

"Let's go home," he whispered. "Let's get the hell away from here."

# 20

**July 2006**

A different sun and a different sand filled their days.

David took Kris to Hawaii, where they rented a beach house and spent their days lying in the waves, or lying in bed. Lying in each other's arms, never separating.

David drank Kris in like he was nectar from God, manna from heaven. Kris felt their breaths sync, felt their hearts beat as one when they lay beneath the stars, when they watched the heavens unfold, endless stretches of eternity and radiance.

*A thousand million stars in the sky would not be enough to count the ways I love you. Or grains of sand on the beach, even if you split every grain in half.*

They kept the TV off and never looked at a newspaper. Didn't read email or download cables to check on. Nothing existed, for two perfect weeks, except for them and their love. If there was a heaven, each moment could have been an eternity spent in perfection. Lying on the beach, facing each other, David laced his hand through Kris's.

He didn't have to say anything. Kris already knew.

Kris's cell phone rang on the thirteenth day.

"*Mr. Caldera.*" Director Edwards called him, personally. "*You did a* hell *of a job in Iraq. One* hell *of a job. I have to say, I'm incredibly impressed with your analytical expertise, and your ability to target and neutralize two of our most wanted targets in the War on Terror. You're the real deal, Mr. Caldera. The president wanted me to pass along his personal thanks to you, and to tell you he's incredibly impressed. And proud.* Very *proud.*"

"Thank you, sir."

"*I have to say... I'm also impressed by the moral stance you took early on with the detainee program. We're cleaning that program up now. Mistakes were made, but they won't be again. Not on my watch.*"

He didn't know what to say.

Director Edwards sighed. Kris heard leather creak over the line, like Edwards was in his office, sitting back at his desk. "*Kris, the reason I'm calling is that I want to talk to you about your future. I realize that you may have a lot of opportunities coming your way soon. But I want you to stay. And, more than that, I want you back on the hunt for Bin Laden. In Afghanistan. Your* country *needs you, Mr. Caldera. The* world *needs you. What do you say?*"

Never, in the history of ever, in his whole life, had he imagined the director of the CIA would tell him he was impressive. That he was amazing. A hero, even.

That the president thought he was something special.

That was a world that didn't exist for him, he'd thought. Sissy gays and men with too much attitude didn't get noticed like that. They got noticed for their clothes or their voice or the way that straight people always made a spectacle out of their existence. They got noticed for being bothersome, or outside the norm.

He cried when he hung up, chest-wracking sobs as he buried his face in David's hip. For a moment, he wanted to call his papi, scream in blistering Spanish at him, throw the president's praise in his face. *I* did *become something, you son of a bitch. Other people see me. Why could you never?*

The impulse faded as soon as it had sparked. He'd given up on his papi when he was sixteen. Instead of a father's approval, he sought the approval of dozens of lovers, mixed with college professors and the thrill of proving people wrong. How that led to the CIA, and then to the president being proud of him...

Dan's voice came back to him, replaying a night years and years before in Pakistan, drinking cheap white wine on the roof. *You blew the door open, Kris. You blew the door for all us gays open.*

Where was Dan now? He'd lost track of everyone and everything while he and David were mired in Iraq. For two years, it had been as if nothing else existed outside Iraq's borders, that the rest of the world was some far-off place, totally removed from the horrors of the day to day.

"What are you going to do?" David stroked his back, broad, rough palms sliding over his smooth skin. "Do you want to stay?"

*I have to stay*, he'd said once to David, in an abandoned embassy in a ravaged country on the other side of the world. They'd been younger, and the war had only just begun. *I have to stay and make sure this never happens again.* He'd been so idealistic, so certain that he was where all the failures had originated, that he'd been the weakest link in the chain of American national security.

After five years and two wars, and horrors he'd never imagined could be real, was any of that true?

He'd still been a child when he watched those planes slam into the Twin Towers and the Pentagon. A college graduate and a junior CIA officer, but still a child where it counted. His world would forever be shaped by that morning, ripples translating in both directions, forward and backward in his life. Was there a life he could live, somewhere, that wasn't impacted, saturated, with the War on Terror? With September 11 and the day's aftershocks? Would he ever be able to live with himself if he walked away, knowing what the world was capable of?

The only thing as monumental to his life as September 11 was David.

"What do you want?" he whispered.

"To stay with you. Forever. Wherever that is." David kissed the back of his hand. "This is your career. You're admired. Respected. I'll follow you to the ends of the earth to support that. And you."

Shit, he was going to cry again. "David—"

David swallowed. Turned fifty shades of magenta, every hue of flushed unease. "There's just— There is something that I do want."

"What? Anything." Whatever David wanted, needed, he'd give him. "Is there something I'm not doing for you? Something I need to change?"

"No, no." David kissed the back of his hand again, lips lingering on Kris's skin.

He dropped to his knees, both of them. Cradled Kris's hand in his palms. "I want to *marry* you," David whispered. "I want you to pick me. I want you to keep me, forever."

Kris's jaw dropped. He was definitely going to fucking cry again. His heart was pounding, tears were erupting, and something was bursting in the center of his chest. "*David—*"

"The Quran says all souls were created in pairs. One soul, one life, that was meant for two people. In this world, we're supposed to find the other half of our souls and join together with them. Rejoin, and find the house of peace that we once knew before time." David moved closer. "I feel that with you. I always have. From the moment we met, it's been like I've known you for forever. Like everything in me is supposed to belong to everything in you."

Tears poured down Kris's face. He couldn't breathe. "*David...*"

"I was incomplete without you. I never want to be that way again. I want us to be together for all eternity." David kissed Kris's hands, the backs, his fingers, and turned his hands over. Kissed his palms, the very center of each. "Will you allow me to marry you? Will you let our souls join together? Forever?"

He pitched forward, falling into David's arms as he nodded, sobbed, gasped, tried to speak, all at the same time. "Yes, yes—" He could only repeat the word between hiccupping sobs as he clung to

David, as he buried his face in David's neck, his shoulders. Kris poured into him, folded into his arms, into his hold.

David carried him to their bed and stripped Kris's bathing suit, tears in his eyes as he kissed his way up Kris's body. He took his time, savoring Kris like they were marrying that moment, like Kris's *yes* was all it took for them to be wed, their souls joined together. He made love to him, joining their bodies as if making love were a prayer, an act of devotion to Kris's soul. A promise for all time in the curve of skin on skin, the thrust and hold, palms sliding up thighs and ribs, and in their curled toes.

Kris was a bonfire, a firework, dynamite that kept erupting, a nuclear warhead that kept expanding along every one of his nerves. There was no end to the moment, to the lightning, to the blaze. And he didn't want it to ever end.

---

Late the next day, when Kris finally raised the white flags, completely spent and physically unable to endure another moment of David's lovemaking, they discussed how to make it all work. How to turn the spiritual into the legal in the world of men.

"I've been researching." David flushed as he ate slices of mango. "I think we should go to Canada. We can get a license and get married right away. No residency requirement, no verification. We can just be married."

Kris sipped his mimosa, his third. The world was soft on the edges, the roar of the ocean an ever-present hum in his veins. "Let's do it. Let's do it right now. I don't want to wait."

"Really? You're sure? About this, and us?"

"It's been five years. I've been sure for a long time."

"I can arrange everything." David had a small smile, a look of expectant wonder on his face. "I'll see how fast we can actually get it done."

Kris beamed. "I will take care of the clothes. I'm only marrying once. So we're going to look phenomenal." He savored his mimosa, visions of white suits with black satin finishes, black bow ties and magenta cummerbunds flitting through his mind. "*Phenomenal*," he repeated.

David smiled. Their laptop had been abandoned on the kitchen table, but he spun it toward them and turned it on, plugged it into the ethernet cable. "I also want to buy you a house."

That stopped Kris's fantasies. "What?" They still, supposedly, lived in Kris's tiny studio, even though they hadn't been there in over a year. The rent had been auto paid. Hopefully everything was still there.

"I made way over three hundred thousand while we were in Iraq. And I have savings from before, when I was in the Army. I want to buy you, us, a home. A palace, just for us."

"A *palace*?"

"Figuratively speaking." David grinned. "I want us to have everything. I want to give you everything you've ever wanted."

You already have." Happiness, security. A man who loved him, and who he loved in return. Stability. Confidence. Empowerment. "I never had a house. I grew up in Manhattan. We had a two-bedroom block, stacked on top of other blocks. Low income housing."

"I loved the house I grew up in in Libya. In Benghazi. There was so much light. You could see the ocean from the roof, and the beach. The sand. When I came to America, I fell in love with trees." He chuckled. "Forests. I always loved field exercises when we were buried in the woods. Everyone thought I was insane."

"What kind of house do you want now?"

"Something quiet. Maybe a bit farther from Langley. Something with land, and trees. Privacy. But most of all, peaceful. Someplace you and I can relax."

"That sounds perfect." He slipped around the table and perched on David's lap. He took another sip of his mimosa. "Okay. I accept your wedding gift."

David laughed. One hand landed on Kris's briefs-covered ass. "This is not how you take a break."

Kris shrugged. One eyebrow arched.

David's laptop chimed. The website he'd clicked finally loaded. An advertisement and a service for gay couples eloping to Canada scrawled across the top. "*Elope in Canada for US$200! Call today! Next Day Services Available*!"

Their eyes met.

"Want to go to the airport?"

---

On the way to the airport, Kris called Director Edwards back. He was owed two full months of vacation after working nonstop in Iraq, hunting Saqqaf, and he was going to take every single day of it. He told the director he accepted the assignment in Afghanistan and that he'd report back in six weeks.

They flew to Toronto on a red-eye and checked into a hotel downtown. Kris dragged David from store to store, looking for the perfect pair of suits. David picked out a pair of fitted smoking jackets, and he looked so perfect in the dark brocade that Kris gave up the hunt and bought two, along with matching dark slacks, French cuff shirts, and bow ties.

David disappeared to buy rings while Kris window-shopped, promising to be back to meet Kris at an art gallery for the evening.

The elopement agency had a small assortment of locations where they could get married. They chose Gibraltar Point, a stretch of sandy beach near a park, for the next day.

They couldn't stop giggling the next morning. From making love with huge smiles to getting dressed in their pants and shirts, to tying their bow ties, they kept devolving into smiles and handholds, nervous and delighted laughs that turned into tiny and lingering kisses. They held hands in the taxi the whole drive to Gibraltar Point, stealing looks until they just stared into each other's eyes. Kris could see the outline of a ring box in David's pants.

A tall man, slender and wiry and dressed in a blue suit, met them. He was geeky and affable, and kept grinning at the two of them, obviously amused by their lovesick adoration of each other.

And then they stepped to the edge of the sand. Waves lapped at the shore. Seagulls cried overhead. Summer sun warmed the early afternoon, turned the sand golden, the sky a perfect azure.

David took Kris's hands. Kris's breath shuddered.

Kris hadn't known what David was going to arrange. He half expected an Islamic ceremony, if there *were* any Islamic imams who would have wed them, two men, and one not a Muslim.

Though, was David a Muslim? What did he consider himself? David's pain was too raw, too poignant, to wade into those waters. Kris would be his lighthouse out of those memories, out of the anguish, his life preserver back to safer shores.

The officiant kept the ceremony short and simple, a standard exhortation on the beauty of marriage and then the exchange of vows, first David and then Kris promising to have and to hold, to love and to cherish, from that day ever forward. David slipped a gold ring, with a channel of diamonds in the center, onto Kris's finger. Kris did the same for David, biting his lip as he beamed.

Kris's breath kept coming faster, his smile kept getting wider. He thought he'd faint, or launch into space. He held David's hand in both of his own.

"Before we conclude," the officiant smiled at Kris. "I understand your groom has something he'd like to recite?"

Kris paled. David chuckled. "I do, yes. It's a poem of Rumi's." He cleared his throat and looked deep into Kris's gaze.

> "Oh Beloved,
> take me.
> Liberate my soul.
> Fill me with your love and
> release me from the two worlds.
> If I set my heart on anything but you
> let fire burn me from inside.
> Oh Beloved,
> take away what I want.
> Take away what I do.

Take away what I need.
Take away everything
that takes me from you."

The officiant wilted. Kris, frozen, tried to come up with something, anything to say that could come near David's love, near his intensity. He scraped his brain, but David's vows kept repeating on an infinite loop, his love drowning everything else out.

Kris grabbed him and pulled them together, capturing David's lips, kissing him with everything he had, every part of his being. David wrapped him up, held him close, and somewhere, they both heard the officiant exclaim, "I pronounce you married! Congratulations!"

There were claps from passersby who had stopped to watch, three walkers and a pair of old ladies. David buried his face in Kris's neck as Kris waved, thanking them. The officiant shook their hands and snapped a few pictures, part of the package, and promised he'd email them as soon as he could.

"Husband," Kris said, squeezing David's hand.

"Husband," David repeated. "*Beloved*."

---

After two more days in Toronto, they flew back to DC. David had already started looking online at houses to buy, and he had a long list of homes ready to check out with a realtor. Buying a house seemed all the better after they returned to their cramped studio, which, shut in for a year without air or light, was covered in dust and musty with disuse.

On the third day, they found their home. Older, with a North Eastern style, it sat on a couple of acres within a dense woodland outside of Leesburg, Virginia. It was pure Americana, the kind of home from sitcoms and television shows. The backyard had a porch and a grill and a patio set, and miles of uninterrupted woodland views. From the moment they walked through the door, it was home. They both felt it, immediately.

"We'll take it."

The seller balked, at first, at a gay married couple purchasing their house. But when David offered to pay cash, they accepted. The house was already vacated, the previous couple already moved on to their new home on the West Coast.

Kris and David moved in ten days later.

For a month, they lived a dreamscape, a fantasy life their childhood selves might have once imagined, but pushed away as unattainable, too far-fetched. Happiness that pure, that distilled, wasn't possible in their lives, they'd thought. Nowhere was there a future with a husband, a home, professional respect. Not for scrappy gay brown boys from the Lower East side, or for an exile separated from everything he'd once known. His home, his country, his family, his faith.

But how life curved and turned and twisted.

Happiness was waking up in their bed together, making love with the windows open and hearing the birds in the trees. David, baking breakfast, cinnamon rolls and French toast and mimosas. Eating together on the porch, walking hand in hand through the trees. David grilling as the sun set. Curling together in front of the fireplace until they were kissing, making love, flickering flames casting glowing light against their sweat-warmed skin. Day after day of perfection.

Kris called his mother, the first time he'd called her not on Christmas or Easter in almost a decade. She immediately, of course thought he was dying, that he had cancer and was in the hospital. "Mi chico, Dios mío, *what is wrong? You're in the hospital, you're dying? You have cancer?* Dios mío, *what is it?*"

"*Mamá, Mamá!*" He'd laughed at her. "*Mamá*, no. *Mamá*, I have a surprise for you."

"*Ay, I cannot take surprises. You know I do not like them. You know!*"

"*Mamá*, I got married!"

Silence. "*Ahhhh!*" She'd cried, a blubber of Spanish and English and exclamations, happiness that blurred into noise over the scratchy call to Puerto Rico. "*But,* mi chico*....*" His mother had hesitated. "Mi chico, *I thought you...*"

"His name is David, *Mamá*. We have been together for five years. He's the love of my life." He couldn't stop the happy sigh in his voice, the joy in his words.

"Cinco años? Ay, ay, mi chico*! You are happy? This man, he makes you happy?*"

"The happiest I've *ever* been, *Mamá*."

She'd clucked at him, telling him she was happy for him, that she kept praying for him every night, always praying for his happiness, his safety. She was happy her prayers had been answered, she said. "*I just want you to be happy,* mi chico*. I love you so much. I couldn't make you happy when you were little. I'm so sorry,* mi cariño."

"*Mamá*, you were great. I love you. I'll always love you."

"*I love you,* mi cariño. *Tell David hello.*"

For not seeing each other in over a decade, and for only talking twice a year, it went better than he'd expected.

David spent a week gearing up to call his mother. Kris caught him pacing in front of the phone, staring at it and mentally composing what he was going to say. When he finally decided to call, they sat outside on their porch, David's favorite spot, and Kris held his hand.

"Mama, *as-salaam-alaikum*. It's me."

"Wa alaikum as-salaam*! Dawood*!" Her voice, warm and rich, erupted from the phone. "*How are you, my son? Where are you? It's been so long since we spoke.*" Her voice held a gentle reprimand.

"I'm sorry, Mama. I'm outside Washington DC now. I've left the Army. I work for a contractor."

"*Oh.*" She didn't say much about that. Contractors' reputations had been hit hard, especially in Arab communities. Most Americans called contractors mercenaries. Most Arab communities called them murderers.

"Mama..." David took a deep breath. "Mama, you've always wanted me to be happy, right?"

"In shaa Allah, *it is what I pray for, Dawood. That you find your way to happiness, and to Allah, again. They are one and the same,* habibi."

David flinched. "Mama... Why did you not remarry? After..."

She didn't speak, not for a moment. "*Because I married your Baba for this life and the next. We were two souls meant to be together,* habibi." She paused. "*Why do you ask me this now?* In shaa Allah, *is there a reason...*"

"There is, Mama." David's voice shook. "I've met someone. Someone who, I believe, is the same for me. Part of my soul is theirs. And I am so happy, Mama. So happy."

"Allahu Akbar! *Dawood! This is a blessing from Allah!* Bismillah, *I have prayed for you to find a loving wife, a woman who can calm your soul! Dawood!* Allahu Akbar!"

David squeezed his eyes closed and clenched Kris's hands. "*His* name is Kris." He held his breath.

His mother stopped. Stopped everything. Stopped cheering. Stopped praying, praising Allah. Stopped celebrating. Stopped breathing. "*You mean... you have found a friend? Not a wife? This is like the friendship of the Prophet,* salla Allahu alayhi wa sallam, *and Abu Bakr*?"

Abu Bakr, the Prophet Muhammad's best and closest friend, and the father of Aisha, Muhammad's most influential wife. The two men had been inseparable, brothers in arms and in faith, a model of friendship for over a millennium to Muslims.

Kris bowed his head. She wasn't getting it. She was *choosing* not to get it.

Cringing, David trembled in Kris's handhold. His expression crumpled, and he curled forward, dragging one hand over his face. "My *best* friend, Mama. My best and closest friend. Kris will be with me *forever*. In this life and the next."

Silence.

"Do you understand what I'm telling you, Mama?"

"*Dawood, I am grateful you have found such a deep friendship. I am. But,* habibi, *do not let this friendship take the place of what you need. The love of a wife, and a family. I will continue to pray for your heart to find its match in a wife.* In shaa Allah, *your wife is waiting for you. It will happen,* habibi. *I know it. You will find your love."*

"Mama..."

*"I can ask my friends about their daughters. If you would like help? I thought you wanted to do things the Western way, but I can help you,* habibi."

"No, Mama." Tears trickled down David's cheeks, rivers that turned to waterfalls at his jawline. Kris squeezed his hand until it hurt, until he thought all his bones would break. "No, Mama. *In shaa Allah,* I will find my soul mate." David squeezed back.

"Ana bahibak, habibi." His mother's love flowed over the phone line. *"I pray for you every day."*

"Mama. *Ana bahibak."*

He hung up before she could say anything else, cutting the line and dropping the cordless phone on the porch. He pitched forward, burying his face in both hands as sobs tore through him. Kris kneeled, holding him as David's tears soaked his shirt. "I'm sorry."

"She'll never accept it. She'll never understand. Even if I brought you to her, showed her how much I love you..." He sniffed, tried to wipe his tears away. More fell. "I wish I could introduce you to my father."

Kris shook his head, unable to speak, and his tears joined David's in a puddle on the porch beneath them. David clung to him, crying as the sun set and the stars peeked through, as the day turned to night, until Kris guided him to their bed and held him for the rest of the night.

## CIA Headquarters, Langley Virginia - September 2006

"Where do I submit paperwork to update my personnel status to married?"

Eight weeks after leaving Iraq, Kris strutted into CIA headquarters and into George's new office. George had been promoted again, now the deputy director of operations, in charge of clandestine field operations around the world. Time had been kind to George; rank advancement even kinder.

Kris couldn't begrudge him too much. George had carried them all alongside him with his rise through the agency. Kris was off to head up a base hunting Bin Laden in Afghanistan again, and Ryan was the chief of station in Afghanistan, just beneath George.

First things first. Kris wasn't going back to Afghanistan without official endorsement of his marriage to David. During the Saqqaf hunt, David had been transferred from contractor status to employee status, a way to bring him on board without having to send him to The Farm, interrupt the Saqqaf hunt. Which meant he was now a CIA employee. Which meant Kris and David could be deployed together to Afghanistan as a married couple.

He held up his marriage certificate, sent from Toronto, like a warrant. He arched one eyebrow.

George's fingers hovered over his keyboard. He blinked. "*Married*?"

"Last month. In Canada. We're married now. I expect we'll be treated like every other married CIA couple."

George blinked again. "I... don't know how that will work. There are no gay married couples."

"Yes there are. We're married. And it doesn't matter if we're gay. We will get the same treatment."

George cringed. "But... gay marriage isn't legal here, Kris. Only a few states recognize it, and the federal government explicitly stands against it. The DOMA—" George frowned.

The Defense of Marriage Act. Kris's blood boiled. In 1996, the same year it was finally legal for homosexuals to hold security clearances, Congress passed the DOMA, defining federal law to recognize marriage as between one man and one woman only. No federal agency recognized same sex marriage or civil unions. "You're the deputy director of operations. You can make this happen."

"I cannot change federal law."

"You can get us stationed together. He's coming with me to Afghanistan. And this time, none of the bullshit about not being able to share housing. We're fucking married. And I don't give a shit what some ridiculous law says. You want me to find Bin Laden? This is my price."

"You're an employee of the CIA, not a mafia boss. You don't have a price we'll pay. You do the assignment or you're out of a job." George's voice turned sharp, his face sour.

"You called me in Iraq. You begged for my help, and I came through for you," Kris snapped. "You going to show up for me?"

George's jaw clenched. Kris watched him lick his teeth, purse his lips. "You need to go to HR if you want to update your marital status," he growled. "I'm not the person to talk to."

---

"Mr. Caldera, there's no option in the system to list you as married to Mr. Haddad." The frazzled HR tech threw up her hands. "If I change your status to married, it asks for the *wife's* name. If I say that the spouse is also in the CIA, in order to give you the joint assignments that you want, it gives me a list of female employees to select. Mr. Haddad isn't on the list of people you can be married to."

Kris blinked. He counted to five, slowly, in his head. He held up his left hand. "Do you see this ring? It's identical to the one on David's hand. My husband's hand. We are married." He tapped their marriage license, laid out on the desk between him and the HR tech, repeatedly. "We're married, legally."

"In Canada." The tech sat back, sighing. "I'm not even supposed to try to help you. The law in the US is clear. The federal government does not recognize marriages between same sex partners. It's not allowed. It doesn't exist in the United States. There's nothing I can do."

"I'm married. Crossing a border doesn't invalidate that," Kris snapped.

"Mr. Caldera, it just can't happen here. Gay marriage isn't legal."

"So you're saying I can't get assigned to the same stations as my husband? Can't put my husband on my health plan? Can't file our taxes together? Can't put him as my inheritor and designated spouse survivor?"

The HR tech shook her head. "No. You can't. Not until the law is changed. And..." She shrugged. "It doesn't seem like that is going to happen anytime soon." She sighed. "I'm sorry."

"I don't fucking care about your sorrys!" Kris's gaze fell on her diamond ring, glittering from her left hand. "You're married?"

"I am."

"To a man?"

She nodded, once. Her expression closed down. Gates fell behind her eyes. She lifted her chin, staring at him.

"How would you feel if you couldn't call him your husband? If you were told your marriage wasn't legal? That it didn't exist?"

"I wouldn't have bothered getting married if I knew I couldn't. I wouldn't try to cause problems." She laced her hands in her lap and glared. "I cannot help you, Mr. Caldera. In the eyes of the federal government and the CIA, your marriage isn't valid and doesn't exist. If the law changes, you can come back. Until then."

She held her hand out to her doorway.

---

He ran into Dan after lunch, outside CTC. Dan looked worn and tired, thinner than before, pale.

"Kris!" Dan beamed and wrapped him up, hugging him for a long moment. "I heard all about Iraq, what you did. Taking out Saqqaf. Amazing, as per usual." He laughed, held onto Kris's arms, as if he didn't want to let go. "How are you?"

"Good!" Kris waggled his left hand. "We did it. We ran away to Canada!"

Dan's jaw dropped as he stared at Kris's ring. He froze. Blinked. Inhaled sharply. "You and David? You got married?"

"We did!" Kris pulled a face. "Not that the CIA or the United States government are recognizing it, but I'm not giving up the fight."

Dan chuckled, the sound wan, thin. "You never do. But they're going to have to give in to you. They don't know what they're facing." He stared at Kris, slowly smiling. "David is a very, *very* lucky man, Kris. A *very* lucky man."

"I'm the lucky one."

"No. He is," Dan said softly.

"What's been going on with you? You look like shit. Are they over-working you?"

Dan snorted, half laughing and turning away. "Thanks. That's what I've always wanted to hear from you." He shook his head. "I was at Gitmo." He shrugged. "After everything, though, I came back to headquarters. I've been working with George. In operations."

"Ooh, on management track." Kris wagged his eyebrows. His voice turned serious. "How was Gitmo? I heard it was bad. Real bad. Lots of abuse, lots of crossing the line."

Dan sighed. He stared at the wall as his eyes narrowed. "It's in the past now. It's all over and done with."

"You okay? I mean, really okay?" Kris reached for his elbow and squeezed.

Dan covered his hand with his own. "I'm all right."

"Seeing anyone?"

"Nah. All the best guys are taken." He winked.

"We'll find you someone, Dan. Someone wonderful, just like you."

Dan blushed. "I'm good. I'm really happy for you, Kris. I'm happy you're happy. Keep in touch?"

"Of course. You too!"

---

At three in the afternoon, Kris barged into Director Edwards's office, fired up and ready for a fight. He fumed, thoughts racing through his mind, a bitter diatribe against the CIA, against their policies, against the federal government, against DOMA, against George and the entire world that seemed pitted against him and David. He kept circling back to the same thing, over and over.

If he was good enough to find the United States' enemies, why wasn't he good enough to be recognized by the CIA or the federal government? Why was his marriage such an abhorrent thing? Was the government that tortured detainees, that had enabled the decisions that allowed Abu Ghraib to happen, actually going to say his love was worse?

Fuck that.

He stormed in, fire in his wake. If he could have killed a man with the force of his glare, headquarters would have been littered with corpses. "Director—"

"Ahh, Mr. Caldera." Director Edwards smiled and nodded to the leather club chairs across from his desk. George sat in one, scowling. "Please, join us."

"Sir, first of all, I have to say—"

"You got what you wanted, Caldera," George interrupted. He held up a manila folder. "It's all in here. Your orders to Afghanistan. And his."

Director Edwards smiled again. "Please take a seat, Mr. Caldera. We need to go over the details of your assignment."

Slowly, he sat, taking the folder from George and perusing the orders. He and David were assigned to the mission. David was to be one of the senior security specialists, and he was being given command of a remote CIA base in the Afghanistan-Pakistan border region.

The orders were addressed to Ryan. He'd be reporting directly to him, in Kabul. Kris couldn't hold back his snort, his eye-roll.

George sighed, comically loudly.

There was a handwritten note, signed by George, at the bottom of the orders. **Assign CALDERA and HADDAD joint living space. CALDERA and HADDAD in committed civil partnership, attested to the CIA on this day.*

Conspicuously absent was the word *married*.

It was a start, though. More than what he had that morning, less than what he wanted. Way, way less.

There'd be time to fight for more. He'd chip away at this, until he and David were recognized. Until their marriage was recognized.

With the grace of a princess, he closed the folder and nodded to the director. "This is acceptable," he said. "*Barely* acceptable."

Director Edwards asked for the folder and countersigned George's note. "We'll get these sent to Kabul station right away. Now, let's talk about your mission."

# 21

## Camp Carson, Afghanistan-Pakistan Border, Afghanistan - Autumn 2008

Seven years after Kris had left Afghanistan, the country looked worse than it had before the invasion of 2001.

The Taliban had surged and faced off against US forces in pockets all around the country, controlling large swathes of territory and subjecting Afghan citizens to their same repressive fundamentalism mixed with tribalism. Women had gone back under the burqa, and girls were forbidden from going to school.

Bands of warlords had poured out of the lawless tribal areas, each snatching a section of the border region for their brutal gangs. They ran weapons and drugs, terrorized locals on both sides of the border, and stood against the United States, the struggling Afghan government, and Pakistan. Scattered border crossings straddled the main roads that passed between the two countries, but goat paths and footpaths crisscrossed the border, smuggling routes for anything and everything. And everyone.

Al-Qaeda, whose fighters and leaders had fled the firebombing of their homes and camps in late 2001, returned, staging a Hollywood-worthy comeback story in the mountainous border region and tribal belt.

As the United States poured men, money, and myopic attention into Iraq, al-Qaeda fighters regrouped, returned and resettled. New commanders were promoted, bloodthirsty and hungry to strike back for every moment following September 11, every death of their brothers and comrades.

*Al-Qaeda,* Kris wrote in his monthly summary cable to Langley, *remains highly organized, highly motivated, and extremely capable of carrying out large-scale terror attacks within Afghanistan, Pakistan, and abroad. Their abilities at the present time meet or exceed their abilities from before 11 September 2001.*

In so many ways, on so many levels, Iraq had derailed *everything.* National security. The hunt for Bin Laden. The destruction of al-Qaeda. The lives of thousands of American soldiers. The lives of hundreds of thousands, millions, of Iraqis, and so many more in the Middle East. The lives and hearts of a billion Muslims around the world.

Seven years after the invasion, and here he was, trying to pick up the broken pieces of Afghanistan and destroy al-Qaeda *again.* But this time the enemy was stronger, more enraged, and had seven years of experience striking back at the United States, the US military, and the CIA.

But Kris had new weapons, too. Back in 2001, drone warfare had been in its infancy. Only a handful had circled the skies over Afghanistan then. Now, hundreds of Predator drones swung in lazy orbits over the skies.

Director Edwards had given him the orders straight from the mouth of the new president: the gloves were off.

The drones were unleashed. *Destroy their safe houses, their training camps, their communication networks, and their commanders, wherever you find them, as quickly as you can.*

It was the evolution of the former vice president's decree. *Find them, stop them.*

But now *stopping them* meant *killing them,* anywhere in the world.

If there was a chance that terrorists were planning the worst attack imaginable, then the US had to proceed like that was *fact*. All of the United States' strategic and tactical decisions stemmed from the vice president's orders, given shortly after September 11, 2001.

Kris fell asleep, finally, after staying up and reading the day's collected phone intercepts from Langley, Kabul, and Pakistan. Every cell phone call in the region was vacuumed up and analyzed by an array of computer servers and then a horde of analysts at the NSA and CIA. Several names had repeatedly popped up around vague references to malls, football stadiums, and bus stops in America. Phrases that sounded like veiled conversations about practice runs and surveillance.

"*Find them, Caldera*," Ryan had barked over the phone from Kabul. "*And kill them.*"

The two named men were several rungs down the ladder of al-Qaeda from Bin Laden, but they were big fish in the organization's rising phoenix. Salim and Suleyman, both on the FBI and CIA's Most Wanted list. Salim had been a part of the 1998 embassy bombings in Africa and had made his way back to Afghanistan to help with al-Qaeda's post-September 11 savagery. After the fall of Afghanistan, Suleyman had been promoted up the ranks until he was in charge of all terror operations in Pakistan and Afghanistan. He'd planned the assassination of the Pakistani prime minister and had organized a multi-year reign of carnage on both sides of the border. His largest attack was the bombing of the Islamabad Marriott Hotel.

For the past week, Kris had been following them with his drones until he finally found their headquarters, their safe house, deep in the tribal belt in an abandoned village. Only Salim was there, for the moment. Suleyman had disappeared. But he'd be back.

"Should we try to capture them? They're in the senior al-Qaeda ranks. Don't we want to interrogate them? Find out what they know about Bin Laden? Zawahiri?" Kris had pushed back against Ryan's order. "These are the most senior members we've targeted. What if Suleyman is with Zawahiri now? Or Bin Laden?"

*"Then you should have kept better eyes-on. Never have let him slip your Predators."* Ryan's voice had been tight, barely controlled anger simmering beneath his words. *"How would you try to capture these two, Caldera? Send Haddad in, guns blazing? An Arab John Wayne? We have no authority in the tribal belt. We don't have the manpower to insert a strike force, render a target, and get them out of there. The costs are too high. Besides,"* he said, his words going tight. *"We don't do that anymore. And how would you suggest we extract critical information from such a hardened al-Qaeda leader?"*

"My track records speaks for itself, Ryan."

*"Find them. Eliminate them. Those are your orders."*

"Yes sir."

Before sunrise, only hours after he'd fallen asleep, David's arm thrown around his waist, the door to Kris's quarters slid open. "Sir, we've got a hit on a target."

He trudged down to the drone bay, a double-wide trailer behind a concrete wall fortified with sandbags, and slipped into the dim cavernous space. Monitors glowed in night vision green, infrared spectrum, cool blue and warm red. Soldiers and CIA operators manned a dozen joysticks before their monitors, flying the drones circling the region.

His deputy, a man named Darren, who had cut his teeth in Iraq as an Army intelligence captain before moving to the CIA, waved him over to the main monitor bank.

"Salim left his hideout in the middle of the night. We followed him as he drove out to a remote village in the mountains where he picked up a man he seemed to know well. They got into his vehicle and returned to his hideout. These are the images we captured of the second man."

Kris flipped through angled shots of the mystery man. About six foot, slender, robed. A turban obscured his face from most of the images. "How do we know it's not Salim's father? Or his uncle? Or his wife's uncle's brother's best friend?"

"It's not his father, and it's not his uncle." Darren, who seemed to tolerate Kris only enough to complete their mission, ignored his third question. "We believe this is Suleyman and that they are together in Salim's safe house now."

"You want to strike."

"Yes sir." Darren loved "taking out the trash", as he called it.

But each strike came with consequences. *Find them, kill them* was almost too easy with drones. Too far removed from the impact, it became far too easy to become a push-button jockey. Innocent civilians had been caught in the crossfire, or had been targeted mistakenly. There was innocent blood on the drone program's hands, but since that blood was hundreds, if not thousands of miles away, no one in the US seemed to mind.

Kris did.

"Tell me the full history of this safe house. How many civilians have entered and exited? Who has come and gone in the past twenty-four, forty-eight, and seventy-two hours? What civilians live in the proximity of the target location?"

Darren and the drone operator ran through the evidence, pulling up images and logs to substantiate the comings and goings of everyone into and out of the safe house. As far as they had seen, it had only ever been Salim, with phone intercepts providing the intel that Suleyman visited occasionally. The safe house was in an abandoned village, far from civilians. Unusual, in the practices of al-Qaeda. They liked to surround themselves with civilians, situate themselves in the worst possible target zones. Make a strike against them a morally objectionable call and an impossible order.

But not this time.

"Are there any women or children in the compound? Does Salim have a wife? Kids?"

"Salim's wife and kids live in Peshawar."

"How confident are you that it's Suleyman with him?"

"Eighty percent, sir."

He held life and death in his hands every day. Kris imagined his decisions like rocks being thrown into a pond, ripples from every decision expanding, striking other decisions, other lives and beings in the pond and the world. Consequence, for every action, every single thing, sometimes beyond the horizon, beyond the curve of the earth, where no one could see. Sometimes the ripples seemed to stretch forward and backward in time, even. Here he was in Afghanistan, seven years after September 11. And September 11 had been decades after the CIA's support to the mujahedeen, decades after Ambassador Dubs's assassination. Ripples expanding, ever outward.

What would this strike create? What consequences?

"Proceed with your strike." He nodded to Darren. "Use every Hellfire. Let's be certain."

Let it never be said that he, a gay man, shied away from ordering a rain of death and destruction. If there was one snide comment others could fling at him, it was not that he was weak, or had a soft stomach.

The drone pilot pivoted his joystick, changing the Predator's orbit until he was lined up for his strike. On-screen, the safe house filled the center of the monitor, black-and-white images in the pre-dawn glow. *They're just beginning to pray.*

The pilot fired, counted down. "Three... two... one... Impact."

A giant mushroom cloud appeared, non-nuclear, but skyrocketing debris and dust and shattered lives into the air.

It took hours for the cloud to dissipate. The drone stayed in orbit the entire time, recording the crater that had replaced the safe house and the removal of two burned and mangled bodies from the rubble. In the intercept bay, Kris flagged anything discussing the deaths of any al-Qaeda commanders be brought to him immediately.

Several hours later, a runner brought him the intercept: Salim and Suleyman were declared dead.

Al-Qaeda vowed revenge.

---

Kris longed for his and David's Virginia home, nestled in the woods, surrounded by nature and peace.

Home in Afghanistan was Camp Carson, a dusty, windswept base of concrete sprawl and HESCO barriers, sandbags and concertina wire, trailers and humming generators. The base perched on a plateau just north of Tora Bora. It was close to where he had manned the radios while David and Ryan and the others plunged into the mountains, shadowing Bin Laden's footsteps, so long ago. Now, instead of the bare emptiness and desolation from before, the base was a fortress guarded by helicopter gunships, massive perimeter fencing, and armed guards in towers, watching everything.

The land was the very definition of austere. Dry desert, devoid of life, stretched for miles, until the plateau bumped into the White Mountains and the slopes of Tora Bora changed to craggy woods and scattered ferns. Even from a distance, the scars and craters of the battle in 2001 were visible, pockmarks on the land, empty of life.

Beyond Tora Bora, Pakistan stretched into the horizon. The border separating the two countries was impossible to see, a line in the dust without marking, without signposts or fences. The peaks seemed to hover in the haze, scarred with sunlight, as if trying to escape the earth into the sky. In the afternoons, when the light burned onto the dead lands, the desiccated, war-ravaged earth, Kris thought the place looked a little like Hell would after the fires burned themselves out. Afghanistan still seemed that far away from the rest of the world.

Life on base wasn't terrible. He and David shared quarters, a privilege only given to married CIA officers. They had a cramped double bed shoved in the same size space as a single officer's quarters, one nightstand, one desk that wobbled whenever it was looked at, and a fluorescent light strip with a dangling orange extension cord.

Compared to being separated from David, it was paradise.

They shared a bathroom with two other officers. The base had a gym crammed full with exercise equipment, donated by every fitness manufacturer in the States. The food was good, and the mess hall served a rotating selection of American favorites. Lobster and crab legs even showed up on the menu. There was nothing as strange to Kris as eating lobster with David by the light of their flashlight at two in the morning, their version of a date in Afghanistan.

A CIA-run lounge served beer and wine, a luxury that the rest of the soldiers in Afghanistan couldn't taste. Football, basketball, and baseball games were beamed live into the base via satellite.

Kris commuted from his trailer quarters to the command center every day, a walk of three minutes. David, more days than not, dressed in traditional Afghan clothes and slipped out, driving a series of loops and switchbacks and changing cars and bicycles and even picking up a donkey, all to avoid being tracked. He, and sometimes others with him, would wander the border regions, crisscrossing into Pakistan and back into Afghanistan, scouting for tracks, hidden weapons, signs of the Taliban or al-Qaeda. He'd joined the CIA's ultra-secretive counterterrorist pursuit teams, hunting on the ground to collect intelligence, and to capture or kill the CIA's most wanted.

They formed opposite sides of the spear. Kris with his drones, David with his clandestine infiltration on the ground. David sparred with shadows and ghosts, always looking over his shoulder, ever mindful of being discovered. Kris battled politics and whispers, a dizzying array of mixed priorities, and constant pressure from every part of the government. The Department of Defense, NATO Command in Kabul, Special Operations Command, and Ryan, each pulled Kris in different directions, wanting different operations, different actions.

The CIA base was host to Special Forces and Delta operators, military royalty who were *never* told *no*, never questioned. Already against the CIA in principle and mocking them behind their back for being clowns, push-button jockeys, and children who hid on their bases, the Special Forces soldiers recoiled hard when they were told Kris was the new commander of the remote field base.

More than once, Kris heard soldiers mockingly refer to Camp Carson as Camp Cocklover. Or to himself as Major Fag. The Special Forces, notoriously tight-knit and cultish, excluded David from their fraternity with a pathological virulence.

Darren, his deputy, had come from the Special Forces world, and he straddled the gulf between the CIA and the military. Darren showed up and he did his job, and he never acted anything less than professional to Kris's face, but his best friends were the loudest of the operators who sneered and joked in the mess hall.

After Salim and Suleyman's deaths, Kris's eavesdropping nets spread wide across the northwestern Pakistan frontier, stretching from the Afghanistan border with Central Asia to almost the heart of Pakistan. The world's best and most sophisticated technology pointed at the globe's most backwater and underdeveloped regions. Drones hovered over every ancient village, every dirt path, every huddle of goats. Computers at the NSA and at Langley hummed, ripping through trunk phone lines, scanning bytes of data passing over the internet, and poring through captured phone conversations vacuumed up by the technology of the most powerful nation on earth.

It was awe-inspiring, how much power they wielded.

The hunt for al-Qaeda's senior leadership usually progressed at a fixed pace. The computers chewed data. Analysts reviewed intelligence. Kris directed their gazes and analysis, focused his team to zero in on certain areas, expand other lines of intelligence gathering. He was in charge of both the drone program and the human intelligence program, managing an army of informants from Pakistan and Afghanistan who traded bits of information, sightings, and rumors for handouts of cash and parcels of food.

But everything came to a screeching halt with one word, vacuumed up over a war-ravaged Pakistan province infested with al-Qaeda and Taliban warlords in the heart of a brittle no-man's-land of terrorism and virulent anti-Western hatred.

*Nawawiun.*

*Nuclear.*

The flash cable came in from Langley: al-Qaeda intercepts in Waziristan Province had captured the phone conversation of two senior commanders debating the Islamic merits of using nuclear devices. The original intercept, translated Arabic, was beneath the summary. Kris read it four times.

*Nawawiun. Nuclear.*

Kris's phone blew up seconds later, Ryan phoning from Kabul at the same time an analyst from Langley tried to get through. He answered Ryan.

"*Have you seen the newest cable?*"

"I have it in my hands."

"*This is a fucking nightmare. If al-Qaeda gets their hands on a nuke, that's a fucking disaster. It's what they've always wanted. Always.*"

"Where could they have gotten one, though?"

"*Pakistan. Old Soviet weapons that have gotten misplaced. There are more than a few very plausible options for how they could have gotten their hands on a nuclear device.*"

"We haven't authenticated this report beyond just a single intercept. We need to know more."

"*You're telling me.*" Ryan snorted. "*You need to get your people out there, now. You're the most forward base, and this threat is coming from your territory.*"

"I'll redirect my people. See what we can find out from our sources on the ground. I can move more drones over Waziristan, but the DOD is going to start complaining about the reallocation."

"*I'll handle DOD. You just find out what's going on in Waziristan, before al-Qaeda detonates a nuke and we're looking at the real Apocalypse.*"

---

The intel came in like an ocean wave, crashing against Camp Carson.

Another intercept, a few days later: three al-Qaeda members talking about a Shura council meeting they had attended where the topic of debate was whether using *nawawiun* devices was Islamic. Was such a device considered something lawful in the eyes of Allah? Or were nuclear devices harmful to creation, to Allah's will?

Shura council meetings were called when al-Qaeda decision-makers needed to find consensus on an action and needed Islamic cover for their choices in combat. Bin Laden had called such a meeting to discuss the September 11 attacks. The Shura had ultimately rejected his proposal, saying the attacks were un-Islamic.

Bin Laden proceeded anyway.

Saqqaf, in Iraq, hadn't bothered with a Shura council. He'd forged ahead, dedicated to his own death cult, his bloodthirsty, apocalyptic vision of jihad as a cleansing fire of wrath that would sweep the world. Only a scattered handful of extreme imams had ever signed on to Saqqaf's vision of Islam. Every major and established religious authority across multiple sects of the faith had denounced him.

What did it mean that a new Shura council was debating the use of *nawawiun* devices? Shura councils were not called for high-minded ideas or what-if scenarios; they were the faithful's most devout form of democracy: what did the people think of a leader's proposed action, and how did such actions line up with Allah's will for humanity?

The possibility that this nuclear threat was real, and imminent, shot higher.

Director Edwards held a conference call with Kris and Ryan, going over every minute detail of both intercepts. What did this word mean in Arabic, in all its permutations? What had human sources said in the past few days? Had there been anything to corroborate the reports?

David and another CIA SAD officer headed out to Waziristan for three days, posing as out-of-work farmers searching for any employment they could find. David came back filthy and covered in shit—he'd found a job making mudbricks out of fresh cow dung—but with ominous rumors and street chatter as well.

Something *big* was coming, the word on the street said. Something not even the Great Satan could withstand. Something not even they could stop.

Kris formally recommended Director Edwards ask to increase the threat level for the homeland. "This is the most serious threat al-Qaeda has presented since before September eleventh, Director. What they're saying, how they're acting. This is serious. Deadly serious."

*"Kris, if you think this is that serious, then I'll take your recommendation straight to the president. Promise me, Kris. We're going to find out what the hell is going on over there and stop whatever it is they're planning."*

"I promise." His vow, seven years old, echoed, a ripple extending forward through time. He would never let harm come to the homeland again, not because of him. Not because of what he did or didn't do. "I swear."

---

His phone rang in the middle of the night.

Kris was still awake, reading daily cables and reports from his analysts, trying to find a morsel of intel to exploit or expand on. David lay facedown on his lap, face burrowed into his belly. They'd made love and David had passed out, exhausted to the bone with his near-daily treks across the border and back.

His phone buzzed on the nightstand, clattering across the cheap laminate and skittering away from his grasp.

The country code showed Jordan. He didn't recognize the number. "Hello?"

"*Mr. Caldera.*" The deep voice, sounding almost as tired and worn through as Kris felt, belonged to Ahmad, one of the Mukhabarat agents Jordan had sent to Iraq to help with the hunt for Saqqaf. "*We need to talk.*"

"What about?"

"*I'm going to send you an email. It has a video clip attached. After you watch it, call me back.*" Ahmad hung up.

Kris pursed his lips and waited. A minute later, his phone vibrated again, an incoming email. *Watch this*, the subject line read.

He clicked the video file.

It was grainy, the shadows too dark and the lights too bright. Men in robes and turbans moved around a crowded room, a mudbrick hut with open holes for windows. Rifles were propped against walls. The men sat on dusty carpets in a circle. The video zoomed out, panned slightly. Refocused. It was obviously shot from something small, something handheld. Something concealed. A bit of robe fell over the lens before being brushed away—

And revealing the aged face of al-Qaeda's number two, Ayman Al-Zawahiri.

Kris stopped breathing. His eyes widened, until he felt like his eyeballs would fall from his skull.

Zawahiri spoke, but the audio was distorted. Kris had to rewind and re-watch a half dozen times. "*Brothers*," Zawahiri said. "*The Sheikh, Allah bless him, sends his love. He has asked that we discuss a most urgent topic today. We must discuss the nuclear devices. Does Allah declare the nawawiun a proper weapon of war*?"

The video cut out abruptly.

The Sheikh. Osama Bin Laden. *Nawawiun*, nuclear. The devices. *Nawawiun* devices. Nuclear devices. A new plan of Osama Bin Laden's, and somehow, al-Qaeda had managed to get their hands on nuclear material.

Kris called Ahmad back. "How did you get this?"

"*We have a mole. Someone we turned in Jordan and sent to Afghanistan. He's worked his way up, and he emailed us that file a few days ago.*"

"Tell me everything."

---

"His name is Hamid, and the Jordanians picked him up when he was agitating for Saqqaf online. Posting in jihadist chat rooms and advocating violence against the West. Raising funds to send to Saqqaf. They traced his ISP and plucked him out of his Amman home. He wasn't who you'd expect. Married, father to three boys. A doctor. He tried to volunteer to travel to Iraq to help as a doctor, but never took the final step."

Kris led the top-level intelligence briefing from the command center at Camp Carson. On the main monitor in his secured conference room, George and Director Edwards, back at Langley, and Ryan in Kabul, each filled a corner of the screen. The president's national security advisor and chief of staff were also on the call, scowling into the cameras from the Situation Room.

"Is he a coward?" Ryan glared across cyberspace. "Willing to talk the talk but not walk the walk?"

"He turned on his old jihadi brothers in Amman at the fingernail factory." The grim nickname for Jordan's intelligence headquarters. "He begged for the chance to make things right. The Jordanians told him the only way they'd wipe his record clean was for him to start working for them. They gave him a thousand bucks and told him to go to Afghanistan, pose as a doctor looking to support the jihad. They wanted him to identify threats against Jordan or any potential jihadist returnees to their country."

"Sounds like a giant gamble." Director Edwards frowned.

"They didn't really care much whether he lived or died. If he bit the dust, they were out a thousand dollars. If he came through with intel, great. He fell off the map for two years, after he sent an email from Peshawar. Said he was linking up with some fighters and making his way into Afghanistan, but that he was going to be offline for some time. That people would be watching him. Said he'd be in contact when he could. After six months, the Jordanians closed his file and declared him dead. There were tons of drone strikes in that region. They assumed he'd been hit."

"What the fuck has he been doing for two years in Afghanistan?" The chief of staff glowered at the camera, his dark eyes picking Kris apart, even from ten thousand miles away. "I don't buy it. He disappears into the badlands, and then comes back with this video?"

"Our analysts have authenticated it." Director Edwards spoke before Kris could.

"Zawahiri hasn't been seen since 2002. Not by anyone outside of al-Qaeda or from the West. There have been zero sightings. Getting him on video, like this, is huge. It just doesn't happen. What has Hamid been doing for two years? Working his way up the ranks, most likely. Until he got something he knew we'd want. And don't forget the reward for either Bin Laden or Zawahiri. Twenty-five million buys a whole new life," Kris said.

"To be clear, the Jordanians have been running him, yes? No American intelligence officer has met this agent? There's no American assessment of his reliability?" The national security advisor jumped in.

"No, sir. Not yet. The Jordanians have said they believe he's reliable. Apparently before sending him to Afghanistan, his handler built a rapport with him. Made him see the light. Hamid was begging for a chance to redeem himself, they say." Kris took a deep breath. "Our plan is to meet with Hamid personally. We do need to get an American assessment of his abilities, his access, and yes, his reliability. Ahmad, his Jordanian handler is flying out. We're working on contacting Hamid and arranging a meeting time and location. We want forty-eight hours with him for a full debrief."

"Is there a possibility that the video is a fake?"

"No, sir. The analysts at Langley authenticated it."

"Could he have stumbled on old video?" the chief of staff asked. "Maybe it's something that he found somewhere and is passing off as his own intelligence?"

Kris shook his head. "I highly doubt that. We have current intercepts that reference the conversation Zawahiri is having with his Shura council. Wherever this video comes from, it's recent. Very recent. And it refers to a threat we have to take extremely seriously. Al-Qaeda may be in possession of a nuclear device, and they are currently debating how to use it."

The chief of staff and national security advisor sat back. They glanced at each other, then at Director Edwards. "What's the CIA's recommendation if this Hamid ends up being legitimate?"

"We track him. We put an active tracker on him and follow him around the clock. He'll give us a signal when he's back with Zawahiri, or if he's taken higher. He's a doctor, and there aren't many of them in al-Qaeda. Both Zawahiri and Bin Laden are in poor health. We've always wanted to pursue the health angle and try to insert some kind of medical personnel into the movement. This is exactly what we've wanted." Director Edwards smiled at Kris, over the screen. "Bin Laden is hiding in a cave somewhere, marginalized. He's a symbol. But Zawahiri is operational. When the next attack comes, it's coming from him. This may be the big break we've all been dreaming of."

"A real double agent inside al-Qaeda." The chief of staff finally cracked a tiny smile. "Don't put the champagne on ice just yet, but..." He nodded to them all. "Fucking *well* done."

---

Ahmad arrived at Camp Carson two days later. He hugged Kris and shook David's hand, both his eyebrows rising when he found out they were married and quartered together. "I didn't realize, in Iraq—"

"We kept it quiet. But we've been together for years."

Ahmad nodded. He smiled at them both. "To find happiness in these days is a great and beautiful thing. *Alhamdulillah*."

Kris and David debriefed him, learning everything they could from him about Hamid. Exactly how *had* the Jordanians found him? *Exactly* how fast did he flip, once Ahmad had him inside the fingernail factory? They went around and around. Where had Hamid been for two years? He'd been a *die-hard* Saqqaf supporter? Had Ahmad and Hamid *truly* connected enough that Ahmad believed he was genuine? Was Hamid really willing to sell out his brothers, his *heroes*, for cold hard cash?

"Twenty-five million buys a new life. Many new lives. Is there something you wouldn't do for that much money? Or does that much money buy your allegiances as well?"

"It doesn't feel right. Not to me. He turned too quickly."

"Zahawi turned during our first conversation at Site Green," Kris pressed. "And how many supposedly hardened jihadis did we flip while hunting Saqqaf in Iraq?"

"And how many we *didn't*. Low-level thugs who treated his movement like they were joining a street gang, who weren't hardened believers in the cause, gave up the ideology. For them, the ideology was a justification for their violence, not the root cause."

"It comes down to whether they can see the writing on the wall. Whether the jihadis can realize what's in their best interest." Ahmad shrugged. "Everyone breaks. Everyone talks. Some are just smarter than others. They talk faster."

"Deep faith, hardened faith, is thicker than that. It doesn't break, not that easily," David said.

"You think Zahawi's faith wasn't strong?" Kris frowned.

"What's Zahawi doing now?" David leaned back and crossed his arms. "He's in Gitmo, and he's the cell block leader for all the other al-Qaeda fighters there. He leads prayers. He says in every one of his tribunal meetings before the military judge that he is still anti-American. He still believes in the cause. He's a true believer and he's never changed from that. Giving up intelligence to us did not change his core beliefs, then or now. And—" David glared. "Torturing him didn't help either."

"Have you been checking up on Zahawi?" Ahmad looked at David like he'd grown a second head.

"I've seen men die for their faith." David held Kris's stare. "Deep, hard faith."

A basketball stadium flashed in Kris's mind, a swinging body. Like he'd seen it, like he'd been there. He closed his eyes.

"And we've all seen men turn greedy and give up everything they can for cold hard cash." Ahmad lit a cigarette and blew smoke across the table toward David. "This guy wants the money. He wants a new life. Wouldn't anyone want to get away from this hellhole?"

---

Hamid emailed Ahmad every few days now. After the video, it seemed that Hamid had reached some kind of level within the movement where he was trusted, where he was allowed to have his own cell phone and travel where he wanted, as he pleased.

*On the frontier now*, he wrote. *Gathering medical supplies. Have not seen Zawahiri since the meeting. Two drone strikes yesterday. Many dead. I set three broken bones. We buried twelve bodies.*

Kris and Darren reviewed drone footage and found two strikes in a remote corner of Waziristan. The pilot, as per his orders, had lingered over the site as al-Qaeda had come for their wounded and dead. All in all, twelve graves had been dug.

"Ask him for a target. Tell him we want him to identify a target for us to strike. To prove his bona fides."

Three days later, Hamid emailed, saying a group of Taliban would be traveling from Pakistan through the mountains to Asadabad, Afghanistan. They'd be traveling at night, in cars with no headlights.

Kris and Darren waited through the long hours of the night, until the drones hovering over Asadabad caught sight of a two-car convoy snaking down the potholed, gravelly Kunar road through the mountains down from Pakistan.

Kris gave the order to fire.

Twin explosions burned the night, and in the morning, the wreckage of the cars was pushed off the road by the villagers. Blackened scraps of metal tumbled down the flinty ravine and came apart in a cloud of black dust.

Hamid had proven himself, at least with the first tests. Kris felt the pressure of Langley, of Ryan, of Director Edwards, and even of the White House breathing down his neck. *Find them, kill them* was the mission, and he'd only had drones to work with for so long.

Now, Hamid had appeared like a gift from above. *Find them... and use Hamid.* Hamid could be an extension of Kris, inside al-Qaeda. Hamid could be his eyes and his ears, even his hands, if he got close enough. Hamid could be Kris's weapons.

God, he hungered for Hamid's access. They all did, from Kabul to Langley to DC. For what it meant. If Hamid was inside the inner circle of al-Qaeda, if he could get back to Zawahiri, they could make meaningful strikes against al-Qaeda. Hit them where it ached, like they'd hit the US. Where it hurt.

After seven years of frustrations, of failures, of devastation, and death, Kris needed a win. He needed something to check in the victory column. The ledger felt woefully imbalanced after seven years of his eyes seeing the worst of humanity crawl up from the darkness.

He could feel the desperation swimming in his veins. Clawing at his heart. *Please, a win, please.* He wanted to get the sons of bitches that had ripped apart the world on September 11, 2001. Do something to fix what had become of the world. Right some wrong, or at least provide the tiniest bit of recompense he could to the families of the three thousand souls who had died that day.

And he wanted to do this for David, too. Rip the men out of the world who had twisted and perverted David's faith, his father's faith, until David was certain Allah was dead. If they could just destroy this evil, crush it, eliminate it, maybe there'd be space for David's faith to return. It was the closest he could get to David's father, Kris felt. Resurrecting David's father's faith and freeing it from the darkness.

To get started, he had to get to Hamid.

Know *everything* Hamid knew.

And then unleash Hamid on al-Qaeda, weaponized by Kris's own hands.

---

*You have told the Americans about me, haven't you?*

Hamid's next message came before Ahmad had a chance to explain.

*I have*, Ahmad wrote back. *And you've made all of Jordan proud. Your king proud. Your nation, and the world, is inspired by you. The ummah will praise your name. The Americans all rejoice over you. And, habibi, you are the one they most wish to speak to you. Urgently. We must plan for your next moves. Keep you safe.*

Hamid went radio silent for three days. Kris paced Camp Carson, from the command center to the runways to the helipads.

David found him at the helipads, walking the empty squares where the Blackhawks landed every evening. The ethereal dust haze hovered in the air, choking off the sky and settling over everything in a fine layer of grit. It felt like walking through ghosts, like some kind of otherworldly realm. The dust seemed heavy, the dust of shattered empires and millennia of history trapped within the borders of Afghanistan. The sun, trying to peak over the Tora Bora mountains, couldn't push through the haze completely. Afghanistan was still on planet Earth, but the sun seemed farther away than it did back in DC.

"I'm not sure this guy is everything you want him to be," David cautioned. "I think he's pulling back because he can't deliver. I think he's been talking a big game with Ahmad and now it's about to get real. And he's not ready."

"You think we're being played?"

"He says the right things. Delivers the right intel. Seems to be in the know. But we don't really know that for certain, do we? And we don't know why he's doing this."

"We know the why. Twenty-five-million-dollar reward."

"You know, I've always thought that reward was a silly amount."

Kris's jaw dropped. "Excuse me?"

"Most people here don't think that much money exists in the entire world. Twenty-five million dollars is make-believe money to them. Their entire lives can be lived on less than a hundred dollars."

"Hamid is Jordanian. He's Westernized. He for sure knows the value of twenty-five million."

"We need to move slowly with Hamid. Carefully. Take our time understanding him."

"No, no, no," Kris sighed. Exasperation weighed down his words. "That's exactly the opposite of what we need. We need to get inside his skull. Understand what he knows and what he can do for us. If he's a con man, then we cut him loose. But we can't just let this linger. What if he's killed? Or worse?"

David took both his hands. Looked into his eyes. "What if this is a trap?"

"A trap?" Kris snorted. "So a mole that the Jordanians inserted two years ago is somehow conspiring with Zawahiri? And comes up with intelligence that matches multiple intercepts, all speaking to the same tactic? It doesn't make any sense. Why would al-Qaeda, or Zawahiri, trust someone who had been sent to infiltrate them?"

"I don't trust this guy's change of heart. I *don't*."

"David, what's more likely? A huge conspiracy, years in the making, using sophisticated tactics al-Qaeda has never used before, trusting someone who was sent to burn them, who Ahmad swears is legitimate, in an attempt to trap us? Or that Hamid has been dazzled by the potential reward and he wants to cash in on his little adventure?" He paced, his hands on his hips. "Look, if anything, I think he's playing a scam for money. Trying to cash in on the CIA's dime. That happens all the time. Could it be happening here? Sure." Kris cringed. "But, Jesus, I hope not."

"I *know* the Arab mind. The Arab soul. Things don't just go away. We're desert people. And the desert is eternal, Kris. The past lives inside the present and shapes every single day. History, the past... These aren't just academic concepts. The past never leaves someone. Never."

"David—"

"You and me, we're CIA. We're American, as American as you can get, but even we've been disgusted by the past years. There are times I have been ashamed to show my face to Muslims, to my fellow Arabs, because of what we've done. If *I* feel that way, then how do others feel? Who've lived every day on the front lines of the disintegration of their world?"

"I didn't know you felt like that," Kris said softly.

David kept going. "Hamid spent more years cheering on Saqqaf than he's been undercover."

"You think he's still sympathetic to the jihadis?"

"I just don't trust him, Kris. And I don't want you to get hurt. I know how badly you want this. Everyone on this base and back in DC seems to have Hamid fever. Be careful."

He smiled and rested his hand on David's chest, over his heart. "You always watch out for me, my love."

David covered his hand. "I always will. Forever."

"And I you." Kris kissed him, sweetly, a peck on the lips, even though they were out on the airfield and anyone and everyone could see them. "But this is going to work. I promise. We started this seven years ago and we're going to finish it. Together."

David smiled. He said nothing.

His smile didn't reach his eyes.

---

Ahmad knocked on their door in the middle of the night. When Kris answered, he seemed morbidly fascinated by their shared quarters, by David sleeping facedown and shirtless in their bed and Kris in his sweatpants and tank top. He grinned so wide his face seemed to split in half.

"What's up, Ahmad?" Kris shut their door firmly behind him.

Ahmad finally focused. "Hamid has emailed. He is willing to meet."

"Excellent. What did he say? How soon can we meet him? What kind of travel is he able to do?"

Ahmad held up his hands. "He is cautious. He says not soon. And he says that he cannot travel far. We cannot fly him anywhere. He cannot go to Kabul."

"Fuck." Kris groaned and slumped against the wall. "You tell him we need to meet him immediately. Or the money is off the table."

Ahmad's eyebrows shot up.

"If he won't come to Kabul, then we'll have to meet him someplace in the middle."

---

"Your base. Camp Carson. Meet there." Ryan, on the video call, stared Kris down. "You're right over the border from Pakistan. He can slip through and you can bring him on base for your debrief. He only has to travel an hour from the border."

"Plus wherever he is in Pakistan." Kris mulled Ryan's suggestion over. "It's a good idea. I'll start putting everything together."

"You make damn sure that you keep everyone safe." Ryan glared, the grainy video connection somehow making his scowl even uglier. "I want your base locked down tight. All nonessential personnel cleared from your meeting location. And you make sure this guy is legit. I don't want to end up with egg on our face in front of the White House. We have enough problems as it is. Looking like giant assholes who can be duped by some goat fucker isn't the image rehab we're going for."

"Cute, Ryan. You always were the culturally sensitive, politically correct one. It's nice to know your concerns are all about how you'll look when this operation is reported up. I take it Kabul station has taken over running Hamid?"

"You report to me on this, Caldera. Everything goes through me, before it goes up. Understand?"

---

It took two weeks of back-and-forth negotiations with Hamid to get him to agree to come to Camp Carson. He refused at first, demanding to meet at Miranshah, a mean border town that sold drugs and weapons and everything else just across the mountains in Pakistan's northwestern frontier. Kris refused and threatened to walk from their association. Hamid relented, but refused to stay at overnight. *I only have seven hours I can be away from our camp*, he said. *Sunrise to sunset. And what will I tell my brothers*?

David put together a local package of medicines and natural remedies, teas and creams, for Hamid to carry back to his camp. "He can say he was picking up medical supplies," David said. "These come from Miranshah. It will all be legitimate."

Finally, Hamid agreed. He would come in one week, for one day. *How will you get me into your base*? he asked. *And how will you protect me? Spies are everywhere. I will not get my throat cut because you let one of the spies see who I am.*

It all came down to Kris.

Seven years after September 11, after his failure to stop the attacks, here he was, asked to create a plan to train and equip an undercover agent in al-Qaeda, the best possible lead they had in finding and destroying Zawahiri and Bin Laden. He could practically taste victory, could almost feel the vindication, glorious, righteous fury singing in his blood.

But first, he had to get Hamid to Camp Carson. Debrief him. Equip him with a small mountain of tech and gear. And then release him, all in just under six hours.

Hamid could get to the border crossing, but he needed an escort across the border and to the base. Using any of the Afghan military or police was *out* of the question. Their ranks were infested with spies for the Taliban and al Qaeda, and blue-on-blue attacks, where an Afghan soldier would kill American forces on a joint operation, were on the rise. The Afghans, CENTCOM and Langley warned, were *not* to be trusted.

Sending Special Forces to meet Hamid was also out of the question. The muscle-bound, dip chewing, action hero stereotypes stood out in Afghanistan, a land of deprivation of privation. Most Afghans were skinny and small, short statured from childhoods of malnutrition. Special Forces soldiers came in big and bigger, and had the attitudes to match.

David. David had been crossing the border for a year now, weaving in and out of the northwestern frontier, in and out of the border towns and villages, crisscrossing farms and rivers and streams. He'd built a small network of human sources and he'd become a familiar face to the scattered communities. Here, he was Dawood, an itinerant farm hand, a laborer for hire. He could pose as a taxi driver and pick up Hamid from the border, bring him back to Camp Carson.

How many people should be at the meeting? Six hours wasn't long. In Iraq, he and David had run informants and human sources as a two-man team while driving around. They traded off who drove while the other sat in the back seat with the informant, driving in circles through Baghdad or Mosul or Ramadi. Whoever was in the back seat led the interrogation, checking for weapons or hidden bombs before launching into questions.

Would that work here? Could he and David handle Hamid alone?

His pride and ego warred with his common sense. He needed his best people. The best analysts. Interrogators. Men and women who could dive deep into Hamid in a short time, turn his mind inside out. Study his body language. He needed the best al-Qaeda expert to corroborate Hamid's information and extrapolate based on the new intelligence he was going to provide. Hamid was going to be bringing them a gold mine.

Technical agents from Islamabad and Kabul were flying in with their whiz-bang gadgets. Kris had been sent a suitcase of flip phones, identical to the cheap knockoffs found on the streets of Pakistan, that could take pictures and text them instantly via a hidden, embedded satellite link. The pictures also had geotags coded within the image, invisible to the naked eye. But once at Langley, analysts could identify exactly where on the vast, vast globe the picture had been taken.

*Get a picture of Zawahiri. Or Bin Laden. Make him smile for the camera.*

Ahmad, as the Jordanian Mukhabarat officer in charge of Hamid, had to be there, too.

At this point, if he did a vehicle meet, he'd need a school bus to keep everyone in, drive everyone around in circles outside Camp Carson.

No, keep the meeting on base. Everyone would be together, maximizing time, expertise, and equipment. Darren, his deputy, would take the al-Qaeda angle. Three interrogators and an analyst were being flown in from Langley. Ryan was sending his deputy. And a team of CIA SAD officers, former Special Forces, would provide security for the meeting, in case anything went wrong.

But nothing was going to go wrong. This was *it*. This was their big break. Hamid was coming to Camp Carson.

What then? Hamid was right about the spies. Afghan national police helped guard the base perimeter, but no one trusted them. More than one was most likely a spy for al-Qaeda. If they saw Hamid's face, they would instantly report back to their commanders, and Hamid would be tortured and killed when he returned to his camp. And, they would lose their chance at getting Zawahiri and Bin Laden.

When David and Hamid approached the base, the Afghan guards would have to leave their posts. Preserving Hamid's identity, his safety, was most important. The guards would leave the gates open, and David would drive Hamid through. David would be in charge of the car, so they wouldn't have to worry about a car bomb. They could skip the car inspection, drive Hamid right up to Camp Carson's command center.

Kris thought of David. What would David put into this plan? What would he suggest? How did the world look from Hamid's eyes? He'd been undercover with al-Qaeda for two years, roughing it in the most inhospitable landscape on the planet. What would David recommend?

*Hamid must be shown the utmost respect,* he wrote. *Hamid is to be treated as an honored guest.*

---

"This is *horseshit*!" Carl, the leader of the SAD team assigned to Kris's debrief, Operation Pendulum, shouted at Kris. "This is the stupidest fucking piece of garbage I've ever seen! Have you ever been in a war zone?"

"I've been in war zones for the past seven years straight!" Kris bellowed. "I've managed war zones! I managed the Saqqaf operation! I killed Saqqaf! Don't fucking talk to me that way!"

"You want to bring an al-Qaeda agent onto our base without searching him? 'Treat him like an honored guest'? This is bullshit! I'm not putting my men on the ground with this plan!"

"Yes, you are! This agent is undercover. He's working for us. He came to us with this intelligence. He's sacrificing a hell of a lot to help us with this. We can show him the smallest bit of respect, not treat him like a terrorist!"

"They're all fucking terrorists!" Carl hollered. "Every fucking one of those towel-headed fuckers! They all want to kill you! Can't you get that through your skull?" Carl snorted, shaking his head. "Or are you too concerned about how he'll feel? Don't want to get his feelings hurt?"

"You are way out of line," Kris hissed. "The vast majority of Arabs and Muslims are not terrorists. Your attitude is exactly what keeps this war going."

Carl held up his trigger finger and squeezed. "The war keeps going because I keep killing hajis."

"Do you even fucking know that 'haji' is a term of respect? It's for someone who's made the pilgrimage. It's a title of deep respect for the faithful."

Carl spat. A thick wad of dip-tainted spit stained the dirt outside the command center.

"This is the plan. And I am in charge. Your men will provide operational support. Or I will ship your asses back to DC on the very next flight."

"Not this plan." Carl tossed the stapled sheets at Kris's feet. They blew against Kris's boots, skittered in the dust. "You want to make him think you're about to suck his cock, fine, be my guest. He can think he's about to get some sweet American ass all the way into the base. But as soon as he steps out of the car, my men are searching him."

"You are not to treat him harshly. He is not a suspect, and not a terrorist. You have no idea of the intelligence that he has supplied!"

"He's a fucking terrorist until I say he's not!" Carl glared at Kris. "And there's way too many fucking people on this op. This isn't a Goddamn parade, or a zoo. No one is worth all this."

"He is. You just don't fucking know." Kris snatched his plan, Top Secret, Eyes Only, before it blew away. "If you harm the asset in any way. Leave any bruises. Bend a single hair on his head. I will make your life hell, I swear to God."

Carl laughed. "Seven years, you said? You've drunk the Kool-Aid. You think everyone just wants peace and cupcakes. You just don't get it. Every one of them wants to kill us."

"Just do your job. And when it's done, you're gone. I want you off my base."

"Suits me just fine. Camp Cocksucker isn't for me anyway."

# 22

**Afghanistan-Pakistan Border, Afghanistan - December, 2008**

David tapped his toes against the footwell of his car, waiting. He wore a thick salwar kameez, heavy robes, and a flat Afghan wool cap. Still, he was chilled. A mass of humanity crowded on the Pakistan side of the border, waiting their turn to be waved into Afghanistan. Pakistani guards had their rifles pointed toward Afghanistan. The Afghanistan guards sat around a fire and drank tea.

Thoughts of Kris helped console him. They'd stayed up almost the entire night, completely unable to sleep. Talk of Hamid and the operation turned to talk of what could be. What would it mean if they really did get Bin Laden?

"*Would it be over after that? For us, I mean*?" David had held Kris's hand, resting his chin on Kris's chest. "*Do you think we could walk away from this war? If he's gone, maybe that would be the end for us*?"

Kris had stroked his hair. "*I think so*," he'd finally said. "*We started this hunt for him. Seeking to end what he'd begun. Bring him to justice and make him answer for what he did. We've got everyone else. Zahawi. Saqqaf. If we can get Zawahiri and Bin Laden...*" Kris gave him a tiny smile. "*It would be nice to go home,*" he'd whispered. "*To our house. Live a quiet life.*"

"*What would you do?*"

"*Maybe stay at the CIA. Maybe not. Something that gives me as much time with you as possible. I've given the CIA a decade. I want to give you the rest of all my decades.*"

David had kissed him, slowly. "*I want to find peace,*" he'd breathed. "*I know my peace is inside of you. I want to spend the rest of my life just being with you.*"

Their whispers turned to making love, languid and serene, until Kris came with a shout, practically crying as he trembled apart in David's arms. David tumbled after him, trying to combine their souls, trying to crawl inside Kris's body and fuse together, never to be parted.

They'd eaten breakfast before David had dressed and driven off. Kris kissed him through the driver's window. "*Be safe, my love,*" Kris had whispered. "*After this, we're going home.*"

"*Home is where you are.*" He'd blown a kiss as he drove off. The rest of the base had been humming, full preparations for Hamid's arrival already underway. His job, in comparison, was simpler. Pick Hamid up. Drive him back.

Finally, at the border crossing, David spotted him.

Hamid was wrapped in thick robes, like David, against the Afghanistan winter. Snows were already on the mountains, and the Panjshir, far in the north, was frozen. Hamid picked his way through the crowd and slid into the back seat.

"*As-salaam-alaikum,*" David said, twisting around to get his first look at Hamid.

Hamid was exhausted, that much was obvious. Dirt clung to his robes, and his beard was disheveled. Dark circles hung beneath his eyes. His face was lean, far leaner than the photo Ahmad had shared from his case file. Two years of hard living in Pakistan could do that, though.

Hamid leaned back in the car and sighed. "*Wa alaikum as-salaam,*" he breathed. "*Shukran.*"

David passed him a soda and a bag of chips. "Please, eat. We won't be long. But make yourself comfortable."

Hamid accepted the chips and the soda with a smile. "*Shukran, habibi*," he said, nodding.

The drive back to base was only thirty minutes, but David stretched it to an hour, taking switchbacks and parking on the side of the road to, ostensibly, check his tires or his radiator fluid. He watched for followers, observers, anyone trailing them. The road bled into and out of the mountains, along ridges and ravines. He passed donkeys and carts led by stubborn mules, refusing to walk another foot. He kept his eyes peeled, scanning the road and the ditches for new dirt or fresh rises in the mud, evidence of burying. The signs of an IED. He snaked into the dusty town that squatted between Camp Carson and the military base, Camp Seville.

All the while, Hamid crunched his chips in the back seat and stared out the window.

Farmland surrounded Camp Carson, fields that had been harvested and left fallow for winter. The irrigation ditches lining the field were low, the waters mostly mud and filled with blown trash from the village. As soon as he started down the straight dirt road that led to the main base gate, he flashed his headlights twice.

That was the signal. The Afghan guards at the base were to open the gates and leave their posts, head to the mess hall for tea and a break.

David watched the main gate rise and stay open.

He slowed as he neared and made his way through the twisting maze of concrete barriers and sandbags.

Ahead, he could see Kris, and Darren, and Ahmad. The analysts and interrogators, all standing in front of the command center, a double-wide cargo container converted into a state-of-the-art technical repository, but from the outside, looking like another nondescript, bland, meaningless building. The security team held their positions in a grid surrounding where he was to park the car. They were small dots at the end of a long stretch of gravel road, paralleling Camp Carson's airfield.

*Once we're through, once we've got them, we can go home. Our part in this will be over. We've given our all. It's time to go home. It's time.*

David kept his eyes on Kris, the love of his life. Home, and the promise of the rest of his days in Kris's arms, safe and secure and wrapped up in love. Kris's love was the closest he'd ever felt to the love of his father. Unconditional, all-consuming, all-encompassing love.

One more mission. One more task. And then they'd go *home*.

When he was close enough, David saw Kris smile, his big, beaming smile, not his sly or snarky grin. The smile David saw most, or Kris only let slip when his emotions couldn't be contained, couldn't be suppressed. David grinned back.

The hardest part of the operation was over. Hamid was here.

For the first time, David actually believed it could really happen. They could get Bin Laden, or Zawahiri. They could end what they had begun together. They could go home, knowing they had finished what they'd promised they would.

David slowed, gravel crunching under his tires. The security team moved in slowly, weapons at the low and ready. He pulled to a stop, brakes on the ancient Afghan sedan squealing, metal shrieking against metal.

Behind him, the front gates were still up. The guards wouldn't return until Hamid was safely inside the interrogation rooms off the command center.

"Driver, exit the vehicle," Carl barked.

He slid out, leaving the driver's door open, and walked away from the car. He wanted to go to Kris. Wanted to hold his hand. Wanted to be with him at this moment. The excitement, the rush that Kris must have felt for the past two weeks had finally hit him, too. Hamid fever.

This was *it*.

But Carl had ordered him to stand twenty feet behind the car after exiting, and he headed to his position, keeping an eye on Hamid and the front gates.

Everything had gone perfectly, according to Kris's plan.

"Sir, exit the vehicle, slowly," Carl barked again, this time to

Hamid. He reached for the back door of the sedan and opened it for Hamid.

Hamid scooted across the bench seat and opened the opposite door.

Carl glowered. He waved to the two men on the other side of the car. They moved in, reaching for Hamid.

Hamid stepped away. "You said you would treat me well!" His head whipped around, searching. He spotted Ahmad. "You said I was a hero!"

Ahmad stepped forward, hands outstretched. "You are. Come, these are just precautions. We are friends, *habibi*." He placed his hand on his heart.

"We don't have time for this," Carl growled. "We have to search him."

"Hey, calm down—" Kris snapped.

"I will show you a true hero," Hamid said. He reached into his robe—

"What the *fuck* is he doing?" Carl shouted. "What is he reaching for?"

"*Drop your hand! Drop your hand*!" Carl's men shouted in unison. All four whipped their rifles up, fingers more than half-pressed on their triggers.

"Don't shoot!" Ahmad bellowed! "*Don't*!"

"*La illaha illah Allah*," Hamid wailed.

David's eyes flicked to Kris's.

It was a trap. Hamid wasn't their savior. They weren't going home.

"*No*!" He shouted. He took one step, running for Kris. Kris was too close, far too close. He was inside the blast radius. "*Kris*—"

He never took a second step.

A burst of light blinded the world.

Hamid blew apart, his body disintegrating as the bomb he wore burst apart in every direction. A blast wave tore through the air, a bubble of flame and fury, ripping through the staging area. The car, the rusted old sedan, flipped over and over, a toy tumbling and sliding on the gravel until it came to a stop upside down, pinning what was left of Carl beneath the roof.

Carl's team, the three others, were shredded in a scatterblast of ball bearings and nails, screws and broken glass, packed shrapnel that flew in every direction. A thousand *plinks* sounded, the rain of shrapnel slamming into the command center's walls, at the same moment the thunderous *boom* of the detonation shook the earth, trembling the ground and the sky for two miles in every direction.

The blast wave slammed into the group waiting to receive Hamid. Eardrums burst and lungs collapsed, the impact equal to slamming a car into a brick wall at one hundred miles per hour. Everyone tumbled, blown off their feet and thrown through the air, landing in a skid of gravel and blood, tens of feet away from the blast.

Silence followed, for a moment.

Then, tiny *chinks* and *clinks* and *plinks* of debris hitting concrete and steel. *Thunks,* the larger pieces falling next. Hamid's severed head, the only part of him to survive, fell to the ground and rolled, finally ending upside down in front of David.

David clawed forward, bloody fingers scraping through gravel as he struggled to breathe. Blood dripped from his lips, stained the rocks beneath his face. Fires raged, the car and two buildings and severed limbs burning. He could just see bodies through the heat haze, the shimmering air. Figures lying on the ground, unmoving.

"Kris—" he called, his voice choked. He coughed, his voice lost in blood pooling in the base of his throat. "Kris!" he called again, trying to drag himself forward.

Shouts rose… from *behind* him.

No. The gate.

It was still open.

David twisted, looking back. Men in dark clothes with black turbans covering their heads, wrapped around their faces, ran onto the base. Two trucks with a mounted machine gun in the bed screamed in behind them. Every man clutched a rifle.

They weren't the cavalry coming to the rescue.

This was the second phase of the attack.

Al-Qaeda had planned this, everything.

Sirens rose across the base. In the distance, through the flames, David saw men racing for them, Special Forces soldiers and CIA officers.

They weren't going to make it. Al-Qaeda was going to get to them first.

David tried to crawl, but his body was broken, his movements too slow. His ears rang, and blood kept dripping into his eyes. He couldn't breathe. His leg wouldn't move, and when he looked back, he saw white bone sticking out of his salwar kameez, ragged edges caught on the torn and blackened linen.

Moments, he had moments before the jihadis were on him. He could hear their shouts, their cries to Allah. The rev of the trucks' engines. Gravel crunching beneath the tires and their boots.

A group of jihadis split off and ran for the nearest bodies. Carl's teammates, and one of the analysts. They rolled them over, shoved their rifles in their faces. Fired.

David roared. He struggled, trying to scramble forward. Damn it, he was too far away from everyone else, too far from Kris.

More jihadis lined up and peppered the command center with shots, firing at the corrugated steel shipping container until the building looked like a cheese grater from the waist up. Everyone inside would have hit the deck as soon as the bomb went off, but al-Qaeda didn't know that. *Please, let everyone still be down*, David prayed. *Please, please.*

Shots fired back at the jihadis from the Special Forces soldiers and CIA reinforcements tearing across the base. They were close enough now to fight back, taking cover in the maze of buildings and shipping containers that dotted the base at the end of the runway. The jihadis' trucks braked hard and unleashed their rifles at the reinforcements, a hail of bullets that shredded the air, the buildings. Shell casings dropped, clattering and bouncing across the gravel. A dozen rolled in front of David's face.

"Retreat!" David heard the jihadis cry in Arabic. "Fall back!"

"Find *him*! Find the one!"

Fighters swarmed over the bodies nearest them, but they were pushed back by more gunfire. David tried to keep crawling, keep getting clear, but he was too exposed. Any moment, they would be on him—

*This isn't how I want to go. This isn't how I wanted to die. Allah, would you be so cruel as to show me what my Paradise would be with Kris and then snatch it away from me? Would you be so cruel, again?*

He gasped, tears and blood mixing on his cheeks, smearing on his lips.

*Better me than Kris. Allah, spare Kris. Keep him alive. Let him live until he's one hundred and twenty, until he's had a long, glorious life. I'll trade my life for his. In shaa Allah. In shaa Allah.*

Hands grabbed his ankles, flipped him over. Pain, pure, agonizing pain, split his soul in two as his broken leg twisted, wrenched against his torn skin. He roared.

They grabbed at his clothes, his head. Forced him to look up, into a half dozen jihadi faces. "It's *him*, it's *him*!" three of them cried together. "*Allahu Akbar*! It's him!"

Tires squealed, the trucks starting to scream away. The jihadis grabbed him by the arms and legs and ran beside the truck, passing him up to a group of men in the truck bed. He felt weightless, torn apart, every ounce of pain he'd ever felt in his whole life concentrated in his leg, in his severed bone. Bullets flew past him in both directions, the jihadis and the base soldiers firing at once. Bullets hit the truck, shredding the metal. Three jihadis fell as he was tossed in.

"Go! Go!" The fighters slammed on the roof of the truck. "We have him!"

Engines wailing, the two trucks roared past the base gate, rear guns firing on the soldiers who tried to pursue, to chase. David watched the base's main gate pass overhead in a blur, the hazy blue sky smear into gray, and a jihadi stare down into his face before darkness poured in and his entire world went black.

---

Everything was too slow, like Kris was stuck in a dream.

Flames shivered in slow motion, enough that he could see every curve and arch of the fire. Someone screamed in his face. He could make out every rounded shape of their words, their letters. See each of the fillings in their teeth. A dull roar had replaced all sound, the inside of a bell that had been rung once and had taken over the world.

He couldn't draw a single breath. His lips moved, gasping for air. The world snapped, racing from too slow to too fast, a dose of adrenaline coursing through his body, his mind, with hyper clarity and a rush of reality.

Finally, he dragged in a breath and shot up. Hands pushed him back down to the gravel. "Do *not* move! Do *not* move, sir! You've been injured! We're getting you medically evac'd now!"

"David—" He pushed at the man, a soldier, a Special Forces medic trying to check him over. He rolled to the side, trying to escape. Looked across the gravel.

Twelve bodies lay motionless on the ground, some mangled so badly they looked like they'd been through a meat grinder or had dropped from an airplane without a parachute. Medics worked on two people, motionless and drenched in ruby blood. Kris watched one shake his head and sit back, wiping at his forehead.

The gravel yard, where they had paced and waited for Hamid and David to arrive, sharing jokes to cut the tension, was *gone*. Blasted earth, flames, and blood-soaked gravel were all that remained. Bullet casings, a thousand of them. Shards of glass and nails that rose like spikes.

"No," Kris breathed. "No, no, no..." He struggled against the medic's hold again, trying to sit up. "David! Where is David? Where the *fuck* is David?"

The medic fought him, grabbing his hands and arms and forcing him back to the ground. "Do *not* move, sir!" he bellowed. "You have a serious internal injury! Do *not* move!"

"How many are dead?" Kris screamed. "How many?"

"Everyone but you, sir."

"*No*!" Kris bellowed. "*No*!"

"And one was taken. Al-Qaeda penetrated the base and took a hostage."

---

The medic strapped him to a board and loaded him into a helicopter forty-five seconds later. As they rose over the base, Kris saw another two choppers taking off from the airfield and circling the base, searching the perimeter, the roads. *Have to find the hostage*, Kris thought. *Have to find him. Who? Who did they take? David—*

His thoughts were interrupted by the slip of meds into his veins, the medic pumping his IV bag full of sedatives. The last thing he saw was a helicopter sprinting away from the base, following the dirt road past the fallow farmland and rising over the village.

He woke briefly in the US Army hospital at Camp Seville as the surgeon was calling out orders to the surgical team. "The patient has a nicked artery and a collapsed lung, along with broken ribs. We stabilize the bleeding, treat the lung, package the ribs. Secondary team, you work on removing shrapnel embedded in the dermis. Any human body parts, bones, teeth, skin, that you pull out as shrapnel, save for identification and packaging for the mortuary team. I can see he's got someone's shattered bone splinters embedded in his thigh. All right, let's begin."

A tear slid from his eye as the nurse pumped his IV bag full of sedatives again. *David, where are you? Are you alive? Please, be alive. Please, please, be alive.*

**Washington DC - One Hour After the Blast**

Director Edwards looked up as a tentative knock sounded on his doorjamb.

No one in the CIA knocked like that unless it was *bad* fucking news.

George hovered in the doorway, looking like he was five years old and his puppy had just died. His hands wrung together. "Director," he started. He looked away. Swallowed. "Director, there's been an incident. He licked his lips. "At Camp Carson."

"The Hamid op? Caldera?"

George nodded. "Sir, thirteen officers are dead. And al-Qaeda stormed the base. They took a hostage."

"*Fuck.*" Rage bloomed within Edwards, a nuclear reaction of despair and fury. "Find out everything. I have to call the president."

## Camp Seville, Afghanistan-Pakistan Border, Afghanistan - Eight Hours After the Blast

Kris woke to a steady beeping.

Bandages covered his chest, tight enough that he could barely breathe. He felt a pull in his abdomen, constriction in his chest. He pushed at the bandages and saw a line of stitches running from his belly button to his sternum. More bandages wrapped around his thigh, his arms. One arm was in a sling. An IV line stuck into the back of his hand.

Where the fuck was he?

Where the fuck was David?

*Please, be alive. Please, please be alive.*

He tore at the IV line and flung the needle over the side of his bed. Ripped the EKG monitors from his chest. The machine's steady beeping stopped, input not detected. He forced himself to the side of the bed, his arms and legs shaking.

Step by slow step, he pushed himself to the end of the line of beds, filled with silent, unmoving bodies wrapped in bandages and casts. Most were missing limbs, legs or arms or both. The ward could have been a morgue. He clutched his belly, his ribs, and kept walking.

An Army nurse spotted him and ran to his side. "Sir, you cannot be out of bed."

"How long have I been here?" he asked the man, a young kid probably no older than nineteen.

"You have to get back to bed, sir. You've been in surgery for four hours, recovering for only another four. You need to rest."

"Fuck you," Kris spat at the young soldier. "I need to get back to Camp Carson." Eight hours since the attack. Eight hours since the blast.

"Sir, you were seriously injured and you need to let your body heal." The soldier tried to push Kris back toward his bed, as if he were an invalid.

"Fuck you!" Kris shouted. His lungs seized, burned. Tears stung his eyes. "I am checking out and I am going back to Camp Carson! I am the base commander, and I will not sit here while one of our own has been kidnapped! Get me the fuck out of here, now!"

---

He pulled rank and threw his weight around. He was the base commander. He wasn't going to be forced back into a hospital bed.

Finally, he was released, and one of the base ambulance helos ferried him back over the village to Camp Carson.

"Carson is on lockdown," the pilot shouted at him over the rotors. "Only one helo is cleared for landing. From Kabul."

*Fucking Ryan.* "I don't care what you have to do, you get me on that base."

The pilot spent twenty minutes talking to Carson's landing officer, but finally, he touched down on the airfield. As they came in for landing, Kris saw the devastation, the destruction, the crater in the ground filled with blood-soaked gravel, the bullet-shredded command center. The flipped and burned car David had driven back to base.

*David, my God, where are you?*

Would he find David in the morgue? Or on the internet, a paraded captive of al-Qaeda? Which was worse? *David, David, my love.*

He forced the pain, the anguish away, and stumbled as fast as he could to the command center. CIA officers huddled outside, numb shock on their frozen faces. Others walked the destruction, taking photos, writing notes.

The investigation had already begun.

Kris badged into the command center. He threw open the door, grimacing—

"What the fuck are *you* doing here?" Ryan blocked his path. "Get the fuck out of here, Caldera."

"No." He gritted his teeth. "I am the base commander here—"

"Not anymore you're not!"

"We have a man out there! And I am not leaving until we get him back!"

"Do you even know who it is?"

Kris shook his head. Tears built, white-hot, in his eyes.

"It's Haddad. The jihadis searched for him, specifically took him."

He gasped, fell forward. Dizziness turned his world upside down, and he clung to a chairback to stay upright. Tears cascaded down his cheeks, Niagara Falls erupting from his eyes. "What do we know?" he whispered.

"You are not a part of this investigation—"

"Don't you *dare* try and shut me out of this—"

"You *failed* to properly secure the Hamid operation, you *failed* to properly vet the source, and you *failed* to protect the lives of people under your command—"

"Don't you dare pin this all on me! You signed off on the operation!"

"You are through on this base, and in the CIA!"

"I'm fucking going to get David back!" Kris shrieked. "Do not push me out of this! That is my husband out there! My husband, kidnapped! We don't have time for this! We have to get him back, before they—" His voice stopped, unable to say the words. His brain skittered forward though, finishing the thought. *Before they murder him.*

Ryan's chest heaved. He glared at Kris, pure fury burning Kris from the inside out. Fine, hate him. Blame him. Kris didn't care.

A hundred pairs of eyes in the command center stared him down, all the men and women who had been inside when the blast happened, when the bullets flew. Did they all blame him too? Broken monitors lay in a heap in the corner, full of bullet holes. Lights hung from their mounts on the ceiling, swaying and dark. He'd allowed the base to be attacked, to be breached. He'd let everyone's lives to be put at risk.

But he only cared about one life. David's.

"What is the status of the search?" He spoke through clenched teeth, his body trembling.

Silence.

"*What* is the *status* of the *search*?" he repeated.

Ryan looked like he was chewing glass, like he'd rather murder Kris than speak to him. "We lost the vehicles that penetrated the base. We think they did a car swap under concealment in the village and then drove Haddad away in a secondary vehicle."

The village around Camp Carson was a warren of mud huts, alleys, and bazaars, perfect to get lost in.

"Have you tracked all cars entering and exiting the village since the attack?"

"Drone pilots were unable to follow all vehicles in the immediate aftermath." Ryan's jaw clenched. "The chaos here was overwhelming, and in an absence of leadership, the base's operations faltered."

Kris felt the rebuke like a slap against his soul. "What leads do you have?"

"Nothing."

Panic clawed at Kris's heart. "Have you sent out the drones? Are you scouring the border crossings? What's coming through over intercepts, over traffic? Any celebrations, any coded transmissions? What do you mean you have nothing?"

"Caldera, get out of here. You're not helping. You're through. Leave, now."

"Don't you dare try—"

"Sir." One of the intercept analysts, three rows of computer monitors away, stood. "Sir, something has been posted to the internet."

"Put it up on the monitors," Kris and Ryan said in unison. Ryan glowered at him.

"Start a trace of the upload link. Where is this coming from?" Kris continued.

On the center monitor, a video appeared. Al-Qaeda's new operations specialist, who had taken over for Suleyman, a man named Al Jabal, sat next to a bound and bloodied David.

"My fellow Muslims, rejoice!" Al Jabal began in Arabic. "We have launched a great strike against the Imperialists, against the Great Satan! The infidels, they believed they could turn one of our brothers against us. But we tell you, a true brother will never turn against his fellow Muslims. Our brother's conscience would not allow him to fall prey to the Great Satan's promises. He would not spy on his brothers for the infidels!"

Kris's heart, what was left of it, sank. *David, you were right.* He watched David sway on the video, tried to will his downturned head to look up. *David, look into the camera. Show me you're all right. Show me you're alive, that you're fighting. Come on, my love.*

"The American devils strike with their missiles and destroy lives in Pakistan, in Afghanistan!" Al Jabal cried. "But now, we have struck you in the heart of your CIA spy nests, your home in Afghanistan. Now, you will taste the blood of your family as your home is destroyed."

He went on, praising Hamid for being a martyr and a true fighter of the faith, promising eternal glory to him and his family.

Kris wanted to puke. Bile rose in his throat, burning the back of his tongue.

"Now, we will try this *kufir*, this false Muslim, this apostate who works for the Great Satan," Al Jabal said, grabbing David's hair. He wrenched David's head back, and Kris saw, finally, his bruised and bloody face. He gasped, his hands flying up, covering his mouth.

David had been beaten to within an inch of his life. He was practically unrecognizable.

But Kris would always know, always, David's soul.

"We will try this apostate for his crimes against the *ummah*, against Allah, and when his sentence is passed, we will carry out his execution for the *ummah* to witness. By Allah, the *ummah* will taste the blood of the apostate!"

"No!" Kris screamed. He turned away from the video, turned his back on it, tried to block out the sound. From the corner of his eye, he saw Ryan give the kill signal to the analyst.

"Any information on the upload?" Ryan growled. "Where did that video come from?"

"Still searching, sir," the analyst called. She and a dozen others were working furiously at the network, trawling trunk lines and diving into ISPs, hunting for the source of the upload.

"Sir, I think I found something. An internet café outside Alizai." The analyst pulled up satellite footage of the village, a settlement of homes and bazaars and weapons markets just across the border, through the mountains.

Ryan's jaw worked, muscles bulging out in time to his furious clenches. "We *cannot* let a CIA officer be slaughtered by al-Qaeda. We have to get him back." He started barking orders as Kris clung to the chair back, desperate to stay standing. "I want two teams ready to go at the airfield in five minutes. Give me everything you have on Alizai. Satellite footage. Drone coverage. Intercepts. Who operates out of there? Who had been identified as working there? What safe houses are in the village? Get me drones overhead covering all angles of the village. Let's move!"

The command center burst into action all around Kris. He sank into the chair, clutching his ribs, head in his hands, as the image of David's beaten face burned itself into the backs of his eyelids.

---

"*ETA to Alizai, eight minutes.*"

Ryan passed Kris a headset. On-screen, the Special Forces quick reaction force was locked and loaded in the belly of their chopper and heading for the border. Kris felt the roar and rumble of the helos pass directly over the command center. A thousand bullet holes in the steel walls made the *whoosh* and grumble of the rotors echo, as if the helo were inside his bones or carving him up as he stood before it.

Alizai wasn't far over the border. North by north east, near Parachinar, the lawless city of the northwest frontier, and the White Mountains, the infamous Tora Bora. Once, he'd worried David would die in Tora Bora. But David had lived, at least in 2001. Was he destined to die there still? Was fate a cruel, cruel mistress?

Or was this, all of this, from the very first moment, all Kris's fault?

Ryan kept up a steady conversation with the QRF team as Kris struggled to stand. Every breath felt like fire ripping through him. His legs shook. His hands were clammy, cold, and sliding off the back of the metal folding chair he clung to. He could feel each heartbeat, each thundering *boom*, from the back of his eyes to the soles of his feet.

"*Alizai in sight. ETA to DZ, two minutes.*"

"We need the identity of the uploader or the delivery man, whoever brought that video message to the café." Ryan crossed his arms and glared at the screen. Live video feed from the soldiers streamed back via satellite, grainy and glitching out in places. "Make this fast, gentlemen. We have exactly no time, and we have no cover for this op."

They saw the helo move into a hover over a squat building with a bright-colored sign hanging from its roof. Ropes being tossed over the side, and soldiers looking over the edge, calling out *good to go*.

The soldiers slid down the ropes quickly, hitting the dusty ground in the center of a wind tunnel on all sides of the internet café and setting up a perimeter in two seconds.

Civilians scattered, racing away from the chopper and the soldiers, clad all in black and swooping out of the sky. In moments, the street was deserted.

"*Breaching now.*" The team leader's video feed showed him and his soldiers stacking beside the front door. Two deep breaths, and then they burst in.

"*Down, down, down! Everybody down!*"

"*Hands in the air! Hands in the air!*"

"*Do not move!*"

Shouts, screams. The guttural bellow of the soldiers, the high-pitched, frantic cry of civilians. There were young men in the shop, a handful of teenagers.

"*Where is the owner? Where is the owner?*"

Meekly, one man raised his timid hand. He was middle-aged and slender. He wore a dark blue turban and had a long beard. The beard made Kris curse. Was he possibly Taliban? Or al-Qaeda? The Americans didn't have many sympathizers in the tribal territories on either side of the border. Would he help them at all?

"*A video was uploaded from this location to the internet minutes ago. A jihadist video. Who uploaded that video?*" The team leader was right up in the owner's face, barking questions.

"*I-I-I do not know,*" the owner stammered.

"*A video was uploaded from this café fifteen minutes ago! An American hostage was shown on the video! Who uploaded the video?*"

The owner trembled, shrinking in the face of the team leader's fury. "*Please...*"

"*Who uploaded the video*? Who brought the video to you?"

Shaking, the owner whispered, "*Farrohk.*"

"*Who the fuck is Farrohk?*"

The owner's eyes squeezed closed. "*He is with al-Qaeda. They are here. They are everywhere. Please, my family—*"

"*Where is Farrohk in this village? Where is al-Qaeda? How many are there?*"

"*A dozen, maybe. They are in the mosque. The mosque! Please, please, my family! My son!*"

The team leader turned away, calling back to Ryan. "*Be advised, target is reported to be in the village mosque. Request permission to proceed to mosque.*"

"Permission granted," Ryan responded. On-screen, the team leader radioed for his men to rally around him and pull out of the shop.

"He's probably going to be killed, you know," Kris croaked. "The shop owner. For talking to us."

Ryan didn't answer. He didn't blink. "Let's get them intel on the mosque. How far are they from it?"

"Half a mile, sir." One of the drone pilots pulled up his imagery, showing the mosque relative to the position of the team. Twists and turns and alleyways led to the mosque. "They have a decent amount of ground to cover."

"And everyone knows we're here," Ryan growled. "Be advised, team leader, distance to target is point four miles. Route is urban. No civilian movement detected." The village looked like a ghost town from the Old West. "Be prepared for resistance en route."

"*Acknowledged. Moving out.*"

**Syed Ishaq Mosque, Alizai, Afghanistan - Nine and a half Hours After the Blast**

"They're coming! They're coming!" Farrohk, young, new to al-Qaeda, but a teen with great promise, hissed.

He'd run down from the roof, where he'd watched the helicopter hover of the internet café and spit out the team of black-clad soldiers. He'd watched them regroup and head for the mosque, twisting down the village's dirt roads covered in chicken shit and feathers and ducking against mudbrick walls to check for fighters on the rooflines.

"Good," Al Jabal crowed. "Let them come."

Wires crawled up the walls of the mosque, snaking into and out of old plastique explosives. They'd been passed around the black market for a while, from Pakistan to Afghanistan, and possibly across the border from Iran, too. But now they belonged to Al Jabal, and he had the perfect use for them.

IEDs and hidden bombs were too simple. The Americans were used to those by now. Blowing off legs wasn't enough, not anymore. He needed something big, something bold, after the CIA had murdered Salim and Suleyman with their drones.

And he'd found it, in Hamid.

The plan was as beautiful as it was simple. Turn the American intelligence system against itself.

Hungry for intelligence, for spies to spill their secrets to their drones and their hidden telephone eavesdroppers, feeding false information to the Americans was stunningly simple. All it took was a conversation over the telephone, certain to be picked up, and then Hamid feeding the same information back to his spy handler in Jordan. The apostate kingdom, allied with the Great Satan, would immediately run, like a dog to its owner, to the Americans.

And Al Jabal, with Zawahiri, had supplied exactly the right bait. What the Americans craved, hungered for most of all. Revenge. The blood of the men who had wounded them, all those years ago.

The video was easy to film, almost like making a Hollywood movie. A scene from a spy movie. They'd joked, before and after, about how their part would look in the eventual movie to be made of their successes. The film of al-Qaeda winning the war.

They thought they'd be able to blow up a car with Hamid and the CIA spies inside of it. But when Hamid was invited to the CIA base, Al Jabal realized how much larger their dreams could grow.

They could strike at the heart of the CIA's secret border base.

They could kill so many Americans.

They could kidnap one of the CIA spies who penetrated the border, the tribal territories, almost every day. A man who called himself Dawood, who played at being a farmer searching for day labor. A man who claimed to be a Muslim, but who was working for the Americans. And that made him a dog, a traitor, a *kufir*. Someone to be tried by the laws of Allah and executed.

Al Jabal turned back to his hostage. The dog was huddled on the ground, bleeding. He'd taken their beating silently, not once crying out. His blood coated their fists, their boots. Stained the floor and the walls. Dripped down the *shahada* inscribed on the wall. It was poetic, he thought. A *kufir's* blood falling from the words of the Prophet.

*There is no God but God.*

**Camp Carson, Afghanistan-Pakistan Border, Afghanistan - Nine and a half Hours After the Blast**

It took ten minutes for the team to work their way to the mosque. Nothing moved in the village. Not a soul stirred. Even the wind seemed to still, the air. Time seemed to freeze.

Again, the team spread out to all four corners of the mosque, picking four different breach points. They waited, searching for fighters, for jihadis. Surely someone would fight back. Or had al-Qaeda already fled?

"Negative on anyone leaving the mosque since you've been on station," Ryan said over the radio. "We have seen flickers of movement inside the windows. Definitely active presence inside the mosque."

"*We go in strong,*" the team leader transmitted to his team. "*Watch your partner. Stay alive, but don't shoot any civilians.*" He heard his team click back their affirmative. "*Breach on my order.*" He counted down, slowly.

The burst in from all sides, two teams shattering windows and tumbling in, snaking left and right. The front and rear teams demolished the doors and dove in, weapons up and ready to fire, shouting at the top of their lungs.

"*Allahu Akbar*!" Gunshots rang out. Bullets whizzed past their heads.

They ducked, diving behind walls and crawling on the floor. The mosque wasn't large. A main floor space for the male congregants, and a balcony for the women, with a rickety wooden staircase. Windows were the only source of light. A minbar rose at the rear wall for the imam to pray, to teach from. A cutout next to it led to another room.

"*Eight hostiles.*"

"*Three on the balcony.*"

"*Three on the main floor.*"

"*No eyes on the other two.*"

The team called out targets as bullets popped and snapped,

cracking into the walls and whizzing through the air. The jihadis seemed to spray bullets in their direction, long bursts of automatic gunfire.

They took their time, zeroing on each fighter before popping off three quick shots.

"*One down.*"

"*One down.*" A body dropped from the balcony above, hitting the mosque floor like a dropped watermelon.

Across the mosque, a fighter raced for the doorway behind the minbar. Shots followed his footsteps, chasing him, but he ducked into the darkness and skittered away.

They tried to follow. More shots rang out, chipping at the mudbrick beside their heads and pinning them back in place.

---

"They're here! They're inside the mosque!" Farrohk, breathless, slid to a stop in front of Al Jabal.

"Good. You know what to do." Al Jabal passed Farrohk his rifle and held out a videotape. Farrohk took the tape and nodded. "*Bismillah.*"

"*Allahu Akbar*, brother," Al Jabal grinned. He pointed to the bloody lump on the ground. "Now, help me move him."

---

"*Do you smell that?*"

Kris's heart seized.

"*Smoke. Something's burning.*" The soldier coughed. "*Fuck, it stinks.*"

He tried to drag in another breath, tried to keep standing. Everything inside of him wanted to collapse, wanted to scream and wail and jump into the monitor, leap into the fight and run to David. Fight with his bare hands, run through the bullets, tear apart the mosque until he found David. Bring him *back*.

"*The smoke is coming from the back room.*"

"*We have to get back there, now.*"

"*Fuck this,*" the team leader growled. "*Grenade!*" He tossed a grenade toward the last of the fighters, clustered together behind the minbar. The team ducked, and seconds later, the minbar exploded in a burst of light and sound, wood and brick flying through the air. Debris pelted the team, bursts of hail battering the command center over the radio. Kris flinched.

The gunshots had ceased. Silence filled the mosque.

The team rose. On-screen, black, thick smoke hung in the air, crawling up the walls and undulating along the ceiling. "*We've got thick, dark smoke,*" the team leader called. "*It reeks. Something terrible is burning.*"

*No. No, no, no, no.* Kris's thoughts devolved to one word. A litany, a prayer, over and over. *No. No. No.*

Slowly, the team moved through the mosque, coughing with each step. The video feed grew darker, hazier. Obscured.

"*Moving to the rear room now.*"

Footsteps, in the smoke. Gunshots. Cursing.

"*Allahu Akbar!*" More gunshots, and a man rushing toward the team, in the center of the video feed.

"*Fuck!*" the team fired back, striking the jihadi in the center of the chest, peppering him with shot after shot. He staggered, a puppet dancing on strings, and collapsed.

"*Sir!*" The camera shot to one of the soldiers, standing near a billowing cloud of smoke emanating from the trunk of a car. Someone had driven a small hatchback into the mosque and parked it. A tarp covered the front, and part of the mosque's broken wall. A hidden access point.

The team leader crept toward the car, toward the smoke.

*No, no, no, no, no.* Burning tears cascaded down Kris's cheeks, fell from the ends of his eyelashes. His heart was a black hole, sucking all of his hope into a terrible darkness. His wedding ring weighed a thousand pounds. David's lips lingered on the back of his neck, on his shoulder, a ghost kiss, a prelude, a prophecy. *No, no, no, no, no.*

The camera attached to the team leader's helmet angled down. A hand swept through the black smoke. White-hot flames rose from a fire raging inside the trunk. The ends of rockets, of dynamite, poked out of the conflagration.

And, a hand. A foot. Blackened and burned. But, recognizable.

A human body.

"*Sir! The place is rigged to blow! We have to get out*!" The panicked voice of another team member broke over the radio. The camera jerked away, the team leader panning the walls. Finding the wire. Tracing them to the explosives.

"*Everybody out, now, now*!"

"No!" Kris shrieked. "You have to get David! You have to save him! Pull him out! Pull him out!"

"*Evac, now, move*!" Boots running. The smoke fading. "*Go! Now*!"

"No! *No*!" Kris screamed. "Go back! Get David! Get him!"

Ryan's arms grabbed him, held him in a bear hold from behind. "Kris, he's gone. He's already—"

"*Sir*—"

A rumble began, and then a burst of light erupted over the screen.

The radio went dead.

# 23

## Kabul, Afghanistan - Four Days After the Blast

A void in the shape of David's smile hovered in the center of Kris.

The act of breathing took too much effort. Inhaling, letting his cells fill with life-giving oxygen, was agonizing. The pain of living, the anguish of carrying on.

He couldn't see. His eyes were unfocused, his mind's eye fixed on the memory of a burned-black body in the bottom of a trunk, silhouetted through billowing smoke.

He didn't know how he was still living. Wasn't it impossible to live without a heart? How then was he still walking, still breathing? Shouldn't the freedom of death come for him? Shouldn't he be gone already? Shouldn't he be waking in David's arms, somewhere where they could finally be together?

Why was he still living? He didn't want to be alive, not now, not after that. Not after seeing what lay beneath the smoke.

He deserved to die. He deserved to die a thousand times. All the thousands of lives lost on September 11. And more. Add in the loss of life in Iraq. The civilians killed in Pakistan and Afghanistan.

And David.

He deserved to die for all of them, over and over again. Like Prometheus, he should be chained to a rock and devoured, day in and day out, for the foolish hubris of thinking he could change anything at all, make any difference in the world.

Everything he'd done, everything he'd tried to do, had only brought death. Death and ruin.

*David...*

He bowed his head. He couldn't cry, not anymore. Every tear he'd ever cried in the length of his life had been wept already, spilled down his cheeks and into rivers that ran through his fingers. His wails had unset his broken ribs, his screams had made one of his bones puncture his lung. Ryan had to carry him out of the command center, restrain him, pin him against a wall as he shrieked like he'd been torn in two.

He had. Half his soul had just been ripped out of him.

*Wherever you are, be happy. Be with your father. Find the peace you longed for in this world. I'm so sorry you met me. I'm sorry you loved me. I'm sorry I killed you.*

"Caldera?" Somewhere, far away, someone was trying to speak to him. He heard the voice like it was coming from a dream, warbling and distant, like a megaphone underwater.

It had been four days since he'd seen through the smoke. Four days since the mosque had blown as the team was trying to escape, a remote detonator set off by someone on the outside. The drones hadn't seen any cars speeding away from the village. Someone nearby, someone watching.

The rubble had buried the team for three hours, until a second QRF team dispatched from the base was able to dig through and extract the soldiers. Four were seriously injured. The Pakistanis were outraged, telling the world of the Americans' violation of their borders and of the destruction of the mosque. No matter how many times they said it had been blown by al-Qaeda, the public believed the Americans had detonated it. Protests raged in front of the US Embassies in Islamabad and Kabul.

The last man the team had shot inside the mosque, in the room with the burning car, was a young man the locals had identified as Farrohk. He'd been shot twenty-one times, destroying a videotape he'd carried in his jacket, over his chest. The mosque falling down on him had crushed the tape further, destroying most of it. Portions were recovered, inches of film that could be restored and viewed.

David's trial. His crimes against Islam, against Allah, read aloud by Al Jabal.

All in all, the recovered tape was a little under two minutes, but it was two minutes of the end of David's life.

Kris watched it and puked, wailed.

Farrohk was probably supposed to take the video to be uploaded to the internet. He was probably supposed to escape, the analysts said. But since he hadn't, and the Americans had recovered it, the tape would never see the light of day. David's last moments wouldn't be broadcast for all to see, for some to gloat over. His memory, at least, would find peace.

There would be no peace for Kris. Never, ever again.

"Caldera?" Again, the voice.

Ryan. Ryan was trying to talk to him. Kris focused, trying to draw back to the world. It was like plunging into a river, diving headlong from a cliff. Reality rushed at him, ice-cold and shocking.

*Everything* was real. *Everything* he feared was right there.

David was *gone*.

"Kris…" Ryan sighed and scrubbed both hands over his face. "Jesus fucking Christ."

He'd been in Kabul for three days. Ryan had dragged him back to the CIA station and put him in the embassy hospital. After a day, he was discharged and put in embassy quarters. He'd been left, abandoned, since. Until Ryan's summons to the CIA station, and to the station chief's office.

Ryan spoke stiffly, chewing on his words. "I have to formally censure you for this. This… entire thing," he sighed. "The Hamid operation has blown up in our faces. Congress has already started an inquiry. The director has launched his own internal investigation. Everything is pointing one direction." He stared.

"It's all my fault," Kris breathed. "All of it."

"They're going to focus on the planning, the prep. How much you vetted Hamid. How much you knew and didn't know, and how much you assumed."

"You were there, Ryan," Kris breathed. "We knew next to nothing."

Ryan looked away.

"We all wanted it so badly," he whispered again. "We were starving for this. Desperate for it to work. Everyone was. Not just me."

David's fears, his words of caution, came back to Kris. *You were right. You were always right.*

"I am relieving you of your command," Ryan choked out. "And you're being removed from the counterterrorism division. Immediately."

"*What*?" Counterterrorism was everything he'd ever done. Everything he knew. He and David had dedicated their lives to the fight. David had been taken from him by the men he hunted. No, he had to stay. He had to continue the fight. Avenge David. At the end of the day, what else did he have left?

There was nothing else. No hope, no home, no love. His heart was gone, shredded, turned in on itself until it was a black hole. All he had left was vengeance. "CT is my life. It's everything I do, everything I know!"

"Everything you know got fourteen people killed, and more seriously injured."

He flinched. Gritted his teeth. "Fire me then." Maybe he'd do it himself. Disappear into the wilds like a bandit of old, like the Punisher, like an action hero or a comic book hero. Or he'd join a gun slinging contractor, blood for hire, and take out his rage through licensed murder.

Or he'd go home and eat a bullet, sitting on the porch that was David's dream.

Ryan glared. "We can't fire you," he spat. "But Goddamn, if I could." He shook his head. "You've been a Goddamn shitshow since the first moment you stepped foot in Afghanistan. Always overstepping your boundaries, mixing yourself up where you don't belong. You were never supposed to be here. Never supposed to be a base commander. Never supposed to be in charge of anything. You should have just taken the hint and slinked away, years ago."

Kris's jaw dropped. "What the fuck?"

"The CIA doesn't need people like you."

Oh. It all clicked. "You mean *faggots*? Gays. Say it. Say it to my *face*. You don't want the gays in your boys' club."

"I don't give a fuck about that. I *mean* bleeding hearts who just want to understand everything. Who want to sit down with our enemy and try to work something out. Who think that we're not in this fight for the life of our civilization. Our way of life."

"You don't have any fucking idea what I think. You reduce the world to black and white and call it a day. You refuse to see the shades of gray, the impossible choices that billions of people have to face. How people pick the best of the worst and hope they survive the night. That everyone just wants to survive."

"You're so fucking naïve," Ryan spat.

"And you've never actually looked at the world. Never understood it, not once!"

"I didn't get sucked into a delusion of Islamic grandeur!" Ryan shouted. "You fell for Haddad, and Haddad's been on a fucking *roller coaster* for a decade! Ever since nine-eleven, he's been unstable! Unbalanced. His sympathies, and his loyalty, have been in question."

"How dare you!" Kris leaped to his feet. The chair he sat in flew backward. "David has only ever been one hundred percent loyal to everyone! He's done everything, absolutely everything, anyone has ever asked!"

"Sit down. We're not through here."

What was the worst that could happen if he just lunged at Ryan? Wrapped his hands around Ryan's throat until he begged for mercy? Until he gasped and choked and the last thing he saw was Kris's face?

He grabbed his chair and sat, slowly.

"As I said. You've been removed from your command and you're no longer a part of the CT division. I've been given the authority to reassign you within the CIA. I've placed you in the Special Activities Division. You'll begin your training in six weeks, after a month on the bricks."

Kris threw his head back and howled. SAD. The paramilitary arm of the CIA. Men who had *hated* Kris his entire life, who resented him commanding them. Carl had been SAD. Ryan had, too.

"You want me to quit on my own, don't you? Wash out of SAD training and disappear. You think I can't cut it there, and so you can get rid of me without having to dirty your hands with a civil rights lawsuit. 'Cause you know you can't fire a gay."

"There's more than enough blood on your hands to fire you. But you seem to have a few friends left in the agency. I know you won't cut it. I know you'll fail. And nothing will make me happier than seeing you get cashiered from this agency and spend the rest of your days knowing what a fucking failure you actually are."

"Fuck you, Ryan. What's going to happen to you? You losing your command?"

"You were in charge of this, Caldera. Didn't you say a minute ago this was all your fault?"

It was, he knew it was, all of it, from the moment the planes had hit the towers until he saw David's body in the trunk. But damn it, he wasn't going down alone. Not for this. "Your hands are just as bloody as mine."

Ryan stared. He folded his hands on his desktop. Looked beyond Kris, eyes boring holes into the back wall of his office. "Haddad's body has been ID'd."

Kris recoiled, as if shot, as if his heart had been struck with a sledgehammer.

"His remains were too burned for DNA analysis. They used some kind of accelerant. The car, the body, everything, was ash by the time they were able to recover his remains. But there was enough DNA in the rubble to make a determination."

"Fuck you," Kris hissed. "You're just going to say that to me? Throw that in my face? That's my husband you're talking about."

"Your husband's remains have been sent to his legal next of kin," Ryan spat, his voice choking.

"I am his legal next of kin."

"No, Caldera, you're *not*. How many times were you told that your marriage didn't mean anything in the US? Or to the CIA? Just because you had someone give you shared quarters doesn't mean the law changes for you. Haddad and you aren't married. Not to the CIA, not to the United States government!"

He hadn't thought he could feel worse than he did, spying the blackened pieces of the love of his life through the billowing smoke. He had thought that was rock bottom, the very end. There was no further he could fall, no abyss he could plummet into, for he'd reached the end of all things. There was nothing more that could be ripped away from him. His heart and soul were gone.

Hearing Ryan tell him his husband, what was left of David, didn't belong to him plowed through the bottom of his black hole. Like a plug had been pulled, he felt himself slipping away.

"David is my *husband*." His voice shook. "His body, his memories. His life. Belong with me."

Ryan kept looking beyond Kris. "Haddad's remains have already been transported back to the United States. His mother, his legal next of kin, retrieved his body from Dover Air Force base yesterday. In accordance with Islamic burial practices, she requested an immediate repatriation of his remains and a next-day burial. Her wishes were granted. He's most likely already in the ground."

His soul plunged again as the bottom fell out of his very precarious grip on the world. "You have no right—"

"No, you have no rights. Not to him. Not anymore."

He stood and spun, closing his eyes. The world was upending, tumbling like a car crash, like a speeding train heading for catastrophe. He tried to walk, tried to flee Ryan's office.

One step, and he collapsed. He gasped. It came out like a wail, a shriek. He screamed again, and again. "You can't!" he hollered. Tears and snot and spit puddled beneath him. "You can't *do* this!"

"It's already done." Ryan whispered. "You're on the next flight out of here. Thirty days' suspension from duty. You'll report to headquarters for reassignment when your suspension is over. Unless you resign first."

Footsteps, Ryan rising from his desk. Padding toward him. Hovering above him. Kris couldn't look up. Couldn't stand to see the smug superiority in Ryan's eyes, the sick victory he knew was there.

"It would have been easier if you'd died with everyone else," Ryan choked out. "You would have been a hero, instead of the one we're all blaming." He strode to his office door. Hesitated. "Take the time you need."

He left, shutting Kris inside. Alone.

Alone, forever. For the rest of his days, alone. Without the love of his life by his side. Without his husband.

Without even saying goodbye for the last time.

David had been ripped from him. By al-Qaeda, and by the CIA. By the world, and by fate. By people who hated them for loving each other, for daring to put their love first, before everything else.

But most of all, David had been killed by *Kris*.

### Pakistan Northwestern Frontier, Bajaur Province, Federally Administered Tribal Areas - Six Days After the Blast

The car bounced and swerved over the rocky ground.

Every bump jolted through his body, sent shockwaves through his bones. His ribs were on fire, broken in so many places. He could feel their pinch against his lungs with every inhale, like he was sucking the bones deep inside his organs. He tasted copper, iron in his mouth. Dried blood coated his lips.

David's memories were hazy, images floating out of sequence. Driving. Hamid crunching chips. Kris's smile. Heat, too much heat. Bones snapping. Kris, whispering his marriage vows. A jihadi grabbing his head, staring down at him. Throwing him into a truck. The way Kris's eyes slowly opened, smile on his lips, after they'd kissed for what felt like hours.

Fists. Kicks. A tarp. He'd known how it would end as soon as he saw the tarp.

His thoughts had gone to Kris, of course, and he'd composed the most perfect love letter he'd never send to him as he huddled on the bloodstained tarp, taking kick after kick into his body. *My love, you are the stars and moon of my life. You are the peace my soul has always sought. You were the last gift of a vengeful God, and the only thing that kept my faith alive. Because of our love. Because you loved me. If you exist, Allah must have created you. Nature could not shape someone so perfect as you are for me. My soul, my love, I will always watch over you.*

The world had gone fuzzy after that. He remembered a speech, a video recording. Frantic shouting. Gunfire, far away. Hands grabbing him and carrying him down, deep down, into a tunnel cut into the dirt floor of the mosque. Darkness and dust, his feet dragging as someone hauled him away, pain like a rake that scraped his brain as he was dragged through a black tunnel that seemed to twist and wind forever. Finally, sunlight had speared his eyeballs, sent lances straight through his brain. He'd mumbled, tried to roll away. Tried to escape, but his feeble flailing did nothing.

The last thing he remembered was being dropped into the trunk of another car and driven away.

Why was he still alive? What were they waiting for? He'd rather it all end quickly.

*Kris, my love. I will always be with you. In this life and the next. I swear it.*

The car drove uphill. He pressed against the trunk's hatch, broken bones grinding. He gritted his teeth, tried to push through the pain, the fire in his lungs. *Let it end, let it all end.*

Finally, he heard brakes squealing, felt the car rock to a stop. A man scrambled from the front seat, racing around the car. The trunk opened, and sunlight stabbed David, arching around Al Jabal's scowling face.

Al Jabal reached for him, hauled him from the trunk.

"What is this?" An older man's voice, shocked, rose from behind the car.

David hit the ground. He landed on his face, on his broken ribs, his shattered leg. He gasped, inhaling dust and frigid, thin air. He was in the mountains again. He could taste the snow, the alpine air.

"Hide him," Al Jabal hissed. "Hide him for me, Baba. I have to go."

"*Habibi*, what have you done? *Wallah*, this is not right! *Astaghfirullah*!"

"He is my hidden treasure, Baba. But he *must* be a secret, for now. I will be back for him. I will use him to end this war. Get rid of the Americans, the crusaders, for good!"

"*Habibi*, no—"

"The bees do not come here, Baba. Keep him hidden. Keep him safe! I will return." Al Jabal spat on the back of David's head. "Treat him like the dog he is."

David watched through his swollen eye as Al Jabal ran back to the open driver's door and slid into the car. The old man's voice came closer, and two wrinkled bare feet appeared before David. He tried to roll away, flinching.

"*Habibi*!" Al Jabal's father called. "Come back here! Stay at home! Do not return to the fighting!"

"Fighting is all we have left, Baba." A car door slammed. The engine sputtered and turned over, shuddered, and finally started. Tires spun. Dirt and a thousand tiny rocks slammed into David's face.

Al Jabal drove off, squealing tires and creaking shocks bouncing over the rutted goat trail sloping and winding its way down the mountain.

He tried to move. Tried to put one palm on the ground and push himself up. He collapsed, a scream dying on his lips as he pressed his face into the dirt. His arm, his ribs, his bones, felt like they were being ripped from his body, like his skeleton had been pulled apart beneath his skin.

Al Jabal's father crouched beside him. He rested a gnarled hand on David's shoulder and brushed his son's spit from David's hair. "*As-salaam-alaikum*," the old man whispered.

"Let me die," David breathed. He spoke in Arabic, his first

language. He repeated his plea in Pashto. "Let me die. *In shaa Allah.* Please."

"*In shaa Allah*, you will not die." The old man got his arms under David and pulled him up. Got him sitting, even though David screamed and gritted his teeth, tears flowing from his eyes. "Please!" he whimpered. "*Please*, let me die..."

Roughened hands cupped his face, and leathery thumbs stroked away his tears. "*Bismillah*, do not presume to know Allah's plan for you, or for the world. Your death will come when Allah decides. He has decided to bring you to my home, and as for me, I will not allow another to suffer. I will care for you, brother. *Alhamdulillah*."

David shook his head. More tears fell, rivers streaming from his eyes. He didn't want kindness, especially not from Al Jabal's father. The father of the man who'd kidnapped him, tortured him. Had planned the deaths of his fellow officers. Was Kris even alive? He'd trade his life for Kris's, had begged Allah to trade. Why was he still breathing?

Was the pain he felt only physical? Or was this what it felt like when a soul was ripped in two? Was this what his mama had felt that night, watching the television in Libya and seeing her husband climb a rickety ladder to a noose?

Al Jabal's father started reciting a hadith. "*Whoever removes grief from a believer, Allah will remove from him one of the griefs of the Day of Judgment. Whoever cares for those in need, Allah will care for them in this world and the next. Whosoever protects a Muslim, Allah will protect him in this world and the next.*"

He laid David's arms over his shoulders and helped him stand, bearing David's weight when David cried out, unable to walk. His leg, and possibly his pelvis, was shattered. He leaned into the old man's surprisingly strong shoulders, resting his filthy forehead against his neck. For the first time, he could see more than the dirt or the inside of a car trunk.

Untouched land spread for miles and miles, the slopes of mountains unblemished by the scars of war, bomb craters from drone strikes or missiles or artillery. Villages dotted the tableau, lazy coils of smoke rising from thatched roofs beside tilled fields. Snow was creeping down from the ridgeline, already covering some of the villages, parts of the dirt trails that wound over and through the mountains. This was a corner of the world untouched by the modern world, unravaged by war. Where did such a place exist? Where on the planet was he?

"I will bring you into my home," the older man said. "It is just there, beyond the fields. You will be safe with me. *In shaa Allah*, you will."

# 24

**Andrews Air Force Base, Maryland - January 2009**

It should be raining. It should be thundering, lightning rending the sky, the world splitting in two. The world should end, like Kris's world had ended.

But the sun was shining and the sky was a perfect blue, a crystal blue. Not a cloud marred its flawlessness. He resented the sun on his skin. The crisp freshness to the air. Why did the earth continue to spin now that David was gone?

Shouldn't his death make an impact in the world? Shouldn't the planet mourn? Where was the rain, the snow, the frozen tears from the sky?

He'd been the only living passenger on the CIA's Learjet back from Islamabad to DC. There'd been no fanfare, no send-off. He had two duffels with him, the totality of his and David's belongings in Afghanistan.

There were four flag-draped coffins in the belly of the jet.

Darren, his deputy, and three of the SAD officers from Carl's security team.

He flew with their ghosts for twenty-six hours. The cabin was as silent as death, and for a time, Kris wished the plane would just plunge into the ocean, disappear, take him down to the depths. He should be dead, he *should* be, and there was no logic, no reason to his continued heartbeat. His lungs continuing to inhale and exhale. He didn't want to be alive.

The plane had landed smoothly at Andrews Air Force Base and taxied to the private corner of the airfield reserved for the CIA. Hearses were waiting, and a smattering of dark SUVs.

Kris spotted George and Director Edwards waiting by the hearses.

When the plane finally parked, no one came and opened the jet door. He was left locked inside the jet as the coffins were unloaded one by one by an honor guard and carried to the hearses.

Director Edwards and George bowed their heads as the coffins passed, closed their eyes. When the last was loaded, they climbed into their SUV and the convoy drove off.

Only then did the pilot open the door for him. Lower the stairs.

He got the message, loud and clear. He was to blame, and everyone—*everyone*—knew it. He was going to suffer for this. He was going to be made to wear his stripes of shame for the whole world to see. He was the pariah, forced away, kept back from everyone else in case his tainted fall from grace infected them, too.

He dragged his duffels down the stairs. David's felt like a thousand pounds, like the weight would break his spine. He kept his head down, blood red eyes fixed on the metal stairs, the dark asphalt.

"Kris..."

At the bottom, waiting by the very last SUV, was Dan.

He was pale, his eyes almost as red as Kris's, and tears ran down his face, dripped from his jawline. His lips quivered, pressed together. "Kris, I am so sorry..."

Kris couldn't speak. He dropped everything and ran to Dan, threw his arms around his friend. Dan grabbed him, squeezed him until he thought his chest would pop, and buried his face in Kris's neck. "I'm so sorry," he kept saying. "So sorry, Kris."

He hadn't thought he could cry again. He'd thought he'd used a lifetime of tears. He thought his heart was gone, incinerated, nothing but ash. He thought he'd be alone forever, however long the rest of his life was. Hours, perhaps. Maybe days. Until it was all over, finally.

But Dan was there, holding him up. His tears soaked Kris's shirt, his skin, and his hands squeezed Kris's arms. Dan was *there*. For the moment, at least, he wasn't alone.

"Let me take you home," Dan finally said. His voice shook. "You shouldn't be alone right now."

Numb, he let Dan load his duffel into the SUV. He kept an iron-clad grip on David's. It was all he had left of his husband. Dirty clothes, a paperback he'd tried to read, a notebook of doodles. His wedding ring, clasped tightly in Kris's hand, that he always took off and left with Kris whenever he went outside the wire or over the border.

This duffel was the only coffin he'd ever have.

"Take me to his grave," he whispered. "I need to see."

"Are you sure?"

"I have to see it."

Dan drove him to Arlington National Cemetery, not saying a word. The middle of the day, and traffic was light. Pedestrians smiled and laughed as they walked along the streets of DC.

It felt like two different worlds, inside and outside the car. Everyone else lived in some alternate reality where there were still good things in the world, while Kris was left in the darkness.

They parked near the new burials, and Kris spotted the fresh mound of earth, the uneven patches of new sod laid over a recent burial. Saw the crescent moon carved into the marble headstone above the words *Staff Sergeant David Haddad*.

A dark-skinned woman in a headscarf kneeled at the grave. Her shoes were to one side and she faced east, crossing David's grave. Her cheeks were wet, but she held her hands open in front of her chest, her lips moving silently.

"It's his mom." Kris stared. "She didn't believe him when he told her we were together."

"What do you want me to do? Want me to leave?"

"She's my mother-in-law. I should..." He shook his head. "We both loved him. We should mourn together."

"I'll wait here."

Kris palmed David's ring and slid from the car. He'd carried David's ring all the way from Kabul, holding it between his hands like a prayer on the long flight.

His legs shook as he made his way up the gently sloping hill to David's grave. The headstones blurred into a spinning carousel while David's flew into perfect focus. He wanted to puke. He wanted to run. He wanted to rip up the fresh grass and throw away the dirt, claw his way down to David, pry open his coffin and lie beside him. Lie in his ashes, let David into his body at an atomic level. Would David stay with him, if he held David inside him?

"*As-salaam-alaikum*," he choked out.

David's mother blinked at him. Fresh tear tracks carved mascara down her cheeks. "*Wa alaikum as-salaam*," she whispered. "Did you know my son?"

He couldn't speak. He nodded, collapsing to his knees. One hand traced David's name on his headstone as he covered his mouth with the other. David's ring touched his lips. He kissed the gold, the promise they'd made each other.

He held the ring out in the palm of his hand to David's mother. "We were married."

She frowned.

"Do you remember when he called you and told you he had found someone he wanted to be with forever?" Kris watched her face morph from confusion to shock, terrible shock. "And he told you his name was Kris?" His lips trembled, his chin. "That's *me*. We were married in Canada a few weeks before. He didn't know how to tell you."

"No..." She shook her head. "No, no, no. My son was not—"

"We were in love. So deeply in love." Damn it, he was crying again. "Here, look." Fumbling, he reached for his phone and pulled up a few pictures they'd taken. They weren't the best, but it was them. In Hawaii, cuddling. Kissing. On the beach, holding hands. In

Toronto, in matching suits. Kissing after their wedding. In front of their new home. Lying in bed together, shirtless. David kissing his cheek.

She pushed his phone away and squeezed her eyes closed. "Allah, *forgive* my son," she whispered. "Forgive him, in your mercy. Forgive him from his sins. Make his grave wide and peaceful. Allah, please do not punish him in his grave!"

"It's not a sin! We were in love!"

"It *is* a sin!" Fresh tears burst from her eyes. "You come to me and tell me my son sinned, that he turned against Allah. You bring me this here, at his grave? What are you trying to do? Hurt me?"

"No! We both loved him, I thought—"

"He will be punished for this! And now I must know it! Now I have to think of him, facing an eternity of agony in his grave!"

"We were in love!" Kris screamed. "I loved him! And he loved me! Why does that need punishing? What the fuck kind of God does that?"

She stood, grabbing her purse and her shoes. "If you loved my son, you would have cared for his soul. His relationship with Allah. Now—" She covered her mouth and shook her head. Then turned and strode toward a parked sedan, her head in one hand. Her sobs floated back toward Kris, echoes that seemed to grow, surround everything.

He fell to his face on David's grave, tears flowing into the fresh grass. He didn't, couldn't understand. Of all the things he was ashamed of, in all the ways he'd failed so spectacularly in his life, loving David was never something he regretted. Never, ever.

Why? Why did the world fight against them? Why was their love so suspect?

Why had David been taken from him?

Why had he lived? Why was he still enduring, when the love of his life was not?

He didn't deserve to live. He'd failed on September 11, he'd failed to stop the vice president and his quest for Iraq, and he'd failed on the Hamid operation. There was blood on his hands, no, he was swimming in blood, an ocean of it, waves that drowned him when he closed his eyes. And in the center of it all, the very center of his failures, was the taste of ashes on the back of his throat.

*Everything* he'd tried to protect turned to ash. Towers to bones, ashes to ashes, dust to dust. His love, in the back of a trunk.

His torment, his torture, was to keep on living.

Only God could be so cruel.

---

Dan eventually picked him off the grass and helped him back to the car. Kris mumbled his address, and Dan made the long drive in silence as Kris pitched sideways and lay on the bench seat, clinging to the leather like if he let go he'd be launched into space, or the tether that kept him leashed to the last remnants of his sanity would break.

Would it be so bad to be insane, though? If he hallucinated David, but spent the rest of his life in a padded room, would the trade-off be worth it? Could he ever imagine David the way he truly was, though? Could he ever conjure up the totality of his existence, his soul? All his perfections, all his imperfections, every one of his deepest thoughts and secrets, things Kris had known and hadn't known. He could never recreate David, not if he spent his entire life trying.

The sun had set by the time Dan pulled into his driveway. The shape of their house made his spine shiver, called up every memory of David's smile inside their walls.

How many dreams had David packed into their house, staring at each room like he was watching a future movie play out. What had he imagined for them there? What was he hoping for when they both came home for good?

He walked the entire house, his hands trailing over walls and cabinets, kitchen counters and the back of the couch. They'd made love there and there, fast and frenzied, happy pouncing after unpacking. Slow and sweet, kissing until they ran out of air and they just kept going, never separating. The garage, where David's old truck still sat. He'd moved into Kris's life in that truck, taking them from weekend sleepovers to full-time partners.

The porch, David's favorite spot in their home. They'd drunk beers and held hands, watching the sun set. Ate cinnamon rolls and laughed over breakfast, listening to birds chirp. Walked the property, the tangled bushes and leaning trees, the rough scrabble of northern Virginia. If David was going to find peace, he'd said to Kris, he'd find it right there, holding Kris's hand.

Where *was* he? Where was David? He'd *sworn*, one night after they'd had too much to drink and war was everywhere, and the fear of dying was a real, heavy thing, that he would come back if the worst happened. He would haunt Kris, find some way to break the barrier between life and death. If there was a way, he swore he would find it. He wouldn't leave Kris alone. Kris had sworn the same, promises drenched in alcohol and tears and kisses that turned to endless lovemaking.

He'd carried David's ring like a totem, like an idol, praying to it as if it were a signpost for David's soul. *Come back to me. I'm here, I'm waiting for you.*

Damn it, he'd *promised*. He'd promised he would.

If there was any place on the planet that Kris would find David's ghost, it would be on their back porch. He'd been waiting, he knew, until the last moment. He wanted to walk out there and see him, see David in his chair. Holding out his hand for Kris to join him.

He'd promised he would come back.

But the porch, his chair, was empty, and David's ring was cold in the palm of his hand.

David wasn't coming back.

There wasn't anything to come back from.

Whirling, he puked, heaving a stomach full of bile over the railing. He hadn't eaten in days, and his stomach had started to turn on itself. He swayed, fell. Landed in a heap, a bag of brittle bones and rancid blood, powered by a broken heart and a soul full of shame.

Kris was alone.

---

He stormed out of the house hours later, Dan trailing behind him. Dan had crashed on the couch, slept for what looked like the first time in days. Dark bags under his eyes seemed etched into his skin, and new frown lines arched across his forehead like furrows and canyons.

Kris kept pacing, trying to bottle up every memory, every moment he and David had spent together. It was too much, the house full of hope, of dreams. Too, too much. He was being smothered by all the broken hope, the ghosts of their love. He had to get out.

Dan took him to a hotel, checked him in. Crashed in the second bed while Kris barricaded himself in the bathroom. He turned on the shower and crawled in, sinking down the tiled wall until he was a heap on the floor, soaking wet, shivering down to the bone. But he couldn't feel it. He couldn't feel anything anymore.

He called his *mamá*, only his second call ever outside of their annual Christmas and Easter calls. The first time, he'd called to tell her he was married. When she answered, she was excited, her voice full of joy, of wonder. "*Am I going to be a grandmother?*"

"He's dead. David's dead."

He heard his *mamá* drop the phone, heard her scream, curse, and then pray. Fast Spanish, breathless prayers rushed together in a long, unending string. He sat on the floor of his hotel room like a rock. His *mamá*'s grief washed over him and around him, but he was an unmovable boulder. Nothing could touch him anymore.

She came back on the line with her voice choked full of tears. She wanted to know how, when, why. He gave her the barest details. "It's been on the news. Haven't you seen?"

"*You never tell me details,* mi chico. *I didn't think it was you.*" She moaned, prayed again. "*What will you do?*"

He swallowed.

"*Come to Puerto Rico. Come here. I will take care of you. Leave all that behind, all of that. Just come here. It can be like it was, yes?*"

For a moment, he thought about it. *Mamá* had run after he left for college. She'd escaped a life she hated, a man who resented her, and a city that had brought her nothing but grief. She'd returned to the island she loved, lived away from the world and all of its hurts. She'd hidden herself away, carving a new world for herself where nothing could ever reach her again. It was tempting to fall into that, to disappear into Puerto Rico as well. Run, and never stop running. Run until he outran himself.

But his life sentence had been issued. He was made to live. He was made to suffer, to endure.

So suffer he would.

His mamá's prayers, her sobs, over the crackling phone line brought him back to Sunday mornings he'd spent at her side, incense and candle smoke in the air as he shifted in his too-tight shiny shoes. The low rumble of the priest's chanting. Jesus's nude body on the cross, his muscles glowing, gleaming by the light of the sun carved through stained glass. Verses read aloud in Father Felipe's deep baritone sank through his mind, the remnants of his soul. Hubris and punishment, God's wrath.

*Because you have done this, you are cursed upon all else. Because you have done this, dust shall you eat for all the rest of your days.*

*Dust you are, and to dust you shall return.*

Ashes to ashes. Dust to dust.

For all the rest of your days.

He wouldn't take any shortcuts, no easy way out. Death would be too easy. Living on without David was a punishment worse than any Hell envisioned by any religion. His sentence was harsh, but just. To live, and to suffer. For the rest of his days, until he too returned to ash, after a million torturous days.

He had an ocean of blood to clean up, thousands of lives to avenge.

He didn't have to find David's killer, though.

His killer stared back at him from the mirror every day.

He sat in silence for twenty-four hours, building a wall around his heart, around himself. David was supposed to come back to him, but he hadn't. This wasn't a movie, and there wouldn't be any reunions, any dances at midnight.

There was a truth in the fact that he was alone, that David wasn't a whisper away, his soul vibrating just out of reach of Kris's perceptions: there was nothing, and no one, for him, in this life or the next.

His walls built higher, deeper. The void in his heart yawned wide, and he threw his hopes and dreams into its bottomless abyss. *I will never love again.*

He went back to the house once, yanking clothes out of their closet and stuffing things in garbage bags. He called a realtor and told them to sell it, as fast as they could, and get rid of everything inside it. He couldn't spend a single second longer in the house, a mausoleum to David's dreams. He couldn't breathe the air that David had imbued with all his hope, all of his love. He couldn't create a future for one in a house that was made for so much more.

Three weeks later, he put a down payment on a studio condo in Crystal City. He spent the first night lying on garbage bags full of clothes and staring out of the floor-to-ceiling glass windows, until the sun rose over DC.

Dan checked on him twice a day, calling, texting, and dropping first by the hotel, then his unit. Kris could set his watch by Dan's visits, his quiet concern. He brought Kris food, tried to distract him.

One night, he brought a file over and slid it across the carpet to Kris.

"What's this?"

"Open it."

Pictures, from a drone strike. Black and white photos with a targeting grid overlaid on the grisly center scene. Close ups of a mangled car, and a body hanging out of the driver's door. A face he'd burned into the backs of his eyelids. "Al Jabal."

"There's been a huge increase in drone strikes over there. Revenge and payback. Kabul station tracked down Al Jabal. He was the one who put all the pieces together. Convinced Hamid, and then convinced Zawahiri of what they could do with Hamid. He's also the one on the videotape, with…" Dan swallowed. "The agency believes that he was David's killer."

Ryan had done it. Kris stared at Al Jabal's body, half blown apart, fallen like a broken rag doll out of the car. He should feel satisfaction, wrath, fury. He should cry. He should wail and feel it all again, relive the moment he saw David's burned and blackened body. He should be angry at Ryan for taking away his vengeance. Or grateful, even though it was Ryan. He should feel *something*.

He felt nothing.

His soul had stretched and stretched until it snapped. All of his edges were frayed, flapping in the breeze. Everything good within him was gone. All that was left were brittle bones, baptized in a thousand lives of shame, and a prisoner's sentence to endure. *For all of your days.*

"I thought you'd want to know." Dan said softly. He seemed thinner, the arches of his cheekbones more pronounced, the square angle of his heart-shaped jaw sharper. His face was gaunt, shadows living under his eyes. "Are you really going to do this? Join SAD?"

"I don't have a choice."

"You don't have to stay in the CIA. You've given them everything. You don't have to do this. Especially when you know they just want you to fail. Why give them that satisfaction?"

"I'm going through with it. I am joining SAD. I am going to make it through the training, and not just by the skin of my teeth. I am going to fucking excel," Kris hissed. "I'm going to be the faggot in their ranks, someone they *can't* ignore. Someone they *can't* get rid of. They think they can make me quit? Ryan thinks this is how to get rid of me? He'll never be rid of me."

Dan's lips thinned as he stared at Kris.

"I can't leave. What would I do? Who would hire me? The man who got his entire team killed. The man who ruined the Hamid op."

"None of that is true. There were so many things against you, things you couldn't know."

"I've seen the Congressional hearings. George has always loved to throw me to the wolves."

CNN had broadcast George's unclassified public hearing on the failure of the Hamid op a few days before, and George had taken great pains to isolate the failures to one individual: the base commander of Camp Carson. According to George, speaking for the CIA, Kris had "*failed to imagine the lengths al-Qaeda was prepared to go to*", and had "*failed to properly conduct a thorough counterintelligence operation*".

Never mind that George, Director Edwards, Ryan, and even the White House had been pressuring Kris to move *fast*, get Hamid operational as quickly as possible, get movement on the Bin Laden and Zawahiri case.

"Kris—"

"I can't go anywhere else," he snapped. "I can't. My entire life is here. Everything I've done. Everything I am. If I lose this..." He waved his hand in the air, let it fall, slapping on his carpet. "It's the only thing I have left."

"I'm here," Dan said softly. "You will always have me."

"You are too good a friend to me."

Dan smiled, sadly. "You're not alone."

*Yes I am. For all of my days.*

He said nothing.

## Pakistan Northwestern Frontier, Bajaur Province, Federally Administered Tribal Areas

He was dying, albeit very, very slowly.

Al Jabal's father, Abu Adnan, had brought David into his one-room home and laid him on his straw-stuffed mattress. Two goats lived inside, sharing the warmth of the fire. The place smelled of wood smoke and straw, musty fur and oats.

Abu Adnan did his best to care for him. He set David's broken leg, pulling until the bone slipped back into alignment. Without an X-ray, it was impossible to know if it was set correctly, but at least it was back inside his thigh. "*Alhamdulillah*," Abu Adnan said. "We have set goats and cows in these mountains, and occasionally a mule. But this is the first man I have ever helped with his bone so broken."

David stumbled through his pain, explaining how to wrap his broken ribs. Abu Adnan finally managed to cut up David's shirt and tie it into strips, wrap it around his chest until he felt like a mummy.

Infection loomed. He felt himself grow hot, burn from the inside. Consciousness slipped away, replaced by a hazy twilight, a flickering montage of images that appeared out of order.

Abu Adnan washing him with water boiled over the fire. Cleaning him, even when he soiled himself. Changing bloody bandages along his leg, his chest, his arms. Praying beside him, the slow movements and soft whispers an almost constant hum in the back of David's mind.

He saw Kris, first standing in Abu Adnan's doorway. He tried to chase him, but Kris disappeared, reappeared across the peak in the farmland of another mountain dweller. No matter how he tried to chase Kris, leaping from mountaintop to mountaintop in his delirium, Kris always seemed to stretch farther and farther away.

"Kris..." he moaned in his sleep. "Come back to me."

Was Kris dead? Was he seeing Kris from the other side? Was Kris telling him to join him? *Soon. Soon I'll be dead, too. We'll be together again, my love. Ya rouhi.*

And then he thought of his father. What had his father thought before being killed? What had gone through his mind? He'd prayed, of course. David could remember the shape of his father's lips, blurry over the television screen, mouthing the words to prayers he'd watched his father make a thousand times before. He replayed the memory again, felt the hands of the Mukhabarat officers holding him still, forcing him to watch his father's execution.

Murmured prayers. Were they the last pleas to a God who had abandoned them? He watched the shape of his father's lips in his memory again, suddenly clear, as if he'd stepped into the past, into the memory, into the basketball court.

His father was whispering his name. *Dawood, Dawood. Grow up with the love of Allah in your heart. Never let anyone take His love from you. Dawood, you are the best of the world, the best of your mama and me. Dawood, I love you, my ibni.*

*Father... How can you love Allah so much when* this *is the way of the world?*

Abu Adnan's prayers continued, as did his tender ministrations. Never, not in a million years, would David have imagined he'd be cared for by the father of the man who tried to murder him, who had murdered so many of his colleagues, his friends. What did he do with that? How did he respond to Abu Adnan? Hatred was too simple. *Father, Baba, you would know what to do.*

His fever spiked. Not long now. Consciousness slipped further and further, and the last thing he remembered was Abu Adnan holding his hand as he prayed throughout the night, asking Allah for mercy for his brother.

## Camp Peary, Virginia, CIA Training Compound, The Farm - June 2009

Not only did Kris graduate SAD training, he graduated fifth in his class. His classmates were Rangers and Delta Force, SEALs and Air Force pararescue men. Physical specimens honed to the peak of their limits, used to pushing every boundary. They breezed through training as it if was a cake walk, comfortable in their position in the class, overly confident in their abilities. Overly confident that Kris wouldn't last, either.

But Kris wanted it, needed it, *more.*

Isolated, left alone by the others, pushed aside like a leper, he turned his rage inward, channeling it into pure drive. Every fury-filled thought he had, every sidelong glare he caught, stoked the furnace of his shattered soul. He spent days and nights in the base gym, repeating his and David's workouts until he puked. And then he did it again.

During combat training, every punch that landed was a punch David had felt. Every kick was a blow that had hit David's body. Every breath he took, every step he walked, every beat of his heart, was for

David. He couldn't let up, not for a moment. He had so much to do. So many lives to avenge, deaths to answer for.

Two thousand nine hundred and seventy-eight souls hung his tattered soul in the gallows. All the dead of September 11, plus one: David.

Graduation day, four months after training began, was a simple affair… for everyone else. Director Edwards shook every graduate's hand, congratulated them on joining the CIA family.

Kris was told not to participate and was given his graduation certificate and new orders the night before. He was instructed to report to the SAD office at Langley directly and bypass the graduation. Like a leper, the director wouldn't touch him, wouldn't be seen with him.

Dan, of course, was there. He smiled for Kris and pulled him in for a hug, then took him to dinner at one of DC's best steakhouses. For two hours, over Martinis with Dan as he recounted the foibles of his training, Kris almost felt normal.

Except for the hole in his heart and the void in his soul, and the ring he still wore on his left hand.

They shared a bottle of champagne after dinner. "To new beginnings," Dan toasted.

"To the dead."

"To never letting anyone else tell you what to do.

"To vengeance."

"To those poor bastards at SAD. They don't know what they're getting." Dan clinked his glass with Kris's for the fifth time. And, for the fifth time, Kris downed his champagne like it was a shot. "They have no fucking idea what I'm capable of. Not now. Not yet."

## Pakistan Northwestern Frontier, Bajaur Province, Federally Administered Tribal Areas - June 2009

Somehow, he survived.

He rode his fever in waves and crashes, burning up until Abu Adnan packed snow around his head and under his arms, and then trembled, shivering while every blanket Abu Adnan owned was piled on top of him. The goats slept by his side, trying to warm him up.

Eventually, his fever broke. His eyes opened.

"*Allahu Akbar*," Abu Adnan prayed. He smiled down at David. "You will live, *in shaa Allah. Allahu Akbar*."

"Where am I?" he croaked. His voice, weary from disuse, cracked, split in two.

Abu Adnan named a town David had never heard of, on a mountain David didn't know. "What tribal area?"

"Bajaur."

He swallowed hard. He was a million miles from nowhere, inside the mountainous, unreachable Bajaur Province. The Pakistanis didn't venture into Bajaur, and neither did the US. It was a land untouched by time, locked away from the world thanks to the sky-piercing mountains, a former ocean's canyon floor now scraping the stars. "Do you have a cell phone?"

Abu Adnan shook his head. "No one here has cellulars. There is no way to use those devices here."

"How far is the nearest town?"

"*Yallah*, very far. Very far."

"I know your son told you to keep me here as a hostage." David's voice trembled. He sniffed. "But please. I *have* to go. I have to get back to my people."

"*Astaghfirullah*, I am sorry, brother—"

"Your son wants to kill me. Please, please."

"My son, my Adnan, is dead," Abu Adnan said softly. "He was killed months ago."

David froze. "*Months*?"

"You have been unconscious for some time, brother. But Allah is merciful. He has brought you back to health. *Allahu Akbar*!"

"I have to go. I have to get back. I have people—" His voice choked off as tears built in his eyes. "I have to go back," he whispered.

"How? There is one road out of these mountains. A goat path. It takes four days to walk it. It takes another four days to get to the nearest village. Al-Qaeda is there. That is where Al-Qaeda found my son. He too wanted to leave these mountains. But he only found death."

"Am I your prisoner now?"

"Brother, you are not a prisoner, except of your own body. You haven't stood for months. How do you expect to walk down the mountain? *Bismillah*, Allah can do a great many things, but *that* would be a miracle."

"Please... help me. I have to get back. I have to go home."

"I cannot make it down the mountain. I would not survive the trip. *In shaa Allah*, the rest of my days will be spent here, in my home."

"Who will come for me? Al-Qaeda? The Taliban?" Had his life been spared just to die again?

"No one will come for you, *in shaa Allah*. My son never told a soul where he was from. He kept these mountains, our home, his deepest secret. He brought you here to be a part of that secret."

Tears slipped free of David's eyes, sliding in sideways tracks down his temples. "What's going to happen to me?"

"As long as you are here, brother, you have a home. You are safe under my roof, and you are welcome to my food. I will treat you like family. Like the son I've lost. *Alhamdulillah*."

Was this the way of the world? Was this Allah's path? A son without a father and a father without a son? Had Allah planned this? His tears seared his eyes, his skin, and he curled against himself as they poured forth.

He'd lived, he'd survived, but he was without Kris, the other half of his soul. But suddenly, back in the arms of a father. What twisted paths, what curving melodies, his life had taken. Was there anything other than the touch of the divine in his destiny?

He was *supposed* to *die*. He'd given his life for Kris's, had pleaded with Allah for the trade. But instead of taking his life, Allah had seen fit to deliver him here, to this mountaintop in the most desolate region on earth, a place lost in time, in space. Abu Adnan had probably been born inside these four walls, had probably never traveled more than twenty-five miles in his entire life. His whole existence could fit on the face of this one mountain, raising his family, glorifying Allah.

Was there a purer form of submission to Allah than this? Living outside of time and living with the prayers of Allah in the center of his soul? If his father were still alive, would he not live like Abu Adnan? *Is this the faith you adored, Baba? Is this the God you loved with all your heart?*

What did it mean? What did all of this mean? To lose his father, to find Kris. To lose Kris, but to find a father. Years and years of carnage and despair, evil and death. Did Allah allow this evil, this anguish, to take place? Had he created life, created everything in their pairs, split David and Kris's souls, and then walked away? Was evil of His creation, or of humanity's, the end result of their wickedness run amok? Wasn't faith supposed to bring everyone closer to Allah? How had the world, and His people, fallen so far?

Was this a test? The faithful, the righteous, were always tested. But how cruel a test! To destroy cultures, families, lives. The deaths of millions. To invade with evil into the corners of every life, rip out their hearts, take away fathers and sons. What kind of God would do such a thing?

Or, was this a second chance? Or perhaps, he'd lost count of how many second chances he'd been given by Allah. *Allah is ever merciful*, the Quran said. *Whisper my name, and I will always be there. My mercy to you is eternal, everlasting.*

*Indeed, we belong to Allah, and to Allah we will return.*

His tears turned to sobs, giant, hiccupping gasps that raked through his still-healing ribs, made his lungs ache, his throat go raw as he screamed. Abu Adnan reached for him, pulled him close. Held him, like he was a child. He felt like a child. He felt small and alone and afraid.

Abu Adnan spoke in his ear, softly, "Every heart that aches, Allah soothes. Every tear that falls, Allah catches. Every sin that is regretted, Allah forgives. *Alhamdulillah, ibni. Alhamdulillah. Allahu Akbar.*"

His whole life, his *entire* life, he'd wanted his father *back*. He'd wanted to cling to him and hear the rumble of his voice, feel his chest beneath his cheek. Ask him questions and listen to his father explain the world to him again. He wanted his father, and his childhood, and their home in Benghazi back. He wanted prayers and the mosque back. He wanted the fire in his heart, the lightning in his soul, the electric connection to Allah, back. He'd *never* been able to fill that void, that yearning for his past. He was an Arab, a Muslim, and he missed *everything* about his past.

"*Allahu Akbar*," David whispered. His hands clung to Abu Adnan, to his arms, his back. He was so weak. How many months had he lain there, wasting away, save for the broth and bread Abu Adnan had been able to feed him. He felt like a shadow of his former self.

Truly, he couldn't make it down the mountain, either.

Not like this.

He felt a decision settle around him, made of choices both within and without his control.

*Kris, my love. My soul. We were united before time, made for each other. We will never part, not in this life or the next. Wherever I am, I will always be yours. I swear it.*

He couldn't go back. Not now. Physically, he couldn't make the journey. But beyond the physical, there was something else, something deeper. A yank in his soul, a pull to remain. To return to his faith, a life he could have lived. The allure of a father's love, days spent in prayer, drenched in the faith and love of Allah. He could have had this life. If only for one afternoon, this would have been his life.

Perhaps this was history shaking off the dust. Did all things happen in their own time? Were all things ordained, and brought to pass? *Nothing will happen to us except what Allah has decreed for us*, the Quran said. *Endure patiently, with beautiful patience.*

But what of Kris? How long had he been lying here, wasting away on the mountain? Had he been written off? If the CIA thought he was alive, wouldn't the military overturn the entire country, every province, looking for him? Why was he being allowed to rest in peace, cared for tenderly by this lonely father?

Was Kris even alive? He'd offered to trade his life for Kris's. What did it mean that he was still breathing? If he came out of these mountains and found Kris's grave, he would shatter. He would shatter and fall to dust, and there would be nothing left of him. He couldn't take losing both his father and Kris.

He knew the limits of his sanity.

Was this his last chance? A way to return to Allah, live a life he could have had with his father before joining Kris in the next life? Their souls were destined to be together.

He would always return to Kris. *All the days of the rest of my life are merely hours to pass until we meet again. Our souls will always find each other. I will see you again. Alhamdullilah.*

"*La ilaha illah Allah,*" Abu Adnan chanted softly. He repeated his words, the *shahada*, the cry of the faithful, the statement of faith. "*La ilaha illa Allah.*"

Choking, gasping, with tears staining his lips, snot running in rivulets down his upper lip, he whispered along with Abu Adnan. "*La ilaha illah Allah.*"

*There is no God but God.*

*Oh Baba, Oh Allah. Find me, please. I seek you, I seek you now more than ever. Help me, O Allah, help me. I am lost. I can't breathe, I can't think. I can't go on. Help me. I have lived in the darkness, consumed with anguish. Help me. Help me, Baba, please.*

Lines from the Quran, words on his father's lips, rose like bubbles in his memories. *Even if you but whisper, Allah will hear you, always.*

"I submit to you," he breathed. "O Allah, I submit to you. Bring me closer to you." He gasped, pressing his face against Abu Adnan's weathered neck. "Take care of my love. Take care of my love while I cannot."

*Kris... You are my moon in the darkness, always.*

*We will see each other again.*

*Someday.*

# 25

**Crystal City, Virginia - May 1, 2011**

Kris had an ice pack on his shoulder and one arm in a sling.

He'd returned from the Baltics that afternoon. The Russians were agitating again, and he'd gone to Lithuania to spy on Kaliningrad, and the military buildup the Russians were engaging in. A quick in-and-out trip had turned into a shitshow. But that was par for the course with the Russians these days.

A pain pill, some alcohol, and he'd sleep the whole thing off.

He slid open the silverware drawer and pulled out his wedding ring. He always dumped it in with the spoons before he left on a mission and put it back on when he returned.

Even over two years widowed, he still wore his ring. Still kept to his vows. He was a monk, celibate by devotion to a ghost.

He wasn't ready. Everything he felt, he channeled into his work. Into SAD. Counterintelligence operations was his specialty.

But not counterterrorism. Nothing anywhere *near* the Middle East, or Islamism. He was kept purposefully away from all things Arab. He spent his time in the Arctic Circle, in Eastern Europe. Chasing Russians and playing spy versus spy.

He was a lit fuse at all times, a hair trigger ready to snap, ready to fight. Ready to launch off at anyone who looked askance at him. In the field, he was a brawler. He'd soaked up Muay Thai and Krav Maga, Jujitsu and even straight boxing, in training. Most nights, he hung around the CIA gym, waiting for a sparring partner.

It was the only way he felt anything at all.

He slumped on his couch, legs akimbo, and stared out his giant windows. DC was lit up, the National Mall, the monuments. The dark spill of the Potomac cut through a thousand glowing lights.

He liked looking at the Capitol. Staring down at the bureaucrats who made the decisions that shaped his life. That made him a hero and then an outcast and then a hero again.

Though, of course, all heroes fall. And every gay story ends tragically. Wasn't that how the world was supposed to work? It wasn't enough to be brown and gay and outside the lines. He had to taste perfection and then have it *all* ripped away.

Kris imagined he was in a tower overlooking the city. Exiled, forced to watch as the world carried on. As his world was shaped and reshaped by assholes, morons, and idiots.

His phone rang.

It was probably Dan, checking in on him after his mission. He wasn't up to seeing anyone, but maybe tomorrow they could grab a drink. Dan was his one friend, his only friend in the whole world.

He probably needed to change that.

His blood boiled and his stomach curdled whenever he was around his straight teammates. They still barely tolerated him, and the reverse was also true. He preferred to work alone. He preferred to *never* see straight people. It was irrational, completely. And yet he resented their happiness. Their ease. How they met and loved and married. How no one told them their love wasn't valid, that their marriage didn't exist because they crossed a line printed on a map. How no one took away their love, their memories, if everything went catastrophic. He just couldn't stand it.

There was a gay community center in DC. He should check it out.

He hadn't seen a play in two years, hadn't been to an art gallery since—

Well, since Toronto, and David.

His phone vibrated, in time with the rings.

Blinking, he stared at it.

It wasn't Dan.

It was *George*.

George hadn't said a *word* to him, not once, since everything had come apart. He'd turned his back on Kris when Kris was locked in the Learjet while the coffins were unloaded, and he'd left before Kris deplaned. He'd never called. Never sent a card. Never left a shitty VM or even sent a text saying he was sorry for Kris's loss.

Kris had called him. One time, drunk, raging, fuming at the world, he'd called George at four in the morning and hollered at his voicemail, at the CIA, at George, at everything that was wrong in the world, over a year and a half ago.

Nothing.

What the hell was this?

He answered just before it went to voicemail. "George?"

Silence. Then, "*Kris...*" He heard George sigh. "*I know it's been a while.*"

"Three years, six months, and twenty-eight days. Since David died."

More silence.

"You didn't call, George. We *always* called each other. Wasn't that what we did? When things were bad? We called each other."

"*Kris—*"

"You never called."

He heard George swallow, like he was trying to swallow back vomit. "*Look, I'm calling about something else.*"

"If you're looking for a favor from me, I am hanging up the phone. No, I'm ripping the phone in half."

"*No. I need to tell you something. But I can't go into details. Just... Look, something is happening.* Tonight. *We're finishing our mission. And, getting revenge. For David.*"

Time slowed. Kris tried to think. His eyes closed. He inhaled, forced himself to ask, "What do you mean?"

"*What we started, back in Afghanistan. It's ending. Tonight.*"

Osama Bin Laden.

Kris's tongue stuck to the roof of his mouth. He shook his head, tried to jumpstart his brain.

"*Stay by the news,*" George said quickly, his voice hushed. "*I'm at the White House. And it's happening. Right now.*" He paused. "*I told the guys to put in an extra bullet. For him.*"

"George—" His voice cracked. Somewhere, his body found tears he hadn't shed yet, and they cascaded down his cheeks, tumbled from his eyelashes. "George, wait."

"*I have to go.*" Muffled sounds. The line cut out.

He moved on autopilot, dropping his phone and his ice bag and drifting to his closet. His studio wasn't large. His and David's old kitchen was larger than his whole unit. But he had a small walk-in closet, stuffed with his designer threads, and on the top shelves, his rifles and handguns.

In the back, the very back, stuffed out of sight, were two old duffels from Afghanistan.

He pulled out David's clothes, three years, six months and twenty-eight days old. They still smelled like him, like Afghanistan. Like woodsmoke and sweat, like David and spice. Like hazy sunshine and Virginia woods, and happiness that had nearly burst him apart. How was it possible to be that happy, he'd thought. How was it possible to love someone *this* much?

He buried his face in David's shirt, trying to fling himself back in time, trying to will the world to stop turning, to reverse course, to return to that morning. He'd do everything different, everything.

Hours later, he huddled with David's old clothes and his duffel in front of his couch, watching the television. Nothing had happened. CNN was still reporting the daily news as talking heads bantered back and forth over domestic policy. David's clothes shrouded him, and he'd buried his nose in the fabric of David's old workout shirt. He held his phone like it was a lifeline, his only connection to a lifeboat and he was about to drown.

*Breaking News* flashed across the screen. News anchors fumbled, flabbergasted. The president was about to address the nation. They had moments, and they blubbered, cut to the White House feed.

The president strode down the entrance hall on a red carpet. He stopped at a podium and stared into the camera. "*Good evening. Tonight, I can report to the American people and to the world, the United States has conducted an operation that killed Osama Bin Laden, the leader of al-Qaeda, and a terrorist who's responsible for the murder of thousands of innocent men, women, and children.*"

The rest of the president's speech spun away, each word, each syllable warbling and stretching until it snapped.

Bin Laden, dead.

*David, you should be here. You should see this. This is what you wanted.*

He kept inhaling, dragging David's scent in through his nose, over and over.

It felt like an ending. This was where they'd started. This was how they'd met. Hunting Bin Laden, chasing him across Afghanistan.

Now, Bin Laden was dead.

And so was David.

*Everything* died in Afghanistan, in Pakistan. In the shadowlands of the mountains, at the ends of the earth. Afghanistan, Pakistan, the tribal regions. They were just lines on a map. The earth in those countries was the same as the earth everywhere else. There wasn't any reason to believe they were haunted, that those spaces on the planet were different, somehow, than all the rest.

Except, they were. Afghanistan was the graveyard of empires, the mausoleum to millennia of men who had the hubris to think they were capable of defeating the land. The soil was made of bones, and only death bloomed. The mountains were the home of ghosts, ghosts that would always remain. The haze over Afghanistan wasn't just dust. It was the remnants of a million lives lost within those dark lines on a map.

Part of David was there, and always would be.

And now, so was Bin Laden.

His phone rang, again. He answered, never taking his eyes off the screen. The president was talking about how he'd directed the CIA to make finding Bin Laden their top priority. That had been him. He'd been given that mission. He'd been in charge of the hunt, in a remote base on the edge of the world.

"Hello?" His voice was hollow. Even to himself, he didn't sound human. He sounded like something that had died and come back from the grave, but was missing something integral.

It was George. "*Are you watching*?"

The president spoke, echoing eerily over the line. He could hear the president speaking somewhere near George and over his television, an echo of a delay. "*As we do, we must also reaffirm that the United States is not—and never will be—at war with Islam. I've made clear, just as the president did shortly after September eleventh, that our war is not against Islam. Bin Laden was not a Muslim leader; he was a mass murderer of Muslims. Indeed, al-Qaeda has slaughtered scores of Muslims in many countries, including our own. So his demise should be welcomed by all who believe in peace and human dignity.*"

"That's what David thought. What he believed. What the president just said."

"*The guys, they did it. They got him.*"

"Did they give him an extra for David?"

"*They gave him* ten *extra.*"

"Show me," he growled. "I have to see."

George hesitated. "*Hold on.*"

A moment later his cell vibrated. An incoming picture message.

Bin Laden, dead. Shot through the head. More rounds in his chest. Dead, undeniably, unequivocally, dead.

George spoke again, his voice faint through the phone's speaker. "*For David. And for everyone.*"

Fury roared, racing through him. "Don't you dare speak his name!" he hissed. "Don't you fucking dare! Not after ignoring him! Ignoring his memory!"

"*Kris—*"

"You're a *fucking* coward, George! You used me when you needed me for your career! Used us! And then you threw us away! You used us and you used us and then you abandoned us! You're a fucking coward!" He was bellowing now, screaming at the top of his lungs.

"*You're right,*" George said. His voice wavered. "*You're fucking right, Kris. I just couldn't—*"

"You are a fucking monster!"

"*I couldn't face you! I couldn't look you in the eyes! Goddamnit, Kris, I* sent *you there!* I *was the one who convinced the director that you were the* only one *who could get Bin Laden. That* you *were the one we needed at Camp Carson.* I *fucking sent you, and him, there!*"

He felt like a plane plunging to earth. Like a passenger on September 11 facing the end. The air rushed out of him. He clung to the carpet.

"You never liked me. You never—"

"*I respected the hell out of you. I knew you were the sharpest mind we had in CT.*"

"You threw me out of CT."

On TV, the president was thanking the nation, reminding them of their history. The pursuit of prosperity and equality for all. The words rang hollow in Kris's empty, dead heart, constricted around the memories of David being ripped from him, in the end. There'd been no equality for him and David, never.

George's voice wavered again. "*I'm sorry, Kris. I'm sorry for everything. You didn't deserve what happened to you. It was my fault—*" His voice choked, died. He sniffed and blew out a rush of air that scratched over the line.

"The part where you didn't call? Where you didn't do anything, not one single thing, to help me? That's your fault. You know, once, I thought we were almost friends."

George took it, his cutting hatred. He stayed silent.

"I didn't deserve to get all the blame for what happened. I didn't deserve to be thrown out in the cold. I didn't deserve to lose my husband, the love of my life. I didn't deserve how the CIA treated us, after. You ripped everything, absolutely everything, away from me. You never let me say goodbye to my husband. To my husband, George. You knew, you knew how much we loved each other, and you let them take David away from me in Afghanistan. Did you want to make it hurt? Did you want me to suffer?"

Another snuffle, over the line. It sounded like George was crying. There were voices in the background. The TV had cut away from the president, back to gobsmacked talking heads on CNN, commentators who didn't know what to say, how to frame the announcement. Kris heard someone call to George.

"You have to go. You're the big man at the White House now. Deputy director of the CIA. Such an important job. Do you ever think about the backs you stepped on to get there? How many times we bailed your ass out of a jam? Do you ever think about my dead husband?"

"*Yes. I do.*"

"Good." He was vicious. He wanted George to hurt, even a quarter of what he felt, every day. "Good. Think about him every fucking day."

"*I'm sorry, Kris. I just hope this helps, somehow. Closure, maybe...*" George sighed. "*I spent an hour in my office after it was done. Just... empty. I don't know what to feel about this.*"

"You should feel ashamed."

"*I do,*" George whispered. "*About you.*"

Someone called to George again. It sounded vaguely like the president.

"Go. Go save the fucking world, or whatever it is you do in CT now. Don't call me again, George. I have no use for your sorrys. Your wasted guilt."

"*Kris—*"

He hung up. He didn't want to hear another apology. He couldn't take it. Not a single one. He wasn't going to absolve George, save him from his bad decisions. Not this time.

In his unit, he had a single picture of David, his official Army photo from his last year in Special Forces. The David he'd met, the

David he'd fallen in love with. David before a thousand souls weighed heavy on them both, and when they spent the best years of their love working for others, for governments and bureaucrats who didn't care, in the end, at all about them.

What if they had just run off into the sunset? What if they had been selfish? Why had the burden of security, of saving the world, landed on their shoulders?

He held the frame, traced David's stern expression. In the back of his closet, David's Army uniform still hung in a garment bag. David had told him once he wanted to be buried in it.

But no one had asked Kris what David's last wishes were.

Kris pressed a kiss to the cold glass. He pitched sideways, lying in David's dirty clothes, David's picture in his arms, and watched the commentators on TV recount the past decade, the War on Terror. He watched his life play over the screen, days and months and years of war and terrible, terrible decisions.

*My love. Wherever you are, I hope you have found the peace that this world never was able to give you. I will always love you.*

## Pakistan Northwestern Frontier, Bajaur Province, Federally Administered Tribal Areas

"It is all right," Dawood cooed. "No need for tears. This is only a little cut." He wiped tears off the dirty face of Behroze, a young boy from the mountains. Behroze had a jagged slice from his elbow to his wrist, almost down to the bone. Somehow, he'd skirted the arteries. He and his brother had been playing, goofing off when they were supposed to be helping their father in the fields.

Behroze's father held him in his lap. "You can help him? You can?"

"Yes, 'Bu Behroze." Dawood cupped Behroze's father's cheek. "He will be just fine."

"*Allahu Akbar. Alhamdullilah*, you are a gift from God." The father kissed his boy's hair and held him tight, offering prayers to Allah as Dawood washed his hands in a bucket of rainwater.

The mountain villagers, those who lived with Abu Adnan,

stretched across the highest of the peaks in Bajaur Province, had banded together and built a *qala*, a central gathering fort, on a plateau on the slopes of the middle mountain. Every week, they met at the *qala*, joining as extended families within the safety of the mud walls. They traded food, stories, and companionship. Each week, they roasted a deer or an antelope, sometimes a hyena, and rarely, a tahr, after Friday prayers.

David had been introduced as Dawood, Abu Adnan's adopted son. He was welcomed with open arms, a brother of the faith.

As the sun set, they lit fires in the *qala* and gathered around the warmth. Children, boys and young girls, played in the shadows, running and hiding and drawing in the dust. The wives and mothers retreated to the women's quarters, relaxing in the company of friends. The men stayed by the fire, watching the stars burn above.

They were so far removed from the world, so distant from any hint of civilization. The stars seemed close enough to touch, jagged diamonds hanging in the sky. They seemed to grow there, like seeds planted in the garden of time. The Milky Way stretched from one horizon to the other, bright enough to turn night into day. When the moon was full, it was as if the sun was still shining.

Dawood became the villagers' medic. He helped a woman with pneumonia, having her sit over a pot of boiling water and inhaling the steam until she was able to expel the infection. He treated cuts and broken bones, cared for newborn babies, after the women helped the mother through childbirth.

There was no war in the mountains, and he never saw a gunshot wound, or the aftereffects of a bomb blast. He saw the best of life, in the face of a newborn baby, and eased the pain of life's end, as the elderly laid down their burdens for their final rest. Children loved to run to him when he was in the *qala*, look at the mountain herbs and plants he'd collected. He had a small garden, and he grew Kava Kava and ginseng, carrots and barley. He collected bamboo and birch, aleppo oak and arjuna bark.

He traded for needles and thread, and was able to close wounds with stitches, perform small surgeries. He taught the children how to wash their hands, though they spent more time splashing in the plastic basin than actually washing.

More and more, he was chosen as the Friday prayer leader. Slowly, he became not just the medic, but the imam for the mountain.

His life was simple. Austere. He rose with the sun and prayed beside Abu Adnan. Every day he set out for the *qala*, and families in need came down to him and his small medical office, made of mudbrick walls with no door. He stopped to make his daily prayers under the sun, and then journeyed back to Abu Adnan. The families paid him in food, in eggs and flatbread and fruits, and he had something to bring home to the man who had become his father, 'Bu Adnan.

They ate together, lounging by the fire, and talked. Talked of Islam, of Allah. Of history, of faith. About the weather, and the crops, and the mountains. At night, they prayed together beneath the burning stars before going to sleep.

Occasionally, 'Bu Adnan wanted to know about Dawood's past. Who was he, and why had his son brought him to the mountains? Dawood told him he had been working for the Americans. That they'd been trying to catch bad men, and he'd been captured in turn.

'Bu Adnan spoke of his son, how he'd been seduced by men with rifles down the mountain. How they'd shouted about jihad and every Muslim's duty to defend the faith. 'Bu Adnan had tried to shield his son.

They were safe in the mountains. Only death came up from the valley.

His son, filled with the passion of youth, had wanted more. It was the duty of all Muslims, he had said, railing at his father. Adnan had disappeared, and only came back to throw Dawood at 'Bu Adnan's feet.

"Perhaps he knew he was going to die, and he wanted me to have another son."

"*In shaa Allah.* That would be good for a son to do. A father should never be left alone."

"Neither should a son."

One night, Dawood told 'Bu Adnan about his father. About the stadium and the basketball court, and his father's prayers. They prayed together, and 'Bu Adnan held him as he cried.

"It is as the Prophet, *salla Allahu alayhi wa sallam*, said. The first three generations that followed him are blessed. And following that, the Muslims will lose their way. They will be confused, and take hold of evil things, and wickedness." 'Bu Adnan sighed. "The Quran says, *the human soul is prone to darkness in the absence of Allah. Man will lose his balance between the good of Allah and the darkness, if he is not focused on Allah.*"

'Bu Adnan seemed to have all the wisdom in the world. The only book he'd ever read was the Quran, and his copy was a well-worn tome from the early 1900s, passed down through his family for generations. It had been handwritten in Pakistan, hand sewn in a leather binding. "*Yallah*, I have no son to give this to," he lamented. "It will go to you, *habibi*."

Was this what having a father was like? Was this what his father would have been like had he lived? Would they have spent their days and nights like this, talking of the world and Islam, of faith and the future? Some days, when he squinted, Dawood swore 'Bu Adnan looked just like his baba. The curve of his back in his loose kameez. The set of his shoulders.

'Bu Adnan loved Allah, and loved his home, his people in the mountains, and he came to love Dawood, too.

At night, after 'Bu Adnan went to sleep, Dawood would gaze at the stars. He watched them fall, blazing through the night sky. This nameless mountain at the end of the world. He didn't feel a part of the world anymore. He felt outside of it.

He stared at the moon, so full and huge he thought he could leap off the mountaintop and grab hold. Hang on to the moon as it circled the world, let go, and fall back to earth, right where Kris was.

If Kris was even alive.

It seemed ludicrous, a complete fantasy, that he lived on the same planet where he and Kris had waged a decade-long war. The

United States had technological superiority over every inch of the globe. There wasn't a speck of land they couldn't see or control, he'd thought. How was this corner of the world possible? Where was he where he was outside of time, outside of the raging, endless war?

In all the vastness of the world, there truly were some untouched corners, it seemed.

If he just picked up a cell phone and made a call, said the right words, the NSA would sweep up his transmission. In days, after it was decoded, someone would know he was alive. They would know where he was.

But there were no cell phones here. Not on the mountain. There were no drones or satellites, no patrols passing by. No informants or human sources. No American presence at all. It was almost unnatural, strange. All of their technological superiority, all of their wizardry, and he couldn't do a single thing to contact home. Not from where he was.

He was encased in silence, in pure, impenetrable silence. The hoarseness before a scream, the void of sound, the absence of American might.

Did he even want to go back? Back to the war? Back to confusion, and darkness, and a life separated from Allah? Did he want to go back to the pain? The constant grinding frustration, the way the world had rubbed him raw? Back to *everything* he'd buried for decades?

Could he go back and find Kris dead and gone? There were some things he could not face, he knew, in the depth of his soul. He'd begged to trade his life for Kris's. Was this exile merely Allah's mercy, His way of sparing Dawood the agony of certainty?

Kris was, by all probabilities, dead.

He didn't know what to do, what to think. So he stared at the stars and spoke to Kris, whispers that he imagined the moon would carry to wherever Kris was, living or dead.

*My love, I stitched little Behroze's arm today. He makes me think of what you must have been like as a child. Always impetuous, never listening.*

*Always trying to have fun and go his own way. He will leave these mountains when he grows up. I can feel it.*

*I dreamed about you again. The same dream, the one I always have. Your smile. Your happiness. Ya rouhi, I hope you are happy. Somehow, somewhere. I pray to Allah that you are happy, with every one of my prayers. Your name is always on my lips. Your soul is always in my heart.*

*There is not a moment that passes where I do not think of you. You are the moon that rose in my darkness, ya rouhi. And I know that I will see you again, my love. I know it, in my soul.*

The moon took his words silently every night. Somewhere, Kris was beneath that same moon. Alive or dead, in this life or the next. They saw the same moon every night, and he imagined it was their one connection, a tether that ran from his heart to Kris's, circling around the moon.

*I* will *see you again.*

*Now*

# 26

**Tallinn, Estonia - September 6**

Kris rolled his neck as he settled into the last seat on the CIA's unmarked Gulfstream jet. The others from the mission took seats up front, leaving a wide berth around his back row.

Just the way he liked it.

Up front, the three CIA officers held hostage by Russian president Dimitry Vasiliev during his war games with President McDonough were smiling and popping bottles of beer as they reclined in the front row seats. Banged up and bruised around the edges, they were no worse for wear. President Vasiliev had waited until President McDonough was *just* about ready to invade before agreeing to release the officers in a pseudo prisoner exchange.

The US didn't release any Russians back across the Koidula border crossing in Estonia.

A dark van filled with balaclava-wearing Russians had screeched to a stop on the Russian side of the bridge and shoved the three CIA officers out. On the other side, a company of Estonia's infantry, a platoon of British Royal Marines, and a platoon of US Marines waited, a strong showing of NATO-aligned military.

Kris, and the rest of his team were there, too, matching the Russians, dressed in head-to-toe black.

He'd almost wished it had gone sideways, that he'd had a shot at the Russians. The exchange had been too simple, too easy. He itched for more.

When they landed in DC, he'd head to the gym, try to drum up a sparring partner. Sweat it out with some right hooks and roundhouses.

Or maybe head out for the night. Mike wouldn't be up for tagging along. He was playing house and settling in with Tom. *Finally*, Mike had found a good man, and if Tom knew what was good for him, he'd keep Mike happy. The trial of the century was over and done with, Tom had come out on his own, and his best friend, Mike, was happy. Things were looking up, for some, at least.

His skin prickled, a heavy weight, like someone was staring at him. People often stared. Being the CIA's pariah came with that side effect.

But this was something different.

Kris caught the gaze of one the younger Marines. All baby-blue eyes, fresh buzz cut, and an earnest little vibe. He flushed when he saw Kris had caught him, but didn't look away. His gaze slid down Kris's body.

Maybe he'd soothe that itch right here, right now.

Kris winked at the Marine and settled back, pretending to sleep. The pilot gave his preflight announcement, calling out the twelve-hour flight time back to DC. Cheers rose from the freed CIA officers. The rest of the team, US Marines and SAD officers, started drifting to sleep soon after the plane lifted off.

He waited, until most everyone was snoring and only a handful were reading by the dim light of the plane's overheads. Standing, Kris caught the gaze of the young Marine again. He smirked. Dipped his head to the back of the plane.

Kris stepped into the jet's bathroom—a significant step up from commercial airliners, with enough room to actually move—and waited, door propped open with his boot.

Thirty seconds later, the Marine appeared. He hesitated.

Kris reached for his fly. "You know what to do," he purred. "Get in here."

The Marine rushed in, dropping to his knees. As Kris slid the lock closed, a warm pair of lips closed around him. He tipped his head back. Groaned. "Harder."

**Andrews Air Force Base, Maryland - September 7, 1100 hours**

Kris downed a double vodka and dropped off into a long, post-orgasm nap for the rest of the flight. He didn't wake until they were already on the ground, already taxiing to the CIA's hangar.

Kris waited while the rest of the team deplaned, stretching and grabbing their gear and shuffling toward the ramp. The returning CIA officers were welcomed like heroes, their families rushing to meet them. Director Edwards was there, even. He shook the hands of every Marine, every SAD officer.

Except for Kris.

Kris threw his duffel over his shoulder and walked in the opposite direction, toward the hangar and his parked SUV. The director liked to pretend Kris didn't exist, and Kris felt exactly the same.

"Hey! Uh, wait up a sec." Footsteps pounded the pavement behind Kris. He stopped, sighing. He didn't turn around.

"Uhh, hey man." The Marine came around his side, a flush on his plump cheeks and a bashful grin stretching his lips. "I was wonderin'... could I hit you up sometime? Maybe we could hook up?"

Kris slid his sunglasses on and smirked. "Sorry, kid. Forget you ever met me."

He left the kid to pick his jaw up off the ground while his unit hollered for him to come back and catch up. A moment later, the Marine raced away.

Kris climbed into his SUV. Watched as the rest of the officers laughed and smiled, welcomed home their colleagues from Moscow. Stood in the sun and were friendly. Happy.

Exhaling, he tipped his head back and closed his eyes. *Push it all away.*

A minute later, he started the engine and drove away, heading for Langley. The drive was simple, the traffic light for a change. He badged in at the gate, ignoring the glare from the gate guard as he stared him down with his aviators low on his nose.

In the political hierarchy of the CIA's parking lots, he'd been relegated to the farthest one. Whatever. He took his time walking in, sauntering with his duffel over his shoulder, slowly smoking a cigarette as he passed by George and Ryan and Dan's parking spots before he stomped it out in front of Director Edwards's space.

He dropped his gear in his cube—the farthest in the SAD cubicle farm—and typed up his short after-action report. The rest of the guys were bullshitting over coffee in the break room and planning a beer run at the local bar.

He, of course, wasn't invited.

He checked his email—reminders about security procedures, range-time information, and a monthly CIA picnic next week—before shutting down his computer. Time to head out. Kris gave the rest of his team a princess wave as he passed by. They glared at him, their conversation going silent.

It would be a wonder if he didn't get a bullet in the back of the head one day. Friendly fire, blue on blue. *He was too gay*, he was sure their defense would go. *We just snapped. It was one wrist swish too many. One perfectly arched eyebrow too much.*

Kris's boots squeaked to a stop in the wide central hallway of the headquarters building. *Should he…*

Goddamn it.

There was a tiny part of him that kept him up at night, that ate away at the base of his brain. He'd been ruthless with himself, shutting that voice down. But no matter how hard he tried, no matter what he did, there was an emptiness inside of him that just opened wider. Some days, he thought he was a skinsuit walking around with a void inside him, nothing but darkness and bones.

That tiny, tiny part of him kept asking, *did it have to be this way*?

He glanced down the hall toward CTC. Dan had texted, of course, while he was in Estonia, telling him to be safe. He'd asked Kris to check in when he got back.

That didn't *have* to be immediately.

He and Dan weren't anything.

Though... Dan wanted to change that.

He'd always known how Dan felt about him. From that rooftop in Pakistan fifteen years before, sharing a shitty bottle of chardonnay when Dan had confessed he wanted to take Kris out to dinner. Wine him, dine him. Woo him. But he'd been two months too late. Kris's heart had already belonged to David.

But fifteen years... Shouldn't the affection have tempered? He'd thought Dan would have moved on, found his own partner, husband, someone to love. But every time Kris asked, Dan always demurred.

He had been Kris's best and only friend, until Kris started going to the gay men's community center events a few years back. Started socializing with other gays again, finally. He'd been like a chrysalis breaking free, a part of his soul resuscitated by rejoining his people. He'd dived in headfirst, desperate for his people, desperate for normality in his life. He hadn't played volleyball since college, and even then, it had only been to check out the guys on the team, but he'd joined the gay men's DC league on a whim.

He'd started going out again, too.

At first, he couldn't quite close the deal, though. Nights out at bars ended with an apology and an "another time" as he slinked toward the door. He'd wanted his people, wanted the energy, the vibe, the thrive. Wanted to be full of the gay life again, have everyone's gayness pumped straight into his veins, as if he needed a transfusion of gay to come back from the dead.

But he just couldn't go home with anyone, then. Couldn't kiss another man and *not* think of David. Couldn't look at another man and feel aroused, constantly comparing him to his dead husband.

Every man competed against a ghost, and every man was found wanting.

One night, he'd met Mike, a new gay from out of town, freshly transplanted to DC. *Everybody* in the bar had wanted him that night, but Mike had zeroed in on Kris. *Uh-uh, honey, you're barking up the wrong tree*. He'd wanted to be rid of Mike, send him spinning in another direction. But Mike was fun and kind, gentle when he had no right to be. He'd wanted Kris, and for a *moment*, a half of a breath, Kris had thought about it. Mike was the only man he'd ever met who reminded him of David, in a way. Who had that same mixture of strength tempered by warmth, and an earnest, honest kindness.

Mike was David without all his ghosts, he'd finally realized.

But he'd told Mike no, no a half-dozen times. Mike asked him out for brunch the next morning instead.

He had shown Mike around DC, given him tips on where to live, what to watch out for, and who the real snakes in the grass were. They'd had dinner, and then drinks, and then that became routine.

Mike never pushed again. And Kris had one more friend.

It was nice, having a friend who didn't know his entire tragic past. Who had no idea he'd once been Director Edwards's hand-picked hero. A hero who had made the president crow with pride. But who then had gotten his entire team killed, let his husband be murdered. Who was the scum of the CIA, a walking scarlet letter of pure shame.

Of course, he told Mike in fits and starts. The first time, five Martinis too deep into a night that seemed innocuous to Mike, a Thursday, but to Kris was the sixth anniversary of Saqqaf's death. Two weeks later, he'd ended up a raging mess in Mike's apartment, six years after David's proposal.

Dan was the only person alive anymore who *knew* him. Who truly knew him, every shadow, every dark secret. Dan had refused to let him wallow, refused to let him slip beneath the waves of darkness that tried to suck him to the bottom of his personal abyss. He was Kris's partner to plays and art galleries, his lunch date, his after-dinner drinks meet-up. It was good. They'd always had an easy friendship.

Four years after David's death, Dan invited him to be his guest to a dinner honoring CIA leadership. By that time, Dan had been promoted fully onto the leadership track in his own right, managing

CTC. He, along with George, the deputy director of the CIA, and Ryan, the new chief of clandestine operations, would all be receiving handshakes and huzzahs from Director Edwards and the president himself.

Inviting Kris to be Dan's date was the juiciest kind of *fuck you*, a *coup de grace* to Kris's personal relationship with the director, with George, with Ryan, and with the whole CIA.

"You sure you want to even be seen with me? I'm the CIA leper. You'll catch whatever I have. Soon you'll be the agency's most hated."

Dan had shrugged demurely. "It'd be worth it." He'd winked. "*Especially* to see the looks on their faces."

It was a black-tie affair, and they'd showed up in matching tuxes and holding hands. Director Edwards shook Dan's hand and ignored Kris, as if he weren't even there. Ryan had avoided them. George had carefully kept to the opposite side of the ballroom for the entire evening.

They'd flirted outrageously, holding hands through dinner and sharing bites off each other's forks. They'd made each other laugh, caught each other's gaze over glasses of champagne.

It was good to laugh again. Dinner turned to dancing, and Dan led him through swings, spins, and dips. He'd loved it, every moment, drank in the way he felt alive for the first time in four years.

He'd never had the chance to dance with David.

When a slow song played, Dan had stepped back, letting Kris go. There had been a heaviness in his gaze, a resignation that hadn't been there before.

Kris had reached back for him, drawing him close again.

"Are you sure?" Dan had whispered. His hands had landed softly on Kris, as if afraid to actually hold him. "You know, don't you? How I feel about you?"

"I know."

"I've never asked you for anything. I never will, Kris. I know, I know how much you love him, still. I can't replace him, I know that."

"Dan..."

Dan had smiled, looked down at the floor. "This is the part where you say I'm just your friend. It's just, dancing with you, like this—" He'd cradled Kris in his arms, so close their noses brushed. "I can't help it. I am *so* in love with you," he'd whispered.

Kris had felt something snap then, the final break of something he'd buried and buried and tried to erase. The bottom had fallen out from beneath his feet, and again, like four years before, he was falling, plunging, a freefall into a darkness that he was already so intimately familiar with.

But, God, he couldn't go back there. He couldn't survive the freefall. He'd known he wouldn't survive that darkness again.

He was lonely, and aching, and four years into a broken heart that hadn't mended. He was riding high on adrenaline, on a *fuck you* to the CIA that had put him there, and on waves of champagne. And Dan was there, warm and alive. He knew all of Kris's sins and he still forgave him, still loved him.

If there was a bottom to the abyss Kris was lost in, if there was something after the freefall... Maybe it was Dan.

He'd nuzzled his nose against Dan's, heard Dan's sharp inhale. Felt Dan's fingers curl on his back, into his tux. Felt Dan's hand holding his tremble.

"Kris..."

He'd cut Dan's words off with a kiss.

They didn't stay long after that. Dan had nearly set a land speed record driving back to his house in Maryland, even in his shitty little electric car. He'd helped Kris out, wrapped his arms around him. Had kissed him, trying to guide him through his house without ever breaking their kiss, their hold.

Tuxes had flown, landing on the carpet and the back of a couch, a table in the hall. Dan had laid him down in his bed like Kris was the last copy of a timeless novel, a priceless jewel recovered from a shipwreck.

For a moment, Kris had hesitated. His wedding ring had been heavy on his left hand.

But David was *gone*.

Dan had hovered over him, his gaze filled with so much desire, so much care. He'd crawled over Kris, their faces hovering, skin brushing. "If I could make it all go away," he'd breathed, "I would. I would do *anything* to make it better. Anything."

"Make me feel," Kris had whispered. "Make me feel alive again."

Dan made love to him like his touch could heal Kris's soul. His hands mapped Kris's body, the long, lean lines of his legs, the taut muscles of his back. The scars on his chest. Kris was more awkward, having to relearn how to love, where to move, how to slide and arch and press into a new lover. Into someone not-David. But, it was easier than he'd thought, tumbling into bed with Dan.

Dan kissed him through it, watched him. Traced his eyes and his lips and his face, captured every gasp with a kiss. He took his time, until Kris thought he was going to come apart at the seams. His fingers had clawed Dan's back, grabbed his hair, his ankles had wrapped around Dan's hips, and he'd *just* managed to not shout David's name.

Dan had buried his face in Kris's neck when he came and breathed, "I love you."

They came together twice more that night, Kris riding Dan and then Dan pounding him hard and fast as Kris screamed face-first into a pillow. They'd been a sweaty, sex-ruined mess when they finally fell asleep.

In the morning, Kris had woken alone, listening to Dan whistle softly to himself as he cooked breakfast.

It had felt wrong, suddenly, all wrong. He was still wearing his wedding ring. David wasn't having sex, not in the afterlife. He'd said he'd wait for Kris. He'd said he'd always be Kris's. None of that seventy-two virgins in paradise for David, they used to joke.

What the *fuck* had he done? What would David think? Jesus, he had to get out of there. He had to go, just go. He'd jumped up, grabbed his pants and his button-down, gotten dressed.

He'd collapsed while trying to find his socks and ended up slumped on the carpet, his back to the bed he and Dan had partially destroyed.

David was *dead*. David was *gone*. And there wasn't anything after this life, nothing waiting for him, for them. David, everything he was, everything they had, was *gone*.

Dan had walked into his bedroom with an omelet and mimosas and had found Kris sobbing.

"I'm not ready," Kris had finally whispered. "I'm sorry. I'm just not ready."

Dan had dumped the omelet in the trash and driven Kris home in silence. Anguish, tinged with anger, had poured off him, nearly drowning Kris.

He hadn't been ready to love again. He hadn't been ready to care for Dan, or anyone. He hadn't been ready to try and resurrect his heart, a heart that wasn't even inside him anymore.

His heart was six feet deep in Arlington.

No, his heart was in the back of a burned-out sedan in Afghanistan.

His heart was nothing but a pile of ash.

But, the easiest way to get over someone was to get under someone else, or so the saying went.

He *couldn't* fall for Dan. But he *could* fuck his way through DC and feel nothing at all.

And he did.

### CIA Headquarters, Langley Virginia - September 7, 1430 hours

"Hey." Kris leaned into Dan's office, smiling. "I made it back in one piece."

Dan was elbows-deep in a red-bordered intelligence file, scouring eyes-only intercepts and source intelligence. He snapped the thick file closed as he looked up. Shock, and joy, broke over his face. "Hey you," he said softly. "I didn't expect to see you so soon."

Kris shrugged. He padded inside Dan's office and collapsed in one of the dark leather club chairs. Dan had done well in his career, surging where Kris had faltered, had failed. He'd become head of CTC. His glass-walled office overlooked the operations bay, the workstations and monitors they had once worked at together, so many, many years ago.

Why was he here, though? Why come see Dan, put that glowing smile on Dan's face? Dan knew his game. He knew exactly how Kris was. Some nights, it was Dan's bed he ended up in after a few drinks, or a long week of hating everyone and everything at the CIA. Other times, months went by before he showed up at Dan's door.

Sometimes, with someone else's fingernail scratches still on his back.

Maybe it was Mike. Maybe his best friend finally finding the love of his life, finally settling down, was affecting him. He'd been happy like Mike, once. He'd had the house and the love. The joy and the laughter. The smiles over coffee in the morning, the warm body to curl into. He'd had it, and he'd loved it.

Maybe part of him wanted that again.

Kris propped his boots on the edge of Dan's desk and crossed his ankles. "All quiet on the Western Front?"

"I wish." Dan snorted. He jerked his chin to the folder he'd closed. "Something strange is rumbling out of Afghanistan. Pakistan. Yemen. Even Iraq."

Kris's mind still went sideways, like a radio channel tuned to static, whenever anyone mentioned Afghanistan. He blinked. "Similar chatter? From different locations?"

Dan rubbed his temples, frowning. "Yeah. Different al-Qaeda affiliates are starting to echo each other. They're talking about someone coming."

"Some*one*?" Kris's eyebrows shot up.

"Mmhmm."

"Think it's Bin Laden's kid? Is he starting to take the reins?"

Dan shrugged. He opened his mouth—

"Never mind." Kris waved him off. "I don't care. I don't want to know. Don't tell me anything." He'd forgotten, for a moment, that he didn't care at all, not one single bit, about the CT world anymore.

Knocks pounded on Dan's door, just before Ryan poked his head in. "Hey, have you looked at the—"

He stopped. Glared at Kris. "What the fuck are you doing here? You're not part of CT."

"Personal visit." Kris slouched in the chair, getting comfortable. "Visiting my boo." He blew Ryan a kiss.

Purple bloomed over Ryan's features, a furious fuchsia. "Dan, we need to get the most recent dump from Islamabad analyzed. They've got something."

"I'll get right on it."

"And, have you seen the FIAs?"

Foreign Intelligence Agents. Occasionally, the CIA hosted officers sent from overseas agencies for six-month training missions. Currently, Israel and Saudi Arabia had sent over an officer each. Not an easy combination to handle.

"Noam is spending time at the satellite bay." Noam Avraham, from Mossad in Israel. "I don't know where Zaiden is." Zaiden Asfour, from Saudi Arabia's General Intelligence Directorate.

Ryan nodded, glared at Kris again, and ducked out.

Dan stared. "Your *boo*?"

He shrugged. "It got rid of him."

For a second, Dan couldn't hide the hurt. He looked like a kicked puppy, quickly turning back to his desk and stacking folders, making sure the edges were obsessively straight. Anything to not look at Kris.

"I didn't mean—"

"Yes, you did." Dan smiled, sadly. "It's okay. I know your rules. I'm just one of your 'boos'."

"It's not like that. I don't..." He shook his head. "I don't know what I want anymore."

"It's been nine years," Dan whispered.

"Some days it still feels like yesterday," Kris snapped. "Time *doesn't* heal all wounds. That's crap. It's bullshit, what they say. You're never over it. You're never fine."

"I'm sorry." Dan held up his hands, surrendering. "I didn't mean it that way. I just..." He exhaled hard, his face twisting. "I wish I could see you smile again. I wish you were happier. And I know I can never replace him. I know I can never be who he was, and I know you can never love me like you loved him, but—" He stopped, drawing up short, like he'd let too much slip free. "I wish you would let me love you," Dan finally breathed. "I wish you wanted to come see me right away when you got back. I wish this wasn't a surprise for me. I wish I was your only 'boo'. I wish we could really *do* this, Kris. And... most of all, *I* want to be the man who makes you happy again."

Kris's jaw dropped. Dan hadn't been that blatant, that direct with him, *ever*. It was *the thing* they never spoke of: Dan wanted more. Kris... didn't know what he wanted, except a good hard fucking, something to numb the pain. But now Dan had *said* it, had actually put words to his feelings in their twisted little dance.

Damn it, he didn't want to know. Knowing made things complicated. Knowing tugged on things he didn't want to feel, didn't want to think about. His eyes darted around Dan's office, hiding, searching for somewhere to look, somewhere that wasn't at Dan. He fumbled for something to say.

Dan ended the conversation for him. He always did. How many times had he let Kris off the hook, accepted the tiny morsels Kris threw his way without complaint? "Look, I've got to get going on this new dump of traffic from Islamabad. This thing, from al-Qaeda... it's getting big. I've got to go."

Kris stood. "You, uh, will probably be working all evening?"

"All night." Dan rubbed his forehead. He looked exhausted. "I might crash here for a few hours and keep working tomorrow."

"'Kay." Nodding, Kris backed out of Dan's office. "I'll see you around."

Dan chuckled, once. "Yeah. See you around."

Kris felt his gaze on his back as he walked away.

# 27

**Kandahar Province, Afghanistan - Three Weeks Prior**

War came to the mountains.

Dawood tucked his face into his scarf as the wind of the valley whipped around the trees, sluiced down a rocky gorge. Towering peaks shielded their valley. Their new camp.

Rickety trucks clambered over the flinty shale roads, carrying the brothers and their supplies. They slid, skidding out, and came to a stop beside an eternally dry wadi, desiccated for over a millennium. The sun, just starting its descent for the evening, glinted through the scraggly trees at the top of the range. Sharp rays cut through the fading daylight, sucking color from the valley.

Kandahar, Afghanistan, was a wild, untamed, vastness. He thought he'd been at the end of the world before, in Bajaur, on the mountain with no name. But, this, in the depths of Afghanistan, was the bitter end. A land of endings, of ghosts, of dead things.

The wind seemed to carry voices, snippets of whispers and soft cries, echoes of screams and laughter, the lives of so many cut short, the voices as broken as the bodies who once spoke. Their valley, for the moment, seemed to shiver, echo like Dawood had picked up the world and held it to his ear, as if he could hear all of the world's woe like holding a seashell and hearing the ocean. Torment scratched at his bones.

"It is time to pray!" Dawood called. He waved to the drivers, to the brothers in the backs of the trucks. "Time for *salah*!"

The brothers hurried to form lines behind him, jostling shoulders. He waited while they unfurled their prayer mats and quieted.

In the mountains and as they crept across borders, they did their *wudhu*, their ablutions, with dust.

"In the name of Allah, the most compassionate, the most merciful." Dawood kneeled, cupping the cold earth and rubbing it over his hands. He let the grains blow away, then rubbed his palms over his face.

He breathed in, the scents of life, of Afghanistan. Allah was in these hills. He was with these men. He'd been with them the day war arrived in their mountain home, in Bajaur, three years before. When the bullets and the bombs fell, and the soldiers arrived, and the sky had burned the mountain to the ground, turning everything to dust.

### Pakistan Northwestern Frontier, Bajaur Province, Federally Administered Tribal Areas - Three Years Before

Pakistan, pressured by the United States, pushed into the tribal territories, sweeping for extremists, for terrorists. Their sweeps were broad, their attacks indiscriminate. The bees, the drones flown by the CIA and the US military, appeared overhead, as did their constant, ceaseless hum.

When the bombs fell, and the fires burned through the farms, everyone tried to hide. Tried to hunker down and ride out the surging violence, the waves of attacks from the military trying to cleanse the mountains of all living souls. No matter who they were.

Bombing the mountain out of existence seemed to be the strategic plan. All night, fire rained, stars seeming to fall, bombs that erased families from the face of the world. Farms. Homes. Lives. Dawood huddled with 'Bu Adnan in the trees, lying on his belly.

He heard every agonizing scream. Every cry from the children he'd cared for, had helped bring from infancy to adolescence.

He heard their cries go silent, cut short, after the blasts, after the shock waves tore through their homes.

One bomb took out Behroze's family home. Another the *qala*. A third and fourth obliterated farms, spread fire to four families' homes.

It was no use staying. It was suicide to remain. They fled, running from the flames, running for their lives. Dawood carried Behroze, burned, but alive, playing in the fields behind his house when the bomb fell. They stumbled down a ragged goat path, hiding from the sky.

'Bu Adnan made it halfway down the mountain.

He stumbled, fell. Cried out to Allah.

Dawood, leading everyone, called for a halt. Tucked his people into dark spaces between the trees, hiding women and children and old men as best he could.

The drones hovered overhead. He could feel their optics, feel the hunting gaze of the pilot. Predator drone. Predator. What an apt name. He felt like an animal. Desperation flooded him, sang in his veins.

He slid to the dirt beside 'Bu Adnan, the man who'd become his baba. Six years, they'd been a family. Six years, he'd had a father again.

"Baba, we must keep going."

"*Astaghfirullah, ibni*. I cannot." 'Bu Adnan clutched his chest. His heart. Six years, and 'Bu Adnan had gone from the man of strength, built like an ox, to an old man, almost paper frail. He'd aged before Dawood's eyes, as if time was robbing him. Robbing them. "I knew I could never make it down the mountain. Even with Allah."

"You can do this, Baba. You can. I will carry you—"

"You must carry Behroze now, Dawood. He needs a father, now more than ever."

Behroze was a young teenager, wide-eyed and wondering, forever slipping away from his family. It was that which had saved him. He had too much curiosity in his eyes, too many questions that wanted answers. He was destined for heartbreak.

"Baba—"

"It was never Allah's will that I leave this mountain, *ibni.*" 'Bu Adnan clutched his chest again. Heaved a ragged breath. His eyes were wet, burning into Dawood, twin rubies shining through the dusty depths of time, strong despite his withered frame. He reached a shaking hand for his Quran, lying in the dirt beside him, the one item he'd carried from their home. "This belongs to you, now, *habibi.*"

"Baba, *no*. We are *all* getting off this mountain."

Gunshots, in the distance. Answering fire from the ridgeline. Fighters on the ground. Military, warlord, jihadist. He couldn't know. The sky was on fire, the mountain was falling, and his father was dying.

Again.

"*Habibi.*" 'Bu Adnan cupped his face. He couldn't hide the pain, the way he curled over his chest. His ragged breaths. But he tried. For Dawood, he tried. "Take our family away from here. Keep them safe."

"There's nowhere safe in the world, Baba. That was it. Our home —" His throat clenched. His vision blurred. Not again, *in shaa Allah*, not again. "What do I do, Baba? What do I do?"

"Follow the Prophet, *ibni.*" 'Bu Adnan gritted his teeth. His hand clasped Dawood's cheek, gripped his face, bruisingly tight. "You know in your heart what your path is. What it always has been. Allah laid out your life for you, *habibi*. You must follow the path Allah has laid out for you."

"*No...*" Dawood leaned over 'Bu Adnan, pressing his forehead to his father's. His path had once been twisted and rotten, full of darkness and pain. His path was supposed to circle that mountain endlessly, live out his days in the light with 'Bu Adnan.

Why was Allah dragging him back to the darkness? To death, and anguish, and war? "Baba, I don't want to."

"Allah alone is charge of our days, *habibi*. His will for you is laid out. And His will for me is to die." 'Bu Adnan shuddered. "*Bismillah*, Allah granted me that you shall be my last sight."

"Baba!" Dawood grabbed 'Bu Adnan with both hands, cupped his face. Held him close. "Baba—"

His father held him, and he held his father in return, as 'Bu Adnan exhaled his last breath.

He shouldn't cry. He knew he shouldn't. Everyone's time on the planet was determined by Allah, and to cry over a death was to subvert Allah's will. But tears built and tumbled from his eyes, dropped onto his Baba's still face.

It wasn't *fair*, losing everyone he loved, *everyone*, in his entire life.

What path was this Allah had laid for him? What point was there to this pain, this anguish, time and again? What point was there to the darkness, the rage in his soul?

Screams rose from the scrub brushes he'd hidden his people in.

Sounds of running, men bursting through the trees onto the goat path they were following. Clad in black, with fighters' vests and jihadist masks, every man carried a rifle.

Dawood laid 'Bu Adnan down and rose. Two strides placed him between his people and the fighters. His hands clenched.

"*As-salaam-alaikum.*" One of the fighters made his way to Dawood. His eyes darted over Dawood's people. "Brother, where have you come from?"

"*Wa alaikum as-salaam,*" Dawood grunted. "We come from up the mountain. The bombs, they drove us down."

"Those dogs are bombing everything! The entire range! They're trying to destroy these mountains, *yallah*!" He looked beyond Dawood, to 'Bu Adnan's still body, lying in the dirt. "*Subhanallah*, what happened?"

"My baba. He—" Dawood couldn't speak.

"*Inna lillahi wa inna ilayhi raji'oon.*" *May Allah give him an easy and pleasant journey and shower blessings on his grave.* The fighter held his hand over his heart. "He is a martyr, brother. Do not grieve. He is already in Paradise, with Allah."

The mountain rumbled, and on the flinty peak above them, fire bloomed, a shower of earth exploding in a mushroom cloud.

"They are trying to take down the mountain!" The fighter reached for Dawood. "Come with us. We will protect you and your people."

What could he do? The sky was falling, the world was burning, and his family was going to die if he didn't move. He had no idea where to go, no plan, nothing but blind fear that guided them down the goat path.

Was his path, instead, to follow this man?

He pressed his hand over his heart. "*Shukran*, brother. But I will not leave my baba."

The fighter handed his rifle to Dawood. "Do you know how to use this?"

Dawood nodded, once.

"I will carry your father. My men will lead us down. Care for your people." He stooped and gathered 'Bu Adnan in his arms, cradling his body. 'Bu Adnan's lifeless cheek fell against the fighter's chest, against his vest and his ammo clips. "*Yallah*, we must hurry! Before more bombs fall!"

Dawood rounded up his people, took Behroze back into his arms. Behroze was a young teen, but still small. Easy for Dawood to carry on one hip with the jihadist's rifle still in his hands.

Together, the band of fighters and villagers crept down the mountain.

## Kandahar Province, Afghanistan

"*Allahu Akbar*." Dawood held his hands by his ears. The brothers behind him repeated the call, the glory to God. "*Allahu Akbar*."

He centered Allah in his heart, his intentions. *Oh God, this is the path You have led me to. Through the twists and turns of my terrible life. You have led me to this place. You give everything form, and then guidance, oh Allah. It is only now, at the end, looking back, that I see the path for what it is.*

He placed his arms over his stomach and looked down. "Praise and glory be to You, O Allah. Blessed be Your Name, exalted be Your Majesty and Glory. There is no God but You. In the Name of Allah, the Most Compassionate, the Most Merciful. You alone do we worship and You alone do we call on for help."

*Remember, Dawood,* 'Bu Adnan had said once. *Every beat of your heart functions only by the permission of Allah.*

Why does he keep me alive? Why keep me here?

*Because he loves you, habibi.*

*"You who believe, be steadfast in your devotion to God. Do not let hatred of others lead you away from justice, but adhere to justice, for that is closer to awareness of God. Be mindful of God! God is well aware of all that you do. Allahu Akbar."* He led the brothers in the Quranic verse before he bowed. "Glorious is my Lord, the most great."

*When you called on your Lord for help, He responded to you.*

Was his whole life a cry to Allah? Had he been too stubborn to see the signs? Had he been crying in the dark, raging in isolation, and had missed Allah's reach for his soul? Days that built from shifting sands, unstable foundations, the hole in the center of his soul always leaking his anguish into the world, coloring everything in shades of pain, in loss?

*Kris...*

Dawood bowed his head.

## Pakistan Northwestern Frontier, Bajaur Province, Federally Administered Tribal Areas - Three Years Before

The fighters led Dawood and his people down the mountain, into the tangled valleys of Bajaur, away from the bombs and the strikes, hidden deep in jihadist territories.

The first dawn, they buried 'Bu Adnan. Dawood led his people in prayer, and Ihsan, the man who'd saved them, brought his fighters to join in. He helped Dawood dig the grave and lower 'Bu Adnan on his right side, facing Mecca. Helped him cover the body in dirt and say the final prayers over the grave.

Later, convoys appeared, long lines of trucks and technicals, pickups with machine guns mounted in the back. Black flags flapped from the tailgates.

"Jihad?" Dawood asked Ihsan.

"It's all we have left," Ihsan said. They were standing around a fire, the first they'd had in days. Dawood couldn't feel any warmth, though. Behroze curled at his feet, sleeping in a borrowed blanket. He never left Dawood's side.

"Time stops for the West whenever they wish it. When they are angry, when they are hurt. But a thousand Muslims die in Afghanistan? A thousand more in Iraq, in Sudan? A thousand, again, in Chechnya? Time never stops us for us, brother. No one cares about our lives. Only we care."

He stared at the fire, memories playing in the flickering flames. His father's execution in Libya by Qaddafi had been the most evil thing in his entire world at ten years old. He'd thought the entire *universe* would react, that everyone would see the evil of Libya's Great Guide, their dictator, that there would be salvation and justice from the world. But the world kept turning, even though the ground beneath his feet had stuttered to a halt. Everyone else kept moving on, following the rise and fall of the sun, kept moving forward in time. In Egypt, there wasn't even a headline about the execution. In America, most everyone said "Libya" like it was a dirty word, a nasty country, and he was just lumped in with everything and everyone that made Libya such a terrible place.

No one came to rescue him, or his family. No one cared about his father's murder. Ten years old, and he'd known a truth then, something he refused to face as a boy.

But as a man, the truth was inescapable. The twisted, horrible path of his life, revealing the same truth to him, a dozen different mirrored ways. Reflections of agony, reflections of evil.

Where did it all end? How? Had the paths of history become so hopelessly entangled that there was no end? Just a ceaseless cycle of violence and death, killer and murdered always trading places? Where was reason? Where was justice?

What was his role in this life?

"*Subhanallah*," Dawood muttered. What would his baba say? 'Bu

Adnan, and his father before him? What would either man have said of Dawood sitting side by side with Ihsan?

"*In shaa Allah*, brother, we must restore the Caliphate. Every battle we fight, we're trying to push the invaders away. Little by little, we must reclaim what was once ours."

"The world is too big now. The Caliphate, a land of our own, is now just a dream. We can never go back to the past, to the Caliphates of old."

"Don't you want a home of our own? *Muslim* lands? Where we can be free? You know, the children of Saqqaf are trying. In the *Sham*. They've taken half of Iraq, half of Syria."

"*Saqqaf*?" Dawood snorted. "Saqqaf was a thug. He was *no* Muslim. His followers were not Muslims. Nothing built in his name is any glory to Allah. He, and everything he brought into the world, go against Allah."

Ihsan sighed. "The children of Saqqaf call themselves the Islamic State. They have declared that they are the Caliphate renewed." His eyes were dark, burning with something that looked like wariness as he judged Dawood. "Al-Qaeda broke with them recently. For being un-Islamic." Ihsan sighed. "I lose fighters to the Islamic State every month. They yearn for that Caliphate. They want to be part of a world where we are not subjugated any more. Where Islam lives and breathes, and our lives are one with Allah."

"They will *not* find that with Saqqaf's children. That is not Islam. That is a death cult. They have turned Muslim against Muslim, slaughtering anyone they wish. Nothing they do reflects the Prophet's teachings, *salla Allahu alayhi wa sallam*. Allah's wrath will fall upon them, swiftly."

"Then *where*, brother? The Arab Spring was supposed to liberate our people." Ihsan shook his head. "Democracy was supposed to be the salvation. *Finally*, dictators would fall. The people would speak! Islam would rise! But, after the people spoke, the military took control, seized the government in a coup after elections brought our brothers to power. Eight hundred brothers and sisters were massacred in Egypt. The

Syrians are trying to rise up, seize their freedom from the brutal hands of their leader, but the world ignores their cries for help. For justice. The world just looks the other way when it's Arabs and Muslims who are dying. What must we *do*, in this world, for our freedom? For our Muslim lives to mean something, to *matter*, to this world?"

"A Muslim is a Muslim no matter where he is or what the world does. As long as he is close to Allah. The more difficult the world, the more a person's closeness to Allah is tested." Dawood swallowed. If he could boil his life down to one statement, that would be it. His words tasted empty, though. There was a war being waged for the soul of Islam, battles that tried to shape their existential reality. Where did he fall on those battle lines?

Ihsan's eyes pinched as he stared at the fire. "Who *are* you, Dawood? You do not speak like an Afghan, or like a Pakistani. Or like a man who has lived his entire life on top of a mountain. You are your people's imam. But how? What brought you there?"

"You do not speak like an Afghan or a Pakistani, either."

Ihsan laughed. "I'm Saudi. I came to join the mujahedeen after the coup in Egypt. We *must* defeat these dictators. And clear our lands of the infidels. Until we have something of our own again."

Dawood took his time answering. "I was born in Libya. I have traveled the world, to all the corners. My being has been shaped by the West. But I was born Arab and Muslim. And I have been pulled back to who I am by Allah for a reason." He met Ihsan's gaze. "I'm still figuring out that reason."

Ihsan smiled. "*In shaa Allah*, perhaps we are meant to meet. Have this conversation. Become friends." He clapped Dawood on the back, laughing.

Overhead, the moon rose from behind the shattered mountains, bloodied and haze-red from the fires, the smoke, the blood in the air and the ground. Dawood's eyes lifted.

*Kris. My bones are exhausted. My soul. I can't understand this anymore. This life. This path. Not a moment passes where I do not wish to hear your voice again. The answers I need are in your soul. But you're gone. What do I do?*

He prayed to Allah, asking for blessings for Kris, for Kris's soul to be at peace. Ihsan caught his whispered *dua*, watched his moving lips.

"Brother, you are not alone." Ihsan wrapped one arm around him. "Come. Join us."

"I'm not a fighter. Not anymore."

"There are many ways to perform jihad, brother. Jihad of the mind. Of the tongue. Of the heart. I don't need to tell you this. You are the imam of the mountain. Come, we need an imam. Ours was killed in the bombing. Is this meeting not meant to be?"

"Joining you would be a jihad unto itself for me," Dawood snorted.

"All Muslims must fight to right injustice," Ihsan said, finger wagging like he was teaching a lesson. "You know this. It's in the Quran. It's required by God."

"Where will my people go?"

"Wherever they wish. We have a camp for some of the families hidden in the hills. It has never been bombed. We stay far, far from it. We can have a guide transport your people there. They will be safe and will be given new lives."

"My people must be safe. They must be cared for."

"Say no more, brother. They will be. *In shaa Allah*."

Dawood stared up at the moon again. *You must follow the path Allah has laid out for you*, 'Bu Adnan had said. But his life had led him down a path that was nothing but death, years and years of terrible death. Was that truly where he was meant to go, again?

Above, the blood moon stared down at him, eternally, perfectly silent.

### Kandahar Province, Afghanistan

Cold wind swept from the ridgeline, down from the haunted mountain passes of Afghanistan. The wind came from Khost, and beyond, from Tora Bora. Passed through Kabul, picking up more souls, more lost dead. Dawood felt the wind lift his scarf, circle around his neck. He heard their whispers, the lamentations, across his skin.

He stood and raised his hands. "Allah hears those who praise Him." Behind Dawood, the brothers rustled, rising and reciting their prayers under their voice. Over his shoulder, he saw Ihsan, eyes tightly closed, fast whispers falling from his lips. Ihsan's faith was hard, desperate, a cry in the dark for what he craved.

"*Allahu Akbar.*" Slowly, Dawood dropped to his knees and prostrated. His forehead touched the ground, the dust of ghosts.

How many ghosts had sought Allah? How many had been just as desperate as Ihsan, reaching out with both hands for hope? How many had died for the wrong reasons, or for choices others had made for their lives? How many ghosts were like his father, who had just wanted to live, to love Allah?

How many were the ghosts of the wicked? He felt the chill on the back of his neck slice his skin, the cold turning razor sharp.

He'd tried, for three years, to convince Ihsan that Allah was not a brother to be hugged, a power to be grabbed on to and seized, or a missile that could be shot at the heart of his enemies. Allah was subtle and hidden, found in the whispers of the world, but only if one could listen. Finding Allah was like spotting a firefly in the corner of your eye. Like seeing the sun break the horizon, and that first beam of light stretch into the night sky and touch a star. Gone so fast, but for the moment, perfect.

*You must follow the path Allah has laid out for you.*

Paths were made of choices, choices that *men* made. Allah had given him, and all men, the freedom to choose their own steps along the path He laid out. Each step drew a man closer or further from God, kept him on his path toward Allah or led him off it. Allah gave each man a key to their life, and it was up to each man to turn that key.

The choice to seek Allah, or the choice to stray from Him.

The choice to seek answers, or the choice to ignore.

The choice to build, or the choice to destroy a life, a soul.

Life was a mystery that stretched to infinity, and only at the end could a man look back and see the pattern of his life.

Dawood breathed in the dust of ghosts as he whispered his

prayers. Even on his knees, even pressed to the dirt, Allah heard his whispers.

He was on Allah's path.

## Afghanistan-Pakistan Border - Three Years Before

He sent the families to Ihsan's safe camp. They kissed his cheeks, cried, squeezed his hands. Thanked Allah for him, for the years he'd been with their *qala*. He prayed with everyone, holding the men's hands, brushing away tears from the faces of the children.

"When you miss me," he told the children, "look to the moon. I am always looking at the moon, and we will be looking together. If you wave, I will wave back. The moon will be our messenger."

They nodded and hung around his neck, refusing to let go of their hug.

Behroze wouldn't leave.

He'd become Dawood's shadow since the mountain, since his family was murdered. When Dawood turned around, there was Behroze. Every morning, Dawood woke with Behroze curled into his hold, lying in the dirt as close as he could get.

"Don't make me go," Behroze whispered.

"Behroze..."

"I want to stay with you." He laced his hand through Dawood's. "Let me fight. Please. I can, I can. *Bismillah*, I can."

"Behroze..." Dawood pulled him close. Hugged him, as if he could merge their atoms. "Fighting is *not* what I am going to do."

"You're going with those men. With the black flags."

"I'm going to be their teacher. Like I was your teacher."

"I still want to be your student." Tears rolled down Behroze's cheeks. "I won't run anymore, I promise. I promise to Allah, I won't run away anymore. I will always stay at your side. Please, please just don't send me away."

There was a unique pain in breaking a child's heart. A very specific anguish that shattered the soul. He felt the moon fall from the sky, felt the sun reverse its course. "You won't be safe, Behroze."

"I'll do everything you say, I promise." Behroze's sniffles turned to sobs. "I promise, I promise."

Dawood hung his head between his shoulders. What was right? What did a shattered child need? Distance, a life far away, safe from war? Isolated, and with a hardened heart, with no family left in the world for him? The *qala* would care for him, of course. But how dark would his heart turn? Left alone?

He *knew*, he knew what that felt like.

But to bring a boy into a viper's nest? Into a war?

Where was the worse sin?

Behroze was on the cusp of teenagerhood. Could Dawood help him cross that threshold, shape him into the man he would become? What did he know about boys becoming men? He'd had to make that journey alone, with only American television and high school to help. A million miles away, another lifetime. What could he possibly do now?

"If you come," he said carefully, "you must never pick up a rifle. Never, *ever*. You are not to become a fighter, Behroze! Your jihad is of the heart! Do you understand?"

Behroze nodded, his body shaking too hard to speak. He pitched forward, collapsing into Dawood's arms. Dawood felt his tears run down his neck, felt his sobs against his skin.

They moved out the next day, to link up with the rest of Ihsan's fighters. They were making a press across the border, heading south.

Into Afghanistan.

Afghanistan was a faded memory to Dawood, pictures in random sequence, scattered like postcards on the floor. He remembered half moments, frames from movies that felt like another person's life playing in half-second loops. The sounds of the drone bay. Ryan's scowl. Helicopter blades whirring, the tremble in his bones as the helos lifted off. Kris's laugh. The light in his eyes. The warmth of his body in their shared bed. Morning kisses tinged with coffee and exhaustion.

A blast that burned his soul. Pain, so much pain. Thirteen still, unmoving bodies on the ground.

Kris. He hadn't moved after the blast. He hadn't moved *once.*

Dawood pushed the memories away, smearing them across his mind.

He was not that man any longer.

Those memories belonged to someone else.

---

Kandahar City was a reflection of the soul of Afghanistan.

The province of Kandahar was an arid, desolate waste, as if the sun wanted to blast the land from the surface of the earth. The homeland of the Taliban was a place of extremes, of blinding light and too-thin air, of choking dust and lifeless, empty horizons.

Kandahar City was a fortress, an outpost in the endless stretch of nothingness. From nothing came a harsh and brutal siege fortress, a city built upon suspicion and the distrustful gaze against outsiders. A city that had turned its back on the world long ago, convinced that only danger came from the outside, that *Others* were not to be trusted. That there was no future outside the city's walls, or in trusting anyone or anything.

Ihsan and his fellow units linked up in the warrens of Kandahar City. The streets were dusty, unpaved, the inhabitants even mistrustful of such things like concrete and asphalt for they were of the outside world. Kandahar City had been a no-go zone for years for the CIA, for the military, for NATO.

Walking through the city felt like walking back in time to Dawood.

With the odd juxtaposition of rifles and AK-47s, RPGs and homemade bombs sharing space with donkeys and bazaar stalls. Women in blue burqas whispered through the streets. Dawood's heart ached for them, for the secrets they kept beneath their layers, for lives they could only half live. There was nothing in the Quran that required women to don anything close to the burqa. The requirement for modesty in the Quran spoke to men *first*, admonishing men to dress modestly as well, and to lower their gazes, to respect, to the ends of the earth, *all* women. Where had this come from, the imprisonment of half of humanity behind silence and cotton?

*The first three generations that follow the Prophet will be blessed. And following that, the Muslims will lose their way. They will be confused, and take hold of evil things, and wickedness. The human soul is prone to darkness in the absence of Allah. Man will lose his balance between the good of Allah and the darkness.*

Dawood followed Ihsan to the jihadist quarter of the city. Held his hand over his heart as he was introduced as Imam Dawood. "I am also a medic," he said.

"*Allahu Akbar*," Ihsan said, grinning ear to ear. "The Doctors Without Borders hospital has pulled out of Kandahar Province, and we have had no one to take our wounded to. Truly, Dawood, our meeting was meant to be."

Ihsan gave him and Behroze a room in one of the many mudbrick homes the jihadists occupied in Kandahar City.

He had no idea what to do for the boy. He hadn't had a father at Behroze's age, didn't have a model for how to take care of him. But he *did* know how the loss of a father shattered the soul, and how a boy without a future, and with the knowledge of evil in the center of his heart, was a crumbling sandcastle, a tree in the desert stripped of its bark by a punishing sandstorm.

He placed Behroze's prayer rug beside his. He bought Behroze a djellaba, the same as the one he wore, day in and day out.

Behroze slept beside him, still a frightened boy in the middle of the night. When mortars fell, or jets screamed over the city, he wailed, terror seizing hold of him as he clung to Dawood, senseless cries of horror as he replayed memories of the mountain burning, of the sky falling.

It took a year for him to sleep on his own.

## Kandahar City - Two Years Before

The day Abu Dujana arrived was a normal one for Kandahar City. Gunshots rang outside the city walls. Military helicopters swirled around the sky. Spies walked the streets, slinking out to report back to the NATO military base nearby. The Belgium forces were in command at Kandahar Air Base, and they left Kandahar City alone, for the most part. Heat and hatred swirled in the air, resentment turned outward from the city walls, against anything and everything that threatened their lives.

"I hear you have a new imam," Abu Dujana said to Ihsan, after greeting him, sharing the bonds of brotherhood. "And that he came from the mountains of Bajaur."

"Brother Dawood, yes." Ihsan beckoned Dawood to join them. "Brother Dawood is a blessing from Allah. Our paths were meant to cross."

Abu Dujana's eyes narrowed. "Tell me. What do you know of a stranger brought to the mountains, years ago, by brother Al Jabal?"

"He's dead. He died in the mountains." Dawood's heart pounded, palms slicking. 'Bu Adnan had said the mountains were Al Jabal's biggest secret. That he would never, ever, risk his family. Dawood was supposed to be a ghost after Al Jabal died.

"Brother Jabal was my closest friend. He confided everything in me. *Everything.*" Abu Dujana stepped closer, frowning. "Your accent, brother, is strange. Where are you from?"

"Libya."

"The stranger in the mountains was from Libya as well."

"Brother Dujana, what is this?" Ihsan interrupted, shaking his head. "What are you saying? What stranger?"

"You remember when Brother Jabal and Sheikh Zawahiri conspired with Brother Hamid to strike the CIA at their base, years ago? You remember the spy Brother Jabal captured?"

"The spy was tried and executed."

"No, Ihsan. The spy *lived.* Brother Jabal took him to the mountains. He hid him with his father, and he told me he'd go back one day. That after the dust settled and the CIA had forgotten about their spy, he would drag him back out and begin the real trial." Abu Dujana lifted his chin, smiled. There was something predatory in that smile, a wolf that had cornered its prey.

"Brother Dawood?" Ihsan's trembling voice, his confusion, spanned years, his gaze wavering over the knife blade of uncertainty, of betrayal, of a thousand questions that had no answers.

"I told you," Dawood whispered. "He is dead. *Maa shaa Allah*, everything that he was, Allah remade. The stranger—to Allah, to the brothers—no longer exists. I swear it."

Ihsan hissed, inhaling like he'd been stabbed through the back. Like his world had been flipped upside down. "You—"

"*Everything* of me is for Allah now. *In shaa Allah*, I exist only for Him. He knows the length of my life, the weight of my heart. My sins. And I have given everything to Him to judge. It is in Allah that my heart now finds rest."

Ihsan swallowed. He looked down. Exhaled, his breath shaking.

Abu Dujana gripped his shoulder. "Brother Dawood. Allah calls you now. There are things that only *you* can do. Knowledge that only *you* have. Will you help us, brother? It is Allah's will."

*You must follow the path Allah has laid out for you.* He held Abu Dujana's gaze. Black fire burned in the depths of his eyes. Black fire that reflected the anguish of the mountains, the distilled agony of a Muslim soul. That promised *change.*

Something inside Dawood awoke.

"What would you have me do?"

**Kandahar Province, Afghanistan**

Dawood rose from his prostration and sat on his knees. "Allah, forgive me," he whispered. "Have mercy on me. Strengthen me. Pardon me." His breath faltered, his whispers dying on Afghanistan's harsh wind.

Abu Dujana kneeled beside Ihsan, whispering his own prayers. Soon, they would move out, cross the border again, head to Peshawar. Ihsan and Abu Dujana were about to embark on their mission.

And Dawood on his own.

For two years they'd planned. Everything came together slowly. Dawood watched the patterns, watched the ripples of history moving forward and backward in time. Watched his path straighten, the steps before him made clear by Allah.

He offered up a final prayer, a private one, the words of an old imam from centuries back circling his heart. "Allah, make the best of my life be the end of my life, and the best of my deeds the last of them. Make the best of my days the day that I will finally meet You."

Looking right, he performed the *tasleem*, gave blessings to the angel on his right shoulder, and then again to the angel on his left. "*As-salamu alaykum wa Rahmatullahi wa barakatuhu.*"

And then he was done. He stayed kneeling, though, for a moment. He'd finished his last prayer service for the brothers. Soon, they would separate, go down their different paths. Find their different ends.

*You must follow the path Allah has laid out for you.*

After he rose, Ihsan and Abu Dujana gathered the brothers around him. Ten in all, young faces, eager to embark on the mission. They wore mismatched camo jackets and cargo pants, black-and-white scarves tied around their necks. He, too, wore the garb of a fighter. Gone were his prayer robes, his djellaba.

Abu Dujana smiled, urging him on. He was supposed to make a speech.

He swallowed. Inhaled slowly.

"To be a Muslim is to live with a pain that sits in your soul. A pain the rest of the world cannot know. It is *Muslim* pain. To have everything of our greatness ripped away. Everything of our history, destroyed. The world once saw us as people to admire. To love. But now, the world sees only ruin." He took a breath, a shaking inhale. "I know what it's like to be hated for who you are. To have your life dictated by others, and your choices, your path, made for you. There is a rage that lives inside us, brothers. There is a rage that screams, 'we will prove everyone wrong'. We are *more* than this."

Murmurs. Ihsan's eyes glittered. Abu Dujana nodded, fury and passion in his gaze, in the way he looked at Dawood. Like Dawood was the answer to his prayers.

"*Yallah, this* is Muslim pain," Dawood whispered. "And we will not feel this pain any longer."

Cheers rose, breaking like waves over the ghost lands of Afghanistan. The brothers fired their rifles into the air. Shots echoed, cries of *Allahu Akbar* mixing with private *dua*, prayers offered to Allah. Abu Dujana pocketed his audio recorder. Dawood's message would go out to the whole world, soon. His stomach clenched. Who would hear his words?

Behroze waited for him, standing apart from the fighters. His big brown eyes stared into Dawood's. No longer was he small, underfed and slight. He gazed into Dawood's eyes as a young man. A scraggly beard, a young man's beard, dusted his cheeks, his chin. "Imam," Behroze said slowly. "I *still* don't understand."

Everyone had their mission, their destination. Except for Behroze. He was to go to Islamabad, stay in a house Dawood had scraped and saved for. Once, he'd had a home on the other side of the world, a place of peace, grand and expansive. What he was able to give Behroze was a one-room square made of concrete and tin, with no running water. But it was a home, and it was what he could do. The rest of his meager savings, he sent to an imam at a madrassa and asked for Behroze to be taken in, taught to be a scholar, to follow in Dawood's footsteps as an imam.

"Your jihad has always been of the heart, *habibi*. To love, when it feels like love is impossible. To love like Allah does, continuously, eternally, with no conditions."

"Why are you leaving?" For a moment, Behroze wasn't a young man, verging on the cusp of adulthood. He wasn't the young man who had devoured what Dawood had taught him. He was the boy from the village again, his lip quivering as Dawood stitched his arm. Held him as he sobbed. As he curled close and wailed when mortars launched, or fighter jets screamed overhead. "Why must you *do* this?"

There were no answers for Behroze, not now. He handed Behroze a piece of paper, folded tight. "Check this email, *habibi*. Check it every day. One day, you will have your answers."

A single tear slipped from the corner of Behroze's eye. "You make my jihad so much harder, Baba. Why—" His lips clamped closed. He rubbed away his tear.

Dawood dragged him close, enveloping him in a father's embrace. "Look to the moon, *habibi*," he whispered. "We will always be under the same moon."

"*In shaa Allah*," Behroze whispered. "Please, *please* tell me when you'll return?"

Dawood stayed silent.

"Your name will always be on my lips and in my prayers." Behroze stepped back. His face twisted, his struggle exposed for everyone to see. His eyes gleamed, shining, wet.

"As will yours, *habibi*." It seemed he was destined to leave, always be separated from the ones he loved. Was this another outcome of the path Allah had given him? Endless goodbyes, endless broken hearts?

"It is time!" Abu Dujana's cry broke over the brothers. "Brothers, it is time!"

Behroze lifted his chin. He clutched the Quran 'Bu Adnan had given to Dawood, and Dawood watched him try to bury his heart. Behroze walked away from Dawood, toward the convoy that would take them over the mountains and back into Pakistan. Into his future.

*You must follow the path Allah has laid out for you.*

*Kris.* Dawood closed his eyes. The moon hadn't risen yet, but still, he whispered to him. *Soon, we will be together again. This life is drawing to a close. This path is winding to its end. And, after everything, my only hope is* you.

# 28

### CIA Headquarters, Langley Virginia - September 7, 1800 hours

Deep breath in. *You can do this.* Deep breath out.

Did he *want* to do this?

Part of him did.

Kris badged back into CTC, a bag of takeout Chinese in one hand. The center hummed, constant soft chatter flowing between workstations in the dim light of the two-story monitor banks along the front wall. He headed for Dan's office, above the rows and rows of analysts plugging away.

Dan stood behind his desk, his back to the door, arguing on the phone. Kris leaned into the doorjamb, blatantly eavesdropping.

"Ryan... *Jesus*, I'm working on it. I know, I know. The dump from Islamabad scares the shit out of me too. Do you think calling me and yelling about it is going to get this done faster? My people are working on it. *I'm* working on it. I will call you when I know more. Hell—Hello?" Dan stared at the phone. "Prick."

"Hang up on you?"

Dan twisted, his jaw hanging open. Shock lined his wide eyes. His gaze darted over Kris, from his change of clothes to his bag of takeout.

"He used to do that to me too. When I was—" Kris flicked his wrist, as if that conveyed all that was the past and Afghanistan and his bitter shame. He shrugged and headed for Dan's desk. Set the food down with a plop. "Hungry?"

"I… didn't expect to see you again." Dan hung up, still staring. "Maybe *ever*."

"I swung by the Golden Sun." Kris shrugged, taking out cartons of rice and egg rolls, lemon chicken and crispy beef. "Thought you might be hungry." He kept his voice light, as much sass as he could inject. As if he just happened to be out, happened to drive by Dan's favorite Chinese restaurant. Happened to have showered and changed into one of his best outfits, his slim black pants and a crisp turquoise button-down, showing off his collarbones. He slipped out of his Gucci trench, draped it over a chair.

His hands trembled.

He couldn't look at Dan.

Not yet.

Dan's confession had haunted him the whole way home, the words circling his mind as he drove, as he parked, as he rode the elevator to his unit.

They didn't mean anything. It was just Dan. Dan being in love with him. That was nothing new.

Home, and his empty studio seemed to swallow him whole. The hum of the laundry machine was as loud as a train.

A bowl of condoms and a bottle of lube on his nightstand had stared him down. Across the bed, on the opposite nightstand, David's photo sat, alone. Other than the photo, was there anything real in the entire condo? Anything that showed the world a human existed inside the four walls?

Kris's gaze had traced David's image, his stern glower, his brawny stance. Why had he chosen *that* photo? Why not a picture of their wedding? Why not something happier, something that showed them, their love?

If he'd had to look at that every day, could he have ever moved on?

*Had* he ever moved on? Was fucking his way through every older man in DC moving on?

It was something. But something wasn't everything.

He'd held David's photo, staring into his dead husband's gaze. Was there anything left of their love? Was there anything left between him and this photo?

Finally, he'd set the photo facedown on the nightstand and headed for the shower.

It was in the shower that he collapsed, clinging to the tiles as he slid down the wall, sobbing, shrieking, falling to his knees as it hit him, *again*, the truth blindsiding him as powerfully as it had nine years before. David was *dead. Gone.* He was all alone.

Kris cried until the water ran cold, face buried in his hands. He'd taken his ring off after six years. Even the tan line had faded. His ring lay next to David's, tucked into the bottom of David's duffel from Afghanistan, in the darkest corner of his closet.

David was dead, and gone, and there was nothing Kris could do to change that. To make that hurt less. Freezing his life hadn't worked. Freezing his heart hadn't worked, either. The hurt still ached, still was an anguish he couldn't possibly bear.

Dan's words kept circling and circling, trying to reach his heart.

*I wish you would let me love you. I wish we could really do this.*

*I want to be the man who makes you happy again.*

*Could* he be happy again?

There were moments he was. Mike, as infuriating as he was at times, made him smile. How had a masc meathead marshal like Mike and he become friends?

*Because Mike reminds you of David.* Parts of him, at least. Would Mike and David have been friends, if David were alive?

Why hadn't Kris said yes when Mike pursued him? Why had he pushed him away, kept it friends-only between them? Would Mike have ended up being a hollow echo of David, sentenced to always be compared in Kris's mind? Would he have lined up Mike versus David for the rest of their lives, had he pursued Mike?

There were other moments when he was happy, though. Moments with Dan. Dancing with him that night. The way their kiss had raced through every nerve in his body, lighting him up from the inside in a way no one else had, no one but David. Moments since, when he tumbled into bed with Dan. When they met for dinner, and he saw the curve of Dan's grin over candlelight, or they shared a bottle of wine and laughed on Dan's patio, watching the stars. Dan's touch ghosting over his skin, over his lips, as he stared down at Kris in his bed. How their fingers laced together, held, as Dan made love to him. He'd always held back, but...

Maybe... maybe he could be happy again.

He panicked in the shower, then tore through his closet for the perfect outfit, putting on his makeup and eyeliner like he was going on the hunt. He was going out, forget the rest of his squad, Mike and Billy and Jon and Carlos and Aaron. He was going to find a man to bring home, fuck this panic, this heartache away.

But he didn't make it past the bathtub. A hollow emptiness in the center of his chest had opened and opened, a zipper inside him ripping apart until he thought he was going to trip and fall backward into himself.

He was tired of it all. He was tired of being alone.

When he knew exactly what not being alone felt like.

When he knew how wonderful, how beautiful, how fantastical it was to be loved. To be in love.

Two hours later, and there he was, in Dan's office with Dan's favorite Chinese food. He finally looked up, into Dan's gaze.

Dan's face was hard, his expression locked down. Eyes tight. "Kris, you don't have to do this."

"Do what?"

"You don't have to try and make everything fine. Pretend nothing happened. In fact, I'd rather you didn't—"

"I'm not— That's not what I'm doing."

"No? What's this?" Dan nodded to the food. "Look, you know how I feel now. I figured if I ever told you, you'd run away, and..." He sighed. "I just don't want to do this anymore. I don't want to pretend."

"I'm not pretending. And I obviously didn't run away."

"Kris..." Dan looked away.

"I'm trying, Dan. I'm *trying*. This." He waved between them. His hand landed on a container of fried rice. "I'm trying, I am." His eyes flicked up. Met Dan's. "Us."

Dan's entire existence formed a question. He didn't move, not a muscle, not a hair. But *everything* changed.

"I'm trying," Kris repeated, softer. "So just sit your ass down and eat your damn food. Before it gets cold."

Finally, Dan sat, pulling out his chair and collapsing like his bones had turned to jelly. Kris saw it hit him, that Kris had picked up his favorite food, from his favorite place. Kris looked down, picking through his lemon chicken as Dan tried to reset back to neutral. Dan had always been a case study in measured calm, an oasis of it, even. He'd been the center of Kris's hurricane, ever since Kris had stepped off the Learjet *without* David.

Maybe even before.

"Ryan giving you shit?" Kris steered the conversation back to safer waters. Shitting on Ryan was practically an Olympic sport for him.

Dan, diplomatically, demurred. "He's ripping his hair out over this new threat."

"You're not?"

"I am. I just don't berate my subordinates about it. I keep my freak-outs all in here." Dan tapped his forehead.

"See, that's why you got the big office. Why you became one of the big boys at the CIA."

"My poker face?"

"You can take Ryan's shit and not want to strangle him. Not vault over your desk and beat him to death with your keyboard. I'd be in jail for murder, I know I would."

Dan snorted. "We all learned from your example. 'CIA Officer versus Vice President' is a teaching module at The Farm now, you know."

Kris laughed, his head tipping back. His laugh echoed, bouncing around Dan's glass office for a long moment. God, it felt good to laugh again, for fun and not at someone or like he wanted it to hurt.

He caught Dan's gaze as he sat back. Warm joy, liquid gold, poured from Dan, seemed to slither through the air and into his skin, down to his bones. Kris's stomach clenched. His heart pounded. Heat built in his blood. He let it. Let himself react to Dan, to Dan's outpouring of love.

Dan cleared his throat. "Actually, I was going to call you."

"Missed me already?"

"Always." Dan smiled. "But, no, this time, officially."

Kris frowned. Froze, with lemon chicken halfway to his mouth. "'Bout what? The intel dump? This new threat? I don't work in CT anymore. You know that."

"There's something in it that I need to show you."

"You know Ryan is going to shit if you bring me in on this."

"I have to." Dan winced, set down his carton of crispy beef and grabbed a red-bordered Top Secret folder from the stack on his desk. "This is the transcript of an audio file uploaded to al-Qaeda's media office and sent out online." He held out the folder.

Kris reached for it. Dan didn't let go, not right away. He held Kris's gaze, worry in his eyes. Kris sat back slowly as flipped the folder open.

Inside lay a statement, first in Arabic, then translated into English:

> *To be a Muslim is to live with a pain that sits in your soul. A pain the rest of the world cannot know. It is Muslim pain. To have everything of our greatness ripped away. Everything of our history, destroyed. The world once saw us as people to admire. To love. But now, the world sees only ruin. I know what it's like to be hated for who you are. To have your life dictated by others, and your choices, your path, made for you. There is a rage that lives inside us, brothers. There is a rage that screams, 'we will prove everyone wrong'. We are more than this. Yallah, this is Muslim pain. And we will not feel this pain any longer.*

"I've watched videos of your interrogations," Dan said carefully. "I know you built rapport with your detainees by addressing their pain. You've called it 'Muslim pain', verbatim, before."

"I've said several things in here verbatim before." Kris flipped the folder shut. Set it back on Dan's desk. Memories clamored from behind the locked door in his mind. He swallowed. "Whoever said this, you think he's a former detainee? Someone I worked over once? Someone we let go who went back to the great jihad?"

"Can you remember who all you said this to? I've pulled the old detainee records, but I was hoping to spare some of my people from having to watch thousands of hours of footage of your interrogations to build a list of suspects. If you can help narrow it down..."

"The records aren't complete, anyway." Kris pressed his lips together. "The first detainee I used this approach with was Abu Zahawi."

When the detainee program came to light, CIA leadership at the time had ordered Zahawi's interrogation tapes destroyed. Everything, from Kris's questioning to Paul's torture, the beatings, the waterboarding. The only remnants of Zahawi's interrogation lay in Kris's notes and in Zahawi's statements to the military tribunal, his public condemnation of his treatment by the CIA.

Dan blinked. His eyes pinched.

"Let me see the list you've got. I'll run through it, see what names jump out."

"Thank you." Dan sighed. "I know this is hard. I know you want to put everything from back then behind you. I appreciate this."

"You can show me how thankful you are later." Kris winked.

Laughing, Dan passed over a printout, a list of detainees Kris had interrogated. It was three pages long, two columns on each page. Jesus. He folded it in half, slid it into his trench.

"So who is this asshole, hmm?" Kris went back to poking at his food. "What's the word on the al-Qaeda street?"

Dan leaned back, his hands laced behind his head. He exhaled slowly, shrugging. "They call him Al Dakhil Al-Khorasani."

"'The stranger from Khorasan'? Interesting *kunya*."

"What's really interesting is the way all the al-Qaeda branches are throwing their support behind him. Sending blessings to Al-Khorasani, wishing him well on his *hegira*."

"His *hegira*?" Kris's eyebrows shot sky-high.

"Yes. One of the reasons why Ryan is going apeshit is... we have no flipping idea what that means."

"Divine direction to go someplace? Or leave a place? The *hegira* refers to Muhammad's journey from Mecca to Medina. Traditionally, it's been used as a call for Muslims to migrate to places where they can live in peace."

"Buuut," Dan said carefully, "Jihadists have been militarizing it. Turning a call to peaceful migration into a military injunction to reshape the Middle East, and then the world, into their version of a militant Islamic state. A renewed Caliphate."

"As part of their apocalypse. Yes, I'm familiar with the eschatology. And so is Al-Khorasani. He's using the Khorasan hadith as part of his jihadi name."

"*Hegira* for the jihadists has become inextricably tied to jihad. The Prophet moved for war. They move for war. It's become *the* call to move to a place to conduct jihad against their enemy."

"So Al-Khorasani is going someplace to wage war. Hardly new behavior for jihadists."

"But *where*? We've got no intel. We've got no idea who this guy is. 'The stranger from Khorasan'?" Dan threw his arms out wide. "We're days out from September eleventh, and you know jihadists all love to try something on the anniversary. But all we have to go on is the hope that you might narrow down this list and we can focus on finding former detainees you identify, then try and track them down around the entire globe. So far, we're running into graves and dead ends. It's like Al-Khorasani is a ghost."

"Ghosts don't exist. He's a man. Which means we'll find him." Kris smirked. "We're the CIA. We find all men."

"Thank you for helping. It might give us an actual lead. We've bumped everyone into high alert. Sent out threat warnings across US Embassies and to all FBI offices."

"I'll look over it tonight."

"If you want..." Dan inhaled, a sharp, quick breath. "If you want, you can look it over at my place. I won't be getting out of here until at least the next cable dump comes in from Islamabad, but..." He shrugged. "I can cook you breakfast when I get home."

Kris looked down. His empty studio, and the ghosts of his pain? Or Dan's home, his modest Maryland ranch house, comfortably lived-in, always open to Kris?

"I think," he said carefully, "that *I* should be the one making *you* breakfast."

Slowly, Dan smiled, like dawn breaking over the ocean, over a snow-topped mountain, a thousand glittering rainbows falling from the sky. He pulled out his keys and twisted one off, held it out for Kris. "You can keep this."

Kris took it. Palmed it, taking a deep breath. "I will see you at home."

"I'll see you at home," Dan whispered. He tried, he really tried, to hold back his joy, his galloping exuberance. "Thank you. For... everything."

"Thank *you*. For not giving up."

"If I knew I just needed to throw a tantrum, I would have years ago." Dan chuckled.

Kris threw his fortune cookie at him. "All right, I'm gone. You have a ghost to hunt and I have bad guys to remember. I'm going to need a drink to jog my memory."

"Have one for me." Dan blew him a quick kiss as Kris grabbed his trench.

He turned at the doorway and blew a gentle kiss back to Dan.

He *could* do this.

---

He drove through DC toward Maryland instead of taking the outer loop. He pulled out at Dupont Circle and drove two blocks, then parked. Walked past the Tap Room, Mike's go-to joint, and went another two blocks to a small jazz bar tucked into the walk-ups and the streetlamps. It was quieter, someplace he went when he just needed to get out of his head.

Before he went to Dan's, this time for something other than a fuck-and-go, he needed to say goodbye.

No one knew him there, not like at the Tap Room or his other go-to hookup bars. He could fade into the background, be nobody. Anonymity was a precious, beautiful thing.

He ordered a Cosmo and sat at the corner of the bar, far from the door. It was too early for the live music, too late for dinner, and he was one of the few crowding the place. Couples lingered over drinks at scattered tables here and there. Candlelight threw shadows and whispers of light on the walls.

*David.* Kris twirled the stem of his Martini glass. Ruby swirls spun, and he stared into the ripples. *Is it okay to say goodbye to you? To your memory? Is it okay to move on?*

His cocktail was silent. He downed a swallow and set the drink down, watching the ripples form again, crash into each other. *Is it okay to look for a piece of happiness again?*

A barstool squeaked next to him. He closed his eyes. Damn it, he didn't want to deal with anyone, not tonight. Ironic, though; the first time he wanted to be left alone, someone made their move. One day before, and he'd have spun with a smile, investigated the man until he determined *yes* or *no*. To fuck or not to fuck.

"I'm not interested," he said, not looking up. *Take a hint.*

A man settled beside him, propping his forearms on the bar top. In the entire length of the bar, not a single other seat was taken. He'd sat right next to Kris. On purpose.

And he wasn't leaving. Kris felt the hot stare of the stranger's gaze against the side of his face.

"Look—" Kris grabbed his drink and twisted. God help this man, interrupting his soul searching, his goodbye to David, on this night. He glared, his eyes sharpened to daggers. "I'm not—"

David gazed back serenely.

David blinked. Once. Twice.

The Martini glass hit the floor. Shattered, splintering into a billion fractional pieces, as many pieces as Kris's heart had broken into, his soul.

Kris's mouth moved, but nothing came out. His mind wouldn't work. Memories erupted from behind the locked doors of his brain: an explosion, the ground shaking. A strike team moving through black smoke in a cramped mosque. Finding an open trunk, a car on fire. A body, burned black, turned to ash. David's smile as he drove Hamid onto the base. David's headstone in Arlington.

David, *dead.*

Except, David was sitting six inches from him, close enough Kris could feel the heat of his body. Could smell him, smell the soap and his skin, like moonlight and sundrenched sand and jasmine, something that had been purely David.

David had changed. A decade did that to a person, especially if they were alive. Lines creased his face, around his eyes, deeper than before. He sported a short beard, dark strands streaked with gray and trimmed close to his skin. His hair was longer, curled on the ends. He wore jeans and a long-sleeved shirt, and a simple green canvas jacket.

His eyes, which had always been event horizons for Kris, the edges of David's soul, rough borders where they merged and became one, glittered. His light was marred, though. Where once galaxies had shone, sorrow tinged his gaze.

Kris's chest heaved, his breaths coming hard and fast, speeding up until he was gasping, struggling to breathe. Was he imagining this? Had he just lost it, his final grip on reality? His gaze darted left and right, landed on the bartender, heading his way with a frown.

"Everything okay?" The bartender's gaze went from Kris to David and back. "You two all right?"

Kris bobbed his head, something between a *no* and a *yes* and a *what the fuck?*

"We're fine," David said smoothly. "The glass slipped. We're sorry."

The bartender stared for another long moment and then nodded. Strode away.

"*David*?" Kris hissed.

That was *his* voice. *David's* voice. But David was *dead*. He was *dead* and *gone* and Kris *knew* that because he'd *never* come back. He'd never reached out for Kris, had never tried to find him. He'd seen David's *body*, for fuck's sake. He'd seen burned bones, piles of ash. A man didn't walk away from that. There was a fucking headstone with David's name on it, just across the river. There were fucking bones beneath the ground. "What the *fuck*?"

"I didn't know you were alive," David breathed. "I didn't know."

"You didn't know—" Kris boggled, almost bit off his tongue. His eyes nearly popped out, and he just barely restrained himself from grabbing David. Shaking him and shaking him, slapping him across the face so hard his palm burned. You couldn't slap a ghost, right? "What— Where— How—"

The bartender was glaring at them again. Kris's gaze bounced from David to the bartender, around the bar. People were staring.

David grabbed his arm, pulled him off the barstool. "Come here," he murmured in Kris's ear.

God, David's *touch*. Kris melted, the very center of him going liquid, just like he had sixteen years ago in the mountains of Afghanistan. David's hand on his body, the too-close brush of their presences. He followed behind David, powerless to stop. Once, he would have followed David anywhere. Would he follow David's ghost, too?

David led him into the bathroom, locked the door behind them.

He took his time turning to face Kris, though.

A million questions formed at once, as soon as David pulled away. *How? Where? Why?* Each clamored to be asked first, demanded to be heard. His breath sped up again. His body trembled.

"I thought you were dead," David whispered. He leaned against the locked door, his hands behind his back. He stared at Kris, sorrow bleeding from his gaze.

"That's *my* line," Kris hissed. "That's what *I* say. Because I saw your fucking body! I saw your fucking corpse! And they took you from me and they buried your bones in the fucking ground!" He heard his shouts bounce off the walls, echo in the cramped bathroom. "You *died* over there! I saw you die!"

"It wasn't me they burned," David said softly. "Al Jabal took me—"

"Were there *no fucking cell phones* where you were?" Kris bellowed. "Have you been living on the surface of fucking *Mars*? You've got both legs! Both feet! Two hands! Was there no possible fucking way you could pick up a phone, or send an email, or walk to the nearest embassy? Crawl to a fucking military base?"

David stayed silent.

"It's been almost a decade," he hissed. "And you never said a word? And now you're here? How the fuck did you appear here?"

"I looked you up. When I arrived. I had to know if you died that day. I never saw you move after the blast."

"I wish I'd died that day!" Kris whirled, his fingers clawing at the tiles. "I was the only one who lived! Do you have any idea how many nights I laid awake begging to die? Because of that day?"

"I thought you were dead," David repeated. A tear slid from the corner of one eye. "I—"

Kris's hands trembled off the walls. He folded into himself, dug his fingers into his arms, the bunched sleeves of his trench. "How did you get here? This isn't some fucking sci-fi show where you can just transport down from your spaceship in the sky! How did you get here?"

David looked away, to the side.

"*Answer me*!" Kris shrieked. "Are you here for *me*? Did you claw your way back from the dead, across the entire world, to come back to me? I fucking would have for you!"

Slowly, Kris pitched forward, drawn to David. One hand reached for him, shaking like he'd frozen from the inside out. His fingers whispered over David's shirt, closed around the fabric. Grabbed, and pulled.

David fell toward him, falling as if he were crashing down to earth, a fallen angel who had lived on the dark side of the moon for the last ten years. He crashed into Kris, arms wrapping around him, so familiar, as if it had only been a moment and not a decade. His face buried in Kris's neck, and Kris felt, God, he *felt*, David's breath, the physical evidence of his life. Heard the beat of David's heart.

David was *alive*.

Kris grabbed him, held on. Ran his palms over David's back and his chest, trying to touch everywhere. He couldn't get to David's skin, not through the jacket, not through the shirt. His hand rose, over David's neck, into his hair.

Their eyes met. *Why?* screamed from every pore in Kris's body, from every shattered remnant of his soul. Why here? Why now? Why for so long? Why hadn't David said *anything*?

He didn't care, though, about the answers, not when David looked at him like that. Not when he was falling into the event horizons in David's eyes, trapped, never able to be free, and not when David leaned in, closed his lips over Kris's. Kissed him like he thought he'd never be kissed again.

It was every one of their kisses, from the first to the last—that Kris never *knew* was going to be the last they'd ever have, through the window of a busted Afghan sedan on the way to pick up Hamid—all wrapped in one. David's hesitancy mixed with his urgency, his need tempered by his love. Power, the depths of David's soul, opening beyond their kiss.

Kris tried to climb his body, tried to disappear into David's arms. He reached for David's waistband, his jeans—

David pushed him away.

Kris's back hit the far wall of the cramped bathroom, next to the urinal.

"I can't," David stuttered. "I'm sorry."

Turning, he fled.

# 29

**CIA Headquarters, Langley Virginia - September 8, 0645 hours**

"Caldera? What the fuck?" Wallace's confused voice broke through Kris's haze, shattered his ironclad concentration. "Fuck have you been doing in here?"

Exhaling, Kris sat back from his workstation. Coffee cups littered the floor, beside a thousand sheets of paper, printouts from the CIA archives, records, reports, after-action reviews. Anything he could access from his workstation, pore through and dissect in minutiae.

David's autopsy, such that it was, lay open on the desk. *Burned bone fragments recovered from the trunk of unidentified vehicle parked inside mosque. Incomplete skeletal remains. X-ray imaging inconclusive. DNA dental or bone marrow recovery impossible.* They'd decided it was David because of David's blood on the outside of the car, in the back seat, and on the trunk lid. The bumper. *Evidence suggests drag patterns and blood spatter. Overwhelmingly, the evidence points to DAVID HADDAD as the deceased.*

But it *wasn't* David.

They'd *missed* something. Goddammit, they'd missed something, for a whole decade.

"Caldera!" Wallace, again. This time, he shouted. Wallace was his SAD team leader, and if there was anyone who hated Kris more than Ryan did, it was Wallace. "I asked you a question!"

Kris's bones creaked as he pushed back from his desk. His chair ground over paper, crinkled reports on the strike team's mission, the recovery team's findings at the destroyed mosque. His mouth tasted like death behind his molars, like burned coffee, worse than Afghanistan's had been. Something was alive in his veins. Rage, hope, or too much caffeine, he couldn't tell.

How long had he been sitting there? All night, since he'd raced back to headquarters, after picking himself up from the bathroom floor? The bartender had wanted to call the cops, certain Kris had been attacked, assaulted. He'd stumbled, fumbled, kept saying no, but no one could understand him through the shrieks, the wails, the body-shaking sobs. He'd managed to slip out of there before the cops arrived, jogging down the street as the bartender bellowed for him to come back.

An hour in his car, screaming, punching his steering wheel. Losing all of his shit, every last bit, like he'd never done before.

Until all that was left was silence and snot, an ocean of dried tears cracking into salt flats on his cheeks. Streaked mascara.

And questions.

He'd turned the key, put the car into drive. Steered toward headquarters.

Somewhere, there were answers. And he'd always been the man to find them, no matter how far he had to dig.

"I'm working, Wallace." Kris stood, grabbing David's autopsy and a list of files he couldn't access, not from his station. He needed to get to the archives, pull the hard copies.

"Working what? Making a fucking mess isn't your job!" Wallace grabbed one of the papers off the floor. His eyes flicked to Kris. "Why are you digging up *this* shit?"

Kris shouldered past him.

Wallace grabbed his arm, spun him around. He shoved the paper against Kris's chest. "SAD lost six guys that day, you know. Because of *you*."

Kris stared. He said nothing. Didn't reach for the sheet. Wallace let go, and it fluttered to the floor, slipping between their boots.

"Why'd *you* live, huh? When good people, good men, died?"

Kris ripped his arm free. He stared into Wallace's eyes as he backed away, files tucked under his arms.

"Gonna make us clean up your shit again, huh?" Wallace kicked an empty coffee cup toward Kris. It flew, skittering and tumbling in the air before veering into another workstation. "You're a Goddamn shitshow, Caldera!" Wallace bellowed. "I can't fucking wait to get rid of you!"

Kris flipped Wallace off with both middle fingers as he backed out of SAD's office.

"Caldera—"

Wallace's shout cut off as the heavy door slammed shut.

Kris ran, racing down hallways, pushing through doors and throwing himself down stairwells until he finally made it to archives. Chest heaving, breathing hard, he hesitated outside the double doors.

What had they overlooked?

How had they let David go missing for ten years? Why hadn't they turned the world upside down, shaking every tree, every mountain, until they found him? *Never, ever leave a man behind*. It was ingrained into the marrow of their bones, engraved on the underside of their ribs. *Never, ever*. How had David been left?

Had Kris missed something? Had he sentenced David to exile?

How had he left his husband, the love of his life, for a decade?

What had *happened* to David, all this time?

What if he found what they'd missed?

What if he *didn't*?

Kris badged his way into archives, bypassing the check-in desk and heading for the old mission records. Archives smelled like dust and secrets, like redaction ink and old tears. The secrets and lies of the CIA were buried in the stacks, in between papers and in between the lines.

His hands trailed over documents boxes, spines of notebooks, bound folders wrapped with string. Canisters of microfilm. He counted down the numbers, the dates, until he got to what he was looking for.

*Afghanistan, 2008. Camp Carson. Hamid Operation*

Three file boxes. That's what the fulcrum of his life was to the CIA. Three file boxes, two of which contained the Congressional inquiry's findings and evidence. Had it been up to the CIA, there would be no file boxes, he was certain.

Kris dragged all three to the floor and flipped the lids. Start from the beginning, the very beginning. He slid to his knees and pulled the first file—

David's personnel folder fell open in his lap. His picture was stapled to the front corner, taken just before their deployment to Camp Carson. At the bottom of the photo, David's left hand was just visible, a gold ring glittering on his finger.

He ripped the photo from the file. Crumpled it, gasping, bending over at the waist as he breathed in, the smells of Afghanistan flooding him from the files, the smells of death and waste. His eyes closed.

*Why did you never reach out? Why did you stay dead? Why didn't you do* everything *you could to come back to me?*

*I thought you were dead,* David had said. He'd repeated it, like a robot, like a ghost. But ghosts and robots didn't feel warm, and they didn't leach sorrow like it was the only thing inside of them. He could still see David's gaze from across the bathroom. A thousand regrets wreathed in a bottomless, aching pain.

Slowly, Kris uncrumpled the photo and set it on the nearest shelf. Propped it against the files so David could watch over him. "I'll figure it out," Kris whispered. "You know I will."

He turned back to the files. Somewhere, there was a truth, a real truth, and Kris was going to find it.

**September 8, 1430 hours**

"Kris?"

He opened his eyes. Fuzzy shapes appeared before him. Shoes. He followed the shoes up, to ankles, pants, legs. He rolled over. A paper stuck to his cheek.

Damn it, he'd passed out sometime between reading the Congressional inquiry and cross-checking the team's findings in the mosque with David's autopsy. He lay on the floor of the archives, in between the stacks, in a pile of folders and scattered papers.

He was a fucking mess. His clothes were ruined. Rumpled, with coffee stains and ink all over them. He could smell himself, the stink of his adrenaline, his desperation. How many hours had it been since he'd been home?

"Kris?" Dan crouched in front of him. Beyond Dan, three techs from archives hovered at the end of the aisle, blatantly staring. "You didn't come home."

Fuck. He was supposed to go to Dan's. They were supposed to—

Jesus fucking Christ, how could he start a relationship with Dan? When David was alive, was actually fucking alive, living and breathing and walking somewhere out there in DC? When Kris had felt him, felt his skin? Heard his voice.

If David was alive, wasn't he still married? *Could* he be married to a legal ghost? David was dead, according to the law.

"Fuck, Dan," Kris moaned. He pulled the paper from his cheek and sat up. Everything in him ached, his bones, his muscles. He fucked up his sparring partners every other week, spoiled for fights with Russian GRU agents in seedy bars, but this was too much. He was pushing on the door of forty. He wasn't a young man anymore. "What time is it?"

"Fourteen-forty. September eighth." Dan swallowed, and his gaze wandered over the files Kris had spread like toys on the floor. "What are you doing?"

Kris rubbed his hands over his face. How could he possibly explain this? Where did he even start? He couldn't tell Dan about

David, not yet. David was a ghost, still, for a reason. Kris had to know why.

But bringing Dan into his quest for the truth about David just stung in all the wrong ways. Kris had done many things he wasn't proud of in his life. But he just couldn't do that to Dan. Or to David.

"What if we missed something, Dan?" he whispered. "What if we missed something that day?"

"What do you mean?"

Kris swallowed. "What if David wasn't killed? What if he survived?"

"Oh Kris..." It was Dan's turn to cover his face. Kris watched his shoulders shudder, heard his deep breaths behind his hands. "Kris, *don't*. Don't do this to yourself."

"I have to know. I didn't— I've never looked at the files. I've never looked at what actually happened."

"Kris..."

"I didn't want to know. I couldn't know. But, Dan, the autopsy. They couldn't definitely prove it was him. Everything was circumstantial."

"I've read it, Kris. He was beaten to death beside the car," Dan whispered. "There was enough blood in the rubble to know he'd lost so much. Then he was dragged into the trunk, where they poured accelerant on his body."

"There was no DNA match to the bones."

"Because every trace of DNA was gone. He was *ash*. Even the bones that did remain... They fell apart when the team tried to recover them." Dan's face twisted. "Kris, they took him out of there with a shovel. His ashes filled a plastic bag. Don't do this to yourself. Don't hurt yourself like this."

*It wasn't David. It wasn't David because I saw David last night, I held him in my arms.*

*It wasn't me they burned*, David had said.

"Kris." Dan reached for him, grabbed his hands. Held them between this own. "Kris, *please*. If this is because of last night. Us. Please, Kris. You need help. I want to help you, but I can't help with this." He nodded to the files, the papers littering the floor. "I love you, and I want you to be happy. I thought I could do that for you, but *this.*" He kissed Kris's hands. "You need help. Have you ever talked to anyone? About his death?"

Kris ripped his hands away. "I'm *fine.*"

"You're not fine. *This* is not fine."

"I am fine! Don't you think knowing is important? Don't you think we should be sure, absolutely certain, about what happened?"

"We are certain! We know! There was a Congressional inquiry, for God's sake! You don't want to go down this path, Kris. You're only going to hurt yourself with the truth!"

He stood, turning his back on Dan as he started gathering the papers, the files, the statements and evidence.

"And you're hurting *me,*" Dan breathed. "What is this? Another reason to not be with me? Another excuse for us not being together?"

Kris sagged. The air punched out of his lungs, like he'd taken a hit right to the center of his chest. "Dan..."

"We can't keep doing this. I can't keep taking this from you. Last night, you made me the happiest I've ever been. I thought, 'Finally, he's letting me in. He's letting me love him. Maybe, maybe one day he'll love me a little bit, too'."

"*Dan—*"

"I can't compete with a ghost. I can't compete with your complete devotion to him. And if last night sent you spinning down this rabbit hole. If being with me is such a terrible, terrifying thought for you that you had to come here, do *this...*" Dan took a shaky breath. "You need to get help. You need to move on. And I can't be a part of that. You have to do that for you."

Kris slammed the lid on one of the file boxes. How the fuck could he move on when David was alive and out there somewhere? How could he ever let go?

But... David had pushed him away. Had shoved him away and then fled. What did that mean?

Did David not want him anymore?

What had ten years apart done to David?

What if he'd moved on?

What if Kris really was clinging to a ghost?

"Kris..." Dan's voice shook. His voice never shook. Kris couldn't face him, not now. "They called me here because you scared the techs. And you're scaring me. Please, I'm begging you. Call someone. Today."

Kris stacked the file boxes, grabbed David's autopsy report and his photo, and strode away.

### Brentwood, Washington DC - September 8, 1500 hours

Brentwood hummed with urban decay, with poverty, with murders in broad daylight. Police sirens wailed at all hours. Steel-eyed residents turned inward, living behind fortressed walls and ignoring the outside world.

Dawood had slipped into the neighborhood, setting up in a run-down motel. The neon sign buzzed, five of the lights busted and one half-sputtering at night. A pool once full was now only algae green, a swamp of refuse and beer cans. Prostitutes brought men to the rooms and gave the owner a cut of their earnings. He heard banging headboards as he made his daily prayers, heard loud moans and cries of orgasm.

His prayers were scattered, his mind a mess. Kris was *alive*. He hadn't believed the news reports, the lists of the dead he'd finally drummed the courage to search for online. *Camp Carson Base Commander, Sole Survivor of al-Qaeda Triple Agent Suicide Bombing.*

How many nights had he lain awake, convincing himself he'd seen Kris's dead body? That Kris had died in the attack?

Fear had kept him imprisoned for years. Fear of finding Kris dead. Fear of losing what he'd found on the mountain. Fear of his sandcastle tumbling down, again.

How many choices had been made because of the certainty of his fear, his desperation?

How many steps along the path taken with false knowledge?

*You must follow the path Allah has laid out for you.*

*Allah, you knew. You knew he was alive. And yet, this is the path you laid.*

He prostrated, his forehead digging into his prayer rug. *Trust, trust.* "Oh, Allah, I have put my trust into you," he prayed. "Whosoever puts his trust into Allah, He will suffice him."

A moan sounded through the wall. Dawood breathed out. A headboard slammed, and slammed again.

*You must follow the path Allah has laid out for you.*

*Trust in Allah*, the Prophet Muhammad, *salla Allahu alayhi wa sallam*, said. *But tie your camel.*

He stood, rolling up his prayer rug and hiding it. If anyone came into his motel room, they'd find nothing but a backpack, some chewing gum, and a few changes of clothes, bought with cash from a Walmart. A bottle of water, a toothbrush and toothpaste. He was nobody. He was nothing.

He pulled a cell phone from his pants pocket. It had been waiting for him when he arrived, waiting in an envelope at the lockers on the wharf, just as promised. Ten days at sea on a cargo ship and then another six with a smuggler, moving through international waters and dodging the US Coast Guard until they slipped into the Chesapeake and rode right up to the waters of DC.

He texted the one number programmed into the phone. *When do we meet?*

*[ Soon. Your partner is on his way. Wait, and don't draw attention to yourself. In shaa Allah, this will succeed. ]*

He rubbed his thumb over the screen, over the message. *In shaa Allah.*

*In shaa Allah*, if only *everything* had been different. If only he'd *known*.

But that wasn't the path. That wasn't the path Allah had set for him.

*You must follow the path Allah has laid out for you.*

Grabbing his money and his motel key, Dawood headed out.

**Crystal City, Virginia - September 8, 1920 hours**

Kris trudged down the hallway to his door. How had everything gone so wrong? How had everything ended up upside down, backward instead of forward?

Where did he go from here?

Dan wanted him to get help. What did he tell a psychologist? That he'd seen his dead husband, had kissed him. But David had shoved him away and disappeared, and he had no proof, none at all, that it had ever happened?

Maybe he should get tapes from the bar. Get a statement from the bartender. Surely, he'd remember last night. It wasn't every day a man came apart like Kris had, all over the bathroom floor.

If he told anyone David was back, without proof, he'd be locked away for evaluation.

How did he find David?

Did David even want to be found?

What did it mean that he was a widower but his husband was alive? And not with him?

He turned the key in his lock, shouldering open the door. He wanted to crawl into bed and wake up yesterday, before all this happened. He'd go to any other bar, any other place. Not see David. He'd go straight to Dan's.

No, he wouldn't.

He didn't know what he'd do.

Eyes closed, he slipped into his unit and shut the door, leaned back against it.

"Hi."

His eyes flew open. His heart stopped, his lungs. His fingers scrabbled at the door behind him.

David sat on his couch.

Blinking, Kris looked from him to the door and back. He'd locked it. Of course he had. He always locked his door. He'd just unlocked it, for fuck's sake. He lived in a secured building. No one was supposed to break in, ever. Certainly not his not-dead husband who didn't know where the fuck he lived.

"I looked you up. When I got here. I thought I would go visit your grave." David looked away, to the empty white wall opposite Kris's couch. "When I found out you were alive, I drove out to the house. But… You sold it."

"Do you think I'd really live there? Without you?"

David swallowed. Kris watched the rise and fall of his throat, the movement of his Adam's apple. "I tracked you down. Property records. Found out you bought this place. There are two parking spots per unit. I found my truck in one."

This wasn't happening. Kris's fingernails scraped over the door, the only sound in the studio between David's soft words.

"I waited until you showed up. And then…"

"You've been *following* me?" Had he watched his unit, watched when Kris had come home the day before? And then followed him to Langley, then out to the bar? "You followed me to the bar last night?"

"I just wanted to see your face," David whispered. "Even in all my memories, every dream I had of you, nothing compares to the reality of you. I couldn't ever remember you perfectly. Not the way you actually are. All your perfections, all your subtleties. The exact curve of your smile. The angle of your jaw. I just wanted to see you again."

"What the fuck did you think was going to happen?"

"I didn't think." Finally, David looked at Kris. His eyes were fireballs, stars blazing in the dim light of his unit, the setting sun over the Capitol casting shadows over everything, except *him*. "I thought you were dead. You, alive… I never thought it was possible you could have lived."

"*I* never thought it was possible *you* lived." Kris ripped David's autopsy from his laptop bag and flung it across the apartment. Papers fluttered, landing upside down on the carpet in front of David. "This is how you *died*."

"It wasn't me they burned," David whispered. "The son of the internet café owner. They took him, as collateral. He—"

Silence. Kris heard David breathe, heard the squeak of his leather couch as David shifted.

"How did you get here? You're dead. You couldn't have made it through customs."

"You know as well as I do there are a hundred different ways to enter the US under the radar."

"Smugglers? Through Mexico? Canada?"

"By boat."

Kris nodded slowly. Licked his lips. "Which means you've been in contact with civilization. Phones. Emails. US Embassies. You didn't think at *any* time to try and reach out? To the CIA? To *me*?"

"I thought you were dead."

"You keep *saying* that—"

"Without you, there was no point in coming back! To the world, to the CIA, to anything."

Damn it, wasn't that exactly how Kris had felt? The world wasn't worth living in without David. It hadn't been, for a decade. He wilted, slumping, and his head *thunked* against the door.

"Ever since I found out you were alive... I can't think." David trembled, curling forward. "Every thought I have comes screeching to a halt, crashing against the knowledge that you're here. You're alive. You've been alive all this time."

Two for two on that. It was like David was saying the thoughts forming in Kris's mind. But hadn't they always been linked in that way? Hadn't David and he always shared a soul, shared a mind? Finished each other's thoughts, each other's sentences. Would a decade apart truly change that?

"Why are you back? Why now?"

David inhaled, shakily. "I had to come."

"But why—"

Knocking pounded on the door behind Kris. He flew forward, spinning, his heart in his throat. He was going to die of a heart attack, murdered by too many fucking surprises. Too many uninvited guests at his home. "Who is it?" he shouted.

"*Kris, it's me.*"

Fuck. Dan. Kris's gaze bounced from the door to David. David frowned, confusion unfurling as he stared back.

But, of course. David didn't know that Dan and Kris were on the cusp of something, that David had interrupted his big grand gesture to Dan, his hanging up of his jock and his condoms and trying to settle in for round two of the good life.

*"Kris... I've been thinking about you all day. This afternoon.... You're scaring me, Kris. Please, let me in. Can we talk? I want to help you."*

"I'm fine, Dan. Really. It's okay."

*"Please."* He heard Dan sigh. *"Please, just let me see you. I'm frantic over you right now. I'm so sick, thinking I pushed someone I love into this. God, Kris, I'm so sorry—"*

Confusion on David's face bloomed, morphing to shock, to realization. To agony.

He had to get rid of Dan. Right now.

"You didn't do anything, Dan. It wasn't you. I promise."

*"Open the door, please. Just let me see you."*

He made sure the chain lock was on. Reached for the doorknob and sighed. He glanced over his shoulder. David had disappeared from the couch. There was no way Dan could see over Kris's shoulder and into his studio, could spy David back from the dead.

He wasn't ready for Dan—or anyone—to know, not yet.

Maybe David would disappear again. Maybe they'd say the goodbye they never got to say. Maybe David was riding off into the sunset and Kris was just one stop on his goodbye tour. What did ten years as a dead man do to a man? Did the same person come back?

He cracked his front door. Pressed his face into the opening. "I'm fine, Dan."

Dan looked him up and down, taking in his same clothes, rumpled and stained. His exhaustion, warring with the adrenaline of finding David in his apartment. "I didn't mean what I said earlier. That I couldn't be a part of your healing. Don't think that I'm walking away from you. I'm *not*. I never will. I just want you to be okay."

"I'm— I'm fine. I'm going to be fine. I will." He nodded, ridiculous bobs of his head up and down. He had no idea what he was saying.

"Kris..."

David appeared, hidden behind the door, out of sight. Rage thundered through his gaze, primal purpose. Lightning flashed in his eyes. "He's *busy*," David growled. He slammed his palm against Kris's door and shoved it closed, right in Dan's face.

Kris heard Dan's gasp, his choked-off shout of surprise, muffled through the closed door. "Why did you—"

David grabbed him, spun him. Pressed him against the door. His hands squeezed Kris's shoulders and his legs pressed against his, from feet to thighs. Every part of David trembled.

He stared into Kris's eyes, every emotion roiling within him laid bare. Like sixteen years before in Afghanistan, when David had finally let Kris see into his soul, had let him see how he truly felt before their very first kiss. Agony, anguish, heartache. Confusion. Anger. *Need.*

Desire. Hunger.

Love. So much love.

Terror. Fear. He saw David's fear spin on and on, heart-clenching, throat-choking anxiety. Was it too late? Was he too late?

Did ten years change a man?

Yes... and no. Kris responded to David like he always had, like part of his soul was reaching for David, like something inside of him needed to be with something inside of David. Like they were two halves of a whole, desperate to be one.

Ten years, and he still loved David with every fiber of his being. Every part of his soul, every shattered remnant of his heart.

And David still loved him.

He grabbed David and pulled him close, as close as he could. David groaned, shuddering as he collapsed against Kris, as their bodies fit together.

Hands were everywhere. Grabbing jackets and shirts, tugging, pulling, freeing skin. On waistbands, undoing pants and jeans.

They were naked in moments, clothes scattered on the floor. Kris's hands roamed over David's body, over his warm, burnished skin. He knew this body, knew it inside out. Had loved it for years, and still loved him in his dreams. But there were new scars, new marks. Burns and cuts, ragged lines where the skin had been torn, healed roughly. Star-shaped bullet wounds. Ten years had not been kind to David.

David ran his rough hands over every inch of Kris's chest. SAD had filled him out, turned his lean body hard, made him cutting. He had scars, too, every one of them earned after David's death, earned because Kris had wanted to feel a fraction of the agony of David's death. He'd been reckless, so reckless. He'd wanted to die.

"Kris," David breathed. Their noses bumped, shared breaths mixing together. He kissed Kris's face, his nose, his cheeks, his eyes. "Kris, *please—*"

"Yes, David, yes. Make love to me," Kris whispered.

David backed him through his studio, through the tiny space to his bed. They kissed and never stopped, hands exploring, relearning, remapping bodies they'd committed to their hearts. Kris's legs hit the edge of his bed, and he scrambled onto the mattress, dragging David by the hand after him.

David surged, covering him completely, his body sliding against Kris's, claiming him, owning him. Kris whimpered. His arms and legs wrapped around David, holding tight.

"You're so beautiful," David whispered. "*Ya rouhi.*" He bent to Kris again, kissing him, caressing him in every way, dragging a symphony of moans and shudders from Kris.

Kris tipped his head back, gasping for air. Everything inside of him burned, everything. His blood, his bones, his heart. His soul was on fire, every shattered piece of his heart reforging in the heat of David's love. Nothing existed beyond this moment. Nothing existed beyond their bodies, pressed so close, locked together. Shock waves erupted from within, earthquakes in his soul that rocked in time with David's thrusts, in time with his grunts, his breaths in Kris's hair, his ear.

"I love you," David whispered. "I have *always* loved you."

"David!" Kris's fingers dragged down David's back, left furrows in his skin. Ran over raised rough ridges, old scar tissue.

David burrowed into Kris's body, into his soul, into that place inside of Kris that had always and forever been David's and David's alone. That part of him that had always held David's soul.

Somewhere inside of David, part of Kris's soul existed, too.

David kissed his way down Kris's throat, cradled him in his arms. Rocked forward, and pressed their foreheads together. Stared into Kris's eyes. David dragged Kris's pleasure out in long, languid lengths, until Kris couldn't breathe, until his back arched and his toes curled and he screamed, yelling at the top of his lungs. It was different, God, it was so different, when there was so much *love*. Nothing could compare, ever.

David held him, after, caressing him as he kept gently rocking into Kris's body, whispering kisses and declarations of love in English and Arabic all over his skin.

Dizzy, Kris tried to hold on to David, tried to keep both hands on his dead husband as the world tumbled, twirled away. Was this madness? He was okay with it, if it was.

"I want to make love to you forever," David whispered. "All night long. And tomorrow. And the day after."

Kris shivered, to the tip of his toes. "Why don't you?"

Above him, David grinned. He kissed Kris's nose, his lips, both of his eyelids. "Okay."

---

Hours later, they finally rested.

The bed was destroyed. Sheets lay in a pooled heap on the floor. Kris's white bedspread was torn, more off than on. The mattress was exposed on one corner, the sheet ripped free as Kris screamed through his third orgasm, as David rode him through his second. Handprints streaked the glass mirror at the head of the bed from when Kris had ridden David slowly, an hour's worth of heat building between them until David tipped him backward and took control.

They lay entwined, one edge of the fitted sheet wrapped around their hips against the cold. Wet spots stained the bed, lube and everything else.

David's gaze flicked to the bowl of condoms beside the bed. His eyebrows arched.

Kris swallowed. Looked down. "I thought you were dead. I didn't know how to deal with that—"

David silenced him with a kiss.

Jealousy slithered up Kris's insides. "You? Ten years is a long time..."

David shook his head. "Nothing. There was never anyone. Never anyone else."

"Jesus, that makes me feel *worse*." Kris covered his face with his hands. How many men had it been? He tried to add up the round numbers, the nights he'd spent, the weeks in a year multiplied. His face burned.

David kissed his chest, his collarbone, his throat. "*Ya rouhi*, it's in the past. Don't think of it again."

Kris bit his lip. "Are you back? Are you here for good? You've just appeared out of the blue twice. What do you want, David?"

David's hand splayed over Kris's belly. "It's Dawood, now," he said softly. "I go by Dawood."

"Dawood." Kris blinked. "Are you... Muslim again?"

"I've always been Muslim. I was born Muslim."

"Are you practicing?"

David—Dawood—nodded. "*La ilaha illah Allah wa-Muhammad rasul Allah*," he breathed, whispering the *shahada*.

"What happened over there? What happened to you?" Kris propped himself up on his elbow, turning toward Dawood. He laced their hands together, fingers entwined. "Tell me, please."

Moonlight glittered into his studio, curving through the windows. Pale light fell on the bed, between their bodies. Dawood held out his hand, as if he could catch a moonbeam in his palm. "Every night, I whispered to the moon. As if it could take my messages straight to you. Every night, I thought of you. Told you what happened during my day. Gave you my prayers. I thought you were with Allah and that you could hear me. I thought the moon was our messenger."

Tears slipped from Kris's eyes and fell into the moonlight.

Slowly, Dawood spoke. About how Al Jabal had dragged him free from the rubble of the mosque through an escape tunnel and driven him north, hundreds and hundreds of miles, to the footsteps of his father, Abu Adnan, in the remote mountains of Bajaur Province. "I was supposed to be a prisoner. In secret. One day, Al Jabal would come for me and finish me off."

"Ryan killed him. Two weeks after your death. Ryan put everything and everyone in Afghanistan into the hunt for your murderer. Two drones obliterated him. I saw his death photos myself."

Dawood winced. He muttered a prayer under his breath, Arabic too soft for Kris to catch. "Abu Adnan told me. And he told me his son's death freed me. That his son had told no one, ever, about his home. That no one in the world knew where I was."

"Why didn't you call? Why didn't you find some way to reach out? Any way?"

"The mountain felt like the end of the earth. Like the oceans had been turned upside down and we lived somewhere entirely off the map. Maybe even a different world. Some days, I didn't know if I was alive or dead, if anything was real. The only thing I knew, for certain, was that if I came off the mountain and you were dead, I wouldn't survive."

Kris squeezed Dawood's hand until his bones hurt.

"Abu Adnan took me in. He took care of me. Nursed me back to life. Gave me a place in his home."

"Al Jabal's father? Your murderer's father?"

"He became a father to me as well. *Bismillah*."

Kris blinked, slowly. "I can't even imagine..."

"I had a father again," Dawood whispered. "I had a father, and I had Allah, too. I thought you were dead, in Paradise, and I gave my prayers to you through the moon. I was just waiting to see you again. That's *all* I lived for."

Hadn't that been all Kris lived for, as well? But he had stopped believing in fairy tales of an afterlife, delusions of heaven or a hereafter. He'd stopped believing because David—Dawood—hadn't come back for him like he'd promised he would.

But if Dawood was alive, then of course he couldn't come back from the dead, from an afterlife, for Kris. Of course not. Why hadn't he thought of this before? Why had he left his husband for *ten years*? Guilt twisted at his guts, slicked up his spine. Shame, the familiarity of it, curled around his heart. It felt like a homecoming.

"I'm sorry," Kris whispered. He cupped Dawood's cheek. "I'm so sorry."

Dawood covered his hand and kissed Kris's palm. "I'm not. It was good, being there. I was alive in a way I hadn't been."

"Spiritually?"

Dawood nodded. He glanced out the window, to the moon. "I need to pray, *ya rouhi*." He kissed Kris's nose and rose, striding out of bed and to the bathroom. Kris watched him, watched his naked body move, the long lines of his legs, the strength in his back.

Water turned on in his shower. Dawood stepped in, rinsed. He could hear him speaking softly, Arabic words, prayers. *He's doing his ablutions*. After intercourse, after any bodily fluid had been spilled, a full washing was required.

Silently, Kris watched Dawood pad back out of the bathroom after the water turned off. Beads of water clung to his skin, the ends of his hair. He'd let it grow long and had brushed it back off his face. A towel wrapped around his waist, covering his hips and his thighs. Dawood lined up, facing east, and began his prayers. "*Allahu Akbar*."

Kris sat up, the sheet pooling around his hips, their releases staining his skin, his bed, as his husband gave his prayers to Allah. Arabic whispered over his studio as Dawood bowed, kneeled, prostrated, and prayed. "*Allahu Akbar*."

He finished with the *tasleem*. "*As-salamu alaykum wa Rahmatullah wa barakatuhu*." Rising, he stretched, the moonlight carving around his body.

"I thought you believed Allah was dead."

Dawood crawled into bed slowly. He lay beside Kris, one hand stroking Kris's leg, his sheet-covered hip. "I believe Allah created you and me out of one soul. That we are meant to be together, before time and after time ends. If I believe that, how can I truly believe Allah is dead?"

"Your father?" Kris whispered.

Dawood blinked. He licked his lips. "I have tried to become a man my father would have been proud of. I try to do my part to make the world a better place."

"There's so much evil in the world. So much hatred. It seems to get worse every year, every day. Where is the justice?"

Dawood's gaze skittered away. "Sometimes, justice is what we make ourselves."

"And evil? How do we fight that?"

"If I have lived for Allah and lived like my baba, then evil will be fought."

Kris lay back on the mattress. The pillows were long gone. His thoughts slid to Al Dakhil Al-Khorasani, the jihadi on his *hegira* for war. Where was he going? What were his plans? Was he coming to America to slaughter Americans, blaming them for the evils of the world? Americans were complicit, or so the jihadist sayings went, in the actions of their government, thanks to democracy. He chewed on his lip. "There are many people who say they live for Allah and fight against evil. But everyone points the finger at each other, saying everyone else is the evil one. Where is the truth?"

"The truth is complicated," Dawood whispered again. His eyes were lost in darkness, only the shadow of the moon reflecting in slivers off his dark irises. "But there are objective evils in the world. Death, before someone's time. Murder. Torture. Oppression. Betrayal. Some things are just *wrong*. I put my faith in Allah to help me find my center, as my baba did."

"What about this?" Kris hitched his naked leg over Dawood's. "*Us*. Doesn't the Quran have a few things to say about people like us?"

"Allah made me this way. He made me, and He is perfect. He does not make mistakes. And, in the Quran, the Prophet Lot was aghast by the cruel treatment of strangers by the inhabitants of

Sodom." Dawood kissed the back of Kris's hand. "If you go into the texts, into the classical Arabic, the meaning is forced sodomy. Rape of men. Specifically, the inhabitants of Sodom attacked travelers, blocked their way, and raped them." He rubbed his cheek, his beard, over Kris's fingers. "The Quran is a book for all time, given by God to us for our learning. It is a book that renews itself, reveals itself deeper as we progress as human beings. How can we ever presume to understand His mind? Allah speaks in poetry, in science, in sunsets and sunrises and shooting stars, in planetary orbits and psychology. But He has made all things possible. If a line in the Quran seems to violate His world, His order, then that line is just more of His poetry. He made me." Dawood kissed Kris's fingers, the tips of his pads. "He made us. Made us out of one soul. He did not do that in error. Sometimes..." Dawood sighed. "I believe Islam has ossified under so many layers of human error. Of fatwas and rulings and dusty old men issuing their rulings. We have lost sight of the truth, and faith has become stagnant in our blood, in our souls. We, as Muslims, must go back to the beginning, to become closer to Allah."

"Isn't that what the fundamentalists say?" Kris whispered.

"Allah detests violence against the innocent. Wickedness. Why is so much of the world in collapse, now? Why has so much evil risen? Allah is trying to tell us something, but no one is listening."

"Tell that to the jihadis. They think they have a straight line to Allah. Dedicated cell service."

"Jihad comes in many forms. But, *qitaf fi sabilillah*. The holy war. That is only to be waged on the evildoers, the ones against God. Anything else is not allowed."

Ten years *had* changed Dawood. The dead weight of his past, the silent scream he'd carried inside of himself, was gone. Something else was in its place, something Kris couldn't quite put his finger on yet. Certainty? Or something else?

"I've *missed* you," Kris breathed. He reached for Dawood's hand as moonlight drenched their bed. "I've missed you so much."

Dawood kissed his nose. Smiled. "I am here now."

"Will you stay? We can figure this out. Go to the CIA, explain everything. You can be declared undead. Not-dead. Whatever it is."

Dawood leaned forward again, kissing him softly. Like he'd kissed him the day they married and the day Kris had said *yes*. Like they'd kissed the morning before the Hamid operation had broken everything apart.

"You didn't finish your story." Kris pulled back. "You were living on the mountain with Abu Adnan. And now you're here. Fill in the blanks." He settled back and took Dawood's hand, kissed his palm.

Dawood looked away, a million miles away. "'Bu Adnan died."

"Oh, *shit*. Jesus, Dav—Dawood." He fumbled on Dawood's name, the shape of it unfamiliar on his lips. "Shit, I'm sorry. I'm so sorry." Two fathers in Dawood's life, gone. "Was it… peaceful?"

Dawood shook his head.

Kris tugged him down until Dawood's head lay on his chest, right over his heart. He wrapped both arms around Dawood, cradled him close. "I'm sorry. I'm so sorry."

Dawood turned, rolling against him. Brought his body against Kris's, their legs and hips and everything else pressed so tightly together. "Make me forget," he breathed. "Make me forget, for tonight." His lips closed over Kris's.

Kris held him close, drawing him in, wrapping his arms and his legs around Dawood as Dawood crawled over and above him. His lips parted, and he kissed Dawood with everything he felt, every moment of loneliness, every night he'd cried himself to sleep, every dream he'd had of waking up with Dawood beside him once again. Every memory of his smile, his laugh. His fingers carded through Dawood's hair as his legs fell open, as Dawood pressed against his thigh, his hip.

Yes, he wanted this, wanted Dawood. Wanted their love and their life back. He wanted Dawood to slide within him again, all the way in, until their souls merged and they drowned in each other, and all the darkness, all the pain, all the agony of every day of the past ten years, was erased. He arched his back, opened himself to Dawood. "Love me," he breathed.

"*Ya rouhi*, I always have," Dawood whispered. He slid inside Kris, into his soul, and shuddered. Kisses whispered over skin, hands, fingers, caressed. "*Ana bahibak*, my love. I always will."

**September 9 - 0710 hours**

Kris woke to Dawood's soft prayers, his calls of *Allahu Akbar* before the rising sun. Squinting, Kris shifted, standing on wobbling legs and heading for the bathroom. He was a mess. He hadn't been loved this much, this hard, since—

Since their trip to Hawaii. Since their wedding night. Since their new house. Every one of his best memories were Dawood.

"I'm going to shower," he called back. "Want to join me?"

"I'll make breakfast." Dawood appeared in the doorway, his jeans on but unbuttoned at the waist. "You still like your eggs over easy?"

"I always like everything you make me."

Dawood smiled and disappeared.

Kris took his time in the shower, relaxing under the heat, letting loose muscles that hadn't relaxed in ten years. He laughed out loud, smiling into the spray. How was this possible? How did happy endings happen? How did dead husbands come back?

He sobered as he washed his hair. What was he going to tell Dan? Last night, Dawood had shoved him away, had sent a loud and clear message to Dan. How had that gone down? He had, in the ancient wisdom of an old TV program, some 'splaining to do to Dan.

This was going to hurt, no matter how it went down. But, in his heart, Dan had always wanted the best for Kris. That *had* to still be true. It had to be.

Between Dawood and Dan, there was no contest, and there never had been. His heart, his soul, had always belonged to Dawood.

He toweled off, fluffed his hair, and pulled on a pair of skinny jeans and a loose sweater. He'd call out for the day, spend his time with Dawood. Figure out their plan together.

Barefoot, he padded out of the bathroom.

A plate rested on the kitchen counter. Two eggs, perfectly fried. A piece of toast. A glass of orange juice sat beside it.

But his studio was empty.

"Dawood?"

Nothing.

*No.*

This couldn't be happening. His heart raced. He spun, checking the corners, peeking under the curtains. His gaze flicked back to the bed. Was Dawood hiding, or lying down, or...

The walls were closing in the faster he spun, the harder he breathed. No, no. Where had he gone? *Where*? And *why*? Why had he left, *again*?

Kris stopped, staring at his front door.

His bag, his laptop, everything he'd brought home from the CIA, was *gone*.

And so was Dawood.

Collapsing, Kris screamed, grabbing his hair, pulling on the strands, screaming and screaming until his voice went hoarse and his throat was raw. He flung himself forward, a mimicry of Dawood's prayers only an hour before.

Dawood had stolen his CIA-issued laptop.

Dawood had robbed him.

Dawood had *used* him.

And he was gone. *Again*.

He had to call Dan.

# 30

**Crystal City, Virginia - September 9, 0845 hours**

FBI forensic technicians crawled over Kris's apartment. Their soft chatter filled the empty spaces, the deafening silent scream that split Kris's head in two. He huddled at his kitchen counter, slumped on a barstool, arms wrapped around himself.

Dan paced behind him, from the stove to the refrigerator and back, talking softly into his phone. "Yeah, it's all gone. His laptop, his access card, everything." Silence. "I have *no* idea what I'm supposed to tell these FBI guys, Ryan." More silence. "Yeah, okay. Okay, thanks." He hung up with a sigh.

He didn't look at Kris.

Fingerprint dust glittered in the air, a dark grit that hovered, that caught in Kris's throat. Techs flipped back his stained bedsheets one by one. Ran their flashlights over every inch of his bed, pulled fingerprints from his mirror, from his bed frame.

A tech with a set of tweezers grabbed a long, dark hair from the carpet where Dawood had prayed. He dropped it in a plastic baggie marked EVIDENCE and sealed it, set it aside.

Kris's stomach twisted, clenched. Bile crawled up his throat. He buried his face in his hands, exhaled slowly.

Everything *burned*. Everything in him burned, a searing shame, a fire that, if he believed in anything at all, he'd call the wrath of God.

He was *so* fucking ashamed.

How had he been so fucking stupid?

Anger bubbled, simmered with resentment, with regret, recrimination. He should have told Dawood to get the fuck out. He should have told him to call the CIA, the FBI, call anyone, and sort out his legal status—dead or not dead—before saying a word to Kris. He should have told him that ten years without reaching out was ten years too many.

He should have told Dawood that ten years changed a man.

Because it had. It *fucking* had.

What had happened to the man he knew? The man he loved?

Kris chewed on his upper lip, memories tumbling. Had that been his husband, last night? Had that really been him? It felt like him. Tasted like him. His soul thought it was his love, his partner, his husband.

But how had his husband, the love of his life, left him... *again?*

And stolen his laptop, his CIA ID badge, and his access card.

Nothing made sense.

Did Dawood love him?

Or was that all an elaborate pretense, a game to get what he needed? Get Kris's access to the CIA, his files, his laptop.

Behind him, Dan cleared his throat. He stood as far from Kris as he could, and looked like he wanted to crawl the walls, stand on the countertop, get even farther from Kris. As far as he could. "Ryan has told the FBI this is a national security incident. Everything about this is being locked down. FBI will report direct to the CIA deputy director on this."

"To George?" Kris picked at the dark granite of his countertop.

"Yes." Dan blew out, slowly. "So... That was *him*? Last night? Who—"

Who had shut the door in Dan's face when Dan had come to see how he was doing. Kris nodded. "I didn't know he was here. He broke in." Kris shrugged. He should have questioned that more. *How? Why? When?*

But faced with his dead husband, he hadn't thought about national security, or any darker possibilities of why Dawood was back in his life seemingly out of thin air.

"All your access has been revoked. Anyone logs into the network with your card, or tries to access the internet from your laptop, we'll be alerted. Your laptop has been flagged, and if he tries anything, its ID will pop up at CIA headquarters. We'll send out a response team. We'll bring him in."

"He's former CIA, Dan. He knows all this. It took, what, thirty minutes to notify tech? He got everything he wanted off the laptop in under twenty." Kris sank against the counter, laying his head on his folded arms.

Hadn't he failed in all the ways a person could fail? Hadn't he fallen as far as a man could fall? Wasn't he already the scum of the CIA? Out of all the ways he'd failed, he'd never let classified material into enemy hands. Was that what he'd done now? Was Dawood one of them, still? Or one of *them*?

Dan inched forward, leaning his hips against the counter a few feet down from Kris. He folded his arms, pursed his lips. He still wouldn't look at Kris.

The lead FBI agent, a woman wearing a blue suit and sporting a brisk blonde bob, marched to Kris. Set her notebook on the counter, a perfect right angle to the edge. "Sir, I'm Agent Spalding. I have a few questions for you, as part of the investigation."

"The CIA will handle the investigation. We just need the FBI to process the evidence." Dan jumped in before Kris could speak.

Agent Spalding cast Dan a cold glare. "We will be conducting a thorough investigation without CIA interference. National security information may have been compromised. This is no time for a turf war."

Dan snorted. "Your boss will be calling you soon. Just a heads-up. This *is* staying within the CIA. Just process the evidence, Agent

Spalding. The CIA will take Mr. Caldera's statement back at Langley."

She blinked once at Dan. Turned back to Kris. "You engaged in sexual intercourse with the suspect, correct?"

Dan flinched and turned away. Kris saw his hands grip the counter's edge, his knuckles go white. "I did."

"We haven't recovered any used condoms in the trash. Were they flushed, or did you not use any?"

"We didn't use any."

Dan exhaled, slowly. Kris felt his exhale like a sword slicing up his spine. He'd never let Dan touch him without wearing a condom. He'd never let anyone else, ever, touch him without a condom. Dawood had been the first, the only, in his entire life.

"We're going to need to take you to Fairfax, to the medical center—"

"Why?" Dan was suddenly there, suddenly right at Kris's side. "Why do you need to do that? Is he hurt?" He turned to Kris, finally looked at him. "Did he hurt you?" Dan looked like he wanted to puke, then wanted to rip Kris's kitchen apart with his bare hands.

"Mr. Caldera needs a sexual assault forensic exam. We can collect the evidence at Fairfax medical or at Quantico, the choice is yours. But we need to do this."

"I'm going to be sick." Kris pushed Dan away and ran to his sink, emptying his stomach of bile and shame. What had he eaten last? Lemon chicken, with Dan. And Dawood's—

Closing his eyes, he rubbed the back of his hand over his lips. Spit dribbled from his mouth.

Dan's hand tentatively rested on his back. A gentle, barely there spread of his fingers. As if Dan didn't want to touch him.

"Why is this required?" Dan's voice could cut diamonds.

"We need to definitively identify the assailant—"

"It wasn't an assault." Kris rinsed his mouth, spat tap water into the sink. "And I know who he was."

"I was under the impression that there was some confusion about who this man was. The CIA asked the FBI to provide a definitive ID.

We need DNA to do that. The fingerprints we're pulling are mostly partials. If a definitive identity is what the CIA is after, this is how it's done." Agent Spalding's gaze bounced from Kris to Dan and back. "But now you say you know who he is? If that's the case, then what are we doing here? Wasting time?"

Dan squeezed Kris's shoulder, hard enough to tell Kris to keep his mouth shut. "We do need a definitive ID, yes."

Agent Spalding's eyebrows arched high. She waited.

Dan didn't give her anything more. "This is a national security matter. We won't be sharing anything further. All evidence recovered needs to be rush processed and forwarded immediately to Deputy Director George Haugen."

Agent Spalding snapped her notebook closed. "Then the only thing left is the forensic exam. Fairfax or Quantico, Mr. Caldera. The choice is yours."

Kris rested his forehead on the edge of his sink. The world was spinning, had spun since Dawood had disappeared, since he'd seen the plate of eggs and the empty studio and his missing laptop. He couldn't drag in enough air through the way his heart had caved in, crushing his chest. "Fairfax."

"I'll meet you there, Mr. Caldera. Go to the emergency room. I'll have a nurse waiting to collect the samples."

*Collect the samples.* He'd showered, but there could still be traces of Dawood on him, under his fingernails.

There absolutely still was Dawood inside of him. Absolutely.

His stomach lurched again. He clutched the edges of his sink, bile racing up his throat.

"I'll drive," Dan said softly.

---

The drive to the hospital was the quietest ride of Kris's life. Not even the flight home from Afghanistan with four bodies in the same plane had been so silent. Dan's electric car, his Bolt, barely hummed, barely made a single noise. Kris picked at the sleeves of his sweater.

Dan sat ramrod straight, driving like he was an instructor at The Farm, solid, definitive motions to every turn, every lane change. Kris finally gathered the shards of his courage and glanced his way.

Dan looked like shit. Like he'd been up all night, maybe drinking. Dark circles hung beneath his red-rimmed eyes. His knuckles were white where his hands clenched the steering wheel. He breathed slowly, in and out, like controlling his breath was the only thing holding him together.

Finally, they arrived, and Dan pulled up to the front of the ER, set out his CIA placard, his 'don't fucking tow this car' sign. Sighed, and sat back in his seat.

"I thought, last night, you'd just picked someone up," Dan breathed. "I thought everything you told me two days ago was bullshit. I thought you were just playing me." He looked down. Toyed with his key ring. Inhaled brokenly. "I thought you'd finally ripped my heart out enough for me to move on."

"Dan—" Tears bubbled up from within Kris, from the ragged parts that remained. "I meant it. I did. I wanted—" He couldn't do this. God, he couldn't do this. Pitching forward, Kris howled into his hands, sobbed into the tear-soaked wrists of his sweater. "I don't know what's happening. I don't understand anything. Any of this."

"I don't either." Dan reached for the door handle. "They're waiting for you inside. And we've got to get back to Langley. Ryan is waiting for us."

He tried to be brave, walking into the ER. Agent Spalding was there, texting someone and waiting with a nurse. They motioned for him to follow them down a long hallway to a closed room in the back.

Kris hesitated. "Dan," he mumbled. "I don't have any right to ask you for anything. Not anything, I know that. But..." Tears streamed down his face, a river rushing over his cheeks, down his jawline. "Will you stay with me?" His hands twisted in front of him, destroying his sweater's wrists.

Dan's eyes slid closed. For a moment, he didn't breathe. It might have been easier if Kris had asked him to carve his heart out with a spoon, offer it up to Kris on a golden platter. "Yes," Dan sighed. "You know I will."

They made the long walk to the exam room together. Dan pulled out his phone and turned it off.

Inside, the nurse asked Kris a lengthy health history, including a list of his recent sexual partners. In front of Dan, he detailed his and Dawood's four orgasms, his blow job from the Marine over the Atlantic, and a one-night stand in Estonia with a drunk British soldier. Dan sat, stone-faced.

The nurse asked him to strip, and then took photos of bruises on his wrists. A bruise blooming on his hip, the shape of a palm, squeezing.

"All of these were consensual," he whispered. "I thought—" He sniffed.

"I need to swab for DNA," the nurse finally said. She passed over a hospital gown, open in the back. "Please take off your briefs and lie facedown. I'll be back soon."

He shook as he undressed, almost fell over. Dan steadied him. Held him up. Guided Kris to the exam bed and helped him lie on his stomach. Grabbed a blanket from a stack on the shelves and spread it over Kris when Kris couldn't stop trembling.

"Thanks." Slowly, Kris reached out with his fingers, spreading them across the cheap plastic of the exam bed, inch by inch, until his index finger grazed the side of Dan's hand.

For a moment, it seemed like Dan was going to break down, was going to split in half and sob, let out every ounce of agony Kris knew he was holding on to. Agony Kris had given him, had dropped into his lap, a giant ball of twisted anguish straight through the heart. He tried to pull his fingers back. What right did he have, reaching for Dan and his care? What right did he have asking for help, for comfort, when all he did was hurt Dan in return?

Dan grabbed his fingers, linked two of his through two of Kris's, holding on like their fingers held the universe together. Kris could feel Dan shaking, trembling, his entire soul quaking within him.

Knocks sounded at the door. The nurse slipped back in. "All right,

I'm going to make this as quick and painless as possible. Three swabs, and then we're done."

Kris buried his face in his and Dan's linked hands.

Dan wrapped his other hand over Kris's head and pressed his lips to Kris's temple.

---

"Ryan is waiting for us."

"Fuck." Kris wilted in Dan's passenger seat. "This day just gets worse and worse."

Dan drove to Langley's executive parking lot, closest to headquarters. He had a spot right up front with his name on it. Why did Dan even give him the time of day?

"Ryan has set up a counterintelligence polygraph interview—"

Kris groaned. He *thunked* his head against Dan's passenger window.

"You *know* we have to do this. We have to know everything, Kris. And we have to be certain."

"*Today*? Right *now*? You know polygraphs are junk science, right? And you know us SAD guys are trained to beat them?"

"I'd advise you don't advertise that to the polygrapher. You're in enough shit as it is right now."

They walked in through the front doors, and as they crossed the CIA seal, Kris stared at the wall of stars, the Memorial Wall to fallen officers. Each star was carved out of the marble, chunks pulled out, each star representing something—someone—missing from the CIA. Dawood's star was up there. He'd spent hours in front of it, feeling the edges, running his fingers through the darkness, the hollow spaces.

But Dawood was alive. He was back. How did a fallen star get put back up?

Dawood was stealing CIA property. Was he working against the CIA?

How did a good man go bad?

*Allah detests violence against the innocent*, Dawood had said. *Wickedness. Jihad is only to be waged against the evildoers.*

*There are objective evils in the world.*

*The truth is complicated.*

Kris's heart, his soul, trembled.

His access to headquarters was restricted to being under armed guard and escort. Dan waited in the lobby with him while a retinue of internal guards arrived, each carrying an MP5 in a neck holster and glaring at him like he was a filthy traitor to the stars and stripes, to apple pie and the American way.

*I was first on the ground in Afghanistan,* he wanted to scream at the hulking guards. *I built this agency's terrorist hunting program. I have more kills than you'll* ever *know.*

But the only thing he'd be remembered for, inside the halls of Langley, was Camp Carson. And now, for breaching national security, for having his CIA files stolen by a ghost, a man who didn't believe enough in *them*, in their love and in what they were, to reach out to him for a decade.

---

It was Ryan's first question, once he was in the polygraph room and hooked up to the reader. "Why *now*? Why is Haddad back *now*?"

"I don't know." The polygrapher stared at her monitor, displaying readouts of Kris's heart rate, the speed of his breathing, his skin temperature, his sweat. A dozen cables wrapped around his chest, EKG pads were stuck beneath his collarbones, and a pulse monitor squeezed his fingertip. A camera stared at his right eye, watching for pupil dilation.

"How long have you known Haddad was back in the United States?"

"Two days. September seventh. I was on my way home—" *I was on my way to Dan's.* "—and I stopped for a drink. He showed up at the bar."

"He showed up?" Ryan's eyebrows shot sky high. "He just... showed up. Out of the blue."

"He said he was following me." Kris shifted. The cable across his chest stretched.

"Following you. Outstanding countersurveillance work there, Caldera." Ryan pushed off the wall and started pacing. "What did he say about where he'd been?"

"In the mountains, he said. He said he was cared for by a man named Abu Adnan. The father of Al Jabal."

"The father of the man who tortured him? Who was planning on murdering him?"

"Yes."

"Jesus fucking Christ." Ryan kept pacing, wall to wall in the cramped room. "What does he want from you, Caldera?"

"I don't know." Kris's voice shook. He felt his heart beat faster, felt his breath speed up. "I don't fucking know. If I knew that, I'd know what to do."

"What the fuck do you mean?" Ryan glared.

"I'd know why he's here!" Kris screamed. "I'd know if I should love him or hate him! I'd know if what happened last night was real or if he was just fucking playing with me!"

"Oh, he fucking *played* with you, all right. All night long, I heard."

"Fuck you!" Kris tried to lunge for Ryan. The cables, the sensors, kept him tied to the chair.

Alarms on the polygraph machine wailed.

"Calm down," the polygrapher snapped. "None of this is helping."

"He's just lost his husband. Again." Dan tried to interject, softly. "Can we be a little more conscious of that? This is a hard time for him."

"He hasn't just lost his husband!" Ryan roared. "Haddad was declared dead a decade ago! If Haddad is alive, then it's on *him* as to why he's been hiding for a decade! What kept him from the US?" He whirled on Kris. "Was he held against his will?"

"No."

"Was he a prisoner?"

"No."

"Was he wounded? Was there any reason he couldn't physically get to a US Embassy or military base?"

"No."

"Then he *chose* to stay," Ryan hissed. "He chose to fucking stay with al-Qaeda. He chose to become one of them. Which makes him a fucking enemy combatant! A Goddamn terrorist jihadi!"

"We don't know that—" Dan tried.

"I told you he was unstable! I told you he was bad news!"

"He's not fucking al-Qaeda!" Kris shrieked. "He's not a fucking terrorist!"

"Then why didn't he come back?" Ryan roared. "Why didn't he come back to you? If you were so fucking in love, so fucking in love that you had to change CIA policy to accommodate you both, why didn't he come back to that?" Ryan pushed into Kris's face. Blood vessels had burst in his eyes, turned his gaze red.

Kris slammed his head forward. He was too far away to break Ryan's nose, but his forehead connected with Ryan's chin, hard.

Ryan flew back, licking a trail of blood from his split lip. In the corner, Dan smothered a tiny smile.

"Fuck you, Caldera," Ryan hissed. "Fuck you. You should have come to us with this right away. But you hid it. You hid Haddad's return, and that makes you complicit in everything he fucking does, from that moment on. Are you ready? For whatever that is? For the love of your life to unleash the next September eleventh on American soil? Because you didn't act when you had the chance?"

Again, Kris tried to lunge for Ryan, tried to rip off the monitors and cables, tried to get his hands around Ryan's throat. Never, ever again, he'd sworn. Never again. Dawood had sworn with him. They'd sworn together that they would dedicate their lives to preserving life, to saving people. To never letting hatred and violence take control of the world again. Their whole lives, they'd fought against the forces of evil, of blind hatred, of crazed vengeances and bloodthirst. No matter who was guilty.

But were they still on the same side in that struggle?

*The truth is complicated.*

No, it's not, Dawood. It's us, together forever. It's us, always us. It's us against evil. That's how it always was. That's what we did, together.

*There are objective evils in the world.*

Do you think I'm evil now, Dawood? Have I become your monster? The Great Satan, the evil CIA?

Is that why you never came back to me?

The polygraph machine's alarms wailed in the silence as Ryan nursed his split lip and Kris wilted, no longer struggling against the cables.

He was going to flunk the polygraph. His emotions were careening, veering wildly left to right, up and down, too much for any reliable reading. He wanted to murder Ryan, strangle him with his bare hands. He wanted to rip the cables off and run, just run. He wanted to stand in the middle of DC and scream until his throat bled, scream and scream for Dawood to come back, just come back to him.

When Dawood did come back—if he came back—he wanted to slap him until his head spun around on the top of his spine. Nail his balls to the ground until he got his answers.

A part of him didn't ever want to see Dawood again. A growing part of him nurtured a searing resentment, a shadow cradling a ball of ice in the depths of his soul. Hatred didn't burn. Hatred was cold, a frozen heart, a frozen soul. He felt it forming slowly, felt his darkness cradling it close.

*Did you ever think you'd hate the man you married, the man you loved with all your heart and soul? Did you ever, ever think he'd do this?*

Three beeps sounded at the door. Someone badging in. Kris mustered the energy to glance up.

George strode in. Kris tried to get a read on him. Who had walked in: former friend or the deputy director?

He stared at Kris, his hands on his hips, and sighed, slowly.

"He's all yours," Ryan grumbled. He pushed past George and ducked out of the interrogation room. George did a double take at his split lip, but said nothing.

"Hello Kris," George finally said. "I never thought I'd see you again."

Kris's eyes narrowed. "You know what office I'm in. You could have dropped by anytime."

George looked down. "Kris, did you know Haddad was alive?"

"*How* can you ask me that?"

"Answer the question, Kris."

"You *honestly* think I knew he was alive, and I, what, lived like I wanted to die for ten years, lived without him... just because?"

"Answer the question. This is an official inquiry. You might spend tonight in jail. Or you might go home. It all depends on your answers."

"Home to *what*?" Kris cried. "My apartment is a *crime scene*! My dead husband *abandoned* me—"

"*Caldera*!"

"*No*!" he bellowed. "I did not fucking know he was alive! If I did, I would have gone and rescued him! I would have found him! I would have crawled through the fucking earth to get back to him!"

Dan looked down, stared at the cheap carpet as George closed his eyes. Exhaled.

"Have you helped Haddad in any way? Have you given him any CIA material?"

"Are you kidding me?"

"Did you give him your laptop?"

"Of *course* not."

"Why did you conceal your contact with Haddad for thirty-six hours? Why did you not report your initial contact with Haddad immediately?"

Kris shook his head, snorting. "I didn't know what to think. I didn't know if I was crazy or not. If he was really there. Or if I'd finally lost it."

"Have you seen things that aren't there before?"

"Yes, George," Kris snapped. "I regularly hold seances with the Easter Bunny and Santa Claus. We talk to the ghost of Saddam Hussein all the time."

Dan choked back a half laugh. George tilted his head from one side to the other, glaring.

"No!" Kris snapped. "I'm fucking sane. I don't see any ghosts or little green men or think black helicopters are following me. I don't think my microwave is trying to send me hidden messages."

"After he approached you in the bar... That's why you went to the archives, isn't it?" Dan, finally, asked a question. It wasn't part of the polygraph, though.

Kris swallowed. Nodded. "I had to know. I had to know if we missed anything."

"Did you find something? Some clue that we overlooked?" George looked like he dreaded the answer. "Did we leave a man behind?"

"No," Kris whispered. "I found nothing."

"Which, again, means he chose to stay away." George pinched the bridge of his nose. "Kris before I came in here, I received the forensic report from the FBI. They were able to positively ID the DNA samples they took from your apartment and from the forensic exam at the hospital. I... don't think I have to tell you this. It's definitely Haddad. I'm about to brief Director Edwards on everything. Do you have... any idea why he's back? Now? And why he'd steal your CIA material?"

Kris closed his eyes. Tried to think. Nothing made sense. Nothing added up. His mind kept jumping, bouncing from Dawood in the moonlight, performing his prayers, to Dawood lying over him, Dawood sliding inside of him, smiling, gazing at him like he was something long lost and beautiful. The way he'd held him, the touch of his rough fingertips against his skin. How his voice had whispered his name right before he came inside Kris's body, everything within Dawood shuddering and trembling. Hadn't that been real? Hadn't that been something?

"I don't have any idea why he's back. Or why he'd steal from me. I thought... I thought he came back for *me*. To me. But that's just not true." Blinking fast, he looked away, staring at the boring walls, the faded paint and the scuff marks as his vision blurred.

George murmured for the polygrapher and Dan to join him

outside. Kris waited, blinking back his tears. He wouldn't give George the satisfaction of his agony. Wouldn't give the cameras, the permanent record, or Ryan, who was probably still watching, the joy of his anguish. Watch the gay boy suffer. Yeah, Ryan would get off on that shit. No. He'd hold his chin high. He'd get through this. Somehow. No matter what.

Eventually, Dan came back with the polygrapher, who unhooked him from the machines, freeing him from the cables and the monitors. He'd dislodged the pupil monitor when he'd head-butted Ryan, but apparently that didn't matter.

"You flunked the polygraph," Dan said, leaning back against the wall and folding his arms. "But it's pretty clear why."

"No shit." Kris shook the pulse monitor off his finger. "Whose fucking brilliant idea was it to polygraph me today?"

"Ryan." Dan shrugged. "You know how he is."

Kris glared Dan down, as if he could murder with his stare alone. "What's the verdict?"

Dan took a deep breath. "Well, Wallace has benched you. You're off SAD. And Ryan wants to start termination processing. He wants you out of the CIA."

"He always has. Polygraphing me today, for fuck's sake. This is a Goddamn gift for him."

"George has held him off from that, for now."

"Does anyone care that my husband is back? He's back? And we don't know why? Or where he is?"

Dan blinked. "Yes, Kris. Yes, we care. I care. I care very much."

Fuck. Kris deflated, his heart taking the punch straight from Dan. "I'm sorry." Two days ago, wasn't he thinking about building a life with Dan? Wasn't he planning on waking up in Dan's arms, making him breakfast, falling asleep with him again? Building an *us*, he'd said.

Now what were they?

Why was Dan even in the same room with him? He had every right to be as furious with him as Ryan was. More so, even. Ryan didn't want *anything* to do with him.

Dan wanted *everything.*

And Kris had shit all over his hopes and dreams.

But it wasn't like Kris wanted this. Damn it, he was saying goodbye to David when Dawood just waltzed in and sat down, exploding Kris's life with his resurrection exactly like he'd done with his death, a decade before.

"I convinced them to let me watch over you," Dan said carefully. "Ryan wants to throw you in jail. George wants to send you to protective custody. I said I'd take responsibility for you." Dan hesitated. "If you're okay with that. If you'd rather do something else, I understand."

Something broke inside Kris, something wound too tight for far too long, twisted and twisted and twisted until he couldn't take it any longer. He didn't deserve Dan's kindness. He didn't, and he never had. Shame rose within him, tides of it, waves and swells that made him dizzy, made him want to surrender to the depths, fall backward into the abyss.

Fall into Dan, and let him fix the world, and everything that had gone wrong.

Let him fix Kris.

After Dawood's death, Dan had been an anchor for Kris within the storms of his soul. Why should his dead husband's resurrection be any different?

He wanted to surrender. He wanted to just surrender this life, surrender to everyone. Raise his hands, his white flags, and let the game end.

Why had it all turned out this way?

How could it all stop?

He held his hand out to Dan, a lifeline, a surrender, a capitulation. A plea. *Rescue me.*

"I'd like that," Kris whispered. "Thank you."

"Come on," Dan said, the hint of a smile quirking up one corner of his lips. "Let's try and think this through together."

### Brentwood, Washington DC - September 9, 1440 hours

"Oh Allah," Dawood whispered. His voice cracked, splintered apart. Tears spilled like diamonds, his breath catching on his prayers. "I seek refuge in you from an anguish that eats me alive." He gasped, tried to breathe through his closed throat. A sob raked through him, and he pressed his forehead harder against his prayer rug. "With your name, I die and live. To Allah we belong, and to Him we shall return."

*You must follow the path Allah has laid out for you.*

His soul *burned* for Kris, to the very center of himself, the center of his heart. Desperation had fueled him. He'd *had* to see Kris, once he'd known he was alive. See his face, just from afar. Then, up close. Just once.

Like a drug, he couldn't keep away. He could *never* keep away from Kris, not ever. Not when Kris carried a part of him within his soul. How could he run from his own soul, half of his being? Memories of their love, their life together spilled through his mind. Kris's hand on his cheek, the glow in his gaze when he stared at Dawood. How his eyes were full of love, always, for Dawood.

Kris had been the moon that rose in the darkness of his soul, reflecting the light of the sun into his pitch-black corners. He'd been half alive before Kris, caught eternally between the boy he'd been and a man he hadn't yet embraced, living in hiding behind a mask of his own creation. His soul had been built on shifting sands, but Kris had helped him form a foundation. Bring order to the chaos within.

Until Kris had been taken from him by this horrible, twisted life. This path.

*Why?* he wanted to scream. *Why, why?*

Why had their lives diverged? Why had they endured this separation? What point, what purpose?

Why was he to know his love, his soul, *lived*, only to lose him again in the end?

*Endure patiently,* the Quran said. *The promise of Allah is truth.*

He squeezed his eyes closed, pressing his face harder against his rug. His fingers gripped the edges so hard his bones hurt. He could still smell Kris, still feel his body against his skin, molding to him in all the ways that had always been so perfect, so exquisite to his existence.

Rushes of anguish crested, self-loathing and bitterness warring within him. He clung to his prayers, reciting the first surah of the Quran, the Al-Fatiha, the devotion. "*In the name of God, the infinitely Compassionate and Merciful. Praise be to God, Lord of all the worlds. The Compassionate, the Merciful. Ruler on the Day of Reckoning. You alone do we worship, and You alone do we ask for help. Guide us on the right path—*"

His voice choked, died.

Everything had shattered when he saw Kris, alive. Everything he'd planned, everything he'd meticulously laid out, for two years. Suddenly he was adrift, a castaway in an ocean of uncertainty. The man he loved, to the depths of his soul, who had defined his existence, who had given him the strength to face the world, and then face his destiny with the promise of their reunion in the beyond, was alive.

*You must follow the path Allah has laid out for you.*

He'd panicked, watching an egg sizzle in Kris's studio, listening to the sounds of his love showering. What was he doing? He was off the path. He was ruining everything, everything he'd sacrificed for. Everything he'd poured his new life into. Could he really just walk away, give up on his plan?

Every prayer felt like his heart was being sliced, divided between his love and his devotion. Uncertainty was a cancer, a poison consuming him from within.

Agony poured through him, filling his heart, circling his mind. His lungs shuddered, his breath quaked, faltering. His chest seemed concave, as if someone had scooped out his heart, ripped it out of him, and he was left with the hollow emptiness.

He couldn't breathe. Gasping, he clawed at his rug, snot and tears and choked breaths pushing against the dusty threads where he'd given so much devotion to Allah. *Why, why?*

Ten years in Afghanistan had changed him in ways he couldn't fully count. The sands of his soul had shifted, resettled. He'd thought his love for Kris had been buried, lost like the ancient cities of old in the sands of history. Something deep within him, and for another time.

Kissing Kris, making love to him, brought everything back. Nothing had ever been lost, ever been buried. He'd never stopped loving Kris, not once. Not ever.

Love wasn't something he'd expected from his life. Not when he was ten years old, staring down a cold, heartless world. Not when he was fifteen, and he'd realized with a dread that filled his entire being, that he was different, he was broken, that he craved the love of another man. His entire world had screamed that he was wrong, oh-so-wrong, and he'd buried that truth next to the memories of his father. He'd never love. Never.

David, stoic, dependable, predictable David, had been formed out of reactions. Reactions against himself, a careful mirage of everything he'd hated covered by something new, something different. Reactions formed by the world, reactions that shaped his identity until he was nothing but a kaleidoscope, shifting and ever changing under different people's gazes.

But Kris had cut through all of that. Kris had found his soul, had delivered his soul back to him.

Afghanistan, the land of ghosts, drenched in death and regret, had to be the center of the universe.

He'd met Kris there.

Fell in love with him there.

And lost him there.

All under Allah's gaze.

His cell phone buzzed, rattling on the table. Dawood inhaled slowly. Rose, and grabbed it.

A text appeared from his contact. *[ You were supposed to keep your head down. ]*

He swallowed. His throat stuck. *I thought it might help. I was trying to gather intelligence. But he doesn't work for CT anymore. His laptop was useless.*

Kris's laptop was in his bathtub, soaking until it was utterly worthless. He'd swiped what he could in under twenty minutes, enough to see that Kris wasn't a part of the counterterrorism world anymore. He didn't have anything for Dawood, nothing that he could use. Nineteen minutes after he'd grabbed Kris's laptop, he'd ripped out the battery. When he got back to his motel, he'd dumped the laptop immediately into the tub.

*[ There's absolutely nothing that we need from him. He's not important. He's a distraction from our mission. And you're fucking up. ]*

*Astaghfirullah.*

*[ Are you still in? Still committed? ]*

*Yallah, of course. Maa shaa Allah.*

*[ Then call Yemen. It's time. We cannot be distracted, brother. ]*

*In shaa Allah.*

The phone was silent. His contact stopped texting.

Slowly, Dawood kneeled on his prayer rug again. Tears dried like paint on his face, a new mask. He turned his head up, took a shaky breath. He was nothing but raw wounds, holes in his soul that had been flayed open. He should never have wondered what Kris looked like now, never have dreamed of the taste of his kiss again.

*Stay?* Kris had whispered. *Please?*

Something fractured inside him, a wall that had held everything back cracking. He'd walled everything off, a lifetime of mourning, a lifetime of agony. He'd always fought it, always fought against his pain.

His darkness, something that had lived within him since he was a boy. At ten years old, he'd been witness to the cruelty of the world, the madness that was to consume everyone, that had slipped into everyone's soul like black oil. He'd tried to fight back his whole life, tried to do the right thing, tried to be one of the good guys, but—

What was the right thing, anymore? What was true? Where was truth in a world full of Qaddafis and planes that slammed into buildings, full of torture and a hatred that lived in the bones, so deep and dark and twisted it poisoned the world. Where was truth in the graves of the innocents, in drone strikes, in car bombs and IEDs that left lives shattered, holes in families around the whole world?

What was true, between the bonds of brotherhood and the bonds of true love? The bonds of Allah and the promise of faith?

Or was truth a cold reality, the promise of retribution? Of justice? Of death?

What was the price of justice?

*You must follow the path Allah has laid out for you.*

Had Allah given him this test, this cruelest of tests, as the bitter finale to this life? His heart screamed, the labyrinth of his soul caving in, the sands of his world collapsing, drowning him.

He closed his eyes. He'd done what he could. His whole life had been lived at the mercy of others' whims, their twisted fates. From watching his father struggle at the end of a rope to feeling the press of an American soldier's boot on the back of his neck. From loving Kris to losing Kris. From finding a father's love again to losing it all, all over again.

*The truth is complicated.*

Was there any truth between the taste of Kris's kiss and the path he had to walk? Was there any outcome, any choice for a future? Any hope, anywhere, at all?

"Oh Allah," he whispered, prostrating himself again. "I seek refuge from the evil of darkness when it settles."

It was evening in Yemen. His brothers would be in the middle of their isha prayer. He'd wait, for a moment, to call.

His mind spun on, possibilities and dreams colliding with reality. Was there *any* way—

The sands of his life kept tumbling, kept pouring in on him.

*You must follow the path Allah has laid out for you.*

This was always his fate.

But, he had a couple of days, still.

A few more days to watch, at least. Gaze upon Kris, the moon in his darkness, the reflection of all the light in the world, trying to shine into his soul.

**CIA Headquarters, Langley Virginia - September 9, 1610 hours**

Kris existed in limbo, somewhere between 'unauthorized personnel' and 'jailbird'. Dan got him a visitor's badge for the CIA and escorted him to one of the secured interview rooms outside of CTC. For the umpteenth time in his career, he was on the outs. Again.

"All right." Dan tried to smile across the table at him. It didn't reach his eyes. Pain hovered there, a knife that went through Kris's chest. "Let's see what we can put together." He slid a cup of coffee to Kris. "Caramel macchiato, sugar-free."

Just the way he liked it. "Thanks."

Dan flipped open a stack of folders he'd brought. Surveillance images from the bar where Dawood had first ambushed Kris. The camera pointed at Kris in the corner. Pure, perfect shock shaped his face. His hand was outstretched, like he was holding a Martini, but nothing was there. He'd already dropped his Cosmo.

From that angle, the camera had only captured the back of Dawood. But it was enough for Kris's heart to race, for his stomach to clench.

Dan spread three photos across the table. Two from the bar: the one of Kris, and one of Dawood fleeing, a shot of his face as he'd pushed out of the front door. The third was a photo from Kris's complex, a shot of Dawood entering the stairwell, looking up, about to make the climb to Kris's floor.

A thousand emotions clamored inside Kris, rocked his soul. His heart was exhausted, but his senses were tuned too high, red alert blaring through his subconscious. The world tilted over like a cartwheel, like he was falling, like he was being thrown through the air, collateral from some explosion he hadn't seen.

Dan's fingers grazed the back of his hand. "I know this is difficult for you."

"For you, too."

"This isn't your fault."

"Is it his?" Kris jerked his chin to the photos of his not-dead husband.

"That's what we need to talk about. I think we should look at this from a new angle. If Dawood Haddad were any other person of interest, what would we do?"

"A full workup. Analyze his background, his profile. Any possibility of radicalization and his propensity toward violence. Retrace his steps, get inside his mind. Understand his life, his motivations."

Dan nodded. "Let's do it. Let's just go over the facts."

They started with Dawood's childhood, his home in Benghazi. Dan pulled immigration records, Dawood's mother's history. "She's American, but she converted to Islam and went to Libya, married Abu Dawood Haddad, and then stayed after the revolution that brought Qaddafi to power."

"They were middle class, probably on the upper end. She had money of her own. His father was an imam." Kris closed his eyes, the memories of Dawood's confession of his father's fate mixing with the sands of Iraq and the scent of blood and stink of terror coming back. "His father was murdered by Qaddafi. He was made to watch."

"Jesus..." Dan wouldn't look at Kris. He scribbled notes down, frowning.

Kris filled out what he could. Dawood's flight to Egypt, then America, with his mother. His rejection of Islam, of his Arabness, of everything that he was. His drive to the military, trying to fit in somewhere, trying to find a new family, a new brotherhood. Trying to find a home.

How September 11 had rocked his soul, started the first chink in the dam he'd built within him. Running from his past had turned into a U-turn, running into his future. Into facing down Islamic radicalism, forces of hatred, evil, and torture. How every step of their lives seemed to mirror something of his past, and he'd circled a darkness deep inside himself that Kris had tried to save him from.

He'd thought he had, when they married. The happiest he'd ever seen Dawood had been that month. His proposal, their elopement. Their new house. He'd thought he could heal all of Dawood's anguish with his love, paint new love over old wounds, old cracks in his soul. That if they came together, their souls could fix the broken parts within each of them. That's how Kris had felt, for so long.

Why wasn't he enough for Dawood *now*?

He stuttered and stopped, coming back to himself as Dan cleared his throat. The dull, plain walls of the interrogation room came back into focus, the dust in the corners, the chipped plastic table. He shifted in the hard seat, folding his arms. "That's him," he said, shrugging. "At least, that was him. Up until ten years ago."

Nodding, Dan kept writing. He frowned, wearing that look of concentration Kris saw whenever Dan was puzzling through something, when he was tackling something huge.

"Okay..." Dan tapped his pen against his notepad. He took a deep breath. "There's no one profile of someone who is susceptible to radicalization or terrorism, no one standard identification matrix. But there are commonalities. Recurrent patterns that have cropped up. Haddad... fits a lot of it."

Kris exhaled slowly.

"Most radicalized individuals are second generation Muslims. They've been well integrated into society for the most part, until they experience a break with society. Prison, a shock to the system, something that radically alters their paradigm. Radicalization occurs after, and psychological pressures build within that individual, until an opportunity presents itself to lash out at what the individual believes are 'evil' entities."

"There are exceptions—" Kris started.

"These characteristics are, on the whole, stable." Dan seemed to pity him, for a moment. "Most radicals are 'born-again' Muslims who revert to Islam after a secular life. There is sometimes a shame component, a desire to wipe away some perceived sins of the secular life. But there's a sudden renewal of religious observances. Prayers, rituals, devotions."

Dawood bowing in his apartment, praying to Allah beneath the light of the moon. Leaving Kris's arms to pray. His voice, murmuring in Arabic.

Kris wiped away a tear that hovered at the corner of his eye.

"There's also the radicals' *hegira*. They typically choose to leave their home. Their family, their country. They separate from whatever society they were a part of, remove themselves to another place, a place where they can practice their pure, idealized form of Islam. The Islamic State and al-Qaeda both capitalized on this from the Quran. 'Migrate for the faith'."

"And then move again, for jihad," Kris choked out.

Dan's phone chimed, and he swiped to answer a call. "Ryan? I'm with Kris. We're working. Yes, I know."

Kris wiped another tear with the back of his hand. Had Dawood thought he'd needed to leave? Had he hidden in Afghanistan, radicalizing away from Kris? He should have gone there, should have crawled through the mountains until he found Dawood.

Why was Dawood back, *now*—

Fuck.

He froze. Inhaled, his spine going rigid. "*Jesus*, no..."

"I'll let you know if we build any leads from our profile," Dan said, nodding along as Ryan growled over the line. "Good luck at the FBI." Dan hung up. "Ryan's offsite, heading over to FBI headquarters to work with them on the hunt for Haddad—"

"It's him," Kris whispered. "Al-Khorasani."

"What?" Dan frowned.

"*Al Dakhil Al-Khorasani*. The 'Stranger from Khorasan', on his *hegira*." Kris's voice warped, twisted by a sob rising within him. "That's why he's here..."

Dan's jaw hung slack as he stared at Kris. "You really think he's capable of that?"

"I don't want to." Kris tapped their notes, the pictures. "If you didn't know him. If you were just looking at the profile, what would you think?"

Dan frowned. His jaw still hung open. "He's your husband—"

"Was. He *was* my husband." Kris swallowed. "I don't think I know who he is anymore. Or what he's capable of."

"But you really think he can do *that*? Attack the United States—"

"He fits the profile. He is a stranger, at least to Afghanistan. To the

West now, as well. He comes from Afghanistan. *Khorasan*. Where he's been for almost ten years." Kris scrubbed one hand down his face, held it over his mouth. "And, Al-Khorasani's message? He was with me for all my interrogations. He was with me for Abu Zahawi. I got that part about Muslim pain from *him*. He's the one who said it first," Kris breathed. "In Afghanistan."

Dan stared. His lips moved, but nothing came out.

"It's him. I know it's him. Dawood *is* Al Dakhil Al-Khorasani." Kris shook his head, even as tears built in his eyes, tumbled from his lashes, blurred out Dan and the world. "He's here for a reason. He didn't come back for me. He didn't even know I was alive. Something else brought him here, this week. And he stole my laptop. He *used* me. *Us*, our memory."

Dan's face twisted, heartache and rage battling for dominance as Kris spoke. His hands made fists on the tabletop.

"Al-Qaeda says Al-Khorasani is here on a mission. It's the September eleventh anniversary in two days. He must be here to pull off some kind of attack." Kris covered his face with one hand, trying to hold back his sudden sob. Tears rolled down his cheeks, dripped from his jaw.

His eyes closed. He couldn't look at Dan.

Just hours before, Dawood had *fucked* him.

He'd fucked Kris, and fucked him over, too. Everything he'd said had been a lie. All his whispers of devotion, of his undying love. His words rang hollow and empty, especially falling from the lips of the man who'd stolen Kris's heart and then his laptop, who'd tried to steal CIA secrets.

Who had *used* Kris.

Who was here to attack them all.

"You need to call Ryan," Kris choked out. "We have to stop him."

Dan jumped into action, not looking at Kris as he made his calls, upgraded the APB and put out an alert for Dawood's immediate arrest. He called for all intelligence on Al-Khorasani, everything that had been found, even if it was just a scrap, a rumor, a whisper, next.

"Dan? Have them bring the original audio recording of Al Dakhil Al-Khorasani's speech. Not just the transcript. We'll know then."

He knew it was true, like he'd known he wanted to marry David, but he didn't want to face it, not yet.

His husband was now the CIA's most wanted terrorist.

His heart was screaming, his soul was shredding, and he just couldn't take this anymore.

Dan's hand covered his, silently.

When the door beeped open, Dan drew back. Kris slumped over himself. A man entered, someone Kris had only met in passing. He wore a sharp suit and had even sharper features, cheekbones you could skydive from, olive skin and dark, wavy hair combed back just so. "Dan," he said, nodding hello. His voice was gently accented. It took Kris a second to place the accent. Israel. Tel Aviv.

"You're Noam, right? The FIA from Israel?" Kris sniffed, loudly. He must look like shit.

The man nodded. His eyes flicked over Kris. "You must be Kris Caldera."

Kris swallowed. So even the FIAs had heard about him.

Noam leaned into Dan, one hand on his shoulder, and spoke softly. "My people have a source in Aden. They sent us these." He set a folder down on the table, flicked it open.

Pictures in black and white. Pictures of three men clustered around the port in Aden, Yemen, beside a moored tanker ship. Saying goodbye, hugging, kissing each other on the cheeks. In the center of the group, there was Dawood.

And then, boarding a tanker, waving goodbye to the two Arab men who'd stayed behind.

"Our sources say this man—" Noam pointed to Dawood. "—is the one they called Al-Khorasani."

Dan's gaze flicked to Kris's. He exhaled.

Noam squeezed Dan's shoulder. Their eyes met, and held. "Thank you," Dan said softly. "This is huge." Noam smiled, something softer than just a FIA, a Mossad agent, to a CIA colleague. Kris blinked, and saw Dan and Noam in a different light. Saw the hand on Dan's shoulder, the small smile on Noam's face. How long their gazes lingered.

He cleared his throat, overly loud. Lifted his chin and stared Noam down when Noam started.

"I'll come by your office later, Dan." Noam strode out, never once looking at Kris.

Dan wouldn't look at him, either.

"You two know each other well."

Dan took his time answering. "Remember when I spent those six months in Tel Aviv? On assignment with Mossad? Noam and I became friends then."

Friends. Of course. Something dark slithered in Kris's belly.

Was he *jealous*? Was he fucking jealous of Dan having someone, something other than Kris? For God's sake, he'd fucked Dawood, a terrorist, after telling Dan he would be his. Shame grabbed Kris's spine and yanked, made him curl over. He was shit. He was a shitty, worthless person.

"I'm glad," Kris choked out. "You deserve to be happy."

Dan stared at him. "Two days ago, I thought I was."

"I thought I was, too."

But not because of Dan. No, not that. He'd thought his husband was back, he'd thought Dawood was back, had come back for him, and they were going to live happily ever after. He'd thought all of his most fantastical dreams had come true.

They didn't speak again, not until an analyst badged in with an audiotape of the original Al Dakhil Al-Khorasani file and played it.

Dawood's voice filled the cramped room, blew out the cobwebs and the dust and the doubt. Filled every corner of Kris's heart and soul with the truth, with an endless, silent scream.

*This is Muslim pain.*

"It's him," Kris said. "Al Dakhil Al-Khorasani *is* Dawood. And he's here to attack America."

**McLean, Virginia - September 9, 1910 hours**

It was strange to be driving his truck again.

Kris had kept his truck, for some reason. Kept the beat-up old pickup, the first truck he'd bought after he joined the Army. The truck was over twenty-five years old, a relic of two former lifetimes ago.

It wallowed beneath Kris's building, backed into Kris's second assigned space.

He had it hot-wired in under a minute.

No one would think to look for a truck that was as much a ghost as he was.

It took him an hour, winding through back roads and driving through neighborhoods, avoiding highways and busy suburbs. But, finally, he pulled up to the mosque.

He spun his keys as he walked in. Too late for maghrib prayers, too early for isha. He'd be the only one there.

Perfect.

As he strode in, the imam, kneeling in *dua* and facing east, turned toward him. He wore a dark dishdashi and a white turban, and he smiled as Dawood approached, his hand on his heart.

"*As-salaam-alaikum.*"

"*Wa alaikum as-salaam.*" The imam spread his hands. "Welcome, my brother. The peace and blessings of the Prophet, peace be upon him, be always with you. How can I help you, *habibi*?"

"I have come to speak with you." Dawood breathed in, carefully. "About jihad."

The imam froze. Stared at Dawood, his gaze going cold. Hard.

"I was sent here," Dawood breathed. His hands trembled. He shoved them in his pants, hid them in his pockets. "I was sent to you."

Silence stretched, long enough Dawood heard dust settle in the corners, heard the creak of the sun slant against the roof in the evening light. He waited. His heart, his soul, quaked.

"Sit," the imam finally said. "And let us speak of your jihad."

# 31

## CIA Headquarters, Langley Virginia - September 10, 0400 hours

"Kris?"

Someone was shaking him. He moaned, pressed his face into the throw pillow. Tried to pull the blanket higher.

"Kris, we should get you out of here." A hand cupped his cheek, thumb stroking softly down his skin.

Dan's concerned face swam into focus, shadowed by the fluorescent lights of the interview room. Dan looked like shit. Haggard, exhausted, like he'd run two marathons back to back.

"What time is it?" he groaned.

"Zero four hundred."

"Have you been up all night? Again?"

Dan nodded. "We're trying to find Haddad. The FBI has mobilized and they're working with local police. We've got an APB out, and we put out the images from the bar and your building. The FBI is getting tips but most of them are junk. Wherever he's hiding, he's staying low and out of sight."

Kris pushed himself up and blinked, hard. His eyes felt rubbed raw with sandpaper. He'd finally cried himself to sleep sometime the night before, locked alone in the interview room while the rest of the CIA looked for his husband before Dawood launched some kind of attack against the homeland.

Kris had been up with profilers for most of the previous afternoon and evening, trawling through Dawood's service record, both in the Army and the CIA. Dawood knew enough, between the two units he'd served in, to be deadly, dangerous, devastating. Especially operating on his home turf, able to blend into American society and hide in plain sight.

Some things had been revelatory. Kris had never known Dawood was an expert in explosives. Or that he'd earned the expert marksmanship award in the Army and was practically a sniper.

No one knew what he was planning. Analysts dissected his past, his service record, his childhood, as narrated by Kris. Picked apart the audio file, his statement to al-Qaeda.

"'To have your life dictated by others'," one of the junior analysts had recited earlier. "Could that be rage directed at the institutions he's served? The military? The CIA?"

"We should definitely consider the CIA a target," Dan had said.

Under the table, he'd squeezed Kris's hand.

They all took what they needed from him and left, and Kris had wallowed in his memories and his fears until he'd sobbed, curled up in a ball on the stiff couch, and finally passed out.

Kris tried to shake the sleep away. "Where do I go?" His apartment was a crime scene. Had it been cleared? Was he allowed back? Was he allowed to be anywhere without Dan's supervision? Or was he off to jail, Ryan's eternal Christmas wish come true?

"Do you still have my key?"

Kris nodded. It was still in the pocket of his trench he'd grabbed on the way to the hospital the day before.

"I think you should go to my place. Not... for anything. But you'll be safe there."

"And out of the way."

Dan looked down. Pursed his lips.

"I know. The CIA can't babysit me." Kris heaved himself to his feet. Everything ached. The sobs the night before, the hard, tiny couch. Dawood, around him and in him. His body wanted to quit, wanted to give up and give in. "I'll crash in your spare bedroom."

"I've got to be here for a while longer, but I'll come home this afternoon. At least for a bit."

Kris looked away. He couldn't tell Dan not to come to his own house, couldn't say he'd rather be alone, would rather sit in the dark and mourn for Dawood, for David, for everything they'd had. Try and trace back through the strands of their entwined lives until he could find the place where everything went wrong, where their paths diverged and they'd ended up *here.*

Dan pulled his car keys from his pocket and handed them to Kris. "I'll get a ride home later.

"From Ryan?" Kris snorted. Ryan lived near Dan, was almost a neighbor. As much as they bickered at work, Ryan and Dan were friends. They hit the golf course together, played the back nine and had a few drinks at the clubhouse in their upscale suburban community.

"He's losing his mind." Dan tried to smile. Failed. "We're all terrified, Kris. We don't know enough about the threat. We don't have any idea what he's planning. What his target is."

"If I knew anything, I'd tell you."

"I know you would." Dan reached for him, one hand on his shoulder. It was supposed to be a squeeze, Dan giving him reassurance.

But Kris didn't want reassurance. Or care. Or comfort. He stayed still, not drawing into Dan's offer of an embrace.

Dan sighed. "Go to my place. Shower, get something to eat. Try and relax, as much as you can. We're doing everything we can here, and if we need more from you, I'll call."

He nodded. He couldn't meet Dan's gaze. "See you later."

"Kris..." He was at the door when Dan's voice stopped him. He hesitated, but didn't turn around. "I'm sorry," Dan said softly. "I'm sorry Haddad made this choice."

"Yeah." Kris ripped the door open, fury igniting a sudden bonfire at the base of his heart. "Me fucking too."

---

Dan's electric Bolt was exactly like he was. Practical, tidy, and clean. There weren't any straw wrappers on the floorboards or spare change in the drink holders. The satellite radio was tuned to classical music.

Kris turned off the radio with too much force. He'd rather listen to hardcore rap, blare rock at the top of the stereo, scream with the windows down as he raced down the highway.

But the Bolt's speakers didn't go that loud, and the top speed of the little electric car was not the least bit satisfactory. He locked his elbows and leaned back against the driver's seat, breathing hard in the silence.

Not even the engine made noise. He slammed the accelerator out of the Langley gate, listened to the hum of the battery spin up slowly as it chugged along to its top speed. At least the window was down. Wind rustled through his unkempt hair, messy strands going wild after a night on the couch.

Dan's house was north, off the outer loop in Maryland. He could get there in twenty minutes.

Kris drove right past the exit heading north. Kept driving west. He stared at the horizon, fingers clenching around the steering wheel.

Eventually, he pulled off at a woodsy suburb, winding through the small downtown and through tree-lined streets, the leaves just beginning to turn, to tumble from branches. Autumn dusted the small town, the quaint charm of apple barrels and scarecrows on display in shop windows.

*You could have had this. Walking hand in hand downtown, watching the seasons change. Year after year.*

He kept driving, into the outskirts. Turned into a neighborhood and wound his way to a house at the end of the development, nestled against the woods.

He parked across the street.

A new family lived in his house now. A minivan was in the driveway, and yard signs in the flowerbeds boasted of a little a girl dancing ballet and a boy playing baseball, little plastic silhouettes of suburban pride.

Dawn's first glow shimmered over the house, a halo of glitter, diffused golden light that turned the woods, the memories, soft.

*I should have told the CIA to go fuck themselves. After Iraq. We should have stayed here. We could have been so happy.*

Headlights appeared at the end of the road. Drove slowly toward him. Stopped at the curb, behind the Bolt.

Squinting, he tried to make out the vehicle. The headlights were high, nearly blinding him. A truck, for sure.

The truck's engine died. The headlights winked off.

Jesus *fucking* Christ. That was Dawood's truck.

No one knew he'd kept it. He'd parked it under a tarp in his building's garage and left it, a mausoleum to memories he couldn't get rid of.

His heart pounded. He couldn't move. His fingers stuck to the steering wheel, squeezing. His arms, his body, shook. He stared at the truck through Dan's rearview mirror.

The door opened. A man slid out.

He'd always know that body, that shape.

Dawood.

Kris sagged in the driver's seat. Had Dawood followed him from Langley? Stolen his truck from Kris's building, camped outside Langley and waited, for hours and hours, for him to leave? How had he known Kris was in the Bolt?

Dawood waited, his hands in his pockets, by the truck's door.

He should call this in. He should text Dan *right now*, call for reinforcements. Get the police, the FBI response team, out here immediately.

Instead, Kris slid out of the car. Faced Dawood.

Dawood looked terrible. As terrible as Kris felt, maybe worse. He rocked from foot to foot, and his shoulders were bunched, clenched tight up by his ears. In the morning light, Kris saw stubble, regrowth from where he'd shaved the beard he'd sported only two days before. His eyes were red, bloodshot, like he hadn't slept or like he'd been crying for hours.

"You followed me. Again."

Dawood nodded.

"Why? Think you can steal more intel from me? Newsflash, hon. Thanks to your little snatch and grab, the CIA is probably going to fire me."

Dawood winced. He turned to the truck and curled inward, pressing his forehead to the window, his hands clenching the door. "I didn't— I wasn't—"

"Please, tell me what you *didn't* do. Because from where I'm standing, you fucked me. You used me. And you stole from me."

Dawood hissed, long and sharp. His breath shook.

"What you *didn't* do was tell me the truth." Kris shook his head. "Do you even care about me at all anymore? Even a tiny, tiny bit?"

"I fucking *love* you!" Dawood whirled, exploding, shouting through gritted teeth. He strode toward Kris, reaching for him.

Kris jerked back, out of his range. He put up his fists, dropped into a fighter's stance.

Dawood froze. "I'll never hurt you," he whispered.

"You already have hurt me. More than you'll ever know. Ever understand."

Dawood's expression crumpled.

"Why did you take my laptop? What are you planning?" It was the strangest fucking interrogation of Kris's life, standing in the middle of his old street with his formerly dead husband, the CIA's most wanted terrorist. He still had Dawood's touch on his skin, could still feel the ghost of his kisses on his shoulder, his thigh.

Down the block, a garage door opened. A jogger appeared, a man heading down the block away from them. He did a double take, though, and ran backward, staring. Strangers in the middle of the street were unusual in this neighborhood. It was quiet, serene. Private. That's why they'd picked it, all those years ago.

"Can we go somewhere and talk? I have so much to tell you."

Dawood's words trembled, his voice wound through with something that sounded like regret.

"You can tell the CIA everything you need to."

"No, I can't do that." Dawood dug in his pockets, pulled out a cell phone. "Kris, I am trying to help—"

"By what? Attacking us? What's your target? The CIA? Or something else?"

"No!" Dawood held out the phone. "Read this! Please!"

"You want me to be the one to push the button? You want me to detonate some bomb? God, you're fucking cruel, you know that. Entrap me in your plan, make me the murderer—"

"No! Do you think so little of me?"

"*Yes*. After yesterday? After the past decade? Yes!"

Dawood's lips thinned. He rubbed one hand over his face. He held his phone out again. "Please," he breathed. "Read these texts. You don't have to push anything."

What did Dawood gain from him reading the messages? Would it matter that his prints would be on Dawood's phone? If he called this in in the next few minutes, no. He could say he was reeling him in, playing along. What would he gain from reading the texts of a terrorist? What manipulation was Dawood trying to pull?

He wouldn't know unless he read them.

Kris snatched the phone. The screen was on, texts from a DC number displayed.

*[You were supposed to keep your head down.]*

*I thought it might help. I was trying to gather intelligence. But he doesn't work for CT anymore. His laptop was useless.*

*[There's absolutely nothing that we need from him. He's not important. He's a distraction from our mission. And you're fucking up.]*

The time stamp for the first message was hours after Dawood had fled his apartment. From when he was locked in the polygraph room, being interrogated about Dawood's resurrection, his reappearance at his home.

Who had known, truly known, that Dawood had come to see him? Had stolen his laptop? Who knew *exactly* what Dawood was talking about, without mentioning it at all?

"Who fucking sent these to you?" Fury crested within him. He blinked, hoping the words would rearrange themselves, that something different would be on the screen. That he'd hallucinated the messages, somehow.

"I don't know," Dawood whispered. "That's what I'm trying to find out. Please," he begged. "Can we talk?"

---

They ended up walking the trails through the woods branching off their old neighborhood. *This is how I end up fucking murdered,* Kris thought. *This is how I end up in a ditch, strangled. Nine times out of ten, the murderer is someone the victim knows.*

Dawood kept his hands in his pockets as they shuffled through the trees, through the autumn brush and the dense undergrowth. Pine needles crackled beneath their shoes, the soft carpet of the forest shushing all sounds, drawing everything inward.

"You're Al Dakhil Al-Khorasani."

"Yes," Dawood whispered. "I am."

"You're the enemy, then. You're against us."

"No. Not *me*. There's a mole in the CIA," Dawood said. "Helping al-Qaeda. And they recruited me to join their attack."

"That's fucking ridiculous. No one in the CIA would help al-Qaeda."

"Just like no one would spy for Russia in the Cold War, or for China today?" Dawood swallowed. "It's what you think of me. That I'm one of them. That I'm working for al-Qaeda."

"You fit the profile. And you just admitted you're Al-Khorasani." Kris's heart burned. "You're not CIA anymore. Ten years in the grave means you're not."

"I'm not against you," Dawood insisted. "I'm trying to tell you that."

"You had ten years to tell us. Why should I trust you now?"

Dawood took a deep breath. He kicked a fallen branch, tumbling it end over end through the woods. "Three years ago, the mountain where I was living was bombed. Do you remember the Pakistani-US sweeps of the FATA? The Tribal Agencies?"

Kris nodded, once.

"I was deep in Bajaur. Weeks away from any civilization, Western or otherwise. There were no drones. It was a part of the country we'd never covered in a surveillance net. To get to the base of the mountain, it was a four-day journey. And I was a broken man when I got there. It took months to heal. A year before I was walking right. Another year before I finally shook off the last of the infections. After a while, I made a kind of life there."

"Talking to me through the moon, yes, you said."

"I thought you were dead," Dawood whispered. "And I was too afraid to come out of the mountains and find your grave."

"So you made me live with yours."

Dawood flinched, stayed silent. He stared at the ground. "Allah opens paths before us, guides our lives. We have the choice to follow His path or turn our backs on Him. I spent my whole life, from when I was ten years old until I was dumped on that mountain, with my back to Him." He squinted. "But on the mountain, Allah opened a path before me. I thought I was doing the right thing, walking it. For my sins, for being away from Allah for so long, I had to pay somehow. I had a father again, but I'd lost you. I thought that was my path."

"How does this lead to a CIA mole? To you becoming Al-Khorasani? Get to the point."

"Three years ago, during the campaign to rid the provinces of al-Qaeda, of jihadi fighters, the Pakistanis carpet-bombed the mountains. They obliterated everything. Our homes. Our farms. We lost everything in the bombs, in the fire. And we had to run." Dawood bit his lip. "That's when I lost 'Bu Adnan."

"Where did you go?"

"Down the mountain. We met up with a group of fighters fleeing as well. We were defenseless, helpless. I was in charge, and I didn't know what else to do to protect my people. I joined the fighters."

"Jesus Christ..."

"We made our way over the border, back into Afghanistan. To Kandahar City."

"Kandahar City? You were two miles from a NATO base. You could have come home anytime."

"I had—*have*—a son."

Kris whipped his head around, staring at Dawood, wide-eyed. His jaw clenched, his teeth scraping together. "You said there was no one else!"

"Behroze's family was killed in the bombing. I took him in. Cared for him, like I needed after I lost my father."

Kris strode ahead, leaving Dawood behind in the pine needles and the silence.

Dawood chased after him. "What else could I do? I was looking in the mirror of the darkest, most terrible parts of my life! I saw a boy who was *me*, brokenhearted, broken in his soul! What would you have had me do, Kris? Tell me, what you would have had me do!"

"I don't know!" Kris shrieked, whirling. "But you could have at least told me you were alive! And we could have figured it out together!"

"I thought I was on Allah's path," Dawood breathed. "And at the end of the path... was *you*."

Kris shook his head. Stared over Dawood's shoulder, at the sunlight winking through the trees. "So you raised a son in Kandahar City. A hotbed of jihadism and al-Qaeda in Afghanistan. Did you fight for them?"

"I was one of their imams."

"Jesus *fucking* Christ." Kris buried his head in his palms. "Are you shitting me?"

"You have no idea what it's like." Dawood's voice trembled. "Burying your friends. Burying children you helped care for. Digging bodies out of the rubble of houses and farms that moments ago were standing. You can't see the drones coming. You can't hide from them.

You can't tell when or where death will come, so you just live with knowing every single moment can be your last." He breathed hard, his fists clenching. "Did you know the kids there, they talk about the drones like they're the Hand of Shaytan? Like Shaytan lives in the sky and reaches out, murdering whomever he feels. How can a child know the difference between their loving father and an al-Qaeda fighter? When the father has been by the child's side their entire life, playing soccer and eating dinner together? When the boy's father is everything to him?"

"They're the enemy. They want to kill us. They do kill us."

"And we kill them. *Yallah*, we are *very*, *very* good at killing Arabs and Muslims all over the world. We've made it an art form. A disgusting, hideous art form. There's so much death, Kris. I am exhausted of death. Of seeing everyone I know dying. Of praying the prayers of the dead, washing corpses and shrouding them and burying someone I know, someone I love, every single day!"

"We're fucking tired of it here, too!" Kris hissed. "Five CIA officers in the past year have been killed in Afghanistan! Five! And almost a hundred members of the military! Do you have any sympathy for them?"

"My soul aches for everyone." Dawood reached out. "Didn't yours, once? You saw this pain, once. Muslim pain."

"That was before they took you from me."

Before Dawood had been kidnapped, tortured, and murdered.

No, before Dawood had been kidnapped, tortured, and dumped on a mountain.

Before Dawood had chosen *them* over *Kris*.

Dawood dropped his hand. He kept talking. "Two years ago, an al-Qaeda fighter came to Kandahar City. He'd been Al Jabal's friend. His best friend. The only one Al Jabal ever told about leaving me with his father in the mountains."

"What's this jihadi's name?"

Dawood stayed quiet.

Kris looked away, squinting. Just where were Dawood's loyalties? What was he giving up, and what was he keeping quiet?

"He said he'd been looking for me. That he'd been looking for the CIA spy Al Jabal had been keeping to execute later. To make an example of him, finally. I told him that man was dead and gone. He didn't exist anymore. But he knew who I was. And he wanted me to help their fight, as a sign of loyalty."

"You didn't, did you? You did not take up arms against the United States..."

"No. I never have. He wanted information. He wanted to corroborate what he was being told by a CIA officer who was passing intelligence to him."

"The supposed mole?"

"It's not supposed, Kris. You said you lost five CIA officers in Afghanistan this year. Why do you think that is? Why do you think you've suddenly lost so much ground against al-Qaeda in Afghanistan? Why are ambushes against your forces worse now?"

Kris breathed through his nose. It wasn't possible. It just wasn't possible. But, his mind whirled, calculating who had known about Dawood coming to his home, who had known about that night.

"The mole has been passing along intel to this fighter. Giving him American intelligence, to attack American CIA and military officers."

"Why? Why would someone in the CIA help al-Qaeda? This is not some MICE scenario." MICE was the counterintelligence acronym for possible motivations for a traitor. *Money, Ideology, Compromise, or Ego*. "Al-Qaeda isn't buying any CIA officer's loyalty. Al-Qaeda can barely rub two pennies together! And, al-Qaeda would be hard pressed to come up with compromise material that would pressure a CIA officer to give up as much as you're claiming. They're not the fucking KGB resurrected. They don't have that kind of reach. And the only person with any ideology sympathetic to al-Qaeda and the jihadi movement is *you*."

"I'm not supportive," Dawood snapped. "I hate it. I hate the ideology. I hate the war. I hate the killing. That's not Islam. That's not the path of Allah."

"I thought you were on his magic path!" Kris shouted. "That's why you left me, isn't it? To follow Allah's yellow brick road!"

Dawood turned away, muttering under his breath. He spoke with his back to Kris, after a long moment. "The mole was building his bona fides with this fighter. He was proving that he was the real deal. That he was passing on real intel. Like Hamid, all those years ago, did with us. It was classic tradecraft. One hundred percent CIA. And everything he passed along panned out." Dawood turned. A tear raced from the corner of one eye. "Do you know how sick I was, watching someone in the CIA pass along information that al-Qaeda used to attack Americans?"

"What did you do to stop it, huh?" Kris spread his hands wide, inside his coat pockets, flaring his trench. "Did you seriously just watch Americans die? Do nothing?"

"I've been trying to figure out who it is. Trying to gather evidence. And then I was asked to join their biggest mission. Their grand finale, when the mole will strike against the United States in the name of jihad. The mole said it would be bigger than September eleventh."

Kris stared. His heart pounded again, harder, faster. He swallowed, his throat clenched agonizingly tight.

"*This* is the path I am on, Kris! *This* is Allah's path. All things happen in time. *Endure patiently*, the Quran, says. *With beautiful patience*. Walk the path Allah has laid out for you. If I wasn't kidnapped. If I didn't stay in the mountains. If I didn't join the fighters, become their imam. How would I ever have found out about the mole? Been asked to join in the mole's plan? Be the one person who could stop this?"

It was too much, too much cause and effect, too much destiny, too many ripples in the waters of time and reality. The long years of their lives stretched forward and backward, choices Kris and Dawood had made, apart and together, bringing them to this moment. Afghanistan was a fulcrum, as was September 11. Ghosts lived between his bones, in the hollow spaces of his soul, his broken heart. Ghosts of the past, of his failures. Ghosts of the innocent, ghosts of the damned. Ghosts of Americans and ghosts of Muslims, of Iraqis and Afghans and so many others. He tasted ash in his throat, felt the grit of sand between his teeth.

His knees buckled, his bones, his muscles, letting go of reality, their grip on life that had kept Kris going for a decade, sheer determination in the face of anguish. His hands flew forward, landing in pine needles and dewy ground, fingers scratching through dark dirt. He kneeled, head down, gasping for breath.

It was madness. It was pure, utter madness. Paths through life, choices made to follow destiny or turn your back on it. Ripples in the water, always spreading outward, crashing into each other, cause and effect, action-reaction, always, ever onward.

His mind churned, slowly at first, then faster, sharper.

*A dead ambassador in Afghanistan leads to the Soviet invasion, which leads to the CIA supporting the mujahedeen. Which leads to the collapse of Afghanistan, the rise of the Taliban, of al-Qaeda and Bin Laden. Which leads to September 11, and the war in Afghanistan, and the war in Iraq. Justifications for war build up a terrorist who unleashes an army in the lawlessness that follows. His children, drenched in war, raised on hatred, build an apocalyptic Islamic State, try to bring about the end times. Destroy the entire world.*

*Promises of retribution on both sides, blood for blood, an endless, agonizing war without end.*

How had everything gone so irrevocably, irretrievably wrong? Was there anything at all to believe in? Any paths, any destiny, any gods? Was there any way forward from this moment? From Dawood telling him it was paths and destiny that brought them to these woods, through the tangled refuse and the agony of the last decade?

It was fucked up, all of it. It was fucked beyond belief, and he hated it, hated every word Dawood spoke.

But most of all, he hated how he wondered if it was *true*.

"Kris..." Dawood hovered before him, crouching in the dirt. His hands fluttered in front of Kris, uncertain. "*Habibi*..."

"Don't," Kris spat. "Don't fucking call me that. I'm not your love."

"You are," Dawood breathed. "You always have been. Always will be."

Kris pushed himself to his feet. Dirt clung to his palms, his knees.

Stained his skinny jeans. "If what you're saying is true, then what the fuck is this big plan? And who is the mole?"

"I don't know. I'm trying to find out. He arranged transport to the US for me two weeks ago—"

"Through Yemen."

"Yes. Through Yemen. A cargo ship, and then a human smuggler up the Chesapeake. This phone was waiting for me in a locker at the wharf." Dawood sighed. "I've been trying to find out who he is. He says I have a partner for this attack I'm supposed to execute."

"Tomorrow? On the anniversary of nine-eleven?"

Dawood nodded. "I haven't met my partner yet. And I still don't know who the mole is." He winced. "I stole your laptop because I thought I could find him. I thought I could figure out who he was if I looked through the CT mission logs, saw who was in charge of those Afghanistan operations. I thought I could prove who he was."

"I'm not in CT anymore. I haven't been since Hamid."

"I didn't know," Dawood whispered. "And I didn't find anything on your laptop. I'm sorry."

"Why didn't you tell me? Why didn't you say something to me? Why did you insist on doing this alone?"

"Once I found out you were alive, I freaked. For two years, I've been solely dedicated to this path. To finding the mole. Taking him out. But you... You derailed everything. At the end of the path, you were supposed to be there. We were supposed to be reunited in Paradise. That's what kept me going. It was okay if I died stopping the mole, if this was my end. Exposing him and preventing this attack. Because I'd be with you again. But—" He shuddered. "Here you are. And you look at me with so much hate in your eyes..."

"Whose fault is that?"

Dawood looked down. "I don't know if I would do anything differently," he whispered. "Because I believe I am on this path to stop the mole. To save lives. I am following Allah's path, I know I am. But I've lost you, again." A sob broke through his voice, shattered his words.

"What proof do you have that this, this story, any of what you're saying, is true?"

"Just these texts. But if I can get into the CT database, I can check the mission logs. I can find out who was in charge of those operations. Who had the knowledge, the intel, to pass on to—" He came up short, not saying the jihadi's name.

Kris rolled his eyes. "You want me to believe this, but you won't say the name of your jihadist buddy?"

"In a way, they became brothers to me," Dawood breathed. "Can you blame me for not wanting to sign their death warrants? I've seen too many drone strikes. I've buried too many of my brothers."

"You sound just like them."

"I'm not. I swear to Allah, I swear on us, I'm not."

Kris paced away from Dawood, shaking his head. He was going to be sick. He was going to vomit until he threw up his heart, his soul. "What exactly is it that you want from me?"

"You wanted me to tell you the truth? That's what I'm doing. I'm trusting you. I'm asking for your help. I'm asking for you to help me find this mole. Help me search the CT mission logs—"

"Jesus, Dawood, you want me to give you classified information now? You want me to become the mole, become the traitor!"

"No! I want to stop him! My heart is broken over what this mole has done. I'm sick—"

"We all are," Kris snapped. "You don't have the monopoly on suffering. You don't own pain."

"Who would have access? Who has access to the drone program? To the Afghanistan clandestine operations? To mission intelligence and to military operations?"

It was only a handful of people. Director Edwards, obviously. The deputy director, George. The director of operations, Ryan. The director of CTC, Dan. The head of SAD, Wallace. The Afghanistan station chief. A few others, analysts and deputy directors who crossed agency lines, liaised with the military.

Who of all of them had also known Dawood had been in Kris's apartment, hadn't kept his 'head down'?

"I can't get you that information. I'm not in CT anymore. And, thanks to your little stunt with my laptop, I'm banned from the building without an armed escort."

Dawood wilted. His spine seemed to crack in half, his entire soul drooping as he pitched forward.

"But there might be another way."

**University Park, Maryland - September 10, 1140 hours**

Kris led Dawood to Dan's house, cursing himself and his fucking stupidity the whole drive.

Dawood parked down the street, well out of sight, and walked casually to Dan's, meeting Kris at the front door. He eyeballed the key in Kris's hand. "You have a key?"

Kris glared. "I don't think you have any business questioning my personal life."

"The other night, he was at your place—"

"And my actions hurt him very badly." Kris turned the key in the lock, shoved Dan's door open. "I shouldn't have slept with you again."

"That night meant everything to me," Dawood whispered.

Kris turned his back on Dawood. "It was a mistake." He jerked his chin to Dan's office. "This way."

Like all senior CIA officers, Dan had a secured home office, modified by the agency's techs to transmit classified data between Langley and his home. Emergencies arose at all hours, and sometimes there wasn't time to get to Langley. Dan's home office was soundproof, swept for bugs once a month, and had a dedicated, encrypted data line going to his computer.

And he had full access to the CIA's database.

"Stand there." Kris pointed to the center of the office, the center of Dan's throw rug. "Don't move. Don't touch anything."

Dawood fidgeted as Kris slipped behind Dan's desk, logged in to his computer.

"It's time for noon prayers," Dawood said softly. "May I pray here?"

Kris shrugged. "I don't care. As long as you don't leave that spot."

Dawood's soft voice filled the room, his deep Arabic swimming around Kris's head, into his soul and around his heart. He bowed, prostrated. Recited from the Quran.

Prayed for Kris, for his happiness. For his soul.

Kris slammed Dan's keyboard on the desk, typed hard and fast. How dare Dawood pray for him. How dare he. After everything, how dare Dawood even breathe his name, think of him at all.

Mission logs appeared, two years' worth of Afghanistan operations, a seemingly endless file. Kris sighed. He'd have to sort them, somehow. He scanned for the operations that had failed. Operations where their officers had been killed.

Was it actually possible? Was any of Dawood's story believable at all?

Could a CIA officer ever work for al-Qaeda?

If he thought it was possible for Dawood, what made it any less believable if the mole were sitting at Langley right now?

Did he have a duty to check it out, explore the possibility?

Or did he have a duty to turn Dawood in, hand his ass to the FBI for interrogation? If a mole did exist, wouldn't someone other than them, a fallen CIA officer and the CIA's most hated, be better equipped to find said mole?

His cell phone vibrated in his pocket at the exact same time the search results came back. *Five missions with dead CIA officers.* He pulled out his cell.

Dan had texted. *Hey. Bad news. There's a fire in Aden, in Yemen. Looks like an oil refinery was deliberately lit up in the middle of the night.*

Kris looked up. Stared at Dawood.

Lines from the hadith came back to him, slammed into him like a shotgun to the heart: *And a fire will burn forth in Yemen, driving the people to the place of judgment, the final reckoning.*

He texted back. *[ It's one of the signs of the Islamic apocalypse. ]*

*Yeah. We think it's part of a coordinated attempt to make whatever attack is planned look like part of the Islamic end times.*

His vision swam. His fingers scraped against Dan's desk,

scratching in the stillness. Dawood's Arabic fluttered, the rise and fall of his prayers moving in a careful rhythm.

"Dawood," he said slowly. "Who is in Yemen?"

Dawood froze.

"Who is in Yemen? Who are you working with?"

"Don't ask me that. Please."

"'And a fire will burn forth in Yemen, driving the people to the place of judgment'," he recited. "There's a fucking fire burning in Yemen right now! And you left two of your jihadi brothers there, in Aden! Who the fuck is in Yemen, Dawood? What aren't you telling me?"

"I have prayed with them!" Dawood cried. "I have lived with them for years, shared tears and joys with them!"

"And I'm just your husband! And this is just your home! Your country! Goddamnit, you haven't told me the truth!" Jesus, he'd brought an al-Qaeda operative into Dan's *house*, into Dan's CIA home office.

He should have called it in as soon as he'd seen the truck. He should never have listened to Dawood, to his lies. He was such a sucker. Dawood knew exactly how to play him.

"They're just supposed to set the fire! I was the one sent to America. I was the one who was supposed to carry out the attack. Me, and me alone, with the mole. I didn't want the others to die! Don't ask me to send them to their deaths!" Dawood started toward him.

"Stop!" Kris bellowed. Lightning fast, he reached into Dan's desk, drew his hidden pistol. "Do not come any closer!"

Dawood froze. His eyes went wide, perfect circles. He held up his hands. "I swear, I'm not lying to you, *ya rouhi*."

"Shut up!" Kris's hands trembled. "Just shut up. I don't want to hear your voice."

What did he do? What the fuck did he do? If he called the FBI, brought them here, he'd implicate Dan in his fucked-up decisions. Drag him into his shit, again.

Damn it, he had no fucking idea what to believe.

Dawood was in front of him, living, breathing, aching. Talking about conspiracies and begging for Kris's help, but he had no proof, nothing except his words and a few scattered texts.

What if those were faked? What if he'd sent them to himself? How easy was it to buy a burner cell phone, create the image of a conspiracy? Convince Kris to get him intel from the CIA's mission logs with a wild story that pulled on Kris's heartstrings.

Where was the truth? Could he believe the words of a dead man, a ghost who had chosen to walk away from him, follow a path that split them apart?

He'd always just wanted to know the truth, know what had happened to his David.

But the truth was unbearable, impossible to hold in his heart.

And what Dawood said, the possibilities he presented...

Kris didn't know how to reconcile the past and the man he knew with his broken heart, his shattered soul. How to take Dawood's confession, his pleas and his reaching out for Kris after ten years and one night and a morning that had broken Kris in ways he didn't know he still *could* break.

He hadn't known that he could point a gun at the love of his life, either, but—apparently—he could.

Could he pull the trigger? If Dawood moved, if he tried anything?

Were there any right decisions in the world anymore? Between love and hate, destiny and choice, death and life and thousands of ghosts, was there anything left that was *right*?

Dawood was still frozen, staring at Kris. His face had gone blank. Acceptance lay heavy in his gaze, the weight of fate and destiny across his soul. "I love you," he whispered. "I love you so much. You have always been the moon inside my darkness."

Kris blinked fast. Tears burned his eyes, his soul. "You have ten minutes to run. Get as far from here as you can. Forget your plans. Forget your apocalypse. Forget everything you came here for. It's the only thing I'll give you. You have *one* chance to get away. Because in ten minutes, the entire world will be chasing you."

"I'm not going to stop. I'm going to find this mole somehow. And

I'll do everything I can to stop this attack. Whatever it is. Whatever they want me to do. I won't do it. I'll die first."

"Get the fuck away from here, Dawood. Go back to Yemen. To Afghanistan. To your son. Just get the fuck away from here, and from me."

"That's not the path I'm on. I must follow the path Allah has laid out for me. I must."

"When they find you, they're going to kill you. You're listed as 'extremely dangerous' in the APB. They will execute you. Just get out of here!" he screamed through gritted teeth.

"I swore to protect the homeland," Dawood breathed. "I swore with you, in your arms, sixteen years ago. *Bismillah*, I will never give that up." Dawood looked away. Closed his eyes. "Kris... after this... after everything... Will you be happy? With— with Dan?"

His throat closed. He couldn't breathe. Couldn't speak. The pistol shook in his clenched hands.

"*In shaa Allah*, all I want for you is to be happy, *ya rouhi*. After me. After everything. If that's Dan..." Dawood hissed, like he'd taken a knife to the heart. "I *love* you. Always."

"Go," Kris whispered. "Go now. You have nine minutes."

# 32

## University Park, Maryland - September 10, 1235 hours

How had it all come to this?

Kris sat in the dark corner of Dan's office, leaning against the cherrywood paneling. He clutched his phone, his forehead resting on the edge of the plastic case. Dan's gun lay on the carpet beside him.

Each breath trembled, made his body quake. He couldn't stop shaking, couldn't get himself under control. He had to move. He had to get up, call Dan. He had to stop Dawood.

All he wanted to do was sit in the dark, in the silence. If he did nothing, could he fuck anything up anymore? Hadn't every decision he'd made just made *everything* worse?

Maybe Ryan was right. He should have been locked up. He was a public safety hazard. He was a mosquito light for Dawood, just like Dawood was for him.

Hopefully the FBI would catch Dawood. Had already caught him.

Hopefully Dawood was three counties away by now, running for his life. Trying to get away from the US, back into the arms of human smugglers. Maybe by this evening, he'd be on a boat back to Yemen.

Would he ever know if Dawood made it out of the US? Or would his husband be an eternal question mark in his mind, forever a *what if?*, the bitterest regret of his life.

*You should have died. You should have died in the back of that car. You should have turned to ash. You shouldn't have turned into* this.

No. He didn't believe that. Could he ever truly wish for the love of his life, his husband, to be *gone*? Wasn't it better for him to be on the opposite side of the planet, changed, different, but alive?

Ten years *changed* a man.

Vibrating shattered the silence, nearly split his skull in two. His teeth clattered as his jaw clenched. He sat back, staring at his phone.

Dan was calling him.

It was only a matter of time. He swiped his phone on. "Dan?"

"*Kris? Are you okay? I just saw the updated intel on Haddad. An anonymous sighting was reported in my neighborhood. Did he follow you? Are you at my house? Are you safe?*"

He pressed his lips together, trying to keep his sob in.

"*Kris? Talk to me. Are you okay? What's going on? Is he— Jesus, is he* there*? Do I need to send the police?*"

"No," Kris whispered. "Not anymore."

"*Not... anymore?*"

His sob exploded out of him, a rush of rage and sorrow, grief that eclipsed his heart. He buried his face in one hand, curling over himself. "Dan, I'm so sorry. I fucked up. Again."

Silence. "*What happened?*"

"Not on the phone," he breathed. "Just... get everyone searching in this area. I called in that tip. He was here."

"*Ryan is on it. He's liaising with the FBI on this. He said he's got a whole unit about to descend on the area. If Haddad is anywhere around there, we're going to flush him out. And we're going to get him.*" Dan sighed. "*Kris,* talk *to me. Why was he there? At my house?*"

"Not on the phone," Kris repeated. "I'll drive back in. I have to tell you in person. What he told me."

"*You* talked *to him?*"

"Not on the phone, Dan. I'm on my way. I'll meet you there."

---

He raced back to Langley as fast as Dan's little electric car could go. His mind zipped from Dawood to Dan and back, from Dawood's trembling confessions, his insistence that he was doing the right thing, to Dan's text about Yemen. About the fire. And Dawood's refusal to give up his brothers.

Was it the bonds of brotherhood only? Dawood not wanting to lose another life, no matter whose life it was?

Once, hadn't he thought the same? Hadn't he argued for the same? Argued for compassion, for humanity, for Zahawi, a man who would rather Kris be dead than interrogating him. That touch of humanity, though, had won out over brutality. *We're all just human.* Could he fault Dawood for not giving up his brothers to their death?

Or was the refusal to give up his brothers in Yemen his Achilles' heel? The weak point to Dawood's master plan, the coordinated confusion of Kris's soul?

*Whose side are you on?*

*Or are you on your own side now?*

Dan met him outside Langley, pacing by his assigned parking spot as he talked on his cell. Kris heard him say goodbye to George as he jumped out of Dan's little car.

Dan grabbed him, pulled him close. Wrapped both arms around him and sighed into his neck. "Are you okay? You're shaking."

"I don't know." Kris gripped Dan's elbows. His fingers felt like claws. He was still trembling. Maybe he'd never stop.

"Did he hurt you?"

"No." Kris swallowed. "He never touched me."

Dan exhaled hard, squeezing Kris against him. Kris could feel his relief, the deluge of it. He pulled back. "We have a big problem. Dawood, he followed me because he said he had to tell me what was really going on."

Dan frowned. "What do you mean? What did he say?"

"He said there's a mole in the CIA. Someone who has been feeding al-Qaeda intelligence. Information on operations, for over two years. That he was brought in by al-Qaeda to verify what this mole was giving them."

Dan turned bone white, every speck of color draining from his face. His jaw dropped. "Holy fuck," he whispered. "Who?"

"He doesn't know. He's been trying to find out." Kris paced away from Dan, one hand on his forehead. "That's why he stole my laptop. He was trying to find out who had been in command of the Afghanistan missions where we lost our officers this past year. And who was the lead on the other missions that went sideways. That were sabotaged from within."

"You don't have that access anymore."

"He didn't know. He's... been gone a while."

Dan blinked. A breeze would have knocked him over. "What proof did he have? How do you know this is real?"

"I don't know," Kris whispered. "All he had was a cell phone number, someone who has been giving him instructions over text. He says the texts are from the CIA mole. But..." He shook his head. "We have to find that cell phone. Who's been texting him."

"I've got to call Ryan. He's with the FBI. They're the ones who can look this up. You know the CIA can't do anything on American soil."

"Dan, wait. If there is a mole, it's someone high up. Someone who could access all the intelligence in Afghanistan, across the drone program, joint military missions, and dig into our clandestine program, our SAD officers. Who fits that description? Who has that kind of access?"

"You think it's Ryan?"

"Only a handful of people have that access. And, think about it. Why do you think Ryan has been on a hair trigger for years? Stress from a double life? Trying to keep his spying for al-Qaeda secret?"

"Ryan *hates* al-Qaeda," Dan breathed. "Why would he spy for them? Pass along CIA secrets?"

"I don't know!" Kris snapped. "I don't fucking know! I don't even know if Dawood told me the truth or not! He's giving me mixed signals. Wants my help one moment, but is keeping secrets the next.

When I brought him to your house, he wouldn't even tell me the names of his Yemeni brothers!"

Dan froze. "When you *what*?"

Fuck. Kris gritted his teeth, groaned. Clenched his hands into fists and looked away, shaking his head.

"I thought he *followed* you to my house. Now you're saying you brought him..."

"I went to our old house first. Just to see it. I was being... maudlin, I don't know. He followed me there. We went into the woods. Talked."

Dan cursed. "And then you brought him to my house?"

"You weren't supposed to know that. I wanted to keep you out of this."

"Why did you bring him there? Why did you bring a possible al-Qaeda agent into my house?"

"I... was going to look up the al-Qaeda mission logs for him."

Dan stilled. "Did you?"

"I looked them up. I didn't give him anything, though. I pulled your gun and made him leave."

"You let him go?"

Kris looked away. He nodded, once.

"Jesus Christ..." Dan closed his eyes. Seemed to try to center himself, pull himself together. "Okay. Let me run through this. We may have a mole in the CIA. You let an al-Qaeda agent into my home. Almost passed along critical Top Secret intelligence. And then you let the nation's most wanted terrorist go. We believe there's an attack being planned for tomorrow, and we don't know anything about it." He opened his eyes. Sighed. "But all I can think about is how to keep you out of jail. Damn it, Kris."

"I'm sorry."

"Were there any laws you didn't break? Any you left that I could try to work with?"

Kris looked down.

"What did you find in the mission logs?"

"Nothing useful. The missions were all headed up by either you or Ryan or Wallace, or signed off by George. There wasn't a pattern.

Nothing at all that broke operational regulations. Nothing that screamed *mole*."

"If there is a mole, whoever it was probably didn't authorize the missions. They probably went into the logs after. Which means we have to inspect the mission access logs. See who looked at the intel, at the mission specs before they went south."

"And we have to track that cell number, the one texting Dawood."

Dan pulled out his cell phone. "I'm calling Ryan. I know you don't trust him. But, Kris. I *do*. Trust me, okay?"

"And if he is the mole?"

"If Ryan is the mole, then this phone call will turn the heat up. He'll know we're on to him. He'll start making mistakes. Try to cover his tracks. Try to get out before the net closes around him. Because while he's supposed to be looking up the number, I'll be looking into the mission logs. See who pulled them, and when. If it is Ryan, we'll know soon. One way or another."

"If it is Ryan..." Kris's voice cracked. "He's already ordered the FBI to consider Dawood extremely dangerous. What if he orders the response teams to shoot on sight? What if he executes Dawood?"

"If Haddad is the only one who can corroborate this, then he probably will give that order. Or, he'll make sure Haddad goes down in whatever he's planning for tomorrow." Dan stared. He licked his lips. "You believe Haddad?"

Kris exhaled. His breath, his body, trembled, again. "I don't know what to believe," he whispered. "If I believe Dawood told the truth, then I'm hoping someone has betrayed us. Someone at the heart of the CIA. Someone who knew Dawood was alive and who kept that secret from all of us. From me. But, if I believe he's lying... Then he's trying to play me, craft a conspiracy that he thinks I'll buy. Why? To send us chasing after our own tails? Turn us against each other? Distract us while he works on his grand plan?"

"Give me the phone number," Dan said softly. "We'll know soon enough."

Kris waited as Dan dialed Ryan's number, as Dan pressed his lips together, waiting for the call to connect.

He could barely breathe. His throat was closing, his lungs refusing to fill. He was drowning, drowning in conspiracy, in potentiality, in possibilities of betrayal, each darker than the next.

"Ryan? It's me." Dan waited, staring at the pavement. "Look, we have a situation. I'll come brief you in a few. But right now, I need you to run a search on a cell number for me, okay? It's tied to Haddad. I'll explain more in a bit." He waited again, then recited the number Kris showed him. Kris had written the number on a sticky note as soon as Dawood had fled Dan's house. His fingers rubbed over the square of paper, over and over. "We need to know who owns that phone. And where it is." Dan listened for another moment, nodding along with whatever Ryan said. "Okay. I'll see you soon."

He stared at Kris as he hung up. "Kris, I don't know what to say," Dan said softly. "I don't know what to think. What to believe."

"I don't either. If he's still playing me, then I'll know for sure the man I loved is dead. That there's nothing left of him. But…" His voice went high and strained. "If there's a one percent chance that what he's saying is true…"

Dan grimaced, shaking his head at the 'one percent doctrine', the guiding philosophy of the War on Terror. That philosophy had been an impossible standard, a weight that had broken the CIA's back. They could never cover all the possibilities, all the permutations. They'd never imagined September 11. They'd never imagined Hamid.

How could they have ever imagined this? A CIA officer helping al-Qaeda. The mole was either someone inside Langley or was Dawood himself.

But someone had broken. Someone had fallen. Someone had switched sides.

Was it his husband?

"Dan, I owe him this, at least. He's my husband. *Was.* I don't know."

At Kris calling Dawood his *husband*, Dan's expression twisted, a flash of pain bursting across his features. He took a deep breath, and it vanished. "I'm going to brief George, too. And Wallace. Same basic idea. If the mole is one of them, we'll know when they start covering their tracks."

He couldn't argue with Dan's plan. It was one of the fundamentals of counterterrorism investigations. Pressure the target, provide them with enough information to get their paranoia going. Watch for after-effects, for their moves to get sloppy.

If there really was a mole. If this wasn't just an elaborate hoax. Dawood's last mindfuck.

"What can I do?" Dan said softly. "For you?"

"I don't know," Kris breathed. "You're the only one I trust."

God, he *wanted* to trust Dawood. He wanted to fall back through time to when he knew Dawood better than he knew himself, when he could understand exactly what Dawood thought and felt, more than he knew his own thoughts and feelings.

"Do you want to stay here?"

"At Langley? Locked up in headquarters like a prisoner? Fuck no."

"Listen to me." Dan took both of Kris's hands in his own. "*Please.* Drive straight back to my house. Lock all the doors, all the windows. Stay. There. Haddad is fixated on you. He might come for you again now that we're closing in on him. He might try and do something." Dan swallowed. "I should get the police to escort you back home, get a patrol unit to sit at the curb. Watch over you. Keep you safe—"

"No. I'm okay. I'll be okay. I'll go straight back. There's a huge police presence in your neighborhood now. I'll be safe. And, I've done enough to fuck everything up. I'm done."

Dan's hand cupped his cheek. He stroked his thumb over Kris's cheekbone, stared into his eyes. In front of the whole CIA and anyone who could be looking, Dan pressed his lips to Kris's, kissing him gently, sweetly.

Kris felt nothing at all.

"Call me if you need anything," Dan said. "Anything."

"Stay safe." Kris's soul yo-yoed, and suddenly, Dawood was standing in front of him, cupping his cheek, smiling sweetly. It was right before the Hamid op and Dawood was about to head out, pick up Hamid, start the mission that would be the end of the line for both of them. Blinking, Kris shook his head. Dawood disappeared and Dan reappeared, gazing at him, concern and an ache that looked like love etched into the backs of his eyes.

Kris's heart screamed, his soul rubbed raw, desperate and aching and wanting. He felt the ghost of Dawood's hands on his body, felt Dan's touch like a brand. He stepped back, out of Dan's hold. "I'll text you when I get to your place."

Dan shoved his hands in his pants pockets. "We'll figure this out. I promise."

Kris walked backward to Dan's car. He should say something, should tell Dan he believed in him, that he knew Dan could do this. He should thank Dan for always, always being there. He should say something, anything, before he drove away.

But his tongue stuck to the roof of his mouth and his throat closed and the words just wouldn't come. As he slid into Dan's car, it felt, for a moment, like the Hamid op all over again, except this time *he* was driving away and calamity would befall those left behind. Dan, the CIA, anyone, *everyone* else.

Had he done enough? Had he done too little?

What was the right choice, the right action?

Dan raised one hand, a silent goodbye, as Kris backed out of his parking spot.

He floored the little electric car out of Langley.

Dread followed him every mile of the drive, suffocating him inside Dan's silent car.

September 11 was only 11 hours away.

### Brentwood, Washington DC - September 10, 1635 hours

*[ You fucked up big time. ]*

Dawood stared at his phone. The number, his contact, was texting again.

*[ You fucked up big time, and now everyone is hunting for you. ]*

*I had to see him one last time.*

Dawood tossed his phone on the bed and went back to shoving

clothes into his duffel, grabbed his toothbrush. He had to hide. The motel wasn't safe anymore. He could feel long stares on his back, eyeballs digging into his skin, lingering looks that lasted too long. Even in Brentwood, where the residents despised the police with a sizzling, searing hatred, al-Qaeda operatives were *not* welcome.

*[ I've worked too long, sacrificed too much, to call this op off. Get to the safe house. Stay there. Don't fuck with Caldera again. You are fucking this up. Didn't you swear you wanted to watch America burn? Wanted to make everyone suffer like you did? ]*

He grabbed his cell, pulled his duffel over his head. He had a new baseball cap and clothes he'd lifted from a street cart. *I wish that everyone could feel an ounce of what Muslims feel. Understand the depth of Muslim pain, of our anguish.* He hesitated. Closed his eyes, for a moment, exhaled. *Should we call this off? Postpone it?*

*[ Nothing is getting called off. The op goes forward. If you're not in, then it goes on without you. ]*

Dawood cursed, a breath of Arabic and a plea to Allah rolled into one. *Of course I am in. In shaa Allah, this will succeed.*

*[ Then quit fucking up. Get to the safe house. ]*

His contact texted him an address, deep in southeast DC, another hard-edged neighborhood where the locals didn't look too closely at what strangers were doing. It would be slow going on foot, dodging cameras and police, all the way across the city.

*When do we meet?*

*[ Tonight. Your partner is here. You'll get your mission together. ]*

His stomach clenched. *Alhamdulillah.*

*[ If you can keep your head down. If you can make it to the safe house. If you're caught, you'll be shot in the face. And this will go on without you. ]*

*I'll make it. I swear to Allah I will. Nothing will stop me now. In shaa Allah.*

Dawood shoved his phone in his pocket and slipped out of his motel room.

*You must follow the path Allah has laid out for you.*

He had a long walk in front of him, and prayers to pray. The prayers of the dead, of the martyr, before their sacrifice.

He was ready.

He'd wondered, once, how he'd feel in this moment. How he'd face himself as he prepared. What thoughts, what regrets, he'd have. He thought he'd console himself with thoughts of Kris, dreams of their future in Paradise, or being reunited at last. But...

In a way, Kris *had* been at the end of his path. They'd had a goodbye, of sorts. He'd tasted Kris's soul, lingered over his lips, felt his body like the sun breaking across the desert of his barren life once more. That was the end, for them. Kris would no longer be with him in the next life, not after this. He had his own path to walk, his own future to forge.

But these memories, the last touch of his love, would be enough to sustain him for eternity.

Goodbye, *ya rouhi.*

# 33

**University Park, Maryland - September 10, 2200 hours**

His cell phone lingered in a puddle of light, a circle falling from Dan's bucket lights hanging over the breakfast bar. The house was dark, eerily silent, other than the kitchen.

Silence, from the CIA. From the FBI. From Dan.

No breaking news alert, no police shootings reported on the news. No press release of a wanted terrorist arrested in DC, a plot foiled.

Was there nothing to report? Had they discovered nothing?

Or were they keeping everything under wraps? Had Dawood been shot dead somewhere in the street already? Or taken alive, brought in for interrogation?

Was the mole real?

Had Dan uncovered their trail?

Had the mole slipped up?

He'd said he'd stay at Dan's, stay out of the way. Not interfere. *Again.*

But a phone call was okay, right? Just to check in. Just to see how the investigation was going. If Dawood was...

If he called Dan, Dan would take it as him checking up on him.

Could he call Dan and ask about his husband, the wanted terrorist? Ask if Dawood was okay? If he was right or wrong, if there was a mole or if Dawood was a master manipulator.

How would Dan react to him asking about his husband?

He tried to care. He really did. But—

Maybe he and Dan needed some time apart, after this. Or maybe he needed time apart from the world, away from everybody.

Where was Dawood? Was he alive still?

Had everything he'd told Kris been a lie?

Damn it, his mind was racing in circles, going around and around and around, over and under itself, tying his soul in knots.

He grabbed his cell, dialed Dan's number.

He had to know.

Dan's phone rang and rang. Kris waited, one foot swinging off the barstool, his toes tapping out a too-fast rhythm. Surely Dan was busy. He couldn't just drop everything for Kris.

But he always had before.

Kris hung up when Dan's phone rolled over to voicemail, his calm voice politely asking the caller to leave a message.

He'd wait a few minutes, then call again. Or Dan would call back.

Five minutes later, he dialed Dan's number a second time.

Again, no answer.

He called the CIA switchboard next, asked to be patched to Dan's office. Ringing, endless, endless ringing. That drone, that buzz, would live in his brain, he thought, a drill bit behind his eyes. Where the fuck was Dan?

"*Hello?*" Finally—

But, that wasn't Dan's voice. His deputy answered, her voice ragged and fraying at the edges.

"Shannon? Where's Dan?"

"*I don't know,*" she sighed. "*I haven't seen him since this afternoon. He said he had to go talk to Ryan.*"

*No.* Dread crawled up Kris's soul, slithered around his bones like ice creeping out of the ground. "Have you spoken to him at all? Been able to get a hold of him?"

"*No, no one has. I can't find him. We* need *him, though. We're getting nowhere in this investigation*!"

"What about the mission logs?"

"*What mission logs*?"

Oh God. Kris crumpled, both elbows on the countertop as he held his forehead in one hand. The mole, he must have *gotten* to Dan. He'd stopped him before he could do anything. Jesus, was Dan even alive, still?

*Who* had Dan told? *Who* had he called?

Ryan, right in front of him.

And he said he'd brief George after.

It *had* to be one of them, Wallace or Ryan or George.

Wallace hated his guts, blamed him for the Hamid op and wanted him out of SAD. The guy was an asshole, was no doubt begging Ryan to fire him—

Memories snapped through his mind, shotgun blasts of time smearing behind his eyelids. Ryan, watching Zahawi die in a puddle of water and blood, frozen immobile. Ryan, always on the edge in Afghanistan. The rage he'd nurtured, the darkness that hovered around him. How he'd *hated* Kris, always. The way he seemed two steps from flying apart.

And, the Hamid op. He'd pinned everything on Kris, had let Kris take the entire fall, all on his own. Had he known, even then, that Dawood was alive? Had he killed Al Jabal to tie up loose ends, keep his secret safe?

How long had Ryan known Dawood was alive?

Had looked Kris in the face and lied to him?

How long had he been planning this?

What had Ryan done with Dan?

"Shannon, have you heard from Ryan at all?"

"*No, he's not at Langley. He left earlier today.*"

"I gotta go." Kris hung up on her confused questions. His trembling fingers hesitated over his phone.

He knew who he had to call. They always called each other when it came down to the wire. That was what they did, wasn't it?

He thought he'd never call him again, not after everything, but...

History was a cruel predictor of the future.

Kris pulled up George's cell number, pressed the call button before he could hesitate.

George picked up on the second ring. Dead air hovered over the line before he spoke. "*Caldera*?"

"George, did Dan call you today? Did he brief you on a cell phone number you had to track? On a possible mole within the agency?"

"*Kris, slow down. What are you talking about? Did Dan do* what?"

If Dan had briefed George, George would have known *exactly* what he was talking about. Goddamnit, Ryan had gotten to Dan, somehow.

*Trust me, Kris,* Dan had said. *I trust him.*

"George, Dawood came to me this morning, again." *And damn it, you were right. You were right, Dawood. And I pointed a gun at your face.*

"*What*?"

"He said there is a mole in the CIA that he is trying to uncover. Someone passing along information to al-Qaeda. That he's still with us, and is working against the mole, trying to uncover their identity. This mole has been feeding information to al-Qaeda, in Kandahar City, for over two years. They arranged for Dawood to come to the US and be the front man for this attack. It's the mole's false flag attack. He's pinning everything on Dawood, but this is coming from a mole. Someone who has been working against us for over two years. He's why we've lost those officers this year. Why everything's gone to hell in Afghanistan."

Speechless, George sputtered on the other end of the line.

"I called it in, George. I told Dan everything. The mole could only be a few people. Ryan, you, Wallace... Dan wanted to try and turn up the heat, flush the mole out. Put pressure on him, see what he'd do. So Dan called Ryan. I watched him call Ryan and tell him to run a search on the cell phone that was texting Dawood information, that the CIA mole was using. He was going to brief you after Ryan. But he's disappeared. Ryan did something to him. Stopped him, or worse."

*"Dan never called me. I haven't heard* any *of this. I'm with Wallace. We've been holed up all day. We're just about to—"*

"George, where is Ryan? Where is he?"

*"Ryan is coordinating the hunt for Haddad with the FBI. He's been out of pocket all day, all evening, following up leads."*

"How do you *know*? Have you seen him? With your own eyes, George? Do you know where he is?"

*"Jesus fucking Christ,"* George muttered. *"When did Dan disappear?"*

"He told Shannon he was going to see Ryan. Now no one can get a hold of him. And no one seems to know where Ryan is, either." Kris sucked in against the stabbing pain in his chest, a knife into his back. All this time, he'd been wondering about Dawood, agonizing over his husband, but Dan had been in danger. Was missing. What if—

Kris heard George moving, heard him tell Wallace to keep trying Dan's phone. Heard him breathe hard as he jogged down the hallway, started running down stairs. He pictured George running from his executive suite, down to the operations units, down to CTC. Heard him shout orders to people, for someone to call the FBI command center, for someone to find Ryan, *now*, *now*.

"I need you to do me a favor, George."

*"Kris,* no. *We need to let this process work. I'll call the FBI. They will locate Ryan. He was with them last. They can track him down. We* will *find him."*

"We *need* to track the cell phone that Ryan has been using to communicate with Dawood! You need to track it!"

*"You* know *we can't do that on American* soil. *To an American* citizen. *That's the FBI's turf. We* don't *have jurisdiction."*

"We don't have time for this! There is an attack planned for September eleventh, right now, in our country! The only one who has the information is Ryan!"

*"Are you willing to blow any chance of a criminal prosecution? If we act and we don't follow the rules, anything we uncover can't be used as evidence. You* know *this."*

"I'm not thinking about a trial," Kris snapped. "We have to stop him. We have to. He's been playing us for two years. Jesus, he's known

Dawood was alive all this time and he didn't tell anyone! Didn't tell me! Trial is the last thing on my mind."

Silence. "*What is it you want me to do*?"

"As deputy director of the CIA, I want you to do a geo search on that cell number. You can create a legal justification, I know you can. Since Ryan has been texting Dawood, and Dawood is associated with an Afghanistan al-Qaeda cell, you've got jurisdiction right there."

"*I thought you said Haddad was on our side.*"

Kris swallowed. "I hope he is. But then that means someone on our side *isn't* with us. *Ryan*."

George grunted. "*I'm walking into CTC now.*" He heard the buzz of CTC, the hum of activity. "*It's a fucking beehive in here.*"

Kris waited as George shouted for Shannon, explained to her that he needed a number traced, immediately. Shannon walked him to the secured data center, the bridge between the CIA and the NSA, the cluster of data points and network access that gave them backdoor intrusions to cell phone networks and internet service providers. "*Give me the number.*"

Kris read it off to him. He'd folded and refolded the sticky note a hundred times since that afternoon, staring at the numbers like they were tea leaves to be divined from.

"*It's definitely a burner. No registration data. It's not logged as being contracted to anyone.*"

Keystrokes, the sound of typing. "*And, it's off*," George said. "*It's not sending a signal into the cell network.*"

"Wake it up, then."

"*Kris, we're crossing a big fucking line here. We're breaking laws* specifically *put in place to stop this, exactly this. Are you* absolutely *certain? About Dawood? About the mole?*"

"I am one hundred percent certain about my husband. And I regret not believing everything Dawood told me, from the very first moment. If I had, maybe Dan wouldn't be—"

He should have brought Dawood in, kept him safe. Should have trusted him. Should have worked with him, searched the mission logs with him. Come up with a plan. Together. They should be doing this together.

Now where was Dawood? Facing Ryan alone? Without help, without backup?

He needed to be with him. Needed to help him. Now. They were supposed to be together forever, and he'd left Dawood to face this alone.

"I trust Dawood. I do, George. He is with us. Do *you* trust *me*?"

George said nothing. Kris waited.

"Sixteen years, George, we've been together. You and me. We've had our problems, I know. But I know Dawood is right. I know he's with us. I know he's trying to help. We need to help him, too."

Keyboard keys clicked, George typing on his end. "*It's pinging the network now. Hold on... It's triangulating...*"

Kris held his breath. Almost whimpered.

"*Deanwood. Southeast DC.*" George rattled off an address, something in the middle of the urban neighborhoods, a tangle of homes and warehouses that bordered Anacostia and the urban waterfront.

"I'm closest." Kris grabbed Dan's keys off the counter. Dan's weapon lay outside the circle of light, on its side. He grabbed that, too. "I'm on my way now."

"*Kris,* no. *Don't go. Wait for the FBI. I'll call them now, get the response teams over there immediately.*"

"The FBI takes at least an hour to coordinate a monkey shit fight, George. I'm not waiting for anything or anyone. They'll be too late. I'm going in. I'm going to my husband."

"*Kris—*"

"I will never leave him behind. Not again." He jogged to Dan's car, turned the key in the ignition. The electric car spun up silently.

"*What about Dan?*"

"I hope he's still alive." Damn it, Kris's heart was screaming. But the only thing he could do was run forward. Face his choices head on. Face destiny. Walk the path. "Send the FBI in. But I'm going now."

"*Kris... Be careful.*"

He put the car in reverse and gunned the engine.

## Deanwood, Washington DC - September 10, 2300 hours

Dawood kneeled in prayer, his hands held open before him, whispering to Allah. "Make the best of my days the last of my days, Oh Lord. The best of my deeds the last of them, and the best of my days the day upon which I will meet You."

He was ready.

He waited inside the decrepit remains of a long-abandoned warehouse, one in a string of industrial black holes on the south side of Deanwood. Just to the south, the urban grit of Anacostia and the shipping channel to the southeast of DC began. He was in the forgotten corner of the capital that languished in disrepair and disquiet.

It was the perfect place to hide in plain sight, and the perfect place to stage an attack.

"*Oh, you who believe, be persistently standing firm for Allah. Be witnesses for justice, and do not let the hatred of people prevent you from being just. For justice is nearer to righteousness.*" He recited verses of the Quran, trying to center his soul. He tried to set his fate in Allah's hands, tried to quiet his mind, his heart. "*He has the keys to the unseen. No one knows but Him. No leaf falls without His knowledge, nor is there a single grain in the darkness of the earth, or anything fresh or withered, that is not written in His heart.*"

His thoughts turned, always, to Kris.

*You must follow the path Allah has laid out for you.*

Even if it broke his heart, shattered his soul, and took him away from Kris.

Even if Kris, in the end, became someone else's, *loved* someone else.

*For justice is nearer to righteousness.*

*I will love you forever,* ya rouhi. *In this life, and the next.*

Outside, car tires crunched on gravel, chewed through the silence of the abandoned night. A car door slammed.

Dawood inhaled.

*I am ready.*

## CIA Headquarters, Langley Virginia - 2300 hours

"I need FBI tactical teams to assemble at the command center *immediately*," George barked into his phone. "We have a hot lead on Dawood Haddad, and possible accomplices, and we're going in. We have to move, now!"

He'd taken over CTC in Dan's absence, trying to coordinate a response while down two of his best men. Panic simmered beneath the surface of his skin, an itch he couldn't scratch. *Dan, Ryan, where are you guys?*

*Don't let this be true. Don't let any of this be true.*

George swallowed hard. It was easier, far easier, to think Haddad was the bad guy, to pour all his anxieties, all his nerves, all his fear and his hate and his terror, into the specter of Dawood Haddad.

*Do you trust me?* Kris had asked.

*I don't know*, he should have said. *I've never known. Half the time, I don't know what I'm doing. I just try to hold on as tight as I can and close my eyes before we all crash face-first into the brick wall.*

"Sir!" Shannon jogged to him, a Bluetooth earpiece in her hand. "The FBI, they've found Ryan!"

He snatched the earpiece out of her hands, shoved it into his ear. "Talk to me. Where is Ryan?"

"*Sir? What the* fuck?" Ryan, pissed as hell and loaded for bear, growled over the connection. "*I was taking a* fucking *nap and an entire squad of FBI agents turned the fucking cot over, dumped me out. They're circling me with flashlights and their weapons drawn, and I need to know what the* fuck *is going on, right* Goddamn *now!*"

George blinked. His eyes slipped closed.

*No. Please, no.*

*It's supposed to be Haddad.*

"Ryan. Did Dan call you today about tracing a phone number Caldera uncovered?"

"*Dan? I haven't talked to him since yesterday.*"

**Deanwood, Washington DC - 2300 hours**

Feet crunched over gravel, over the broken glass of the warehouse's shattered windows. Two years of agonizing waiting, trying to string clues out of breadcrumbs, trying to track a ghost whispering through Kandahar City, trying to find out who was slitting the throat of the CIA from within. Once he knew about the mole, he couldn't leave Kandahar City, not until he could prove, beyond all doubt, who it was. Not until he could do *something* about it, stop the killings, the betrayal.

He would finally have his answers.

*True patience comes from complete trust in you, Oh Allah, when the trials and calamities are at the highest.*

Footsteps, closer, closer.

*There is no God but God.*

Dawood rose, slowly. One hand reached behind his back, gripping the handle of a pistol he'd bought from a twelve-year-old in Brentwood the first day he'd arrived back in the States. It had been easy to acquire weapons in Afghanistan. Easier still in the United States.

The mole thought he was on their side. He had the element of surprise.

*Kris. Ya rouhi, my love. Forever.*

"Hands up, Haddad."

He knew that voice.

*No...*

"I *said*, hands up. I can see you. And I have my weapon trained on the center of your forehead, so if you don't want to die, this very moment, put your *fucking* hands up."

Slowly, Dawood let go of his weapon. Lifted his hands until they were next to his head. He stared at the darkness, the blackness from where the voice had come. "Show yourself."

The barrel of a handgun appeared first, then hands clutching the grip. Arms, legs, a face cast in shadow. And—

*Kris, I am so sorry.*

"Finally, you can follow instructions," Dan purred. "Let's see how well that continues. On your knees."

Dawood didn't move.

"*Now*." Dan stepped closer and took aim, right between his eyes. "Don't make me tell you again."

He kneeled, his knees digging into the cold, broken cement of the warehouse's cracked floor. "Why, Dan? Why did you do this?"

Dan circled him slowly, weapon aimed for the center of his head. Dawood's breath shook, trembling over his lips as Dan's boots crunched against the dirty ground. *Bam*. Blinding pain streaked through his skull, made his vision streak and smear. A boot slammed into the center of his back, shoving him forward, face-first. All the air in his chest *whooshed* out, and he gasped, struggling to breathe. Hands grabbed his arms, wrenched them backward.

The cold steel of handcuffs closed around his wrists.

"Quiet. You don't get to ask questions. Not after the trouble you caused. Just keep your mouth shut while I fix your mess." Dan pushed hard off his back and moved away, holstering his weapon.

Dawood struggled to his knees. "Why are you turning against the CIA? Why have you betrayed everyone?"

"I am a *fucking* patriot!" Dan snapped. "I care about this country! About the world! I'm going to wake everyone up again! Wake them up to your fucking barbarism again. Of you and your kind."

"My kind?"

"Fucking *Islamists*. You and your brothers who bow to your Allah, who worship a camel fucker from the seventh century and want to return the world to the backward bullshit of the medieval times. Who think that the only laws worth following are Sharia laws, which, by the way, would see you stoned to death for being a fucking sodomite."

"That is *not* true Islam, or the true love of Allah—"

"*Spare me* the preaching. I've heard enough preaching, in the gutters of Islamabad, from the mouths of Zahawi and Khalid Sheikh Mohammed and all the other al-Qaeda fucks we threw in Guantanamo Bay and Abu Ghraib. I've heard enough about your fucking death cult to last the rest of my life."

Nothing made sense. Nothing added up. "And you decided to *help* al-Qaeda? Decided to betray the CIA?"

"I'm *helping* the CIA! I'm reminding *everyone*—the CIA, the president, the American people, everyone—just how dangerous your kind truly is. The world has slacked off, let the fucking Islamists regain ground. ISIS making land grabs in Iraq and Syria, in Egypt, in Africa, and back in Afghanistan. The world has taken their eyes off the ball, and it's time they realized how wrong that is. It's time to remind everyone that this is a war for the soul of humanity. Against you, and your death cult, your God of murder. It's time that everyone remembers that we have to destroy every last one of your kind."

He couldn't breathe. Dan spun in and out of focus, Dawood's vision fracturing into a billion shards, the world collapsing all around him as he struggled to hold on to reality. What had happened to the world? To the man he'd known, the soft-spoken, gentle analyst, Kris's friend... and lover? Dan was supposed to be the happy ending he couldn't give Kris. The safe harbor for Kris's heart, the arms that cradled him close after.

Dawood blinked. Tried to inhale. Tried to form a thought, a prayer. *Allah, what is this? What path is this?* He'd put his faith in Allah, in the path he had to walk, had clung to his determination in the face of everything. In the face of Kris, the other half of his soul. His jihad had always been about the soul, about keeping to the path of his life, holding fast to Allah, like his father had begged him to so many years ago.

Was this what clinging to the path led to? What faith delivered? Was this, in the end, all that was left? He'd run his race, fought his wars, lived more lives packed into one lifetime than any man had any right to feel in his heart. And for what? What did the end of the path lead to? Where had his faith brought him?

*Like father, like son*, the proverbs always said. *The apple does not fall far from the tree.* His father had been murdered for his faith.

So too, it seemed, would he.

What did he have to show for this life, this dedication to his faith? His father had, at least, had him, his mother, a happy home, a life of love and light and peace, submission to a loving God who breathed radiance into all things.

Dawood had a pit in his soul, a hole carved in his heart in the shape of Kris's smile. A void, dead space within him that hummed, that threatened to overtake his mind, his soul.

And he had a husband who had thrown him aside, who had lain in the arms of another man. A traitor.

*Allah, what am I supposed to do? I thought this was your path.*

*Endure patiently*, the Quran said. *With beautiful patience.*

*Endure.*

His heart folded inward, collapsed on itself like a star surrendering to the last shudders of its inevitable descent into darkness. Shame pulsed from him, waves and waves of shame thrown off like a dying star shedding its corona. Shame warred with rage, wrestled with the sting of failure, of self-recrimination. Self-wrath. He hadn't done enough, he hadn't. Not if this was the end. Not if Kris was still in danger.

Dan was right about one thing.

He did not fear death.

He welcomed it. Welcomed the release, the shedding of this terrible life.

*Every moment that passes from this one is dedicated to stopping you. To ending you. I am already dead. I only await my reunion with Allah.*

His soul settled heavy around his heart, squeezing like chains against the broken shards he'd cobbled together, had tried to coax life out of. But it was impossible. He'd died that day, ten years ago, the moment he'd realized he wouldn't see Kris again. He'd died, the best part of his existence carved out of him, and nothing could replace that.

He breathed for one purpose, now.

One purpose alone.

Dawood stared into Dan's gaze. "What have you planned?"

Dan finally lowered his weapon. He glared at Haddad. "You know, you were supposed to be my golden goose. The gift that keeps on giving. A perfect patsy. A perfect fall guy. Who *wouldn't* believe that

David Haddad, lost to time and Afghanistan, *wouldn't* come back to America bitter, enraged, and hostile? After ten years with al-Qaeda?"

"You knew it was me? For two years?"

"Of course I knew it was you. As soon as Abu Dujana bragged about 'the stranger from Khorasan' who used to know everything about the CIA and was al-Qaeda's secret weapon. Of course I knew it was you."

"And you never told Kris?"

Dan laughed, his head tipping back. "Why would I do that? I finally had him right where I wanted him for so long. In my bed. In my arms."

Dawood flinched.

Dan grinned. "Hurts, doesn't it? Seeing the man you love in the arms of someone else? You have no idea how much joy I got making love to him, knowing you were living on dust and the trash of American bombs in the wastes of Afghanistan."

"You weren't like this before, Dan. Something changed in you." Dawood ached for Kris, for the love Kris had thought he'd had. *Kris, ya rouhi, I wanted it to be* anyone *else. I wanted you to have an ever after.* "What happened? Why are you doing this?"

"Sixteen years of war changed me!" Dan bellowed. "Made me into this! Sixteen years of facing your kind, and your hate, and your fucked-up God! Sixteen years of staring into the worst of humanity, fighting them every tooth and fucking nail." He grinned. It was a dark thing, like a knife glinting in moonlight. "But I broke them, all of your brothers before you. I broke Zahawi after you left Site Green."

"What?"

Dan snorted, shaking his head. "You know, Kris could have been something amazing if he hadn't been tied to you. You fucked up his mind, filled him full of bullshit, until he didn't know who the enemy was anymore. You fucked him for life when he pulled out of the Zahawi interrogation. You fucked his whole career. He and I could be running the CIA now, if it weren't for you."

"You didn't stop the Zahawi interrogation..." God, Kris had clung to that, to the knowledge that he'd left Zahawi in the hands of his trusted friend. That Dan had picked up where he'd left off, doing what was right, what was just. That Dan had been a good man in a miasma of moral failings.

"Of course I didn't. I took over. Paul was a heavy-handed oaf. He didn't know what he was doing. I *did.* I broke Zahawi in twenty days."

"Ryan—"

"Ryan couldn't stomach it. He always thought he was some big badass, but when it came down to the wire, he bailed. He's had to live with his shame, knowing how weak a man he really is. I kept his secret. How he couldn't take it, couldn't watch the interrogations. Couldn't watch me."

"You're a monster," Dawood breathed. "You've become a monster."

"Look in the mirror!" Dan shouted. "You're talking about yourself! *I hunted the monsters*! For years! *I* am the one who built the detainee program! *I* am the one who built Guantanamo! Who trained *everyone* at Abu Ghraib! *I* was the nightmare to your brothers, your jihadi fucks! *I* was the end of the line for the real monsters, the animals like *you.*" He inhaled, a ragged breath. "Until the world started to forget. And lost its nerve. And *look* what happened. The monsters hid in their rat holes and regrouped. *ISIS,*" he snarled. "Left to your own devices, you and your kind will *always* choose barbarism. It's in your nature."

Dizzy, he was dizzy, the world was spinning, upending. Everything he and Kris thought they knew was wrong. The knowledge they'd built their world on, their reality. That Dan was a good man. That he'd stopped the torture, had worked in the grinding bureaucracy to put an end to dark things, to evil.

Instead, Dan had stoked his own evil, burned his own rage until his soul collapsed, until everything he had been was lost to the purity of his hatred.

When had Dan tipped over the edge? How long had he been living without a soul? There was nothing left of the Dan he'd once known.

What was he truly capable of, without any of his morals, any ethics, and driven purely by hate?

"What is it you have planned? 'Something bigger than nine-eleven', you said to Abu Dujana. Something so big you wanted me to pull it off. You specifically asked for me, Al-Khorasani, to come to America to execute your attack. I'm just your convenient terrorist, is that it? Pin the crime on the Muslim?"

"Your ignoble death was supposed to drive Kris into my arms for good. The shattering of your legend, of your mystique, your final hold on his heart. God, I *hated* you so much. Even in death, you had a stronger power over Kris's heart and soul than I ever could dream of."

"We were made for each other and you couldn't come between that. You could never compete, not when our souls were paired by Allah before space and time began."

Dan laughed. "Don't think *that* highly of yourself, Haddad. Before you fucked up, he was finally mine. He'd finally let you go."

*You have a key?*

*My personal life is none of your business.*

Dawood swallowed, and it felt like a thousand knives of betrayal, a thousand days and nights of longing, of yearning for Kris with every breath in his body. "You've twisted him around so badly he doesn't know up from down, left from right."

"He was following the script *perfectly*," Dan snapped again. "But you had to reach out. Had to make contact. Had to confess everything. Don't tell me you weren't all in on this, Haddad. That you didn't want to make America suffer, make Americans bleed. Make them taste the death and the stink of terror and horror you've lived with every day, for ten years."

He closed his eyes. Swayed, smelling diesel fumes and burning mudbrick homes, heard the sounds of children screaming. Heard Behroze wailing, kicking and clawing in the middle of the night. Felt the heat of an incandescent fire blazing off the rubble left behind from a drone strike, so hot they had to let the flames burn themselves out while they listened to the screams of the dying within the shimmering flames. *Do not kill with fire*, the Quran said.

*For that is of Allah, and you shall not take the power of Allah for yourselves.*

*Stay close to justice, for justice is nearer to righteousness.*

There were moments, in the darkness, when he'd felt something close to hatred. When he'd stared at the hand Ihsan always held out for him, a silent offer to join his brothers. When he stood at the cliff edge and looked over the abyss of American foreign policy and felt the anguish of a billion Muslims cry out in rage. He'd wondered if it was possible to go too far. Where the line was. Where his rage tipped him over the edge.

Where he risked turning into what Dan had become.

The thought of Kris, the memory of their love, of everything Kris was, kept his soul from spinning off, splintering into the winds and withering to dust and ash. Kris, and his love, his commitment to justice.

*Stay close to justice, for justice is nearer to righteousness.*

For Dawood, that meant staying close to Kris, and to his memory.

"My path has always been to expose you. To *destroy* you."

Dan laughed again, gesturing between them with his handgun. Dawood was still on his knees. "Working out well for you, huh? How did it feel when Kris threw you out of my house? When he didn't believe you?"

"My path is mine to walk alone."

"He didn't believe you. No one is coming for you, and no one is going to help you. You're on your own, Haddad. And you're mine."

"Whatever it is you're planning, I won't help. I won't participate in the slaughter of Americans. Or push your twisted evil, your intolerance, your justifications for hate, in any way."

"Yes. You will."

---

Kris ducked beneath a broken window outside the decrepit warehouse at the address George had given him. Voices murmured from within, rising and falling on the still night. Above, a crescent moon carved through the clouds, casting a faint glow over the dead end of the capital.

Dawood's deep tones carried in the moonlight. "You've thought of everything, haven't you?"

Dawood. Kris closed his eyes against the crash of his heart, the scream in his soul begging him to throw caution and everything else to the side, to just leap through the window and go to Dawood, be with him. Be by his side, like they were supposed to be, for all time.

He was here now. For Dawood.

He'd parked two blocks away, out of sight on a dark residential block abutting the abandoned industrial park. He'd zigzagged through back lots and alleys, Dan's gun in his hands as he jogged low and fast. His skinny jeans, long-sleeved pullover and his trench coat flapping behind him were not the tactical uniform he would have preferred. But nothing would stop him, not now. Not ever again.

At the warehouse, he'd circled twice, taking in emptiness, the urban destitution, the way the night seemed to collapse around the neighborhood. Collapse like the warehouse was some fulcrum of evil, the pivot point of destiny.

Outside the warehouse, a dark older model SUV was parked in the shadows by the warehouse's side freight doors. Two silhouettes within were carved in the light of the SUV's headlights.

One standing, a holstered gun on his hip, gesturing as he spoke. Ryan. He gritted his teeth, tried to breathe through the surge of rage.

One kneeling, his hands behind his back, like he was cuffed. Dawood?

Another figure lay on the ground, still, unmoving. His throat clenched. Dan? Was he too late?

Muffled voices carried on a soft conversation, punctuated by harsh laughter that grated down Kris's spine.

Time to end this. Time to confront Ryan. He eyeballed the inside of the warehouse over the edge of the broken window. Ryan had his back to the SUV, to the freight doors. That was his breach point, keeping to the shadows as he slipped in.

Kris moved, and then waited at the edge of the doors, listening to Dawood's voice.

"The death toll will be astronomical. This will ignite a fury that cannot be contained, that cannot be controlled. You will unleash hatred and wrath on the world, and all for what? A *lie*?"

"It's not a lie. It's a revelation. It's showing the world exactly what you truly are. Your Quran, your hadith. Your jihadi brothers, your ISIS fighters, they *beg* for this, for the apocalypse, for the end of the world. They beg to meet their God."

Kris's blood turned to ice, freezing solid in his veins. A thousand spiders tap danced down his spine, the pitter patter of pure terror.

That *wasn't* Ryan's voice.

"I'm just giving your kind exactly what they want. A holy war, and the apocalypse. The end times. It just won't turn out the way they want."

"You have become what you hate," Dawood said. "You have become exactly what you hate."

Kris felt every beat of his heart, heard the rush of blood in his veins. His thoughts tumbled, swirled, coalesced.

Truth stared him in the face, at last.

*He* didn't *call Ryan. Everything he said, it was a* lie.

*I gave up Dawood,* right *into his hands.*

*He covered his tracks, threw suspicion off him, from the* moment *I brought Dawood's confession to him.*

*Straight to* him, *the mole.*

"And you don't understand. We will always win. *I* will always win." Laughter, suddenly so familiar to Kris, a laugh he'd heard hundreds of times over the years, a laugh he'd come to rely on, a sound he'd set the compass of his heart to when all his moorings had come undone. "I already have won. Especially where it really matters."

"You're going to break his heart."

"I'm going to hold him close and kiss away his tears when he mourns the memory of who you were. When he rages against what you became, and what atrocities you are about to commit. He's going to give his heart to me."

Fury crackled through Kris. How long had he been played? How long had this been going on? How blind had he been? His vision swam, narrowing until all he saw was the dark silhouette before him, the shape of a man, a shadow outlined in headlights. The back of a head, the very center.

Where he'd put his bullet.

He pushed forward, striding out of the shadows as he raised his weapon. "Dan. *Freeze*, you son of a bitch! *Hands up*!"

Dan gasped. He could hear it, in the stillness of the warehouse, Dan's quick little inhale. He kept his back to Kris and raised his hands, slowly.

Beyond Dan, Dawood kneeled on the ground, hands behind his back. A trail of tears glittered off his cheeks. "*Habibi*—" he started.

"*Shut up*!" Dan growled. "Suspects don't get to speak!"

Kris advanced, digging the barrel of his gun into the back of Dan's head. "Take your own advice, Dan. I will pull this *fucking* trigger if you move one single muscle."

"Kris—"

"Try me. *Please*. Give me an excuse."

"You're confused, Kris. You don't know what you're seeing. You walked in on something that can't be understood, not like this. Let me help you."

"*Shut the fuck up*!" Kris bellowed. "Keep your fucking mouth closed! You've spread enough lies!"

"Kris, you're *wrong*. You don't understand—"

"*Habibi*, it's him. It is." Dawood sighed. Fresh tears poured from his eyes. "I'm sorry."

"Who the fuck is that?" Kris jerked his chin to the body on the ground, a man lying on his side, his back to the headlights, to Kris. His burnished skin suggested Arab, and his unnatural stillness, the way his limbs lay loose and unmoving, clawed at Kris's guts.

"Haddad's partner," Dan snapped. "Like I said, you don't understand what is happening here—"

"*Habibi*!" Dawood shouted, panic shredding his voice. He tried to stand, his eyes wide, crazed. "*Look out—*"

A pinch, a hot prick, stabbed Kris in the neck. He whirled, but the world smeared, and shadows turned to darkness as everything tipped sideways.

He felt hands on his arms, catching him as he fell, and the last thing he heard was Dawood's voice bellowing his name.

---

Dan lowered Kris's unconscious body to the warehouse floor, cradling his head before it hit the cold ground. "You were supposed to keep a lookout."

"I was working on the timer." Noam glared at Dan as he yanked the syringe from Kris's neck. "He appeared out of nowhere. I barely had time to duck so he wouldn't see me."

"He's SAD. You're Mossad. Aren't you supposed to be better than SAD? Isn't that your point of pride?" Dan cursed. "He may have seen too much. Why the fuck is he even here?"

Noam wagged the empty syringe over Kris's body. "This beauty will wipe his recent memory. He won't remember anything. He won't even remember how he got here."

"You better be fucking sure."

"I *am*. I use this all the time."

Dan glared. "Is everything ready?"

"Almost. Converting from a switch to a timer takes a while." Noam glowered at Haddad, cuffed and kneeling. "Would have been better if he hadn't fucking turned on us. I thought he was the anchor of our plan?"

Dan grinned, all teeth and raw hatred, his fury pouring from him, crackling off his being, the very center of his soul *finally* unleashed. "Haddad has always fucked everything up. It's his legacy. I shouldn't be surprised about this."

"I need a few more minutes on the timer."

"Get back to it. And don't worry about Haddad. He's still going to fucking help us."

"I won't." Haddad swayed on his knees, as if he were about to pitch forward. Everything in him screamed, reaching for Kris. Dan had to see how he barely held himself back from crawling across the dirt to go to his husband. "I won't murder for you. Ever."

Dan cradled Kris's still face in one hand. Kris was so stunningly beautiful. He'd always been gorgeous, from the day he'd walked into CTC nearly twenty years ago and had pressed pause on Dan's life the first moment he'd seen him. How he'd stolen Dan's breath, had captivated Dan's mind. He'd nurtured long fantasies of their lives enjoined, the happiness they could have, as soon as he worked up the courage to ask him out. How he'd craved Kris, nurturing his desire in the silence of CTC, watching Kris in his formative years.

Nearly twenty years ago. How long their lives had been entwined, had been shared.

They were destined to be together, in every way.

Until Haddad. Until Haddad had fucked *everything* up.

Dan pulled his gun from Kris's limp fingers. He rolled Kris's head, turning Kris's face to Haddad. Dirt and grit dug into Kris's cheek as he pressed the barrel of his gun against Kris's temple.

"No! *Yallah*, no, no. *Astaghfirullah*, no. *No,* please. *Please…*" Haddad's voice, his breath, trembled. "*Please…*"

He begged beautifully. His tears glistened, each a drop of joy in Dan's soul. Naked terror danced in Haddad's gaze.

"Please… Don't do this. Don't…"

"You want him to live?"

Haddad's eyes closed. "Don't do this," he whispered. "Don't make me choose."

"I thought I would have to spell it out for you but you jumped the gun, Haddad. Good boy. So. Do you want to see Kris's beautiful, beautiful brains all over the ground? Or do you want him to live a long, long, happy life?"

Haddad doubled over, screaming through gritted teeth. He pressed his forehead to the ground, anguished sobs crashing through his chest.

"*All* your *paths* lead *here*, Dawood Haddad! Every choice you made in your life, every pitiful, desperate, stupid choice you made, built your road to this! It's *always* been your destiny! You're nothing but a filthy Muslim!" Dan's bellows bounced off the warehouse walls, echoed in the darkness. "You were always, *always* going to go out like this. Worthless. Meaningless. But I have given your death meaning, Haddad. You should fucking thank me. You should thank me in your prayers for delivering the end times that your fucking psychotic God and all his followers begged for. Because this will be the end. And you're all going to fall. You're all going to die. You will always fall to us. To me!" Dan hissed.

Haddad's sobs seemed to tear him two, seemed to rip his soul into tatters.

"It's so fucking poetic, don't you think? I will beat you, and I will kill you, and I will take everything that is yours. Exactly like history is supposed to go."

Haddad rolled his face against the ground. Dan saw a puddle of snot and spit, the ocean of his tears. "Allah," he moaned. "I cry out for you in the darkness..."

"Your God is dead, just like your people will be. And you will be remembered as the man who brought about the end. Who ushered in the end of days and woke the might of the American people." His thumb dragged over Kris's lips. "Because you're going to do this. You will never, ever let him die."

Haddad's shoulders shook. His prayers turned to a low keen, a wail that sounded like a soul dying.

"If you care about him, at all, then you're going to make this right for him." Dan pushed off Kris, standing and tucking Kris's gun into the small of his back. Kris rolled, limp and boneless as a rag doll, his cheek dusted with grime, but still perfect. Still utterly perfect. He was wonderful like this, pliant, limp, open to Dan in all the ways he never was. Why had Kris sealed off the deepest part of himself from Dan? Why hadn't he ever let Dan into his heart, his soul?

Fucking Haddad. It was always, *always* Haddad. "You're going to write him a confession. You're going to confess everything."

Finally, Haddad sat back. His eyes were vacant, shattered orbs that bled sorrow and hollow acceptance inside every tear. Snot and spit and dirt stained his face. He was a filthy animal, nothing but a filthy animal. How had he ever captured Kris's love?

"You're going to tell him this was your plot. That you wanted it, that you dreamed of it, hungered for this. That you planned it, all of it. You're going to give him a future in my arms."

Haddad shook his head, like he didn't understand. A line of spit dribbled from his lips, stretched to the ground.

"Yes, you are. As long as you play along, as long as you do your part, he lives. And he lives with me. In my arms." Dan pointed his gun at Kris's face. "Or he dies. Now."

"Dan." Noam appeared at his shoulder. "We're all set." He nodded to Kris. "We have to move. If he's here, then reinforcements are likely on the way."

"He loves to buck the system. And I made him believe I was the only one he could trust. Kris wouldn't have called anyone. He tries to be the Lone Ranger, always. He probably wanted to save the day on his own."

"Still. We have to go." Noam headed for Haddad's partner, the last component to their plot. The Arab man lying on his side, unnaturally still. "Help me move him."

Dan caught the latex gloves Noam tossed him. They snapped as he tugged them on. No fingerprints, not on the bodies, and not on the SUV. They'd wiped it down a week before, had driven it to the safe house wearing gloves.

Dan grunted as he hefted the Arab. "He's heavy."

"A dead body packed full of shrapnel is." Noam winked.

The man's arm flopped down, the back of his hand dragging on the ground. Dan stared at his face, still, expressionless, locked in death. In the moonlight, he looked like wax, like a doll.

Save for the bullet hole in his temple.

He'd been an ISIS fuck, executed by the Israeli military when they caught him planting IEDs on their border. He'd been one of the millions of Middle Eastern ghosts, unknown men who could be

Syrian or Iraqi or Palestinian, or *Who Gives A Fuck*, who had no home and no hope and no future. He'd been a body without an identity, a human who didn't exist to the multitude of bureaucracies in the world, someone who'd been born and had lived and had slipped through the cracks of everything and everyone.

And that made him valuable.

Noam, at Mossad, had taken ownership of his corpse for research purposes. He'd faked an autopsy, filed a report, and marked the body as disposed.

Mossad would never know just how far off the reservation Noam had wandered.

And then Noam had come to America for his six-month exchange with the CIA, flying diplomatic transport and skirting all checks, all inspections. No one questioned the refrigerated crate he'd brought with him.

Over the months, Dan had built a profile in the system for their mystery man. ISIS, young twenties, an exchange student from Iraq, supposedly here on a student visa, but he'd never shown up for classes. How the American people would rage, demand a change to their open borders. *Look at the terrorists pouring into the country*, they would scream.

All for an electric ghost and a man who had never existed in the world.

Dan heaved the shrapnel-stuffed body into the rear of the SUV. Noam had packed the vehicle with explosives, built to ISIS specifications, using ISIS blueprints. He'd wiped his own fingerprints, had meticulously spent hours pressing their corpse's fingers on each block of plastique, each wire. In the end, only fragments and ash would remain, scattered traces of DNA, but the hint of one partial print would be all they needed.

One dead ISIS member, one SUV packed with explosives, and Haddad, detonating the bomb on the anniversary of September 11.

There was no better start to the end of days.

"I'll pack up." Noam shut the trunk. "Haddad and I will head to the staging point. What are you going to do with Caldera?"

"I'll keep him with me. He's our insurance. If Haddad balks in any way, call me. I'll send video of Kris eating a bullet to get him back on track."

Noam snorted. "*You'd* kill *him*? You?" Noam stared at him, the edges of his gaze pitch black, as if his eyes were sucking in the moonlight, the starlight, taking the light out of the world.

Dan swallowed. "Is there anything you wouldn't give for this?"

Noam had spent nine months undercover inside ISIS ranks, had been a part of the migration from Syria to Iraq, the first months of the war. He'd seen the butchery, the bloodlust, the calamity unleashed upon the world. When Dan had met him in Tel Aviv, Noam had been hovering on the edge of eating a bullet or ten, one shot of vodka way from ending it all. He'd dreamed in screams and the roar of gunfire, in crimson blood and bodies burned alive.

He'd seen the future, the end times, the way the world would go if they didn't act. If they didn't right this wrong, *now*, put down those animals once and for all. All of them. Every last one.

Their plan had been born then, in whispers of rage, in drunken bloodlust, in sweat-and-sex-covered delirium, a hundred nights of perfecting their shared wrath, their bitter fury.

And now they were here.

"Haddad still has something to do." Dan tore out a page of the SUV's manual from the glove compartment and stalked back into the warehouse.

Haddad hovered over Kris, his lips pressed to Kris's temple, tears falling like rain on Kris's smooth skin. "I love you," he whispered. "Forgive me, *ya rouhi*. Forgive me my love for you."

"Get the fuck off him!" Dan kicked Haddad, the flat of his foot slamming into Haddad's face. Bones crunched in the darkness, Haddad's nose, his cheek, and he went flying, landing on his cuffed hands in a skid across the ground. "He's not yours anymore."

Haddad didn't move. He lay on the ground, his chest shuddering, face to the dirt.

Dan tossed the torn page and a pen on the ground in front of him. He pulled out his handcuff keys. "Time to write your confession."

# 34

**Deanwood, Washington DC - September 11, 0043 hours**

"There's no one here." Ryan cursed, his bloodshot eyes scanning the empty warehouse. Red-and-blues flashed, lighting up the dark corners, the empty spaces of the abandoned industrial dump. "Whoever was here is long fucking gone."

"We found Dan's personal vehicle two blocks away." George swallowed back his bile, his rising vomit. "It's what Kris was driving. And the FBI is lifting tire tracks from an unknown vehicle that was parked by the side doors now. Looks like an SUV."

"There are a *million* SUVs in DC." Ryan's face pinched, his emotions battling his control. "Has Dan answered any of your calls?"

"His phone is off. He's pulled the battery. We can't get a location trace."

Ryan spun away, both hands over his face, his eyes squeezed closed. George watched him pace, watched his shoulders tremble.

Techs swarmed over the warehouse, FBI agents looking in every crack and crevice with their flashlights, CIA analysts shadowing their moves, working in concert with one another. George and Ryan stood with the FBI deputy director, managing the hunt that had just shifted, twisted from hunting for a terrorist to hunting one of their own.

What would a CIA officer on the run do? Where would he go? They were staring their own playbook in the face, trying to track an enemy that knew all of their moves, that could play everyone against each other. Who knew their defenses better than even they did.

If there was anyone who could pull off a September 11-style terror attack and pin the blame on someone else, it was Dan.

"Sirs!" One of the FBI techs shouted, waving her flashlight. "I've found something!"

George, Ryan, and the FBI deputy director jogged to her, clustering around her outstretched gloved hand.

A cell phone lay in the center of her palm. "It's on," she said. "It's still making a call."

"To who?"

She swiped through the screen, pulling up the number. "To itself, sir."

"Oh my fucking God. *Voicemail.* It's recording everything." Ryan hung up the phone, jabbing his gloved finger on the button to end the call. "How long has it been going?"

The battery indicator flashed. It was low on juice. "Almost two hours, sir."

"Let me see it." George gently took the phone from her. His gloved fingers swiped to the home screen, then to the messages. The phone was a burner, a knock-off smart phone that looked fancy but was no more powerful than a cheap calculator.

The message inbox loaded. One message was on top, unread.

The phone's owner had sent it to himself. He clicked the message icon.

*To whoever finds this phone. This is the record of CIA officer Dawood Haddad meeting with an unknown CIA officer who has been passing intelligence and information to al-Qaeda for over two years. Please turn this phone immediately over to the FBI and CIA. A recording of the meeting will be lodged within this phone's voicemail. Make sure this gets to the right people. Make sure justice is done.*

"Holy shit," Ryan breathed. "Someone get a phone charger! *Now*! We have to listen to this."

"Haddad..." George's throat clenched. "Well done."

# 35

**September 11, 0740 hours**

Sunlight stabbed into Kris's brain, bleached out his eyeballs, even through his eyelids. He groaned, trying to roll away from the light.

His head felt like a gong had been struck in the center of his brain, like his skull was a watermelon that had been split in two. He pressed his face against the cushion, smelled carpet cleaner and car upholstery—

Voices out of context, words without meaning.

*Habibi!*

*You don't understand what's happening here.*

*It's him.*

*Shut up! Suspects don't get to speak!*

*I am so sorry.*

*Habibi.*

*I will pull this fucking trigger if you move one single muscle!*

He blinked, struggling to make sense of the flutter of images whirling through his mind. *Driving, a dark warehouse. Dawood on his knees. A prick of pain, his body going heavy. Dan...*

He tried to sit up. His body ached, like he'd gone ten rounds with an entire frat house, or had spent the night in a cement mixer.

He couldn't move his hands. He tried again, tried to pull his wrists out from behind his back.

He was cuffed. Why?

"You awake?" Dan spun in the front seat of his car, slowing as he braked. Morning sunlight streamed through the windshield. Dust rose around the car, like they were driving off-road, deep into the woods on a rocky, dry track. "How are you feeling, Kris?"

"Why am I cuffed?" Kris rose slowly, slumping against Dan's back seat. His eyes darted around the car, outside the window. Trees surrounded them. Where were they? Where were they going?

"I didn't know how you'd be when you woke up. Do you need some water? How's your head?" His concerned gaze bored into Kris.

Kris groaned, squeezing his eyes closed. He shook his head, more fragments of memories going off like fireworks.

*Shut the fuck up! You've spread enough lies!*

*You walked in on something that can't be understood.*

*Habibi... It's him.*

"What do you mean, how I'd be when I woke up?" Kris stared at Dan. "What happened?"

"What do you remember?"

*Dan. Freeze, you son of a bitch!*

He blinked. Licked his lips. Looked at the trees, the dirt track they were deep into. "I was coming to help Dawood," he said slowly. "Against the mole."

Dan nodded. "You found him. But you walked in on something you didn't fully understand."

Kris stayed still. Silent.

"I found Haddad, too. I was trying to negotiate with him. Get him to turn himself in. Work with us. I offered him immunity if he'd just come in and reveal what he knew about the mole."

*You're confused, Kris. You don't know what you're seeing. You walked in on something that can't be understood.*

"What happened?"

Dan twisted in the seat, all the way around, and showed Kris his black eye, his swollen jaw. "Haddad said no."

Kris threw his head back against the seat. Closed his eyes. Tried to stop the pounding in his head, the train barreling through his mind.

The car started moving again, rolling forward. Dirt and rocks crunched beneath the tires.

"Kris... the plot about the mole. It was all a lie. It was all just a smoke screen. Haddad was playing you." Dan reached into the passenger seat and grabbed a torn sheet of paper. He tossed it behind him, into Kris's lap. "He left a confession."

*Habibi... It's him.*

The words swam on the page, Dawood's slanted handwriting staring him in the face. He squinted, tried to focus as the car lurched.

*Ya rouhi –*

*Forgive me, for what I am about to do. Everything that happens now happens because of me. Because of my choices.*

*If I set my heart on anything but you*
*let fire burn me from inside.*
*Oh Beloved,*
*take away what I want.*
*Take away what I do.*
*Take away what I need.*
*Take away everything*
*that takes me from you.*
*La ilaha illah Allah wa-Muhammad rasul Allah*
*Allahu Akbar.*

Kris shuddered, reading the words. *There is no God but God, and Muhammad is his messenger. God is Great.* "Where are we?" he choked out.

"Just getting away for a while. I've got to keep you safe. They're still trying to find Haddad. But it's September eleventh. I have to get you out of here, in case he's trying to hurt you."

He stared at the back of Dan's head, lines from Dawood's poem repeating in his memories, from a different time. "I *know* what I saw last night, Dan."

Dan sighed. "No, you don't, Kris. You were confused. You walked in on the middle of something, and I knew you wouldn't understand."

"I *know* what I saw. What the fuck did you do to me?"

"Damn it, no you *don't*!" Dan slammed his palm on his steering wheel. The car leaped forward, accelerating. "I'm trying to save you!"

"Dawood was right. About everything." He shifted. "About the mole."

Dan cursed. "Is that what you believe?"

"I believe the truth."

"The truth is staring you in the face!" Dan shouted. "Haddad confessed! He said everything that happens is because of him! And that he's doing this for the God he loves, his Islam! His brothers! Christ, you are *obsessed* with him, so obsessed!"

Kris laughed. "This confession? This is a love letter. Our marriage vows are in this, you dumb piece of shit! Dawood is telling me he's doing whatever he's doing for *me*. That he'd do anything for me. Even something he was forced to do, something abhorrent. Something the mole was making him do against his will."

In the rearview mirror, Kris watched Dan's gaze darken, his face tighten. Watched him mutter curses as he gripped the steering wheel.

"I should have believed Dawood from the first moment. I should have gone with him, helped him with everything. I should never have listened to you!"

"I'm not the one who fucked a terrorist! I'm the Goddamn patriot here! I am helping the country! I am waking everyone up again!"

"You're a monster, you sick fuck!" Kris kicked the back of Dan's seat, both feet slamming hard, once, twice, three times.

Dan reached behind the seat, punching at his legs. "You told me once you wanted to blow open the entire detainee program. Call the newspapers, be a whistleblower. You remember I asked you if you thought you were willing to be the one person to make that call?

Make choices for the world, the whole government, decide what is and isn't worth it? For everyone?"

"What the fuck are you talking about?"

"I've been thinking about that moment for *years*," Dan hissed. "And *I* am the one who can make that call. Who can make the sacrifice. Who can make the hard decisions, for the right reasons. I always have been. That's why I succeeded where you failed, Kris. That's why I have the job you should have had. I could do things no one else could! And that's why I'm doing this. I'm saving everyone!"

"You want to murder thousands and thousands of people. You disgust me!"

"I'm a hero! You should fucking worship me! One day, everyone will thank me!"

"You're fucking delusional! Everyone is hunting for you, you fucking terrorist! I called George! Before I came for Dawood. I fucking called George!"

"*What*?" Dan's gaze flicked to his in the mirror.

"I called George. I had to know if you'd briefed him. At first, I thought Ryan had got to you. That he was exactly the asshole I thought he was. You covered your tracks well. But, you can't hide from the truth. It's *you*. You are the mole, Dan. You've been betraying the CIA for two years. And now everyone knows!"

Dan's gaze burned through the mirror, sudden, pure hatred flowing from him.

"You've known Dawood was *alive* for two years. You looked me in the *eyes* and you *knew*!"

"What the fuck did you expect I would do? Tell you the love of your life was alive? Fuck no! We were finally together! Haddad wasn't going to fuck that up!"

"We were never *together*, Dan! I fucked you, like I fucked a lot of men! But only one man has ever had my love!"

"Fuck you!" Dan roared. "What the fuck did you tell George?"

"Panicking?" Kris shifted, sliding across the seat, moving his legs. "Worried your lies are about to be exposed? Worried that everyone is going to know it was you?"

"What the *fuck* did you tell George?" Dan bellowed. Gone was the controlled, rational man Kris had known for years. Dan punched the steering wheel again, seething as he glowered at Kris in the rearview mirror. The car jumped ahead again, rocking over the uneven ground.

"He geotracked the phone you used to text Dawood to the warehouse. "I was closest, but the entire FBI was swooping in. Did they make you run and hide? Did you panic and flee? Is that what this is about? You on the run?"

"The FBI never showed up," Dan spat. "No one showed up." His hands clenched on the steering wheel, leather squeaking, groaning. "You're lying. You didn't call him."

"I did. How do you think I knew where to go, asshole?"

"What the fuck did you tell him?"

"Enough that he knows the mole was meeting Dawood at that location, in the warehouse." He kicked the back of Dan's seat again, shifting quickly. "And who did Dawood meet? You. The game's up! Everyone knows you're the traitor!"

"No..." Dan's lips thinned. "No, only you know. Only you were there."

"You're so fucked, Dan. Betraying your country. Giving intel to al-Qaeda. You're going into a black hole so deep, no one will ever fucking see you again. You're going to disappear. I almost hope they fucking waterboard you, you son of a bitch. For what you've done."

"You know," Dan growled, reaching into the passenger seat again. "I thought it would be hard, blowing your fucking brains out. I did love you, you know." He gripped his gun as he slammed on the brakes. "But it's not going to be hard at all." He twisted, gun in hand, aiming for Kris—

Kris lunged, throwing his cuffed hands over Dan's seat back and around Dan's neck, yanking hard. He'd slipped his handcuffs around his legs while Dan wasn't looking, bringing his arms in front of him.

Dan squawked, gasping, gagging as he tried to grab Kris's handcuff chain and shoot at the same time. He fired, aiming wildly, and two bullets shot holes in the roof of the car. Another shot. The back window exploded.

Kris yanked harder, digging the chain into Dan's throat. Dan thrashed. Dropped his gun, both hands rising to the handcuffs. He gagged, mouth open as he struggled to breathe. In the rearview mirror, Kris saw panic race through his eyes. Saw his face twist, grimacing, desperate.

"I hope you burn in hell," Kris hissed. "I hope you suffer a fraction of the anguish I suffered! I hope you feel one tenth of what I felt, losing the love of my life!"

Dan's hands scrabbled at Kris's face, fingers trying to gouge his eyes, grab his hair. The car fishtailed, veering left and right.

Grunting, Kris heaved, jerking his handcuffs back and up, trying to snap Dan's neck, collapse his trachea. Kill him, destroy him.

Dan's foot slammed on the gas as he grabbed Kris's hair and yanked, tried to haul him off, throw him sideways.

Kris screamed through clenched teeth, his arms shaking as he pulled and he pulled, and he felt Dan's bones crunching, the delicate cartilage in his neck bending, snapping. Felt Dan's body tremble and seize, watched his mouth gape open and close.

The car accelerated, weaving across the dirt track and heading for an open space, a break in the trees. Kris saw a sign flash by. They were headed for a ravine, a drop off the track, a hundred feet down to the bottom of a wooded gully, coming up fast.

"Shit!" Unhooking his hands from around Dan's neck, Kris threw himself into the rear passenger seat. He grabbed his seat belt in both hands and yanked, rolling into it.

Dan gasped, a ragged, choking inhale. His hands flew forward—

The car raced off the edge of the track, hanging for a split second before tilting, twisting, tumbling in midair as it plunged toward the ravine.

*Crunch.* The bone-shuddering crash of impact, the car slamming into tree trunks as it careened downhill. Airbags deployed with a bang. Glass shattered, showering Kris in a million tiny fragments.

They tumbled, rolling end over end, jerking left and right, ricocheting and skidding through underbrush and dirt.

A long creak and a slow slide gave way to the bottom of the ravine, a gully tangled with vines and dead branches and a trickle of runoff in the bottom of a creek bed. The car groaned, wheels spinning as it lay on its roof.

Kris let go of his death grip on the seat belt he'd wrapped himself in. He fell to the roof, landing on his side in a puddle of broken windshield shards. Winded, wincing, he tried to breathe, tried to stop the shaking in his arms. Tried to make sense of the images, the voices, the whispers, roiling through his mind.

It all coalesced into sudden, startling clarity as he spotted Dan's gun lying in a mess of dirt and shattered glass.

He lunged, scooping the gun up in both hands, and twisted, landing on his side as he aimed for Dan's head.

Dan hung upside down in the driver's seat, motionless, arms limp over his head. Blood dripped from his temple, the ends of his hair, pooling rapidly.

Kris scrambled out of the car, sliding feet first through the busted passenger window, keeping his eyes on Dan. He crawled through the dead leaves and the debris of the gully, getting away from the car, and then rolled, pointing his gun at Dan.

Nothing. No movement. Dan's head hung at an angle, twisted unnaturally to the left.

Kris swallowed. He breathed in. His hands shook, trembled.

He could hear everything. The sound of leaves settling, the tumble of rocks skittering down the ravine, unsettled by their crash. Birds, flying away, fluttering and cawing high above. His heart, the blood roaring through his veins. His breath, the hollow sound of it rattling through his lungs, his throat. Passing over his lips.

He *had* to move. He had to find Dawood. He had to stop whatever was going to happen. Whatever Dan had planned, today.

His mind churned, trying to put the pieces together. Memories fluttered just out of reach. The touch of sedatives lingered inside him, trying to confuse him. Someone had drugged him. Someone working with Dan.

He breathed deep, closing his eyes. *Grab the memories. Push through. You know what's true in your heart. Remember.*

The SUV, parked outside the warehouse. Large enough to be packed with explosives, enough to devastate a city.

A body on the floor. Haddad's partner, Dan had said.

Dawood's confession, his love letter. What was Dan forcing him to do?

What day was it? September 11?

Kris crawled back to the car, his eyes glued to Dan's body. Blood dripped from his face, from his nose and the corner of his mouth. Kris stilled, waiting, watching to see if his chest rose or fell. If he breathed.

Nothing. Dan was gone. Dead.

*Good*. He shuddered. *Good.*

He set the gun down in the leaves and reached over Dan, trying not to touch him as he fumbled in Dan's pockets for the handcuff keys. They tumbled free, clattering to the roof. He reached—

Beneath the deflated airbags, trapped at the end of the dashboard, Kris spotted a cheap burner phone, identical to the one Dawood had shown him.

Dan wasn't stupid. He'd have smashed the phone George had tracked him with, destroyed it and hidden the remains. Dan was smart, damn it. He'd covered his tracks well, had hidden his betrayal for two years. Had lied to Kris's face for two years.

This must be a different phone.

Was it the phone he and his partner used? Whoever had knocked him out last night?

Kris grabbed it, dragged it free, and shimmied out of the car.

Handcuffs first. He dropped the phone as he wiggled the key into place, twisted, jimmied the lock until the catches released, and the cuffs dropped in the dirt.

The phone vibrated when he picked it up, and the screen winked on when he pressed the home button. One unread message.

He opened it.

The thread was a back-and-forth of location data and times, starting just after one in the morning.

*[ 0745. MMU. Heading to AMB. ETA 0810 ]*

*Dawood.* If it was him texting, or if it was someone with him, the partner Dawood had said Dan was providing, Kris didn't know. But these texts had to be from them, location and time stamps on their way to their final destination.

*MMU.* He closed his eyes, tried to think. MMU. A landmark, a hotel... A museum? Nothing fit, nothing was the right acronym—

Marymount University.

In northern Virginia, near Arlington. Which meant—

*AMB.*

Arlington Memorial Bridge.

*ETA 0810.*

He checked the time. 0749 hours.

He had twenty-one minutes.

But he had no idea where he was.

Kris grabbed Dan's gun and started running, heading down the gully as he pulled up the phone's GPS mapping software. The screen flickered, and the program loaded as slow as a glacier. It was a shitty burner phone, and it had shitty burner phone GPS. "Come on, come on."

Finally, a splotchy map of Washington DC appeared, blocks appearing at random, fuzzy and distorted. A pin appeared deep inside Rock Creek Park, in a gully beneath one of the horse trails that went up to the low cliffs overlooking DC.

Had Dan wanted a high vantage point, when whatever was about to happen went down? Some view over DC? What could be seen from the cliffs they'd been driving on? Georgetown, Foggy Bottom, the landmarks on the National Mall—

The Nine-Eleven Memorial service, the Patriot Day gathering, which began every year at 8:46 AM with the ringing of the bells and a moment of silence, and then the recitation of the names of those murdered in the attacks.

Victims' families, their loved ones, the president, members of congress, the cabinet, military officials, and thousands and thousands of civilians were there every year. Crowding the National Mall.

That must be what Dan planned. Magnifying a tragedy, squaring the worst attack on US soil in the history of the nation, trying to incite the end of days with a spike of pure rage to the heart of the nation's mourning.

Kris tasted ash on the back of his tongue.

He was seven miles from Arlington Memorial Bridge, through Adams Morgan, Dupont Circle, and the West End, in the middle of rush hour traffic. Most of DC came to a standstill for the September 11 anniversary. But not everyone.

He followed the map, jogging through dense underbrush and scrambling up the sides of the gully, trying to climb out of the ravine. If he followed this gully, he should pop out on—

Asphalt appeared, dark and cracked. Ridge Road, running up the northwest side of the park. He jogged onto the street, his back, his legs, his entire body screaming.

Tires hummed over the pavement, coming from around the bend, heading his way. *Perfect.* Kris stood in the center of the road, spreading his legs and taking aim.

The driver screeched to a stop, brakes squealing, almost side-sliding to a stop. His hands rose, hovering by his ears as his jaw dropped.

"CIA!" Kris bellowed. "*Get out of the car!*"

A man in a jogging suit poured out, falling over himself in his scramble from his SUV. He stared at Kris, hands held high, and sputtered. "*You're* CIA?"

What a sight he must be. Dirt stained his jeans, the pullover he'd borrowed from Dan after his shower. He wanted to rip it off, throw it on the ground, shoot it until it was nothing but threads that blew away. His trench coat fluttered in the morning wind, flapping behind his thighs. His hair stuck up at every angle, and grime stuck to one half of his face.

"CIA business. I need your car."

The jogger frowned. "I need to see some ID—"

Kris pointed his gun at him, right at his chest. "*This* is my ID."

The jogger backed away, all the way off the road, until he slipped onto the dirt shoulder. "Take it," he snapped. "Just fucking take it. It's insured."

"The government will contact you." Kris hopped in, slammed the door. The jogger glared at him, flipped him a double bird, but stayed on the shoulder.

Kris threw the car in reverse and slammed on the accelerator, yanking the wheel hard to the right. Tires squealing, the car spun in a slick turn, until he shifted gears and straightened the wheel.

0755 hours.

*Fifteen minutes.*

---

He dialed George's number as he came out of the park and skirted Adams Morgan on Rock Creek Parkway.

"*George Haugen*," his gruff voice answered on the fourth ring. He sounded like he hadn't slept, not once in his whole life. Like the entire world was about to crash down around him. Like he'd failed, everything and everyone.

Kris knew exactly how he felt.

"It's me."

"*Kris*!" George's tone changed instantly, sheer shock and amazement laced with terror winding through each consonant. "*Jesus Christ, where the fuck are you*?"

"Heading down Rock Creek Parkway toward Arlington Memorial Bridge. I think Dawood and whoever Dan's partner is are on their way there. I found a text on a burner phone of Dan's, with a location and an ETA."

"*Where is Dan*?"

"Where I left his body, in a ravine in his crashed car in Rock Creek Park."

Silence.

"He was about to kill me."

George exhaled slowly. Kris heard everything he didn't say, couldn't say, in his shaky breath. "Later, George. Listen, last night—"

*"Haddad recorded everything on his phone. We have everything. We know what Dan did. We think Noam Avraham and Haddad are together in an SUV. Older, with remanufactured tires. We don't have a make or model."*

Noam. Kris swallowed. *Noam.* "They're coming in from Marymount University, so if you have any units in that area, tell them to keep on the lookout."

He heard George repeat what he'd said, bark it out to the analysts and operators around him. In the background, he heard Ryan's gruff voice ask, "*Is he okay*?"

*"Where are you, Kris? Where are you going?"*

"To the bridge. I'm going to my husband."

*"We're right behind you."*

---

0804 hours

Traffic backed up for a mile off Arlington Memorial Bridge, onto Rock Creek and Potomac Parkway. The Watergate rose on his left, overlooking the river. Ahead, the Kennedy Performing Arts Center gleamed in the morning light. And beyond, miles of snarled traffic, gridlock on the roads, stretching across the bridge in both directions.

Fuck this.

Kris grabbed the cell phone and his gun and jumped out of the SUV. He weaved between the vehicles, ignoring the honks, running as fast as he could southbound on Potomac Parkway, past Easby point, past the sand volleyball courts. The Lincoln Memorial rose ahead, sitting on a hill overlooking the bridge, gazing at Arlington National Cemetery on the opposite bank of the river.

He jogged up the cloverleaf, rounded the bend, raced past the Arts of Peace statues.

Pedestrians clogged the walkways, the sidewalks on either side of the road. Cars sat bumper to bumper, exhaust fumes heavy in the air.

Honks sounded up and down the bridge, angry drivers frustrated at the gridlock. He tried to see, tried to crane his neck over the crowds, reach around the mass of humanity—

Impossible. It was fucking impossible like this.

Kris clambered onto the hood of the nearest car. The metal warped beneath his boots, groaning. The driver honked, horn blaring as a window rolled down and a man screamed, "What the fuck?"

Kris jumped from the hood to the trunk of the next car. He jogged over the roof, jumped off the hood and onto the rear spoiler of a low-slung white sports car. It rocked, and he leaped sideways into the bed of a pickup before running forward, jumping to the hood of a sedan. Horns blared, following his every move.

He kept his head on a swivel, scanning every car coming in from Virginia, searching for an SUV, an older model, dark. It would be low on its tires, weighted down with explosives. Heavier in the rear, sitting back—

Sunlight glinted off a midnight blue Chevy Blazer, late nineties model. Something almost obsolete. Something that could be bought for around two grand, cash-only in a back-alley deal.

Its back end sat heavy on the tires, its suspension weighted down.

He ran forward, jumping from hood to hood until he was a hundred feet from the SUV, close enough to see.

Two people in the front.

One driving, clinging to the steering wheel.

One beside him, something in his hand, outstretched toward the driver, hidden beneath the dashboard.

The sun gleamed, winking off cars and the river. He couldn't see, couldn't make out—

*Dawood.*

Dawood sat in the driver's seat, staring at Kris like his bedraggled, dirty ass was an angel sent from heaven, like he was the Prophet Muhammad come back to life, Jesus Christ resurrected. Like he was every dream Dawood had ever had, standing on the hood of a honking sedan in the middle of Arlington Memorial Bridge.

Kris raised his gun. Took aim. The wind shifted, blew his trench to the side.

*I've come for you, my love. I will* never *doubt you again.*

Dawood closed his eyes. Smiled, bruises on his face stretching.

Four gunshots split the air, cracking the DC morning.

Three bullets slammed into the Blazer's windshield, pummeling Noam in his chest, one dead center through his throat. Blood arced against the windshield, the passenger window.

And one bullet slid sideways, from the gun concealed in Noam's hand, through Dawood's side. Kris watched Dawood double over, clutch the steering wheel, grit his teeth as he screamed.

"Dawood!"

He ran, jogging over cars and leaping from hood to hood. The horns had stopped. Drivers had their cell phones out, recording him, his wild sprint to Dawood. Sirens rose in the distance, from both sides of the bridge.

Good luck getting to them, through the gridlock.

It was just him. Only he could get to Dawood.

Through the cracked windshield he watched Dawood sit back, press one hand to his side. Cringe, before the sun obscured his view.

"Dawood!"

Dawood threw the Blazer into reverse. The SUV rammed the car behind it, flattening the front end, sending it crunching into two cars behind it. He roared forward, shoving three cars out of his way. Again, and again, until he had maneuvering room, until he was able to turn the SUV.

Aim it toward the walkway.

The edge of the bridge.

"No!" Kris bellowed. "No! *No*!"

Dawood honked, over and over, his fist pounding the horn as he crept forward, enough to get the message across. Pedestrians scattered, shrieking, racing out of the way.

"*No*! Dawood, no, *stop*!"

Dawood turned to Kris, only twenty feet away. Kris saw his

battered and bruised face, his swollen eyes, his busted lip. Someone had beaten him. *Dan.*

It wasn't supposed to be like this. Dawood was the hero, and he was supposed to live. There had to be something, anything they could do. Anything other than *this.*

"*No!*"

The Blazer roared. Jerked forward, and then barreled over the empty walkway, crunched through the old concrete barrier on the side of the bridge.

The SUV hung in midair, suspended like time was paused, like Kris had grabbed the hands of a clock and frozen the seconds, the moments that would bleed forward. Kris exhaled. Too slowly, he was moving too slowly, trapped in a nightmare, locked in a reality where he was always too slow, too late, too wrong.

The SUV tipped forward, the back end rolling over the front, tumbling as it careened toward the glassy surface of the Potomac.

Kris made it to the edge of the bridge in time to see the Blazer slam into the water's surface, in time to see the nose and roof of the SUV hit the river as one.

Water poured in through shattered windows. He saw the outline of an airbag.

Saw Dawood's still body deflate against the airbag, slump sideways in the driver's seat as the SUV began to sink.

Not this time. He wasn't losing his husband. Not again.

Kris peered over the edge of the bridge, over the broken concrete and shattered rails Dawood had driven through. It was a thirty-foot drop, give or take a few feet.

He didn't think. He didn't question. He shoved his gun in his trench coat pocket and ran.

People screamed as he jumped, pointed his feet and plugged his nose and closed his eyes.

He hit the river like an arrow, like he was being stabbed everywhere in his body, like his soul had just been punched out of his chest. Disoriented, he flailed, first sinking before kicking up, swimming his way to the surface. As he broke the water, gasping, he heard someone shriek, up on the bridge, "There he is!"

Dawood's SUV was sinking, and he was too far away. Dawood was still inside, still not moving. Blood smeared across his face, marred the side of his head.

*No, not you. Not you. Not like this.*

He kicked, swimming harder than he ever had in his life, racing the sinking SUV and all of time, watching as the water rose, creeping over Dawood's chest, up his neck. Closed around his lips, and then his nose.

He screamed as the water covered Dawood's head, and the Blazer gurgled, slipping beneath the Potomac's muddy waters.

He took a deep breath and dove with the sinking Blazer, pushing through the water. Just a few more feet, just a few more. Dawood was still limp in the SUV, floating like a mannequin in the driver's seat. Blood haloed him, a river of it dyeing the waters red, staining the Potomac. Beyond Dawood, Noam's limp body slumped against the passenger door, his face mangled by the airbag, body bloodied and hovering lifeless in the cabin.

Finally, Kris gripped the broken glass of the driver's window. He reached in, yanked on the door handle, practically ripped the door off.

Handcuffs glinted in the river's fading light, catching a sunbeam from above. Kris's stomach clenched.

Noam had cuffed Dawood's right hand to the steering wheel. When the airbag deployed, it had shattered his cuffed wrist, his arm, his elbow. Dawood's right arm seemed to have four extra joints.

And Kris couldn't get him out of the Blazer. Not until those cuffs were off.

He fumbled in his pocket, pulled out his gun.

He'd get one shot at this. The back blast in the water would break their ribs, if they were lucky, and probably break another bone in Dawood's arm. But he could live with that, if it got them out of there.

Kris lined up the barrel of his gun against the chain of Dawood's handcuffs.

His lungs burned, and his brain started to panic, started to demand more oxygen.

Time to go.

Kris pulled the trigger.

Back blast from the shot created a shockwave in the water, spreading out and behind the gun, catching Kris in the chest. He tried to absorb the full impact, tried to take the hammer that had just been thrown through the water into his ribs completely, sparing Dawood. He screamed underwater, curled forward. Almost breathed in, reflexively.

The bullet had shattered the chain, burying itself in the SUV's dashboard.

Dawood was free.

Kris grabbed him and *pulled,* pushed off the sinking Blazer with both his feet. Dawood was deadweight, motionless, completely still. Blood floated in front of Kris's eyes as he tried to push for the surface.

Burning, burning, his lungs were screaming, collapsing. If he just opened his mouth. If he just breathed, just a little bit. But there was no air, not here. His brain was trying to trick him.

He had to hold on, just a little longer.

Darkness haloed his vision, the water, the surface going blurry. No, no. Just a little longer.

They broke the surface together, erupting into a world of light and sirens, of people screaming, shouting from the bridge. "There! There! There they are!"

"Help me," Kris croaked. He gasped, chest heaving, but could barely drag in any air. Water lapped into his mouth, and he coughed, sputtering into the Potomac. Dawood lay heavy in his arms, dragging him back down.

Splashes, nearby. His head dipped under water. He couldn't breathe, couldn't see.

"We got you, we got you." Hands lifted him, helped him get his head out of the water. More hands hefted Dawood.

People, in the river. Men who'd come to help him, swimming from the banks by Ohio Drive and the Lincoln Memorial Circle. They dragged them both back to shore, where a crowd waited, civilians on cell phones recording every moment, police muscling their way through, firefighters and paramedics racing to get to the riverside.

"He... he's CIA," Kris sputtered. "He's CIA. He's one of the good guys. Just saved us all."

They dragged Dawood out first, up the muddy banks and onto the grass. Blood trailed behind him, staining the ground a watery red. Kris shook off his rescuers, scrambled up the muddy slope. Slipped on the grass and crawled the rest of the way to Dawood's side.

Paramedics hovered over Dawood. "I've got no pulse. Asystole."

"No breathing. Starting compressions."

"Dawood, you have to come back," Kris whispered. He reached for Dawood's hand. "You have to come back. You have to come back to me. This isn't how it's supposed to go. This can't be the end. I cannot lose you again!"

"Airway ready."

"Intubate."

A second paramedic dropped Dawood's jaw, tipped his head back, and slid a breathing tube down his throat.

"Resume compressions."

A third paramedic slid a needle into Dawood's vein, an IV line and a bag of saline. He held a syringe in one hand, poised over the access port for the IV. "Ready with the epi."

"Go."

He slid the needle into Dawood's IV, plunging epinephrine into the line, into Dawood's body. Kris lunged for Dawood as they did, cupping Dawood's cheek, pressing his lips to Dawood's icy skin, willing him back to life. "Come back to me!" he screamed. "If you die, I'm coming with you!"

"Get back!" One of the Paramedics shouted. "Get back! We have to keep working!"

"Dawood!"

Hands grabbed him, yanked him, lifted him bodily off Dawood. He tried to beat them off, tried to fight, but he was carried away, down the grass slick with river water and blood, until they both collapsed, falling into the mud.

The man's arms wrapped around Kris, holding him close. His face buried in Kris's neck. "Let them do their job, Kris," Ryan grunted. "They have to save him. They have to."

He watched the paramedics pump his husband's chest until his vision blurred and his throat went raw, and his screams were drowned out the sirens, by the roar of the helicopter that came to take his husband away at 8:46 AM on September 11.

# 36

---

**George Washington University Hospital, Washington DC - September 16**

Kris's entire world had been reduced to a series of beeps. Every two seconds, another soft beep. Every forty-five seconds, the slow flow of oxygen restarting. Red and green and blue, washing the hospital room in dim lights, dancing lines whispering over the still bedsheets.

He sat at Dawood's bedside, listening to the hum of modern medicine. Watched the IV lines and arterial catheters, the oxygen lines, all snaking from his husband. Monitors traced the steady beat of his heart, measured his oxygen levels.

Kris's touch ghosted down Dawood's still hand, skirting the IV needle and the bandage, following the bones in the back of his hand down to his ring finger.

A gold wedding band, inlaid with a channel of dusty diamonds, was back where it belonged. Dawood's ring, on Dawood's hand.

---

He'd flown into a rage after the helicopter lifted off from the traffic circle outside the Lincoln Memorial, flying Dawood across the capital to George Washington University Hospital. Ryan had let him go, let him run after the helicopter, screaming, crying, shrieking at the top of his lungs until he fell again, a soaking wet pile of adrenaline and terror.

While George weaved in and out of the police, the FBI, trying to control the scene, trying to stop the thousands and thousands of cell phone videos streaming the incident live to the internet, Ryan had grabbed a paramedic and brought him to Kris.

He remembered being loaded onto a gurney. Being strapped down, and the pinch of an IV line in his elbow. Hands, pressing on his ribs, and what felt like lava erupting through his chest. "Broken ribs," one of the paramedics had said. "Gotta get him—"

He'd woken up in a hospital room, in the dark.

Someone sat at his bedside, though. Tall, lanky, and with his reading glasses perched on the end of his nose. Messy brunet strands. One leg was crossed, and he was reading from a legal file.

"Tom?" Kris had croaked. He'd tried to swallow. "Is that you?"

Tom had dropped his files and leaned in, one hand brushing back Kris's hair. He'd smiled, the warm, wonderful smile Tom had, the one that lit Mike's soul on fire. "Hey Kris. How are you feeling?"

"Where's Dawood? Where's my husband?"

"He's in ICU. He's in pretty bad shape."

His chest had caved in, and every fear he'd felt that day in Afghanistan, the day after the Hamid op, came roaring back, a thousand times sharper. "No, no, no," he'd whispered. "No, he has to be all right. He has to be okay."

"They're doing everything they can." Tom had leaned in, pressed a kiss to his forehead. "He's got the best care in the nation. He's a hero."

He'd laced his fingers through Tom's and let it all out, every sob he'd held in, every fear, every anguish, every impossible dream, every second of the last ten years he'd endured without Dawood, pouring out of him like a dam had broken. "I can't be without him again," he'd finally choked out. "If he's gone... I don't want to live without him again. Not again."

"It's early." Tom had wiped his tears away. "It's only been a day. Give it time."

Groaning from the floor had made him frown. Tom had looked down, smiled.

Mike had appeared, rising from the sleeping bag he'd unrolled on the floor of Kris's hospital room like a bear coming out of hibernation. His pompadour was a ragged mess, standing up on one side of his head, and his eyes were dark, sunken into his face. But he saw Kris awake, saw his tears, his broken soul.

"Kris..."

Kris had sat up as Mike crawled into bed with him, both meeting in the middle, arms wrapped around each other like they were trying to combine lives, like Mike was trying to give him enough of his heart to keep Kris's going. Kris had felt it, and he'd shuddered in Mike's hold. Collapsed, falling into Mike, and had let Mike hold him up as his tears restarted, as his fears raced in, and he imagined the world without Dawood, the love of his life... again.

---

Five days later, and he sat by Dawood's bedside, a constant, uninterrupted vigil.

He'd been discharged after a day, his broken ribs wrapped and bandaged, and had gone home to change, shower, and dig out his and Dawood's wedding rings from the duffel in the back of his closet. They were dusty, the gold spotted and dull. But they were theirs.

At the hospital, he'd kissed Dawood's ring finger before sliding his wedding ring back on like he had eleven years before when he'd vowed to be Dawood's for all time, for every day of his life.

The ring was loose on Dawood's slender fingers. He'd lost weight in ten years. Lost weight and gone gray in places. Silver streaked his temples, and strands peppered his dark hair. It was longer than he'd ever seen, soft waves that came almost to his ears, combed back. It was a good look on him. A gentle look.

His own ring fit, sliding on like he'd never taken it off. Like it was supposed to be there, always, for eternity.

*Never again. Never ever will I take this ring off. Never will I be separated from you.*

The doctors had removed Dawood's breathing tube two days before, and they weren't cautioning Kris to prepare himself, to expect the worst, as often anymore.

Noam's gunshot had shredded his liver, and the surgeons had removed almost three quarters of it. He'd lost blood, almost too much. But it was the crash into the Potomac that had killed him, at least for a few minutes, underwater. He hadn't breathed, and his brain had swelled, a massive concussion from the crash. How many minutes had he gone without oxygen? Would he ever wake up? Would he be the same if he did?

"We need to be realistic," one of the doctors had said. "There's a fifty-fifty chance he won't wake, ever. It all comes down to him now. How he responds. We've done all we can, but he experienced significant trauma."

"He's coming back." Kris had laced their hands together, had cupped Dawood's left hand in both of his. Kissed each finger, slowly. "He's coming back."

He *had* to. This was their second chance, their impossible happy ending. This was *theirs*, their love story, and it *didn't* end here. Not after everything. Not after Dawood had fought back from the dead, not after Kris had put an end to Dan, to the betrayals, to the twisting of everything Dawood held dear.

*If you are gone, my love, then I will follow you. I won't let you go again. Never, ever, again.*

*If you breathe your last breath, the very next will be my last as well.*

He kept his vigil through the long hours of the day and night. Mike and Tom came every evening, bringing him food, sitting with him, sometimes talking, sometimes in silence.

At night, he slept in the cup of Dawood's left hand, cradling his face in the hollow of his palm. Sometimes he traced Dawood's veins, the muscles in his arm. Kissed his wrist, and imagined what their future would look like.

Together. They would be together, and that was all that mattered.

---

It was the afternoon, seven days after September 11. Kris held Dawood's hand, watched the rise and fall of his chest. Physically, he was getting better, slowly. The medications the doctors were using to keep him sedated were being weaned back. Everyone was waiting, wondering.

Would he wake up?

Knocks sounded at the door. Kris and Dawood had been given a private suite, VIP level, and CIA guards traded shifts with DC police. No one could just stop by, just turn up. Even Mike and Tom had to be cleared three times before they could visit.

Kris turned his bleary gaze to the door.

George and Ryan hovered at the opening.

Both seemed condemned men, like they'd lost something irreplaceable in the last week, something they didn't know how to live without. Ryan was half in and half out of himself, like he wanted to escape reality. Escape himself.

Kris knew that feeling.

George led the way into Dawood's hospital room. He had a brown folder in one hand, and he held it out to Kris as he stopped at the foot of Dawood's bed.

"This is from the CIA, Kris, and as you're Dawood's legal next of kin..." He trailed off, shrugging.

"Last I heard, I *wasn't* his next of kin."

"June 26, 2013, you became his next of kin." George slid both hands into his pockets, looked down. "United States versus Windsor. The Supreme Court struck down Section 3 of the Defense of Marriage Act as unconstitutional. Which meant the CIA, and the entire federal government, recognized same sex marriages from that moment forward." He swallowed. "I watched the case, and I thought about you. And Haddad."

"Little late for us, don't you think?"

"Not anymore."

He opened the folder. Papers tumbled free, across Dawood's legs. A USB drive landed on the sheets.

"A recording of what happened in the warehouse. Between Dan and Dawood. You were there, too. It seemed right, giving you a copy. So you could know... what happened."

He flipped open a folded sheet of heavy paper, cream linen, with the CIA seal embossed at the top of the page. A letter from Director Edwards.

*Officer Dawood Haddad,*

*You have the gratitude of a thankful nation for your dedicated service, your commitment to excellence, and your many, many sacrifices over the years. While we cannot turn back time, we will do everything we can to make your sacrifices right.*

*From a grateful nation,*

*Director Ken Edwards*

"Haddad is a hero. The papers, the news, everyone has the story. He was undercover within al-Qaeda for years, working to prevent their largest attempted strike on American soil since nine-eleven."

Kris frowned. "That's not entirely true. What about Dan?"

George's gaze pinched. "Dan... died tragically a few days ago in a traffic accident."

They were going to bury it. Bury it and hide it forever, a secret that would never see the light of day. He shouldn't be surprised. The CIA buried their skeletons, their secrets, deeper than they buried their dead. Part of him was disgusted, wanted to be sick. But he'd been a part of those secrets they'd buried. He'd been a skeleton in their closet. "And Noam?"

"Mossad has officially denounced him and has labeled him a rogue element and called his actions criminal in the extreme. That's the classified version. The unclassified version is he, too, tragically died in a motor vehicle accident."

Kris closed his eyes.

"We dredged the Potomac in the middle of the night. Brought up the SUV. There was a dead body full of shrapnel and enough plastique explosive to put a fifty-foot crater in the National Mall. Kill thousands. When Haddad drove that SUV off the bridge, he shorted out the circuits in the homemade timer. He saved everyone's life."

The dead body. Dawood's partner.

Kris flipped the letter from Director Edwards over. The gratitude of a grateful nation was all well and good. But there was ten years of bitterness in the water under that bridge. Ten years of isolation, of backs turned on him and the memory of his husband.

The next sheet was a reinstatement into the CIA, signed and sealed by the director, for Dawood Haddad.

Kris was listed as his official spouse.

It included his salary information from a decade before and the automatic promotions he would have been eligible to receive. Every year was there, added and tabulated, with interest calculated. *Total back pay to be disbursed,* the last line read. *$2 million.*

"This belongs to him. And to you. To both of you. No matter what." George fumbled, trying to find the right words.

Kris shook his head. "This is the right thing to do. He's always been with us."

"I know. It's only a start, though. If he wanted to continue, if he wants to come back… He's welcome." George cleared his throat. "As are you."

Kris laughed, hollow and empty. "George… I think I'm done with the CIA."

He was, finally, just done. The guilt that had seized his life, that had propelled him forward. The certainty that he had to toil, for his entire life, to undo the failures, the wrongs of September 11.

But he'd given his *all*, and then more, until he was stripped raw. He'd given the CIA, the nation, everything he had to give, and then he'd kept going. He'd lived with ghosts for so long, the heavy weight of their lives hanging off his bones, grinding the spaces between his joints, that he'd gotten used to the pull of their shame.

And when they'd gone, he'd replaced their haunting with his own self-shame, his own recrimination. The noose around his neck wasn't of the past, or the dead, or his failings anymore. It was only him, only his own deluge of anguish and the stifling suffocation of his deepest self-loathing.

He'd failed, before. He'd failed to stop September 11. He'd failed to stop Hamid.

But he'd done some things right, as well. He hadn't lost his soul, hadn't hijacked the hatred of al-Qaeda, of ISIS, and started living in their twisted brand of hate. Hadn't hitched his soul to a black hole and ridden the collapse until he'd perverted into whatever it was that Dan had become. Something ugly and evil. Something that was against the world and everyone in it.

The balance of his life was set. His deeds were done. The days of saving the world were beyond him. Someone else, someone younger, would have to step up, step into the void and fight the good fight. Fight the battle between losing your soul over the edges of inhumanity and stopping the rise of evil, from all corners of the globe, looking to hurt. To kill. In any way evil could.

Nietzsche once said, *Beware when fighting monsters, you do not become a monster yourself. For when you stare into the abyss, the abyss stares back into you.*

Kris had stood on the edge of the abyss and peered down. Dan had plunged headfirst, as had Noam. As had Saqqaf, and Zahawi, and Bin Laden, and so many others.

Dawood had been his anchor, his fixed Northern Star, keeping him grounded on the firmament, keeping him from tumbling into the darkness.

Memories and ghosts and promises lived in his bones. He'd carried them for half his life. It was time to let them go.

It was time to start living for *him.*

Him and Dawood.

Ryan hovered behind George, staring at Dawood for a long moment before flicking his gaze to Kris. "Can we… can we talk?"

Part of him didn't want to. Ryan and he had history, sixteen years of animosity and snapping at each other, and the disastrous Hamid op that had sealed the uncrossable gulf between them, an impenetrable divide.

But, Ryan had held him as he'd come undone on the banks of the Potomac. And he'd hunted Al Jabal until he was dead, until he was nothing but ash, had devoted his entire being to hunting Dawood's torturer and killer. There were redeemable moments in his life. Was there more Kris couldn't see?

"Sure. I need a coffee anyway."

"I'll buy."

George took Kris's seat beside Dawood, watching over him with his hands pressed together, fingers against his lips like he was praying over Dawood. Maybe he had his own confessions to give, his own words to say in the silence, for Dawood's ears alone.

Ryan shuffled to the door and held it open for him, looking as uncomfortable as hell, then fell into step as Kris headed on autopilot for the hospital's cafeteria. There was a coffee stand there that made a decent sludge, enough to keep him awake for a few more hours. Ryan bought two cups and guided him to a table in the corner, settling in the chair backed against the wall.

Ryan batted his coffee cup back and forth as Kris crossed his legs. Sipped his coffee and stared at Ryan.

Ryan licked his lips. Pressed his lips together. "I'm sorry," he breathed. "For… everything."

"Everything is pretty big." Kris shifted. Sighed. "What do you mean?"

"I thought I was doing the right thing. I thought we all were. Dan… he was one of my best friends. I don't understand—"

Kris looked down. The CIA, and Ryan, George, and Edwards in particular, were going to have to take a long hard look in the mirror. How did one of their own turn against them? How had Dan, long a rising star in the agency, become so twisted? Turned so evil?

"The Dan you thought you knew has been gone a long time. Same with me. The man I thought I knew? He was just a fake. A fantasy. The real Dan is the one lying in the morgue, right now. That's who he was, at his core."

Ryan buried his face in one hand, hiding from Kris. His shoulders shook. "If Dan can do that, then who else can? How far does this go? Is he an aberration? Or is his hatred... normal?" Kris heard what Ryan didn't ask: could Ryan slip and fall into the darkness, slide down into the abyss after Dan? Was he, too, capable of something like that?

"Something in between, I think." Kris played with the lid of his coffee cup as Ryan stared at him, his dark, bloodshot eyes boring into the center of his forehead. He'd never seen so much fear in Ryan's gaze, a fear that danced deep in the back of his eyes.

"Dan hijacked the hatred he claimed to loathe. He became exactly what he despised. He hijacked ISIS and al-Qaeda's destinies. He became the most devout believer of their twisted ideology."

"Dan was *not* a Muslim—"

"No, but he was a nihilist. He wanted to watch the world burn, tear everything down, destroy anything in the way of his vision of the perfect future. That's exactly what ISIS and al-Qaeda believe as well. And—" He glared at Ryan. "You should know better than that. ISIS and al-Qaeda do not represent authentic Islamic beliefs."

Ryan swallowed, looked away.

Would Ryan finally listen? Actually hear him if he tried to really speak? They'd been using the same language but talking past each other for sixteen years.

"Dan, Noam, George, and you, yes, *you*, Ryan, have all had the same problem for sixteen years. You look at Islam and all you see is al-Qaeda, ISIS, Boko Haram. You see the loudest, worst parts, and you erase a billion other believers who don't share any of those beliefs. You don't see nuance when you look at The Other. You just see an enemy."

Ryan stayed silent.

"Al-Qaeda and ISIS are the right-wing fascists of the Muslim *ummah*. They rose to prominence like all fascist groups do. In response to failures of nationalism, of governance, in response to people's fears about the future, worrying economics times, and a fragile world teetering on the edge of all-out war. Fascists are rising everywhere, from the US to Europe to Asia. They're *all* playing on fears, trying to control the world through terror, through hatred. They pull lines from the Quran to justify their evil, and twist everything to their own ends, just like fascists everywhere justify their actions. Why can't you see how al-Qaeda and ISIS are exactly the same as fascists rising within the West? It's fascism, and it's hatred, pure and simple.

"The failure of the Arab Spring to bring any lasting change, any democratic reform, led to the resurgence of these fascists in the Middle East. To ISIS, and their satellites. Al-Qaeda, trying to come back after Bin Laden's death. They're tapping into fear, amplifying terror, feeding hopes and dreams like a drug. ISIS and al-Qaeda are just the fascist, right-wing Islamic response to the yearning for a bright future for the Muslim world.

"No one over here seems to get that. There are fascists in Islam, and they're hated just as much *there* as the fascists rising in our communities are *here*. And there are people fighting against them inside of Islam. It's not just the Western world versus ISIS versus al-Qaeda. This isn't the clash of civilization that so many people dream about. It's just another fight against the return of fascism. And we need to fight that, yes, but we need to support the progressives, too. Not tar every Muslim into shades of evil." Kris exhaled, holding Ryan's gaze.

"What about Haddad? I mean... Dawood?" For the first time, Ryan used Dawood's Muslim name.

"Dawood?" Kris smiled, sadness tugging down the corner of his lips. "He's a hippie. He always has been. Gentle in his heart, his soul. He just wants to connect with the universe, find the good in everyone. Just like his father, I assume. If his father had lived, I think Dawood and he would have been as happy as they could ever be living in the desert, herding camels, and living a simple life of prayer and family love." He chuckled. "Maybe smoking some hash, too. But Dawood is an Islamic hippie. He's always just wanted to love and be loved." His thoughts turned darker, turned against themselves. "This war has shredded him. Sixteen years, and almost a decade out in the cold. I can't believe he held on to himself."

"Did he?"

Kris nodded. The night they'd had together, and Dawood's confession in the woods. He'd seen the truth of Dawood, the light of his soul, the inner strength of the man he most loved, most admired in the whole world. "Ten years changes a person. It does. For Dawood... He's like a diamond that's been compressed out of ashes. Gold that's been through fire, all the rough spots, the wreckage, burned away. When I look at him, I'm breathless." Kris closed his eyes as his throat clenched. "He's the best of all of us. And he always has been."

"And you?" Ryan asked. "Did you change?"

"For the worse," Kris whispered. "Without Dawood, I forgot how to love."

"Where do we go from here?" Ryan swallowed hard, both hands clutching his coffee cup.

Where did Ryan, and the CIA, and the world go from here? Kris hadn't a clue. How could anything change? How could the hatred ever stop? Would anyone so hateful, so twisted, so full of vileness and malice, like Dan, like Noam, like the fighters of ISIS, ever reconcile? Ever find a way through the madness to peace?

Dan had given up peace long ago, had surrendered to cold expediencies. Peace through victory, Dan must have thought. Peace through death and destruction, laying waste to the enemy. Peace through circumnavigating justice, avoiding the trifles of conscience and human rights. If Dan had believed he was fighting monsters, then it was only a small leap to accepting that monsters didn't have human rights. He could follow Dan's warped logic down into the abyss, the rationalities and explanations for torture, for murder. For using terrorism as his own weapon of political persuasion, to galvanize the masses to his will.

He had become *exactly* what he despised.

"In a way, we lost this war when we lost Dan." Kris cleared his clenched throat, tried to speak through the memories, the pain. "When we lose ourselves, when we become what we hate, we've lost everything. Defeat came, and we lost the war, and we never even saw it. But now we're sitting in the rubble and ruin and trying to make sense of the future." Kris exhaled slowly. Ash sat heavy on the back of his tongue.

What was left, after all that?

How did Ryan reconcile his best friend to the abyss? Ryan's fingers scratched over the cardboard sleeve of his coffee, picked at the overlapping edge. His bloodshot eyes stared at a point on the laminate table between them, somehow gazing a million miles away, into the past, into all of the paths that had led them to this point.

"This world is full to the brim with agony and grief and rage. Everyone is searching for something to hold on to, Ryan. Searching for certainty. Who is the enemy and how do we destroy them to make the world safe again? Searching for hope, that there is still goodness in the world, beyond the hatred, beyond the pain. But we have to face the world as it is, and not try and force it to be something it's not. There *is* evil in this world. There are fascists, both in the West and in Islam. There are terrible things, and terrible people, and terrible choices. But we have to find some kind of light through the darkness. Something that cuts through that."

"I was always so..." Ryan's expression twisted, like he was about to jump off a skyscraper, like he welcomed it. "I *hated* how certain you were. All the time. You were so fucking certain of yourself, of your morals. This was right and that was wrong. I didn't know how you held on to that, with everything..."

"You couldn't watch what Dan did to Zahawi."

"But I didn't try and stop it, either. Not like you." Ryan's voice broke. He looked away from Kris, visibly fighting for control.

This war had robbed them all of their empathy, their ability to see reason. Hatred was a smog that hung in the air, that colored the world in shades of blood and fire. That let men be tortured to the brink of death and beyond, that let Dan build an entire program, a machine dedicated to breaking men, to anguish and suffering, all in the name of expediency.

"I was lucky, Ryan. Dawood has always been my rock. My light in the darkness. You once said he compromised me. That being close to him led to me making wrong decisions. You almost called him, and me, traitors to the CIA."

Finally, Ryan looked up. Met his gaze. "I was wrong," he whispered. A single tear slipped from his eye. Ryan wiped it away with the back of his hand, turned to the side. Hid his face, his shame. "About... everything. And for far too long."

*Now he recognizes what he's done.* Kris was exhausted, almost too exhausted, for this conversation. But he could see Ryan's agony, see his pain bleeding out all over the table, flowing across the hospital's cafeteria. See a soul-weary ache, and a desperation for something that looked like salvation.

Ryan's wounds went soul-deep, fissures on his heart and his conscience that he'd have to reconcile with. Choices he'd made that had fractured who he was, until he was a man barely hanging on, clinging to rationalities and his rage. George, too, was lost in his own psychic wounds. A lifetime of playing politics and fighting a war, and losing both, forever destined to make sacrifices and compromises for the worst of all sides, did that to a man. He'd been a politician more times than not, trying to please everyone, but when the hard calls had to be made, George had, at least, been able to call people who could get shit done. Kris. Dawood.

And what about them? Dawood was fighting back from choosing to die, choosing to sacrifice himself for everyone, and Kris didn't know if bringing him back was the right or wrong choice to make. After forty-seven years of an anguished life, did Dawood deserve his peace? Did he deserve to meet Allah face to face, and rest, finally, in the arms of his creator? He was a hero, an undeniable hero. Should he be given the hero's send-off?

Was it selfish, holding on to him?

He wouldn't live without Dawood again. He'd come to that simple truth days ago. What happened would happen. But his choice was made.

"We all lost ourselves in this war. Some more than others." *Dan... How did you spin so entirely out of orbit?* "Every choice we make, we choose to either cut out a piece of ourselves, sacrificing what we know is right, or we make the choice to be better. But it all comes down to us. How each of us faces the world, and our choices in it. And after that..." Kris sighed. "It's up to our conscience to make peace with our souls. Because it's us who will build this future, Ryan. Us. Individuals. Men and women and people who think and feel and make decisions. So are we going to make a world of hatred? Or are we going to look at ourselves, at what we've done, and try to make something better?"

There weren't any answers to that, not yet. Answers didn't lie in reports or CIA briefings, in Congressional testimony, or in destroyed videotapes.

Answers lay in everyone's souls, deep inside their hearts. The greatest battle they would endure would be to face the world and *feel* it, *see* it, through someone else's eyes. Through someone else's heart.

"I don't know if I can live with this," Ryan grunted. "Dan, he was my direct report. He was my friend. My only real friend. I didn't see this? I didn't see what he'd—"

"Don't take Dan's sins onto your soul. They're not yours. Dan duped everyone. *Everyone*. I was just as close to him as you were."

Ryan crumpled over his coffee cup, hiding his face again.

"We all have a past. We all made choices. Dan made his. Dawood made his. Those choices set them on a collision course toward each other. Two shooting stars bursting apart on impact." Kris reached across the table, pried Ryan's clenched fingers off his coffee cup. He squeezed. "What matters is what we do *now*. How we live with our past. The choices we made."

When Ryan met his gaze, Kris saw shades, echoes of Ryan's decision. A bullet, a gun. A lonely house, and a bottle of whiskey.

"Don't *do* that, Ryan." He squeezed hard, until Ryan's bones shifted in his hand. "Don't take the easy way out. We need you. The world needs you. We need to make this right."

"I don't know how..." Ryan breathed.

"Don't drag your past into your future. Don't hold on to that pain. Leave your history where it belongs. In the past. Learn from it. Take it out and look at it, turn it over. But put it back where it belongs. Don't let those ghosts live with you in the present." He shuddered. Swallowed. "I... carried nine-eleven with me. I've carried it all this time. Because I felt responsible. Because the hijackers' names crossed my desk. Do you remember the Nine-Eleven Commission? When they were done, they recommended thirty-six CIA officers be censured and terminated, because they knew about the hijackers entering the US and they didn't share the intel with the FBI. *I* was one of those thirty-six." He licked his lips, swallowed hard. "Director Thatcher said there was enough hurt to go around, enough self-blame and self-castigation. He didn't fire any of us. But that doesn't mean we weren't responsible."

Ryan frowned.

"Did that give me the drive I had? The fire to live this life? Did my moral failing, at twenty-three years old, shape my ethical certainty for the rest of my life? A commitment to doing the right thing, no matter what? Maybe." Kris shrugged. "But I also let those ghosts dictate my life. Keep me tied to what I felt was my sacred duty. I couldn't separate the good from the bad. Couldn't learn from my past without feeling the shame, spiraling into the agony all over again.

"We've done terrible, obscene things. The CIA, and each of us, individually. And in this world, there are appalling things, appalling people whom we've fought, darkness that we've come up against. But they're people. Just people, making terrible choices from their own places of darkness and horror. We can slide into the darkness with them, or we can fight them and their horror, their terror. Some days it feels like we're just killing machines, trying to take out as many bad guys as we can before more crop up. But maybe there's something different we can try. Maybe there's a new direction you can lead us through. You and George."

Ryan nodded slowly. He squeezed Kris's hand. "You could have gone the other way. Decided the ends justified the means. You'd do anything to stop another nine-eleven."

"It was a moral failing that caused nine-eleven. More moral failings, more abandoning what's right? That wouldn't solve anything." Kris shook his head. "You're at a crossroads, Ryan. You're at the center of fate and destiny, where all paths have converged."

Paths upon paths, choices made that carved destinies, changed the course of time and reality. What if Dawood hadn't been lost for ten years? What if there had been no one to stop Dan?

Ryan closed his eyes. Took a deep breath and let it out slowly. When he opened them again, the certainty, the finality, was gone, replaced by someone else. Something that looked almost like hope.

"What you do next, the choices you make, will impact the lives of millions. Billions. Make your choices for them. For everyone else. Walk the path that will save lives, and you will change the world."

"Like Dawood did?" Ryan, finally, smiled, just faintly.

"Like my husband, yes."

"I never said..." Ryan breathed, red washing his cheeks. "Congratulations on your marriage, Kris. On finding the love of your life. I mean, that was such shit timing in the middle of a war. But, thinking back, that had to be fate, right?" He chuckled, once.

"Thank you." It was eleven years late, but it was something. Kris let go of Ryan's hand, sat back. Sipped at his cold coffee. "And you? Any wife at home?"

"I haven't been able to connect with anyone. This job..." He waved his coffee cup, trying to encompass the enormity of their lives. "I stopped even trying to meet people. The last few dates I went on were... years ago. I don't know, maybe something is broken in me."

"It's not. Not anymore." Kris smiled, his lips thin. "You are going to be okay, Ryan. Don't eat a bullet."

Ryan took his time answering, fiddling with his coffee cup, staring at the plastic table. But when he looked up, Kris saw certainty in his gaze. "I won't. Because of you."

---

Kris returned to Dawood's bedside, needing to ground himself in Dawood, take over George's vigil. George stood up, and they exchanged a long, silent glance before George pulled him into an awkward hug. Kris felt his trembles, heard the words George couldn't say.

As the sun set, and the last of the daylight bled from Dawood's room, Kris pulled up his phone. Opened an app he'd installed days before, sitting by Dawood's bedside.

Daily verses of the Quran appeared. He'd been reading to Dawood as often as he could in the stillness, in the silence. He laced their hands together and recited, whispering from the Al-Furqaan surah. "*In the name of Allah, the Most Gracious, the Most Merciful. The servants of the Most Merciful are those who walk the earth in humility, and when the ignorant address them, they say, 'Peace'.*"

Oh, how deeply that described Dawood, in almost every way. Kris felt a hot blade slide through his heart as he tried to breathe.

Next to read was the Al-Imraan surah. "*In the name of Allah, the Most Gracious, the Most Merciful. O Allah, Owner of Sovereignty. You grant sovereignty to whom You will, and You strip sovereignty from whom you will. You honor whom you will, and You humiliate whom you will. In Your hand is all goodness. You are Capable of all things. You merge the night into the day, and You merge the day into the night, and you bring the living out of the dead, and You bring the dead out of the living, and You provide for whom you will without measure.*"

He studied Dawood's face, the stillness. The stubble, dark brown mixed with silver. *Wake up, my love. Wake up.*

Kris flicked to the next verse, from the Al-Araf surah. "*It is He who sends the wind ahead of His mercy. Then, when they have gathered up heavy clouds, We drive them to a dead land, where We make water come down, and with it We bring forth every kind of fruit. Thus We bring out the dead—*"

Kris dropped his phone on Dawood's bed and pitched forward, resting his forehead on Dawood's thigh. "Oh Allah," he whispered.

"I'm not ready to let go. Please… *please* don't take him. Not yet. Please."

Fingers brushed his hair. Ghosted over the back of his neck.

Kris sat back, staring up at Dawood—

At Dawood's open eyes, at his soft smile. "At the end of the path…" Dawood whispered, his voice hoarse, dry, unused for a week.

"*You* were there," Kris recited in unison with him. "You were there," he repeated, rising, rushing Dawood, cradling his face in both hands as he kissed him, kissed every inch of his skin, his eyelids, his lips, his forehead. Dawood held him, his left hand squeezing his arm. His right arm was immobile in a full cast and sling, propped on a pillow.

Dawood reached for Kris's left hand, brought it forward. Stared at his wedding ring, and then up at Kris, his jaw slack.

Kris lifted Dawood's left hand and kissed his ring finger, his wedding band. Dawood hissed, and then smiled, the same smile he'd worn the day of their wedding.

"I married the love of my life for all time," Kris said. "Nothing will ever break that."

Dawood pulled him close, until they were kissing again. "*Ya rouhi*," he whispered. "You are the moon in my darkness, *habibi*. Always."

"You are my love, my light, my guiding star."

They kissed, and kissed, and kissed, until the nurses bustled in and gently separated them, moving Kris to the side of the room as they got to work checking Dawood over.

Their gazes stayed locked together, fixed on one another, the entire time.

Nothing would ever break them apart.

Not ever again.

---

When the nurses finally left, Kris crawled into bed beside Dawood, careful to keep away from his stitches, the still-healing bullet wound in his side, and not jostle his broken arm. Dawood folded into him, their heads resting together, lips trading kisses as they held hands.

"Weird question," Dawood asked, after an hour. "Do you have a phone I can borrow?"

"Of course." Kris dug his phone out of his pants and held it out.

"Can you go to Gmail? I need to check something."

Kris pulled up the internet browser and typed in the email address and login information Dawood recited.

A single email waited in the inbox.

*Re: Confessions*, sent by Behroze Haddad.

"Is that your son? The boy you adopted?"

Dawood nodded. He swallowed hard. "I told him everything the night before I met Dan. Who I really was. How I came to the mountain. He was just a child when I arrived. I was the stranger who showed up and became the healer, and then the imam. I stitched his arm closed twice, cleaned and bandaged so many of his cuts and bruises. He was the only one of his family to survive."

"Where is he now?"

"I sent him to Islamabad to study to be an imam. I made him swear he would never pick up a weapon, never follow the path of violence." Dawood exhaled shakily. "I told him about you, too. About my husband."

Kris blinked. "I wonder what he's said."

"Read it to me?"

Kris clicked on the email. He started to read, but his voice choked and he stopped, unable to continue. Tears blurred his vision. He held the phone for Dawood to read.

*Baba,*

*I am filled with a thousand questions.*

*I knew you always had secrets. When we were kids, sometimes we would make up stories about where you came from. Since you always stared at the moon, I told everyone you were from there and had fallen to earth, and you were trying to climb the mountains to get back home.*

*I think, in the end, I was the closest in our guesses.*

*You have always told me my jihad is of the heart. That my challenge, my entire life, will be to love unconditionally. To love like the Prophet, peace be upon him, when all I want to do is rage. Be angry, or hate.*

*I thought I was angry and struggling when you left me in Islamabad. I kept to my studies, and I've tried to follow your teachings: my jihad is of the heart. I should always* love.

*You did not tell me that, in time, answers would arrive. That I would understand one day why I have loved as hard as I have, even through the pain, the anger. Why still, to this day, you remain a fixed point in my heart, a man and a memory I constantly turn to for guidance. Your absence has been a wound that I have not been able to close, Baba.*

*I want to know more about who you are.*

*And I want to know Kris, too.*

*Teach me, Baba. I have so much more to learn.*

*You said you may never respond to my email if the worst were to happen. If you are reading this, know that I have prayed for you every day since you sent your email, and I will continue to pray for you every day going forward. Your name will always be on my lips for Allah.*

*You have my love, Baba. Always.*

*Behroze Haddad*

Dawood turned into Kris's neck and wept.

# 37

**McLean, Virginia - September 23**

They walked hand in hand down the soft trails of Pimmit Run Stream Park. The leaves were turning, gold and ocher and tawny umber, rust and cardinal floating above them, beneath them on the damp earth of the park. A stream trickled through the center, babbling over stone and fallen logs.

"What will happen to your brothers in Yemen?"

Dawood sighed. "I'm sure they've seen the news reports. I'm now officially known as an undercover CIA officer who'd penetrated terrorist cells for years. I sent Ihsan an email. Tried to tell him I had to stop Dan. That he was ruining Islam, was just as terrible as ISIS. That we weren't like that. *I* wasn't like that. That my jihad was to preserve the best of our faith."

"Did he reply?"

Dawood shook his head. "I gave their names to the State Department. The ambassador in Yemen is quietly asking to track them down. They'll be arrested. Ihsan will be deported to Saudi, go to one of the deradicalization camps the Kingdom has established. After that, he will have his life back. And hopefully he can find his peace in this life. Abu Dujana…" He sighed again. "I hope he finds peace, but I doubt it will be in this life."

Kris squeezed his hand, wrapped his arm around Dawood's waist. "You were right to keep their names hidden. Dan would have had them executed."

They walked in silence, letting the stream babble, the leaves crunch beneath their feet as Dawood whispered a prayer to the men he once knew, men who had been a part of his life, not quite friends, not quite enemies. Human beings he'd walked his path with. Brothers.

"I officially resigned from the CIA this morning." Kris leaned his head against Dawood's shoulder. "I was offered an early retirement by Director Edwards. I accepted."

"I didn't expect what they did for me." The back pay, the letter of commendation, the public glory as an undercover officer. Though the public face was to blur over Dan's heinous betrayal, the CIA had worked overtime to turn Dawood Haddad into the nation's hero. It was nice, for once, to be the good guy.

Even Dawood's star on the Memorial Wall had been filled in with gold, commemorating a returned hero once thought lost.

There wasn't going to be a star for Dan. His body had been buried without fanfare in a municipal cemetery in Maryland. Only George and Ryan had watched the casket go into the ground.

"We're free." Kris squeezed Dawood's hand. "Free to do whatever we want. Wherever we want. Do you want to move overseas?" Would Dawood like it better in the Middle East? Would he want to go back to Libya, if the civil war ever settled down? Would he want to live in Dubai, or Kuwait? Or go to Behroze in Islamabad? "I'll come with you."

"You have a life here, Kris. You've lived in DC since you were eighteen. More than half your life."

"More than half my life has been lived in war zones."

"What about your friends? Mike and Tom?"

They'd had dinner at Tom's house two nights after Dawood was released from the hospital. Tom was a gracious and wonderful host, and he'd fed them a banquet of Middle Eastern and American foods. Dawood had eaten half his body weight in burgers and hummus, in kebabs and shawarma. Mike had acted like he'd met a superhero, like he'd met Captain America himself. Wide-eyed and starstruck, he'd hung on Dawood's every word, all night long.

"They are wonderful people," Dawood said softly. "I like them. I would like to spend more time with them."

The park petered out, returning to the suburban bustle of McLean, to a shady street that boasted homes and churches and a café on the corner. Dawood turned right, heading up the street.

Kris frowned. "Will living here be enough for you?"

Dawood stopped outside a white building with a squat minaret, a short tower that blended in with the trees and the other buildings on the block. A sign on the fence read "*The Al-Fatiha Masjid. An MPV mosque.*"

Dawood lifted Kris's fingers to his lips. "I wanted to bring you here. Show you this mosque." He kissed Kris's fingers, slowly. "I want this to be my home. Where I worship for the rest of my life."

"So you do want to stay? Here, with me?"

"I do. Especially with you." Dawood nuzzled Kris's fingers against his cheek. "And I want you to be a part of this. A part of my life here. I'm not asking you to convert. But I want you to feel welcome here, with me. In every part of my life."

Kris shifted. He swallowed. "Are we welcome? Won't we have to hide?"

Dawood smiled. "Come. Let me introduce you to the imam."

Hand in hand, they walked into the mosque, passing beneath a canopy of magnolias and a cypress tree, the leaves whispering on the DC wind. The mosque's foyer glittered with inlaid mosaics, and along one wall, the *shahada*, done in a rainbow of colors.

"*Habibi*!" A voice from the masjid cried out. Footsteps, rushing toward them, the imam coming to them both. Dawood squeezed Kris's hand, refused to let go.

The imam wrapped both arms around Dawood gently, avoiding his right arm in its sling, and kissed both his cheeks. "I have seen you in the news! You saved everyone, *habibi.* Undercover CIA hero saves the nation from terrorist cell! *Bismillah*, you are a hero, and truly, Allah has worked through you."

Dawood flushed. He turned to Kris, lifted their joined hands. "Imam Youssef, this is my husband, Kris."

Imam Youssef beamed, and he pulled Kris into a hug, kissing him on both cheeks three times. "Your husband spoke about you. He did not do you justice, *habibi*. You are more beautiful in person."

Dazed, Kris blinked, his jaw hanging open. He looked from Imam Youssef to Dawood and back.

Imam Youssef grinned. "This is an MPV mosque. Muslims for Progressive Values. There are only a dozen in the United States, but we are growing. We accept everyone. All Muslims, no matter what. We embrace women, and gays, and lesbians, and anyone else as leaders in our faith. One of the leaders of my prayer groups is a woman. Another is a gay man, married, like yourselves. We welcome absolutely everyone here."

"I came to Imam Youssef during the incident." They'd taken to calling the week of Dan's scheming, his plan to destroy DC and ignite a war to engulf the world, *the incident*. "I had questions. I didn't know what my jihad was anymore. I didn't know if I should keep on the path Allah was showing me and then die, exposing the mole. Or, if I should abandon the path, go to you, be with you. Forget about everything else."

"You *didn't* choose me?" Kris's eyebrow arched high.

Dawood flushed. "Imam Youssef helped me see that following the path would lead me to you. In this life or the next. That the battle I was fighting against Dan wasn't just of this world. But it was a battle for the next, as well. And for millions of souls. Millions of lives hung in the balance. Especially yours. If I died, I would wait for you in the next life. But no matter what... We would be together again."

"He did choose you, *habibi*," Imam Youssef said, smiling. "He always chooses you. For this life, and for eternity. And he chose to save so many lives."

Kris tried to swallow. His vision blurred. "He is a hero." Kris smiled, and kissed Dawood's cheek. "He's my hero."

"Imam, I want to show Kris the beauty of our faith. Everything good. Everything that is love. We've both been in the darkness for too long. We've been around too much hatred. We've walked our paths, and now we want to rest. I want him to see what I see, feel what I feel, from Allah."

Imam Youssef turned to Kris. "Is this what you want?"

"I want to understand. I want to walk with my husband. Be a part of his life in every way."

Imam Youssef beamed. "Then I will expect to see you both make a home in this mosque. Kris, you may join in prayers, or you may watch. Whatever you are comfortable with. But you both will *always* be welcome here."

---

They stayed for tea, and Imam Youssef gave them a blessing for their new life. After, Kris stood on the masjid's steps and turned his face up to Dawood, kissing his husband as the setting sun beamed down on them.

"We'll have to buy a new house. Somewhere around here." Dawood wrapped his arm around Kris's waist.

"I'll sell the studio." They'd been staying at Kris's place for now, but it felt wrong. Dawood didn't belong there, high in the sky in the ultra-modern studio with the white leather lounge sofas. They needed something new, something that was theirs, again. "And I have savings, too."

"And we have my back pay."

Kris laced his fingers through Dawood's, behind his back. "Do you want Behroze to move here? Come join us?"

Dawood's eyes glittered, joy bursting outward. "I would love for him to study at our mosque. Learn to be an imam from Youssef. I want to work there, too. I want to help people, Kris. For the rest of my life, just help people."

Kris smiled. That was his husband. The hippie. The lover. The soul of the universe and all that was good in the world inside his bones, inside his heart. Like his father before him. And like Behroze would be, after him. "Let's ask Behroze to come to the US. Move in with us. Let's be a *family*." He hesitated. "A Muslim family. I'm... not ready to convert, but I want to support your faith. And Behroze."

"*Laa yumkinu lilkalimati an tasifa hubbi laki*," Dawood breathed. *Words cannot describe my love for you.* "*Ya rouhi.*"

"I love you, Dawood. Always."

Dawood kissed the top of Kris's head as they started walking, arms laced around each other's waists. Kris closed his eyes, letting the sun, the warmth of Dawood, the peace of the late afternoon, fill his soul.

Sixteen years of war.

A thousand decisions made, creating a path that carved through time. Connections upon connections, the waters of reality spinning onward, ripples from the past and the future finally syncing. More patterns would emerge, more destinies. More paths to walk.

But for today, they had this.

The sunlight.

Each other in their arms.

A new life.

The future, their path together, belonged to *them*.

# AFTERWORD

> *"Indeed, Islam began as something strange, and it will return to being strange just as it began. so glad tidings of paradise be for the strangers, the ones who are righteous and are guided by Allah."*
>
> *~ Prophet Muhammad, salla Allahu alayhi wa sallam*

Palestinian human rights activist, political scientist, and philosopher Iyad el-Baghdadi (not *that* Baghdadi, as he is fond of saying!) remarked on Twitter, "*The focus on Jihadism studies without a wider interest in Muslim and Arab culture, history, art, and native agency makes me very uncomfortable. Someone is* ***really*** *interested in us, but only in our warts and boils.*"

When I started writing this novel, I set in my heart that I wanted to write an honest, heartfelt depiction of Dawood's Islamic experience. His journey into and out of the faith, explored against September 11, 2001, the greater War on Terror, and the existential shock that has pulsated through the Middle East since. I wanted to delve deep into what it means to be a Muslim, to love Allah with one's whole being, to live to the rhythms of Islam. To embrace an Islamic and Arab identity.

I hope my attempt has succeeded, at least in part.

One of the most frequent questions I am asked by editors and proofers, following Whisper, is, "Are you Muslim?"

No, I am not. However, to dive deep into the soul of Islam and attempt to portray the faith with any shred of justice, I felt it was only appropriate to go to the very center of Islamic studies. To that end, I enrolled in an Islamic seminary as a visiting student. The imams and scholars have welcomed me as a seeker, opening their arms, their hearts, and their minds to my journey of understanding. I like to think, in some ways, we have helped open each other's minds in certain areas.

I have found that to be a Muslim is to be at peace with the universe. To have internally surrendered to Allah, to be in a *constant* state of surrender to Allah, to His love and compassion, and to the universe. To be in harmony with what *Is.* To be in a state of Islam is to hold the faith of Allah in the center of your soul.

Islam today is experiencing a revolution, one as existential as the Reformation was to Christianity. Muslims and non-Muslims are struggling to answer questions about Islamic identity, the intersection of Muslim faith, politics, and society, and how to reconcile Islam's past, present, and future. One of the best books I have read on this topic is Shadi Hamid's *Islamic Exceptionalism – How the Struggle Over Islam is Reshaping the World.* For the reader who wants to understand more of the political history of Islam and how the faith is examining itself as it moves into the future, I **strongly** recommend this book. It was my favorite of my research materials, and one I've read multiple times, each re-read finding something new to explore.

The second most asked question I have received is, "How much of this story true?"

A lot of it. Possibly, more than could be believed. I have retained as much historical fact as possible, up through Chapter 22, and have consciously placed my fictional characters within a true historical world and setting.

Kris's interrogation of Abu Tadmir in Chapter 2 is based on FBI Agent Ali Soufan's interrogation of Abu Jandal in Yemen on September 13, 2001. FBI Agent Soufan was the first individual who provided evidence corroborating al-Qaeda's link to September 11. Agent Soufan successfully used Islamic arguments to convince Abu Jandal to cooperate and to identify the hijackers as being al-Qaeda operatives. The lines from Chapter 2, where Kris tells Abu Tadmir that it was Tadmir who told him al-Qaeda was responsible for the attacks, are accurate representations of what occurred in the real-life interrogation. That is *exactly* how Abu Jandal relayed to Agent Soufan who was responsible for the September 11 attacks.

Following the interrogation, Abu Jandal, Bin Laden's former bodyguard, renounced al-Qaeda and became a witness for the United States in federal court, turning against his former terrorist brothers. "This is not right," he said. "This is not the Islamic way. The Sheikh... he has gone crazy. This is not right."

The CIA's war in Afghanistan, the invasion after September 11, is true. Details for this section were collected from CIA records, archives, the CIA museum, and declassified memos of the invasion. The officers who went to Afghanistan on Operation Jawbreaker are some of the finest in the agency, and were more prepared and more culturally sensitive than I have shown my very fictional George and Ryan to be. Many of the struggles that the team encountered in this novel were encountered on the ground. They also faced additional struggles and political machinations. The invasion was a grueling endeavor, with successes and failures across the board.

The fight in Tora Bora is likewise accurate, though scaled to fit within one chapter. Entire novels have been written about the Battle in Tora Bora, as well as multiple military and intelligence analyses. Ultimately, the failure to plug the passes over the Spin Ghar Mountains by US Army Rangers and by the Pakistani military allowed Bin Laden to slip into Pakistan and into the remote tribal regions, where he hid for several years. At one point, the US military fighting unit in the mountains was within fifty feet of Bin Laden's position, but was unable to move forward and capture or kill al-Qaeda's leader.

The CIA's detainee program, and the arrest, capture, and torture of Abu Zahawi are based on the arrest, detainment, and torture of Abu Zubaydah. Working from classified materials, the Senate Intelligence Committee Report on Torture, military tribunal records, Red Crescent Society investigations, and Abu Zubaydah's diaries themselves, I reconstructed a fictional representation of the CIA's imprisonment of, and decision to torture, their first high-value al-Qaeda detainee.

Declassified memos reveal the CIA made the decision to keep Zubaydah "*...incommunicado for the rest of his natural life,*" after deciding to torture him. Zubaydah voluntarily gave up information to his interrogators for two months prior to any application of torture. In DC and at Langley, it was the fear that Zubaydah was holding back critical information that pushed officials to turn to torture in a blind attempt to double-check that Zubaydah had given up all that he knew. After torturing him for almost one month straight, and subjecting him to waterboarding over eighty times, the CIA determined that Zubaydah had "no new information to provide." He had shared all intelligence he would ever share prior to the beginning of his torture.

Abu Zubaydah, to this day, remains locked in Guantanamo Bay, and all his requests for a trial to be set or for a decision to be made about his fate have been postponed indefinitely.

Trainers from Guantanamo Bay, who helped build the detainee program and the CIA's torture apparatus, were sent to Abu Ghraib Prison to train and instruct military and private contract prison guards. Most of the training centered around how to "break detainees" and how to "soften them up for Military and CIA interrogators".

For more information on the CIA's detainee program, please check out *The Senate Intelligence Committee Report on Torture: Committee Study of the Central Intelligence Agency's Detention and Interrogation Program*; *The Convenient Terrorist: Two Whistleblowers' Stories of Torture, Terror, Secret Wars, and CIA Lies*, by John Kiriakou and Joseph Hickman; *Torture and Truth: America, Abu Ghraib, and the War on Terror*, by Mark Danner; and *Torture Taxi: On the Trail of the CIA's Rendition Flights*, by Trevor Paglen.

Another book, written by the architect of the CIA's torture

program, Dr. James E. Mitchell, is *Enhanced Interrogation: Inside the Minds and Motives of the Islamic Terrorists Trying to Destroy America.* Dr. Mitchell is a strong advocate for the use of "enhanced interrogation techniques" that he helped craft. Dr. Mitchell's experience, up to that point, was as a consulting psychologist for the US military's Survival Evasion Resistance & Escape (SERE) program, the military's training environment for personnel who needed counter-interrogation training. This training included tactics and techniques taught to withstand torture, and as part of the training, US military personnel were subjected to several "enhanced interrogation techniques", under medical supervision, to simulate the experience of torture at an enemy's hand. Dr. Mitchell was instrumental in pushing the CIA to move from rapport-building interrogation to his methods, which have been called "torture" by multiple human rights organizations, US government institutions, and international NGOs.

All branches of the US military, in the early 2000s, decided to eliminate waterboarding from the SERE curriculum entirely.

In 2009, President Obama ended the CIA's use of "enhanced interrogation techniques", and in 2014, President Obama made the unprecedented admission that the US, and specifically the CIA, had tortured detainees they'd captured. President Obama went on to say, "It is important, when we look back, to recall how afraid people were after the twin towers fell, and the Pentagon had been hit, and the plane in Pennsylvania had fallen and people did not know whether more attacks were imminent... We did a whole lot of things that were right, but we tortured some folks. We did some things that were contrary to our values."

The confrontation between the vice president—Dick Cheney, at the time—and a leadership team at the CIA in the run-up to the Iraq war over conflicting intelligence conclusions actually took place. Connecting Iraq to al-Qaeda was a foundational goal of the Bush Administration, with the express desire to rid Iraq of Saddam Hussein. The book, *The One Percent Doctrine*, by Pulitzer Prize-winning journalist Ron Suskind, brilliantly dives into the Bush

Administration's response to September 11, 2001, the lead-up to the Iraq War, and the intelligence community's crisis during that era.

Saqqaf is a fictional representation for Abu Musab al-Zarqawi, the grandfather of the present-day Islamic State. *Black Flags: The Rise of ISIS*, by Pulitzer Prize-winning journalist Joby Warrick is a phenomenal deep-dive into Zarqawi's history, psychology, and his disastrous shredding of the soul of the Middle East.

Muammar Qaddafi was the dictator of Libya for over thirty years. He brutally repressed his people, his authoritarian regime violated human rights and was a strong state sponsor of global terrorism. He was at odds with Islamists for the majority of his tenure, as he sought to bend Islam to support his political system, rather than bring Islamic practices into Libyan daily life. He violently clashed with Islamic clerics and was at odds with many Islamic scholars. Recordings of executions carried out in basketball stadiums have been recovered in post-Qaddafi Libya.

Hamid, the Jordanian mole within al-Qaeda, is based upon Humam al-Balawi, a real-life Jordanian double agent who infiltrated al-Qaeda in 2008 and then turned against his Jordanian handlers. In 2009, at Camp Chapman in Khost, Afghanistan, Humam al-Balawi blew himself up at a meeting with his CIA and Jordanian handlers, killing seven CIA officers, his Jordanian handler, and an Afghan security officer. Those killed were: Jennifer Matthews, base Commander; Scott Michael Roberson, base security chief; Darren LaBonte, Amman station case officer; Elizabeth Hanson, Kabul station targeteer; Harold Brown Jr., case officer; Dane Clark Paresi, security officer; Jeremy Wise, security officer; Sharif Ali bin Zeid, Jordanian intelligence officer and Balawi's handler; and Arghawan, an Afghanistan security officer entrusted at the meeting.

Balawi worked with al-Qaeda to manufacture video evidence of his penetration into the highest ranks of al-Qaeda. The plot was sanctioned by Ayman al-Zawahiri, who knew the CIA would seize upon any chance to gain access to al-Qaeda's inner circles. "Balawi Fever", the rush to grasp the opportunity Balawi presented to strike at the heart of al-Qaeda, was blamed as one of the significant failures of the pre-operation workup. In Whisper, Kris has taken on the role of Jennifer Matthews at Camp Chapman. He, unlike Jennifer Matthews, lived.

Chapter 22 is also where I begin to weave a wholly independent and fictional story. Al-Qaeda never attacked Camp Chapman with a second wave attack and never kidnapped a CIA officer to put on trial and execute. Executing a CIA officer *was* their original plan, when they thought Balawi would only be meeting with a handler or two in Miranshah. But when Balawi was invited onto Camp Chapman, their plans grew larger.

David's capture, beating, and exile in the mountains of Pakistan are entirely fictional. The sweeps of the Federally Administered Tribal Areas (FATA) for fighters after Bin Laden's death, and for the next several years, are not.

A mole within the CIA, working in conjunction with al-Qaeda and planning an attack on American soil, is also fictional. The CIA mole's motivations are based, in part, upon the motivations of former FBI Special Agent Robert Hanssen, who betrayed the FBI to the Soviet Union and to the Russians for twenty-two years. He is currently serving fifteen consecutive life sentences at a federal supermax prison, in complete isolation form the world. Hanssen's betrayal was one of the worst in the United States' history. At his arrest, Hanssen stated that he was trying to help the United States through his betrayal, to make the US stronger.

Muslims for Progressive Values is a real organization, small but growing, and is an important voice in progressive Islam. With chapters around the world, MPV is a "human rights organization that embodies and advocates for the traditional Quranic values of social justice [bringing together] an understanding that informs our positions on women's rights, LGBTQI inclusion, freedom of expression and freedom of and from belief." (www.mpvusa.org) MPV's vision states: "[We] envision a future where Islam is understood as a source of dignity, justice, compassion and love for all humanity and the world."

Dawood's use of the phrase 'you are the moon that rises in my darkness' is inspired by the Palestinian poet Mahmoud Darwish.

*Baraka Allahu fika! May Allah bestow his blessings upon you.*

Thank you for reading.

Additional thanks to my editors and proofers, Rita, Justene, Charlotte, Trisha, Lindsey, and James.

For readers who want to know more, selected books I read during the writing of Whisper were:

- *Inside the Jihad: My Life with Al Qaeda*, by Omar Nasiri;
- *The Exile: The Stunning Inside Story of Osama bin Laden and Al Qaeda in Flight*, by Cathy Scott-Clark and Adrian Levy;
- *Hunting in the Shadows: The Pursuit of al Qa'ida Since 9/11*, by Seth G. Jones;
- *Dijihad et la Mort*, by Olivier Roy (Jihad and Death: The Global Appeal of Islamic State);
- *Misquoting Muhammad: The Challenge and Choices of Interpreting the Prophet's Legacy*, by Jonathan A.C. Brown;
- *Our Last Best Chance: A Story of War and Peace*, by King Abdullah II of Jordan;
- *In the Footsteps of the Prophet*, by Tareq Ramadan;
- *Living Out Islam: Voices of Gay, Lesbian, and Transgender Muslims*, by Scott Siraj al-Haqq Kugle;
- *The Road to Mecca*, by Muhammad Asad;
- *The Impossible Revolution: Making Sense of the Syrian Tragedy*, by Yassin Al-Haj Saleh;
- *The Holy Quran*

# ABOUT THE AUTHOR

Tal Bauer is an award-winning and best-selling author of gay romantic thrillers, bringing together a career in law enforcement and international humanitarian aid to create dynamic characters, intriguing plots, and exotic locations. He is happily married and lives with his husband in Texas. Tal is a member of the Romance Writers of America.

Drop Tal a line at tal@talbauerwrites.com. He can't respond to every email, but he does read every single one.

Check out Tal's website: www.talbauerwrites.com or follow Tal on social media.

facebook.com/talbauerauthor

twitter.com/talbauerwrites

amazon.com/author/talbauer

bookbub.com/authors/tal-bauer

## ALSO BY TAL BAUER

**The Executive Office Series**

Enemies of the State

Interlude

Enemy of My Enemy

Enemy Within

**Executive Power Series**

Ascendent

**Stand Alone Novels**

Hush

Whisper

A Time to Rise